With an Ocean Blue Sky

a novel of the future

by

ROBIN MATCHETT

Piercemore

First published 2003

10 9 8 7 6 5 4 3 2 1
Copyright © Robin Matchett, 2002
James Piercemore Books ®
www.piercemore.ca

*Publisher's note: This book is a work of fiction. Names, characters, places and incidents
either are the product of the author's imagination or are used fictitiously, and any resemblance to actual persons living or dead, events, or locales is entirely coincidental.

Printed and bound in Canada

National Library of Canada Cataloguing in Publication
Matchett, Robin
    With an ocean blue sky : a novel of the future / by Robin Matchett.

ISBN 0-9730798-2-7

I. Title.

PS8576.A7996W48 2003 C813'.54   C2003-900145-8
PR9199.3.M3935W48 2003

for Tess, and family

Judging from the past, we may safely infer that not one living species will transmit its unaltered likeness to a distant futurity.

–Charles Darwin

Dedicated to who is entitled to it –

With an ocean blue sky I go,
Wearing it like a shroud
Across the field into the maple wood,
Resigned to muse beneath a surfeit of leaves
That murmur fecklessly against the fiery sun,
Spun in shadows slain by night,
An unbelievable tale -
Wherefore a mosaic of stars
Like dreams do glimpse fantastic children,
Who glow in the dark calling mommy earth
To sit down beside them
And tell the science fiction story
About the boy who traps a star in a box
And would not let it out -
But mommy steps into the Stone Age
As an avenging angel
Compelling the boy to let it out
And behold the pie in the sky,
Then sing magically with the silver birds
Humming precisely
Like the wind in the trees
Waving invisible wings
Good-bye

                                        –Jimmy Pidgeon

one The Pyramid

With an ocean blue sky I go,
Wearing it like a shroud
Across the field into the maple wood
                                    –Jimmy Pidgeon

The monitor beeps, then beeps again, jarring his sonic silence. But the man at the console, Cephren, ignores it caught in a reverie, gazing out his large window to patches of fleeting blue between colossal broken clouds. From his loft in the peak of the Pyramid, he watches them race by in the frontal winds, one of which seems to tear its underbelly in a gaping slash by the point of the apex, submerging his view in a fog. The monitor beeps again impatiently, indicating a call on his private link. In spite of it, he puts his fingers to the console and begins.

Aug. 31, 2395

A terrific thunderstorm this morning with torrential rain really fired me up again, dear reader. All that cloud ripping ionization seems to placate the spirit; it must be the depressurization – a freedom-breathing release such as the Sacred Stones. How I cherish the fierce wind buffeting against this grand old edifice – and how impregnable we seem to be, though the wind pummels like an arrant spirit, bringing on the future, relentlessly.

I decided, just now, to begin writing my notes again after a lapse of many months, due I think to a spell of atrophied time among other distractions, partly a recent flurry of UFO sightings around the world: discs mainly and one gigantic cigar-shaped craft. Also, in spite of the UFOs, there has been coincidentally a resurgent Chicago full of their imperial conceit; but before I get into that, permit me as your leader to preamble.

Prudence will be the axiom of this charter; and, henceforth to the best of my ability, what modest imprint I leave as the Hereditary Chairman of our beautiful little autonomous 'province' Sunsetwind (our province of the world), shall be a testament to my time as leader. On that point, time and history as I have discovered, are like a sea by which the effluxion indeed compels one (in my position) to prescribe some direction, especially in view of prevailing winds. But metaphorically speaking, to sail into a headwind thinking one could arrive sooner at their port-of-call so-to-speak, is rather foolish and credibility may founder no matter how sound or proven one's well-meaning intent. New scientific discovery, for example, may not waylay old perceptions that often retain a stubborn sense of righteousness. So, dear reader, in this spirit I must tell you that as of late, due to foreboding winds of change, a potpourri of impressions have pervaded my thoughts: a sci-fi bonanza if you will, spurred perhaps from recent sightings of those ubiquitous UFOs and inspired by my 21st century mentor, the writer-scientist James Piercemore, (aka Jimmy Pidgeon – only Redman and Chromolox believe me that they were quite possibly one and the same). Just the other night, very late, a UFO was reported by numerous people hovering silently over the Pyramid. Why do I always miss them? It was apparently discoid and emanated a virtual Aurora Borealis of colours. How do they do that? Suffice to say the reality of alien visitation, according to the sceptics, is absolute fantasy, even with the incontrovertible evidence of videography. My own convictions aside, I would usually defer to the Sunsetwind Board (Sunsetwind – emphasis on the second syllable – foreigners have to be reminded), who more often than not subscribe to the press to eke out the truth – which sometimes signifies a convenient impartiality – meaning 'truth' usually can *take on a life of its own. Of course, my personal autocracy is a gentle push this way and that to find out exactly what that is. I should point out that the witnesses to the UFOs were all sound in mind and body. And so I set out on my journey here, armed with a whole mythology of evidence but nowhere to go. Alas, let me digress upon our circumstances. Chromolox, our elected President . . .*

There is a beep at the door. Cephren views the door monitor on his desk to see Chromolox. 'Chromolox,' he says, calmly. 'I was just thinking about you. Do come in.'

'Good morning, Cephren,' she speaks gingerly into the monitor outside his study before opening the thick oak door. 'How do I deserve your thoughts?'

Looking up, Cephren watches Chromolox enter in her weaving red, white and blue linens. She has wild premature grey hair, a tan complexion, long body, feet, fingers, nose, yet is blithely striking with sparkly, sharp green eyes. One gets the distinct impression her sensitivity is charged with such high voltage, one could look but never touch.

'Your humility is touching,' he replies. 'But issues are the order of the day.'

'Deserving as your loyal servant, Cephren, ever dutiful,' she teases playfully, doing a silly flourish. 'Could you be more precise?' she adds, cocking her head.

'Chromolox,' he says pre-empting the reason for her intrusion, 'so glad you ask; I have a serious question for you. I hope you don't mind my asking about a touchy subject. You see, I have been reflecting on next month's World Symposium that we've agreed to host, because I know how most of the Board want so much to meet everyone...' He lapses momentarily into one of his reveries. 'Anyway, I really must know where you, as President, stand with the issue of our judicial sovereignty, which we all know has been under scrutiny lately, and for that matter, every ruling family so-to-speak on the North American continent.'

Cephren raises his hand, as Chromolox is about to open her mouth. 'Please forgive me,' he goes on, 'I want you to know that I do very much appreciate your fealty towards the Path line, but it seems in this day-and-age, the larger issue of greater multi-regional autonomy, even nationalism seems to be at the fore, hence, our simple ways may be fast approaching relative extinction. There are movements afoot; are there not? Please be frank.'

Chromolox shakes her head. 'Cephren, for nature'sake, must you be so ridiculous? But before I get into that, Redman left an urgent message with Mobius to tell *me* to tell *you* to please meet him this morning at the bunker at your earliest convenience – something about Jimmy's Chip.'

'Jimmy's Chip?' Cephren wonders aloud. But he knows it well: the rare computer chip known to have originated in the 21st century containing a poem written by an obscure fellow named Jimmy Pidgeon, and hours of documentaries about the 21st century.

'Yes . . . '

'So that was him,' Cephren interjects, recalling the earlier beep. 'I was busy at the time. I don't know why he must always leave messages with Mobius.'

'Perhaps, because you never answer your link, Cephren, but you know Redman: he's as recalcitrant as an old goat. And as for Mobius, Redman knows he can always rely on him. He never calls *me*,' she pouts abruptly. 'I am the depraved *Trashie* who 'must've done good' I recall him saying once. He's so damned austere.'

Cephren laughs. 'Be thankful; what's this about Jimmy's Chip?'

'I don't know; he's quite beside himself, I understand. Mobius also mentioned an "echo" . . . '

'An echo? Is the old man going batty?' poses Cephren.

'Nothing new there,' she remarks, shaking her head in exasperation. 'Now about this revolution: I realise that you must have some horrible vision – but yes, of course we all speak about it; it's in the air, on the waves, in the links; you'll be strung up tomorrow at sunset! I'm always hard at work thinking up ways to trash the system! Especially the likes of you and Redman!' The twinkle in her eye reveals her mockery.

Cephren sighs and she has a laugh on him.

'We like it here, Cephren!' she exclaims. 'No one wants the Chicagos or Mississippis or Americans to hold the majority in *our* homeland. We are Sunsetwinders and Sunsetwinders we'll stay over my dead body!' Chromolox's beautiful slender arms flail about, as she expresses herself like a weird six-armed diva. She terms herself, like many, a descendant of an "unrepentant Trashie" (her joke). She has been educated, refined and trained to a perfect pitch. She speaks three languages, could fight, could farm any ground worth tilling, was wilderness trained, fusion smart and generally a walking trust of capability, hence her meteoric rise to the top of the Sunsetwind hierarchy and election to the Presidency. She now stands there holding up her hand to block the blinding sun beaming into Cephren's study window at the very apex of the Pyramid.

Cephren opens the link on the monitor and turns to face her with his magnetic smile. He is eight years older than Chromolox and of mixed blood (most Sunsetwinders are of mixed blood which constitutes any variation of African American, Native American, Anglo-Saxon, or Asian), but looks almost equal to her forty-three years. Though admiring him for his purported intelligence, his detractors think him naïve, even dopey. And thanks to unfavourable commentary by the Chicagos, there seems in Sunsetwind a growing antipathy towards him. Though well-meaning, his introverted ways are not the leadership qualities exalted in the changing world; therefore his dependency on Chromolox and the Board make his position all the more questionable. His demeanour is affable, and looks, handsome, with short, well-cut, dark blond hair, physically large and tall over 180 centimeters (six feet). Though well proportioned, his features show no outstanding attribute other than his blue watery eyes, which appear innocent, but rather more mysterious. Together with his short strong nose, well-shaped forehead and mouth set in a square face and decent cheekbones, leaves one with the impression of his being a great happy-sad clown or a big koala bear. He usually wears the customary soft, earth-tone linens of loose fit (if rumpled) with a hemp belt, low-cut collar shirt and brown synthetic all-weather ankle runners.

'Thank you, but you know what happened out west last week,' declares Cephren. 'Besides, you know that Cleo thinks I'm weak, at least "ineffective" was the word she last used.'

'Cleo would have us flexing muscles we don't have; anyway, Hoyle deserved it. That was simply a case of toppling a tyrant. The man was demented. He was found to have subjected his victims to all sorts of horrid abuse like some King Shaka redux.'

'I met the man once, not King Shaka,' he laughs. 'They should have committed him to an asylum. There were some collateral relatives, but the people chose to destroy their constitution. Now they're in chaos.'

Chromolox ponders a moment. She has moved to the wall out of the brilliant sun. Cephren stands up, walks to the window and lowers the blind. 'All I can say,' she goes on, 'is that in the west they're many little regions that still operate feudally, given their geography. The last time I went there, they desperately needed some progress; governments, when pressed, must evolve I admit. They do have their snow boarding, logging, mining and water. I suppose tourism's making a comeback.'

'We could all use a little of that,' comments Cephren. 'I find young people today rather disillusioned. Have you spoken to Cleo, our friendly terrorist? Any progress in the investigation?'

'No. But you know I had a notion that perhaps the accident was caused due to some inadvertent anomaly in the electromagnetic harmonics by these UFO's. They shut down numerous reactors.'

'You may have a point there,' he broods. 'If we could only communicate with these beings; I suppose we're not to their liking. I have to admit, nothing intrigues me more than these elusive phenomena, yet I've never seen one other than in the videos.'

'Neither have I,' says Chromolox. 'It bothers me they do not make an effort to communicate, yet they don't appear to have hostile intentions.'

'As I indicated, they must then think us positively primitive and choose not to interfere.'

'Perhaps they're frightened, as you said. I would be, with the likes of Hoyle around.'

'You're right,' sighs Cephren. 'They should avoid us like the proverbial plague.'

In reference to the investigation, two people had been found as good as dead the previous month during the Summer Fête. The extraordinary nature of the incident stunned all of Sunsetwind, whose domestic countenance had heretofore been so congenial crime was all but non-existent, consisting of a general smattering of domestic upset, fraud, theft, intoxication. Ten Mile and Penny Luck were both popular of mixed racial background upwardly mobile in the hierarchy, Ten being in Fusion Development and Penny in Logistics. There had not been a single lead, or motive, or anything. All that was found were two bodies gripped in coitus, frozen solid in liquid nitrogen. Numerous experts from around the world had offered their services, believing it was possible to bring them back; however, since the two lovers had almost no chance of surviving, the authorities decided to leave them where they were until a decision could be made. In part, their reluctance was due to the fact that there had not as yet been a reasonable explanation for their demise; it seemed impossible, yet there they were apparently frozen in ecstasy. People surmised that their affair had gone somehow very wrong.

Supposedly, the much maligned sub-space chamber created strong neuro-stimulous conditions for meditation and even sex and was used notoriously as a pad by those with access. Cephren, Cleo, Chromolox and the rest of the Board sort of winked at it. Some, including Strange Honey, the prominent sculptor, even suggested that she could make Ten and Penny into a statue of black and white ripple marble. Cleo Path, Security Chief of Sunsetwind, was not having an easy time of it, as Ten Mile had been her boyfriend, and suspicions abounded that she found out about Penny Luck.

'Cephren, I think you must check up on Cleo; she's seemed a little troubled, and you're the only one who can get through to her. You know how everyone looks at her funnily. Though we certainly have our differences, I support her opinion that it must have something to do with Chicago: I believe it was Trinny Burnamthorpe attempting to sow the seeds of a revolution here.'

'Unlikely, if I know Trinny; doesn't seem right; I can't imagine that she'd order such a senseless murder. Through her channels, Cleo told me yesterday that she was overheard commenting: "At least they died well", which seems to me an inferred accident. One would have to agree, dying well that is.'

"Hell, if we can bring 'em back, they'll have had the world's longest orgasm.'

'*Chromolox*,' intones Cephren, though it was his dry sense of humour.

'Hey, you have to look at the up side.'

Cephren shakes his head. 'No one can explain how they ended up in the liquid nitrogen vat!'

'You mean what happened was a transpositional-neuron-electrical-freak-out? Well, that leaves Chicago off the hook, doesn't it?' quips Chromolox, quirkily.

Cephren often wonders about Chromolox's weird side; it is as if she is trying to get something off of her mind, or exfoliate some peculiar need beneath her official life. Their working relationship is sound, but any closeness beyond what her abtruse comments seemed to consent to had an invisible wall. He stands up and looks out his window behind his desk, and sees the rolling green hills of the Niagara Escarpment to the west from high up on his promontory of the Pyramid.

'Maybe, maybe not,' he replies. 'The sub-space chamber has been shut down for years, but everyone with clearance has been tampering with it and Ten and Penny were doing their thing like everybody else, except the cheating on Cleo. I suppose it's belated, but did anyone think to check whether the conversion panel had been tested for prints?'

'Cleo would know,' she pipes. 'But that might implicate half the Pyramid.'

'Call her for me, would you Chromolox?' He sighs. 'Tell her to come by this evening. I also want to discuss the World Symposium. Be there too, Chromolox, thanks.'

'Cephren, Cleo is in the Kawarthas for the day surveying the Chicago war games in the Neutrals, but I'll get a message to her. What time?'

'Of all their territory, must they intimidate us and the Neutrals?' he says sadly. He had known of the war games, but as usual retreated into his condo to ignore them.

'And how many formal complaints have we made to the EF (Earth Federation)? Even George Washington assured us he would do something, but drags his feet,' imparts Chromolox frustrated.

Cephren says nothing, but bows his head in thought. His friend George as the EF Chairman and President of America has made many promises that have not been kept, but Cephren remained loyal to him.

'Three or four,' he finally says, referring to the complaints.

'Could we meet at six this evening?' asks Chromolox, tilting her head. '*Politica Prophylactica* opens tonight at the Mellow, and I for one am going to be there. It stars *Anna Gram*,' she says ribbing Cephren, by raising her eyebrows and softening her voice. She knows Cephren is infatuated with Anna Gram, the sensual superstar.

'Mmm, maybe I'll go,' he says, seriously. 'Six would be fine. It might be amusing to see Hollywood do that particular Piercemore.'

'You're welcome if you want to join . . . the *women*,' she emphasizes. 'I'm going with a friend.'

'And who might that be?'

She hesitates, but complies quietly. 'Season Honey.'

'Well, let me think about it,' he says indecisively.

Chromolox laughs as she exits, adding, 'Don't forget Redman.'

Cephren then disregarding Redman's urgency, thinking the old man was just exercising his usual self-importance, goes back to his writing and continues where he had left off. 'Yes, Chromolox,' he muses aloud, getting back to his notes, then writes:

> ...Chromolox had risen from the very poorest of Sunsetwind. Her ancestors had survived the Horror by living like beavers at the edge of a swamp eating bulrush shoots. Before long they joined with others who eventually came to appropriate land for loyalty to my ancestors who were generous though prudent enough to have retained some hegemony over a large land base. It was here that Flower Child, the great demi-mythological matriarch of Sunsetwind, had originally proffered security to those who desired it on the condition of allegiance. However, all Survivors were grouped historically as both Heavies and Trashies, which names originally termed as slang became the formal nomenclature. The Trashies were made up of small malevolent bands of marauders and their enslaved women and children, who as a tribe usually kept to themselves but killed and stole indiscriminately for their own survival, whereas the Heavies comprised just about everyone else who sought harmony and common sense. Common sense unfortunately had little in common with their apocalyptic predicament. The Heavies were more socially responsible, but through no fault of their own by way of desperation did at times resort to thieving other's hard-toiled spoils, but in like response. Chromolox had descended from a tribe of Trashies, who allied themselves to the Paths and their little benevolent though authoritarian oligarchy, Sunsetwind. At the time, many of the Trashies were ultimately wiped out or forced to integrate. In the early years, the more Heavies the merrier: many people were needed to help build a better world for all.
> Throughout the 22nd century, after the Horror, neo-feudalism arose and ruling families jockeyed and manipulated for power, and there evolved an underlying sense of democratic observance in that life being as precarious as it was, able-bodied, educated men and women sought to recreate a just society in the tradition of the great democracies of the twentieth and twenty-first centuries – the Atomic and subsequent Fusion Age (sometimes referred to as the Secret Age). This was after that fateful day when doomsayers after thou-

sands of years of issuing bogus warnings finally got their due on August 14, 2126 (the cataclysms of 2012 and 2078 hardly count). The Big Asteroid – a five-kilometer diameter rock was seen to be on collision course with earth. Astronomers predicted it would miss by its trajectory; well, it didn't for some unknown reason. The Armed Forces of China, France, Britain, Russia, India and the U.S. in a heroic joint effort managed to detonate nuclear missiles beyond Saturn in the Asteroid's path in the attempt to alter its course before it hit our planet. Most of them were ineffective, but one missile impacted just enough to pulverize the Asteroid into smaller pieces, some as large as football stadiums, and one chunk the size of a modest mountain impacted on the coast of China, while the remainder (though less lethal, if it mattered at that point) hit east-coast Russia and the north-west Pacific. The asteroid was calculated at a speed close to 79,000 kilometers per hour, which translated to approximately 22 km. per second – not an easy target by any measure. The result was simply the most catastrophic event in the hard won history of humanity, even more so than that of the demise of Atlantis, assuming its reality. The collision was estimated to be equivalent to the detonation of twenty thousand 10-kiloton nuclear bombs. The ensuing shock waves set off immediate massive earthquakes worldwide and reactivated once dormant volcanoes. The atmosphere then heated up with trillions of tons of red-hot dust and ash producing sulphureous gases, and for weeks vast tracts of the surface of the earth burned everything flammable where even certain areas of the oceans boiled at the surface. Most people and life forms were all incinerated where they stood (if they remained in the open), especially on the impact side of the earth, but no side was exempt. All flora was denuded of its greenery. Survivors ascertained that a series of thousand meter tidal waves rushed across the Pacific and were stopped only by coastal mountains, otherwise swept inland for hundreds of kilometers. The sun then disappeared for many months as an ash cloud pervaded the entire atmosphere raining a bituminous blackness as deadly as battery acid, finally burying the precious earth under varying depths of ash. In the decade that followed the apocalypse, it had been estimated that over 99.9% of the human race perished leaving miraculously a world population of no more than 25 million to scrounge through the remains. At the outset, there were the 60 plus Celsius temperatures, which melted the remaining ice caps, then in the year following the apocalypse, temperatures plummeted to a minus 10 mean average. Nothing grew. Everything went dormant or died like the dinosaurs. Nowadays, of course, what had happened to the poor earth so long ago, seems almost forgotten, or simply perceived as the greatest cataclysm in the river of humanity. People today don't have generally any real idea of the deprivations and horrors of that time and subsequent century, known in history as the Horror. It made the Black Death seem like a bad year for the flu. Sorry, dear reader, I just thought I should remind you, lest we forget.

Now back to Chromolox: in a way she's my catalyst to power, my intuitive wonder. She has a finger on the pulse of the people. Old Redman even hinted once, he wasn't sure what her sexual preferences were; that's to say: she felt compelled to hide it, when we are so free in our society; but that is her prerogative, and she seems happy, if intense. Personally, I am blissfully unfettered, especially after the unmentionable hellfire of my ex-wife, Trinny Burnamthorpe. To think it took an EF Judgment to get her off my back, at least overtly. Her power is enormous; she's another hereditary leader like me, but of the vast State of Chicago: all hardware, weapons, biotechnics (genetics), and good ole bible thumping. She has since our time together (now that was a merger), proclaimed herself to her many admirers in the developing world, the "Lady Godiva, the Avenging Angel of Piety", an Omega Pointer, (those who believe that theoretical physics and blind faith amount to the same thing) whose explication for human well-being is the militant upholding of monotheism. We apparently cannot survive without its purification, her purification rather; she of course being the feral will of God. I prefer simply, individual rights.

Her father, Sam Burnamthorpe, a religious man in the Christian mold, was otherwise more sensible and saw to both the social and historical context of faith and religion, especially in the case of his champion, the Essene, Yeshu David (Jesus); he being literally the dynastic descendant and true heir of the old kingdom (King David's) as revealed in the Dead Sea scrolls centuries ago.

Essenic dogma, Sam argued, was essentially what we had come to call Christ-ian, which invariably set Yeshu bitterly apart from some of his compatriots, morally and ritualistically. It was this, Sam would advise me (he would often engage me in his philosophising) that demythologised Yeshu's godliness that had been heretofore literally transcribed in pre-Horror Sunday School. Although a "riddle of metaphors", Sam claimed the correct translation of Yeshu's ancient language deciphered the "mythology of miracles" to bring "Jesus" online with the future, thanks to the scrolls. We in Sunsetwind, to Sam's relief when I married his daughter (don't ask me why), have always been broad-minded with the old stories and put great stock in them for social education and his-tory. We give all religions the same importance: Islam, Hindu, Buddhism, etc. I remember once I told Sam that I thought perhaps Yeshu was part extra-terrestrial, as he purportedly claimed himself to be. Sam laughed and just said that I made his case in point. 'You see what I mean, Cephren? You speak of metaphors and supernature.' I suppose he had never seen an UFO. Neither had I for that matter, yet I responded by saying that we too must then be supernatural, at least our technology was.

Trinny Burnamthorpe, need I remind myself, dear reader, rules the sover-eign State of Chicago as the true autocrat. Allied with America (as it stands today), Chicago now comprises most of the Great Lakes watershed and bio-regions, including the Minnesotas, Wisconsins, Michigans, Iowas, Illinois, Indianas, Ohios, Upper New York and North Pennsylvania. I should now re-acquaint myself with its general history to remind myself of how two coun-tries that sprang from the same tree turned out so differently and opposite.

It came to be that Trinny's distant ancestor, Elias Burnamthorpe (the General, as he was known) and his family survived the Horror in one of the many government bunkers. This great leader of the remnants of old Great Lakes America less Sunsetwind, "re-established" most of those aforemen-tioned lands whose people "invited" him to assist restoring order with his small but organised army. He was stern and "vested with the mandate to survive" though he liked to think he was "judicial", with the price being the people's undying allegiance "if order was to remain restored". The fact of the matter was, there were so few people, disorder was hardly the appropriate term to describe the country; it was more like utter helplessness in the most dire configuration of human suffering ever conceived. However, the General was the right man for the job, and in a matter of time basic needs were supplied as the fledgling state emerged. Within the decade, regional geopolitics held sway over former nationalistic ideology and soon enough a new map of North America demarked itself and even the old U.S.-Canadian border was regarded as a thing of the past. Old southern Ontario less Sunsetwind eventually merged with the Chicagos and all their geography. The Burnamthorpes proved to be master controllers and within a generation held unquestionable autonomy over any other authority. Their manipulation of "judicial sovereignty" under the thick coating of a fervent nationalism in the name of freedom has for over two hundred years been deemed an impregnable cultural institution. In the early years, however, border disputes were about as far removed from their reality as Alpha Centauri. Food, shelter and order took precedence over everything. In our history programs, this theme is a compulsory subject; however, I'm not about to indulge you too much, dear reader, because this of course is evident, in terms of our problems today.

Great Blue Lake (formerly Georgian Bay) and North Lake Superior are the exceptions to Chicago's sovereignty over the Great Lakes bio-region, Great Blue being divided between Sunsetwind to the south and Anishnabe to the north. Sunsetwind's surviving sanctity was long ago attributed to Ezekial (Zeke) Burnamthorpe's marriage to David Path the Younger's daughter, Emily, who claimed to have descended from Flower Child herself. Anishnabe encompassed a vast sovereign wilderness region extending from the west in Kenora through North Superior to Ottawa in the east, and reaching Moosonee to the James Bay watershed to the north. They were a hodge podge of various ethnic groups, predominantly aboriginal. The Anishnabe are our friends though we do not see them often, due I think, to the cold war with Trinny Burnamthorpe and Chicago, or more possibly, the re-emergence of our more complex and interdependent society with greater and greater trade issues as well as geopolitical problems. But, I do trust the

Anishnabe, nevertheless. Certainly Johnny Fish, who played for the Sunsetwind Storm, was one of the greatest hockey players that ever lived.

So I ramble on here, dear reader, so excuse me while I get my stride, which I will. Cleo, my sister teased recently, "Cephren, you could be only one of two things, a benevolent despot or the village fool!" I replied peremptorily, "You lack mysticism!" and she exited the room in a pall of thought. She has definite insecurities, I think. When she came back a half hour later, and I said even more callously, "Did you find some?" Then I didn't see her for three days. Finally, she hit me back: "There is no such thing as mysticism, anymore! It died like the dinosaurs during the Horror!" And I remarked, "The truth is: mysticism is the quiet effusion of ego." We had a truce then, to my relief. Laughter is not so easy with us. Old Redman sees us as a check and balance of sorts; he is wise and very old, even older than my long deceased grandfather who built the Pyramid.

Why am I saying all this, dear reader? I suppose I must recapitulate for my own digression, not to mention your own understanding. I believe it is my responsibility to define our extraordinary position in the world. But, I keep thinking of Chromolox and Cleo and how dependable they are, knowing about everything worth knowing in our government it seems. I recall Chromolox once pointed out that only Redman, Cleo and I have eluded her "class" as she terms it. Her ambition and self-confidence run aground, I think, not knowing what to make of a hermetic Hereditary Chairman-Treasurer and a quirky old scientist, or a cagey amazon for that matter. Yet, she really knows how our little province ticks, neo-feudal as it is, or used to be. The hegemony of blood is perfectly acceptable to her and everyone for the most part at present, but I can feel the times are changing. There is a natural propensity for humanity to fold back on itself once quid pro quo sets in after centuries of peace. Anyway, I feel that she hasn't the same respect for me, because I'm Hereditary, which is not so great any more, but I believe she values my inbred leadership and search for knowledge.

As I said before, our province and all the others: the bio-regions, states, sub-states are once again becoming interdependent. We have survived *against stupendous odds the Horror so long ago. And now we have never been so free, although there are stirrings afoot that would have us give up my judicial sovereignty for some kind of grand neo-American country as they used to call it. Then of course, some traditionalists would like to see the Commonwealth of Canada coalesce again, which I believe unlikely. Regionalism now has absolute autonomy (Perreault was right after all) and roots so deep nothing short of conquer or cataclysm would change anything. At every World Symposium someone has to raise the issue. Old world dreams die hard. And peace is the ever-minder . . .*

Cephren's monitor beeps again. Cephren sighs and responds this time. He engages the link and sees an irascible Redman staring at him on the screen.

'I thought you'd be on your way by now, Chairman!'

'Redman, I was just finishing my notes . . . '

'Are you procrastinating, son?'

Redman always knows what to say to make Cephren feel guilty.

'I'm on my . . . ' Cephren is cut off. Redman escapes the link. 'Damn him,' mutters Cephren, deciding to finish his notes. He continues . . .

I love being innocuous, but politics, politics, politics! How I hate politics! Some things never change. But literature, science and honest history are the true marks of civilisation. If Sunsetwinders could know me in this regard, they should respect me for my political improvidence. Fortunately, that's unlikely; they see me as the sole keeper of the key – the code key to my precious files and all Sunsetwind – and above all, the autocrat. O woe is me the innocuous one – a political phantasm, a benevolent gargoyle.

We, of Sunsetwind, pious agrarian fools, a hundred years behind the times, accused by Trinny Burnamthorpe (therein lies a sacrilege with a name like that for a she-devil – some believe she was named after that first atomic bomb) of subversive co-opting! We the co-opters? We, who invented lunch box sized fusion generators to power everything from emops to homes? We, who developed anti-viral units, and a potential sub-space (anti-matter) chamber, though need I repeat, we don't know how to do that yet. Everyone's sceptical about that big breakthrough, but it seems all so random and obvious in the end and redemptive. I say, send your spies Ms. Burnamthorpe and we don't care who they are, because frankly we don't really give a damn! You can have the damned technology, at a price! But I refuse to be libeled at the World Symposium for co-opting and delegated to oblivion!

Today, Trinny Burnamthorpe casts a shadow over enlightened Sunsetwind (Old Sam, oh how you must roll across the metaphors to see your great State of Chicago careen into the rocks with your daughter steady at the helm, careening steadily). She claims we have made new emop advances and were in secret negotiations with the Muslim Chinese in the Kush under O'Reilly al Khazzami to turn them against her allies, the Mao Chinese. What fear mongering! What advances? Is it because O'Reilly freed Tibet? And what of the Mao? They're a world minority, who for over two hundred and fifty years since the Big Asteroid, have lived separately from their Muslim neighbours. Dim Sum has yet to be improved and fermented mare's milk for that matter, so why should our fusion be held up to scrutiny? We should be grateful for the way things are. The Secret Age, however, was a long one with dark shadows and a burgeoning mythology that truth must ferret out, especially regarding aliens, yet we have not quite come out from under the veil of our terrible past, though I think we are ready. The thought sometimes haunts me that we of the earth are the oblivious subjects of an eternal experiment conducted in this colossal terrarium – our very own biosphere.

Cephren Path exits the Pyramid using the west tunnel. He walks away from the landing where numerous emops (electromagnetic out-phasers – airborne vehicles powered by an anti-matter reactor that rides its own gravity wave as a controlled surf out of phase with planetary or solar gravity) and emop transports come in and out softly with their reactors humming at a low intensity. He had his own emop, an '86 Experimentor, in his personal port near the Pyramid summit. Although Redman lived a few kilometers from the Pyramid, Cephren would have taken his own emop had he been in a hurry, which was rare, but it is too nice a day and he wants to exercise with his Siberian Husky, Blondy Boy. He comes to the kennel, a six-hectare compound, where the keeper lives with numerous other dogs. Cephren releases Blondy Boy from the invisible containment with his pocket code-key, giving him a hefty pat and hug, and then keeps to the trail that leads down into a forested swale. At the other side along an ancient cedar rail fence, the trail winds around a hay field. There he stops to look around as he always does at the old ruins of his Barnett ancestor's red brick farmhouse. He can see far to the north and the expanse of pale, blue sky cutting Great Blue Lake across the horizon, and turning to the northeast he surveys the Pyramid high on its hilltop plain with its flashing beacon at the apex. It stands massively covering a forty hectare square (about ninety-six acres) rising almost two hundred meters (six hundred and fifty feet), built in the 2330s by Cephren's grandfather Jonathan Path with the view that it would stand eternally as a monument to a better world and a just one, free from the ignorance and madness of earlier ages.

Built of stone, adorned with surrounding glass on just about every level emitting lots of light, the Pyramid was erected with three-meter thick giant slabs of light grey-red granite, tongue and grooved, cut to perfection, and five subterranean levels with eight main entrances, north, south, east and west. Above ground, there are twenty-nine levels of varying areas culminating in the executive level at the top with the Chairman's loft at the very apex. At every level, windows surround the building, as well as exterior walkways not unlike the look of ramparts so solid was their construction. The foundation and sub-structure were also granite, designed to easily support the massive weight. In fact, a full fifth of the internal area was constructed of dense granite. A single fusion reactor that emitted almost zero waste powered this architectural wonder of the world.

On the main level in the center of the Pyramid stands the main support bearing pillar thirty meters in diameter as well as a series of secondary bearing pillars half way between the center and the outside perimeter. Located on the ground level is Survivor's Walk, a vast promenade and foyer with a Reception Area, Grand Salon and Banquet Hall at the west end, as well as other areas that provided food depots, supply stores, health facilities and general needs including restaurants such as La Petite Vache and Nori, and entertainment facilities such as the Mellow. The various departments of the province's Administration, Information and Business are generally above ground, and Research and Logistics (application) are below. In the Logistics section, there is a huge space four levels high and a three hectare floor area specifically for engineering, design and construction of prototype emops, generators, industrial equipment and reputably the most advanced space program anywhere in the world.

Cephren stands mesmerized, as he always does, when looking at this awesome edifice. The pride he felt piloting its course and thinking of the grandfather he never knew, makes his heart swell as he breathes in the fragrant air. Blondy Boy, he notices, comes and looks eagerly in the same direction. Cephren turns and heads into the meadow and woods, which descend into the valley where Redman lives.

Old Redman is one part Temaugauma Anishnabe aboriginal. His father, Richard, was an adventurous blond Minnesota who trekked his way into Sunsetwind almost one hundred years before with a dog sled team, of which Blondy Boy is one of the descendants. He claimed the only reason for his coming, besides trade and salvage, was because of the extremely cold winter that froze the St. Clair river, now pure, enticing him to cross, only to find the ice breaking up following a great thaw shortly afterward. He thought he'd go back the long way around Great Blue; however, he met Bird-in-the-Sky, soon to become Redman's mother. At an early age, Redman became a good friend of Cephren's grandfather, and subsequently showed great aptitude and intuitive knowledge, which earned him considerable prestige in the fledgling research program to which he had been attached ever since. Though no longer fledgling, the program rivaled that of California, Japan, Russia, America and Texas, not to mention Chicago.

Cephren approaches Redman's abode, a renovated bunker, apparently built before The Horror. Blondy Boy had already arrived having stirred Redman's old mutts. Delmira, the mulatto housekeeper, is hanging laundry between the trees, as Redman likes his clothes forest-scented. He appears at the door slightly crooked, with that air of calm diffidence somewhat resembling the Confederate General Robert E. Lee. His white hair is slicked back in his customary fashion; his brown eagle eyes and smooth dark skin like well oiled leather give him an almost youthful look. Redman could have been a grand old chief of a nineteenth century tribe, despite his modest neo-aboriginal repertoire of almost twenty-fifth century technical knowledge. He is tenacious, and short-fused.

'Cephren, my son; where have you been?' he asks with his eyes piercing. 'You make me impatient. I called all morning. When was the last time I asked you to come here with such urgency? What gives, eh?'

'Redman, I think last spring. You wanted to tell me about that "thinking" isotope, you named "Huck". Remember?' recalls Cephren, hoping flattery might distract Redman from his own tardiness.

Huck was the name given to a fusion isotope that held its energy ten times longer than previous types. A modified reactor had been incorporated into the latest emop prototype, the Volcano.

'That was important, eh? And obtaining those alien alloys?' Redman's eyes twinkled, appeased.

'Probably the most important discovery in recent memory,' says Cephren pursuing the flattery, knowing Redman had a weakness for it. Then it occurs to him something out of the ordinary is happening: but what indeed was truly ordinary? The supposed alien alloys had been procured from the DVI (Death Valley Institute) of the sub-California bio-region in accordance with a trade agreement exchanging Huck and other electromagnetic technology. Many states, especially the Chicagos, thought the whole deal was a scam, but now the Chicagos were contravening trade agreements and stealing them from the DVI.

'Please, let us proceed,' says Redman leading the way into the interior of his den. Cephren follows, his curiosity peaking.

The dankness of the bunker could never seem to be expelled, although his home is warm and comfortable with soft furniture and original light oak-paneled walls. The living area has one large single pane window with a view into the forest ravine. Bands of sunlight emitting through various openings of the dense and green canopy of maple leaves shower the forest with enchantment. Cephren only glances that way as Redman hobbles quickly past into the kitchen and by the bedroom and bathroom, then down the passage into the large recesses of the bunker where he has his lab and study. There is a well-lit main area six meters high packed with old apparatus', some still blinking on and off, which they had been doing as long as Cephren could remember. There are shelves stacked with ancient books and junk, mostly personal collectables. Most of the floor space has been collecting dust for fifty years, as Redman's scientific forte had been more theoretical than practical.

Up the rickety old stairs at the end of the workroom they enter Redman's "office". Here at his old oak desk is where he spends most of his time. His monitor is an original Venus made of maple, plastic and the electronic components. Its million-gigabyte capacity was considered ridiculously superfluous fifty years before, and now, is relatively obsolete. It is no bigger than a pre-Horror desktop. Its thin screen is still the standard liquid mirror, hardly improved upon. Its imaging is so fine, the naked eye could not tell the difference between realities save the hardness of the screen.

The screen shows weather formations as the usual holding pattern over Sunsetwind as viewed by the satellite. On the close swoop, the Pyramid appears and some heavier cloud cover is forming again to the west over the escarpment and across the High Plains down to Lake Huron and north to the Peninsula, which divides Huron and Great Blue. The view then swoops across Great Blue to Indian lands (Anishnabe) and south across the

Ten Thousand Islands to Huronia, west to Kawartha and south and west in a final sweep to the pastoral Clearview and back to the Pyramid. They can see an emop transport gently hover and land at the south gate, a fruit and vegetable shipment from one of the Peninsular Hot Houses.

Redman sits down in his wooden swivel chair. Cephren pulls up another chair beside him. Redman reaches over and picks up an old 21st century plastic yogurt container filled with tiny obsolete chips. 'You see these?' he says.

'Yes, salvaged antique industrial chips,' replies Cephren.

'Yes, and what have we done with them?' quizzes Redman.

'They're filed in Archives. We've gleaned much information from them. They've been essential, in fact.'

'But mostly of historical significance today, wouldn't you say, Cephren?'

'Yes, but in the early days they were lifelines to the technology of the past. We wouldn't be who we are today without them. The early generations were really salvage operations, the sum effort of which now resides in a yogurt container, a odd measure of our success, wouldn't you say, Redman?'

'Right, Cephren,' says Redman in his patronizing manner. 'Did you know that in the Region of California, they now use Resonant Scanners to forecast weather?'

'I had heard something about their discovery. I had no idea they could forecast weather. What's wrong with their satellites?'

'In the June issue of our Science Bulletin, I wrote an article about that,' remarks Redman looking sardonically at Cephren.

'I must've overlooked it,' says Cephren, knowing Redman's admonishing impatience.

'Well, Resonant Scanners can actually measure the various levels of resonance, both radiation and otherwise issuing from the sun and planets or unknown sources. This so-called discovery of "small import" according to a critic's response, because it just reads weather is actually a huge leap, which I believe will become apparent soon, quite soon. It may be possible to control weather with this technology. I may not be around to see it happen, but I believe it will.'

'I thought Jimmy's Chip and some echo were what you called me down to talk about.' says Cephren calmly, wishing he hadn't opened his mouth.

'I'm not your messenger boy Cephren, hell no! Do I have to keep you on the ball, to know what in the great-blue-yonder I'm talking about? Bear with me, Chairman!'

'Pardon me, Redman, please continue,' he responds calmly, thinking what a snide old bastard he could be. He has a self-righteous side to him that pontificates a superiority complex as if he was the only force behind Sunsetwind. He once claimed (it is general knowledge that Redman is eccentric) that when he was twelve years old, he and his mother had had an alien experience in which the supposed aliens surreptitiously left behind a small alloy container which contained a unique pellet the size of a ball-point. This object once investigated, was discovered to be a unique computer chip subsequently known as Jimmy's Chip – so named by the author, Jimmy Pidgeon, of a strange poem inserted rather ambiguously, as per the chip's historical content. Growing up on a farm in Huronia, Redman had witnessed late one evening (once his memory returned – the aliens had controlled their subject's minds with a form of energy field effectively shutting down any memory of the experience, also known as missing time) a metallic-grey discoid aircraft hover quietly around their property and then stop above their wood-frame house. The childlike, somewhat haunting grey and luminescent, dark almond-shape-eyed visitors (known hypothetically as the Greys) with over-sized craniums, descended in a bluish beam seemingly as if by magic. They were very passive and took some interest in young Redman and his mother. The story goes that Bird-in-the-Sky had made strawberry-mint tea in which the aliens dipped their long, strange fingers. After Redman and his mother 'woke up' they discovered the container and with it the fragmented memory of the encounter. Once convinced their minds were not playing tricks on them, they sought out the proper authorities to tell their tale and handed over the mysterious container, fearing the contents. The authorities ignored their story and assumed the father had salvaged it before he died earlier that year, because he had been known to be a salvage trader.

'Yes,' continues Redman, 'Resonant Scanners can pick up various levels and types of resonance, some thought unheard of because we had no yardstick to measure them; therefore we chose to ignore the possibility for centuries. Clement Reesor of the DVI – have you heard of him?'

'The name rings somewhere.'

'He accurately predicted to the day and even hour all the hurricanes in the Caribbean, major storms, anything of consequence last year and this year, *months* before they occurred. No one believed him, of course, but they do now. He discovered most weather originates not on earth, but out there in space, which is not new of course. What is, is the resonance patterns, understood after years of study with this device he had rigged in a satellite – some kind of electronic field pattern stimulator with a proton pulse – once scanned, corresponded to certain atmospheric criteria. Well it turned out to be almost one hundred percent accurate – one hundred percent! We can now know when next year's big blizzard will come, or twister, or whatever. Now as fascinating as this is, this is not the reason I called you down here. Along with his studies, Clem Reesor developed a little gadget to scan for viruses in a computer. We have our own, of course, but it is not a Resonant Scanner. Rather than send a neutron pulse at variable intensities, the Resonant Scanner seems to do the same thing, but with calibrated protons at octave harmonic levels with the same objective – to clean out any "hubris" in the system. But what's interesting: if you put your search modem on a capacity frequency, the scan creates a shadow. As we know, a shadow in our system indicates a PCC (percentage capacity capability), which tells you whether your cleanout has done any cleaning; anyway, with the Resonant Scan, echoes of non-accessible information appear in the shadow. What the echoes reveal, especially in salvaged chips, or otherwise, is which chip has buried information. We can therefore, separate those chips which have or have not buried inaccessible information.' Redman pauses for a minute to access his monitor.

Cephren is still assimilating what he has just heard.

'I didn't know we were sitting on inaccessible information,' says Cephren finally, as his imagination is already probing the possibilities. Redman had said a "huge leap". This was profound for Redman. Redman for all his theoretical eccentricity is beneath his exterior a severe sceptic who put more scientists to shame for impractical hypothesis. Nonetheless, he has had an uncanny ability throughout his life to hit on very important breakthroughs, such as Huck the Isotope.

'You got it, but on one chip only.'

'Yours truly, Jimmy's.'

'Indeed.'

'Does this have anything to do with aliens?' queries Cephren thinking about Redman's dubious alien story and skittish UFOs.

Redman laughs in his characteristic way and then somewhat mysteriously says: 'I should hope so, but I think you've been watching too many Reptoid episodes, my friend.'

Redman breaks into more idiotic laughter after his banal comments that everyone finds such an aberration to his dour nature, then stops as suddenly as he began. It was always considered odd that once integrated, the 'alien' chip revealed only earth documentaries. But Redman is not one to mince words. 'You are right in supposing one thing, Cephren: we have a whole new dimension here. Resonance is something we know little about. Mass and energy? We know them sufficiently, I think; but resonance between the two is relatively unknown. I want to renew the sub-space program. With this new technology, there may be something more we can discover.' Redman brings up one of the Archive files. 'Do you recognise this?' he adds.

'Of course, that's from Jimmy's Chip. What's the connection?"

'The connection is that we've been sitting on a treasure chest all of our lives. This chip has a very big echo.'

'Can we get in?'

'Clem and I have been in communication for years. He's a man in his sixties. I first met him at the California Earth Show about twenty years ago.'

'I was not aware . . .'

'You're not aware of a lot of things, son; let me finish. He sent me this kit, a program and device that was easily adapted to the old bitch, my monitor, and since early spring, I've been scanning all the original chips. Only one came up with an echo (that has been analysed by his program) and has a huge shadow at least somewhere in the 99th percentile of this chip. Jimmy's Chip, according to Clem, has been suggested to be one of the old government series that we believe originated in Area 13, the underground facility within Area 51 or Dreamland, as it was known, in the old Nellis Air Force Test Range out there in Nevada. I thought of you immediately with your history studies and that you should have a go at it, first. Of course we have no way of getting into this chip without a code key or it may self-destruct, as Clem found out with another chip, one of the B400s.'

'B400s. They were government bond chips – self-destructing if tampered with – highest grade; the best all-in-one memory drive, and prototype for implantation,' comments Cephren barely holding his composure. 'I know the Chicagos have a few B series in their archives, which no doubt has spurred some activity, knowing Trinny.'

'Yes and so might every developed power in the world with the new race into space.'

They both sit there contemplating for a moment. Cephren thinks of reasons why a poem by an obscure fellow named Jimmy Pidgeon would be on this odd-one-out chip squeezed between a lifetime of topical news and docu-history of the 21st century. It must've been a good cover, he supposes, adding fuel to his pet belief Pidgeon and Piercemore were one and the same person. What did the aliens know, he wonders? And were their recent sightings coincidental?

'I must ask you,' continues Redman, 'to keep this under your hat until we can divulge the nature of this buried information. It may be nothing or it may be something very potent.'

'Does Clem Reesor know you have found any shadows?' asks Cephren.

'No.'

'Has he found any of his own?'

'He told me when I last spoke with him it was all the rage in his part of the world to scan old chips and programs. Treasure Hunts, he called them. Most of what had been retrieved was of little importance. He did say he had a chip that seemed impenetrable, but got in with a decoder program. It was a B500 and apparently an older type of chip. In it there are references to an X13, which must have been a super secret chip or place, because nothing was divulged. He also said his chip was recovered from the former mysterious Area 51. I do know that what was accessible was very interesting. Clem sent me a dozen files containing information about aliens recovered from this chip. Before the Horror, as you may know, the United States conducted a massive program regarding the sighting, recovery, and study of UFOs including reverse engineering programs, and apparently how and where they happened actually to meet aliens face to face and perhaps exchange information. It was the most highly classified program in their history. Clem surmised there might have been some hostile intent by these aliens to warrant the extreme secrecy. These files, however, only record places and dates with very little information as to what they actually discovered. References to Area 51 or Dreamland are made, however, and he feels the shadow and echo in our chip may contain the whole shootin' match. He invited me to try to get in as they had some success. They tried millions of code combinations as well as password combinations before getting through. The combinations are endless, unfortunately, if indeed the code is at all what we imagine it to be.'

'We may never get through,' says Cephren rather morosely.

'That's a cruel possibility, Cephren.'

Redman jacks in the accessible program and keys in the directions. The old newsreels appear as clear as the day they were made with the exception of two lines that slightly obscure the mirror at intervals. On the screen the news-anchor-woman spoke out the headlines almost four hundred years before: *Perreault has done it! Danielle Perreault has just been elected Prime Minister, the first woman in Canadian history, and with a huge majority! Perreault, only 45 years old, had entered federal politics only four years ago as leader of the Opposition of the new party, her very own CDs (Conservative Democrats) to take the country by storm . . .* News clips of this cool charismatic, light skinned woman, with elegantly arranged dark hair flash across Redman's screen. The crowds are all going wild, seeing in her the demi-goddess who would bring about the revolution that could resurrect Canada from a divided and indebted nation into a super-power. The year was 2026.

Later, back in his loft, Cephren sits at his large pine desk staring attentively into the liquid mirror screen of his own monitor, a Mars 2. He just stares, emblazoned in static energy; his mind burning with an array of possibilities. Yet none come. He had inserted Jimmy's Chip into the adaptor and the monitor brought up all the information that he had seen a hundred times before: the news flashes covering the long political career of Danielle Perreault, the Water Summits of 2031 through to 2041, the polarising of Western politics, the various terrorist and disease rampages of the century – TB, cholera, small pox, malaria, aids, the ozone nightmare, the murderous al-Qaeda, starvation, the sterility epidemic, the ECD (Earth Crust Displacement), other natural disasters on a scale never seen in human history, and of course World War III brought on inadvertently by rampant terrorism building to critical mass. On the positive side, there were manned space missions to the outer planets of the solar system, excursions into deep space (though amounting to little), the rejuvenated environment, the development throughout the world of thermal fusion power and gravity propulsion by the amplification of anti-matter – a major step in the evolution of human achievement.

These leaps of technical progress, however, precipitated a growing gulf between burgeoning global cultural movements, specifically the United Front and the Righteous (formerly an outgrowth of the Radical Right originally supported by New Republicanism). The rampant exploitation of biotechnology, the shrinking margin of benefit for society under capitalism, and the overwhelming cost of global social disparity had fomented a revolution, which ignited with the assassination of the President of the United States, a Democrat. Tragedy culminated in the mayhem, which like an insidious cancer unwittingly brought on World War III in 2078 through to 2083. It was really an epic struggle between the interests of global business and the old establishment of predominantly New Republicans against the social union policies of the United Front – a buzzword for the Democrats – who had been swept to power with a slim majority. Both sides were utterly convinced of each other's justification for survival, thus stimulating and perpetuating the madness of a crisis with no solution in sight. However, cooler heads prevailed and in the interests of a unified America, leaders were forced to battle the uncompromising Righteous, who had secured Cheyenne Mountain and numerous states with a large fully equipped armed force led by Colonel Jeremy Blaine. There were numerous frightful battles as the government tried to subdue the Righteous. Meanwhile, the causes that had long boiled over into full blown war around the globe, and spread uncontrollably like a prairie fire, where everybody was fighting it seemed for their own survival, specifically in South Asia, the Middle East and ultimately in North America. Then escalations went nuclear. After a half decade of unequivocal destruction, a unified America finally defeated the Righteous, who had refused to capitulate in the wake of at least two hundred million dead worldwide and many North American cities destroyed, especially in the Midwest where the Righteous had taken hold. Chicago, Detroit, Buffalo, Cleveland, Indianapolis, Cincinnati, St. Louis, Kansas City, Memphis, Denver, Dallas,

Houston and countless small places were nearly destroyed. It was initially considered "containment", but ultimately went ballistic, when on April 19, 2081 a "crazed" Colonel Jeremy Blaine of the Righteous nuked New York, Atlanta and even Mexico City from their stronghold under Cheyenne Mountain before one of his own men shot him, sparing Washington, which was next. The world reeled in horror and disgust. The Chinese then used the opportunity to assert control over almost all the East Asian markets, simply filling demand where the U.S. lost its influence, but for India and Pakistan, who almost nuked each other into annihilation. Europe remained relatively unscathed for once. The Middle East, however, fought it out to the finish in a Holy war that literally destroyed the entire region, leaving it barely habitable for the survivors who thankfully made a lasting peace. All in all, the result of the war made the whole over-populated world undergo a major sea-change in the bid to survive at a time when life was pure hell on earth. The historical significance of the war demarked the end of nationalism, big business and to a certain extent the free enterprise system. It was recognised that the needs of the many took precedence over the interests of the corporate state, in order to construct an equitable global society. The old order died and with it the power and wealth of the corporate state, which ironically had done more for a higher standard of living than their successors could subsequently, but such are the winds of change when overwhelming issues produce critical mass. Looking back from Cephren's time, the outcome of the war was the beginning of a new era with a new powerful global system in control, delegating justice and equality for all people.

Cephren contemplates this precise general history of the 21st century in these many documentaries with graphic footage and commentary. The documentaries almost seem to him too well laid out, as if someone had highlighted a compendium for posterity to show the glaring idiosyncrasy of Pidgeon's elusive poem as a kind of induction to a great reckoning. There is something unusual here, feels Cephren, yet he is at a loss to determine what that really is. There are too many questions: who was the narrator? The producer? Was it Pidgeon? If it was, he would have had to have someone do it for him, because Pidgeon was supposed to have died in 2047 in his 67th year, and that would have left more than half the century unaccounted for. Cephren knows there is something definitely weird about the documentaries if Pidgeon had anything to do with it.

Cephren, unable to think coherently for the moment, stands up restlessly and walks to the window. He changes his mind and opens the sliding glass door on the east side of the apex. There he stands out on the granite balcony, distracted, watching the harvesters in the fields surrounding the Pyramid buzzing through the oats and barley in wakes of dust. Once their hoppers are filled, they would cumbersomely lift up like giant laden bees to unload at the storage terminals. *How do you get into that chip!* thinks Cephren, returning to his fixed focus. He goes back impatiently to his monitor and begins looking for something that might lead him in the right direction. Redman had said millions of combinations of letters and numbers had been used in the attempt to break into other chips with modest success, but he had none himself with such a sophisticated decoder program. Cephren then wonders whether the key could be something simple. He thinks of sequences of documents put through as passwords, and considers whether indeed the whole batch was the password. He sets up the program as one might have when it was created. He enters and codes all the documents. Nothing. He tries various sequences. Still nothing. He tries to retrieve a direction that might have been lost. He punches in the question in desperation without expecting a response: *How do I get inside this infernal program?*

To his amazement the monitor actually responds and words appear on his screen: *You are inside the infernal program.*

The program has a sense of humour, muses Cephren surprised. He realises excitedly that it must indeed be the Synaptic Memory Chip. He rises to the challenge by playing along: *But I can't get into the shadow. How do I get into the shadow?*

The monitor responds with a question: *What is a shadow?*

Strange, thinks Cephren. It even asks a question. So he punches in: *A shadow is what we term an inaccessible document or program. Please let me into the inaccessible documents. Do you have inaccessible documents? And how do you ask questions? And why not before now?*

The response: *no.* Then after a pause: *no comment.* Then: *no one ever asked.*

Cephren tries another tact; he writes in: *Is there a passkey, code key, password or some such fun and games?*

The response: *yes.*

An enthused Cephren punches in: *What is it then?*

The response: *This program is not programmed to know, use, or receive the key. It is advisable however, not to tamper internally with the chip or program because the contents will dissolve.*

Cephren bows his head in dejection. He lamely asks: *How does one use the key if you don't receive it, use it or even know it?*

The final response: *The program is the key. The key is the program.*

Great. Great, thinks Cephren, this damned program is a mind game. He punches in: *I don't play mind games!*

No response.

He punched in: *What must I do?*

No response.

Have you lost your voice?

No response.

Cephren stands up again, goes out of the sliding glass door and walks around the parapet to the west side. A steady breeze helps to clear his head. He looks up at the beacon on the peak. A high-speed guerilla emop comes out of the sky and circles about silently. Its underside glows that bluish corona emitting for split seconds the spent epic (electromagnetic pulse inhibitor charge). The emop signals by dipping at him; it is Cleo. She then angles her machine down to her western bay beneath him at her condo and disappears inside. Cephren goes back inside without sitting down. He stands there and wonders whether he has made any progress.

The program had said it was the key, but that it didn't have any access to it – an oxymoron. He considers then that the owner of the key knew what to do with it because . . . mindgames. Mindgames from the 21st century, the secret West, which now was actually a requisite psychology course in the university (Great Blue U.) *The Secret History of the Pre-Asteroid West* covers all the misapprehensions from the Elizabethan times through Shakespeare, the American and French revolutions, Napoleon, the Industrial Revolution, the First, Second and Third World Wars, Cold War Politics, Vietnam, the Kennedy assassination, Islamic terrorism, the Perreault years, Piercemore, the suppression and dissemination of extraterrestrial visitation which is still controversial. A thought strikes Cephren: the monitor had revealed that the program was the key. It was the key. Or at least perhaps a person was the key. What person was outstanding in the accessible program? Jimmy Pidgeon. Who was Jimmy Pidgeon? Why Jimmy Pidgeon? Why a poem by Jimmy Pidgeon? Was he the key? Or maybe the dedication, thinks Cephren; it's also asking the reader to dedicate it to someone entitled to it. Cephren brings it up on the screen. This part of that page had been damaged somehow and the words were badly faded, but still visible under keen scrutiny. Cephren rereads carefully what the dedication says: *Dedicated to who is entitled to it.* Cephren had spent many intensive moments pondering this cryptic dedication. Up to then he had settled with the thought that the verse had been dedicated to anyone who understood or at least felt harmony with the strange concepts it illustrated. Contemporary English scholars mostly ignore the poem as an obscure scribble by an even more obscure poet. The only thing known about Jimmy Pidgeon is that he supposedly wrote that one enigmatic poem, which just happened to be inserted to induct numerous documentaries pertaining to the 21st century. As a willful twenty year old, Cephren had written a thesis comparing Jimmy Pidgeon to James Piercemore, the author-scientist. He claimed the idiom, phrasing and general style of the two were one and the same. However, no one took him seriously, especially having based his theory on one poem. In his studies, however, with access to all historic files in Sunsetwind and the State of Chicago (in which the city of Toronto was now situated), using his code-key, he had been able to trace a few tags on a James Pidgeon who lived in North York (a municipality within Toronto), until the year 2031, then left a forwarding address with Bell Canada to Leghorn, Box 884, Las Vegas, Nevada 89104. Furthermore, having put a trace on Pidgeon's social insurance number, he came up blank, which confused Cephren, as everybody back then had a number, even Danielle Perreault. Cephren nevertheless concluded Jimmy Pidgeon wasn't a nobody although it appeared he was literally nobody. Cephren knew that if you didn't have a number in the Secret Age there was usually a good reason for it, although no way of finding out why. Then one spring day years later came his breakthrough, after completing a university psychology course called Remote Viewing, in which psychic capacities were stimulated. Consequently, he believed he had had a vivid experience claiming to have envisioned a teenaged Danielle Perreault with a friend whom he had presumed to be Piercemore. It was a long shot, but spurred Cephren to pore over all information relating to Danielle Perreault's childhood thinking that he might have found a connection to the elusive Piercemore, and by extension to Pidgeon. He learned that she had lived in many parts of Canada at one time or other, because her step-father was a self-employed programmer who had contracts with the government and private sector. Her natural father, an apparent biker gang member had died mysteriously, presumably killed by those to whom he had been indebted. Biographies claim she had never known him, at least publicly she never revealed anything about him. Despite her mysterious past, the author of one biography written in 2056, mentions in passing numerous high schools she had attended, one of which was North York High where she had spent a full year. This was of note, as she had obviously undergone some kind of dramatic change there, because during the following year in Calgary she had become the school leader in every facet of school life and succeeded similarly for the remainder of her life. All that was known of her pre-Calgary days was that she was once quoted as saying she was a "border delinquent" and "hated life", having been exposed to its ghastly side in her difficult childhood. Cephren didn't have any information on North York High, but during his marriage to Trinny Burnamthorpe, he had been given access to more historical documents possessed by the Chicagos. After an arduous search, and much abuse from Trinny, citing his "total uselessness" and obsession with "absolutely meaningless pursuits", he did come up with the yearbook documents in the old school computer log and even the year in question, 1995-96. And to his utter surprise there at the back of the yearbook in a collage of random photos stood a sixteen-year-old Danielle Perreault with two friends both boys, one white and the other black. She and the white kid seemed together, though disregarding the camera. They were about the same height, the white kid slightly taller, both dark-haired. The boy had his hair cut short; he seemed relaxed, alert and lanky with a wry smile. Danielle had her long black hair tied in a tail; her appearance was striking with the contrast of black hair and very white skin. Her well-known features were not so apparent in the poor photo; there was a coolness missing, a mischievousness that had made her more interesting in later photos; in this one, her usual bright eyes were dulled and her face almost flaccid, though her famous beauty was still apparent. Her taut body exuded that powerful mystique even in the ill-fitting baggy jeans and sweatshirt. In Danielle and the boy, a quirky symmetry was visible; yet how well did they know each other at the time, wondered Cephren? The black kid standing next to white kid was smiling and turned toward him. They could have been buddies.

Cephren had looked for class photos in order to identify the two boys, but there were none. However, in the Herbert Akins Junior High that fed into North York, Cephren struck gold: there were much younger identical white and black boys standing in the back row of their graduating class photo. Anxiously, Cephren had read off the names. He reread them over and over not quite sure or believing what he was reading: James Pidgeon and Roderick Fleming. Cephren then went on to trace Roderick to see if there were any subsequent connections to Jimmy. What turned up was that

Roderick had lived in North York most of his life before dying in 2074. Half of his working life was spent as a Philosophy professor at Glendon College. What really convinced Cephren that Pidgeon must have been involved secretly with Perreault was what he uncovered in the paper's obituary on Fleming: there was a long article relating to his running for public office in the 2020s to the '40s and winning his seat five times. He served in Perreault's cabinet as Minister of Defence in the second and third terms, and Energy in the fourth and fifth. In the first term he worked on special projects, ranging from water export to energy and mines. Cephren noted it was unusual that a person with a philosophy background was involved in Defence and Energy. One would have thought he should have been more suited to social issues. Not only had Cephren dug up a connection between Danielle Perreault and Jimmy Pidgeon, but their mutual chum Roderick Fleming was close to Prime Minister Perreault for twenty years of public office. As a personal friend of them both, what better cover for Pidgeon to carry on his secret scientific work under the matriarchal eye of Perreault. Cephren for years up to the present time had reasoned that Jimmy Pidgeon was subsumed in the name James Piercemore as his cover. But nobody at the time knew who he was!

The traditional belief and conventional course of study had Piercemore as a penname for Maxwell Light, Danielle Perreault's personal secretary and body guard who on account of his position hid his identity to insulate Perreault from unnecessary exposure. Whole courses were devoted to Piercemore, one of the greatest scientists who ever lived, not to mention his poetry, plays, novels, and even paintings and music. He was the 21st century's renaissance man, a model of Leonardo da Vinci, but probably more so. He was credited with the invention of fusion and wrote the pioneering masterworks *Fusion and Applied Technologies* and *New Harmonics of Electromagnetic Gravitational Fields*, which sat up there with Darwin's *Origin of Species* and Einstein's *Theory of Relativity*. But then there were his literary works, novels such as: *Woman From the Crypt, Earth Tone Seven, Renée Antionette, Mount Serious, The Race Machine, Politica*

Prophylactica, Amore in Nero e Bianco, Coq au Vin, The Pleidian, The Cocktail, Picnic In Algeria and reputedly his greatest work, *In the Universe* a thousand paged pseudo-biblical tome about almost everything. And of course there were his poems, and his paintings, and music. Most of his estate worth untold millions by the end of the 21st century, was given away by the Barnett family (to whom Perreault left the estate in trust) to aid organisations. But who was he? Was he really the affable technocrat Max Light, who proclaimed simply in his suicide note after Perreault's assassination that *Piercemore is dead.* Yet no one up to then even knew he had existed! That was the first the world had heard of Piercemore, but not the last: in fact, *In the Universe* and numerous other works appeared posthumously years later thanks to the Barnett family. Perreault had been a good friend of the family, as she was known to spend holidays with them years before. Some of Piercemore's works were piled neatly in CDs on a table near Light's corpse. But why was Piercemore not revealed or uncovered in real life? And why was Pidgeon erased from the record? Cephren knew he was onto something. He could feel it humming in his monitor and blowing across the Pyramid.

Cephren now reclines on his sofa thinking about Piercemore, who seemed to be saying, "Bend the rules". Then to nap blissfully with the thought that Jimmy Pidgeon must have meant *someone* rather than *anyone* being the dedicatee of his poem. That particular someone could just as well be himself, if he could only find the key.

Hardly twenty minutes of absolute blackout sleep, is abruptly interrupted by Cephren's monitor beeping. He had neglected to redirect any calls to his reception unit and cringed in his delirium at such a rude awakening. He wouldn't have answered had it not been the nagging possibility that it was Redman again. He sleepwalks to his desk and with half open eyes that refuse to focus, speaks into the speaker an inebriate 'Yes'.

'Have we stirred the somnolent wonder of the world? Hello dear. Have I called at a bad time?'

Not only is Cephren half-asleep, but now that unmistakable sharp flashy voice of his ex-wife has abruptly invaded his sacred sleepy sanctum. There she is, as spooky as ever, emanating that mega-maniacal aura of power. Her dark hennaed hair falls gingerly down to her shoulders, her long nose pointing into his liquid mirror, and her small set mouth hiding little rabbit teeth. But nothing can hide those deceptively innocent marine blue eyes that warn him only too plainly: turn it off. In a sluggish shock of the worst kind, Cephren slowly comes to his senses and the slight delay mercifully gives him a moment to recover. He reaches for the escape.

'Don't do it, Cephren.'

That voice checks his impulse. He sighs.

'Trinny. This is indeed an affront to my somnolent repose. How do I rate your time?' he says impatiently.

'By bearing with me for a moment, I have decided this day to inform you of a matter of which I believe you might have a fervent interest.' She is sincere. Cephren at least knows that.

'Fine.' He waits.

'Two things: I understand through Clem Reesor that you have found that the X13 has some buried treasure. Would you like to make a joint effort in deciphering the code?'

Cephren goes numb all over. She can see him squirm. He tries to hold his composure; this is a blatant drive for something she desperately needed. But how could she know it is something that important? How could she know? Redman and Clem Reesor hadn't any idea the X13 was even a chip. Cephren resolved that she was making an inquiry to see if he had made any discoveries, an intuitional trick.

'It seems funny, Trinny, that you make an inquiry, out of the blue, after at least three years of incommunicado, about something you always considered "a waste of time".'

'That was before Resonant Scanners.'

'What could you possibly be looking for in a chip from the 21st century?' he asks attempting to turn the tables as he was coming fully to his senses.

'Buried knowledge, what else? Pidgeon must have had more secrets up his sleeve than ten Houdinis. Clem and I have an understanding. We seek more light. I just hope in the spirit of the Earth Federation, free and easy access to knowledge is still of paramount importance to little Sunsetwind. Is it not?' She smiles cynically showing those little character teeth. Her hypocrisy among those close to her is notorious.

'What makes you think Jimmy Pidgeon had anything to do with this chip?'

'Oh come on Cephren; you have the synaptic memory chip. Everyone knows it.'

'Of course I have the chip. We've had it for decades; it's just that we never knew what was really in it, and may never know. What are you driving at, Trinny? What do you propose to share, or why a "joint" effort?'

'I thought you'd never ask. We have a B480, and according to Mr. Reesor a very important chip, next best to yours; it's a Washington chip – NSA, Cephren love, from the old days, a full shadow so-to-speak dated early 22nd century. Mr. Pidgeon was held in some esteem. We don't know exactly what he did, but as a result, some policy directives seem to have held him still accountable over half a century after his death, which for your information, they reveal was in 2047, the same year Perreault was assassinated. Do you parlay?'

Cephren, who already knew when he died, deliberates a moment to negotiate an exit. On one hand he is surprised something had turned up about Pidgeon, and on the other, the cat is out of the bag regarding his chip; and there is no way in hell she would ever get inside his chip. It occurs to him he would have to think like Pidgeon to get into it. She knows something about Pidgeon and in fact had derided him about it; but was there any connection to Piercemore? Did it matter?

'I don't think we have anything to work with, Trinny,' he says. 'These chips will self-destruct if tampered with an atomic probe. A "joint" effort would be of no use, certainly impractical, and we do have an agreement, remember? In fact, an EF Judgement specifies a no contact clause.'

'Other than something pertaining to our security.'

'Our security? What threatens our security? A 21st century chip? It's redundant.'

'Is it? And how would you know?'

'I am assuming it has no bearing on today's world.'

'Do aliens have any bearing on today's world?'

'Good question; that, I don't know.'

'Well, if I must enlighten you, Cephren, and your plodding ways that so infuriate me, according to our B480 they certainly exist and by all accounts the NSA had their hands full having expended much time and expertise to deal with them. It is frustrating we have only pieces of the picture and policy directives for secret containment etc. – the recycling bin for public inquiry – without the nitty gritty.'

'How did Jimmy Pidgeon die?' asks Cephren.

'They don't say, only that he'd been taken care of; it seems he ran afoul of the authorities.'

'Any word about Piercemore?' probes Cephren carefully, half expecting a sarcastic response.

'Piercemore. What does he have to do with this?'

'Just curious, Trinny.'

'There's no mention of Piercemore. Now he's redundant. But, I have a question for you: what of your recent relationship with the Chinese?'

'The Chinese?'

'O'Reilly's Muslim Chinese.'

'That's his business.'

'And ours.'

'So what?'

'He dictates what he terms the Kush, one of the largest geo-political areas in the world today: Northern India, Tibet, West China, Afghanistan, parts of Russia, and our allies the Mao Chinese feel threatened by him. Why do you deal with him?'

'You don't like the Chinese; do you Trinny?'

'The Mao are our friends.'

'Can't we all be friends?'

'Just answer my question Cephren, please.'

'We are free. O'Reilly is not the monster everyone believes him to be. His people are hopelessly backward. We sold them technology for minerals.'

'Aren't you forgetting something – arms.'

'We don't need arms, yet; or do we, Trinny?'

'Don't even think about it.' She smiles.

'Are you assuming we deem you a threat?'

Trinny breaks out laughing in her debauched way. 'I hear the Kush is a wonderful place to visit,' she comments facetiously.

Cephren recalls his exotic trip there last winter. O'Reilly had a number of young women waiting on Cephren for his personal care. Cephren, somewhat surprised, had declined their help and privately criticised O'Reilly for his callous treatment of his subjects, which O'Reilly thought was the funniest thing he had ever heard. He remarked Cephren was insensitive to send the girls away when they were specially chosen, as they felt shamed. Cephren, therefore, took them all hiking in the foothills of the Himalayas, and said the one who could best keep up with him could stay as his companion while he was there. The girls immediately became excited and rose to the challenge, but along the trails it turned out he was the first to drop. A tragedy was averted and they all became friends.

'Fine. I would . . .'

'I should hope so, by all accounts,' cuts in Trinny shaking her head flippantly. 'Five virgins?'

Cephren couldn't be bothered to get drawn into that one, but it irked him somewhat on account of her sarcastic accusation that the one young woman he did actually sleep with wasn't even virgin. Besides, they had been intoxicated by an exotic punch.

'Trinny, I would like to thank you for your interest in my affairs, but really, I don't think there is any way we can do a joint venture pertaining to Jimmy's Chip. Now I must say good-bye.'

'Don't you want to know the other reason I called you?'

'Not particularly.'

'It's a trump card I've always been meaning to play; I want to introduce you to . . .' She motions to someone in the room. A young boy about ten years old comes into the screen from behind and sits sullenly beside her. 'Meet Sam Burnamthorpe, and Sammy, meet your father, Cephren Path, Chairman of Sunsetwind.'

A stone silence pervades between the two liquid mirrors. Cephren, at first assumes this is some terrible hoax; well it is a shock no matter how one looks at it, but once the initial impact had penetrated and Cephren had looked as closely as possible at the sullen boy through the mirrors, he saw the resemblance, the Path eyes, dark blond hair, the shape of his face; yet he can also see Trinny's nose, an irrepressible genetic trait, he presumes. Cephren wants to shout his frustration and anger at her for doing this to him, yet restrains himself because of the obviously, at least visibly, indifferent boy in front of him. He doesn't know what to say, but the words just came out: 'Sam, how do you do?'

'Hi,' the boy says meekly.

Cephren senses the boy is not so indifferent as repressed.

'I would very much like to speak with you, Sam, but I must speak with your mother for a minute. Would you mind leaving us for a bit? Then afterwards, I would very much like to get to know you better.'

'Okay,' says Sam, as he quickly disappears.

'How could you do this to me, Trinny? How do I know he's my son?'

'Simple. I was four weeks pregnant when we parted. I never told you. And I think you know he's yours; he's a Path through and through.'

'What have you done to the poor kid? He seems depressed; has he always known me as his father?'

'Yes. I told him you had gone away and would not be coming back because your position wouldn't allow it. Politics, you know.'

'Has anybody been a father to the boy?'

'Of course, he's had a variety of fathers who are all great pals. So now do you want to cut a deal? How about his visitation in return for access to your chip, should you get into it of course?'

'It may take years, or never; are you prepared to part with him? Although, I think you should in any event; you've been very cruel and devious; I still haven't forgotten all the technology you've stolen from us. You owe us, but since we're neighbours and we've learned to live with you, and so long as we continue to live peaceably and freely without any more interference, including war games around us and the Neutrals, perhaps some arrangement can be reached. So we will let bygones be bygones and believe me, as I think you know, there are some here in Sunsetwind with whom I have had to pull all my formidable vested power to thwart considerable opposition to my pacifist ideology. But, yes, I would indeed like to see my son as soon as possible, and I would be willing to impart whatever can be gleaned from X13's shadow *if* it can be of use. However, I want to retain the right to withhold anything that might be used against us in a hostile way either politically, industrially, militarily or otherwise.'

'Now that wasn't so difficult, was it?' she poses obnoxiously.

'You agree, just like that?'

'Why not?'

Cephren thinks about it. It seems too easy, but he isn't about to argue that point; he is too anxious to speak with a son that he never knew he had.

'When will you send Sam along?'

'When would you like to see him?'

'How about this weekend?'

'All right,' she says.

'Fine, you drop him off and I'll return him. Now I'd like to speak to him,' asserts Cephren.

Sam is once again seated by his mother's monitor. Cephren begins by explaining to him why he had never spoken to him before. He conveys that this is the first time he had even heard he existed. Sam looks back in that repressed way saying very little, a "yes" or "no" or nothing. There is something peculiar about the boy: he definitely looks like him, but perhaps his environment suppressed his natural inclinations; a lack of positive bonding with one's 'parents' could severely curtail one's emotional character. Furthermore, Trinny Burnamthorpe was an autocrat of the old school; only strict adherence to the chain of command was tolerated. Her world is really a viper's nest of intrigue and corruption. The poor boy must have seen and heard everything. He might be inadvertently dangerous like a pawn to be played. Cephren has to meet him and see if he is for real. It is a well-known fact that the Chicagos have refined genetic engineering to an art. They have created whole classes of individuals, some for combat, some as bureaucrats, some as breeders etc.; they even went so far as to sell their people for specific jobs around the world. An Earth Federation injunction had prohibited this practice, but there was no way to enforce it. The trade leverage was just too lucrative. Even O'Reilly al Khazzami for his chauvinistic and Emperor-style rule is very much opposed to the Chicagos though perhaps to ingratiate himself to Sunsetwind for their lucrative trade agreement. The great flaw, of course, is that the genetic prototypes (genos) for all their strength and intelligence were devoid of solidarity and had to be told what to do. Free genos around the world, however, had put together an association to curb further slavery as they called it. The cause had been organized by a runaway Breeder named Impala who lived in East Africa and had risen to rule the entire Horn, comprising old Kenya, Ethiopia, Somalia and Tanzania. Cephren knew him well and held him in some esteem. Years later, Impala actually apologised to Cephren after Trinny had been unfaithful to him, because he had been one of her lovers. Cephren knew the man must have had integrity to approach him. When Trinny requested a lover, one did his or her best to be acquiescent, or else be sold "down the river" is the euphemism. There are many regions all over the world that gladly purchase technical people. A hundred and fifty years before, even Sunsetwind had traded in this way. But in those days people sold themselves to the highest bidder. Knowledge and information was power, power was security and security gave one a high standard of living in a dangerous time when the infrastructure of the early feudal states was thin indeed, where going hungry and even starvation was a fearful blight on the psyche.

At any rate, poor Sam has to be shunted over for better or worse. Cephren must do his best to reassure him that his welcome was long overdue and that he would have the time of his life in Sunsetwind, the home of his ancestors. Sam simply shrugs and says, 'Okay' in a Tiny Tim consumptive-like tone. He comes across as so pathetic, Cephren wants to just reach out and comfort the little fellow.

Cephren sits stunned at his console when Cleopatra, his tiger-hearted sister, softly pads in. She comes up to him and puts her arm around his shoulder. He can feel her gentle touch and the vibrant energy that flows beneath it. Cleo is a Ninja woman, all action; her idol is the great Bruce Lee, whose cheap B films still abounded keeping alive his spirit; she even looks a little like him except her hair was brown and complexion lighter, though not so light as Cephren's. She is strong, sinewy and supple, only thirty-three years of age, and stands 170 cm and weighing close to 55 kilos. Cleo's features are hard whereas Cephren's are soft. Her eyes, smaller and brighter have the same angularity over the strong but stout Indian nose and naturally ruby-red lips. Cleo is the eyes and ears of Sunsetwind and she has in her impulsive way admonished Cephren more than once about his 'old world' attitude regarding security. During the past century, Sunsetwind had been predominantly a peaceful, charitable country – once the Horror saw some light, after more than a hundred years of horrible strife and usurpation due to feuding powers – yet only in the last decade has the need for greater security arisen, resisted by those whom believe in a better world, which Cleo feels is tumbling imminently around them.

Cleo has created a small elite force of men and women who are in top shape and alert twenty-four hours a day; nevertheless, she knows that any concerted effort by the Chicago's with their genos and vast superiority in numbers, would spell her failure to effectively protect Sunsetwind. There is an ultra sensitive electronic invisible security system surrounding Sunsetwind that covers a swath of borderline three kilometers in depth to account for natural transgressions of old farms and winding rivers and hills that are connected to both Sunsetwind and Chicago or Anishnabe to the north. Of course, the natural barriers of the vast forests that now cover the Neutrals are the best defence; but even here land is being cleared. Traffic between most provinces, states and bio-regions (sovereign areas with autonomous farms, towns and communities having allegiances to one or more provinces or states) by footpath or emop was free and open to the extent that an increasingly serious problem arose concerning the infiltration of undesirables and criminals not welcome elsewhere or who had escaped detention or prison. In the Neutrals, Foragers are free to eke out their existence from nature or whatever came their way. Prisons are usually loosely secure, as the penalty for the most heinous crimes when they occurred (though rare in the recent past but growing with an alarming frequency), is death by instant vapourisation in the fusion incinerator after being put mercifully to sleep to avoid due episode.

Cleo's world is one in which she was caught between the knowledge of their inherent weakness in an increasingly hostile world, and the fact that they as a society are simply not mentally prepared, nor even capable of doing much about it; the people are just too complacent. The relative utopia of the past two centuries appears to have ingrained a genetic improvement in the human temperament, and any reversion to a more cruel and militant society was seen as the most degrading and humiliating, if not impossible change. Cleo is a devolutionist, one who believes for all their good intentions only chaos and deprivation are the end products of humanity, hence her vigilance.

Cephren raises his head and put his arm around his sister's waist. 'Cleo, we have a problem; it seems that we are getting an even greater rash of problems these days. You are not going to believe what I have found out, on a couple of counts . . . '

Cleo disengages herself from him and casually extends herself across his divan. 'Cephren,' she interrupts quietly, 'I thought I was the purveyor of ill tidings; what is it?'

'I just got off the monitor with our 'friend', Trinny Burnamthorpe; she claims I am the natural father of her son, Sam Burnamthorpe, whom, I gather was four weeks incubated when we separated almost ten years ago. The poor boy, with whom I also spoke briefly, seemed timid and is going to visit us this weekend. I have . . . '

'Wait a minute, Cephren! Before we go any farther with this charade; you invited that bitch Burnamthorpe's son, here, without speaking to me? Are you out of your mind?'

'I know he's my son, Cleopatra; I have a son and you a nephew; he looks like me; we have a member of our family residing in the Burnamthorpe Bungalo; your nephew needs us. I think the boy is suffering.'

Cleo, with tremendous restraint, which at times was one of her cool virtues, takes a deep breath and begins to pace the room, only to stop at the north window and gaze out to Great Blue Lake. Cephren, wary of her control in view of what he revealed to her, holds his tongue for a moment to give her a moment to absorb what he had said. With a level voice in her soft tenor, with only the barest hint of emotion, she finally speaks: 'She'll twist this Cephren. I accept your judgement concerning the child, but she will twist this and you know it. This is a trap; she must have been licking her catty chops for a long time . . . poor child, he wouldn't have any idea what is going on. Cephren, we must protect our province; we cannot be drawn into a fray with Ms. Burnamthorpe until we get some assistance in the way of our own ability to protect ourselves, or at least formally ally ourselves with America who I think are strong enough to deter any hostile action, which I believe must be in the works, or she would not have any interest in giving you your due time with your son, if he really is your son. You know what the Chicagos have done with genetic technology. They're perverted; you know I've told you their new geno prototypes are part silicon, for nature'sake.'

Cephren sighs. He knows all too well what they are about: hegemony and dominion.

'In return,' he continues unfazed, 'she wants Jimmy's Chip, at least what's in it,' says Cephren, subdued to the common sense of his sister. 'I agreed, because there's nothing in it that we know of any value, in terms of technology . . .'

'What on earth could she want with Jimmy's Chip? It's full of historical documentaries from centuries ago!' she utters incredulously, her demeanor uncoiling slightly. 'And the Pidgeon poem,' she adds cynically as an afterthought.

'She also claims the aliens are definitely here according to a B480 they cracked.'

'What else is new?'

'I met with Redman today,' says Cephren, now standing and going to the window before facing Cleo. 'He called for me to come and see him. I obliged him of course; his requests are not to be denied, as you know. At any rate, he told me about Clem Reesor of the DVI; newly affiliated with California by it's allegiance.'

'Yeah, sure, Resonant Scanners; I've heard of him.'

'Well, you're more up on some things; anyway, you can now scan old chips for shadows and echoes which indicate the presence of more information beneath the surface that we never knew to be there. Jimmy's chip is apparently the only surviving chip we have with a large echo and subsequent shadow. Clem claims to have or had one, which may still be intact; you know the self-destructing programs of many of those chips if tampered with . . .'

'Where is the chip now?' demands Cleo.

'In my Mars 2.'

'We must hide it; it's too valuable not to; I insist, Cephren. Trinny wants it so bad she's pawning her own kid to get it. This is our ace. We will control her with Jimmy's Chip,' says Cleo with regained coolness and authority.

'Now wait a minute, Cleo; nothing is going to happen to us; this isn't war . . .'

'Oh, that's where you're wrong, Cephren; this *is* a war that is heating up so fast we won't know what hit us. Don't appease the Chicagos.'

'Then, how could we hide the chip and protect Sunsetwind if they're planning to come in anyway? I think you're being too alarmist.'

'This is her way of inveigling some pretext to invasion, Cephren,' she states flatly.

'Invasion!' retorts Cephren. 'Now you're paranoid.'

'Am I?'

'Do you really think their war games in the Neutrals are just exercises? Through all history those kinds of dictatorships always mobilize for war. The first thing we must do is hide the chip, perhaps implant it.'

'Listen, I'm not going to implant it,' he declares adamantly.

'Who said we should implant it in you?'

'I'm not giving my chip to someone else. This chip belongs to me. If it has to be implanted, a big *if*, I will be the implantee.'

'Then we shall have to devise a plan to get you out . . .'

'Get me out? Cleo, let's just back-track here; I think you are going a little overboard.'

Cleo summons a response: 'I'm not going far enough, Cephren; we stand here at the threshold of a new era and Sunsetwind may not be on the map in the near future. You're going to see the whole bio-region of the Great Lakes from Superior to Great Blue with C-H-I-C-A-G-O spelt across it. Call me a hawk, but I know this to be true! I came here because Chromolox called me, but I was coming anyway. Do you know what I saw today? War games in the Neutrals of the southern Kawarthas, in the forest of Peterborough; in fact, they were blowing up ruins and trees and even some of the Foragers who happen to be in the way, those genos – big bastards with lasers. They were making planks out of two hundred year old maples while they were shooting at each other, even killing each other, the morons. After it was over, I walked through some of the destruction. The Foragers were already collecting anything of value that was left. I left as they were burying their dead! The Chicagos are *Trashies* all over again! *Cephren! Do you read me?*' Her whole body is shaking in pent up frustration.

The outburst leaves both of them momentarily shocked. Cephren lowers his head and sighs. Tears come to Cleo's eyes. Chromolox suddenly appears from the lift. She stands there a moment; the room is animate with an emotional charge. She smiles and enquires: 'Are we not a happy family today? There is *something* in the air. Cephren? Cleo?'

When they don't answer immediately, Chromolox's smile fades. She understands that no sibling trifle could have transpired here. She knows it to be the nightmare they have all neglected to address seriously. This was the beginning of the end of the world.

two Hullabalooza

Resigned to muse beneath a surfeit of leaves
That murmur fecklessly against the fiery sun
— Jimmy Pidgeon

'Chromolox,' says Cephren, collecting himself, 'would please you call an urgent meeting of the Board?'

'What has happened?' she asks, dismayed.

'A security matter: Trinny Burnamthorpe again and her son.'

'What son? What has she done now?' Chromolox looks at Cleo feeling a tingle go up her back.

'It may be premature,' pronounces Cleo more calmly, having regained her composure, 'but we have reason to believe the Chicagos may be planning an invasion, or at least some sort of covert action using her son.'

'What son?' she asks again.

'*You* have reason to believe, Cleo,' corrects Cephren.

'Why wasn't I informed of this?' queries Chromolox.

'The Peterborough rampage could also be a prelude to a hostile take-over, coup d'etat, or war,' continues Cleo impatiently. 'You have known about their mock battles.' She is in no mood to deal with civilian reticence to the notion.

Cleo and Chromolox are not close friends and they, to their credit, keep their respective responsibilities autonomous, although Chromolox is technically Cleo's superior; in effect they are more like equals in the ruling hierarchy because Cleo has the benefit of her blood. But usually, Cleo defers security issues to her without compunction. Nevertheless, Chromolox is reluctant to pull rank, yet there is no love lost between them.

'Yes, but what on earth is this all about? On the basis of her juvenile war games? Or this kid?' asks Chromolox, disbelieving.

'Jimmy's Chip may have buried information,' says Cleo.

Chromolox looks at Cephren who is engrossed in a cloud of thought. 'That old thing?' she asks doubtfully. 'What did Redman find?'

'Yes, that old thing, Chromolox,' says Cephren coming to his senses, 'Redman discovered something in it, and Trinny Burnamthorpe wants it all; I do believe we need some intelligence in this matter, as difficult as that may be for us . . . '

'Would someone be so kind as to explain to me what in the world is going on?'

'Chromolox,' interjects Cleo, 'we will, but first let's convene the Board. I believe it is urgent.'

Chromolox goes to the door. 'Certainly, but need I remind you that Ms. Burnamthorpe is an expert in provocation? We have spent considerable time and resources dealing with her intimidations.'

'There's more, Chromolox: please call the board,' demands Cleo impatiently.

Chromolox glances at Cleo then back at Cephren who looks at her with a terribly worried expression. She turns and exits the Loft. Her usual tranquil spark is lacking. There are times when the Paths really get her fired up, but this time it is different. Who is this kid, she wonders?

Cleo goes outside for some air; Cephren follows. On the balcony facing north to Great Blue, they stand silently. The rolling hills of their cherished homeland extend beneath them from the base of the Pyramid to the water fifteen kilometers away. Villages and farms are seen scattered among the valleys and manicured fields. Only tracks and farm lanes connect the tapestry as many of the ancient roads and highways have long since been reclaimed by nature or ripped up to reforest and farm. As well, long has it been since there was any overhead electrical transmission lines, as they live in a bucolic wireless world. Forests complete the mosaic, lining the fields, hilltops, glens, and filling the swales and steep river valleys. The pastoral serenity from their vantage point makes the present crisis all the more surreal and unrelated to their cozy world.

Cephren and Cleo stand in the late afternoon sunshine. The sun is relatively high in the sky to the west and the combines are still flying; they are able to harvest the grain using their emop power, otherwise with the old fusion-powered wheel types the ground would have been too wet in places from the early morning thunder storm. The hot, dry west winds that day had sufficiently dried the standing grain. Both Cephren and Cleo can feel the strain in their hearts and knots tighten in the pits of their stomachs. Cleo's sudden revelation had profoundly affected the both of them. And Cephren realises that he has had his head in the sand.

'Maybe I mistook a revolution,' comments Cephren, 'yet I knew something was in the air. Now we must surf or crash. I apologise for being such a fool.'

'Cephren, should we be surprised? The teacher is history. Over and over civilisations who let down their defences have been invariably destroyed or overrun by a conniving neighbour, either economically, politically, or martially, or all of the above. And you're no fool.'

Cephren hesitates to respond; he feels a swelling in his chest, for his ideals and that of Sunsetwind seemed to hang in the balance. Then softly with the strength of conviction, he utters the words that he himself needed to hear. 'I feel we are an advanced culture here, Cleo, and I will not see that demolished or impaired in any way. The spirit of our enlightenment must prevail at all costs. It has taken centuries since the Horror – which too many people have callously written off as a merely lamentable episode in our history – to emerge blessedly and achieve the greatest harmonizing of humanity and nature ever known. We have even shed the perversities of religious fanaticism, because we have sought the highest calling of scientific truth. It is this truth that succeeds with reality, not a brainwashed piety (as blissfully ignorant as that may seem to be) polluting our senses and closing ones eyes to the real universe. Sunsetwind is our living entity and reflects our highest selves rather than gods that we had traditionally feared to emulate. Charity, truth, knowledge and service to wisdom have expiated mythical idolatry and biblical parochialism which promoted ignorance. This is fundamental to the way most of us perceive life in Sunsetwind and it sets us apart; and that's what casts us above and beyond backward countries like the Russias and Mississippis and needless to say, the Chicagos with Trinny's religious hypocrisy. She once called Sunsetwind the "death of passion": nothing could be farther from the truth. Our passion is love of life and search for truth as spelled out in the *Sacred Stones* established by her own ancestor, Elias Burnamthorpe, and ours, David Path the Younger as well as Yellow Tooth himself. Her brand of passion seems to equate with power and manipulation. Some people in the world think us heathen because we celebrate universal existence under a non-denominational subtitle! Oh woe betide their spiritual stupidity.

'Cleo, we must stand by our principles and yet not attempt by force to provoke or attract conflict. The world is a better place in spite of the many disparities and I believe our allies would stand by to see such a torch bearer of higher ideals be knocked down: America for one.'

'That's where you're wrong, Cephren. Everything you say is correct; I agree with you on every point, even the 'non use of force' you promulgate, because we have not much of a force to use. But where I disagree is where the world stands. The Earth Federation hasn't any mandate except through the International Court, which is supposedly upheld by powerful countries like Chicago; nor does it have the power to prevent hostile takeovers. Look at O'Reilly al Khazzami: no one stops him from invading another region or autonomous province though in fairness hopelessly backward. The Chicagos are no different; they would simply say: we seek to "harmonize relations" or "consolidate business interests". Then the lawyers establish some legal framework. We can yell and scream, but it's not even in our nature to do that! Most of us would humbly submit as long as our world remains for the most part intact – in the spirit of research: science, space, and the philosophy of life: the food and wine, entertainment, luxury to love in peace, and all the accoutrements of Sunsetwind except for us personally, of course. It's you and I who have most to lose. We must reconcile ourselves to that fact. We don't want to let our people die for us!'

'Nobody's going to die on account of us,' says Cephren sternly. 'Sunsetwinders will die, if need be, for Sunsetwinders! I know I am a pacifist, but over my dead body will Trinny Burnamthorpe steal our province! Enough hypothesizing! Enough proselytizing! Enough wind-bagging! I am going to stand for affirmative action! If Sam Burnamthorpe is my son, he will be welcome here and we will work something out. If Sam Burnamthorpe is a pretext to invasion, so be it: we will resist, in the forests, in the towns and cities, in the lakes, wherever we can!

'I will carry on out of great curiosity my research into Jimmy's Chip, implanted or not, until I find out what's in it, and also what seems to have captured the imagination of Trinny Burnamthorpe. But you know, I think we're missing something there. How could she take such an interest in the chip unless she knows something we don't? Cleo, I want you to take your emop and pick up Redman. He knows Clem Reesor who may know more; in fact, with Redman we can call Reesor with the Board present and meet him for ourselves to perhaps find something out.'

'I'm on my way. And Cephren?'

'Yes.'

'I'm glad we had this talk.' Cleo then pecks him on the cheek and spins on her heels. Cephren watches her round the corner of the rampart. Then he turns to again watch the harvest.

Seated around the council table sits all of the Board except the Trade executive, Seven Moons, who is in Europe and LeRoy MacGregor for Agriculture who is on his way from the busy harvest. Cephren sits at the head of the oblong, maple wood table. To his right is Chromolox, the President; on his left is Cleo and next to her going around clockwise are Mita Waterman for Health, who at fifty-nine is the top surgeon and diagnostician with experience in world herbology, as well as homeopathic drainage. She is slight of build with long, beautiful grey hair kept in a ponytail. Her face and general elan remain youthful and alert. Cephren has always been infatuated with her; he really likes her glib coolness. To her left sits Seymour Psabo of Culture who oversaw entertainment, sports and travel. He is a short, strong pugnacious sort with a beard and jolly features. As a well-known personality and former hockey player, he had made a great stir by capturing the hand of Sunsetwind's internationaly acclaimed artist, Strange Honey, who sometimes accompanied him to the meetings and had three daughters: Season, Reason and Treason from an earlier marriage. Their father, Dick Honey (one of Cephren's best friends) had died tragically in an emop accident when his children were small. Seymour was a wonderful replacement, and all Dick's children love him. He plays Santa Claus every Christmas. Christmas is held on December 25, but no longer to celebrate the birth of the Christ, Yeshu David, whose birthday was discovered to be March 1, 7 BC, but rather the advent of the Festive Season, which continues into the New Year. In the new calendar January 1st begins at the winter solstice. Consequently, April 1st for the spring equinox, July 1st for the summer solstice, and October 1st the fall equinox, was deemed to be the natural way to divide up the year and seasons.

To Seymour's left sits Bill and Yani Deerhill a dynamic young couple in their early thirties who had been elected to the prestigious Education and Research portfolio on a strong recommendation from Redman. They are a perfect couple who not only resembled each other, but have what Olivia Lee calls a karmic signature in their composite astrology. Each has blond hair and tanned complexioned, and sometimes referred to as "the twins". Yani is not a native born Sunsetwinder, but moved from Lebanon at birth, her parents both Sunsetwinders. Beside them to their left at the other end of the table is the indomitable powerhouse of Logistics and Engineering, Vince Fuchs. "Rhymes with Fox," he invariably says when his name is pronounced incorrectly. Behind his back, detractors call him the more vulgar connotation of the word. At any rate, Vince has an attitude: he is sarcastic, brilliant, pragmatic and knows it. He has good looks and health for his fifty-two years and uses them rigorously. He had been married once and divorced once and on the prowl ever since. Usually clever, voyeuristic women attracted him and those who treaded his turf were not disappointed, but more often chagrined at his polymorphic philandering. Yet for his shortcomings, Vince is the genius behind the phenomenal advances made in emop technology over the past twenty years. His hard titanium-bismuth-chromium alloys and electromagnetic pulse viscosities are the most coveted anywhere. Emop stability, manœuvrability and speed are fast approaching a whole new dimension in Special Projects. To his left coming around toward Chromolox is Seven Moon's empty place and to the left sits Gabriella, the executive for Law and Sovereignty. She is a black buxom woman who stands for fiduciary purity in every way: she has a deep resonant voice that usually makes people accept her judgments without question. She is never wrong, and if the evidence does not measure up, she was a staunch defender of rights. Her office also issues passports and presides over immigration. To Gabriella's left sits Olivia Lee, the Senior Psychiatrist in many ways. Of Chinese-American descent, she has long legs, long black silky hair, and is a little older than Chromolox, her loyal friend. She has soft eyes and expressions and smiles easily. If there is such a thing as a pontiff for Sunsetwind it is she, or rather more a bodhisattva. And last to complete the circle is the empty place held for LeRoy MacGregor, the litterateur-farmer, who as the executive in charge of Agriculture, is deemed a key pillar of the province. (The cruel history of the Horror had embossed into the general Sunsetwinders's consciousness the crucial necessity for a strong food-producing infrastructure.) LeRoy is the organic purveyor from heaven. His huge department oversees a year-round supply of everything from traditional staples like meats, grains, fruits and vegetables to olive oils and condiments, including tropical and semi-tropical fruits grown in the massive domes on the Peninsula. His is an unrelenting responsibility, and he does it with at least a quarter of all Sunsetwinders under his general direction. So in all, there are twelve members: six women and six men who preside over the neo-feudal province. And finally to the left of MacGregor's empty seat and next to Chromolox sits Redman who in his indomitable way is immersed in a stern reverie of contemplation. Redman enjoys a special status as a non-elected member of the board.

With the exception of Cephren and Redman, all have been elected on their own merits as they moved up through the hierarchy to their present positions. Cephren, upon his father's early death had naturally assumed his position as the hereditary family member in line and took the mantle for which he had been trained from his earliest recollections. Failing him, Cleo or either of their eldest offspring would be next in line.

In that moment all those faces, even Redman's, now wait apprehensively in silence after the initial hubbub. Cephren raises his hand to begin the proceedings. Already events had spun out of proportion. He had even overheard Yani say to Vince, 'The Chicagos are entrenched in the Peterborough forest and creeping on the Kawarthas like Birnam Wood.'

'I'll remind Cleo, Yani,' replies Vince, acerbically.

Cephren assumes it is a joke.

'So Cephren,' speaks out Seymour brightening, 'Ms. Burn and Warp has thrown down the gauntlet, has she?'

'It seems,' interjects Vince, 'we should have invested in some old-fashioned hardware. I recall being given the cold shoulder on that one. Cleo, you know what I mean.' Vince had been snubbed by Cleo whenever he hit on her and everyone knew it, to the point it had become a rather humourous matter of quid pro quo. As such, Cleo permits herself to upbraid him unmercifully after he had seduced most of her friends.

'I recall, that was the one time we actually agreed, Vince,' quips Cleo cheerfully. 'Listen up, everyone,' she goes on seriously, 'we have a suicide mission here, any takers? All you have to do is get inside the Bungalo and find out what they are planning against us? Now let's hear Cephren.'

Everyone laughs at Cleo's saturnine humour, and whether in relief or nervousness is anyone's guess.

'You're killing me with suspense; get on with it!' grunts Redman speaking in his typical taciturn voice and glinty eye.

'I thought I would let Cleo make a speech,' announces Cephren, 'but in deference to Redman and his famous hearthstone wisdom, I shall proceed myself. Please relax. Let me recapitulate the rumors into one concise dose of reality. In a nutshell, Trinny has informed me I have a ten-year old son, Sam Burnamthorpe, whom I have just met briefly on the monitor; and in exchange for visitation she has demanded that I give her access to Jimmy's Chip or the mythical X13, as it's now generally known, presuming it's the real one. Most of you all studied its contents during your level one history courses at university. Am I correct in assuming that?'

There is a general nod around the table. They all seem to be leaning Cephren's way wondering what on earth he is getting at.

'What do three hundred year old documentaries have to do with the threat of an invasion by the Chicagos?' asks Gabriella.

'I'm sure you have asked that for everyone, Gabriella. And that is the very thing we don't know. But first, there is no invasion that we know about and secondly, I can tell you that this morning Redman asked me to visit him regarding this very X13 chip. By using this new Resonant Scanner that Clem Reesor of the Death Valley Institute . . . '

'What's a Resonant Scanner?' interrupts Mita Waterman quickly. She looks intently at Cephren, her eyes always penetrating.

'A Resonant Scanner is a kind of laser device set up in a satellite that maps out a sector of the sky using variant electrons, then positrons, which annihilate one another in a matter-anti-matter sweep; then the process is repeated and the residuals of the first sweep show up somehow in retentive neutrino ripples which indicate through the conversion rate the basis to make resonant calculations; am I right Redman?'

Redman nods his head approvingly. Having arrived before the others, Cephren had been given by him a more thorough briefing on resonance after Cleo and Chromolox had informed Redman personally of the "crisis".

'This scanning device having been used for a number of years amassed millions of statistics. Over time, patterns emerged; experiments were conducted and conclusions drawn – some with uncanny accuracy with emop tuning and weather, for example. By certain fluctuations, it was calculated that storms and severe weather were easily forecast months in advance by repetitive levels that crescendoed and patterned out. Soon, they may be able to manipulate weather, depending on the landmasses involved. Anyway, Reesor adapted this technology to scan computers for viruses and other anomalies, one being old computer chips, to test their health or impairment in such a way that wouldn't permit tampering or cause them to self-destruct like those extremely sensitive B400s. He has been quite successful. He discovered that in many of the old B-types, echoes and shadows seemed to indicate there was more to the chip than previously known. He knows this because he managed to break into a B480 U.S. government bond chip circa 2100 – an apparent lesser cousin to the supposed mythical synaptic memory type with 'liquid crystal' all in one memory and drive still as yet unverified – that revealed much about the super-secret space research program in the United States. We don't know much about this chip, only that Clem Reesor has said our very own Jimmy's Chip, the X13, could be the very liquid crystal synaptic memory chip referred to. Unfortunately, I just learned from Redman that we may never get into this chip because it was made virtually inaccessible to anyone but the original owner who possibly had some genetically engineered custom made DNA codekey, meaning it could have been an implant.

'Anyway, Redman scanned the X13 and it was discovered to have a huge echo and subsequent shadow indicating, according to Clem Reesor, "buried treasure", as he puts it, or simply a motherlode of inaccessible information.' Cephren stops there to drink some water. Others, as if on cue, do the same.

'What's the connection to Trinny Burnamthorpe?' asked Vince, beside himself with excitement.

'Somehow through Clem Reesor, she knows about the significance of our X13 which means she knows Redman had scanned it with this Resonant Scanner,' says Cleo.

'Where do I get one?' demands Vince.

'If I may be so bold as to take the table for a moment,' speaks out Redman, 'I do believe that's the principal reason I'm here, Vince; and I can certainly lend you the one I have. The priorities, must therefore be to find out: one, what is the connection between Ms. Burnamthorpe and Clem Reesor? And two, how it can be regarded as a threat to us, when we don't know what the hell's in that damn X13, if it is the synaptic memory chip –which I think likely in view of its origins?' Redman clears his throat and looks about the room for dissenters. 'And thirdly, if beyond reasonable doubt, Ms. Burnamthorpe is up to something, what in God's name can we do about it? Thank you, Cephren; now could you switch on the overhead monitor; I think it's time to call Clement.'

'What's his code?' asks Cephren, his fingers ready at the council monitor. Redman pulls out his pocket monitor.

'ClemDVI,' Redman states.

The screen in the wall behind those on Cephren's left comes alive. The DVI satellite comes into sight, at least a portion of it. The giant earth radiates below its intense blueness, but no Clem.

'He's been beeped,' says Redman. 'It sometimes takes a while for him to respond.'

'Well, meanwhile, shall we field some ideas, input or sarcasm?' pipes Chromolox. 'You know, we've been here before with the same tension regarding Ms. Burnamthorpe. On the up side, I don't believe she has the guts to do what we fear most.

'And remember, she has common ancestry who also survived the Horror due to our mutual charity and trust. Then again, on the down side, she has been warped considerably over the last decade, which I think has made her pathologically power mad.'

'Her biotechnically implanted cast system has destroyed her credibility,' says Bill Deerhill, 'not to mention these new part silicon prototypes. The Earth Federation has denounced the use of biotechnics in humans except for medical reasons, which she wantonly disregards, although she's not the only offender; most just don't admit it. Nevertheless, we should definitely have the support of the majority of sovereign countries and seek a non-violence injunction.'

'I believe she suffers from delayed paranormal paranoia,' said Olivia in her quiet relaxed way. 'Her mobilisation of technobiotic armed forces is really a time bomb ready to blow up in her face, unless she uses and controls this unharnessed energy with extreme caution. In my opinion, we should take every precaution. In other words, we are now living next door to a psychotic. Furthermore, her professed religious sanctimony is completely in character with paranormal disorder. When will she go over? I think perhaps she has. These provocative war games are proof.'

'Wow, that's optimistic!' says Seymour. 'Anymore positive ions? Hey, if we're the sitting ducks, why don't we strike first: let's spike her ventilation with helium! Better still we'll start a revolution! How about turning her genos on to sex, drugs and rock n' roll? You know, like in the twentieth century! Tune in, drop out sorta thing.'

'I think maybe you have a point there, Seymour,' speaks out Gabriella, humourously. 'With an Earth Federation wink, we could infiltrate their biotechnic operation and sabotage their geno production with time-released LSD!'

The members of the board are not particularly in high spirits and fail to laugh but smile, except Redman who lets loose a few childish peals. The sobering reality, however, is a well-known fact that the Chicagos have dominated human achievement in many areas, for instance, sports. For the last six years because of their biotechnics, six Stanley Cups in hockey, six World Series, six Hoop titles and six Super Bowls in football were won among other events; it was something never done before by any region, state or country anywhere. The Sunsetwind Storm had won the Stanley Cup for the last time seven years before thanks to the great Johnny Fish who retired the that year and moved back to Anishnabe from where he originated. There is some animosity towards Chicago, because they had turned sports from a strictly entertainment business back to a serious take-no-prisoners undertaking, as it was in pre-asteroid times.

'And who might so infiltrate?' asks Cephren. 'Who could get into Chicago today and return with impunity?'

'Chicago's closed its boundaries to free passage,' says Cleo. 'Burnamthorpe spends most of her time at the Bungalo; she protects the place as if it's under perpetual siege.'

'Someone who's had access in the past and might not necessarily be suspicious,' says Chromolox, answering Cephren. 'Certainly, we can do something.'

'Look into it Cleo, would you?' insists Cephren. 'We need some intelligence.'

'Meanwhile, we must set up defenses,' offers Vince. 'As difficult as it may be for us to convert from a pacifist regime to a military one, what choices do we have if we wish to remain sovereign?'

'We must not send out the message of panic to either Sunsetwind or the world,' states Cephren. 'The World Symposium is upcoming on October 1, the fall equinox, which is of course the traditional Peace Day. We must eschew any show of force. Our boundaries will be open to the world, as is our responsibility. We are leaders and must show ourselves to be so.'

'Trinny Burnamthorpe, whatever she has planned,' concurs Chromolox, 'would never hold the world at ransom on such a day for the duration of the Symposium through to Canadian Thanksgiving. She needs political support. No, she would wait until later, but something must be in the works, or we wouldn't be here this evening.'

LeRoy MacGregor walks in briskly and takes his place.

'How's the harvest, Roy?' asks Mita, smiling.

'She's going well in Clearview, but Huronia and Kawartha are still too wet. From here to the Peninsula, it's coming off well. Now what's the trouble?' he enquires.

Chromolox quickly explains the situation to LeRoy. His only comment afterwards is to suggest that Ms. Burnamthorpe's forthright proposition might well be honoured. In other words, if they can access the chip, would it be so bad to give her what they found? What had they to fear from a four-hundred-year old chip? And even if it was the mythical Synaptic Memory chip, as Reesor had suggested, was it really worth the trouble to invade Sunsetwind?

'Of course it is,' plugs Cleo. 'This is just her way of saying, "Whether you like it or not, I'm coming, so get ready, fools." We shouldn't cauterize our memory. Do you all recall what she said when we came out with our new emop line in 2390? She said, "I'd love to check it out." In Paris that year our prototype was stolen. In the past three years all Chicago emops have since been refitted with our new technology.'

'Yes, that was brazen, but falls far short of invasion,' remarks Gabriella. 'And a cheap trick that many at the time relegated to marital fallout, needless to say. But I'm no pushover when it comes to our sovereignty, and I've consistently supported increased security, as you know. Foragers, Chicagos and even the occasional Anishnabe and others have trespassed illegally with increasing regularity. Our inability to take affirmative action is what makes them so bold.'

'We cannot forget the past,' says Cephren, 'and the precedence that has accustomed our tolerance. Freedom of passage has been a great liberty bestowed. Naturally, our reticence to change such an ingrained policy should be made quite clear. Yet, we do live in more complex times. There is greed and intolerance about.'

'And we shall not martyr ourselves as the sacrificial lamb of high ideals!' exhorts Cleo.

Cephren is taken aback by his sister's sudden outburst, but holds his composure. He lets Cleo take the reins on issues from time to time in deference to her loyalty to the Sunsetwind cause. Her defiance is a needed element to stir his own natural complacency. And concurrently, in this instance, he knows that she is right.

There is a general approval around the table as all vent themselves in a humdrum of voices. Cephren puts up his hand and announces, 'We will raise a modest army to protect ourselves on one condition: it will be a covert army, whose leader will be Cleopatra. Her present officers will each create their own regiments and report to her. At present, we have how many active militia, Cleo?'

'Five hundred-eight.'

'This is what we must do: pick one hundred of your best and recruit one hundred new people for each of these. We shall create a guerilla army of ten thousand. Does everyone agree?'

Assent is unanimous. Vince, however, voices some concern. 'Ten thousand guerillas will have little effect on a few hundred thousand brainwashed genos; I think we should review the strategy.' Again there is a general nod.

'The strategy is simple,' counters Cleo. 'If prevention is impossible, we will passively resist and ally ourselves with those noble nations who would support us. At the upcoming World Symposium we will make a stand for peace. Resistance, if necessary, will take the form of clandestine operations, which we have already prepared. We'll strike at the heart of Chicago. We'll have some advantage in emop mobility. Vince, how far are we away from upgrading our present systems?'

'I have one prototype being assembled as we speak, the Volcano, I call it. It may take up to a year to do the whole line; though with this Scanner, it may not be too late to make further modifications sooner.'

At that moment, the overhead monitor beeps and Clem Reesor appears. He is haggard, thin, with blue washed out eyes and wispy red-grey hair. His fair complexion is pock marked from acne in his youth.

There is a slightly disturbed expression on his face. One couldn't be sure whether he is annoyed at being interrupted from some task or is basically a worried man. He wears loose white cotton.

'This is a surprise, Redman,' he drawls in a tired voice. 'And I see you're not alone.' The monitors are two way liquid mirrors. Each side could see the other's environment. 'You know how I feel about . . . security.'

'Clem, I apologise for this sudden imposition, but I must convey to you the urgency with which we need your help. First of all, all seated here constitute the Sunsetwind Board. And they asked my assistance in a matter concerning your recent, or perhaps not so recent communication with Trinny Burnamthorpe of the Chicagos. She has just made a request to involve herself in the quest to decipher what we believe to be the X13. We would like to know whether you have had any contact with her or anybody that may have been working with her.'

'Trinny Burnamthwarpe. Quite a gal, I understand. I heard she recently signed some kinda no-hassle pact with the Mississippis. Now there's trouble. Seems to be the thing these days: no-hassle pacts. I figure if ye gotta sign a no-hassle pact, it just means ye got trouble on yer mind; and then everybody's signin' them so they don't get ostracized and stinkin' like fear. No, I don't know Miss Burnamthwarpe, but I do know she's an Omega Pointer and participated at the convention in Tahoe last year. Pardon me ladies, but she had herself a ball, if ye get muh drift.'

'Are you an Omega Pointer, Mr. Reesor?' asks Mita.

'I most certainly am . . . Miss...'

'Mita Waterman M.D.'

'Well, Miss Waterman, we are passive believers in the physical reality of omniscient life – a Hindu-Christian thing, but to a scientist, the afterlife is of utmost interest. Would you like to hear my theory?'

'Clem, pardon me, my name is Cephren Path . . . '

'Mr. Path, it is an honour, sir.'

'Thank you, Clem; first of all, I want to congratulate you on your success with your Resonant Scanner; this is an absolutely wonderful achievement.' The whole Board claps. 'Secondly, I just want to ask you whether you've revealed your findings about your B480 chip to anyone other than Redman.'

'Well, thank y'all. And yes, there are numerous people who are aware of my findings. Mostly at this institute, but some in Washington, one in Paris. You may extrapolate that. Hell, it's no secret, everybody's scannin' somethin' these days.'

'But, what about what you know, or at least what you have suggested that you believe to know about this so-called "Synaptic Memory chip", which could be our very own X13?' queries Cephren.

'The only thing I told Redman, was that in our B480 there are precisely three references to a quote-unquote "synaptic memory chip" – *a* memory chip, i.e. one, solomente, uno. We know there are numerous B-types, but only one of the synaptic type. During the late twentieth and twenty-first centuries, the U.S. intelligence had apparently obtained a number of alien space vehicles mostly from Zeta Reticula, a double solar system (two stars in close proximity), not binary, almost forty light years from here. In the specs for that craft which we have obtained through the B480, there is mention of a craft called the Meteor which duplicated the alien technology through the work of a fellow referred to as Pidgeon . . .'

'Jimmy Pidgeon?' exclaims Cephren, unable to contain his surprise.

'Could be, Mr. Chairman,' says Clem. 'But the reference is just Pidgeon.'

'Sorry for interrupting,' says Cephren. 'Please continue.'

'Well, this Pidgeon was obviously in charge of that piece of hardware. Now this is interesting, because to this day, we still cannot understand the specific electromagnetic frequencies and harmonics of that technology; yet he, this Pidgeon succeeded apparently with the help of the aliens, all according to this B480. He wrote the damn manual, but that's lost, too. There is no other reference to him; in fact, I think it's down right shabby they didn't reward him in some way; but you how it was back then – all so hush hush – a bunch o' bureaucrats. An' they did a great job in getting rid of the crafts. If we could just have one today. Everything's gone. Where did they go? I swear, they musta flew 'em away, or buried them down some dummy bunker; God, there's enough of 'em out here, hundreds of miles of 'em in fact. But I mean, after the Horror, who cared?'

'Maybe they were destroyed, so no one could get their hands on them after the Asteroid?' suggests Vince.

'Could be, you know,' says Clem. 'But I think the little freaks took 'em back.'

'What little freaks?' asks Vince with a wry smile.

'The little Greys; pardon me ladies. You know, the Reticulans, or whomever.'

Cephren and the Board can hardly contain their enthusiasm. Talk of real aliens is still considered paranoid, except among those more informed. But Cephren is more interested in the reference to Pidgeon, a very conspicuous mention tying Pidgeon conclusively to the X_13; it must have been his after all. Cephren keeps thinking: *Dedicated to who is entitled to it* . . .

Redman won't be astounded, however, at these revelations and duly presses. 'You never mentioned Pidgeon to me, Clem. Did you mention him to others?'

'I might have. Why? Do you know anything about this Pidgeon?' he asks.

Cephren plays coy. If Reesor had leaked that information unwittingly, which in all likelihood he had, any knowledge about Pidgeon might have really stirred Trinny Burnamthorpe to pay very aggressive attention to the possibilities; she knew about Jimmy's Chip and its implications, which now must spell imminent rather than possible invasion. He realises that she had inadvertently tipped him off by using her son to get at Cephren. No good would come of it, but Cephren couldn't deny his son visitation and had to go along with whatever lay ahead. The chip, therefore, has suddenly become the most powerful little weapon in history. Without it the Chicagos would never control space, or the potential technology for years to come.

'In fact, no, Clem,' interrupts Cephren smiling sheepishly. 'Not much.' He feels like a dog who knows he is bad having wolfed down a stolen shrimp or two off of a banquet table. He can feel Redman's eyes boring into the side of his head, yet thank heavens, he didn't admonish him. The truth, thinks Cephren, has tumbled. His final notion in that millisecond is that he really hopes he hadn't sunk Sunsetwind on the shoal of damnation by lying. 'Very curious, this Pidgeon,' he continues. 'I want to thank you for your time, and please keep us posted on anything that might turn up regarding access to this chip. We are at loggerheads; it is imperative.'

'Good luck. And I don't envy y'all sittin' up there in Trinny Burnamthwarpe's sights. Nice t' meet y'all.' He then reaches for his escape sensor and is gone.

Chromolox is the first to respond. 'Cephren! What an outrageous lie! How could you do that? We know now that without a doubt we have the X13. Maybe Clem can help us . . . '

'I've known hypocrisy, son, a bad influence,' says Redman. 'But well done! I'll hold my peace until we know what in hell we have here in that varmint chip!'

'Absolutely,' interjects Cleo, 'Cephren did the right thing. We don't want to advertise that we have the big enchilada. Let's pretend we are under a state of siege; and we're holding the ace. It would be suicide to reveal the escape pod . . . '

'I agree,' says Mita softly, and her timing makes everyone turn and give her the table. 'But first, I need to see a replay of Mr. Reesor. I want a zoom in on his eyes. Please.'

Chromolox does as she requests. Clem Reesor's face looms large. Focus is refined and the frame frozen. Mita walks up to his eyes and studies them with her thumb massaging her chin. She turns and sits down.

'I've seen enough,' she says. 'Turn it off.'

'What have you seen?' they ask in unison.

'Clem Reesor has an implant,' she says calmly. 'The iris lines are too pronounced from extended dilation. He either takes prodigious amounts of Mescaline or has an implant. It's probably a typical Chicago cerebral cortex prosthesis better known as a Triple-c (trip-c). It's probably an accelerator type. I'm sure most of you are familiar with it. It enhances and stimulates synaptic activity in a benign way. I have implanted them in elderly people who needed the stimulus. Another Chicago product. I think we may have solved our mystery. Trinny Burnamthorpe is one step ahead. She probably eavesdrops on his mind. He wasn't aware that he got a special package.'

'Holy hell!' exclaims Cleo. 'Then Trinny knows everything we know as we speak! She already knew that Pidgeon's poem was in that chip. And now she must know that Reesor has asked about Pidgeon . . . and knows Cephren lied.'

'She knows we have *the* X13,' declares Cephren quietly.

'On the face of it,' continues Cleo, 'but at least she's not going to advertise it; she wants it for herself, no competition.'

'Well, I've done my part,' says Redman rising out of his chair slowly. 'I think I'll get that ride back to my Hobbit hole and take my evening whisky. Cleo, dear, shall we?'

'Certainly.' She rises.

'Cephren,' says Redman in a parting word, 'Keep me informed about the chip. I think Vince or Bill may be able to assist you. Do the right thing.' And he shuffles out with Cleo on his arm.

Cephren is smarting. He always seems to fall short when it counts most. If anyone in Sunsetwind knows the value of truth, it is he, but whose truth? Redman's, Reesor's or Burnamthorpe's? He must hold his course; he feels it in his bones. If the chip is indeed the synaptic memory chip, an implant would probably be the only possible way to access it, as hard and antithetical as that may be for him, not to mention dangerous. It is no longer a personal mission, at least in the main, but a critical one with the possible future of Sunsetwind at the brink. The ace must be concealed. If he could access it, could he contain it? What powers would it unleash? Cephren looks up and sees everyone's eyes on him. They are compassionate.

Nothing needed to be said. In his own mind he is numb with elation; he had found Jimmy Pidgeon and perhaps the shadow of Piercemore. It simply has to be. He adjourns the meeting.

'Oh, ahh, Cephren,' says Vince quickly, walking out. 'Listen, call me; let's crack this bug. We'll make Trinny Burnamthorpe sorry she invaded our space. Easy, out.' He exits. Cephren shuts off the lights.

Outside, Chromolox waits. 'Do you want to see the movie?' she asks hesitantly. 'I didn't want to go without asking you after we spoke this morning.'

'Thanks Chromolox, but I think I'll pass. I need to process some of this. Anyway, my head spins.'

'The chip.'

'Yes, a fine mystery. Something I had always thought a private one, yet now involves . . . the world, or more.'

'If you are going to implant, I want you to know we're all behind you.'

'Thanks.'

She looks at him with a smile. She is radiant. For a moment Cephren thought she was going to hug and kiss him, but she turns away like she does when one gets too close. 'I'll give you a rain check,' she says to the air in front of her.

Cephren takes the lift to the Loft. He believes that Chromolox is just not the kind of woman he could be comfortable with. But he has other things on his mind.

Sept. 16/2395

Things are happening, definitely happening. I'm so beside myself with anticipation, I haven't until now been convinced, dear reader, of this phenomenal
piece of work: Jimmy's Chip must be an alien chip! It has to be! Everything I
intuitively felt is coming true. I have a feeling nothing will ever be the same on
account of it. But should I bring it up at the World Symposium? I think not,
just yet. I need more information. Besides, the Chicagos are ready to kill for
it. I must be very careful. Everyone smells its authenticity.

   To the day, two weeks to the World Symposium. I can't seem to get it off
my mind: so many things, like my speech to the world. Poetry is the only thing
I can read at night to calm my nerves. I read from Flower Child's great work:
Maidenhead. Various lines never fail to haunt me . . . pluck me, pluck
me not...I tempt the dandelions springing from your grave . . .
you still live in me, but I must love again . . . spring water I drink
freshly bled from the mortuary earth . . . the world grows in me a
vacuum of necessary sin . . . clinging dizzily to the tendrils of your
body's fire, I abandon in the quickening . . . friend, let us harbour
hope for the haunted children . . . nature revels in my super-eye,
but I reserve my astonishment . . . my assignation with spirit has
been submitted to the sky people, they pity me as I pity myself . . .
I must live . . . the unspoken is my maidenhead . . . they are in me,
these feelings, that speak of wonders beyond the arc of the sun . . .
Her varying images and twisted meanings make sense to me. Otherwise,
anything straight forward from journalism or prose is lost on me these days –
my concentration fails.

   Did spend an interesting evening last night on the Peninsula at LeRoy's
place on Lake Huron. I had a great ride on LeRoy's chestnut gelding, along
the beach too. He and his wife Lena then cooked up a feast: marinated lamb
with mango chutney and yoghurt, wild greens with a Nuits St. George Burgundy '79 and for dessert, pureed chestnuts with maple syrup and vanilla and
Amaretto whipped cream. Friends of theirs from India were staying too,
Jamal and Hani Barimjee. Very deep. Seemed to understand our situation.

They made the suggestion we ally ourselves more closely with America, for they have "a big agenda" to regain their former power. My response to that was what most sovereign states promulgate: power is in the hands of us all. Nationalism was buried with the old order before the Horror. Yes, but these are unsettled times, he says; it is necessary to rally around a "touchstone". What touchstone? I say. The touchstone of democratic ethics. We are democratic, but nationalist democracies failed, I say; remember the 21st century: mass corruption, ignorance and hysteria begat war and destruction. They had no choice, he says, the starvation, dehydration, disease bade civilization good bye – survival of the fittest. Do you believe the Asteroid was Divine Intervention? I ask. Natural Destiny and Divine Intervention are one and the same, he says, therefore a redundant question. I laughed more in a relief of stress. They laughed too. Jamal then went on to say that the "touchstone" was a guide only. What was relevant to the founding fathers of the American Constitution, or Parliamentary democracy may not apply so conveniently today, but the "ethos" must. You above all must understand this, as a benevolent despot. That's where I took some offence. I said our Rules and Laws declare all the freedoms democracies had, the only difference being I was the referee with all of the qualifications. I cited Chromolox as an example of someone who descended from the poorest order, the Trashies, to be elected to the Presidency. I simply hold the code key to access all Sunsetwind and preside over the Board and Bank. It was incumbent upon me to represent the natural destiny. Not divine Intervention? Jamal says. Redundant, I say. We laugh again. Departing last night, I said George Washington would be at the World Symposium and we would indeed be talking. Not to worry. The Chicagos would be there too, he says. I left with the thought that he hadn't any idea what was going on. I declined to raise the issue of involving the chip and my son, Sam, in our discussions.

Sam. Sam has spent two weekends with me. All went according to plan. No complications at the prearranged pick up and drop off point in the town, Beeton, in the Neutrals between us and Chicago. I showed Sam the whole of Sunsetwind from the vantage of my emop, which he enjoyed. We gave him a medical. Mita declared he was indeed my son and free of implants and given a clean bill of health. The second weekend we spent alone on my island, The Winds, on the east side of Great Blue Lake half way up the coast. Sam would sit quietly on the pink granite rock and gaze across the blue horizon just out of reach of the big crashing swells of clear, fresh water. He talked very little, but we got along famously. He is warm physically and needed my comfort. I would put my arm around his shoulder in the kitchen and he'd lean into me. I believe he desperately wanted to stay with me. He was noticeably saddened when I took him back. The first weekend we spent almost the entire day together in the Pyramid. He was fascinated with the rock and kept going up and patting it to see how solid it was. We walked the Foyer and Atrium and had lunch under the statue of Flower Child, which depicted her as a child with flowers and her dog Roughie. I told him what we knew about the orphan, Flower Child, the founding spiritual leader of Sunsetwind and the sole survivor of her family murdered by Darabak, the notorius Trashie. I told him Flower Child was his ancestor; and only seven when she ventured alone into the woods to escape the Trashies and fortuitously found Scratch Rainbow, an old hermit. It is said that Scratch took her in because her parents were killed and she, the story goes, would not have it any other way; it is presumed she had known him already. Years later Scratch was thought to have been killed by Darabak, and Flower Child was enslaved by Darabak's trashies, but she killed them and escaped with others to start their own government. Eventually they took over the whole region and by about 2160 one of Flower Child's sons named David Path was born who was our ancestor, of course. I had to explain to Sam that Flower Child never married but had about seven children from different men. The man she really loved, someone known only as Remy, was apparently killed in one of the feuds. It is believed David Path was his son, though we're not certain. Sam then asked why Flower Child had such an odd name. I replied it was unknown who she had been originally or where she came from; there were many orphaned children during the Horror. Scratch called her Flower Child presumably because she liked to stop and smell the flowers, and the name stuck. People began to write about her long after she

had died. Sam was impressed and even commented on the fact that Flower
Child was his ancestor, though to whom everyone in Sunsetwind claimed to
have been related.

Cephren shuts off his monitor and swings around in his hardwood
swivel chair. He is dressed in his rough biking sweats. The weather is
getting slightly cooler as the weeks go by and the inevitable long winter
approaches. He takes his Strider mountain bike down the lift and
notices Chromalox and Cleo and numerous staff hectically prepare for
the Symposium and the new guerilla army. Having been briefed the day
before, Cleo reported all the officers had been chosen and were recruiting their own men and women for various positions. She also picked ten
of her very best as generals for each one thousand guerillas. Therefore,
each division would have ten captains with one hundred guerillas in
each company. Already, the guerillas had acquired the spirit of the challenge and are adding their own creative flair by naming their companies
the Hoods, Rats and Dogs, etc. Plans and counter-plans are being drawn
up for review. Cephren had spoken personally to O'Reilly, self-pro-
claimed emperor of the Kush to obtain munitions. Cephren is hesitant
to involve America or Texas or anybody but the Kush for fear of intimidating the Chicagos in their own region, nor imposing on their continental friends, at least until his people were ready to conduct a covert
war. They had also evolved a chain of command and supplied each
recruit with a bracelet monitor. Each bracelet was functional only with
the compatible genetic DNA of the original owner so it could not be
easily transferred or stolen for enemy use.

Cephren gets off at the main foyer and walks his bike to a little deli-
catessen where he purchases an avocado-provolone sandwich and juice.
He puts them in his little saddlebag to the rear and under his seat. The
owner of the shop asks him where he's going that day. Cephren says up
the escarpment.

Once on his way down the path with Blondy Boy, his husky, running happily at his side, Cephren feels such a relief to escape the Pyramid which had become so manic with preparations. The whole program, from banquet to entertainment to speeches to recreation to meetings to socials etc., was not to his liking, whereas Chromolox and Cleo and their subordinates seemed to relish the task. Many people in the lower echelons of the provincial hierarchy are very excited to host this once-in-a-lifetime event. People do not travel much, although they are free to do so, because tourism is not nearly so much an industry in the world as it was before. It is a daring adventure to go abroad where facilities to house tourists were scarce and expensive. Hotels and resorts were a luxury of the distant past, but are fast becoming a new reality. Usually, tourists stay at people's homes on exchange arrangements, or they simply camp out in their emops. There is limited international transportation. People use emops to travel but one had to be wealthy to own one, which could cost an average person's lifetime savings or credits that could only be transferable through some commodity, for instance: a service, technology, food, or mineral etcetera. Currency is also a thing of the past, although one has the opportunity to become wealthy with credit. This was achieved through service or merit, meaning, an entrepreneur could take his or her product, invention or service to the market and sell it to the highest bidder. The market was made up of various consortiums, agencies and individuals who enjoyed a type of control or share of the economy. But since the population of Sunsetwind is only a little over a million and trade with other countries, states or regions still minimal (though growing quickly) markets are limited in what they can absorb because demand is limited and wealth is something not measured in currency. Land holdings are the standard yardarm for wealth, but also noted prestige in some scientific, sports or artistic pursuit in which success was achieved. The central idea to the system is based on the ability to share wealth, because throughout the Horror, survival depended on it. Money is still used for small transactions, and coins are minted in limited amounts. In other words, one could not "cash in" their credit, but could exchange credit with whatever they can offer. The value of a sandwich was replaced with a credit towards the vendor in the bank; and there are numerous banks; this could represent a service or commodity owed and held accountable at various quarters of the year. They could be traded or deferred, or even saved up to a year. Food is the cheapest commodity and up until recently had been free. Health is considered the most important physical virtue; for example, it is deemed poor ecological management to let one's health breakdown. If it does, then one must enter a program to rehabilitate it. There is a wonderful health security net for any chronic physical or mental problem. The sick are treated as symptoms of a sick society and must be given the utmost care so they all benefit. The people are imbued with this from an early age that before the Horror most of the world was considered sick: physically, ecologically and mentally, which brought on their insurmountable apocalypse.

Naturally, of course, it had evolved that their neo-feudal system needed someone, Cephren in this case, to be sovereign and all enterprise, ownership and culture extenuated from his central authority as long as the government remained elected. His family had always been prominent since Flower Child herself ruled Sunsetwind. Neo-fuedalism is unique in the sense that only in the particular circumstances of their history could this type of society function well, as long as the supply and demand of goods and services remained stable for a static population. This entailed the strict ecological observances and health laws that are keys to survival in the long run. Every enlightened age evolves a system that they think works best for the advancement of survival of their particular civilisation. Sunsetwinders are free: they can say what they want, do what they want within their economic limit, write what they want, think what they want. Everyone has the opportunity to be impeccably educated, which was the unspoken foundation of any superior civilisation. Here is no dictatorship like those of past civilisations, such as Communist or Fascist, where greed, racism, ignorance and stupidity ruled the day. Mob rule spelled disaster as there was no just political solution to the overpopulation and endemic chaos of the 21st and early 22nd centuries, until, of course, the Asteroid. One wonders what would have happened had the Asteroid not come. It is presumed nature would have probably invoked some other draconian measure to reinvent the earth.

Cephren huffs and puffs up the steep escarpment trail and reaches the half way point of the three hundred meter rise. The lane would level and then ascend and level again. He knows the trail well and so isn't exasperated as each level failed to bring him to the top. Finally, boiling in sweat, he sprints that last sharp rise to emerge at the top onto the cool, rocky, forested plateau. From there he coasts through the still-green canopy of fragrant air with the decaying scents of autumn to come, and settles into an easy rhythm. A few kilometers farther, the land opens again into the sweeping grain and hay fields of scattered farms. He heads north through more farms, waving at those people he sees in the fields and gardens. He enters another forest and proceeds to an old highway that still offers a winding trail through broken concrete and roots. Through a village, past a tavern, he comes to the small lake where Bill and Yani Deerhill live.

Cephren props his bike against an old maple in the yard and enters their old fieldstone farmhouse. Cephren loves that house; it is over five hundred years old and solid as the day it was built in 1880. It had a clean, earthy smell; the old field-toiled stones remained cool in summer yet impervious with good insulation to the bitter winter blasts.

Bill Deerhill is heavy-built like Cephren with a warm generous disposition. His eyes would light up with the challenge of new ideas; he was both a scientist and an optimist, which is a welcome reprieve from Redman's way. Bill has taken over Redman's old position when Redman "retired". He provided a much-needed change at the time a decade earlier from Redman, who with all his success and accomplishment, had alienated some good people too authoritatively.

Once inside, Cephren walks straight through to the study. There is Bill poring over his monitor that is quite different than Cephren's. His is a Prometheus, which had been imported from Texas. It is super-attenuated to scientific hypothesis, prognosis and diagnosis and equipped with bioptic sensors, electro-magnetic simulators and a whole sluice-full of accessories including a 10 to 100 exponential teraflops per second capacity – each neuron of the brain when fired was equivalent to a flop, therefore 10 with a hundred zeros following was phenomenal. At any rate, Cephren had given Bill the X13 chip to analyse. And Bill had been working on it day and night.

'Hello, Cephren,' he says not looking up.

Cephren walks up behind him to see what is on Bill's screen. All there is are millions of intricate interconnected fibers ranging in colour from blue-grey to red-purple moving ever so slowly in a coagulating porridge.

'How's it going, Bill?'

'You're not going to believe what a time I've had with this mischievous little critter here.'

'Oh, I'd wager you on that. Has it been speaking to you?'

'Not a word.'

'Not a word? Strange, it spoke to me,' says Cephren.

'Yes, I'm sure it did.'

'What do you mean, and what is that you're looking at?'

'Those are the innards of our chip. Have you seen anything like it?' asks Bill, as he breaks away from the screen and turns around to face Cephren. 'You've been riding. Would you like some refreshment?'

'My goodness, you got inside the chip? It looks alive. No thank you.'

'You're in better shape than I thought,' remarks Bill.

'So you got into the chip?' reiterates Cephren.

'Not really. I performed a biopsy.'

'A biopsy?'

'Think about it: all these years, we have this little nub-like thing no bigger than a fat ball point on a pen and we are duped into thinking that it is simply a memory vat for a hundred hours of documentary and media coverage in the 21st century, with the exception of course, of the obscure poem by someone named Jimmy Pidgeon; and now we finally decide to analyse it, thanks to the Scanner, so I put it into the adapter program and did a simple diagnostic. No results, nada, it just wouldn't cooperate. I mean what I say: never have I put a chip in my adapter and had my monitor be rejected! Oh, it will play those documentaries for me, and I reread that weird poem enough times, but it simply would not be analysed!'

'I don't understand. What is there to analyse? I thought we just wanted to see if it was safe to implant.'

'This damn thing shut down my electromagnetic relay! And I don't know how. So for the hell of it in spite of the risk of damaging it, I did a biopsy with a microscopic probe and wouldn't you know it: bingo, I'm in. Not really in, but at least able to see what the heck this thing's made of.'

'It didn't self-destruct?'

"Destruct? This thing in indestructible!'

'Really?'

'The casing is different than plutonium. It looks the same, and its chemistry is similar to plutonium, but I call it tripium. I think it has boron, titanium, beryllium and cobalt, maybe a tiny bit of silver.'

'How does it move?' asks Cephren, watching the stuff churn slowly on the screen.

'Are you really sure you want to implant this, Cephren?' wonders Bill suddenly with a sobering expression.

'You don't know what it is?' queries Cephren.

'No, but it's not toxic; human cells are not contaminated by it. I do know that.'

'What's that grey-reddish stuff?'

'Those are the brains, if you will. Now this is what blows me out of the water. You're right; this thing is alive! The inside of this chip is a liquid crystaline substance, according to the biopsy. But look at that stuff move around!'

'Amazing!'

'Look on the screen; it's moving ever so slightly. Whatever it's made of, which I haven't a clue, moves; therefore it's active and alive, somehow.'

'So,' says Cephren elatedly, 'do we have proof that it is indeed the mythical synaptic memory chip?'

'Absolutely. I wouldn't want to guess what its teraflop power is: just awesome. I even find it hard to believe that someone invented it, or programmed it; its just too perfect, too strange.'

'But we still haven't any idea how to get into it.'

'True,' agrees Bill. 'But if it spoke to you, it must have a mind of its own. It appears that it doesn't mind your odour or something!'

Laughing, Bill shuts down his monitor and disengages his adapter. Once out, he pulls out the little insert sleeve built specifically for the X13, closes it and hands it back to Cephren. They walk outside to the patio overlooking the lake. There are some children hiking along the shore with Blondy Boy who has made some fast friends.

'When I last spoke with Mita,' says Cephren, now sitting with a tall glass of lemonade after changing his mind about a drink, 'she said the most likely way to implant was to fuse it to the cerebral cortex with a micro grounding inductive coil in a synthetic epineurium attached to the neurolemnal sheaths, most prominently connected to the cerebrum. She claims with this special grounding microcoil there would be no risk of burnout if the chip should be too "dynamic", her word, for the spinal induction charge, in which case, I might be permanently lobotomized.'

'The Chicagos,' says Bill, 'for all their malignancies, have done a lot more research than anybody on implants. It is my understanding that inert implants, that is, the normal ones like Reesor's (other than the bug in his of course), are quite simply activated after incubation by the spinal charge alone. What worries me about this one, is that because it is alive, so-to-speak, there may be a very different generative capacity; in other words you are really a guinea pig, Cephren. I would not be doing my job if I didn't tell you you were out of your mind implanting. I am sure there could be hundreds of people who would do it for you.'

'I know, I know the risks, but I refuse to relinquish the chip. I don't want to come across as being selfish, but this chip has been my life interest, at least what I had perceived it to be, the Pidgeon-Piercemore thing. Now I want to see it through.'

'Everyone realises now that Pidgeon, whoever he was, was deeply involved in the U.S. ultra-classified projects, and perhaps he was Pierce-more. I believe he was, now that we know he was a scientist as well as a poet and had the same initials. But let the scholars work on that; we're just concerned about your life here.'

The children come bounding up the lawn. Drake and Diane, twelve and eleven respectively, are Bill and Yani's well behaved brood, although Blondy Boy, looking ragged and wet up to his belly, does not seem so. The children politely say hello and go into the house. Blondy Boy, not so politely, wets and muddies Bill's leg, before plopping on the lawn in the shade.

'Hey, Blondy!' mimics Cephren imitating Tuco, the man who named the-man-with-no-name in Serge Leone's film classic *The Good, the Bad and the Ugly*. 'You're a bad boy!'

'No matter, when will you implant?' Bill adds as he wipes his leg with a tissue paper.

'Not until after the Symposium; and certainly not until after Mita has prepared the chip and me for that matter.'

'She will obtain a sample of efferent impulse nerve filament bundles from you to see if the chip will adhere,' says Bill, 'then with the synthetic neurolemnal sheath inject a sample of your own cerebrospinal fluid, then transplant it as you accurately stated, once any risk of rejection has been ascertained. The micro-inductor will activate the chip once the brain tissue has healed. I understand it takes from two to four weeks. Severe migraines are common symptoms of discomfort; but once it has healed, the chip's program should be felt, if it works like most implant chips with a specific job. However, with this chip . . . only you will know; you may have to do a conduit adaption through a monitor hookup to plug in the code-key; but maybe this chip just needs some mental note or oral delivery to turn it on. Have you gotten any closer with the code-key?' Bill is looking across the lake. The question is designed to deter Cephren from putting himself at risk when so little is known about that chip. He is right in supposing the chip could be impervious, in which case the risk would be in vain.

And he knows the risks involved with anyone Cephren's age. Implants are most successful on recipients between eleven and fourteen, not fifty.

'I managed to communicate with it, Bill; it said *it* was the key or words to that effect. This must imply that an implant could be the answer, or at least a means to the answer.'

'Could be. But still a gamble.'

'Yes. I know.'

Taking a different way back to the Pyramid, Cephren stops in a meadow by a creek to eat his sandwich. Sitting on a shelf of rocks he watches the water flow lazily by in its ceaseless arc and ripple. It is a little frequented spot, yet that day there is a family of four picnicking in the distance. The father and daughter come by and seeing the Chairman, make a quick introduction, saying he is an electrician who at present is in need of work and whether the Chairman knew of any. Cephren replies that he doesn't but would ask Mobius, the chief of Maintenance in the Pyramid, if he needed any help in the upcoming weeks. The man, named Grant Wall, is profuse in his thanks and leaves to tell his wife. Cephren contemplates the growing problems associated with employment and the economy. More and more businesses are floundering under stagnant market conditions. The quality of certain products will decrease if trade value doesn't improve. Market stagnation is a serious problem due to global trade difficulties as most countries are self-sufficient. Certain products and commodities are difficult to obtain, for instance, a specific high-grade lithium, or certain medicinal herbs. Cephren makes a mental note to see Seven Moons and prepare a thorough list of objectives to address at the World Symposium concerning these very problems. Grant's daughter then appears carrying a piece of apple pie on a copy of the latest *Foreign Affair*, Sunsetwind's international paper put out by Chromolox's international unit. Cephren thanks the girl and eats the pie. She stands there a moment and asks whether he likes it. He says he does and she says she made it before running off.

'Good men and women of the world, nations far and wide, I welcome you to Sunsetwind and this year's Symposium, and also this Peace Day. As I presume most of you know, I am Cephren Path, Chairman and host for your visit. There will be many speeches, meetings and agendas set to resolve the growing complexities of our time, so I shall not belabour you with a long overture, but get on with it . . . ' Cephren stands in the sun-light emitting from the huge skylights at the podium of the enormous Ampitheater situated in the west end of the Pyramid adjacent to the Grand Salon, Banquet Hall and Path Foyer, which adjoins Survivor's Walk through the Atrium and Waterway. He speaks to the twenty-five hundred or so heads of state and their trains of delegates, men and women attendant to their mistresses and masters. No weapons concealed or other-wise were allowed in Sunsetwind, but if it was deemed necessary, they remained in their emops in orbit high above.

Cephren had been quite nervous before speaking, but as he opened his mouth, he thought that only being himself could mollify his adrenalin rush. He relaxed in the view of the mass mosaic of humanity in front of him. A virtual kaleidoscope of colour and texture painted a pretty sight indeed. He recognises many individuals whom he had met on previous occasions. All are garbed in their cultural glory: robes, leathers, silks, linens and adornments of jewelry glimmering and rustling in a soft ululation of mixed whispers and general melee. Spirits are high and happy. The nov-elty of individual entrances are to be paraded to the maximum. The agen-das are to be prioritized and socials attended with acquaintances renewed. Cephren speaks at length about what his expectations will be from the Symposium. He reiterates the ideal of the Symposium concept and emphasizes that it must be respected with zeal if humanity is to benefit. He looks at Trinny Burnamthorpe who sits back a few rows to his left. Her smug expression gives no indication of any compliance to the con-sideration expressed. ' . . . And next on my list is the touchy one of geo-political hegemony of powerful neighbours and their needs.' The audience turns a notch more silent. Trinny even smiles. 'Today's world is one of a growing industry of fear, fear of losing power and sovereignty over territory no matter how small or free. In the past, nation states like our own Alma Mater, Canada, or the great U. S. A. and those of Europe, foundered on the shoals of greed, corruption and power that accompanied excessive secrecy, and blindness, the cancer of democracy; there is an old middle eastern saying: *the golden rule is: the gold rules.* Must we devolve to such baseness? Must we corrupt the painful cleansing that humanity has come through in the Horror? To be honest, I believe we are perched on a terrible dilemma. There is a silent motion these days to regard challenge as complicity, for example: to meet the challenge of developing new technology; one is then suspect of ulterior motivation. I see the North American continent on the verge of a nationalist revolution. Who are your allies? Do you want a no-nonsense pact? Should America not be unified again? Some would argue that it is the inevitable and natural destiny of regional powers to consolidate their resources. I say, bogus; the power must remain in the hearts and minds of the individual. The ancient Vedas say the highest calling of anyone can only be the process of self-realisation. This is not an institutional calling. This is the calling of knowledge, what the Chinese refer to as the Servant of Wisdom: humanity is enlightened through individual thought, not the programmed hysteria of religious or political dogmatism. I see these latter tendencies on the rise in disguised forms, hidden agendas and desperate measures that serve to justify the archaic and selfish mottos: from each according to his ability, to each according to his need, or god helps those who help themselves. This is misleading, because we all contribute something different: the scientist seeks answers; the entrepreneur seeks profit; the farmer seeks bounty in produce; and in a larger sense various countries are in parallel; we believe our people are altruistic, but teeter once again on the abyss of material and genetic exploitation. We must be cautious. We must be peaceful, so that change may come gradually without war and upheaval. Let's not be graphically reminded of that terrible legacy of bloodshed of the past. We owe it to ourselves and to humankind. The dead are watching very closely. Thank you. Shanti. Shanti.

'I now would like to have two minutes of silence to remember the dead and those who gave up their lives in the past for the cause of freedom and who lost their lives in the Horror, thus giving life for those few who survived.'

The Ampitheater now casts itself into a submissive acknowledgement. Few individuals appear disdainful of the sanctity of these moments. Some are preoccupied with their own problems and others bowed in solidarity. Trinny stares begrudgingly at Cephren.

'Now in closing, before we get underway and introduce the Chairman of the Earth Federation and President of America, George Washington, I would like to quote from Piercemore, In the Universe, Comedians 23:16 . . . *They would have us commit genocide taking as many of us as we were able. This mounting insanity would culminate in the detonation of nuclear devices that would destroy The Promised Land, our earth. Their credo: if we can't save it, no one can. What a means to an end! Literally. This is surely apocalyptical. But there's more. The perpetrators prescribe it must be nature's will, as morbid as that may be. And who's to question the morality of nature? Morality has no place in nature it would seem. Yet, the perpetrators have decried our ecological suicide yet begat a policy called Blue Phoenix – our suicide! This can be extrapolated as humanity is wont to do: righteousness in human affairs cannot be held forfeit to alien reason. Universal Law: accountability is our right. We all differ in experience: this is a cruel fact as intelligence and experience are racially common, and all are equal in nature: black, blue, white, pink, red, yellow or green, thus the myriad combinations of nature in the universe are both self-serving and socially common. Then evolution, or devolution has an agenda in attrition alone. In human terms, survival is not a question of beating extinction, but of hunger, in which all life feeds the stomach of nature. So let it be known then that these perpetrators serve only to impose nature's ultimate power in that it will destroy quickly what we have already begun to do. It remains up to us to prove them wrong and that we can and will survive our self-destruction.*

23:38 In religion, we serve the spirit of godliness, whether through Krishna, Christ, Mohammed, Buddha or any deification of human vision; all are common, no one more exclusive than the other, for these are personal embodiments of spirit. And they inspire our respect because they disembodied themselves, though divined ultimately in the convolution of truth; as we, the living body, must now pursue its remedy to mortal being, whereby reason is simply the common assumption to ascribe our sanity. Those titans of spirit were comprised too of nitrogen, hydrogen, oxygen, sulphur, and carbon and have attenuated from their immaculate combination: the resonant being. The resonant being, however, offers no resolution in spirit, as silicon proffers no resolution in soul. Only with the rationalization of scientific discovery in the advent of furthering creation can life be understood, hence reason is resonance and resonance reason, therefore spirit must be sanctified through this ethos. The stars, and our own, the sun as the life force, are blind. Through them we have eyes to see. This is our dynamic purpose. Thank you. All else is immaterial. May this Symposium bear fruit. Thank you.' There is a modest applause. When it abates, Cephren resumes. 'Let me introduce one who needs no introduction, George Washington. George.'

The applause continues unabated as George Washington shakes hands with Cephren and moves to the podium. Washington is a big man, black, and tough. His tenuous hold on the remaining states and bioregions that call themselves America is a true testament to the old patriotism that originally forged the country over six hundred years before, not to mention the integrity of the past George from whom the present George was namesake. The *Declaration of Independence* still stands at the core of their propriety. The government, like all governments, has gone through massive changes: the senate is a council with life Senators who preside over the governing body. The Presidential candidates are nominated by the Senate and elected by congress, whose representatives are elected by the people. The President's term of office is seven years, as is the governing body. George Washington, now in his second term, had been before his political career the founder of Eco-Systems, a high-tech business which made life support for emops.

The political reforms had been in place since the Constitution Act of 2201. They have been successful in that they served and appealed to the conscience of that old America that had gone through so much trial and tribulation not only since the Horror, which destroyed the Western world as we know it, but even before World War 3 of 2078-82 when America had been terminally polarised. And the name synonymous with that was the fanatical Righteous headed by Colonel Jeremy Blaine, the monster who nuked his own country.

The America of 2395 consists of New England (unified as a bio-region, Vermont, New Hampshire and Maine inclusive), Lower New York, Massachusetts, Rhode Island, New Jersey, Maryland, Virginia and the part of Pennsylvania east of the Appalachians. Carolina had allied itself with America, as did Kentucky, Tennessee, Alabama, Georgia and Florida, otherwise all are autonomous as are the regions in the rest of historic U.S.A.

The Mississippi region has allied itself with Chicago, which controls the original Corn Belt surrounding the Great Lakes. Problems facing George Washington are not unlike those facing the original George, the difference being the present George has to live with the legacy of failure to rally Americans as one nation, a condition borne for a long time in the minds of Americans. He, naturally, wants to be the one to change all that. This, however, is not the gist of his speech to the world. George, being such a likeable person, has also been elected to the Earth Chair (Chairman of the Earth Federation), and so is doubly burdened by recurrent opposing interests. The Earth Chair, however, is the most powerful position in the world, having been assigned sweeping powers to deal severely with chaotic regions, either from war or other disparities. His greatest contribution is the proliferation of mobile courts in emops to insure justice based on International Law. No tribal, religious, cultural or antiquated system could stand up to EF law. There are nevertheless some gaping hypocrisies in this system; powerful developed countries such as America itself, are not held necessarily accountable to these laws, their own systems happening to be models for EF law.

Nonetheless, Washington makes it very clear that the commitment to peace is the only important theme of that Symposium. He claims all else is scenery. 'It must be a spiritual understanding, as Chairman Path has demonstrated. We must suppress the desire of hostile takeover. Amalgamation must be free-to-choose and to the benefit of all. To rebuild the nations of the past, we must first consider the environment and freedoms we now enjoy.'

Washington has made a safe speech, but Trinny Burnamthorpe, who speaks afterwards, not only nominates herself again for the Earth Chair elections to be held the following April 2nd, but speaks of the "dilemma of peace" in which sovereign nations "collude" to betray the "spirit of progress" in that freedoms are "bought and sold". She claims only unification would suffice to control avarice which "insidiously finds its way into each power's own terms". About freedom, she says elusively, "que sera sera" and adds curiously in reference to Cephren's quotes that Piercemore has no place in our age; he was a "Darwinian hobgoblin" who celebrated the "passion of chaos" of the 21st century. Cephren expected as much, knowing she meant it for him.

There were numerous other speakers including Willy Five (King William the Fifth of England), O'Reilly al Khazzami, Impala, Wu Chen Eng and Queen Jodi of Queensland, who in a shocking incident, being nine months pregnant, had her waters break and gave birth abruptly ten minutes later.

However, it is during the afternoon social when an event took place, which would alter what appeared to be a stellar beginning to the '95 World Symposium, and subsequently the history of the world. Cephren and Chromolox are approached by Impala near one of the many buffet tables of superb delights. Music gently cascades over the crowds from an ensemble of musicians playing various pieces by such artists as Mazzeppo and Amy Sinclair, who had died the year before a great-grandmother. The sounds are pleasing in their melodic dissonance – an almost Baroquian sound, yet with acoustic guitar, duduk and harpsipiano as the dominant instruments. Cephren has one ear to the music which he loved, and the other to the rapid, even anxious voice of Impala.

Impala had been subjected to a tri-c chip implantation as a boy by the Chicagos. He grew up in Windy City, having being raised by the Gospels a powerful Chicago lobby and became one of Trinny's prize studs. Cephren, had been cuckolded by Impala years before, but held not a hint of animosity; in fact, he felt more sorry for Impala than himself. He even caught Trinny in the act when Cephren had made a call to her on his monitor from the Pyramid to the Bungalo. Her monitor had been left open in her passion and Cephren had the unfortunate experience of seeing her splayed across the sofa with Impala thrusting gracefully from behind. Eventually Impala stole away from Chicago with a huge emop transport carrying a full load of munitions and reconnaissance emops. He went to America expecting to be taken in with open arms, but the Americans would have nothing to do with him or his payload. Eventually, George Washington and the EF turned a blind eye when to Trinny's chagrin they refused her demands to return her precious geno and his cargo.

Impala then tried other places around the globe, but settled peaceably near the headwaters of the Blue Nile, which he claimed was the Garden of Eden. From there he struck a deal with the EF and over time manipulated through guile, wit, and bribery to secure the horn of Africa for himself and his partner Sheba (originally Avril Brynne from Cleveland – one of his breeding mates). He took with him several others of mixed race who became his lieutenants. He modeled his empire on Sunsetwind and last year held his first elections, and remained Chairman. Surprisingly, most of the warring factions put down their arms and accepted his rule with the help of George Washington, which was hailed as a shining example by the EF supported by the Mobile Court. Subsequently, a thriving economy evolved from a revitalized East Indian community that had been living prosperously in East Africa for nearly a thousand years. Impala was nicknamed Tsavo after the famous man-eating lions. His rule is as tough as Sunsetwind's was soft. But he stuck to the letter of the law and no one was exempt.

Two years before at the World Symposium in Ethiopia at Lake Tana, Impala had made a private apology to Cephren concerning his affair with Trinny. Cephren learned that Impala had been forced, but that he hadn't done his utmost to resist. Cephren expressed the same thing about his own marriage. Impala felt obliged to apologise because after he stole away from Chicago, Trinny had used Cephren as a foil when she said he was going to kill Impala no matter where he was located. Cephren, meanwhile unaware, had moved back to Sunsetwind, (not that he ever really moved away) and tried to mend the damage to his reputation that had been insidiously exploited by the Chicago press, which had always characterized him as that "buffoon" or "impotent wonder". The "political" marriage had been a failure, because Cephren was not "man enough" for their great matriarch, Trinny Burnamthorpe, who was seen and revered by much of the Third World for her "economic miracle". But the damage was done and Cephren was cast as a cuckold to the West bent on revenge. At the Sunsetwind World Symposium and at the three before then, any such thoughts were well laid to rest, as Impala and Cephren were often in one another's company having a laugh or two. They had become genuine friends. There is that special connection which brought them together, but this time there is an urgency in Impala that Cephren can't help but notice.

Chromolox is speaking with Sheba who with her eldest son are presently gorging themselves on cherry-smoked Atlantic salmon at the buffet tables. Cephren and Impala are sampling other delicacies.

'Cephren,' he says, as quietly as he can above the din, 'we need to speak in private. I have some informa–'

Sheba comes within hearing.

'Of course, Impala…'

'When I get old,' Impala speaks as if continuing small talk, 'I want to give all my material possessions to the young who are best able to receive them; then I will retire to a mountain spring and pass my days in abstention and contemplation like an old tribal medicine man.'

'And will not Sheba accompany you?' smiles Cephren.

'Sheba? She will maintain our household . . .'

'He will be back for a warm bed at night,' interrupts Sheba coolly. 'He knows no other habit so well.'

Laughing, Cephren catches a studied look from Trinny Burnamthorpe across the salon standing with the Mississippi delegation led by Mercer Wilsun, the Evangelist.

On a more serious note, Cephren says, 'Impala, why don't you have your implant removed? Mita Waterman would do it for you.'

'Too dangerous,' he says looking about. 'I wear it like an old shirt; can't let it go even if I could.'

'It drives him,' purrs Sheba, detachedly. She then moves off again.

'I know the shock of removal can be fatal, but we would use a modulator that would gradually return your natural hormonal levels to a normal equilibrium once the implant is removed. What kind do you have?' asked Cephren.

'A P300 tri-c, why?'

'The high test one.'

'Yeah. But listen…'

'I really think you should see Mita while you're here, Impala. Confidentially, I know Burnamthorpe bugs her implants. If she's bugged yours, everything you say and think could be monitored.'

'Are you serious, man?'

'Absolutely.'

Impala then rolls his eyes in a peculiar fashion revealing the whites. Sheba returns.

'What's wrong?' she exclaims, curiously.

'My head . . . it hurts.' Impala is having some kind of seizure. 'My . . . head!' He holds his head in obvious pain.

Sheba goes to him. 'What is it?'

'Ahhhhhhh!' he screams deliriously in pain. The crowd abruptly stops speaking and clears a swath around him.

His head then literally implodes. Part of his skull seems to cave in as he leans onto Sheba who tries to hold him up. His body goes limp and he crumples to the floor. Sheba feels his depressed cranium in bewildered mortification. Cephren, stunned, can only look on at this monstrous deed, confused by the reality. One moment his friend is there and the next a grotesque death mask on the marble floor. Cephren doesn't hear the shrieks or see the crowd clear away from the tragic scene; he just stands there numbly with the thought emerging that whatever or whoever did this must have had planned it to cast a dark shadow over this Symposium and Sunsetwind. Trinny Burnamthorpe comes to mind, of course, but Impala could have had any number of enemies. The next thing Cephren knows, Cleo appears with a number of her security people and quickly cordons off the area with Impala's own security and has the Salon emptied of everyone. Cleo is very efficient and doesn't so much cast a single glance at Cephren sitting with Sheba and their son who would not leave Impala, before being persuaded by Cephren.

So much for Peace Day, October 1, 2395. With growing alarm, Cephren knows the world is at a dangerous new threshold, and neither speech nor act in the name of peace would alter the seeming irrevocable fate of these times. If the will of humanity wants war, so be it and cry. And Cephren does just that.

three The Blizzard

Spun in shadows slain by night
An unbelievable tale –

–Jimmy Pidgeon

L eaning against a tree on a mound of forest turf in a sunny glade, Cephren stands soaking up the heat of Indian summer in mid-November. A few leaves still cling desperately to their bare stricken parents, allowing the glorious sun to penetrate the moldering ground. The geese have long flown; the terrestrial kingdom with larders full waits patiently for the long arduous winter ahead. And Cephren feels the comfort of solitude.

The World Symposium had taken place over a month before, and still the reverberations of Impala's death are uppermost on Cephren's mind. He had been unwittingly cast as suspect to complicity in the foul deed due to an unremitting international press egged on by the Chicagos who under the long arm of Trinny Burnamthorpe had hoped permanently to tarnish Cephren's reputation as well as Sunsetwind's. Even Cephren's allies such as George Washington had cooled relations to still the political climes. A delegate from Washington's entourage had complained among other things about Sunsetwind's slow change for improved markets. Only O'Reilly spoke up in his defence after Cephren made an impassioned speech following Impala's death. At the time, Cephren had pleaded with the world "to continue the Symposium in the interests of peace, prosperity and human rights, and not to draw lines and retreat to the posturing ignorance of earlier ages." He had announced that Cleopatra Path was conducting a thorough investigation, leaving no stone unturned in hope of discovering whether Impala's death was accidental or otherwise. So far nothing conclusive had turned up other than the possibility of a defective implant, which the Chicagos had already pre-empted by revealing a 99% success rate, the highest anywhere in the world. Unfortunately, Sheba, mysteriously, would not allow an autopsy and insisted that they be allowed to take his body and return home. Cephren was not prepared to insist on their withholding, though it contravened the law. Gabriella felt Cephren could have averted some of the fallout had he stuck to the letter of the law; nevertheless, if he had been set up to take a fall, it had been successfully implemented, hence the growing ostracism towards him in the world community. The problem with Cephren is that he really does not know how to fight the truculent innuendo directed against him; he is just too prepared to ignore it and retreat from the attention. One thing in his favour owing to his retreat from retaliation, is that there were few photos and little footage of him so that many people had no idea what he looked like – the political phantasm, they wrote, sitting in his ivory tower. On that day in the sunny woods, it seems to him only Blondy Boy his husky is his friend.

The World Symposium had gone on according to plan in spite of the tragedy, though in such a tainted atmosphere little was accomplished. The entertainment and other events were poorly attended. It is presumed the world leaders and their delegates spent more time in their huge emops in the air above Sunsetwind for fear of some other tragedy. Sunsetwind's lax security became the focus and crucible of blame. To it's supporters the times seemed to impart a tragically orchestrated passion play that Sunsetwind be cast as the victim and martyr to the greater good of civilization, represented by the ploy of Chicago's plea for unity. And there is nothing Cephren, Chromolox or Cleo or anybody can do about it. The fallout just keeps moving onward like a runaway train, where the fates all conspire to do what needs to be done. During the World Symposium at night, Cephren would look up at the sky and see the hundreds of emops sitting about like fixed bouys. He had heard that some aloft, including the Mississippis and Chicagos, were engorged in blatant debauchery while making ugly conversation and intentional slurs toward their hosts. What kind of sea-change had traduced upon Impala's death? How could the hosts have averted or mitigated the consequences? This is something that had expended all their wits since the Symposium. The mood is as if a cloud had descended and in a single burst a toxic wash putrefied almost two hundred years of enlightenment. Yet in spite of their present state, Cephren will not be thwarted in his determination. He must rectify the wrong, and cleanse the damned world of this perfidy. He still has the ace, Jimmy's Chip and until he finds out what is in it, he would die trying.

There is another reason Cephren has taken this sojourn on this fine November day. Tomorrow he is to be implanted. The surgery had been set up with Mita a month previously. After reviewing Bill's formal report on the chip and deciding to go with a new Swiss device called a Micro Relay which transforms the spinal kundalini impulse into a stable nerve stimulator, it became apparent the Micro Ground Inductor attached with synthetic fibers was still necessary to artificially fuse with the brain. In effect a benign cyst would form to protect both the brain and the chip. The risk, of course, is whether this chip would adhere. The casing is impervious and made of a substance tripium, as Bill coined it, yet non-toxic as his analysis had predicated. All this biotechnic implanting is at the outset a risk for someone of his age even with a simple standard pituitary implant, the tric, which had been the tried, tested and proven; but this alien thing as Mita had described it, borrowing from Clem Reesor's contention that it had been originally recovered from an alien space vehicle in the 21st century by Jimmy Pidgeon, was foolhardy and only the Chairman of Sunsetwind was stubborn and influential enough to go through with it.

Having rested there by his maple tree long enough, Cephren stands up and stretches. Blondy Boy is back and eyeing him for adventure. Cephren slowly works his way up the easy slope and crosses the creek that is again running after the past week's rains. Coming to the footpath that leads back to the Pyramid a few kilometers distant, he sees across the meadow old Redman standing like a gnarled ancient tree. Redman waves him over in his impetuous way. Cephren approaches with the feeling that he couldn't care less what Redman is going to say; Redman, however, true to form and as enigmatic as ever smiles as Cephren comes up to him. During the past month or so since the Symposium, Redman had not volunteered a single word of reproach nor encouragement. He was all but mute concerning the events that had transpired. Chromolox had said a few weeks past that she had seen him at the market buying cod. They had spoken briefly about nothing in particular, but she couldn't get over his cheery demeanour. While the rest of the Board were in a kind of somniferous mourning, there was Redman carrying on as if he had just won an old time lottery. In parting he had said, "Not to worry, it's all for the best." Chromolox was at a loss to know what he meant. Cephren knew better.

'Good day to you, Mr. Chairman,' exclaims Redman. 'Getting your solitude?'

'A little,' replies Cephren. He can't help noticing how pleased Redman is.

'I'm glad we came upon each other, son; you know I've been thinking how happy I am that you are the leader of our country in these troubled times. I have contemplated the demise of our civilisation and how technology is once again running rampant with those who are incapable of using it properly. So be it, nothing new there. We are surrounded by chaotic beings who are at war with themselves. We are an anomaly, Cephren; we at least have put technology into the hands of someone with understanding and care.'

Redman now grasps Cephren's arm and squeezes. 'Cephren, you are the best damned Chairman this province has ever had. You're doing the right thing. Don't lose heart, even if, heaven forbid, you lose Sunsetwind. No one must get into Jimmy's Chip but you, and when you do, which you will, you must do whatever is necessary to turn the tables.'

'I'll try my best, Redman. Thanks.'

'We are a unique culture, ahead of our time; what chance would we have against the petty ignorance of mob rule? None. The whole world now watches us. Thanks to Clem Reesor, most of the powers that be want that chip of yours, but they wait because they want to see what you can do with it; so I'm warning you, the minute you find something out, they'll pounce, the Chicagos first, then America or whomever; just keep out of reach. Take the new Volcano with you; the Anishnabes will help, O'Reilly will help, so will the Yellow Tooths, maybe the Europeans, or Texans, but stay ahead of them all. Even now they watch through the eyes of others unwittingly. It has been naïve of us to let this happen, but inevitable. Now go and remember what I have said. I have faith in you, boy. Go.'

Redman lets go and shambles away scrunching leaves in his old foot-falls. Cephren wants to speak but no words come. He actually loved the old man. When his own father, Ramses, died thirty years before from injuries sustained in a terrible emop crash that also claimed the life of his mother, Nefertiti, Redman became his father-figure. They had had their differences, as both were strong willed. Cephren watches Redman until he is out of sight. Redman never looks back.

Back in his loft, Cephren picks up his copy of the *Foreign Affair* and reads the front page. There is news about the previous week's untimely death of a Polish leader from a suspicious embolism in the brain similar to that of Impala. There was some talk of it being an assassination, because there was no indication of any health problem in his last physical. Some believed his non-aggression pact with Russia led some of his own people to doubt his ability to lead. Already the new government had made inquiries to the Chicagos about helping to build up their weapons arsenals.

On the second page, there is an article by Sunsetwind's Washington corre-spondent who had received word from an unnamed source. (Cephren knew the source to be a Senator's wife, as Chromolox had informed him.) He never liked the secrecy involved, which the correspondent had insisted for her own "integrity". Supposedly a delegation had arrived from Chicago that was conducting "high level" meetings with George Washington, which dealt with the carving up of North America. The details were not available, but "sources" had speculated that borders similar to the "old democracies of the U.S.A. and Canada were being drawn up." How outra-geous, thinks Cephren, not just because of what they were doing, but what right had they to do it in the first place without any participation by other sovereign states. Cephren wonders what the Chicagos had to offer the present America in return for their own control of the entire Great Lakes region that formerly belonged to the U.S.A. Chromolox who just steps off the lift, however, interrupts his thoughts.

'What on earth is this all about, Chromolox?' says Cephren pointing at the article. She moves closer to look at it.

'We're not really sure; that's why we put it on the second page. Flora said not to headline it in case it turned out to be some kind of "disinfor-mation".'

'I can't believe George Washington would go along with something like this. It's ludicrous. It's tantamount to war. Texas, California, the South, the Sierras – they'll all resist . . . '

'Unless, the deal is so loosely structured, their respective sovereignties are unimpeded; it could be an economic union.'

'I suppose. Are the Mississippis involved?'

'I would think so, if the Chicagos are involved. Perhaps that's what got Washington to the bargaining table. The Mississippis allied with Chicago are a force to be reckoned with.'

'It appears the old Righteous have become the winners by attrition, having waited like vultures over the carcass of old America. Trinny Bur-namthorpe certainly fits the mold of a leader of the Righteous, with all her sanctimonious posturing, except they have joined the Trashies with their biotechnics,' says Cephren.

'Maybe they're just working out a non-agression pact,' comments Chromolox. She stands there holding some papers looking tired and worn.

'You need some time off, Chromolox,' states Cephren.

'We all do; Christmas can wait. Cephren, the reason I'm here is that we, Cleo and I, came across something that I think you should look into.'

'Oh, what's that?'

'Take a look at this.' She hands Cephren a list of people. 'This is a list of staff who helped with the reception the day Impala was killed.'

'So you do think he was killed?'

'I do now. See these names? We have done a thorough check on each and every person working with us. All come clean regarding their history, birth, etc., except one.'

'Who's that?'

'This thirteen year old girl named Cassandra Wall.'

'I remember. I helped her father get some work in the Pyramid under Mobius during the Symposium. Was he not cleared? Besides, what harm can a thirteen-year-old girl do with a tray of hors d'oeuvres?'

'Oh yes, they were cleared all right, but where are they now? Nowhere. We checked out their address and found none. They were spies, Cephren.'

'Spies? For whom?'

'The Chicagos no doubt.'

'But what's there to spy on?' asks Cephren still unbelieving. 'We have nothing to hide.'

'I don't think anything. They were an assassination team.'

'Really? Does Cleo agree with you?'

'Yes, she's quite upset that her security files must have been tampered with. This Grant Wall and his family are no Sunsetwinders.'

'But how were they involved with Impala's murder?'

'We don't know yet.'

'We need evidence, Chromolox. The obvious cause of death was an imploded implant. It has been known to happen.'

'Yes, but Cephren, did you know that Sheba has taken over East Africa? We heard yesterday that Sheba took into her palace Impala's "best" friend Simba Nyerere, a descendant of Julius Nyerere the Tanzanian statesman from the 20th century.'

Cephren remembers his history. Julius Nyerere, although well-meaning, was one of the foolish socialists who nationalised and expropriated highly productive farms owned by Asians and within ten years turned them into wastelands.

'I just don't get it . . . '

'I do,' says Cleo Path as she exits the lift.

'Cleo!' says Cephren. 'This is all becoming very . . . '

'Complicated,' interjects Cleo, who is smiling and dressed unusually in a flowing sari of burgundy silk.

'Yes, that'll do,' affirms Cephren. 'You look terrific; are you celebrating something?'

Cleo does a pirouette, which brings a big smile to Chromolox. 'Do you like it?' she asks, modeling her silks.

'Yes,' agrees Chromolox and Cephren in unison.

'So what do you know, Cleo?' asks Cephren, wondering what on earth has gotten Cleo out of her khaki all-weather hemps.

Sitting down and stretching like a diva across his chaise lounge, Cleo takes her time responding. 'We're dealing with a whole new pan o' fish, dear brother. Get this: I believe the Chicagos have used our forum for the World Symposium as a jumping board, if you will, to extend their domination not just over us, but over all North America and eventually the entire world.' She stops to let that sink in. Cephren lets her continue. 'And,' she goes on, 'she is doing it by bearing the fruits of her massive implantation program. Coincidentally, she is of course, building up a veritable army of genos to underwrite any resistance to her expansion. The only explanation for Impala's death can be that his implant, the tri-c, imploded as we know, causing the top of his head to cave in. This was done by a transmitter carried unwittingly by Cassandra Wall who walked by him the moment he popped. We studied the floor of the salon over and over; that is the only possible explanation. It seems as if the minute you and he were alone together, her father directed her to beeline for you. And you mentioned that he had something important to tell you – probably someone he knew in Chicago got word to him about their intentions in Ethiopia, or elsewhere, even here. We lack conclusive evidence, but the circumstances are just too coincidental; and when we discovered that the Walls were spies, we had our connection. Cassandra must have some kind of implant with a transmitter emitting a frequency that detonates or disrupts in some way, specific implants . . . '

'How can you be so sure?' quizzes Cephren.

'Through a source of ours in Chicago we discovered that Cassandra Wall at the age of four was stricken with a rare form of muscular dystrophy. She received in the Windy City at the age of six a corrective implant to genetically enhance her. Her father, whom we presume to be a Chicago, has no birth record there at all, nor the daughter. I am nevertheless convinced Cassandra was given a special implant that besides her corrective prosthesis, works as some kind of relay switch that triggers certain other implants to implode. This device is both a receiver and detonator. If an individual is jeopardizing Trinny's plans in some way: poof! She'll send in a team like the Walls. I wouldn't be surprised if even Queen Jodi of Queensland, Australia, had her baby on cue to create an atmosphere of chaos and disruption. Remember the way Trinny Burnamthorpe jumped in to help, all dressed in her purple leathers and pink cross-trainers. She makes me sick. I almost throw up when I think about what she is really up to. Then there she was, holding that little baby up to the world. Mother of the world!'

'I had suppressed it from my memory,' recalls Cephren, dejectedly.

'And do you know what she said to me after Impala's death?' adds Chromolox. 'She said, "This is quite a show you're putting on babe – a real hullabalooza!" then walked away swinging that tight little ass throwing back her hair, just for my perusal. When I think of that and what I know now . . .'

'You'd have ripped into her, after me,' declares Cleo regaining her usual sobriety.

'Just think how many Chicago implantees there are around the world,' comments Chromolox.

'She can exterminate whom she pleases, when and where, with impunity.'

'So why the silks?' queries Cephren to Cleo, changing the subject which he finds too unsavoury to contemplate.

Cleo sighs, then smiles, grateful for the personal attention, not to mention a respite from their onerous responsibilities.

'Should I tell him, Chromolox?' she teases.

'He may not like it,' says Chromolox, looking down with her own brand of taboo in her voice.

'Like what?' pipes Cephren, humoured.

'Like, well, I wanted to tell you before...' speaks Cleo hesitantly. 'I had an affair with O'Reilly al Khazzami during the Symposium. I was very careful not to let it interfere with my responsibilities. It just happened. He sent me this sari a while ago. There it is. I think maybe I kinda like him.'

Cephren is stunned and can't think of anything but his friend, the polygamous emperor, with a harem of "virgins" availing his notorious affections on tough Cleopatra, the proud warrioress who once proclaimed, "No man has the guts of a woman and this woman is too good for any man." Cephren is trying not to smile, which he can't help but do when he notices Cleo's guerilla ankle runners underneath the gathered folds of her silk. She is indeed the empress if ever there was one in that day-and-age.

'What are you smirking at?' complains Cleo turning a little red in the cheeks with sparks coming out her ears.

'A good match,' he quickly responds to avert an indignant Cleo.

'A what?' She doesn't hear.

'A great match,' he repeats. 'Come to think of it, if you could rein him in . . .'

'Rein him in?'

'You know, mutual fidelity.'

'He wants me, Cephren!' she fumes. Her pride and honour are not to be trifled with. 'I let him, of course; he is a wonderful lover.'

Cephren wants to say: yes, he's had some experience with his numerous wives.

'So,' he says instead, 'Where is it all going? He lives . . .'

'I know where he lives,' she retorts.

'No need to be defensive; I think it's wonder . . .'

'Cephren, I have told you this only as Security Chief; otherwise, it's none of your business.'

'He's my friend too, and an ally to Sunsetwind.'

'Well, I think I'll get back to work,' interrupts Chromolox, with her head bowed. She turns and exits.

'Of course he is,' continues Cleo ignoring Chromolox. 'Do you think I'd let myself fall in love with an unknown? I trust him. I know him, and his faults. There is a powerful bond between us, and in spite of the madness at the Symposium this year, we hit it off and found time to . . . get acquainted.'

'Is it going anywhere?' reiterates Cephren hoping he said it as casually as possible so as not to set her off again. Cleo in love is not the characteristic cool she normally exudes; in fact, she seems more like a wild tigress in heat.

'I'm thinking of going there at Christmas.'

'Is that wise being as we are, I think, in a state of emergency?'

'I would only go for a weekend, if everything is stable. I might offer a little diplomacy, you know, that could assist us. O'Reilly is a benevolent authoritarian; he actually believes in democratic freedoms; his empire is built on economic union and trust, but woe betide those who deceive him;

he is ruthless but compassionate – my kinda guy.' She smiles half-joking. 'He even talks about his legacy as being one who brought democracy to the Afghans, Pakistanis, Tibetans and Indians within his control.'

'I trust your judgment, Cleo; I'm happy for you.'

'Did you know that his mother was a Hasidic Jew?'

'Yes, and his father an Irish-Afghan Muslim.'

'Isn't that wild?' she exclaims in awe.

'Certainly when their families turfed them out.'

'Love rules,' she avows wistfully.

'I wish.'

Cleo jumps up and valiantly pronounces, 'We are ready to defend this land. Our secret armies are organised and prepared. The Chicagos may want to take over, but they won't want to stay.' She turns and leaves with her sari flowing, to stop at the lift and turn again to face Cephren.

'Good luck, tomorrow,' she adds seriously. 'I'll see you after.'

Cephren flies his emop in a wide loop over the escarpment and out over Great Blue before descending at Mita's private clinic which is situated at her home in a protected cove on the Peninsula with a beach surrounded by dolomitic limestone cliffs. Here she has a full compliment of supplies and equipment that any hospital would carry, but she normally spends most of her time running between the main health centers in Sunsetwind at Barrie, Peterborough, Collingwood, Midland, Owen Sound, and Hanover. There are numerous smaller clinics and hospitals such as Alliston, Lindsay, Parry Sound, Dundalk, Kincardine and Wiarton, which she frequents less often. At her private clinic, she usually takes in special cases. There isn't any prerequisite for her special attention; it is just her own discretionary research.

Having kept his health an optimum priority most of his life, Cephren rarely needed a doctor. He had, however, known Mita since he was an adolescent, she being nine years older. Their relationship, which began thirty-five years before in and about their cottages on the east coast of Great Blue (Mita's parents used to own a cottage near the Path's), was at best always a little mysterious. Cephren had his first major crush in life for Mita when he was fifteen and she, twenty-four. For a couple of years in the summers he would go to great lengths to make himself available to her: he worked for her parents, looked after their boats, and acted as if he was twenty-five. She never seemed to give him the time of day and treated him like a kid. He became terribly depressed once, when she brought an older man to her cottage, and found himself in the unenviable position of being near them all the time. Mita had used his mood change in an attempt to mollify his adolescent yearning by giving him some physical attention such as putting her arm around him as if he was her little brother; however, he knew that in order to redress his pride, he must quit there and then. Subsequently, fate saw to it that he wouldn't see her again until he was twenty-one.

The summer of '66 was to remain embossed in his memory like a super nova. To his surprise, they had struck up a friendship on a remarkable new level. They would engage in rather frank and unusual discussions for hours at a time. He discovered that the elusive Mita was then single and the doctor in charge of the anti-viral unit in Barrie. This was considered to be one of the most coveted positions in her profession, as the anti-viral unit was probably one of the greatest breakthroughs in medicine since the mapping of the gene and DNA which led to the cure of many terminal diseases. At any rate, Cephren, unbeknownst to him at the time, was within a month to become the next Chairman. His parents had died tragically not three weeks after his affair with Mita. (An intoxicated driver of another emop entered a cloud formation going the wrong way in a corridor and collided with his parents killing them instantly). But that summer on a hot breezy day, he took Mita for a sail in his small Sunspray out to the stark, rocky isles on the open water. They pulled the boat up in a protected shallow area and wandered over the isle looking for a place to swim.

Finding the desired place, Mita, to Cephren's shock, flung off her shorts and t-shirt and dived in stark naked. Mita today, at almost sixty, is still considered a beautiful woman, but in her youth, her beauty even preceded her talents, which was to dog her for much of the early part of her life. And her beauty on that magical summer day so long ago projected Cephren into hyperspace. Her smooth light skin, long blonde hair and graceful motions had utterly transfixed him. 'Come on, Cephren!' she called to him. 'It's so delicious!' Cephren dived in, having flung his clothes too. He could see the rocky bottom as he swam a great distance under water. It was so clear, the water's depth at thirty feet seemed only half that. They rolled and cajoled in the water like two otters. Finally they emerged, anointed in paradise, and lay on the hot rocks stomach down. They spoke of their youth, their dreams; Mita deftly lifted the air of hurt that surrounded Cephren that summer a few years back by saying he was one of the most unique men she knew. He revealed that he had had such a huge crush on her. Mita faced him and they kissed. It was so spontaneous and delightful Cephren hardly knew how to contain himself. His exuberant youth coupled with her more seasoned cool caused those hot pink rocks to almost pulse with erotic longing. The fragrance of the lake mingled with their sweat as they hungrily explored each other as if having been suddenly released from the suppression of forbidden passion. After a preponderance of playful teasing and more kissing, the final consummation came as a surprise to both of them. There was no stopping. She ended up on top enveloping him with her damp hair, moaning and sighing. Later, after the magic had waned and her feelings seemed to retract to her earlier posture, they sailed back silently reveling in a corona of mystery that prevailed to the present day. For Cephren it was the only sexual experience that he ever really ordained as love. There were urgent calls, even letters, but out of fate and circumstance, they were never to be together again. Mita fell in love with Rao Tempe, the famous psychologist twenty years her elder, who specialised in, above all, divorce and to a lesser extent, alien phenomena. He traveled constantly all over the world, but had died a few years back from a sudden heart attack that Mita took very hard. They had a daughter, Chantelle, who lived in France.

So the mystery surrounding Cephren's and Mita's relations has aged and receded into a compartment kept for the luxury of reminiscence. Cephren never brings up the past, and in his own maturity, Mita has given him her deep respect. She understands his need for solitude and study, and never doubts him when others sometimes alluded to his idiosyncrasies. During his horrid divorce with Trinny Burnamthorpe, she had Rao delicately deal with the issues, which ultimately became political and out of his hands, but nevertheless effected the transition. Mita, at least, gave a guiding hand by proxy to her old friend. These memories pervade Cephren's mind as he lowered his emop onto the pad adjacent to her house and garage.

At the front door made of clear glass, Cephren can see through the bungalo-like structure into the living room and beyond the large, bay windows to the cold blue of Great Blue Lake in the distance. The house is made of a limestone exterior and pinewood floor interior with a varied assortment of foreign rugs. An antique Steinway piano holds center stage at one end of the living room and a pleasant mix of old and new furniture is sparsely arrayed. A woman comes to the door and lets Cephren inside. She introduces herself as Mary, an apprentice, who bids him follow her downstairs.

The clinic is set up in a wing of the house with its own entrance, but Cephren had assumed he should ring at Mita's front door, as he wasn't told otherwise. Downstairs, numerous naturally sunny rooms are mostly unoccupied. There is nothing sterile or sanitized about the appearance of the place, though immaculately clean. Here beautiful Afghan and Persian area rugs cover the wood floors lightening the utilitarian medical features. Many unique paintings and other art pieces adorn the walls, creating a warm atmosphere.

Mary leads Cephren into a room and tells him to remove his clothes and put on a blue smock. She returns in a few minutes and they exit the room.

Two men, both in their late twenties or early thirties, introduce themselves as apprentices and they all walk down the hall to a lounge area with another scenic view of Great Blue and a cross-section of a rugged limestone cliff with those tenacious cedars eternally clinging to their existence out of the rock. Inspiring, thinks Cephren. He is told preparations are almost complete and that he must just relax and enjoy the "panorama". Mary gives him a small glass of spiked juice to drink.

'Spiked?' utters Cephren, amused.

'Yes, Mr. Chairman,' she says without revealing the spike, 'a requisite tincture to alight the synaptic nerves for medical reasons of course.' She smiles beatifically.

Cephren no sooner complies as she leaves, when Mita enters. She walks to him and pecks a kiss on his cheek, which she never did publicly or at council meetings.

'Delicious, spike,' he declares enervated. What's in it, Mita?'

'Clear guava-strawberry-kiwi with two drops of pure opium.' She too smiles beatifically.

'An curious induction into my brave new headspace.'

'A necessary one,' she says searching his eyes more seriously. She is dressed in light burgundy doctor's linens. Her thick silver-white hair has not yet been tied up and bonneted. 'Cephren,' she goes on in a more solemn tone, 'I want you to know, I cannot be one hundred percent sure this will be successful, but we will closely monitor you here for the next three weeks and if there is even the slightest nuance of rejection, I will remove the chip without your permission, and that my old friend, is final. Are we kosher?'

'Is that really why you are addicting me to opium?'

Mita laugh and takes his hand. 'You are adorable, Cephren. No, that's not why we are addicting you. I don't want you to suffer the post-trauma – the headaches and nausea, although some nausea will accompany the drug, but will go away; this slight addiction will be tightly controlled. Opium is the best drug that chemically administers the optimum sensory discharge to make the formation of the chip's cyst to adhere to the neurolemnal sheath. With an artificially induced electro-encephalogrammatic rhythm, the mind is not only going to accept the device more easily, the actual healing process is hastened tremendously.'

'I see,' says Cephren looking at Mita. 'Well, what are we waiting for? I can feel this stuff rushing me to the destiny ward – it's quite uncanny.'

Mita turns to face him. Her light, brown eyes search his and they are both reminded of their mystery. Nothing is said as the memory dons silence. 'Come,' she says, 'let us begin.' She leads him by the hand into the operating room in an adjacent room. The apprentices are waiting quietly ready to assist. Mary leads Cephren to a reclining wheelchair. He is eased into it and told he would be given a general anesthetic, then removed to the table, then moved back again, so he would wake up exactly where he sat. One of them turns on some music, an old classic, while the other inserts the introvenous line. All Cephren remembers are the first few bars . . . *Let me take you down 'cause I'm going to . . . Strawberry Fields . . .*

. . . Consciousness first makes its presence known in a dull, analgesic nausea that has neither space nor form. It seems to evolve from a colourless infirmity to an audible hushing. After an indeterminable time the hushing transforms to a feeling of expanding space expanding to the point when consciousness forms a strange cosmic pressure as if he is being spun in a centrifugal device at the speed of light yet fully solvent. Vague impressions are slow to visualise as little more than dark chasms of nothingness, before stars appear as little streaks compiling a chaotic mosaic that clarify ultimately into an entire universe with crystal clear constellations. The stars twinkle brightly and the nausea evaporates. There is comfort in their familiarity. Thus consciousness gazes for eternity upon the universe. Thinking he is waking, Cephren sees the pattern of waves rolling into his mind like a three-D Dali with a woman standing on the beach as the waves wash up on the pebbles. He blinks and she is gone. He is reclining in the special wheel-chair looking out the bay window towards Great Blue in the clinic lounge feeling his head has ballooned to an immense size, yet light and strange. He cannot recall for how long he sat there; moments were hours and hours moments. He feels the intravenous course through him like a warm internal bath. Not a thought occurs and bliss is absurd as a gentle voice is speaking which he hears vaguely. It resonates into a jumble of chords like bubbles in his balloon head, vowels and consonants mixing perfectly into syllables. The syllables collate into a puzzle that makes them known by working the balloon's orifice as he speaks and bursts the bubble, which expands again. He speaks some more.

'Cephren,' says Mita sitting beside him holding his hand, 'can you see me? Do you recognise me?'

What comes out of Cephren's mouth is unintelligible. Mita smiles and crouches down in front of him. She looks directly into his eyes and softly repeats her question.

'I think I'm okay,' he says more intelligibly looking at her, his words understood though drawled and distorted.

'It will take a few days for you to regain control of your motor skills, Cephren. You're doing just fine. I'm going to look after you. I want you to know that. I care for you very much. In a week you'll be walking and in two, running. In a few days we will disconnect the intravenous and begin withdrawal of the opium very slowly for two weeks until you're absolutely perfect! How's that?'

'I want you to know how good I feel,' he replies working his mouth with difficulty, 'and that you being here puts light into my eyes.'

Mita smiles and stands up to give him a kiss on his cheek. 'Cephren, use this buzzer to call us if you need anything. I'll be here twenty-four hours around the clock. Now, all you can do is rest.'

Cephren returns to Great Blue. He senses a kinship there in that massive tonnage of water churning blue on blue to the horizon. He doesn't know what he is all about yet, but he can feel it coming. The balloon ascends heavily and he drifts into sleep as the curtain of darkness slowly materialises late in the November afternoon.

Dec. 12/95

Thirty more centimeters of snow this morning. A month has passed since the operation. I feel amazing, dear reader. The implant has caused almost no side affects and my thinking processes have, I think, clarified, which may be wishful thinking. I have as yet made no progress whatsoever breaking into Jimmy's Chip. I really don't know where to start, as I must get the password or program directive, which is unlikely. The B400s at least had complex number codes that a program could duplicate over a period of time, but this thing inside me seems as inert as ever – its strange biomass revolving oozily within. Nevertheless, I feel newly made and devil may care. The world can watch me twitch and turn under their voodoo pin; it doesn't matter, because I have the power, imaginary as it may be. It would appear I play into their hands by being the guinea pig. They must be watching with a keen eye. I may have to bolt for awhile, literally; and if I do, I do not wish to be trespassed against in some coma-tech state. I think I'll take Cleo up on that offer to get a body-guard. Sounds so damned old-fashioned, like something Perreault would do. My ancestors would approve, the early Paths with their for-your-own-good autocracies and pseudo-democracy-martial-law rules, their motley army and traveling court entertainment center. Judge Path would hand down the sentence: you will die for your heinous crimes because we don't know what else to do with you! Menace! Trashie! Ad nauseum. Then there was Jed the Great who conquered Kawartha with the motley force confronted by hair-brained men, skinny mothers and haunted children. They will probably call me Cephren the Implant. I spaced out and gave away Sunsetwind. I can see Trinny Burnamthorpe having kittens with glee and spreading the good word of my tragic demise. She actually called the other day to see if I was feeling better. What a joke! Those double-wink blue eyes flashed an expression so

cynically sympathetic, she'd make Hoyle confess and Flower Child murder.
She did at least give me an option to see Sam again. After the Symposium,
there was a rude silence regarding his access. The simmering political gruel
was thickening. Double double burst the bubble. Slow cook the stew and add
to the brew: Sam will visit over Christmas, because his mother is going away .
. . to Tahiti? With her friends? What friends? A few unlucky genos and a
silicon breeder or two. Spare me and Sam the details, please. Then there was
our little deal that was put off, I thought. No. Remember we are responsible
democratic politicians. Really? Have you seen anything, she asks. Stars,
I say, millions of stars. Stars? What on earth for, she asks. I say the tribal
panacea: it's in the stars. You know, there's Ursula Major, the one with the big
tits. No, I don't say that. I say my head is a balloon. What do I know? I'm
trying to keep it from popping every time I see stars. Keep me posted, she
says. Escape, and she's gone. I must be playing into her trap. So I will play, to
see my son. Small price, so far.

I'm back in the saddle. All the particular plagues of this position are upon
me. Three weeks of prescribed do-nothing and buzz are behind me. There are
exactly one hundred and one memos on my monitor. Even George Washington has once again availed himself; O'Reilly too, with an apologetic note saying: 'Delicacies are numbing – forgive my insouciant ways of the flesh. I have
taken the oath of monogamy. I have shaved my beard in honour of your sister.
I will retire to the Llasa Monastery if my vows are breached. All the Kush
will be Cleo's. I love Cleo, Cephren, with a passion, and I think you know
what that means. She is my queen, empress. Cephren, you are my brother. I
will defend you and Sunsetwind if I can. You must reach me as soon as you
are able to discuss these issues. I just heard America and Chicago have made a
North American ally-pact. Outside interference will be met with force no
matter whose borders have been encroached! My hands are tied! Please see
you soon. Get well.' Poor O'Reilly must really be suffering. What's that old
saying? Seperation makes the heart grow fond? I think it's more like sick. He
even shaved his hasheen beard. Cleo must be suffering too. They really are
nuts. But oh, I must not pass judgement; I have been too far removed from the

material. The reins of power are in my head notwithstanding my heart, yet the practical business of rule is too removed from my mind. Then these demonstrations have begun again while I've been incapacitated. This Del Barker and his Free Radicals taking such liberty! They have no idea what lies out there beyond our borders: the new technocracies, selling themselves to the highest bidder, and now I have joined their ranks with this device . . .

The monitor beeps. Cephren answers and Mita appears on the screen. She puts her hand up to the mirror and Cephren reaches to touch her from his side. 'Good morning,' she says, her hair tied up with strands hanging down provocatively. She is wearing sharp navy linens with silver brocade.

'Good morning, Mita,' he says smiling. During his convalescence, Cephren and Mita had rekindled much of their mystery. It was as intriguing as ever and more. Every evening they would sit at each end of the sofa to watch some entertainment, or relax in each other's silence, or more often, conduct quiet conversation regarding everything including her dear departed Rao. Mita had become cerebral to the point of sublimity in her middle age. She revealed she no longer craved or coveted physical pleasure. Cephren responded by saying he too had foregone sex, but he wasn't at all sure whether he believed her. There is enough of it about, she said with an almost imperceptible tinge of remorse for what may have been a sentiment aimed at their youthful passion. Every evening she would personally massage Cephren around the neck and back accompanied by chiropractic therapy. This was done to assist the body's regenerative "spirit" and alleviate his muscular trauma due to the healing nerves in his cerebral cortex. She enjoyed touching him although she never forgot her strict protocol. Cephren, naturally was completely resigned to her care and let her know by the occasional sigh of relief-with-pleasure. Her mysterious smile would emerge with the hint of flush in her cheeks from the exertion-with-pleasure.

'How are you today?' she enquires with that smile on his monitor.

'Saddled with toil, Mita; I miss those long lapses by your window.'

'I, too,' she says. 'Have you seen any more stars?'

'Yes, the usual. I saw the big dipper last night.'

'Do you think it was a dream or something in the chip?'

'I never used to dream about stars, and they keep coming back.'

'Have you dreamed?'

'I had a strange dream last night about Flower Child.'

'Now that's a typical Sunsetwinder.'

Olivia Lee had done a paper on Flower Child dreams, which were a common theme even amongst the diversity of her clients.

'I suppose you're right, but I never really dreamed of her before. She was reciting a poem, the one about her mentors.'

'Go on. I'm interested.'

'I...I don't know how to explain it really; it seemed as if I was reciting the poem, but it was really she; and it's not as if she was actually reciting it . . . '

'Was she writing it?'

'Maybe she was; it was all so vague. The words just came. You know, I can still hear them in this marvelous voice, with perfect cadence.'

'Tell it to me, Cephren.'

'You must know it: *The Mentors*. I think she had an alien experience.'

'I'm afraid I don't.'

'Really?'

'I've never heard of it.'

'I assumed it must be in some anthology.'

'I am quite familiar with her work. I thought I had read everything,' says Mita. 'Can you please recite it for me?' she reiterates.

'I don't know . . . you must know *The Mentors!*'

'I *really* don't.' She is getting a little impatient.

'Okay, I'll try to recite it. I believe it goes like this; it's kinda strange the way it stuck in my head:

They were there at the accolade for the wrong stuff
The applause went on for generations...
They were astounded at the public eye
Who had presided with the media in the bleachers
Cheering madly for themselves
And praying a lot without umbrellas in the rain
Though my heart went out to their problems...
And I was sorry about the sterility
Then sulphuric ash poured down to cover the bodies...
I am also sorry about the jammed freeways
But envious of the t.v.s and radios full of sexy music
That served up one heck of a party...
We are different like happy haunted mutants
But for them I envy in me a fertility
Like those festive Pompeians frescoed on walls forever
Arm in arm
I am like a green spring shoot...
Envy in me wrapped with my knees under a tree in the forest
Alone on a cold dark night with the coyotes...
I grip my headless Barbie doll
Wishing upon a star when in a flash of blue light
These little skinny fantastic children gather round
With a weird girl who looks just like Sailor Moon
And gives me this memory thing
And super-charges my eggs . . .
I just know that I remember my being there
As if I was as old as the hills
Though I was only seven...'

Cephren sighs relief with his eyes still shut. Mita has her mouth open
in awe. She can hardly believe Cephren had remembered the entire poem
with such prolific ease. It had emerged from his vocals with such a profound

subtlety – each phrase and image a suspension precisely delivered. Cephren opens his eyes.

'Cephren, you dreamed that? You remembered exactly?'

'It all came back to me just like that.'

'Cephren, it's incredible. Somehow you have dreamed up a lost Flower Child piece. And not just a piece but a bonafide abduction experience! What can it mean? Is there a connection to the chip?'

'Good point.' Cephren is impressed with Mita's exuberance. 'I must write it down,' he adds.

Mita studies him. Cephren is acting distantly as if he had discovered some lost self-realisation. His usual relaxed countenance is lacking, replaced by some foreign perception. Mita still smiles enjoying his predicament. Her intuition knows that Cephren would land feet first, but for the life of her, this Flower Child poem couldn't have been farther from what she even remotely conceived as a possibility; it simply had no relevance to what they had hoped for in the chip. 'Oh please do write it down; you can't know how much this means to me,' she says gently, almost imploringly.

'Are you thinking what I'm thinking?' suggests Cephren.

'I don't know. What are you thinking?' she responds a bit vacuously.

'Flower Child had the same chip, Mita – the so-called *memory thing*.'

'Perhaps, but who was Sailor Moon?' she asks, lost on the possibilities.

'Someone who looked liked that historic carton character, I suppose.'

'I don't know the implications here, Cephren, but keep trying to remember more, then record them; and we'll send them along to Great Blue U. for analysis and verification.'

Cephren is too surprised to delve too deeply with the possibilities. He sees in the allusions of the poem a vague outline or pattern that he can't quite put into words. His mind is different; there isn't any doubt about that. With a sudden impulse he perceives that in Flower Child's poem a possible schematic link to Pidgeon could be evident – a bit of *a science fiction story*. But is it to be believed? He must thread the needle if indeed there is a thread, or even a needle, and where is the haystack?

The week before there had been an alarming disturbance in Barrie, Sunsetwind's largest urban community, situated in Huronia at the edge of Lake Simcoe, which separates Kawartha. The disturbance was headed by a man named Del Barker who is a trader in the Barrie market. He works as a senior executive for the Nottawasaga Bank Line which couriers funds for all the banks, as well as operates an extensive public transport system; and he also began a private transit company that has of late been lobbying hard for greater access to foreign markets and travel credits. Barker had been in the news on numerous occasions in the last year or so. He had become the central advocate in the need for change. Although well-to-do, he is a notorious figure because he attracts a radical riff raff and knows how to agitate the status quo. Most Sunsetwinders have not taken him seriously believing Barker to be a harmless but perhaps necessary anomaly. This latest escapade has changed all that. Political lines have been drawn and crossed.

Del Barker and his select group had besieged the local municipal offices and refused to leave. They called out for new rules regarding foreign access and selling off private hegemony. Chromolox went immediately to speak with them and they only gave in to her after immunity and a public promise to "hasten the process". But these things take time and this radical group had gained an important political victory. To diffuse the crisis, Chromolox had said publicly that she and all the Board are "one hundred percent" behind the initiatives espoused by the Free Radicals (so named because the "cancer" they cause would kill the old order to make way for the new), but were hampered by foreign intransigence, except Chicago. Old Sunsetwind loyalties prevailed at that point and people went about their business. Yet, the Free Radicals had promised to stage random demonstrations all over Sunsetwind to keep up the pressure.

From previous ground-swelling sentiments regarding various policy changes, Gabriella had been issuing passports for business and recreational ventures at an unprecedented rate, but the tide is rising for employees without personal emop transportation to use Barker's Line as it is called to go elsewhere in North America as well as in Europe and the Far East. Chromolox and the Board have agreed in principle, but foreign bureaucratic implications and costs continued to stem the tide. At a council meeting, which Cephren had missed, there was division amongst Board members as how best to accommodate the average person who wished to travel without the government having to pay. The problem is that the Chicagos have blitzed the airwaves with all kinds of propaganda regarding wealth and relative exotica offering wonderful government funded package-tours and investment opportunities. The average Sunsetwinder has a superb education and finds employment in most fields; however, because of the very limited market, the accrual of wealth is rare. Every aspect of the economy since the Horror is controlled by private interests held traditionally as a sacred trust for the preservation of life. The neo-feudal state has unfortunately outgrown its original purpose and is crying for change, especially in the markets, where entrepreneurs are being stonewalled by bottled up consumer demand and intransigent industrial monopolies which worked their way down through the system. Only new agreements with other sovereign states can expand the market needs and growing demands of the consumer. Society is transcending itself in spite of bureaucratic resistance and the government's genuine concern for the country's well-being.

Cephren's problems on the political level are coming head to head with the domestic reality of his time. Chromolox is trying to juxtapose both realities and getting nowhere. Now Del Barker and his Free Radicals are in open revolt. This is inevitably spreading throughout the population. The only sector that seems stable at present is agriculture which of course is the foundation of both the economy and constitution of Sunsetwind. Cephren's worst nightmare has caught up with him forcing him to set aside his private agenda and face the realities or succumb. All history and culture of Sunsetwind are on the line. Despite the latent threat of a full-scale invasion by the Chicagos, this revolt seems to confirm those fears regardless of what remedy the Board envisages. Their old ways could well be doomed after all, a paradise lost, indeed. The wave of the future has met a wall after a two-hundred-year leap five steps forward, but threatening three back.

In Chicago and elsewhere it is reported that Sunsetwind is in the midst of a revolution. At the last Board meeting, which Cephren also missed, it was discussed and proposed by Seven Moons that the initiative be taken to announce changes including the holding of a referendum and lottery to get both the public's approval and appeasement. What could be more democratic than that? So a whole roster of proposals are being circulated through the papers to inform the public what lay in store for them. Chromolox has been very careful in her public appearances to warn the people that their sovereignty was not something to be trifled with. The Chicagos are a fascist society who held Sunsetwind's geopolitical importance with the utmost contempt. There is no telling what might happen if the flood waters of "economic union" submerged this province's fertile and freedom loving country.

And what is Cephren doing about the looming chaos in his country? This has also become an issue. The Chicagos have once again insinuated in various newspaper articles that Cephren "…is in therapy in Mita Waterman's exclusive clinic for the Sunsetwind elite . . . " The *Des Moines Religious Review* even goes so far as to say " . . . the fallen monarch who, as good sources had uncovered, lost his mind and was going under the knife to correct a mental imbalance…" and "…Cephren Path has made a pact with the devil, and is now in arrears, and bankrupt. The price exacted has yet to be disclosed. A man with little faith can only expect the wrath of God sooner or later." Cephren, typically, remains oblivious to their kangaroo journalism. His mission is certainly not to be politically expedient to a corrupt oligarchy. Nor is it the blatant militancy of aggressive power. It is nevertheless a time when societies and cultures seem to turn a blind eye to the values of the past, forgetting that hard-earned freedoms come with a very steep price. Yet these insinuations seem to strengthen his resistance. His very enlightenment long removed him from even the concept of devil and god; so what emerged is ironically something akin to a biblical tragedy. And the literature of the bible has become so obscure, that old paradigms of behavioural ethics based on fear of God are beyond his grasp as well as most Sunsetwinders. And so fearlessly he faces these changing times.

Stepping off his private lift onto Survivor's Walk, Cephren briskly walks towards his favourite restaurant, La Petite Vache. As he passes the Atrium and Waterway entrance facing the statue of Flower Child, the general commotion of people turns into a gathering. Someone notices Cephren, and yells, 'Chairman Path! Are you with us?' The crowd instantly parts and surrounds Cephren. There are some jeers and approbation mixed. He realises he is amidst a gathering of Free Radicals. Shaken abruptly out of his worried thoughts, he is at a loss for words. He smiles and must have looked stricken. The first thing that comes to his mind was the idea Seven Moons had left on his monitor concerning civic unrest; do the lottery: free credits for tickets. Cephren pulls out a dollar coin and flips it. On the back of his hand is the sweet face of Flower Child. 'Heads,' he says loudly, 'for a lottery!'

There is little response. Most of them are looking at him as if what the Chicago and Mississippi papers said is true that Cephren Path has lost the grasp of power and is sinking beneath the wheels of "progress".

'And tails!' He looks at the other side of the coin and sees the Pyramid with the Niagara escarpment and Great Blue behind. 'The rape of Flower Child!' he exclaims, pointing to her statue appealing to their loyalties. 'That's what will happen to us! I must tell you the truth. And the truth is cruel. The Chicagos are waiting for moments like this. This is their success! They would enslave us! Please . . . '

A tomato hits him square in the face. A dozen eggs are thrown simultaneously, half of which hit him in the head and body, one in the groin. Someone yells: 'Down with the impotent bastard!' A terrible scene follows in which an emerging group of Cleo's guerillas and duty officers clash severely with the Free Radicals. Her force, using stun guns, incapacitate at least a dozen men and women as the guerillas remove a prostrate Cephren in agony from the granite floor. He refuses their help and with difficulty stands up to face his adversaries.

'Let them go!'" he yells to the guerillas. 'They cannot have meant it! It was a mob mentality relieved of their senses! Propagated by unseen influences! We will forget this incident! Now everyone go home!' Then he shakes off two men and departs for the lift.

The incident becomes known as the Egg and Tomato Riot. It gains worldwide attention in which Cephren is portrayed as the 'impotent leader getting a reality check . . . and insulting his people by letting the perpetrators go thus demonstrating his autocratic ego. He has created the worst type of monster – a moral vacuum . . . ' The image of Cephren cringing in pain covered in egg and tomato is unfortunately the perfect metaphor for his downfall. It is mercilessly personal and yet political dynamite. Any sympathy for him among his friends on the Board is offset by the growing internal malaise of the political climate. Cephren has become the butt-end joke. His victimization has become the symbol of weakness from which everyone wanted to disassociate. The new ethics of a supposed people power has been set in motion by the seductive policies of a new world order emerging out of scientific and economic collaboration with the only means to an end being control. Social values adjust to the harsh realities. People are being teased by the promise of material success. Fashion becomes culture and culture fashion, all underwritten by faith, any faith as long as it is religious – at least a fashionable piety. All the big cities such as Chicago, Toronto and New York are once again Meccas for the sensational dream of enlightened pleasure. And Cephren has become a symbol for the tragic dinosaur of the godless past.

Still Cephren plugs on. He meets with Vince Fuchs in Engineering and Logistics the very same day as the Egg and Tomato Riot. He jokes about egg on his face and Vince doesn't have a clue as to what he is talking about. It isn't until Vince sees the evening news that he realises what had happened. He actually beeped Cephren on his monitor and left him an angry message saying he was out of his mind not to press charges.

When they met earlier, they have some very candid discussions. Vince vents his feelings about Cleo's involvement with O'Reilly and Cephren has to remind him to mind his own business. Among other things, they make a thorough inspection of the new Volcano, which has at least a twenty percent greater reactor charge than previous models. Vince explainsd that without a denser element to irradiate than high grade platinum, there is little more they could squeeze out of their reactor, which is standard for most emops around the globe with and without their patent, which is impossible to enforce. Vince explains that unless they discover something like the mythical unumpentium (UUP), an element with an atomic density of 115, they would never be able to travel beyond the solar system with their present form of technology. Unumpentium, if real, is considered to be unavailable on earth, as it was referred to as an extraterrestrial element in many of the B400 programs from the Secret Age. It is apparently found in Red Giant star systems, in which planets were formed under far hotter circumstances. It is a well-known theory that UUP has such a density that one kilo of it is able to detonate 50 ten megaton hydrogen bombs. When UUP is bombarded with protons and heated to its melting point at 1,740 degrees celsius, it generates element 116 that discharges anti-matter at a far greater amplitude. Such an annihilation in the reactor between matter and anti-matter creates an electromagnetic gravity field estimated from a hundred to a thousand times more powerful than their present reactors. And as gravity propagates itself easily in space, it is believed the manipulation of the time-space continuum is possible, thus making the linear light year distance to neighbouring star systems shrink or warp in a gravity fissure that actually bends, or contracts space. For example, during an eclipse it is possible to see stars directly behind the sun because the sun's gravity caused the star's light to bend around the sun. Gravity also distorts time. If there are two equally synchronized atomic clocks and one is taken up in an emop or up a mountain, on returning they would be out of sync because the clock that remains at sea-level is in a stronger gravitational field.

Vince then shows Cephren his new improved gravity amplifiers. The ameliorated reactor in the Volcano's transmitter is tuned to the three amplifiers (30 centimeters in diameter and sixty centimeters long) forming a triad around the reactor as receivers of the generated gravity wave in amplitude, wavelength and frequency. As the amplitude increases, gravitational waves bend around the oblong disc (the same dimensions as the Experimentor – seven meters long, four wide and four deep). The disc itself is a bismuth-beryllium-titanium inject molded hull with a zinc alloy surface coat. Heat and high pressure resistant windows are installed fore and aft with all the controls, propulsion and eco-system interior.

The Volcano is equipped with a foldout kitchenette, toilet, sink, and foldout bunks. This amazing piece of new Sunsetwind technology could exit the atmosphere and do a loop around the moon and back in under an hour. It can submerge safely underwater to a depth of five thousand meters for extended duration unlike the older models, which could submerge down to five hundred meters only for a short time.

Needless to say, Cephren is impressed, questioning whether or not he should be the one to take it. 'Maybe Chromolox or you, Vince, should have it,' he says.

'Nah, take it, Cephren, take it. For nature'sake, we all know you deserve it.'

Cephren doesn't argue with him; besides, now that the prototype is complete, they can produce many more at the plant in Alliston.

They walk over to a lift that takes them up to Vince's office. There, a pretty assistant brings in some mint tea and shortbread cookies of which Vince devours all but one and when Cephren doesn't want it, devours it too.

'Cephren,' he says in his brash voice, 'you know, we believe everything's going to hell, ever since Redman figured Jimmy's Chip was some mutant monster and now you wear it with some kinda vain hope that its secrets will change our predicament. Well, horse piss! You know and we know that ain't gonna happen. Even Cleo, bless her sweet…pardon me, isn't going to stop what seems to be going down. The floodgates are opening, man! Sunsetwind will be done in by that rat-faced bitch Burnamthorpe and her head games. Dammit, how in the hell are we to stop the unification of North America? We are one damned stick-in-the-mud to those powers that would see it happen! George, bless his black arse, is a great guy, but he's not going to sit and wank the dog when Chicago talks turkey! What I'm trying to say, Cephren, is being as the powers are arrayed against us, let's try surfing for a change. None of this self-right-eous-sovereign-destiny-crap. Hell, I wish we could just keep on trucking the way we are, but you know and we know that ain't playing the game. This is old time snakes and ladders, man! Appease the bitch; dish out the same medicine; let's not stand on scruples here. We have to put our finger to the wind to see which way it blows, not the index up yours!'

Cephren laughs to himself. Vince is the embodiment of perfection in practical affairs; the trouble is this affair isn't any simple conquest, though Trinny would sure find him an easy lay. Vince is read a mile away. His redeeming quality is that he comes by it naturally. There is nothing devi-ous about him in the slightest, which is why so many women warm to his gregarious appeal. Yet loyalty is something to be desired; his concept of loyalty is fun and games. Cephren doesn't suppose he'd feel that way if a platoon of genos absconded with his precious emop technology and he was put out to pasture to upgrade his particular genotype, or maybe he would. Cephren gives him the benefit of the doubt.

'Cephren,' continues Vince, 'in my opinion there's only one thing you have to do. Don't worry about this country for a while; I mean, Chro-molox is elected to do that with the rest of us. All you have to do is get into that damned chip and find that damned unumpentium; we know they had it. If we can get some of that, we've got the world by the short 'n curlies, man. No one could come close to our technology. And that, my friend, is the order of the day: technology. We have risen from the dead

and now it's pay back time! Now take that Volcano and boogie! It's been
test driven over and over in orbit, in Lake Superior, around Mars, deep in
the Pacific. It's hot! Go for it! '

⟨◦◦◦⟩

By the time Christmas comes around Cephren finds himself almost apathetic in regard to the parade of events. His own sense of failure to plum
the depths of the implant underlines this, as well as mounting social
unrest, not to mention the Chicago threat that quietly simmers. This is
an unusual state for him because his modus proceeds from an ineluctable
intuition, but intuition is not indemnified; therefore, nothing can be
more indignant to his sense of self than a supercilious apathy of intuition.
He feels as if he is stagnating like a slow weather system that refuses to
move on. And the current charade of political correctness is the symptom
of this malaise.

That week Sunsetwind had directed a vehement official objection to
the Earth Federation with a long list of grievances aimed at punching
holes in the Chicago's bubble of superiority and obvious abuse of their
once fraternal relations. The earlier EF Path-Burnamthorpe judgement of
2389 regarding Cephren and Trinny personally was failing obviously to
curb her use of diplo-immunized avenues of covert terrorism.

The primary grievance is the presumed assassination of Impala that
seemed to set off a well-orchestrated chain reaction, which has victimised
all of Sunsetwind in an embroiling crisis; and specifically Cephren Path,
who has obviously been targeted personally for discrediting and degrada-
tion. A meticulous report outlining the probable sequence of arranged circumstances that led up to Impala's death, including Cephren's insinuated
complicity by the Chicagos, is the central abridgement to the whole grievance. There is a history of abuse, a proven means to an end in respect to
the Chicago's designs on the continent. There is also a chronology and pro
forma as to their political success with recent economic and geo-political

agreements that ignore Sunsetwind and a few other states completely. The reaction of the Earth Federation of which George Washington is Chairman and Cephren a life member, is unprecedented. Sunsetwind is now to be reprimanded publicly for not taking steps to "beef up" their involvement in world affairs and specifically the unification issue that any "responsible" country would realise is the only way to maintain peace. Chromolox is then soundly booed by her own constituents at a rally to promote self-determination. The Free Radicals are seen as the ones gaining currency once again, as they, under the cagey leadership of Del Barker, are harvesting the smut of an infested time. But what really hurts is the notion and abomination that only as a substitute for war is the Earth Federation permitting the growth of militarism in national agendas. It is absurd, argues Chromolox at the rally that to no avail we must be seen as the *provocateurs* in the 'distemper of the times'. The times could not see the forest for the trees, and the forest was dark. Sunsetwind was once again stymied in her attempt to rein in a world gone mad. Hence Del Barker played on this opportunity.

Cephren, somewhat reluctantly, has been steadily retreating from the public forum, not that he really ever strove to be there in the first place, having taken the advice of Vince, Mita, LeRoy and most of the Board. The X13 is taking up all his thoughts and waking hours. It seems even in his sleep the stars would again materialise like a computer holding pattern. Yet he could not penetrate the surface. Occasionally glimpses of what was beneath came, he presumed, as in the amazing Flower Child dream. Nothing he does before or after bed is significantly different from what he usually does in the evening and morning. Presumably, if Flower Child's dream came from the chip, there must be something he did to access that information, but who knows what? Cleo has suggested that perhaps an outside scan aimed at Cephren on an untraceable frequency might attempt to read any electromagnetic transmission emanating from his head. But again there is no way of knowing for sure, because when Bill Deerhill tried it, nothing happened. They try it again when Cephren is sleeping, and

Cephren does claim he saw a shooting star but some clouds moved in. Then again, he has never experienced that before. He concludes that scanning does have some influence but not an important one. The chip's secrets would remain so. It seems that the mind as a vast untapped reservoir of information is as illusive as this chip and the two were not necessarily inclined to form a partnership, at least without the *open sesame*.

'*Open sesame!*' says Cephren to himself as he packs a few belongings for his trip with Sam to Kawartha through Christmas and New Year's. Outside his bedroom suite in the loft adjacent to the kitchenette, dining room and study beyond stands a new addition to Cephren's world – a one hundred and thirty-five kilogram one hundred ninety-five centimeter (three hundred pound, six foot six) ex-New England Patriot fullback turned guerilla, the indomitable black Sunsetwinder, Runaway Dumptruck. And Runaway could run the hundred meters in ten seconds flat. He was especially feared on kickoff returns when he came down full throttle like a herd of buffalo, not to mention "sweeps" and "through the line", he liked to say confidently.

After the so-called Egg and Tomato Riot, Cleo had marched into Cephren's study with one of her best officers, Runaway Dumptruck, and left him there. Others were posted below and outside in an emop that now hovers about the Pyramid. Enough is enough, she had said sternly. Cephren has gotten used to Runaway, now five years retired from pro ball. They rarely speak and have a comfortable silence. For all Runaway's fantastic symmetry, he is an accomplished Kung Fu adept and flexible like a gymnastic bear. The two have a great thing in common. They are both cerebral, albeit coming from very different backgrounds.

Within the hour they are up and away, Cephren in the Volcano and Runaway in the Experimentor. Flying a hundred feet above the tree line they take the south central corridor through to Beeton. There waiting with his happy stunned expression is Sam surrounded by a small flotilla of menacing genos, but no Trinny. The exchange takes place amicably and Cephren and Sam with Runaway following, head east towards Kawartha.

All the world beneath them is covered in a brilliant white blanket of snow. Sparse grey forests and green snow-clad conifers rush by as they follow the south perimeter east. Farms and villages in the Neutrals appear sporadically, their fires smoking profusely in the frigid, blue sky under an ample panoply of swiftly moving clouds. The silent hum of the emop and Sam's gleeful presence puts a wide smile on beleaguered Cephren's face. Little Sam is excited as the wild lands speed beneath. They cross Lake Simcoe, flying low as the expanding ice along the shore and bays passes along. Then come the little drumlins, farms, lakes and rivers of Kawartha. Peterborough, to the south, is on the southern perimeter and partly forested since the Horror. Its people are both Sunsetwinder's and Neutrals. It is a little like a frontier region, both wild and unruly. They head for The Honey's farm that extends down to the lakeshore. There are numerous cabins in the woods along the shore where Cephren would sometimes spend his holiday season and had being doing so since he was boy, as his mother was a Kawarthan. The lake is fully frozen over and the dark ice can be seen where the snow has blown clear.

Waiting for them on the drive are Strange and Treason Honey. Strange Honey had been a child prodigy in fine art. Her early paintings and later sculptures were sold worldwide as well as her contemporary work. Hers is one of those phenomenal successes. A mixed race blue-eyed mulatto from Cleveland who moved with her Forager father to Lindsay at the age of three began to paint. The father sold her paintings first in flea markets, then the big market in Barrie. Her rise to prominence was one of those miracle success stories that happens every few generations. Out of the bingo of life an amazing talent makes its presence known.

'Oh Cephren,' gushes Strange emotionally, 'I have been so worried, like never before.' They hug and she kisses him on both cheeks; then bends down to do the same to little Sam who responds in his limp way. He looks up to her submissively and smiles in a way that Cephren had never seen him do before. He makes everyone giddy with delight.

'Don't worry, Strange,' says Cephren. 'We are blessed with good intelligence.' He then hugs Treason who puts her head on his chest. 'How is my little Treason,' he declares, as he kisses her black wavy hair.

'Treason is not so little, Cephren,' she replies confidently, looking up into his eyes. They are electric blue, which defies her mulatto skin like shining orbs.

'I can see that,' he says, profoundly affected by her new mature voice and vibrant womanhood. Cephren had not seen Treason in four years. She had been traveling around the world, and apparently conducting an affair in Chicago that was still burning embers, and for a time roughing it in the bush beyond the perimeter. 'I am so overjoyed to see you here this year,' he continues, 'and want to hear all about your exciting times.'

'Well, we will be spending a lot of time together, Cephren; don't you know?' she asks with a mischievous smile.

'Having not seen you for such a long time, I should hope so.'

'Treason is a guerilla,' reveals Strange, sighing.

'A guerilla?' he exclaims surprised.

'Don't be so surprised, Cephren; I've been around and I'm going to be around while you're here, as your personal shadow.'

'Cleo assigned her personally, Cephren,' informs Strange.

'It's good to know everyone close to me is looking out for me. Let me introduce to you . . . ' Cephren looked around for Runaway. Treason gives Sam a kiss. Runaway is still in the emop circling around the area getting the lay of the lake and land. 'Runaway Dumptruck is still checking out the country.'

'Runaway Dumptruck? Are you kidding?' utters Treason excitedly.

'None other, I hope,' he answers.

'Impressive.'

'So between the two of you, I shall sleep soundly.'

'Sounds cozy,' she teases.

'Please, show Cephren to his cabin, Treason,' says Strange. 'And Sam, are you going to have the time of your life! Well, you'd better come with me. I want you to meet my grandchildren. Jacob is not much younger than you, but he's pretty tough, 'cause he's growing up in the woods and on a farm.' Strange leads him into their huge dovetail log house situated on the rise overlooking the lake. There are cows and horses about and Sam goes along in open-eyed wonder. 'Come up as soon as you're settled, Cephren,' says Strange in parting. 'Seymour will be back from Lindsay in an hour or so.'

'I brought some vintage Beaujolais,' he calls out.

'Great,' she responds from the door.

They begin with that old time celebration that brought so much happiness to the children and adults alike. Seymour dresses up as Santa Claus and puts on a show. Even Cephren is touched by his magical presentation. Seymour is after all the real Santa, Sam was told. Though for all his bonhomie, Seymour is a sad fellow. The love he gives out is not returned, at least by the woman closest to him. Strange has specific terms regarding their communal pact. After the loss of her husband Dick, an alcoholic, whom she loved fiercely for his wit and looks, Strange would never allow herself to love in the same way again. She demanded her independence even including romantic liaisons with others. Her artistic expression was her *primum mobile* and nothing could interfere. Seymour having lost at love previously, accepts her terms because he idolises her and her art, which he had collected before he knew her. Seymour subverts his ardent affection for Strange to her family and grandchildren as well as putting Strange on a pedestal that demands his sacrificial adulation. Seymour is too enamoured of being taken into Sunsetwind's most prominent artistic family to let fidelity get in the way; besides, she wanted her own bedroom and studio to be her private space. In defence of Strange, however, she gave him ample warning and never slept with Seymour before he moved in. In fact, in the advent of sexual relations, which happens between them infrequently, the circumstances are likely contingent on some artistic whim of Strange's, calling him her Frodo. But his love is unconditional. One time he discovered her and a young male apprentice in the studio covered in paint. Apparently, her purported lover had been subjected to being painted then made to satisfy her sexually. Seymour accepted her as the consummate artist, though remaining her favourite doormat.

Strange's daughters on the other hand, are not only beautiful like their mother with that blue-eyed mulatto combination, but talented as well. Season, the eldest and divorced, runs a farm and raises horses. She has two children, Jacob and Robyn and had published two books of verse as well as a children's book that won international acclaim. Her sister, Reason, follows in her mother's footsteps and lives nearby in her own studio with her lawyer husband. She did the illustrations for Season's books and has a toddler named Zack. Then Treason, of course, is the guerilla.

For Christmas eve and subsequent days and evenings, they all feast stupendously on Strange's vegetarian meals including exotic curries from the Gujarat, marinated tofu roast, coconut salmon (made by Season), Bali ginger bean curd stir fry and delicate salads. Reason had them over for Traditional Cranberry Duck and pumpkin pie.

Young Sam learns how to cross-country ski with his new friend Jacob and simply glows with happiness. Strange paints a portrait for him portraying an amazing juxtaposition of his expression, both cheerful yet melancholy that only Strange could achieve.

Cephren, all the while enjoys the quaint comforts of his cabin and general scene that strikes memory chords from his past, though becomes increasingly frustrated at his failed attempts to make any progress with his implanted X13. He is beginning to wonder whether the whole exercise is futile, as he had been forewarned. Also, nipping at the edges of his tolerance is Treason who watches over him tenaciously. He has let Runaway go home for a few days as he feels he is more than looked after by Treason. Yet he is not comfortable with Treason's guardianship, as she all but sleeps with him at night. Runaway, for all his size, seems to disappear and appear at appropriate intervals. Undoubtedly Treason is using her very youthful looks and new sexual maturity in little ways that could not help but both titillate and intimidate Cephren. She suddenly would hug him from behind without invitation and one time when Cephren was stretched out on the bed she flopped down and lay her head on his tummy with her knees up and talk of banalities that bored Cephren to the point of distraction. He angrily rebuts her lingering kiss goodnight and shoos her away. She would return apologising for her lack of professionalism and go to her bunk without a sound. She hardly mouths a word to him for a day, but before long it is the same as before. She is in the difficult position of seeing him as a father figure, of which he is her favourite and also as a possible lover about which she could not admit defeat to herself. So she comes across as being the little girl she had always been to him.

The evening before New Year's would inauspiciously become the turning point in Cephren's quest for a breakthrough with Jimmy's Chip. After he had read Sam a bedtime story, he is restless and paces in front of the fire. He is at a dead end and knows not how to proceed any further with the inscrutable chip. Feeling hot, he goes to the door and opens it. He takes in deep breaths of the pine and cedar scented air. It is positively frigid. The thermometer reads minus 28 degrees celsius. Frost sprinkles are gently dusting the boughs and hard surfaces and silently alight on the window. He is to take Sam back to Beeton the next day to be picked up. Trinny had decided it would not be in Sam's best interests to be around the "dissipation" of Strange Honey's New Year's. Cephren had decided that he would agree to her terms. Runaway will be back the next day, of which Cephren is grateful. Treason had been gone a while scouting in his Experimentor, and for all her peculiarity, she is resolute and determined in her guardianship. She keeps in close contact with her commanding officer, Captain Dave, and even Cleo once who had gone to the Kush to be with O'Reilly over New Year's. Cleo came onto Cephren's monitor luxuriating in her newfound dimension like a sun-basking tiger. She, nevertheless, in her authoritative way warns Cephren to be vigilant, but all is calm. Cephren thinks about Chromolox who arrived earlier that day for a couple of nights. She had become close friends with Season Honey, who is ten years younger and had invited her for New Year's. She is staying in the distant cabin out of sight down the shore of the lake. Cephren hears the humming of an emop somewhere above the trees in the darkness. The Experimentor appears and Treason flashes her lights at him as she descends beside his Volcano in the clearing by the lake. Out she gingerly steps in a change of clothing. She is wearing her new winter survival suit – a thick white synthetic one-piece with heated lining and water and windproof shell – open to the navel with navy linens underneath. She is carrying a bottle of Champagne and a CD that she waves saying, 'Guess what I have?'

'I don't know. I wondered where you disappeared.'

'You missed me? How beautiful. And I was doing my rounds. I stopped at mom's and brought this.' She shows him the little round disc. 'Renée Antoinette,' she announces opening her eyes wide. 'The one starring Anna Gram.' Then she hustles inside with Cephren in tow. 'Brrrr, it's cold!' She stamps her boots and begins to take off her survival suit, which is the type that could be used in the water. It has inflatable air pockets and even energy pills. 'So what do you think about that?' she asks shaking her mane of air and tucking it behind her shoulders.

'A great movie,' he replies. It is in fact one of his favourites. Strange had obviously suggested it, since she knew about his lifelong interest in Piercemore.

They watch it together. The romantic thriller was allegedly based on events in Danielle Perreault's life. Anna Gram had won an Oscar for it a few years back. The movie is a shockingly candid presentation that portrays Antoinette's (Perreault) intense affair with Joe Pirelli (Piercemore), a graphic drama about two passionate people, one a public figure, the other private, and how they are both consumed by the circumstances.

They sit on the sofa, with Treason invariably snuggling up to Cephren. The sex scenes have her literally pulsing against him. She is flushed and he feels not the least bit relaxed. The Champagne, however, soothes him enough to enjoy the movie. At the end she bows her head to his chest and puts her hand onto his thigh. Cephren stands up proclaiming the time for bed.

'Is that all?' She looks up.

'I really enjoyed the movie, Treason.'

'I mean, after all the quality time we've spent together, you can't even respond to me as a woman for even an instant?'

'I . . . I can't love you like that, Treason; you're like a daughter to me. I think you're wonderful and beautiful and very . . . talented.'

'If you thought I was so great, you'd want me. All men want me, but I don't want them. Can't you see, I want you?'

'Believe me, I know how you feel, Treason; it's just that I have too many burdens; having an affair with you would be too disruptive . . . '

'You can't know that if you don't find out. We're alone here in a cabin in the woods. For Nature'sake!'

'And you're my bodyguard . . . '

'I know,' she says seductively. 'I'd be so much more to you, Cephren,' she purrs as she slides her hands down his sides. Cephren stands there a moment passively as one hand slips into a large pocket in his flannel-lined linens. She dexterously reaches his genitals, but he quickly removes her hand without resistance. They stand there looking at each other. She realises that there is only firm resolve in his eyes.

'I'm sorry,' she says, coming to her senses. 'I don't know what's come over me. I really am sorry.' She then turns and exits to the bunks where Sam sleeps.

The following morning they awake to a very heavy snowfall. Treason again is on her best behaviour in a happy-go-lucky mood. Cephren has awakened with a curious sensation that he has forgotten or misplaced something. The thought had occurred to him while watching the movie the night before, but Treason's body language had sufficiently interfered with any salient thought, pushing it back into his mind. On the top of his mind is his responsibility to get Sam back to Beeton, but Sam has become uncharacteristically vociferous in his beseeching to remain for New Year's eve. And the weather is getting worse. The wind picks up to gale force readings. It would be stupid to take him back that day. He beeps in a message to Trinny's personal line in Chicago, but receives only her haughty recorded greeting. He explains the situation and can only hope she would receive his message. At any rate, they stay on to Sam's infinite relief and have a great repast and party.

After midnight and all the hoopla, Cephren, Sam and Runaway, now back, trudge excitedly through the drifts and blinding snow to the cabin to settle in for the night. The snow is flying with increasing velocity and it is very cold, their little journey seems like an expedition. Both Runaway and Sam snuggle into their bunks (Treason stays at her mother's that night) and Cephren sits at the window to watch the sheets of blinding snow buffet ferociously against the walls and window panes, making the cabin vibrate in response.

Cephren is about to nod off when he perceives faintly the resonant hum and static of an emop over and above the fury of the storm, the static being caused by the snow colliding with the gravitational field and spitting. Cephren, looking up through the window can see nothing, so he goes to the door, opens it and looks again. He still can't see anything, but hears clearly the unmistakable sounds of emops, lots of them, flying just above out of sight. Somebody's party lost their way home, he supposes and he closes the door, although still apprehensive. Unsatisfied, he then calls the main security monitor at the Pyramid, but gets no response, just a blank on his screen. His heart leaps. Can it just be the storm? Or could it be what they all feared most, an invasion. But in a blizzard? Unlikely, but not impossible; the perimeter defences could have been compromised in the severity of the storm. And no one would ever expect an attack on New Year's eve in such a blizzard! Cephren suddenly has the notion to speak to Chromolox. He calls her on his monitor; there is no response. He then puts on his boots and jumps into his own survival suit to brave the elements and drifting snow. Runaway then appears having sensed some alarm. Cephren explains to him the cause of his fears and what he is doing, but Runaway insists he should remain with him in the advent of an emergency. Cephren won him over, however, when he suggests that he fire up the reactor in the Volcano in case he must make a getaway. Runaway considers that and relents thinking the other emop, the Experimentor, would at least act as a decoy, if they are to evade capture. Once outside, Cephren clears the drift building up to the door of the Volcano and opens it with his remote wrist monitor. As he engages the reactor, the thought suddenly occurs to him what he had misplaced when he had been watching the movie. Anna Gram. That's what was nagging him this past day; after seeing that movie, it strikes him that something about the actress Anna Gram could be the clue he is seeking. *Anagram*. Maybe the password to the chip's program is an anagram. And if it was, it must be in that Pidgeon poem! It had to be, he thinks. In Elizabethan times messages were encoded in anagrams within poems. He has the intuitive revelation that that was the purpose of the poem. Meanwhile, he struggles up to his waist in snow as he drags himself up to Chromolox's cabin. A drift had mounted half way up the door, so he goes to the window seeing the light of the fire. He is not sure what to do looking in and seeing in front of the fire Chromolox and Season entangled in a scrum of passion. Cephren backs quietly away, and retreats to his cabin. He thinks perhaps he should wait until later. He goes back to Runaway and tells him to stay with Sam so he can reconnoiter in the Volcano. They both hear the unusual emop traffic around them and know something is wrong. Runaway protests and having tried to reach the Pyramid again to no avail insists that he should be the one to go up and investigate. But Cephren is adamant. The plan must be for him to get away in case of an invasion. They probably would have found him already if it hadn't been for the storm. He would therefore use the storm as cover to get away; where, he isn't sure, but he would be in touch as soon as possible.

Cephren quickly grabs a few belongings and his monitor, then goes back outside and enters the Volcano. Although protected from freezing, he carefully engages the amplifiers, which make a whirring sound from the reactor charge. He has to wait a few moments to gain the required temperature before securing the gravity field. In the extreme cold, it is taking its time because the amplifiers had been shut down. Then he sees the lights, hundreds of them converging on the cabin through the raging blizzard against the darkened forest. Laser guns are aimed at his machine. Cephren quickly raises his defensive shields, then attempts lift off, but the amplifiers are not one-hundred-percent ready. A few more seconds . . . they are diving through the drifts to get at him, serious genos in white fatigues fully decked out with weapons and emop wave disruptor beams, but all are deflected by the Volcano. Cephren lifts finally as one geno almost slams a jammer onto the Volcano's hull only to be blasted away with others as his gravitational field collided with the snow in a blind flurry.

Cephren's Volcano shoots straight up like a rocket and in seconds pops up above the clouds at four thousand meters. There before him across the white, fluffy mass of clouds and the star-spangled cosmos are thousands of emops sitting like dark, silver pellets, waiting to rain down upon defense-less Sunsetwind. Cephren chokes back his tears as he plunges back into the blind cloud mass. Sunsetwind has been helplessly betrayed.

four Hot Dog Ice Cream

Wherefore the mosaic of stars
Like dreams do glimpse fantastic children
                                    –Jimmy Pidgeon

For a fleeting desperate moment as he plunges through the dense blizzard, Cephren fancies ending it all by letting go and crashing; it would be painless, sightless and not a little gratifying to die as a martyr. As he plunges, there is a grim, yet electric thrill in his meteoric nosedive, but at three hundred meters he engages the pulse inhibitor and levels to turn in a westerly direction towards the Pyramid. Being a martyr, he knows in this case, would be a cop-out. In his charred remains, they would find the X13, and that would be that – no hope for Sunsetwind. And what of Sam? Worse still, through such a forced obliteration, his life would be erased forever from the record and re-written to appease the oppressors – all so damned medieval. He flashes on the scenario: they would denounce him as a "coward" who tried to "steal" an innocent boy from his mother and in the ensuing pandemonium and revolution caused by the release of his "fanatical" grip on his people, Sunsetwind would be "liberated" and law and order restored. Del Barker would be installed as president-elect and his Free Radicals appointed to the Board, or it would be annulled completely. Chromolox and the others would be denounced as enemies to the freedom and unity of North America. They would be discredited as corrupt and perverted. Furthermore, both he and Cleo (fortunately she was out of the country) would be marked for death anywhere anytime via clandestine means.

And what of America? Its present impotency would derail any serious counter-threat to the Chicago invasion. War is not an option, especially if Chicago has made a non-aggression pact with them and who knows what else. Each region would salivate as they carve up Sunsetwind, especially stripping the province of its coveted technology. What is it all about, Cephren muses? Are we really a cancer at the heart of North America that must be cut out? They can't be doing themselves a favour. They would be literally cutting out the heart and soul of an honest people who stand for enlightenment and freedom of individual rights. Is this disaster a natural inclination for humanity – mother nature simply exercising her true accordance to life? Are individual freedoms ultimately an antiquated notion of ethnocentric morality? Cephren is confused, yet stubborn in his resolution to do what had to be done to set things right. Redman was correct in assuming the worst as a means to overcome such odds. It is either stay alive and fight, or martyrdom.

Cephren flies at 1000 kilometres per hour in the blinding blizzard. Through his curved windshield, nothing can be seen but a blur. Only a slight reflection from the corona of blue light emitting from the machine's underbelly can be seen in the wall of snow and darkness before him. He notices on his auto-control panel about thirty blips converging toward him. On the simulated display screen he can see Barrie pass beneath him and the Pyramid's beacon flashing far in the distance to the west. This is one of the modifications of the Volcano, a high-tech gyroscope to simulate a virtual reality when flying blind. The monitor is equipped with a global topographical and geographical sensor chip based on longitude and latitude as projected by the gyroscope and actual photographic memory of landmarks. Older models have similar devices but they are not so accurate unless one travels quite slowly with ground or satellite relays. Cephren then assumes that the emops on his tail are taking huge risks. He decides to dare them by flying low above the trees as they approach the escarpment. They stay with him. Good, he thinks. Then he accelerates to 5000 km/hr as he passes the Pyramid and heads for the rock bluffs. Quickly ascending at the last second, one, three, eight, thirteen, twenty blips disappear behind him. He smiles, thinking that was easy. He tries an open channel to reach the main monitor at the Pyramid. Still nothing; he assumes they must have shut down everything including the satellites, which may have been how they came in undetected. But who could have stopped them anyway?

Now there are at least a hundred more emops converging all around him. He can see laser flashes outside now; they are trying to shoot him down. Cephren, too, could direct a laser pulse but there is little point as he is so out numbered. They fly a little higher than before as they catch on to his tricks. Enough is enough, thinks Cephren; those laser flashes are too close; he must take some evasive action or be taken out. He darts north over Great Blue Lake and is about to dive into the water when a multiple laser pulse penetrates his defenses and jams his gravitational field. Cephren goes into a freefall. He is thrown back. Luckily he has on the seatbelt. He manages to feel for the auxiliary bypass and feels the craft automatically level itself not fifteen meters from the cold, black water beneath. He slows as he lands on the water and submerges, engaging the gravity inversion. He gently sinks to the bottom, only about forty meters deep. There he follows the lake bottom north about fifty kilometers to deeper water and stops. It is a curious feeling being there in those eerie silent depths in the middle of the night beneath a raging blizzard. The blips disappear although hovering a while where he had submerged. Hopefully they had gone, thinking his craft had been hit and sunk.

Trinny would not be happy with a messy underwater salvage operation. And so the next day as soon as the storm clears he knows they would be there with a salvage emop and underwater module searching for him and his treasure, the coveted X13, making him think that he must find some safe place to work on the chip. Anishnabe comes to mind. He could possibly set down in some remote wilderness region and sit things out for a time. And once secure, he would try to contact Cleo. To go to her immediately might put her at risk not to mention himself. O'Reilly would see to her safety for the time being, until she felt it prudent to return somehow, incognito. Cephren is reluctant to make a transmission for fear of giving away his position not to mention his being alive. Being dead, of course, is very good cover.

The Volcano had performed immaculately. It is a good thing only one existed; however, it wouldn't take much time to figure out that he had some kind of superior machine, once they realise he has disappeared. They are probably looking into it at that moment. Cephren hopes Vince had buried the new technology. But Vince was most likely at home warm in bed. And what of poor Chromolox? Only now does he have a moment to consider what must have happened to her and Season. They would have been rudely interrupted in a most uncompromising situation. He just hopes that Runaway, Treason, or especially Sam had not been hurt.

Cephren would also like to call Mita, but again he restrains himself knowing all the Board members would now be held in detention. They would be expecting his call through the Board's private channels if they thought he was alive. But once out of Sunsetwind, he presumes he could risk calling both Cleo and George Washington. Washington's response or lack of a response would give Cephren a good idea as to how the world was reacting to the invasion. For that matter, he could fly to Ottawa, the capitol of Anishnabe, and get some news firsthand or perhaps even appeal to the global links, which are not the most reliable of sources unless the news has been screened and cross referenced from non-partisan interests.

Cephren rides across Great Blue skimming just above the bottom. He comes across startled schools of whitefish and lake trout darting out of the way. He sees an enormous trout that seems to be almost two meters in length and he guesses 60-70 kilos. It moves rather lugubriously, unfazed by the foreign intrusion.

Coming to the northern shore well ensconced in Anishnabe territory,

Cephren stays submerged in a deep bay. There he settles down to get some much needed rest. A few hours later he wakens from a surprisingly good sleep. Again he has been comforted by the presence of stars, in fact, whole constellations. Unconsciously, the stars are so very familiar and unique in that the vast distances between them are of little consequence; it is as if like a navigator he somehow understands their configurations, precessions and dimensions.

He washes, then boils water to make raspberry tea from the few provisions in the Volcano. There are grains, dried beans and vegetables, soy products, dried fruits and a mineral tonic. He cooks some oats and spoons a little honey on them. With soymilk, the porridge is delicious.

Rising to the surface, he finds that the weather has improved, but not completely; the wind and clouds are still dominant, but the blizzard has ceased. Yet it is a viciously cold, grey winter's day. The water has not frozen due to the tremendous winds and the waves crashing against the emop causing great wafts of steam to rise as the repelling hull heats the frigid surf. Bobbing around, Cephren decides to lift off and head for a remote place from which to plan his next move.

He soars over the shield country of Anishnabe at a low altitude in order to stay beneath the low, angry cloud cover. The forests, lakes and rivers below are covered in a rippled blanket of snow that blows in swirls at the slightest current of wind. Isolated homes and occasional villages pass below until only the vast Precambrian world lay before him in a daunting, stark marvel of pure wilderness. The terrain begins to rise as he draws deeper into the Temaugauma region. He comes to the various high points of land and decides to put down under a low rock face near the summit of Spirit Mountain as indicated on his virtual map. The topography is very impressive in its ruggedness. The mountain, though rounded and rocky at the top with stunted trees around the edges and in the protected hollows, is much higher than the surrounding dense woodlands and lakes. From his perspective, his defensive scanners would give him fair warning of any intrusion. The sudden quiet accompanied by the mesmeric buffeting of the severe wind releases in Cephren the pent up shock of his ordeal. He shudders as he put his hands to his head, bowing over his monitor at the helm of the Volcano. He experiences a spine tingling sensation that produces a wave of hot flashes to his face. The delayed shock overwhelms any cogent sense of purpose. He feels helpless and inert. His mind boils in a staccato of incoherent images that cannot be calmed. Cephren stands up and then collapses onto his bunk that folds out from the wall of the craft. He lies there immobilised. The trauma that has set in would take time to ease. He knows what had to be done, but does not have the strength or will to see it through. Although he had slept at the bottom of Great Blue, a lethian tiredness weighs down on him like a drug as he closes his eyes and groans. Mita flashes through his mind, and Sam, Cleo, Vince, LeRoy and Chromolox and . . .

Cleo wakes up that New Year's day 2396 with fragrant wafts of cool, Himalayan air blowing through the open window. They had come from Llasa to a village high in Jammu two days before. Her lover lies beside her dead asleep, the scent of their love still redolent. The erotic magic of the previous evening is residual only in the tired ecstasy of her present languor. Looking over at O'Reilly makes her think how tame and wasted he appeared in comparison to his great ardour scant hours before. She contemplates his power, or illusion of power, and how such a man could actually rule his vast wild regions as he did. That notion kindles a vibrant reminder of her love for him; she is thinking that their sexual glory is really an extension, a metaphor, for appeasement and confirmation of her dynamic needs, specifically the tensions of the past few months. She is not an idealist, nor is O'Reilly. Dreams are for those blessed fools, as are poets. Her brother is one, an idealist, a dreamer. Yet ironically, her love for her brother transcends her own selfish predatory affair with O'Reilly. Yes, she decides, she cannot get enough of him, and must now practice her famed discipline by separating herself from this gratuitous flesh. Despite the sense of guilt working at the edges of her tingling loins, she reaches for him and tugs gently. He is soon rekindled, even alert like a spirit arisen from its nocturnal depth. O'Reilly stirs and his dark hair tumbles about his face with that cruel lip curled in a smile.

'Darling, I must use your monitor,' she whispers in his ear, biting.

'Use it well,' he murmurs.

'I need your code-key, babe.'

'Ali Baba, my sweet . . . '

She bounces up and goes to his monitor on the desk at the other window. She looks out and down that beautiful valley high in Jammu, where mists lurk about clefts and steep forests cling to mountainsides. A guard on a promontory sees her naked through the window, but from that distance she can't care less. Cleo punches in Chromolox's access and waits. It is still early evening in Kawartha and she expects that supper might still be under way. She connects as she hears the beep, but there is no response from Chromolox. She leaves the channel open and goes back to O'Reilly.

'You bitch,' he murmurs endearingly and reaches for her. 'I thought you wanted Ali Baba.'

She laughs and straddles him taking him all the way in.

'I now know the secret of your empire,' she purrs, slowly moving on him. 'Only you would name your code-key after your Wilbur,' she whispers.

The monitor beeps again and when Chromolox appears on the screen she sees them making love. 'Pardon me,' she says quietly, then more cynically, 'It didn't occur to me that you would esteem your love to be state business, Cleo; or is 'love' your New Year's message?'

Cleo covers their nudity, 'Sorry, Chromolox, bad timing,' replies Cleo, hardly embarrassed. 'I do apologise – I was just checking in to say hello; your New Year hasn't quite arrived.'

'Everything is fine, just fine,' quips Chromolox, trying not to gloat. 'Listen, if I may say so, Cleo: watch that man, he's just another unwieldy gun.'

'I declare diplomatic immunity!' utters O'Reilly, defensively.

'I'm out; keep in touch. Happy New Year,' says Chromolox smiling and signing off.

'Have you no shame, Cleo?' exclaims O'Reilly.

'Chromolox is lesbian,' answers Cleo unmoved, but still moving.

'Are you sure? I think she's envious,' he teases.

'I think it was me she was looking at. She's always checking me in sub-tle womanly ways. Do shut up.'

'Do you trust her?'

'With my life, though we do square off from time to time.'

'Who wouldn't with you,' he urges, exerting more gusto.

'I am the cutting edge of evolution . . . oh.'

'Sunsetwinders . . .'

That afternoon amongst the evergreens in the headwaters of the Indus, Cleo tells O'Reilly that she must get back to Sunsetwind. She explains that she feels uneasy that she isn't attending her defences; also the weather reports show a terrible storm. O'Reilly is a little upset, though feigns his response half-heartedly, conveying only that she must do what she must do, then adds more stoically that that is how they must love, on the "edge of evolution". He loses his reserve, however, when she says she could no longer return his affections unconditionally, because after spending almost a week in the Kush, she believes his brand of "empirical democracy" is repressive in the extreme. He retorts that in this part of the world, he is considered "benevolent". People need his repression because various clans resist a universal system of justice that isn't partisan to the local war lords; and he qualifies repression to mean equality, i.e., 'an eye for an eye,' he says, meaning he subscribes to EF law and uses it to justify his repression of those who reject it. Cleo asks why the EF does not become more involved and he proclaims that the people are fearful to exercise their rights, but then adds that the EF is involved; indeed, if there is a problem the international mobile courts are called in and he is obliged to enforce their decision, or someone else will. With eyes flashing fire and a furrowed brow, he asserts, 'But we have no serious crime! We have no endemic corruption! Muslims are honest and seek enlightenment.' Nevertheless, Cleo does not back down, although she does say she would miss his "energy and honour". He broods on that and smiles. There remains, in spite of their different points of view, a genuine compatibility between them would indeed make the heart grow fond with absence.

Airborne in her Cougar with her escort, Captain Dave, flying his own Cougar, they take no time going straight up into orbit. It is 11:38 PM eastern standard time and Cleo thinks she can still make it to Kawartha for her second New Year's eve given the time difference to surprise Chromolox and Cephren.

Cleo calls in on her monitor. There is no response. She tries again. Still nothing. She tries the Pyramid. No response. She puts Dave on.

'We're not getting any response from Sunsetwind, Dave. Could a storm cause that much interference?'

'Unlikely, Cleo . . . '

'Then we have a problem, Dave,' she interrupts. 'I suspect intervention here, which can only mean the Chicagos. We must re-enter with extreme caution.'

'They might be waiting for us.'

'We will scan . . . '

'Holy Hell!'

Simultaneously, a seeming dot matrix of emops appear on both their surveillance screens. There would not have been a chance they could escape had they re-entered the Sunsetwind airspace. Tears come to Cleo's eyes. For a moment she considers going in anyway and taking out as many as she could before bailing out and going underground, but with so many of them, that would be suicidal and there is little good she could do dead.

'By pass! By pass, Captain Dave!'

'Where to, then, Commander?'

'Washington. Our only hope is to rally the Americans. George Washington must be apprised by now. Next sweep around we'll re-enter over the Atlantic east of Washington. There's nothing we can do here. I can't believe this! I should have known it!'

'Don't blame yourself, Commander. Blame Burnamthorpe.'

'The bitch has made her move. Turn on the Chicago news link.'

They tune in to Chicago.

. . . The Earth Federation has already received a statement from our esteemed Head of State, Trinny Burnamthorpe that reads: Due to the instability of the Sunsetwind province, and their abduction of our beloved heir Sam Burnamthorpe, we have undertaken to take control and depose the ruling elite who have by their autocratic ways, failed to bring an oppressed people the freedoms that we all cherish. We have indisputable evidence of a massive upheaval within the ranks of their society, which would have led to violence and threatened the fundamental stability of all North America . . .

Cleo has heard enough. She shuts it off.

'We blew it, Dave; we really blew it!' yells Cleo holding back tears. 'But to tell you the truth, the way things have been going for us lately, a good percentage of the Western world believes Burnamthorpe, in effect; so an ineffective countermeasure would not work to undo what is happening. Oh poor Cephren! I have failed us! I have failed Sunsetwind!' she cries.

'Our secret army will resist!' exclaims Dave choking back his own emotions.

'Oh yes, we will, but not when the full force of the Chicagos is upon us. We must for now disappear like birds in the forest, until they believe us passive, at which time pounce back when they least suspect it. And no fury on earth will ever be seen so devastating or fatal as our fight to save our land, and indeed the future of the human race.'

'But this invasion is against EF law,' says Captain Dave.

'Then let us hope that George Washington will support our side, and not bend the rules to accommodate the Chicagos.'

Cephren lies back on the foldout bed of the Volcano gazing out the side window at the grey masses of frigid clouds. Little dabs of blue appears with greater frequency as the clouds break up. The silence is daunting. He can only focus on his terrible sense of loss. How is he to proceed with so little intelligence? He reconsiders calling Mita but again instinct relays patience. Yet he must risk calling Cleo. In all probability, she now knows about the invasion and would be blaming herself for not being there to defend Sunsetwind. Fate strikes them a stroke of luck realises Cephren: her being out of the country likely saved her life. He sits up and pulls the modem toward himself. He switches it on and scrambles his receiver so his position cannot be traced immediately if the Chicagos are monitoring Cleo's position. He enters her code. The screen becomes fuzzy, but some vertical lines begin to straighten out and soon a picture forms. The image is her emop but no Cleo. Cephren adjusts her viewing screen. The liquid mirror moves ninety degrees. He sees trees and something beyond the trees, the corner of a building. He moves it another forty-five degrees. Cephren's heart leaps. It is the White House in Washington. Cleo the noble heart! exalts Cephren. She is doing the right thing. But why isn't she responding with her beeper? Cephren does another sweep around the emop. On the other side there are guards, not just guards, but fully equipped armed forces. In the distance he can see hundreds of them patrolling the White House lawns. After a few minutes he disconnects, because Cleo is not responding, even with her wrist monitor.

In a quarter of an hour he tries again. Still nothing. This time he keeps it on. 'Cleo, where are you?' he calls in exasperation.

'Chairman Path, is that you?' comes a voice through Cephren's speaker.

'Is this a friendly voice?' replies Cephren taken aback.

'Indeed, sir. Captain Dave, sir. Am I ever glad to hear your voice, sir . . .

'Where are you? I can't see you.'

'I'm under the Atlantic, sir, near the mouth of Chesapeake Bay. I'm interfaced with Cleo's monitor. She said she would report back to me and it's been over five hours. They must be restraining her, sir. Can it be that the Americans have allied themselves with the Chicagos?'

'Why didn't you respond when I called earlier?' asks Cephren.

'I tried to trace your call but couldn't get through due to your scramble. Wise move, sir.'

'Okay, Dave, you're doing commendably. As you know, there has been an invasion from which I barely escaped with my life. Cleo's life may be in danger, if she's found flying around in her machine, as well as yours and definitely mine. If I know George, it seems he is playing it safe with Cleo and has had her incarcerated for her own protection, as well as his own perhaps, until things settle down. Politically, we have drifted apart, but personally, George is an old friend and would not harm her in any way. Now this is what we are going to do: I want you to hold your position until I get back to you after I speak to President Washington. I have his personal code. If for some reason I don't get back to you, go back to the Kush until further contact. Is O'Reilly aware of the situation?'

'Yes he is, sir. Cleo called him before landing. He tried to dissuade her from going in and urged her to come back to the Kush where he would help us, sir. He called four times before you called. Do you want me to tell him you are alive, sir?'

'Only when you see him in person. Have you heard anything about the Board and Sunsetwind?'

'O'Reilly told me he had contacted the Pyramid to ask for Cleo. Apparently, he couldn't get any information from the male operator on line in the Pyramid, who by his attitude appeared to be a geno warrior. He was told there had been a "systems failure" and everyone was incommunicado. He then asked who was in charge. The reply was Del Barker and the Free Radicals! He was then disconnected.'

'I suspected as much. And the Board?'

'That's all I know, sir.'

'Okay Dave, I'll be in touch. Thank you. And remember, this is only a temporary set back. Trinny Burnamthorpe is a Trashie and Trashies don't last long. Out.'

Cephren is seething. Del Barker! That lowlife cad! Mr. Salesman with the dreams of decadence. Cephren had spoken to him once on the monitor after the Egg and Tomato Riot. Barker was sickeningly sweet. Chromolox had warned Cephren about Barker being the old school politician – ingratiatingly earnest but deceitful. In fact, integrity is played like another card. Barker is lacking in the concept of upwardly mobile enlightenment. His vision of society expands no further than organised crime and cheap gratification. Cleo had also informed Cephren that Del Barker was a "virtual pervert" who scammed the middle wealth to aggrandize his own sensational pitch for "freedom and morality". This situation has to be the most hypocritical disinformation since centuries back in the Secret Age when the "responsible" media debunked and ignored credible evidence regarding alien visitation when for fifty years the government had been studying, communicating and exchanging with aliens. Cleo also claimed that Barker had a fetish for teenage girls, who seemed to enjoy his attention. Gabriella once had him arraigned on charges of sexual misconduct that were initiated by the concerned parents of a fifteen year old, but the girl remained loyal to Barker and refused to testify against him. The charges were subsequently dropped for lack of evidence. But Gabriella gave him a tongue lashing, nevertheless.

How ironic historically that people such as Del Barker stand in line for power as if it has their name on it; his stint as a destroyer of the inherent principles of truth that Cephren stood for could be rationalized only within the context of the chaos of the human experience. No wonder, thinks Cephren that the Greys and other alien races who had purportedly visited earth were so hesitant to make official contact. Our absurdity could only make them see us as emotionally undeveloped. Cephren shakes his head. He wonders whether the strange epiphany of their visitations had anything to do with our development. Redman thought so. Cephren isn't so sure. Some of the mythology revealed genetic manipulation from various abductees. It has been suggested that the Horror may have indeed been their doing. A major correction was a prerequisite to our continued survival, and quite possibly their use of us. On the other hand, Cephren muses, most people (even some Sunsetwinders) think the alien thing is something the old democracies created to bolster unity through fear; and all the scientific study was clever disinformation to the extent that when something real came along, people were so inured to scepticism nothing could convince them of the truth. Alien contact was a pathetic off-shoot of the Secret Age. And now Del Barker works to reinforce the big lies that two centuries of truth had sought to expose. Cephren can't see the average Sunsetwinder buying into Barker's world; yet, for example, if the overwhelming majority of continental North America wants unification, the chips would fall where they may and he would submit. But Cephren cannot believe that. Big government was proven to be devastatingly wrong in the 21st century. And World War 3 was testament to that, when one arm of the government took up arms against the other and each side believed fervently in their cause, each having enough military to back up their punches with knockouts – a futility words cannot summate. And futility is something creeping into Cephren's vocabulary as he ponders in anger. What kind of a race are we? He thinks of James Piercemore aka Pidgeon lambasting humanity in Renée Antionette: 'What a devil are we that puts a make on it too!' Futility, he concedes, promotes a devil-may-care attitude which sometimes offered a surprising result.

Cephren plugs in George Washington's personal code. Soon the Oval Office comes into view. George's unshaven face, with a look of awkward astonishment appears. The astonishment turns to outright shock when he views Cephren's face through the liquid mirror screen, every detail of his countenance looking so real one could touch it and almost feel its anguish. But it is Cephren who wants to touch the skin, George's skin, with a wake up clout on the head. That beautifully preserved mug of George's: smooth and black with a full head of grey hair and a physique like that of a twenty year old on a seventy year old frame. His usual smiling eyes have a haunted look that obviates the present situation. Times are not sitting well with him, either.

'Holy Smoke!' utters George. 'Everybody thinks you're dead, man.' His eyes lighten. 'And thank the good Lord they're all wrong. Cephren, where are you? Are you all right?'

'George, greetings. Do you remember that weekend you spent at The Winds on Great Blue?'

'Why, yes . . .'

'We sat on the rocks and watched the sun go down.'

'And what a sun it was . . .'

'The sun was Sunsetwind, George.'

'Yes, no, listen . . .'

'We have both been sitting on our behinds, George; where is Cleo?'

'Cephren, where are you? We have to talk, I mean talk, big talk; there are things going on that have created a runaway train. In a nutshell it's going to crash into the station or we have to build a new track to divert it. Do you follow me?'

'I'm listening, but where's Cleo?'

'She's fine . . .'

'I need to see her, now.'

'Okay, okay, just a moment.'

The monitor goes on hold. There is a visual sweep of America from New England down through Virginia. George comes back on. 'She's in the Pentagon, Cephren. Put on your three way.'

Cephren complies and his screen divides.

'We can't trace you, Cephren,' says George. 'Your receiver's scrambled.'

'I know.'

'I know you must be terribly upset, Cephren, but let's put our heads together and work through this or nothing good can come of it. You don't fight killer bees; they just get crazier.'

'Does that mean we must succumb to the killer bees?'

'Hell no, we must dilute the strain, man, through EF law; that's the only way.'

'By letting them get away with it? And how long would "diluting the strain" take, if we were able?'

'A while: the EF feels we must wield a carrot; the Chicagos are too formidable to consider war.'

'I should have listened to Cleo . . . '

'You should listen to her now!' interrupts the President. 'She wants me to give her our army so she can start World War 4 . . . '

'If that's what it takes, *yes!*' interjects Cleo.

'Cephren!' she blurts out upon seeing him suddenly. 'You're alive!'

'Cleo, I'm okay; I barely escaped,' says Cephren calmly. 'They came in a blizzard late on New Year's Eve. I haven't any news about the Board, Sam, Chromolox, or anything other than the Free Radicals who have taken over the government . . . '

'Cephren, they have detained me. Our friend George says it's for my own good . . . '

'Cleo,' interrupts George, 'you are distraught and apt to do something rash . . . '

'I am a trained professional, George. We could put an end to this invasion if we act now!'

'As I was explaining to Cephren, Cleo, these Chicagos are not worth the fight; it would perpetuate . . . '

'Is unification worth it, George?' speaks up Cephren endorsing Cleo's view. 'Can you live comfortably with someone whose sole purpose seems to be absolute power at any cost? How long can you hold out, George?'

'Listen!' demands George angrily. 'We have a crisis . . . '

'That you helped bring about!' retorts Cleo.

'I bear some responsibility there too, Cleo,' says Cephren soberly.

'Cephren, there was little more we could have done,' states Cleo. 'We must be thankful for our lives. We don't know how the others fared, though. We haven't been able to get past the Chicagos in the Pyramid.'

'George,' says Cephren, 'I ask you to contact Trinny Burnamthorpe and tell her to unconditionally cease these war games in the name and spirit of the World Symposium. And if she refuses, you must convene an emergency EF session and resolve the issue through sanctions and force if necessary. It's the only way, George. Chicago must be dealt with under the strictest terms or civilisation will fall to tyranny. Don't think America is exempt.'

George sighs. He is thinking that he just can't bring himself and America and the world to the precipice of war over little Sunsetwind. He also knows any compromise on behalf of the Paths would be unacceptable. As an old friend of the family, his honour as such would have to be sacrificed for what he deemed to be the greater good. The stakes are simply too high at present. All along, he could feel it coming: the demands of the Chicagos to force change was a tide impossible to stem. It seems that the will of the world at that time is ill-prepared to deal with the power of a military powerhouse. And all for what? Are they really the enemy? Is reunification a good enough reason to bring down an old ally, even if they were slow to come around to speedier notions in the modern world? And are the Chicagos really on the level? Is the freedom they promulgate really as free as that which they subjugated? George is not the man to make a stand just yet; besides America and its allies like Carolina and Florida are satisfied that there is nothing wrong in setting on the straight and narrow what is perceived as of late to be a wayward Sunsetwind. George is of the minority who knows the particular beauty of Sunsetwind, but unfortunately there are ulterior motives or deep politics that hold sway. He knows, as well as Trinny Burnamthorpe, what the X13 could mean. Their own salvaged B400s confirmed this and more. There are issues he knows that just can't be revealed at present to his friend. After all, isn't it really an old U.S. chip and rightfully theirs? He hasn't even bothered to argue the point with his Generals and Admirals knowing full well what they thought. The recovery of the most powerful knowledge and intelligence ever known to humanity resides in that chip and all the niceties and smokescreens of the recent months in utopian dreams are now lifted. He knows what he must do to save America.

'Cephren, our friendship has been a great boon to my life. However, you know what it means to run a country, indeed the world; there are bigger issues than personal friendship. I cannot concur with your demands. You must give yourself up and I will protect you; and I think, in time, Sunsetwind, will once again be your country . . . in a compromising way. Change is hard, Cephren; damn it, I know the meaning of fealty and honour. Look at the oath unto my office!'

'Have you thought about your oath to uphold EF law?'

'To the letter of the law there are provisions, of which you are aware, that allow for certain exceptions . . .'

'And you feel we are an exception?'

'Personally, no, but the executive committee will not support armed retaliation, yet. A compromising way must be found.' Washington sighs.

Cephren remains silent fully comprehending his own predicament . . . a compromising way, yes indeed, he thought. Jimmy's Chip. He decides to play along. Instinct, for better or worse is a wonderful and strange companion.

'Okay, but let Cleo go, George,' he says.

'What guarantees do I have that you will cooperate with us, Cephren?'

'Cephren,' contends Cleo, 'don't make any deals. I don't need to go anywhere. I asked to come here. Admiral McKee is an old friend of mine and quite sympathetic. If George wants to hold me hostage, he must have very good reasons.'

'We're not holding you hostage, Cleo,' objects George.

'Why haven't you contacted Captain Dave, Cleo?' asks Cephren.

'I've been held incommunicado; I gave him orders to go back to the Kush if I didn't call.'

'Well, he's beneath the ocean waiting for you . . .'

'Well, he ignored my orders.'

'Are you coming in, Cephren?' asks George impatiently.

'No, George. And be held incommunicado?'

'It was for her own good until she cooled off, Cephren.'

'Okay, okay; I'll accept that as you're my friend; we must remain cool.'

'What will you do?' queries George somberly.

'I think you know the answer to that. Isn't that why we're here today talking deep politics?'

'No, I'm thinking of your life.'

'And what would you know about that?'

'That your life isn't what it used to be.'

'But what's in my head is?'

'Let's put our heads together, Cephren; without us you'll never see Sunsetwind again. Please, for the benefit of all.'

'Cephren,' comments Cleo, 'he has a point. Maybe he's right. Better America than Chicago. The risks are enormous.'

'I understand the risks. Cleo, I order you back to the Kush,' commands Cephren peremptorily.

'No, Cephren, I won't.'

'What do you mean, you won't? You must. Don't you see what is happening here? I thought you wanted affirmative action! We may be able to instigate it there with O'Reilly.'

'I do,' she replies calmly, 'but we can't take on the world. George is correct on that point. Listen, Cephren, that chip is not worth it. That's what this is about, isn't it? Will it be Sunsetwind or the chip? Well?'

'The chip is Sunsetwind, Cleo. Don't you see?'

'No, I don't.'

Silence. George lets the sibling steam chill for a moment. Neither he nor Cleo realise what kind of determination Cephren channels.

'Cephren, what would the Board think?' asks Cleo.

'Unfortunately, we do not know that, but I hope they would support me on this. I know Redman would.'

'Do you realise what you are doing?' she continues, 'You are sacrificing any hope we may have. Everybody will hate you for this.'

'Are you so naïve to think we will get Sunsetwind if I turn myself in?
Wake up Cleo!' he exclaims.

'I am just trying to make the best of an impossible situation!'

'Nothing is impossible within the realm of the imagination, quote
unquote,' states Cephren.

'Well, it'll take a lot of that to get us out of this one, Cephren,' she
relents gloomily, knowing her brother.

'I'm out, Cleo. George. You'll see.' He escapes.

Chromolox indeed is rudely interrupted. She sees the lights first through
Season's hair. It takes her a moment to disengage her lover from their
momentous pleasure; the circumstances couldn't have been worse, but she
is up on her feet covering herself with Season stunned beneath her. Their
affair had been building for years during Season's marriage to her ex-husband, and only when they were divorced did Season seek out Chromolox's
reassuring friendship and, ultimately, love. It had been an unspoken thing,
yet inevitable. Chromolox had taken the initiative the summer before during the Fête. She never really intended it to become sexual, just intimate.
Chromolox has always preferred unencumbered self-gratification for pleasure, for mutual pleasure is too emotionally charged to be shared with the
responsibilities she felt she shouldered. She is Saturn's mistress. Redman
had told her that when she was still Director of the Pyramid, before she
ran for the Presidency. In those days, she would sleep with almost anyone
commitment-free and it almost destroyed her: her love is too deep and vulnerable. Redman set her on the path to power – blessed power, to do as
angels might. Yet, over the months, Season had touched her innocently
more than once in ways which proved to be devastatingly erotic. It was a
playful provocation. Season, ironically, is the epitome of "straight" when
her mother was wired. It was an awesome challenge for her to consummate
her deepest needs with Chromolox, who also had inadvertently fallen into

this vortex. The temptation was sacred like a trust. And now they are exposed. Who would disturb us? Chromolox fumes. She assumes Treason, Season's pesky little sister. Chromolox hasn't completely trusted her since she had come back from Chicago. Chromolox believes that perhaps Season had told Treason about them. Just the thought mortifies her! No one must know!

All at once, when Chromolox looks at the window, she sees these war-demons, covered in snow, huge and fully armed, crash through the door. For the first instant she actually breathes a sigh of relief; these monsters at least appear to be devoid of interest in their nakedness. Season sits up alert and looks as if she was basking by the fire, before reaching for her large woollen sweater. Chromolox cringes behind her pink night-dress. For an eerie moment, the genos all stand surrounding them with hardly a glance, before ushering them into the bedroom to clothe themselves. To Chromolox, the safety of their secret for all intent seems redeemed amongst these sexless morons, yet, the realisation of what truly had transpired within their inner cell of desire quickly ruptures into the nightmare that they had all feared, but could hardly begin to accept. Their inviolate world was shattered – Sunsetwind. How dare the Chicagos or anyone else even contemplate it! Chromolox was the perfect President. They were the perfect world.

The whole entourage, including Seymour, Strange, Sam (now Sam Path, he insists) and Runaway Dumptruck and others have been congregated in Strange's house. They are not allowed to speak, but all note the curious but foreboding absence of Cephren and Treason. She had been on her way to check in on Cephren and hadn't been heard of since. Her disappearance aroused their suspicions, especially Strange her mother, who vehemently opposed her lifestyle in Chicago. The thought of betraying Sunsetwind is so foreign to any of them, they are at a loss to understand what on earth transpired.

Hours go by and everyone dozes until morning finally comes and the storm has subsided. Chromolox is then escorted into a waiting emop that swoops her away into the grey, cloud mass.

Later another emop comes for little Sam, who kicks and screams, while being picked up by a commanding officer who tries to mollify him by saying, 'It's time to go home.' But Sam yells pathetically at the top of his lungs, 'This is my home! Let me go!' Then something miraculous happens: Runaway, who had been quietly chomping at the bit since the night before, springs from his seat like a cape buffalo from a bush and takes out two huge genos, knocking them senseless, and then straight arms the officer's head, before he drops the boy and crumples to the floor stunned. Runaway, pleased with what he has accomplished, further immobilises the three Chicagos, stripping one of them of his gear, then picks up Sam and deposits him inside the emop. Once inside, holding a gun to the stunned guard's head, he instructs him to remove the officer inside. As soon as the emop is free, Runaway starts it up and takes off. Seymour meanwhile holds the guards at gunpoint for fifteen minutes before giving up knowing enough time had elapsed for Runaway to escape into orbit. It happened so fast, with barely a word spoken. The officer and his genos are so livid they take Seymour out into the snow and kill him with their lasers. Strange runs out hysterically and dares them to do the same to her, but restraining themselves they drag her back inside, a stricken woman.

After Runaway and Sam have escaped, the next few minutes become crucial to their safety. They ascend quickly above the clouds and blend into the pack of emops above Sunsetwind. Undetected, they fly inconspicuously upwards into orbit and away. Runaway goes immediately to the Kush to seek Cleo. O'Reilly, however, is not his unflappable self. He quickly sends Sam off to a Tibetan monk's mountain retreat near where he had stayed earlier those few days with Cleo, and then chafes Runaway on the folly of his risky action, but congratulates him nonetheless. Runaway had entered the Kush in a Chicago emop without warning or open channel. Only because O'Reilly happened to be at his command was the emop allowed to land. Chicagos are strictly off limits – personas non gratas. Furthermore, seconds before, had O'Reilly not gotten off the monitor with Captain Dave, learning of Cleo's disappearance into the Washington web, he probably would have shot down the emop. Yet over the surprise of this serendipity, O'Reilly curls his lips in his characteristic smile. His dark, but friendly eyes light up. He relishes holding an ace. He really holds an ace. Perhaps he could threaten Trinny Burnamthorpe with the life of Sam, but decides against using Cleo's nephew. But if he could lure Cephren there, he could strike a deal concerning the X13. By getting Sunsetwind back for Cleo and Cephren in exchange for the X13, Cleo would always be in his debt, which she may not like. It is however just the sort of intrigue that would keep her interested, on the edge as she was fond of saying. He laughs at such a foolish and inappropriate thought. Even he knows the importance of the X13. Naturally he hasn't any intention of giving it to the Chicagos. If only Cephren and Cleo could see things as clearly as he did! But they are Sunsetwinders.

Jan. 2. 96

Dear reader, I write today with great elation; I am thrilled to announce that I've finally made a breakthrough! I believe I have discovered the key to Jimmy Pidgeon's universe, thanks initially to Anna Gram starring as Renée Antoinette. How extraordinary! So shocked am I that I actually discovered it, these three hours now I have been too apprehensive to even engage it just relishing my surprise! I keep reviewing over and over the inane process of discovery to reassure my peculiar fortune-destiny-luck-trick! I knew it, I just knew it; I could feel it coming, guiding and revealing all at once . . . like a cartoon episode in which a sequence sends a projectile fortuitously to its mark in a multifarious contraption.

There I was, still in my survival suit, covered in melting snow, back in the Volcano; the abominable snowman at my monitor writing Pidgeon's Maplewood poem backwards, forward, sideways, to decode a plausible cipher. But first give me leave of my senses, dear reader. Permit me to indulge you in the wayward process beginning with my silly anger earlier today – perhaps just the needed embroiling that prompted my cause and infused my lagging spirits. I was ready to fling myself over the cliff nearby, snow driving me blind in the razor-blade wind, teeth clenched, fingers numb, the hot pulse of life pitted against the sub-arctic bitterness. Oh, what a sight it would have been to see that large red-faced man flailing in the drifts and then falling into that shallow crevice in the rocks, struggling in seeming bottomless snow, twisting, lurching, groping and finally, remain quietly prostrate to look placidly up at the snow above, sweeping beneath broken clouds, removed from himself, laughing at his own absurdity, laughing with the selfish gene which revels in the absurd, some dispassionate alienation. Then out of the blue, recalling Anna Gram do that part when Renée Antoinette falls from the superhuman grace that she characterised, saying: 'This freakish frame, imbued with senses too honest to endure, has foreclosed on love. Look at this shapely torso, these slender arms, soft breasts, supple legs, doubly entwined; look therein through my blue eyes and into my soul down through my loins, ready to be sprung with the seed of my devil! I divine in the notion, my love, so be off! Be off! I can no longer bear you suffering the trajectory of my love!'

And who is she to be trifled with? Danielle Perreault! Or he: James Pidgeon! They were like anti-matter. Then: 'Oh Renée, what beguiles you so to suffer these secrets to the grave? Have you no faith in me, love, your first and last?'

'First and last, Joey, first and last: these are numbers, composites, combinations. Our secrets are wrought in our innermost parts; our faith is our crucible. We are the host and must purge us from art.'

'Renée, you speak in riddles, subsumed in metaphors, buried in history; if not us, tell me what then is first and last? Tell me!'

'First, what good are myths? They are better not to be understood. And at last, contained. We are the contained!'

'Contained by whom? What do you mean?'

'You and I, my love, we rule the earth – we, the containers.'

'You are mad, Renée, mad! How can we be both?'

'I am both, the tempted and temptress . . .'

Pidgeon, you knew something really big but perhaps were not prepared to say it, just hint at it, like a myth hides a truth. Are we containers, but for whom? What did you really mean? 'Numbers, composites, combinations'. And then it hits me: you are my host and must purge me from your art. 'First and last'. So with nothing better to go on, I came up with an anagram out of the first and last letters of each word in the third line (I could not derive anything from the first two) of the opening couplet: a,s-t,e-f,d-i,o-t,e-m,d derived from 'Across the field into the maplewood'. From those letters I got the very Pidgeonistic anagram: atom deeds fit. But nothing happened. Fit what? I say. Nothing more? I try more anagrams from the remaining lines, but nothing made sense. Pidgeon was proving himself to be beyond obscure. I tried grounding myself to the monitor by touching the Volcano's auxiliary ground sensor. Still nothing. Leaving myself grounded, I reread the poem inserting 'atom deeds fit' before each line. Still nothing. I knew that it must have made some sense, at least to Jimmy Pidgeon. I was getting frantic; I thought I had had it for sure. Desperately, I reread it beginning with other phrases in the poem such as: atom deeds fit a mosaic of stars then atom deeds fit a science fiction story, etc., then ready to give up I tried: atom deeds fit the pie in the sky . . . and BINGO! My eyes went double and I felt a power surge begin at the base of my spine and shoot into every nerve like an electrical grid pattern running up my back straight into my brain. Almost blanking out and frightened, I touched the auxiliary ground sensor and shut down its electro-magnetic relay. Within a few moments, I recovered my former equilibrium. I lay down and relaxed. That was three hours ago. The selfish gene theory for evolutionary spirit reigned supreme! It had to be: most, if not all invention came to be through singular dogged obsession; minds that refused to give up in spite of the odds against them. I had gotten angry! Not at Cleo, thank goodness, nor George Washington thanks to my built in temerarious Chairmanship. I am still Chairman, you know, dear reader, on top of the world, in a round obloid can in the middle of a rugged northern cordillera with the key to the universe! James Piercemore, you and I are now best of friends. Jimmy, we will go to the breach once again soon, as soon as I leave this testament to us,

if I *manage never to come back; but* I *must.* I *will find a way to come back.
That should be easy,* I *hope, once* I *get used to it.* I *have been doing enough
internalizing with my success.* I *just haven't dared take the plunge under the
circumstances.* I *don't know if it's a one-way ticket!* How *can* I *know when to
pull the plug so-to-speak if it is life threatening? Yet* I *won't know unless* I *try
it out.* I *have made up my mind now to proceed having come so far. So much
depends on it.* I *am alone. What better way to find out without being interrupted and possibly hijacked. So now* I *bid you adieu, world;* I *must be off!
Cleo,* I *forgive you; Chromolox, Redman, Mita, remember me. Sam, be
proud! Good-bye!*

Actually, they are a few other factors at work on Cephren that impel
his fatalistic plunge into the netherworld of Jimmy's Chip. He has at
length spoken to O'Reilly on the second of January and blithely resists his
uncharacteristic imploring to come and join Sam, who had miraculously
escaped with that phenomenon Dumptruck who was presently and presumably awaiting orders along with Captain Dave. Cephren then speaks
to Runaway requesting that he and Dave watch the boy while Cephren
"figured" things out. Cephren also gives Sam an unnecessary morale-
boosting talk, as he is having the time of his life. Apparently Sam is
treated like a bodhisattva and lavished with affection by the many nubile
women O'Reilly keeps for his domestic ambiance. O'Reilly, although
somewhat ill at ease with this political "hot curry", sees himself as the
bachelor uncle of sorts with the potential of a possible blood-linking to
his fantasy with Cleo. O'Reilly is in fact, shielding himself from the precarious position he had been put in. For all his reputation as the fearsome
warlord, he lacked the strength to properly defend himself from a great
power like the Chicagos. If they get wind of his harbouring Sunsetwinders, especially the newest addition, little Sam, he isn't at all sure
he can realistically defend himself. Just the day before, Trinny Burnamthorpe who has been strangely silent during those tumultuous days,
had called O'Reilly in a vituperative mood decrying the abduction of her

"sweet Sammy" by that "pedophile football player, Dumptruck". Although knowing that Cleo had been seeing O'Reilly, she proceeded to threaten his life if he didn't come to her assistance calling him in the same breath an "impotent weasal of a human being". Trinny had once been snubbed by O'Reilly years before at a World Symposium, when he dumped her for an Ethiopian. O'Reilly, coolly and humourously countered her threats with subtle snippets aimed at her ego which suppressed her aggressiveness. 'Congratulations, Trinny, I couldn't have done it better myself,' he said poker-faced referring to her conquest of Sunsetwind. She even smiled for a moment, then retorted, 'Should I expect your vote, April 2nd?'

'You can count on it,' he said showing his best white teeth smile.

She liked that and softened her tone. He then probed her about Cephren and how he should be treated with the respect he deserves. She begged off saying, 'Cephren and I despite our differences, have always had an understanding. I wish him no harm; it's just that he needs a kick in the head from time to time.' She had said it limply as if it was old protocol. O'Reilly had never felt sorry for anyone until he met Cephren.

Before Cephren had written the entry in his journal on the fourth, he had listened to the EF News Report, which did not even mention the recent invasion. The day before, he had heard King Willy Five lambast the Chicagos for their "Trashie diplomacy" and "phony freedom". "Wake up world!" he said, but nobody was listening. The new world order carried on in somnambulistic wonder, stoned at the wheel in a utopian trance, and the Chicagos were the unspoken leaders paving the way to a new parking lot. The good earth need not tremble anymore; genetic prototypes would secure the future. There would be no more chaos, no more politico-scientific accidents. Eco-free enterprise is unimpeded – just follow the rules. The genos would gladly impress them upon you, surmises Cephren.

And what gene pool would you belong to? 'Well,' says Cephren, impersonating a technocrat, 'we are sorry there has been a mix up.'

'But,' says the victim, 'my child was supposed to be built like a gymnast, but was rehabilitated as a breeder because her hips were too big. And I became a poet because I soiled my pants when I was a little kid. And now you want me to imitate the heroes of earlier ages – rather a new foolish gene theory!'

This is a static world, muses Cephren, in which the appearance of greatness is a complete delusion. It is no wonder he finds solace in the selfish gene theory and the X13. Ethos and great precepts are merely the mental ornaments of civilisation, which had to be constantly brushed up to maintain appearances. Unfortunately, it is a widely held view that the real future holds little place for artistic renewal. Individual passions are to be ultimately transgressed by a passionless homogeneity akin to a social collective devoid of vision or colour as all races evolve blessedly into one. Only a telepathic link will suffice in their ultimate victory over nature. All secrets of the universe would be discovered. Little shock or surprise could be expected. Food will be as basic as plankton and bodily excretions like sweet-smelling rain, or fresh compost. Life will be long and vegetative. Solitude will be no more; only the ritual of procreation holds any promise; but even there, the newborn are simply lesser versions of their progenitors, mute and indistinguishable as if cut from a cookie mold.

In his mind Cephren has mulled over many of these themes: the demise of Sunsetwind had struck home in a small way acute similarities of their fate with past civilisations. Ultimately, sheer numbers of migratory peoples had brought down the Roman Empire already complacent at the edges by civil influences. All that show of law and order became an empty shell of its former dynamic enterprise. The great aqueducts, roads, temples and colosseums were built on the belief in superior gods of a tempestuous ardour.

The British Empire was founded originally in the hot-tempered spirit of the English feudal lords, underscored, imbued and heralded with the truth and virtue of mercury-tongued Shakespeare. That very icon of English mystery became the effectual torch-bearer of the human condition, to shine immortally as a supreme epitome of martyrdom. And short-lived, there was British colonialism – an ethnocentric attempt to civilise, yet laying tenuously the foundations of interest bearing democracy.

Then the Americans with their independent religious fervour carried the message of their star-spangled power enthroning enterprise and pride. Uncoveted, unwanted, they bore the burden of their power hurtling through the spiral of time unable to understand their own destiny. Eventually it came crashing down in self-destruction like an old patriarch harbouring too many skeletons and refusing to admit his disease – consumed by what they thought worth protecting – the ingenuous naïvety of absolute freedom.

But they're still with us, concedes Cephren; Cleo will look to our defences. And I will look to mine. Cephren lies back on the fold-out bed and touches on the auxiliary ground relay. He then punches in the codekey on the monitor beside the bed: *atom deeds fit the pie in the sky* and waits. Some tingling begins at his feet and works its way up through his body to his head when he feels a nausea and his consciousness slip away from his present world: then like waking anew, there is a transformation into a new world.

Stars. Multitudinous stars. From whence to whither knows all – a brilliant dusting so splashed with cosmic light knowledge is superfluous, yet there is comfort in the vast spectrum synonymous with pure omniscience. To probe any meaning becomes pain, a terrible anguish almost pulsating in a corporeal form. This is reduced further into simple intelligence that seems to coalesce into a fearful darkness. Further still, the awakening transposes itself into the sights, smells and sounds of a deep forest at night. Utter terror overwhelms the incomprehensible reality of the immediate environment and even the warm Rhodesian Ridgeback's sympathetic whimper nudging against her tightly held knees. The old, headless Barbie doll is held in her left hand so tightly her fingers are cramped. The dog, Roughy, stops his friendly nudging at the permeation of a brilliant blue light from the moonless black above and beyond their position atop a steep vale. The light grows brighter and changes from florescent blue to blinding white to blue and purple before going back to white. It moves above the trees alighting the deep greens of late summer into a strange panoply of embroidery. Above them through a slight gap in the trees, a blue laser beam projects onto Roughy rendering him unconscious with a whimper and a sigh. Another slightly different tint of blue beam alights numerous small figures gently to the ground where they quietly stand together in front of the little girl. When she looks up puffy-faced and traumatised, there stand before her a half dozen little people. Their lean, luminescent bodies and hairless oversized heads are in sharp contrast to their large, black pineal eyes staring mutely at her. So traumatized is little Terrie Barnett, the sight of these creatures, if anything, is one of solace or remission; besides, they speak to her telepathically in soothing words saying not to be afraid that they have come to help her. And not caring who or what they are, she cries in relief but lets them tenderly raise her up and walk to the beam which they had descended in and by which they now ascend. Inside the craft, it is warm and filled with other Greys all wearing identical one piece suits without seams as if they could not be removed. One of the people, a female, appears more human and even speaks to her in a sweet little voice. She is very kind and shows her around the craft as it rises into the atmosphere so quietly not even a hum is discernable. She points to a star cluster and conveys to Terrie that it is their home. The female seats her on a low metal table and explains that they would like to give her something, but that she must sleep for awhile because it is so special. Terrie doesn't think this is unreasonable, as if it was like a game. The idea occurs to her that she might awake and find mommy and daddy. So they make her sleep with the wave of a metal rod that directs a beam and then put in her head a little device that contains things she might one day know, as a promise kept by these Greys to another human and great friend who had lived before. This is to bestow great knowledge upon a descendant of his so that people may prosper in the future. The female Grey had decided it must be Terrie as she is the only one, and they truly sympathise with her hopeless condition. They seem to know an inevitable fate either by her very charisma and blood, or have delineated a fate suited to their passive purpose. It is the beginning, as posterity would mythologise, of the magical though checkered destiny of a demi-goddess, known as Flower Child.

And Cephren within the compact of his present omniscience, though unable to extricate himself – to even know himself, searches throughout the periphery of his vision all the details of his experience. He can even sense the slight sulphur-ammonia smell of the aliens and feel the entrapment of their powerful eyes, and observe the marvelous discoid machine, so precise and stationary, yet cutting through the atmosphere like an emop never could. But foremost, it is his ability to see through Flower Child's eyes and feel all that was there like a child himself.

She awakes the following morning with Roughy licking her face. The forest of early autumn is familiar and not so fearful. They wander down the vale to the spring where she has gone before with her mom. There is an opening in the trees where blue sky above has somehow attracted her, remembering a reassuring presence that she is at a loss to recall.

While the dog busies himself running in and out of the bushes, she picks some flowers, goldenrod and purple vetch, before continuing. A little further on they come to a wild cow path that cuts across the gurgling stream with deep little eddies and fallen log falls. A little way down, the path rises up to higher ground. She sits on the bank and looks across where she notices old Scratch, the woodsman, sitting on a log in his camp cutting some wild apples into a large pot. He hears the dog in the brush and turns about to see her standing holding the flowers. On her face is a haunted look without her usual irrepressible buoyancy. There is nothing left for her to do but stay there. She is dirty, hungry and scared. Roughy comes up from the woods behind and sits at her side grumbling a bit to let Scratch know who is in charge.

'Well now, if it isn't a little Flower Child,' he says, using the name out of the blue for the first time. 'Why d'ye stare so sad, Terrie? Have ye lost yer way? Where's yer mom?'

He turns away and goes back to his chores assuming Mrs. Barnett is nearby. She remains without a word.

After a while, when she doesn't leave, he turns again uttering gruffly, 'Go home, girl; you're due home no doubt.'

But still she doesn't move or speak.

'Where's your mom, girl?' he asks, looking about.

The dog barks unable to restrain himself at the sight of food. There is a skinned rabbit on a spit.

'Where's yer tongue, child?'

She looks at him strangely. He can see two streams of tears drop from her eyes.

'Are ye lost?' he asks, concerned.

She nods.

'Why did ye come 'ere by yerself?'

'My mommy told me to go into the woods,' she blurts out tearfully.

'She did, did she? Why in hell would she say that, eh?'

'They were shooting guns.'

'Guns? Who did that, child?' he exclaims alarmed. He jumps up and walks closer to her on his side of the river-stream.

'Those men with Remy,' she begins in an outpouring. 'They were eating supper my mommy made. My mommy came outside and said to go to the woods with Roughy and find old Scratch Rainbow. She told me to run. I cried and said I was scared and she pushed me and said she would meet me. Then she went back in the house and I went to the shed. I heard my mommy scream, so I went to the woods and stayed there in the night, but my mommy never came. Then these little people made me not afraid. Please, take me home, old Scratch.'

'What little people?' inquires Scratch scratching his head.

'The little people with big eyes in the woods.'

Scratch just stands there wondering. The child has obviously been dreaming. The terrible implications of her story now dawn on him. 'Yes,' he mumbles. Indeed he is old Scratch, although he hasn't thought of himself much since the Asteroid. He used to be Father Frankie Rainbow before quitting, but that was a long time ago. He never thinks about that life, because when he had faith he came to decry it. Father Frankie, they called him and loved him, the children especially. He preached, which began as a cautious resentment towards the conventional God-fearing of his denomination in place of an esoteric one, the God of all life, good and bad and how It resides in us, because we make It whatever we want. This is acceptable to him, because in the early 22nd century before the Asteroid, Christian doctrine had become so ossified that the authorities were no more than corporate technocrats presiding over social issues; moreover, he saw his faith as a way to administer his good will on all people of all cultures. The downfall came when he was accused of adultery having had a platonic affair with an unhappy young wife of a devout member of congregation who happened to be a political leader. Subsequently, he was exonerated, but notoriety was brought to bear on his 'mayfair' parish by the press and his Superior Grace the Bishop had himself quoted in Canada's national magazine that Father Frankie was a "recusant demagogue" who "lusted spiritually" and "was not acquitted in the eyes of the Lord". These words vilified his reputation. Father Frankie Rainbow then "retired" to the halfway mission in the hills of Clearview in present Sunsetwind. There he farmed with young offenders and learned the ways of animal husbandry, hunting and survival. He ceased preaching and degenerated into a kind of holy hobo character. He so disregarded his health and hygiene that he earned his new identity "old Scratch". During the cataclysm after the Asteroid, he spent a couple of years in the Barnett's bunker, as a friend, just before Terrie was born. They survived together almost five years of winter cut off from almost any communication. Eventually, Old Scratch "needed to migrate" to his find his own "calling" as he termed it and hardened himself for the "mission". David Barnett, Terrie's father, was a tough, practical man who kept things going on the farm. Luckily, with fusion technology, everybody was basically self-sufficient and a community grew up with a local militia and many of the amenities of life intact. However, over the years an alarming rise in Trashies, as they were called, made easy prey of the lone, unprotected farms. The militia were slow to react, and good people hesitant to abandon their farms for the security of a compound were especially vulnerable. Tragically, the Barnett's two older sons, sixteen and seventeen, had been killed in such a fray when Terrie was still a baby. And the other youngest son, James, had died of tuberculosis during the long winter. Old Scratch had loved the boy and railed to the heavens as a broken man over the frozen corpse awaiting burial, after which he struck out on his own to die, but that was not to be the case. On this "mission" he wandered far and wide in a grizzled torpor witnessing a human calamity too unspeakable for words. There were frozen, starving masses too weak to help themselves or migrate south where conditions were no better. Government reserves were long used up or hoarded by the armed forces, which had disintegrated into chaos. He helped where he could: his sympathy and comfort for the dying – his philosophy morphing into an emotive rendition of absurd wisdom. Cannibalism was common as most food supplies were scarce and survivors held on to their own stocks for dear life. Scratch's ability to live off rats, rabbits, ground hogs, wild pigs, cattle and the occasional deer kept him alive; he never succumbed to human flesh. Summer thaws were just mild enough to find wild leeks, dandelions, potatoes, apples, bulrush shoots and a few other palatable delicacies. Yet after two years had passed since living with the Barnetts when he had had enough of the dying, he was surprised to find himself still alive. It came to him as divine intervention as he straggled through the wastes of Toronto, empty homes and gaunt towers, wild dogs and bones, occasional fires with surreal people in huddled clans, who fought, killed, laughed and rutted amongst themselves. Some were bad and some were good, but it was a depraved life in which his mission had little impact, so again he decided to wander north to his home in the country.

Now it is with some trepidation that Scratch left Flower Child (as he called her in the attempt to cheer her) and her dog in his camp with course bread, rabbit, wild apple butter and make-do shelter, to go that kilometer up the hill and forest across the well-kept fields to the Barnetts to see what had happened. He takes a circuitous route using cover between him and the open ground. He sees the smoldering house on coming through the brush to the north. The antique red brick structure had been torched, yet it seemed to not want to burn that well as if taking offense to the indignity. The attic had been destroyed but some of the windows below looked intact. He could see no movement about as he waited and watched. He carries an old gun, a 20th century Smith & Weston semi-automatic and holds it ready. He had used the gun to kill wild cattle, turkey and deer, the odd pig and once a rabid dog.

After a while, he creeps forward through the hayfield and comes to the paddock fence within the compound of the house and shed; the old barn had been burned in the fray when the two boys were killed. The horses, sheep, cattle, old fusion tractor and wagon have all disappeared. It seems the Trashies had left with their plunder. Old Scratch braces himself as he approaches the premises. The two hundred-fifty year old house is a ruin. From the distance it had appeared to hold itself in a stoic manner, but is completely gutted from the inside out. He can detect the charred remains of David by the boot on one foot that is recognisable. He pokes through the smoldering carnage but can't find any trace of Ida, Terrie's mom. He looks again at David, when something shiny catches his eye from a different angle. Near the back door by the kitchen behind the burnt pantry, he sees her hand groping lifelessly for the charred door, fallen from its upper hinge. He lifts the door, and drops it in horror. Her head and torso are recognisable, but the lower body is burned to nothing. Most of her hair oddly is not burned, but only singed, and she wears no clothes. He turns away to collect himself and leans on a nearby maple tree, its one side of foliage singed brown. Steeling himself, he goes to the shed, finds a shovel and begins digging a hole in the lawn to bury their remains. Speechless, with tears and sweat running from his eyes, he looks to the sky and swears to his old God, 'Damn you!' Then he mumbles to himself: 'Hadn't they suffered enough? You just had to finish them off! Trashie!'

Cephren for all his new found omniscience cannot for the life of him place these proceedings. Only a faint recognition of the absolute necessity of his being there propels his intuition to proceed further.

Through the striking green eyes of Flower Child, her strawberry blond bangs, little nose and gangly gait, he can experience her childish intelligence in fear and wonder. In his vision she sits on a log with Roughy in the shade alert to every subtle noise of the wild woods. And it so happens, Cephren finds himself able to rise out of her mind and observe the landscape as it existed more than two hundred and fifty years before his time. He can also see Scratch up the hill and beyond at the ruin. Cephren then looks even beyond and sees Great Blue Lake to the north in its wide horizon and the glorious countryside looking overgrown except for little pockets here and there where people eke out their living from toil on the land. He seems able to keep ascending high into the atmosphere and see the stars, but uncertainty then presents itself, so he allows the movement to fall back to earth. Once returned to that rural oasis, he can see three men with the stolen tractor and livestock roped to the wagon. They are crossing the river-stream and having difficulty with a cow that becomes tangled in her rope. The cow thrashes about in the water sending stones and mud in a swill around her. Not far down the valley where Flower Child sits, the curses and perfidious ranting rise to a screaming crescendo resolved in a series of shots. Startled, Flower Child jumps up and goes back across the stream towards her farm, as it seemed in a safer direction. Hot and tired, she collapses at the top of the hill in the shade at the edge of the forest. Roughy sits at attention panting with his tongue hanging. He barks at something running across the field, which turns out to be old Scratch waving his gun in one hand. Scratch had just finished backfilling the grave without leveling and packing the earth, when he heard the shots ring out down the valley. Dropping the spade, he bolts in the direction of the shots, which sounded near his shack. He then hears Roughy's bark and goes to that location to find Flower Child. Sweating profusely, he tries consoling the little girl, but she is unfazed, having seen him running to her defence, yet too proud to show her fear. Scratch is the only link she had to her mother whose words are now embossed in her memory, *Go to the woods with Roughy and find old Scratch Rainbow!* Scratch very quickly has become her hope and haven.

'Are ye okay?' he puffs.

'Yes.'

Scratch sits under a tree taking off his ratty, old Bluejay cap. His rheumy, light brown eyes stare into the trees, his pudgy face and round Santa Claus nose are red from his exertions, and sweat-drenched clothes dirtied with antiquity; his lips are pursed stiffly not yet able to bring himself to tell the girl of her parent's demise. His stocky, short-legged body is fully out-stretched but for its barrel-like upper third, which fits snugly into a concave nape of the tree trunk like an extension of a root.

'Where are mommy and daddy?' asks Flower Child fearfully.

'They're . . . ' Scratch can't say it.

'I want to go home,' she says pitifully.

'Flower Child,' he says, 'we must go away for awhile.'

'Why?' she wonders, teary-eyed.

'We don't want trouble with those Trashies. Do you know who they are?'

'They asked Daddy for work,' she replies. 'But one of them I know; he's nice. He helps Daddy on the farm. His name is Remy.'

'Remy Path? The young lad?'

'Yes.'

'What was he doing there?'

'He came with those men.'

'He could have been brought along as a foil, so Dave and Ida would let them in,' mumbles Scratch into his beard. It was a known ploy for strangers to find someone familiar to neighbours and ingratiate themselves to solicit for work and board, though usually not with such dire consequences.

'I can't hear you. Why do you talk funny?' she asks.

'Mmph! No matter, child. How long were they with you?' quizzes Scratch.

'Not very long.'

'Did they do any work?'

'Remy said they would work for food.'

'Yeah, go on.'

'I was playing outside.'

'Did ye hear a shot?

'Yes.'

'When your mommy ran outside did she say who was shot?'

'No.'

'What did she say?' he presses.

'She said to go to the woods with Roughy and find you. Then I heard them call my name.'

'Who called your name?'

'Remy and those men, but I was scared and kept going.'

Scratch pulls at his beard.

'Did you know the names of any of the men, besides Remy?' he asks.

'No. Where's my mommy?' she demands more forcefully, as if she is challenging Scratch with the truth. 'I want to go home.'

'Flower Child,' he begins slowly, inevitably, 'I must tell you . . . your mommy and daddy are dead. Those Trashies killed them. We must go to my other place up in the cliffs until they leave. They might find my camp here; they must be down below somewhere; I should never have left you at the camp. We'll have to be more careful. You are so brave, Flower Child.' Scratch thinks that by continuing to talk it might defray the shock to Terrie about her parent's death.

But Flower Child sits motionless picking at the ground. Her face has turned slightly. Scratch can see that with tremendous effort she is trying to keep her composure and be brave, but the tears well up and her face breaks, her little hands falling limply to the ground. Even in Cephren, his emotions plummet into a head-reeling sorrow. She suppresses a moan still struggling to contain herself, but to little avail; it all comes tumbling out like a burst log jam on a river-stream. Scratch reaches hesitantly to touch her gently with his dirty hands, saying over and over, 'I'll protect you, child; I'll protect you, child; Flower Child, Terrie girl, I'll protect you.'

After a time of indeterminable silence, Flower Child lifts her swollen, damp face to Scratch and says shakily, 'I'm never going to see them again, am I? Just like Lassie the dog . . . except I never make it home.'

'You will go home, one day, Flower Child, I promise. So what do ye say girl? Shall we get some ice cream?' he suggests stupidly, not realising he doesn't have any.

'Ice cream? Where?'

'Up in the cliffs at my safe home.

'You have ice cream in the cliffs?'

'Yeah.'

'What kind?' she queries, disbelieving.

'Ah . . . hot dog ice cream . . . the kind Lassie would like.'

'Hot dog ice cream?' she replies curiously.

'Yeah,' he says trying to look quite serious.

Flower Child even stirs to the makings of a tearful laugh. 'Okay,' she says. 'I'd like some.'

'Well, let's go,' he says, standing and stretching with a groan. 'It's a long walk.'

So off they go back down through the forest, Roughy in front, then Scratch and Flower Child, across the stream to gather a few things at his camp. Then careful not to stumble onto the men they venture up the hill on the other side, through ravines and meadows until almost three hours later they cross a rocky wooded plateau and come to a cleft at the edge grown over by thick cedars. Scratch helps Flower Child down the cool damp rocks through a secret entrance in some shrubs into a dark crevice that leads to a cavern. Beneath the cavern, at least to one side of it, are mounds of old granular snow in the crevices and dark holes that the sun never touches. It is a unique phenomenon that the snow sometimes lingers there throughout the year. The mottled and pitted crusts of snow are blackened from dirt, but serve as a natural refrigerator. In the cavern, Scratch keeps a stockpile of supplies. Adjacent to it, built into the cliff covering the mouth of a cave, is a cozy little shack with a woodstove. Inside, he has a pipe jammed in the rock where a trickle of cool, spring water emerges. Flower Child drinks her fill and then momentarily forgetting the tragedy almost gleefully scoops up the hard snow and throws it in the air. Scratch digs down in the snow at the base of the cliff and uncovers a box. Opening it, he brings out a bundle of hard naturally smoked, venison dogs. He throws one to Flower Child who hesitates at first but soon makes fast work of it. Roughy, too, gets one and wolfs it down.

'What d'ya think?' asks Scratch. 'Good, ain't it?'

'Yeah,' pipes Flower Child, mimicking Scratch. 'Where did you get them?'

'You can cook 'em too,' he says, ignoring the question.

'Where did you get them?' she insists.

'Oh, I made them a long time ago.'

'Mommy said you lived with us,' she announces.

'Yep, with your brothers.'

'They were killed, you know,' she says matter-of-factly, intoning her familiarity to the notion of death.

'Yeah, I know, I wish they weren't.'

'Yeah, me too, I don't remember them much. I was a baby.'

'Flower Child, I have to go back to my camp for a while by the creek, to get some more things. I want you to stay here with Roughy. I'll light a fire in the stove and give you something warm to put on. There's lots of food. Here's some seed bread and more hot dogs. Now get some rest. If you want to climb up that wooden ladder there to reach that rock outcrop, you can see the valley and your old farm across the way, but be careful.'

'How long will you be away?' she asks quietly.

'Until dark.' He makes a fire with some birch bark and twigs from a huge pile of wood in another cavern. 'It's warm and dry in the house, girl; sleep on the bed. The outhouse is down that way,' he says indicating with his head before he is gone.

Scratch makes his way down the valley again and heads north of his river camp. He intends to intercept with the route the Trashies had taken just to know which way they went and to see who they are to report to the local militia. He is surprised, in fact, that no one including himself had seen the farm house burn, especially from high up on the hill. But the farm is isolated and it had been overcast. The country in that region had been so depopulated due to the extremely harsh winters the past decade, few working farms remained, most of which had grown over into scrub-land. Because of their relative isolation, until recently, the Trashies had not found the area to their liking and stayed away. Some of the inmates of the halfway house where Scratch had at one time worked and resided had long gone, but it is possible some of them have returned. There is one person, whom he particularly feared who said he would come back after the Asteroid. Scratch had no doubt about his survival. That was Julius Darabak, known simply as Darabak. He was so bad, thought Scratch at the time, it almost made him believe in the devil. Scratch had always been a pragmatist who upheld the virtues of his faith: forgiveness, charity and compassion, and freely served those scruples to others. But with some people, their quick execution was the only right course given the present circumstances, and he would willingly do it without hesitation. Darabak was both bad and smart, an insidious combination, a thief, rapist, extortionist and murderer with a keen intelligence, brawny strength and penetrating dark eyes that bore holes into his victims. Nothing was beyond his sordid imagination.

Scratch is correct in assuming those Trashies had taken that road. Signs of animals passing are obvious by the occasional sheep droppings and wet cattle manure. He moves along carefully at a good pace and before long nears Sunset Lake atop the valley. They are encamped close to the road watering the animals. Scratch stealthily approaches along the shore hidden in the bushs. To his shock, he almost reveals himself by nearly stumbling into one of the men urinating. Some foliage in front of the man's face blocked his sight. Retreating slightly, Scratch almost doubles up when he sees standing looking in his direction finishing his business, his worst nightmare, Darabak. It would seem Darabak actually saw him, by the look in his eye glaring into the green bushes where Scratch holds his breath as if concussed like prey before a snake. But Darabak turns back to his party. Scratch, immeasurably relieved, takes a deep breath and inches his way back. In hindsight, he wished he had pulled out his gun and shot Darabak, though he prevailed on the wisdom of restraint so as not to put himself at risk for Flower Child. From the distance he does not recognise Darabak's other menacing cohort. The boy Remy certainly looks out of place and depressed. He is undoubtedly their prisoner or hostage in the advent of a contingency plan.

Not allowing himself to reflect too much before distancing himself from that evil presence, Scratch finally realises the seriousness of the threat. He must get back without hesitation and seek the militia's help and if possible kill Darabak, otherwise they were all in serious trouble. Scratch remembers the sham of Darabak's incarceration at Midway House. He basically had the run of the place; the superintendent having thought he had made a friend was found murdered after the Asteroid. Dying he had exclaimed: 'There must be some mistake!' Although Scratch was not on Darabak's vendetta list, he had departed just the same. He went to the

Barnetts who had befriended him after the scandal with the poor bishop's wife, Jessie. He always thought Ida didn't like him much, because of her coolness towards him, though it was David Barnett who was the charitable one; nonetheless, Scratch understood that she must have had some confidence in his nature by entrusting her daughter to him on that fateful day, though little choice. Now considering what best to do for Terrie, and whether she could be better cared for elsewhere, it somehow turns his stomach. He believes he has been chosen to be her guardian now; destiny has given him this redeeming honour, besides he knows the family secret which one day he would have to impart to the girl. He knows John and Betsy McKinley, the Barnett's nearest neighbours, would push to adopt her and probably have the support of the general community; it would be difficult to keep her, unless Terrie herself insisted.

Back at his camp by the river-stream, all had been destroyed. Darabak had come across it, because the old road was not too distant, and he had left a fire smoldering. He is at least thankful for Flower Child's safety. It would have been too much to bear to have lost her. He swears to himself that would never be the case. That moment he hears vehicles, one airborne, then voices on the road. They come closer. The large ruddy face of Bud Hamilton and about ten other Heavies surround him. Bud is the Captain of the militia and a decent fellow. Scratch is pleased they had come on their own, as he was now tired and didn't relish hunting for them.

'You're just the fellow I wanted to see, Bud,' says Scratch beneath his scowling eyes.

'And you're just the man we're lookin' for, Scratch.'

'Little Terrie's safe, Bud. She's at my mountain retreat. The men you're after are up at Sunset Lake; they've got the Barnett's tractor and wagon and livestock and supplies. They did a thorough job. I recall that the leader was from Midway; Darabak's his name; don't take chances with him, just kill him on site and be done with it; he's . . . '

'Scratch, we have a real situation, here. The murdering bastards are well armed.'

'Yeah, it figures; what of it?'

'The McKinleys are dead as well as Ben Silva, and the young Path kid who started up at the old McCutcheon place is missing. You actually knew this guy, Darabak?'

Scratch shakes his head bowed. They'd all known death. Finally summoning his speech he remarks, 'I know he's bad, real bad. An' they got the kid.'

The men are getting agitated. Scratch could sense their rage.

'The girl's okay; she came to me this morning early after spending the night in the woods. She says Ida told her to find me. From what I understand, they fed the bastards hopin' to move 'em along, I can only guess. They raped Ida. Anyway, I buried 'em this morning.'

'We know,' says Buddy, shaking his head. 'Some of us weren't too sure about you, Scratch; but I just want to say thanks . . . anyway, we best get goin'. You better get back to that girl; we'll work somethin' out later. Let's go, fellas!'

'Be careful, Bud. And don't miss.'

'We'll get 'em.'

Those were Bud's famous last words, as well as of most of his militia. Scratch found out a few days later from a family moving south that Darabak had ambushed the militia with a fusillade from an Electramatic stun gun he had somehow procured. The Electramatic was the latest new army weapon developed before the Asteroid. The arsenals had been emptied during the long winter and everything distributed to able men. But many of the guns got into the wrong hands. The Electramatic, based on a tiny fusion reactor, sent out a highly refined lightening rod that immobilized vehicles and electrocuted victims. It seems to Scratch that Darabak was sitting on a heap of munitions. Furthermore, Scratch realises that Darabak could well have seen him in the bushes, and by pretending not to notice, backed out of a possible ambush in that he didn't know how many were hiding. When nothing happened, Darabak prepared himself for an inevitable attack by taking the offensive. So shocked is the community that they appeal far and wide to raise an army to get this Trashie, but to no avail as everybody everywhere are beset by insurmountable problems; besides there are no overriding authorities. The reality of their predicament is all too clear: get out while you can. People then resort to moving away and Darabak feeds their fears with a bolder and bolder attitude luring anyone who stayed with the promise of protection only to swear their allegiance like a feudal tyrant. Within the year, he leads a community living by Sunset Lake. He presides over a subservient mix of men, women and children, some so depraved in their fallen circumstances that most cling to his brutal power. Any proof of disloyalty brings to the individual public torture and death by Darabak's notorious lieutenant, Gus, who does his master's bidding with a religious zeal. Darabak the Great he calls himself, and over time many an innocent family actually sought his protection at Sunset Lake. His hold on Clearview becomes so pervasive that his legitimacy is undisputed. Any resistance or opposition is mercilessly destroyed. Darabak knows how to wield ruthless power. And his "Holy Compassion" becomes the by-word for unassuming migrants. They believe Darabak could protect them from the perils of the Horror.

Not only does Darabak assume law and order, he sows the seeds of a new order. It becomes law that everyone has to contribute to the collective whereby to improve technology was the objective. Vehicles of all types are rehabilitated, including the early prototypes for emops. Schools are set up, material comforts made available and health facilities created. Darabak even goes to war with neighbouring townships which he soundly defeats and quickly annexes. All of this Scratch watches carefully from his hermit hideout with his young orphan, Flower Child. In time, Scratch trades and mixes with some of the Trashies, which he justifies as being the establishment of a "crude civilisation". In his youth, Scratch had attained a high degree of scholarship, although one wouldn't know it from the vulgar vernacular and rough exterior to which he had devolved. He feels nevertheless it is appropriate that he should use his knowledge to teach Flower Child to at least read and write. And not only does he teach her, but as she gets older he rekindles some of his former intellectual skill, bestowing on her a knowledge of history, literature, physics, chemistry and philosophy, not without a sprinkling of religion. He teaches her to hunt and farm, make clothes and be self-sufficient, and miraculously always seems to find new shoes and clothes for winter. He is a good provider. This is all accomplished not ten kilometers from Sunset Lake, now Sunset City, a place that Flower Child had remembered fondly from picnics with her parents, but is now strictly out of bounds.

Cephren, meanwhile, with dizzying recognizance of all this life growing within Flower Child, speeds ahead hurtling through these many years heading for some rendezvous with his own circle of destiny and particularly that of old Scratch. With maturity in Flower Child, now nineteen, Scratch begins feeling a strong purpose achieved and great sense of accomplishment for his life. At the periphery of his mind is the looming specter of mortality. He is an old man and Flower Child would someday seek to break out of her wilderness cloister.

Cephren through this mnemonic window gains the ability to choose for himself a semblance of control in these lives, to the extent that he can transmit his burgeoning vitality into an innate accumulation of knowledge. He still does not know what he is really searching for: only the intuition of some elusive thread in his quest for an answer to the riddle of the X13. Though exhilarated to say the least, he does not feel any sense of urgency. The memory chip is serving up a feast for his eyes and mind.

In the old mirror that Scratch had given Flower Child years earlier, she would look into her face and perceive there the curious inquisition of fate and yearning. For years she had felt a giddy passion from the strange notions of her developing sexuality. Her breasts have swelled and hips filled out, and she feels awkward awareness about her maturity. Scratch, despite his renewed enlightenment and love of his foster child, never once broaches the subject of her sexuality. Even when she begins to menstruate, he ignores her need to understand. He supplies her with rags and teaches her how to boil them for re-use. However, his responsibility to guide her founders on a shoal of sexuality; all his life he had denied the procreative drive that propelled the essential in self-perpetuation. His one deviation with Jessie, the politician's wife, blew him right out of the water. At the time, their mostly platonic affair and consummation of kissing and petting at her rather seductive quest had shocked him out of his spiritual miasma, and he experienced that spring, a happiness never before conceived in his life of piety. He came to revel in their spiritual joining, and they spoke of marriage. But Jessie retreated when they were found out making their weekly rendezvous. Eternal damnation was served by the jealous husband and his own brimstone ire. So what Scratch had divined during his life from a spiritual journey (though flawed by his inability to express an understanding of sexuality), he bequeaths to Flower Child a silence of these matters. She in turn has been created the most innocent, naïve and natural phenomenon ever assembled in the human repertoire.

The time befell one day out and about in the vicinity of "that Babylon" Sunset City, as Scratch would pronounce in that crotchety hermit vernacular: that Flower Child finds it exceedingly wonderful to watch from the distance the men at work in the fields. Their tanned skin and glistening bodies catch her eye and with no clear definition of purpose she becomes attracted to them. To Scratch's horror, while he is looking up from one of his rabbit snares to see where she has gone, Flower Child walks gingerly part way across the field to the men now resting in the shade by the tractor and hay wagon. There she stands ten meters away in a stance with her hands on her hips, saying with brave eloquence, 'You men have laboured well in honest work; can it be you who've raped and pillaged?'

The men are too stunned to respond. Her wild beauty has captivated them.

She continues: 'How is it that what I see feels contrary to what I know about you? Darabak raped and killed my mother, a hard working woman, and killed my father, a hard working man, and left me orphaned, but for Scratch. How can you rationalise this hypocrisy, you hard working men?'

The men, excepting one, are of a perfidious and base nature and decline comment in a sullen incomprehensibility, as the impact of her appearance or apparition swirls in their vacant brains. However, one man does speak to her, 'These are terrible crimes that you speak of and by my own contrition as witness to many crimes, though fearfully innocent, I am guilty of powerlessness to take action against them. In my defence, though I hold myself a coward, I have suffered much abuse and beatings for my speaking out against them, though but a boy at the time. Looking back I wish I had died.'

Flower Child looks at this young man though perhaps ten years her senior and instantly sees him as some underdog worthy of great redemption. 'I am sorry too,' she says quietly. 'But your dying would have made my loss all the more wasted. We survive like you with heavy hearts.'

'Who are you?' he asks amicably, stirred by her sympathy, something unknown in his life.

'Flower Child.'

'I am Remy Path,' he says, seeming to divine in her appearance as if there is something about her that he recognises but cannot place, the many years having obliterated their long gone acquaintance.

'Flower Child,' he repeats. 'There is something familiar about you . . . how do you know Scratch?'

'I live with Scratch.'

His face goes ashen. 'You're little Terrie,' he presumes. 'You must leave here now; it is dangerous. You must go.' He looks around furtively. Gus happens to be approaching from the far side of the field. 'Go, before that man comes! He is a bad man. Go!' he demands forcefully.

Flower Child holds her ground. 'We must speak further of these things, Remy.'

'Where do you come from, honey?' interrupts one of the others who walks up to Remy.

'Shut up!' demands Remy, turning to the man. 'Please go,' he pleads to Flower Child who stares at Remy now as if he is some kind of magic being that has unlocked the secrets of her existence.

'Any bets she's virgin!' says another man.

'You mean like Mary?' she asks, her face lighting up.

'Yuh get fucked yet?' trolls the man.

Remy turns and strikes him across the face. Gus is now running towards the fracas.

'What is 'fucked'?' she asks Remy innocently.

But before the others can demonstrate, Scratch comes bounding out of the woods, his old stubby legs moving with such alacrity that the men can only gape at this spectacle. Without a word, Scratch yanks her to him and bids her to run as fast as her long legs can manage. She looks at Remy once more as she's hastened away. Gus comes upon them yelling, 'Stop them!' and Remy stumbles and trips Gus. Cursing, Gus shoots Remy before he and the men take off after their prey. Remy still alive drags himself to the edge of the field. After Scratch and Flower Child manage to escape, the men leave Remy for dead at the edge of the bush, carrion for the coyotes.

To Cephren the incident had always been known in local folklore as The Visitation. The story goes that when Darabak heard about the incident, he sent out a massive search party that hunted high and low for a month. He wanted the "angel" for himself. They were not successful however in finding as much as a clue to her whereabouts, thus fanning the mystery of the event. Some suggested she must be the angel who would destroy Darabak and his tyranny. Others claimed she was an apparition of an ancient deity, perhaps Venus, and the scruffy old man was jealous Hephaestos (Vulcan) taking back his wandering bride. But to know that The Visitation took place within his grasp and he could not have her, rankled Darabak more than anything he had known in his diseased mind. All his cold logic failed him when he was told of her exquisite beauty and exalted bearing. If downfall in the human experience wasn't in the weakness of a man's loins, no drama on earth was worth recording, short of a woman's forbearance. Yet Darabak was not a real man, he was a Trashie; though in fairness to the historical recording of his time, his influence was instrumental to the founding of Sunsetwind. And Cephren can see that. He also sees himself. His search has stepped up a notch. He grasps the truth. He sees the parameters expanding beyond his immediate vision. He knows that somehow in Flower Child is the link in his quest. Her search is his and of all Sunsetwind and that of the earth. She must lead him as a guiding light into the underworld. The awesome reality of this consciousness in the chip does have some method and purpose. There is a physical property to it all; the technology of nature is being used and enacted through her memory by the chip. What a miracle! And he is there breathing the very air Flower Child respires! He knows Sunsetwind will overcome its desperation through Flower Child. This knowledge is the X13 and the X13 is God.

five Heyoka

Who glow in the dark calling mommy earth
                                    —Jimmy Pidgeon

B y the time the days have turned to weeks and the weeks approach
a month, the windowless storeroom in the bowels of the Pyramid have become something of a prison cell, not the type with
bars or laser barriers, but the rock solid warmth and familiarity of a home
of sorts where Chromolox begins to imagine the outside world and recreate its nomenclature. For example, she now sees herself as the President of
Silence, and the platoon of wooden-faced genos outside her door are the
Faceless Public, whose will propounds that she be incarcerated. She is
important, of course, and the more sonic the silence the more intense the
realisation. She contemplates that all her training, knowledge and experience are representative in some respect of the universal survivor who really
made it and she will get through this. In a more poignant sense she symbolises the burden of legitimacy in that the heritage of her own people and
ancestors had ascended from their roots in the bulrush paddocks of St.
Marie in Huronia, and bore out without compunction the requisites of an
unabashed cultural elite as due natural process. She is never ingratiating,
nor does she stoop to feign a role. Like the Paths, she accepts her demise
fully unrepentant in her righteousness. In a world of cyclical battles

between hard won civilisation and the tyranny of superficial 'progress', honour, common sense and pride are the only remains of integrity. She has no doubt this *coup d'etat* was evil. In time, she wonders if in the distant future there would be a kind of perfection or enlightenment so powerful that no second rate intelligence could usurp, and no technology or ideology worth coveting.

In her confinement there is a simple mirror, a toilet and a deep utility sink in the corner. A cot had been brought in with a sleeping bag, and a small wooden table and chair grace the center of the small room with a bright overhead light. Chromolox will sit alternatively in the chair, then lie on the bed, then pace and do a stretch-callisthenic routine, then jumping jacks and sometimes a wall-sit. Meditation and yoga are her only form of cerebral exercise as they refuse her a book, monitor or pen and paper. There are the long periods from one disembodied stupor to another. The isolation might destroy an average person restrained as such, yet Chromolox seems to thrive on it as the days go by. She has been so toughened from the adversity of her rise to power that only the word invincible could describe her character.

On this particular day, January 30, 2396, she receives her noon meal and hungrily eats the soup, a thick green calaloo (pigweed – a Sunsetwind staple). Dipping the cornbread in the hot soup, she encounters a lump. Thinking it a large piece of crabmeat, (one of the ingredients), she takes her spoon and scoops up not crabmeat but a tightly folded piece of paper. Without finishing, she licks off the paper and opens it. Once it is open, she licks again the remaining green film and reads the barely legible printed longhand:

> *Without mentioning names, we believe you are here.*
> *Because there is no way to verify, we must make a leap*
> *of faith. Thank you for being here. We need your*
> *silence. Dubious as this note may seem, does its*
> *authenticity strike you as possible or unlikely? We will*

say this: no high ranking member has clearance. Del must
be our glorious hero. Thanks. Stay in touch. Keep flush.

Sue Bommorf

Upon rereading it for a second time, Chromolox almost has it memorised. Her crossed sense of elation and shock at such a cryptic communiqué leaves her unable for the moment to make anything of it. Yet she has that famous intuition that its authenticity is probable. It is unlikely that such a ruse by the Chicagos would be that clever. And certainly hero Del is too ignorant to even conceive of such an idea. What purpose would it serve? She is unable to respond, in any event. But who is Sue Bommorf? She spells it backwards: *frommobeus. Mobius!* The superintendent of the Pyramid! Mobius, of course, would be in a position to observe and know some of the action without casting any suspicion; he is a maintenance man, the head janitor, yet with a perspicacity to boot by the look of it. What does he mean by no high ranking member has clearance? Can it be that high ranking means the Board. The Board is incommunicado? Or under house arrest? Likely. But in another sense it contradicts the fact that high-ranking members have clearance. Obviously, the Board has been incarcerated as well, so why mention it? It's a riddle. Unless . . . what is it? She thinks. He says 'we'. Who could be 'we'? Mobius is in touch with someone, but who? Redman? No high-ranking member has clearance. Perhaps he is a high-ranking member that doesn't have clearance. An oxymoron! Unless . . . he means a high-ranking member who escaped . . . or, is not considered a high ranking member. Chromolox muses on that for a moment; then it hits her. Redman. He has to be Redman! Redman is retired from the Board but remains honourary and may not have been subjected to arrest like the others being old and isolated, and technically he does not have automatic clearance but has access if he wants to. But there is Cleo who is out of the country; could she have made it back in? Unlikely. Who else besides Redman? Redman and Mobius and possibly Vince who spends all his time inside the Pyramid and could have been there in his condo on New Year's and before the Chicagos infiltrated the whole complex; maybe, just maybe, he managed to hide in the confusion. Vince. Vince is smart. And Mobius could have helped him somehow. It could be. Probable, she realises. *Keep flush*. She immediately goes to the toilet and flushes the paper down, then casually goes back to her soup.

Chromolox then believes with a leap of faith that probably Redman, Vince and Mobius are not under arrest, at least not yet. Also, Del Barker is in charge, *our glorious hero*, or figuratively, sooner or later he would send for her because once some stability and order had prevailed, he would presumably have to deal with her, one way or another. And in all likelihood, he would at the very least, as a parting courtesy, speak to her, as she did to him during the riots, though under very different circumstances. *Stay in touch, meaning:* hang in there – pure Redman, now that she thinks of it. The whole enigmatic note was probably written by him, as Mobius the signee and messenger to protect the source, and obviously his access to the kitchens, not to mention his undying fealty to Sunsetwind.

Not until four days later, do the genos guarding her cell open her door and announce that she is to meet the President. She is rather humoured by the idea, and bounces off her bed cheerily still dressed in her worn and wrinkled linens from New Year's. She primps her wild hair that refuses to obey and with an eager stride exits her nun's penance chamber.

Along the hallway, she recognises the Logistics Section. She hadn't known where she had been put since arrival because she had been blindfolded and shunted in without anybody seeing her. An elevator is reserved that takes her up through the various levels including Survivor's Walk which she glimpses briefly through the windowed shaft. She sees that it appears to be business as usual. There are many people out and about, shopping, supping and entertaining etc., which mildly hurts her as she could not see any sign of tension or resistance, but on second thought, it mollifies her knowing that it was hers and Cleo's plan that people would carry on passively, so trust could be established which might enable resistance to build innocuously and when the time comes to resist: wham, the

Chicagos would not know what hit them. The hope is that world opinion would have sufficiently realigned itself to support the self-determination of a country, hence restraining the Chicagos from a repeat offence. Anyway, they wouldn't get another chance, blizzard or not. She still can't understand how they got through the perimeters without detection.

Once up in the executive suites, Chromolox is led to the Loft lift and put in alone. There she is, going up to the Loft as she had done thousands of times before. It occurs to her that if it is indeed business as usual, she must play along as well as possible under the circumstances, even if Del Barker really aggravates her to the breaking point. She must be water rather than fire and fill all those blank places so she can be subjected and resigned to the cause, whatever that is.

Stepping out, she keeps her eyes squarely ahead refusing to acknowledge the tacky makeover Del had created in Cephren's Loft. She smiles as she approaches Del behind the old oak desk with Cephren's Mars Two. Del is riveted to the monitor in stern concentration. Without looking up, he says, 'Hello Chromolox, please sit down.'

'Thank you,' she says looking curiously at him.

Finally with a sigh, he signs off whatever he is doing and looks up with his toothy smile and blue eyes – blue deadpan eyes, emitting not one bit of depth or compassion, but the glaze of a fanatic. His tanned, model face and wavy brown hair give the very *coup de grace* to his vain, empty, technocentricity. His background in banking and promotion is in no way any prerequisite to power of the old order, yet a perfect fit in the new. Chromolox almost has to suppress a cynical laugh. This idiocy is sublime, yet she knows that she must succeed to emulate his meritorious march.

'Yes, well, how are you, Chromolox?' he asks in his deep authoritative voice that so impelled his audiences to listen to its seemingly resonant sincerity. 'I trust your accommodations and fare have been adequate. I do hope you understand the strain we have all been under. You must realise that the Free Radical party, only with the greatest contrition through duty to Sunsetwind, have obligated themselves to rule in your demise. We did not ask for it, or covet it, which may come as a surprise to you; we have simply taken this opportunity to rehabilitate a great country. I would have you know, as I said to you once before, I have the greatest respect for you and the Board and wish you no harm and truly am sorry for what has happened to you. In regards to your incarceration, I had no choice. The Chicagos, namely our new ally, have on the whole been very cooperative, but insisted upon a few conditions during this transition. The people of Sunsetwind, naturally, have been very upset at the turn of events, but on the whole, submissive to the process, thanks to our civilised and conciliatory nature. Now before I give you the retirement conditions that the new Board has devised for you, is there anything you would like to say?'

'Thank you for asking, Del, and I'm fine, and congratulations on your promotion; I think the Chicagos, Trinny rather, has made a very good choice. The Free Radical party was never given the credit due for their patriotism. You believed, as we all believed, change must be forthcoming; and as you say, "your obligation" is to the highest calling: the good of Sunsetwind. But let me ask you first, Del: what news? How are Cephren and Cleo and the Board . . . I mean old Board? And the world, is it satisfied with the present arrangement and your rule? Do the Americans accept the new order? How about the Europeans? What is the commentary? I am very curious; I have been without news.'

'Yes, I'm sorry for that; Trinny insisted on the conditions of your incarceration; we had nothing to do with that. But to answer your questions: Cephren, we believe, is in Ottawa. There was a picture of him in yesterday's news gambling in the Parliament Casino, with of all people, Anna Gram, the actress; he seems to be quite jolly and true to form – a fitting place for the man, as he was a problem and symptom of all this. His true nature and karma have finally been revealed, wouldn't you say?' He looks at her intently.

'I have to say I'm relieved he wasn't hurt in the invasion,' offers Chromolox, 'but it is a little disappointing to hear of him . . . cavorting with an actress in our time of need. I wish only the best for Cephren, however; he is a kind man, if flawed.'

'Quite right: to a fault and the expense of us all.'

'How did he get away?' she asks casually attempting to feign disinterest, but suppressing tears of happiness in his deliverance.

'He escaped the Chicagos in the Volcano, which as we now know is a prototype model emop. At first, it was thought he was killed because he crashed into Great Blue that awful night, but was nowhere to be found with not a scrap of wreckage. He went missing for three weeks before turning up in Anishnabe, Ottawa in fact, about ten days ago.'

'And Cleo?'

'That bitch was found to be slumming with the enemy, O'Reilly al Khazzami, whose infidel Kush is now on our hate list. Foreign policy is my newborn baby, Chromolox, and we can't be seen to have friends like that bastard, can we?'

'O'Reilly is not really my type of fellow,' she offers.

'Which begs the question, do you have a type of fellow, Chromolox?'

The question catches her off guard; she just hopes she doesn't turn colours on him. 'Why, I don't have a fellow at present, and it hardly begs the question.'

'Would it be impertinent to confirm one way or the other what the papers have been (not recently mind you) saying about you?'

'I don't know what the papers have been saying, Del,' she says guardedly.

'They say, to quote the Chicago papers, that you're a closet lesbian and an abomination.'

'Well, ah . . . that is impertinent, Del; my private life is private and I will not dignify any response, one way or another!'

'A little touchy, aren't we?'

Chromolox would not get drawn into that line of discourse. She is practicing water and smiles, wretchedly.

'No matter,' he lectures smirking, 'the damage is done; the old order have proven themselves true to form. You know we're bringing religion back to Sunsetwind. And I suggest you get some psychotherapy for your deviance from the norm.'

'Oh, I never realised we were so deprived; people are free, are they not? And I'm not a deviant, Del; love is love; 'nough said.' She swallows the gander rising in her throat.

'I'm afraid not, my dear. We will purge any deviants from our society. As for religion, some of us felt persecuted for our beliefs. I was raised as an atheist and when I rejected that doctrine and became an Omega Pointer in the Buddhist-Judeo-Christian mold, I was chastised for being rigid, me rigid? Ironic, isn't it? The one who actually has the balls to make changes to a corrupt society.'

'Who was doing the chastising, your family?' she wonders, tersely.

He visibly hesitates at the mention of his family, but follows through quickly. 'My family had nothing to do with it; but yes, they were sceptical of my leanings.'

'It was your great-grandfather who was publicly remonstrated against by the Paths, wasn't it? He was an avowed atheist, was he not?'

'You know your history, Chromolox. Impressive. Perhaps you should try for a position at Great Blue U. or one of our many elementary schools.'

'Perhaps.' Chromolox is seething under his patronizing.

'My family was a powerful force in Sunsetwind until the last few generations when the system failed us. My ancestors began the Nottawasaga Bank Line and were the wealthiest in the country by far, but didn't have the land that the Paths had. We wanted to develop new markets long ago but were suppressed and hence our slide from influence. It was my distant ancestor Julius Darabak, notorious as he was, that founded what was to become Sunsetwind. We are some of its greatest progenitors, and now destiny has finally paid our reward. Amazing how things come in circles; wouldn't you agree?'

'Yes, yes of course.' Chromolox knows his true philosophy is that of a dynastic tyrant, and Sunsetwind is now his sole possession. He is so blinded by his own importance, she is reminded of Commodus the corrupt Roman Emperor who sold out the Empire to renewed repression at a pivotal time when he had the chance to build upon the trust gained from old enemies by his predecessor and father Marcus Aurelius whom sought democracy. Commodus symbolised the inner rot of an empire doomed.

'Also, isn't it ironic,' he goes on, 'how I, with my privileged background . . .'

'We all have privileged backgrounds, Del,' she interrupts.

'Yes, well, I have overcome the greatest odds to be President. And you, with your elitism, which is noble in its own way – many of my friends are elitists – struggled and brought yourself into favour with the ruling class and was even elected President, but to be deposed in disgrace. The sanctity of blood is finally sorting itself out, I guess. The gods have set the tables clean. True proponents of freedom and expression are once again in control, thanks to Trinny Burnamthorpe.'

'When are you going to be elected, Del?' she asks with that trusting smile. She really wants to remind him of the history of Trashies, from one Trashie to another.

'As soon as the people are ready,' he replies confidently. 'Don't you see, there has to be some house cleaning; people aren't ready for real freedom just yet. And the Chicagos must go home first. It will never do to have them standing around in our malls.'

'Good point. Then we may run against each other some day.'

'Not quite, Chromolox, the system we envision will not allow just anybody to run for public office. You have to pass the party test. The Free Radicals want to ensure that laws will be upheld, laws that will protect Sunsetwinders from people like you and Cephren. We are a one party system with more checks and balances than any system yet devised.'

'I see. Maybe I really should look up a history position. I might specialise in 20th century Totalitarianism.'

'Very good, Chromolox, I could put a good word in for you. You could be a true representative of rehabilitation with a little counciling. You could set a great example having led the old and riding the crest of the new; what do you say?'

'Thank you, Del, but I need to take some time to adjust: you know, go home and collect my thoughts. But please, tell me more about Cleo; you were saying she was . . . '

'Fucking that asshole O'Reilly. Pardon me, I always had a terrible crush on her, you know; but she's a slut. And now she's stirring up trouble for the Mississippis down in Tennessee.'

'What on earth is she doing?' quizzes Chromolox nimbly.

'She sweet-talked George Washington into staying there in the Pentagon of all places. You have to wonder what she does to get what she needs. All we know is that the Yellow Tooth Cherokees have started a guerilla war in Western Tennessee with the Mississippis who have made many justifiable inroads in the South. You know the South; they've got their independence and be damned with it! The Chicagos have stepped up their pressure on the Mississippis to take big action, of which we are in full support. It's really something; you should see those old confederate flags fly; the strange thing is, the Mississippis are flyin' the stars n' stripes and the Yellow Tooths and their allies, ole Dixie.'

'What's so strange about that?' She urges him on.

'Well, we just got word yesterday that the Americans are backing the Yellow Tooths. They even had a confederate flag raised outside ancient Abe's memorial! I tell you if they're leaning to defend the damned Yellow Tooth Cherokees with the military all hell will descend. Who needs war? George Washington and Trinny Burnamthorpe had a meeting in which Cleopatra's involvement with the Tennessee situation got Trinny so pissed off, she walked out saying, 'We will count the votes April 2, George! Then we'll talk!' She is, of course, referring to the EF election for the Earth Chair, if she wins, which looks likely at present. Africa, Japan, China, Russia, Slavic Europe, most of Latin America and us of course are all tightly connected economically with the Chicagos.' He nods his approval of the thought.

Chromolox has to change the subject; he had become so repulsive her water was turning to ice and melting fast.

'Del, I was wondering,' she drops the question, 'have there been any revelations as to the X13?'

'The X13?' he laughs. 'Who cares about it? Sooner or later Cephren will trip up and give it back or die and that will be the end of it. But I believe it's of no value. It's a piece of junk, that's all! All that UFO stuff is baloney, disinformation designed by the old governments to control their people with terror. Little green men!' He peals away uproariously. 'Don't tell me you got suckered by that crap!'

'No, I was just curious; it was a strange chip.'

'Strange, pah! You know how they were back then; who wouldn't be strange with their ignorance; they were sick in mind and body – a damned good thing that Asteroid. God was merciful.'

'There were some great minds and billions of dead people.'

'Hot blooded fools most of 'em. Well, that just about sums it up, Chromolox.' He presses a monitor button. 'You will be fitted with a wrist-band that cannot be removed. It is a DNA tag so-to-speak, monitored from the Pyramid. We insist for a few of you. We can locate you anytime anywhere, and hear what you have to say, so be careful. Any meeting with former Board members is strictly forbidden, punishable by further incarceration. Repeat offences will be dealt with by life termination. We're designing a new facility to deal with any transgressors of our new order. It may seem harsh for now, but you will see that in time people will be much better off. We're looking at greater public transportation, holiday packages, joint international space ventures, business agreements, trade deals, the hosting of a Technological Fair, the rebuilding of a strong military – so many things – you will see the greatest prosperity ever. Chromolox, we are going to turn this country around. Now you are free to go. Best wishes, dear. Try to fit in. Help us and some day you may get your old job back.'

'Well, then what would you do, Del?'

'I'd be Chairman of course.'

'Of course, how stupid of me.'

'You're not stupid, Chromolox; you're one of the best and brightest we've got. By the way, your condo has been expropriated and your personal belongings taken to your family's place in Midland. It was the best we could do.'

'Thank you so much, Del, best of luck.'

Chromolox stands up, goes to the lift and enters. Raging within, never in her life has she been so cool and yet so angry. She feels lucky to have maintained her composure, as she could have killed him. Del has to be the biggest moron Sunsetwind had ever borne. And one day, she portends, his ignorance will save Sunsetwind. Now that is irony. At least she is almost free. Once off the lift, a geno puts on the wrist band. Tagged, she takes the main lift down to Survivor's Walk and disappears into the morning crowd.

For many days after she had spoken to Cephren, Cleo has felt too incensed to admit to herself that he was right by remaining inaccessible. She knows he would be of no use around Washington, and contrary to George Washington's pleas, it would be politically unsound to be seen to protect him from the grasp of the Chicagos, when most Americans are moving towards the idea of unity. However, that is the least of her worries; the X13 could contain something spectacular and it should be kept out of the political melée. Besides, her anger, she realises, is not so much directed at her big brother, but at her own failure to protect Sunsetwind.

She would take long walks along the Potomac and wander through the old monuments and memorials of the heady days of the USA, that huge force that once controlled the ebbs and flows of the global village. The vast parks and lawns are not that well kept and grow wild in places. It is a veritable jungle around the Vietnam Memorial and vines covered Abe Lincoln. During the Horror, squatters lived everywhere including the White

House, and even Congress was a shambles. Yet the Potomac River is clean and drinkable as are most of the old polluters. Even the Hudson River up to Manhattan, which now runs through a veritable wilderness, is as clean as the day Henry navigated its shores. After the bombing, the entire rubble pile that was Manhattan had been gradually excavated and landscaped, and most of the island was since reforested as a memorial to the war.

That January in Washington the weather is warmer than average. It rains continuously day after day for a solid week. Then it turns cold; the Potomac freezes and the ground is like coarse marble. Cleo lives in the old Pentagon in a tiny room off the Naval Intelligence wing. Naval operations are for the most part no longer marine, but pan-orbital or Solar Ops as they term it, which has absorbed the original Air Force. Their emop technology is a patented Sunsetwind design for propulsion. It is considered to be neck and neck with that of the Chicagos, who don't pay much attention to the original patents, some of which are over a hundred years old.

From the outset, Admiral McKee, with George Washington's blessing, brings Cleo into the top-level operations. Admiral McKee is an old friend of Sunsetwind, who once holidayed with Cephren and Cleo at The Winds on Great Blue. He is a medium-build compact type about sixty years of age. He has sharp brown eyes, a light complexion and cropped grey hair. He never seems to be perturbed, or stressed and has a very positive affect on his command. He can cut through the hubris in any situation and believes firmly in the old adage of the American Dream, but not to the tune of any sell-out to the Chicagos. If unification were to happen, he wants it to be through American leadership. He is also Sunsetwind's strongest supporter. He does, however, agree with George Washington that to provoke Chicago into war over Sunsetwind would be foolish at this time. Admiral McKee has a different plan that requires the cooperation of General Dennis, a cagey chief-of-staff and confidant of George Washington. The General is more of a political wind-sniffer and not greatly admired by Admiral McKee, though the two make a good team.

Privately, McKee informs Cleo of a little innuendo one night in his old

Annapolis house over an aromatic Burgundy and tasty French cuisine cooked by his Moroccan wife, Giselle. It takes him almost two weeks to persuade Cleo that a frontal assault on Chicago would fail, and Cleo knows it would, but argues for it anyway, holding out for a better alternative. Admiral McKee explains to Cleo that in West Tennessee, which is autonomous, the Mississippis are engaged in a similar takeover, though not with blatant military force, but through business. All business in the Mississippis is controlled through the Bureau of Mutual Bipartisanship or BOMB. BOMB is really a front for absolute control over all commerce in the region from the border with Chicago to the Delta. West Tennessee, a poor disparate region, does most of its business through Mississippi but they are rather prickly about their autonomy. Their economy belongs to Mississippi, whose lands consist of most of the Mississippi watershed. But ever since the Chicago-Mississippi alliance, BOMB is calling in its debts, which are in arrears, to pay for its government's huge new joint space program with Chicago. They want to be in control of the Solar System, and have been increasingly hostile to exploratory resource expeditions to the outer planets in search of heavy elements, above all Mars, Saturn and the moons of Jupiter. As a result of this legal bullying, West Tennessee defaulted on many of its loans and have forbidden the Mississippis to claim what they deem to be their state possession. What began as a sporadic problem has become a serious impasse. Admiral McKee even suggests that Cleo stir up the Yellow Tooth Cherokees who live in East Tennessee in the mountains to defend their brothers in the western lands, because if West Tennessee capitulates kicking and screaming to Mississippi, East Tennessee and even the Yellow Tooths might be next. He goes on to say that General Dennis is from Nashville and people there are very upset. The General would certainly look the other way and even get some credit for whatever the Yellow Tooths could do. Nevertheless, it cannot suffice for the Americans to get involved, at least overtly. But Cleo, by clandestine proxy has an axe to grind, and by distancing herself from the Americans with a little help from Navy Intel, (the CIA being long

obsolete) she could begin nipping at the heels of the Mississippis and indirectly, the Chicagos.

As it turns out, General Dennis' support is adamantly forthcoming,
the main reason being that Cleo would be out of his hair. He can't tolerate
the guilt complex she holds over George Washington and his inability to
withstand her. But the General is not a politician, nor is the President,
which at times by his actions have been admonished on occasion by his
supporters in Congress, though to the voting public considered a strength.

Washington has his own course of action, besides sitting on the fence.
He has been of late playing the role of a "love referee", which he secretly
enjoys, steering two hot-headed lovers or ex-lovers (it doesn't matter to
him one way or the other) on their respective trajectories. He is of the
mind that this kind of geopolitical power-broking could be very effective
if exasperating. Cleo and O'Reilly, Sunsetwind and the Kush and now the
Yellow Tooths for that matter: keep them occupied in these theaters away
from America. O'Reilly has made several calls to Cleo and George in
respect to his tenuous situation regarding Cleo and Sam.

One day O'Reilly speaks to Cleo.

'Your nephew, Sam,' he stresses, 'is one political hot potato!'

'I'll send for him when I'm ready,' she replies unmoved. She is about to
head down to Yellow Tooth City, near the Cumberland Pass in the
Smokey Mountains.

'He is very demanding!' he exhorts. 'He asks for you!'

'Stick him in school,' she proposes.

'There are few worthy schools. Everybody works.'

'Isn't he in a monastery? Isn't it like school?'

'Yes, yes, I suppose. My Tibetan friends are in my debt.'

'You must be a genius,' she utters cynically. 'Out.'

Then O'Reilly speaks to George Washington . . .

'Who does she think she is?' he complains to George.

'I don't know, O'Reilly, but Cleo thinks of you as a warlord, an
Emperor, maybe an Irishman.'

'Do you think so?'

'It must be, what else?'

'She is such a . . . such a . . . an amazon! I would do anything . . . anything! I'll make her Empress!'

'Then why not loan her a part of your army and emop force?'

'You have a point.'

'She's going to Nashville to mobilise a force with the Cherokee guerillas.'

'Nashville? The Country Music Hall of Fame.'

'Yes, that's the place.'

'Do you like country music, George?' asks O'Reilly.

'I like Shannon Pearl and the Pearlenes.'

'Yeah, she's all right. How 'bout Tima Deli?'

'Exotic, lovely and strange. But my old favourite is Dylan.'

'Yeah, I've seen some of the holograms – Memphis Blues – or was that Elvis?'

'Yeah, that was Elvis,' corrects George, authoritatively.

'We'll have to get together and listen to some music when this is all over.'

'Sure thing, O'Reilly. Maybe over some unumpentium.'

'Unumpentium?'

'Yes, orange gold.'

'Ahh, yes, the mythical element; is it possible?'

'Indeed, and you hold some leverage – the boy.'

'That may curry favour with Cephren.'

'A hot curry indeed,' avers George, 'but not to my liking.'

'Spiced with little Jimmy Chip.'

'Let us speak further on this.'

'I'll send along a battalion...'

Cleopatra Path has the shock of her life when she descends into the vast Yellow Tooth quadrangle, the traditional epicenter of Cherokee society. There are the seven clan buildings surrounding it, not on the old acre site but rather on a ten-hectare square nestled in a wide, high valley looking down west whence they had come two hundred years before on the Trail of Smiles – the great migration back close to their original homelands so rudely and tragically uprooted in the long ago days of Andrew Jackson and the Trail of Tears. Cleo lands alone on the frozen earth to be surrounded by gleeful children, not a handful but at least a thousand. Their cheers reverberate all around her, the children not touching her, but crying out in the most heart-lifting jubilation dressed in their cottons and leathers displaying American and Confederate flags, wampum belts, bells and ancient totems. There is not an adult among them, as they sit back in the various clan houses to enjoy the spectacle of children. The Yellow Tooth Cherokees, or Kentuckees as they were also called (because Yellow Tooth himself actually came from Kentucky), are really a rag tag bunch of assorted aboriginals. Their descendants were Pawnee, Choctaw, Creek, Huron, Omaha, Mandan, Commanche, Kiowa, Lakota and other indigenous tribes all living together under the Cherokee name. It had been one of the great movements of people since the expansion of the west centuries before. Yellow Tooth, who, like Tecumseh, Pontiac, Sitting Bull and others, brought together many of the native people under one unifying body, but in his case moved back east to reclaim lost land after the Asteroid. This happened during the Horror, when the economic and political infrastructure of the Western world had collapsed into anarchy and the Cumberland Plateau was all but abandoned. It was easily achieved, and many whites and blacks in those early years joined with the Yellow Tooths to become a huge conglomerate through the Smokey and Pine Mountains. States like Virginia and what was once North and South Carolina, (which now comprises the autonomous State of Carolina), even have a loosely held border agreement, as does East Tennessee, with the Yellow Tooths. They seem to be able to come and go freely without prejudice. A couple of centuries before, it was Yellow Tooth himself, in fact, who presided over the creation of the original Confederation of Sovereign Municipal Operatives (COSMO) which eventually evolved into the first Earth Federation sixty years later. Yellow Tooth, Elias Burnamthorpe and David Path (the elder) became fast friends and shared any and all the technology they could lay their hands on. The Yellow Tooths at one time were one of the most advanced new sovereign states. And their present leader is the elusive Heyoka Yellow Tooth, a curious mix of Cherokee, black and white. She is the young thirty-year-old matriarch of their sub-region. Cleo and Cephren have never met her, because she refuses to travel and lives quietly alone. She is mysterious, whose parents are both deceased. She holds the undying loyalty of her people and rely on their elective assembly to deal with local and regional matters, much like Cephren has. It is no coincidence that the Yellow Tooths and Sunsetwinders were similar. Both Yellow Tooth and David Path devised their systems based on ancient tribal, American revolutionary, and British Parliamentary systems that germinated into their own unique neo-feudal elective assemblies. The systems work well as long as the principals of enterprise and freedom are geared to the highest ideals which have been constitutionalised and promulgated as *The Sacred Stones and Laws Bound Thereof*:

> The People of North America herewith uphold these tenets indentured in their constitutions: as sacraments to the well-being of all people the first observance is the promise of our *Creation and Spirit* in the *Universe* whereby in return it is our sworn duty to preserve *Pure Water, Pure Air, Pure Earth* because we believe in the premise that *The Land Owns The People* and to maintain our *Resources* for our children in perpetuity to *Preserve* our *Free Economy* so that we may exemplify a society based in *Justice, Freedom and Prosperity. David Path Elias Burnamthorpe Yellow Tooth* – 2161 AD

These precepts, these *Sacred Stones* is the keystone to their laws and adopted by many other constitutions such as Sunsetwind and even Chicago, though over time the innocent idealism of it has been corrupted by the Chicagos. In time, as the Earth Federation evolved into the political arena it became apparent that these *Stones* had become lost in the complicity of power struggles and variant cultural attitudes. The *Stones* were termed simplistic and naïve, yet few would dare challenge them, as in the middle ages few would challenge the power of the church. In Yellow Tooth however, they still pay strict observance to these precepts. Even in Sunsetwind, the *Sacred Stones* are held close to the heart, although the original manifesto is now encased in a museum display and deemed archaic.

Cleo is led by the throng of jubilant children to a delegation at the perimeter of the open square. A large black man, Harvey, adorned with the many vestments of his office, as chief of Council, greets her warmly. His smile shines munificently along with the gold and silver studs that encircle his arms and covered his back and shoulders on a black leather jumper suit. Wampum belts hang around his neck and he holds a pipe in his hand. He states in deep vibrant voice that he is the Keeper of the *Stones* and hands her the pipe, who takes a puff. He introduces Cleo to his large, white wife, who then kisses and hugs Cleo. Soon they are sitting around a huge fire in a warm building made from stone and wood. All the structures seem to have the same architecture and design. The floor is made of finished hardwood and the air gives off earthen scents from long use, sweaty summers and many fires. Cleo is introduced to the leaders of the Yellow Tooth Cherokee one by one, except for Heyoka who rarely comes out of her mountain retreat. There is some commiseration concerning Sunsetwind's plight and general voice to call-to-arms against the Mississippis who were encroaching on Tennessee lands in the west. Although there are cautious voices, most are eagerly awaiting an organised initiative to help the Tennesses. After some traditional Sweet Grass tea, Cleo is led back to her emop by Sunning Snake, the chief warrior, who is to fly with Cleo as her guide. It is understood that after a tour of their lands, she would visit with Heyoka who would make a decision for the people.

They tour the high Smokeys and river lands through broken cloud, snow and sun. The lands stretch for hundreds of kilometers to the Cumberland Plateau far to the east of Nashville, an ancient metropolis still intact and spared from World War 3. Like Sunsetwind, Yellow Tooth is a rural economy, but without the research and technology. Its people are poor in comparison, but healthy and happy on the whole, although they too faced increasingly difficult problems. Many people are dissatisfied with the opportunities available to them and look to neighbours America and Carolina for alternatives that are however met with little consideration. Indeed, they are a motley sort whom without new emop technology, fly decrepit models keeping the few they had together with incessant repair. They are big users of fusion Four Wheelers and most of the security team drive in these, but roads are not kept up and their machines are unreliable. Heyoka, herself, like most of the million or so Yellow Tooth Cherokees, doesn't operate a vehicle of any kind but has many at her disposal. All-terrain vehicles, however, are a tour de force.

They descend through a cloud-bank in a slow, oblique arc that whooshes over some peaks surrounding Yellow Tooth City. There, in a notch beneath a ridge of rock and stunted trees, is a small mountain lake with some old log buildings nestled against the leeward side sheltered from the bitter prevailing winds. Cleo lands in a clearing between some sheds and the main structure. No one is about and the snow whirls around covering any tracks that may have been there. As she shuts off the reactor, the other emop comes alongside and hovers. Sunning Snake motions in the window a spiral with his finger that he will be around. His emop then lifts and he disappears. Cleo watches them climb, then looks for the entrance.

She finds a door that seems to be in use as the snow is tramped around it and the footpaths converge there. Suddenly three big husky dogs come running from around the side of the building. They jump around her but don't come close, except for a good sniff. An older man follows and he speaks to the dogs gingerly. He scrutinizes Cleo standing there awkwardly. He then laughs and indicates that she may enter. Cleo opens the thick grey, aged door that swings in without resistance or squeak. Inside, the building is light and warm. All the wood has been bees-waxed and smells delicious. The place has a cozy, rambling feel. The hallway leads into the kitchen area on one side and storerooms and bunks on the other. A wood fire blazes in a living area straight ahead. She walks to it and peers out of the large windows onto the little frozen lake. The wooden furniture is sparse though comfortable. There are artifacts and photographs on tables and shelves. Books line the walls. An authentic set of bows and arrows are mounted above the mantle of the fireplace. To the left of the room some steps descend to another room, which she can see contains a pool. It is, in fact, a small deep bay of the lake and the house structure had been built up around it. There are flat rocks and boulders on one side and around the back. On the open side of the lake, a typical indoor pool construction suffices with large bay doors that lead out to a stone deck and the lake itself, where the deck is drifted over with snow. Cleo walks to the edge of the enclosed part of the lake and feels the water. It is warm and clear; there would have to be a partition and recycling system that heats the enclosed lake water, presumes Cleo. She can see the bottom, but not in the deep center. How marvelous! The inside part is half-moon shaped and is actually hot on the rocks like summer from a very sophisticated heating system, no doubt fusion. Cleo turns around, having felt a presence and there standing behind her is a slight strangely striking woman.

Heyoka smiles pleasantly, but in her light brown eyes is a seriousness that belies her age though a few years younger than Cleo. She is not simply beautiful, observes Cleo who still feels awkward in this rarefied place, but astonishingly so, as Heyoka exudes an ethereal persona like none she has ever known. Her shoulder-length brown hair is singed with reddish even blond tones that complement her smooth skin, which isn't just light brown, but glows with a surreal incandescence; and her eyes are like brilliant windows to a mysterious, almost unsettling aura. She has pale red lips, yet firm with resolve, and when she opens her mouth in a simple smile her pearly teeth are perfect. The natural reverence she commands no doubt is absolute among her people.

'Hello, Cleopatra,' she says in a clear, melodic voice, each syllable equally articulated with a distinctive Native American inflection.

'Heyoka . . . I am honoured.' Cleo wishes she hadn't sounded so startled, slightly intimidated by Heyoka's sudden appearance.

Heyoka walks softly down to Cleo, who stands there speechless. The word mystical comes to her mind and mysticism is rare in that day and even considered to be egocentric, yet Heyoka seems inclined to humility as she bestows her guest a little hug and kiss on the cheek, which Cleo warmly returns.

'How wonderful it is to meet you,' says Cleo. 'I must say, you have a unique home here.'

'Thank you, let us sit on the rocks, Cleopatra,' suggests Heyoka. She sits immediately in her loose, embroidered cottons and leather slippers. Her slim legs are brought up to her chin with long arms around them. 'It is good to sit here feeling as it is in the summer, and look out there to see winter,' she says nodding in the direction of the lake, as Cleo sits beside her.

'What a beautiful lake, inside and out,' comments Cleo relaxing. She doesn't quite know how to deal with this sprite of a woman. Cleo's tough guerilla exterior does not open up to close sentimental relationships with women. Her one protégé, Treason Honey, although young, is as tough and sweet as she, but as close as she could get; yet this Heyoka looks as if she never stepped out of the cocoon of her home, far from the distant drums of current realities.

'I have heard of you,' declares Heyoka.

'Well, I hope good report.'

'Mostly good.' She smiles.

'But some bad?' asks Cleo, a little self-conciously.

'No, some superb.'

'Oh . . . thank you.' Cleo is taken aback at her surprising wit. Maybe I will like her, she thinks.

'No need to thank me; your reputed power precludes you and is the pivot from which we must deploy our efforts. I know this; I have seen it.'

'What have you seen?' asks Cleo warming up.

'I have seen war, Cleopatra.' And her brow and eyes sadden.

'Does it surprise you?' presses Cleo gaining her usual control.

'It does not matter. I am confident that we will do the right thing.'

'I hope so,' says Cleo for want of a better thing to say.

'Yes,' Heyoka agrees quietly, looking at Cleo with an elusive penetration.

'May I ask what you think is the right thing to do?' queries Cleo with a hint of impatience.

'We must fight and save the universe,' she replies enigmatically.

'What do you mean?'

'Just that: you take my warriors, ill-equipped, into a modern war. The Americans will cheer us on, because we do what they cannot, just yet. How brave! And many braves will die saving the universe. And they will die willingly.'

'Is there any alternative, Heyoka?' plies Cleo undeterred in this resolution.

'No. Our deaths will not be in vain. The Chicagos will fail ultimately, though not because of us, in spite of us.'

'I don't follow you.'

'We must do as our cousins, the Sunsetwinders, ask of us. It is a necessary honour. But the Chicagos will fail because they haven't the will or the means to destroy the world that we were born into. Trinny Burnamthorpe is flawed and scared. She cannot control her thirst for power. Nor can she accept rejection. But this is not why they will fail. I had a vision: your brother Cephren, who I think is a very good man, is on a journey that few of us have ever taken: it is to the stars. On this journey he will bring a force to bear down on the Chicagos that will tame them like fawns.'

Cleo thinks for a moment; both Cephren and Heyoka would make a good team: two incorrigible dreamers; but she reflects on Heyoka's words so as not to betray her trust.

'How do you know this?' is all she can ask.

'I will tell you, Cleopatra, so you may decide for yourself. It may serve to make you wise with our people on the battlefront, to know that this war must be contained like a decoy action, to buy Cephren a little space. I would like you to stay with me a few days, so we may be friends as our ancestors were friends. I have been in communication with Redman. He sends you his regards.'

'What? You've spoken to Redman?'

'Yes, on an old frequency that dates back to the time of Yellow Tooth. Using an obsolete shortwave that fades in and out of range, Redman sent a message into our monitor. He told us how and when to send a reply.'

'What does he say?' exclaims Cleo exhilarated. She had thought the communication blackout was absolute.

'He says it's a short wave band that rides the Chicago's own links without their knowing. We cannot reach each other on the screen, but speech is audible. I told him you were coming here. I told him I had heard nothing about Cephren, when he asked me. I said I knew he was safe by the news from Washington, though I do not know where he is. He said Del Barker has assumed the Presidency and that all the old Board is being tagged with a wrist monitor. All their communications are being monitored as such. Even Redman has been monitored, but he found a way to jam the signal with his Resonant Scanner and communicate with Mobius, a janitor in the Pyramid. He believes Chromolox is being held in detention in the Pyramid. He has been hiding Vince Fuchs in his bunker. Vince is the only Board member besides Cephren who is unaccounted for. Seymour was killed trying to help Sam Burnamthorpe escape . . . '

'Seymour is dead?' asks Cleo with a wave of despair rushing through her.

'You did not know. I'm sorry. This is what he told me.'

'Not Seymour,' cries Cleo. 'There is no man alive so unthreatening and lovable as Seymour.'

'It can be so sad, death; it comes like an eagle, swooping. I was born in death, held in the last warmth of my freezing mother, hemorrhaged of life, born prematurely by one month not three k's from here. My father was attacked and killed by a cougar while hunting, leaving my pregnant mother alone in a cabin. She tried to walk back, but went into sudden labour. Never Waits, our good helping man, whom you met, found me. He saw me in his mind, born in the snow. It was cold and clear. There were long shadows across the bloody snow in the late afternoon sun, January 22, 2366.'

They sit in a sad comfortable silence. This woman-girl looms larger than life. Cleo, in shock with the news of Seymour's death, nevertheless feels with deep empathy Heyoka's tragic nativity.

Recovering, Cleo asks Heyoka how she knows so much about Cephren, or at least what he must be doing.

But in lieu of answering, Heyoka appears to talk about unrelated things. 'There are many stories about the Horror and Yellow Tooth, my ancestor. There are many stories of stories from before, when the earth was sick. Yellow Tooth as an old man told his family a story he had heard once from an elder who had lived during the Big War. This elder had heard this story from another credible source in a reservation out west. This reservation, and I do not know which it was or where it was, was adjacent to a test range for the U.S. Air Force. But it was said, there was never any testing done, as far as they knew, at least with conventional aircraft of their day. One of the band wandered into this area one night as they were apt to do and fell asleep in a canyon. He was stirred awake by a brilliant light coming from below him in the valley. He crawled to the edge of the gorge to witness a magnificent sight. There was an aircraft shaped like a round emop that sat quietly in mid air. Many colours emanated from this ship: predominantly a bluish-pink corona surrounding it like a halo. It had a powerful beam of light that searched the ground for something, but otherwise it remained stationary. After some time the craft moved towards the man and shone the beam onto him. He felt paralysed and remembered only that he seemed to be lifted off the ground as if lying on a cushion of air. He was drawn inexplicably towards the craft into an open hatch beneath. There, a little grey being met him and told him he would be all right and that he had nothing to fear. This being had long wispy, dark hair with these strange, dark navy eyes that spoke to him without sound. She said she was a hybrid human. He could tell that it was female because of little protrusions in the chest and the curve of the creature's hips and she seemed very gentle and kind and youthful. The native man was led to the main control area, where a human sat in a rocking chair, a wooden rocker or slider! Yes, it seemed strange, but our abducted friend was apparently no fool and had the respect of his people who believed him. Anyway, the man in the slider stood up and introduced himself as Jimmy. They shook hands. Jimmy apologised for his rude capture. He added that the political landscape had not been favourable to the native North American, but that now everyone was suffering the same demise. He wanted to speak to the Indian man, because he felt that he might not be able to speak to another human for a long time. He wanted the man to know that there were things going on that were beyond human comprehension. He cited the example of the big-eyed girl, who he said was named Lilly and was a cross between a Reticulan and a human. He explained that the Greys were a species from the Reticula Solar system many light years from earth and that he might be going there. He said he hadn't any choice because if he were to remain on earth, he would be killed by either the U.S. security or some renegade aliens. He said that they had already killed the mother of his daughter, who being an informed and politically powerful person was about to expose the truth of the alien presence here to the public. He also said that one day he would return and die on earth and leave for posterity all the information and technology gleaned from Reticulans, Pentit Sine-sians (a highly evolved human-type alien), and other races who traveled in space. Jimmy gave the man a token of his word, a little memento, a medallion made of a substance not found on this planet, which we call orange gold. And above all, Lilly the hybrid gave this man a baby to give to his wife, Cora, since they apparently knew she couldn't have her own.'

Heyoka then pulls a silver necklace from her neck and attached to it is a strange medallion, which looked something like gold but glowed a more brilliant orange in colour. Cleo could not help but see that it had not been manufactured on earth by the very foreign symbology of the cryptic letters. Its luminosity and weight gave it an even more other-worldly quality.

'It is heavy,' Heyoka says holding it up. 'We call it the Sacred Stone of the Yellow Tooths. Yellow Tooth was the recipient and gave it to his heirs saying that one day Jimmy would come back to tell his story as he promised. I think it is doubtful that Jimmy himself will come back, but I believe Cephren has the key to Jimmy's story and knowledge. From what I understand from Redman, this X13 we all hear about, could be that story. We will do whatever is necessary to hear that story, because it is the cure for the illness today. We stand at a great threshold in the world. We can go back to the sickness of the past or step into the universal light, which we have tried to live here with moderate success. This story was told to me by Never Waits who raised me like a daughter with the help of my grandmother, Running Water. They tell me, I must always keep the medallion and pass it on to my children.' Then looking down, she says, 'Sometimes I see myself childless. I have a gift for seeing.'

They sit by the still water and gaze upon the strange contrast between summer and winter outside. Cleo is not one to dabble in what she presumed to be old myths and their purported significance. She believes, however, that there must be some truth to Heyoka's story. Jimmy Pidgeon had once again popped up in the most unlikely of places. But she allows the implications of her story, if true, to be processed in her mind. Vince, Redman, Cephren and even Chromolox have spoken of it. If it was true, and a big if, just maybe they could generate some form of reaction that would have some significance today, for instance, the power to black out Chicago and reduce them powerless. Any such device would be worth fighting over. Virtually every power in the world seemed to be sniffing for this mythical substance and here it is around Heyoka's neck.

'Why are we looking elsewhere, Heyoka, when you have the orange gold?' she asks.

'This amount is very small,' she answers, 'but I'm willing to give it up for experiments. It's just to whom and where?'

'Sunsetwind is out of it for now. Vince and Redman could do it. But they're stuck. Bill Deerhill would be another good choice, but he's confined too. It's also a time factor. How long will it be before they locate Cephren and steal the chip?'

'We will preoccupy them in the meantime. I have given my blessing to the council and they are voting on it. But that is a formality. Even if they lose the vote, many will go, for it is their right under our law. Sunning Snake is the leader of the War Party and they pray for a fight. Tomorrow, go to him and make your plans, then come back and we shall discuss them. There is no reason for undue haste at present. You must minimize our vulnerabilities. Meanwhile, let us enjoy this day while it lasts. Please take a swim and clear your mind, then we shall eat. A meal is being prepared. I will swim with you, if you like.' She then slips quickly out of her cottons and enters the water naked. Her freedom is immaculate. Is it magic or wisdom, queries Cleo? Self-consciously, she undoes her fatigues and lets herself into the soothing waters of the lake. Heyoka has swum to the other side and floats on her back, her little breasts bobbing out of the water. Cleo dives deep and emerges smiling: convinced this is indeed a treat and a revelation.

Flower Child begins to write one of her most famous poems sitting on a promontory cliff overlooking the valley :

This is my fantasy:
I'll love that man,
Then I'll kill the bad one,
Before I moan with the wind
Riding the good man,
Breathing honeyed summer air on my bridal bed
And mock the dead.
No virgin shall I luckless be devoured:
I'll have my eggs sunny-side,
Or I'll fuck to terrible ghosts,
And bleed to venerable hosts,
Eating fabulous fruits like mythical mangoes,
And sing prophesies of times to come:
You who now read me
I enjoy your life
And you must try to understand mine –
My love will sweeten like ripened fruit,
And burst forth the seeds of times to come
Like a milkweed pod...

Cephren can feel the old ballpoint move across the cardboard both pausing and writing those seminal virgin thoughts. For a couple of days since the hayfield incident, or what is known to posterity as the Visitation, she has rebelled in earnest against old Scratch who never so much as hinted in all her life that there was anything called sex. Even when the issue cropped up in her studies, he sidestepped any direct interpretation, preferring to say, 'Procreation is the will of nature.' Nature's will, however, is no match for Scratch and his attempts to constrain her natural will; he is reluctantly drawn into Flower Child's intense desire to know what she had intuited in literature and by meeting those men that day, principally the one that put himself at risk on her account. All she had been told was that evil men raped girls like her, so she must steer clear of men altogether. Scratch failed to comprehend the necessary wisdom in explaining the process of procreation based on love. To him, there had only been loss and there was no place in this new world for love, at least the kind that makes children. Most of the children that he knows of in Darabak's compound, he tells her, were not conceived in love, but lust and rape. And any pretensions to the former are false. Flower Child gets a serious talking to when she suggests it doesn't matter because the children are at least born. 'How else could they be born?' she asks with her long, straggly strawberry blond hair blowing across her face. Scratch strides back and forth in their living area, having built it years before in the rocky gorge below the crevice; it joins the cave where they have a woodstove and an old fusion Camp King, which gave them power to heat, light and cook. There is a decent wood floor with insulated walls, stripped from abandoned buildings. 'They must be born . . . properly!' he fumes.

'But how, Scratch?' she persists.

'A woman and a man must mate for life. They can love better that way. You must see that children need stable parents!'

'Then how do they do it better? I want to know.'

'Don't you get it? Love is gentle . . . and a sacred trust, Flower Child.'

'How do you know which man is gentle in love?'

'You just know, that's all. He will be your best friend.'

'Will it hurt?' she asks sincerely.

'It may hurt, but love will overcome, my dear; do not torment yourself over this. It is as natural as . . . as eating.'

'As eating?'

'I don't know,' he says angrily, 'it's just natural!'

'Okay, so when can I try it?'

'Try what, girl?'

'Fucking.'

'Do not say that word! It is terrible! Flower Child, listen to me; what those man said was rude, very rude and vulgar; they were evil and would hurt you, except . . . '

'That man who I spoke with in the hayfield?'

'I know who he is,' admits Scratch reluctantly.

'He was kind and warned me away from the others.'

'That was Remy Path, Flower Child. He was there when your parents died, though I believe he had nothing to do . . . '

'I know,' she intervenes again so quickly Scratch has to sigh: nature has defined its purpose. 'Remy Path,' she adds wistfully. 'I remember he worked for daddy.'

'Flower Child, be patient; he is a good man, but was shot, sorely beaten and left for dead.'

'Shot? Beaten? Why didn't we stay and help him?' she cries out.

'And get you raped and me killed? We had no choice in the matter. Your safety is my prime concern, Flower Child.'

'We must find him and help him escape! And if you won't, I will!' she declares defiantly.

'I will help you,' concedes Scratch, 'but my way. Agreed?'

'Oh Scratch, thank you!' She hugs him.

'As I said, you should know he was there when your parents died. He tried to warn them, but was helpless to do much about it.'

'I would like to see him again,' she says, subdued.

'It's too dangerous at present; Darabak's combing the area like a mad hound. We must move,' he presses on. 'Not far. Across the valley back to the farm. I know where the bunker is, grown over with trees, mind you. I helped bury it years ago. We shall find it. There are things you must know about it, but not yet. You must farm your family's land, which has grown over in disuse. I will teach you. The people at Sunset City may not bother you there, yet there will be contact sooner or later. And when that happens, you will have to be very careful. Darabak will come for you. Be vigilant and carry this weapon in your pants.' He pulled out his handgun. 'Darabak must die! It is the will of my God, so help me!'

'I will gladly kill him,' she avows though with other things on her mind.

'If I cannot, you must or he will . . . I cannot die until I know you are safe. I will not! They're Trashies!' Scratch maintains.

'They must not be all bad,' she contends.

'No, some are there . . . well, because there is no other place to go . . . and, well for all Darabak's malignancy, he has created at the least a center of social activity, which in itself is enviable, but we can never go. We are outcasts.'

'Then let us leave and find a center somewhere else, more favourable,' she suggests.

Scratch sighs. He is old. He knows the time will come when Flower Child would be alone. His foraging far and wide for food and grains has been strenuous. Flower Child is capable of carrying on by herself, but what kind of life would she live? She must integrate somehow. And he knows what that means – enslavement, at least with Darabak. Still, there is little incentive in an alternative. She must one day claim her land.

'Should I not find a mate?' she queries quietly.

'Be patient, someone will turn up, like a dog sniffing the wind.'

'So how do you know Remy isn't dead?' she wonders.

'He saved your life; so I went back the next day to find out what happened to him.'

'Poor fellow, I would like to see him again,' she repeats.

'He is alive, dear.'

'He is? How do you know? Tell me, Scratch; tell me what you know!' Flower Child is beside herself.

Scratch takes a deep breath and reveals what had happened. He tells her that he had gone back to the hayfield the next morning, and not seeing anyone had made his way carefully to Sunset City. There he spotted some boys swimming at one end of the lake away from the "city" and asked them if Remy Path was around. They said they hadn't seen him for a while, but heard that he had gotten into trouble. Scratch then thought that if there was a chance Remy wasn't dead and he wasn't at Sunset City, there would be only one place left for him to go, and that was back at his original homestead near the Barnetts . . .

He walks all the way back, then up the hill past the Barnett ruins to Remy's abandoned frame farmhouse. And sure enough, there he finds him, half dead from his beating, yet he had managed to grope, crawl and limp his way home. He can barely move, for the broken ribs and the bullet lodged in his shoulder. He can barely talk for his broken jaw and bent nose. And he can barely see through his one puffy eye. The other is completely swollen shut. But he manages a quarter smile through his cracked lips crusted with blood. He is a mess. All he can do is drink water and force painfully in his mouth a thin gruel from old grain and husks, which simmered over a fire in a rusty pot. He is one tough, resilient young man. Needless to say, it is a pitiful sight, but Remy has made the best of it. He tries to speak through his pulverized lips. Scratch leans near and hears him mumble.

'They let me go; left me for dead,' he winces. 'I made it home. They won't bother me for a while.' He tries to laugh, but cringes in pain.

Scratch sees how the man had suffered and survived, but would die before long unless he received medical help. His heart goes out to him.

'You must come with me, Remy, or you will die' says Scratch. 'We'll nurse you back to health. Your wounds are severe.'

'I want to stay, Scratch, thanks anyway. Just visit me.'

'We'll make some broth for you, son, and bring greens, but I think you are stubborn and foolish. Come with us,' he reiterates.

'It's too dangerous,' says Remy. 'I'll get you in trouble; they'll find Terrie.'

'Not where we're going, son.'

'Please, I'll be alright. I've been stashing stuff around here for years, though some milk and bread would be nice and maybe a few eggs.'

'Don't you worry about a thing,' says Scratch, in a comforting tone of voice.

'They know about you and Terrie,' says Remy.

'What do they know?'

'Darabak knows it's you; it kind of shocked him. He didn't say any-thing, but made the men leave me; they were happy to do so because some of them were my friends, not the ones at the hayfield.'

'Did you tell him who I was? It's all right if you did; I'm just curious.'

'No, he knew and said Father Frankie has been keeping Clearview's best kept secret.'

'And what did he say he was going to do?'

'Nothing. Then he let me be.'

'But you must've suspected he'd come looking for you.'

'I should think so, but Darabak never said whether he would.'

'He's smart, Remy. He'll wait and watch you. If I know Darabak, I know he wants to find me and Flower Child, if it's the last thing he does.'

'Promise me, Scratch, that Terrie won't come here.'

'Believe me, I'll deal with her; that's why I'm here in fact; to ascertain whether or not you're worth the trouble.'

'Please, don't hesitate to leave me be; there will be trouble, sooner or later.'

'Let me worry about that, son,' reassures Scratch. 'But first I must remove that bullet.' Scratch had found some required medical supplies including antibiotics and novacaine from the bunker fridge hoping they were still active. He injects the novacaine and then removes the bullet from Remy's chest with a sterilized knife. The bullet had luckily deflected from the breastplate into his upper chest area beneath his shoulder not a cen-timeter above his heart and left lung. After cleaning the wound with disin-fectant and crudely suturing and bandaging it as well as tending to other injuries, Scratch rushes back to his cliff retreat to tell Flower Child.

Scratch and Flower Child then move into their new home, the Barnett bunker, built in the twenty-first century before the Asteroid, dug out of a steep vale in the forest, with poured reinforced concrete and proper drainage about a half kilometer from the old red brick ruin that used to be her home. It is wired to a fusion generator and spring water is gravity fed through pipes from a source up the hill. It has a flush toilet, kitchen and amenities of a comfortable home, albeit underground. The interior has been finished with foam insulation and wood paneling. The one outside door built into the slope had being insulated and covered with earth and grown over with brush. They leave the door covered as it is and use the trap door up the hill in the forest. Scratch knew exactly where it was; it had been concealed by forest debris and a portion of a rotten log. The small trap leads down a cement well casing with a ladder lagged to it. At the bottom the corridor exits out of a false panel into the back recesses of the bunker where there is a repository of boxes full of books, dried foods, old clothing, furniture and miscellaneous items. Flower Child cries out with delight. And Scratch mumbles under his beard that that was not the half of it. But she lets the matter drop; she just wonders why they hadn't moved there sooner. Scratch explains that he had been terrified the bunker might have gotten into the wrong hands, especially Darabak's. But in recent years, things had settled down a bit in the area, and that hill was off the main travel routes. Besides, he adds, she must make claim to her land.

In the twelve years since the murder of Flower Child's parents, the abandoned farm and bunker had been on Scratch's mind a great deal. Only now did he risk moving back, not only to better living conditions (although he was happy with his mountain retreat), but to make sure Flower Child claimed her due possessions, and above all to remain safe; it is a last resort. And in recent years there had been an influx of people taking up the plough on many abandoned farms to eke out a living, so long as they paid a tithe in produce to Darabak who policed the area. But these responsibilities are being delegated. And it has now come to pass that one of Darabak's first hostages, the Path boy (he was seventeen when first kidnapped), had gained some credit with Darabak (before the beating incident) due to his knowledge in matters of animal husbandry. And in spite of the beating incident, Remy had been free to go back (albeit half-dead) to the farm from where he had originally been taken near the Barnetts.

As soon as Scratch and Flower Child hastily moved into the bunker using the trap in the forest, he begins to take broth, comforts and food-stuffs to the recovering young man. He forbids Flower Child to go until things cool over. She is beside herself with elation, not so much at know-ing her land is hers again, but that Remy Path when recovered could farm it with her. This was a dream come true; however, she would really have preferred to nurse him back to health with Scratch keeping watch, but Scratch true to his word will have none of that and she, with increasing impatience, must live up to his terms.

Before long as the weeks roll by, Remy is healthy enough to get up and about and begin to clear the fields on the entire hill, including a portion of the Barnett's land. He rehabilitates a salvaged fusion tractor and imple-ments making them ready for tillage the following spring when the brush that had overgrown the fields had all been cut and piled. Th job is an arduous and time-consuming task as the brush consisted mostly of young hawthorn, elm, ash and maple. Once piled, they are ready to be set ablaze later when sufficiently dried out. Afterwards, Remy and Scratch have to dig out the little stumps and roots with the aid of the tractor and loader bucket.

Fall passes, then winter. Scratch still maintains that it is still too dangerous for Flower Child to be near Remy's farm. Then one hot spring day, Scratch and Remy sit at the edge of the field in the shade of the forest, and Remy who does not quite seem himself, appears to need to get something off of his mind. Scratch senses his anguish and thinks that once again it has something to do with making the acquaintance of Flower Child.

'It's too dangerous for you to see her, yet,' says Scratch, confident that he is still on the right track, as a few of Darabak's people show up from time to time and would obviously by now have informed Darabak of Remy's survival and industry.

'Oh no, I would not hear of it . . . not that I haven't thought of it . . .'

'We will arrange a supper one of these days in the bunker. You are one of us now, Remy.'

'You have no idea how much that means to me, Scratch, but what I really wanted to say . . . '

'Yes. Go on, boy.'

Remy shakes his head despondently.

'You're thinking about that day, aren't you?' asks Scratch.

'How could she ever forgive me for not doing more to prevent that tragedy and all the suffering he has inflicted on this region? I was too weak to resist!' His features droop in remorse; the pudgy nose and large blue eyes give him a unique look, if not striking; Remy's big frame, however, is slouched in guilt. His sweaty face still shows scars from the beating and his ill-fitting clothes seem to symbolise the present day poverty for all those people who survived not only the Asteroid, but Darabak.

'Nonsense,' replies Scratch. 'You survived. We the living have all suffered to survive; besides, you are here now. And I see how it is meant to be; we must be stronger than Darabak.'

Remy wants release from his debilitating guilt. At first, his memory teeters on the tip of his tongue and stalls, then as his inhibitions subside, the words just tumble out: 'A day doesn't go by when I don't think about it. If I could have only been . . . stronger . . . I did whisper to Mr. Barnett, 'Get your gun', I said. He understood, but Darabak then put his gun to my head. Mrs. Barnett, who was in the kitchen made like she didn't see anything and went outside; then Darabak turned and shot Mr. Barnett in the face without provocation. I was so shocked I didn't even see Gus smash me in the face with his gun . . . by the time I came too, they were finishing with Mrs. Barnett. It was horrible . . . horrible . . . horrible . . . the things they did . . . I did not have the courage to escape...all these years . . . until Terrie . . . '

There is a long pause.

'There was food and shelter and things got better. I traveled and salvaged, you know: shoes, tractors (this very one too, which I hid up here), cars, trucks, animals, fuel, anything that wasn't tied down. I never stole nothing. I left people alone. I never dishonoured a woman or hurt nobody. I kept to myself and hoped that one day I could reclaim my land. With Sunset City by the lake, we became a community, but no one dared mess with Darabak, and Gus and their militia; he was just too smart, and he kept out of people's way as long as everyone did as they were told.'

'Did Darabak know what happened to little Terrie Barnett?'

'Not really. After the . . . murders, he looked everywhere in and around the house and down to the bush well into the night, with no luck, except he thought he saw some bright lights. I remember when he returned a couple of hours later he and Gus argued because he took so long. Darabak said he was gone for only half an hour. Anyway, they burned the house and called out that if she was hiding inside she'd better come out or else. When she didn't, they figured she died in the fire or ran off and the coyotes must have got to her. I had no idea what happened to her, but I always hoped she got away. When I realised it was her in the hayfield last summer, I felt this great sense of ease . . . sort of a premonition that the dark days would soon be over.'

'Why do you think he did that to the parents?'

'I don't know. The man is a monster who will play with children one moment then kill someone the next. I think he envied their situation, or anybody who had a refuge like a farm; so he burned the place to erase the deed in his mind. He could be reasonable if one gave him his soul in undying loyalty.' Remy turns away not wanting to show his silent tears.

'Do not grieve, Remy,' tells Scratch patting him on the back. 'Darabak's days are numbered. You did the best you could, and I bless the Lord you are here today.'

'I'm glad you're so optimistic.'

They shake hands. A big smile comes over Remy; he seems to be thrilled to have found such a friend in Scratch. His big shoulders and happy-sad face heave a giant sigh.

'Well, I best get to work on Miss Barnett's land.'

'Do you have any seed grain, Remy?' asks Scratch.

'Not nearly enough for the land we've cleared.'

'We have all the seed you'll need: oats, barley, wheat, corn, rye, beans and most vegetables.'

'Where on earth did you find that?' quizzes Remy, surprised.

'Just let me know what you need, son.'

'I will, tomorrow.'

Then they both sit there quietly under the dense canopy of the maple forest. The leaves rustle in the breeze.

'For far too long we've been living off wild life and it's getting more scarce,' says Scratch, finally. 'You know there's an abundance of wild Jerusalem artickokes and potatoes among other things that have grown around the ruins of the Barnett homestead. We also need fences to tame a wild cow or two. It's about time we got domesticated, eh? I see great things happening here, Remy,' says Scratch as his eyes beam onto the green alley vista.

'I really hope so, Scratch,' agrees Remy smiling.

In the days that follow, Scratch finally sends Flower Child off with food for Remy. She would take some meat, bread, cheese or wild vegetables. But as it turns out, she is too shy to introduce herself and just left the food on his old kitchen table. She would sometimes browse around his ramshackle place, seeing where he slept and cooked. However, intimidated by her own lack of courage to meet him, she would run off and hide. It is ironic, as her ignorance and curiosity had gotten the better of her having made such a bold stand in the hayfield, yet her new-found understanding of the shocking reality of the facts of life make her more apprehensive at the notion of man, even a good man. She realises all her fantasies are but illusions and the real thing is something she isn't quite ready to accept.

Later, when Scratch presumes Flower Child has already made Remy's acquaintance, (she lied to him in this regard) he meets up with Remy one day when he is weeding some burdocks at the edge the oat field. They speak at length about his injuries, the relative peace, the weather and how it is getting generally warmer since the long winter. The summer had been the hottest in twenty years. Then the conversation comes around to Terrie Barnett of whom Scratch is all smiles, saying, 'She's so pretty, isn't she?' And Remy replies, 'Yes, but she doesn't like to communicate very much, not that I don't appreciate her . . . fear.' Before long, it occurs to Scratch that both these relative youngsters are not very adept at social graces. He discovers to his utter surprise that they had yet to even meet. Remy has in fact not seen her since the Visitation. Then and there Scratch walks off in a huff, finds Flower Child keeping watch at the edge of the field (they would reciprocate the lookout) and had to virtually drag her out to meet Remy, where after formal introductions they have nothing to say, and would not even look at each other. Old Scratch had been celibate all of his life, and thought even he could have done better than these two nincompoops. They are as green as the first day of kindergarten. Remy, being the elder by nine years, finally asks if he could come and visit them, looking pitifully at Scratch, who hums and haws for fun, then reluctantly agrees. And so, the next Saturday the date is set. Remy would come for supper to the bunker. He was to meet Flower Child at the ruin, and she would then walk him down to the secret bunker.

At the appointed hour, Flower Child sits in the ruin of her old family home. It is a glorious late spring evening in June. The lilacs are in full bloom and send wafts of scented air her way. The sun has a few hours before completing its day's work and the minutes slipped by until she realises he is more than half an hour late. She stands atop a section of brick wall but cannot see him. She decides to head towards his house not a kilometer away. Unfortunately, or fortunately as fate would dictate, Scratch has waived his lookout at the edge of the field rather to keep an eye on his stew instead.

There is still no sign of Remy up on the old gravel road, which had mostly grown over. That's odd, she thinks; with a sigh, she trudges along the field taking a short cut to his farm. She enters a bush using it as cover. Her old dog Roughy who had died years before, comes to mind. Never a day goes by that she doesn't think about him. It haunts her too that Remy might be another impending loss. So much had been lost in her life already leaving little to depend on in her world. Although he is the only man she had ever known besides Scratch, Remy seems just right for her. She can hardly think in terms of fate; things just happened, as there is little alternative to reality. Her heart is pure and simple, yet her mind knows what threatens: death all around. Wisdom gained through heartfelt loss are the strands of maturity when youth is fleeting and Flower Child is still very young.

She sees the house through the brush. It is run down and overgrown by the dense cover as most standing farmhouses are. There is a wide path leading from the road. The drive shed has a good lean to it, but she can see the tractor inside. There is no sign of activity. She walks quietly up to the side of the house and hears voices. One is sharp and commanding, while the other resigned, though steady. She looks in the window and sees a raw, brawny dark-eyed man with a brush cut dressed in leathers of medium height gesticulating with ease as he speaks. His words are crisp and sardonic. Remy sits in a chair looking straight ahead. 'Remy, Remy, you are a real asset to our enterprise. You have done well for yourself here: planted crops, and vegetables too. Why then do you protect these people when we protect you?'

'Your men nearly beat me to death, Darabak.'

'You were seen with the old man. Tell us where he lives with the girl.'

'I repeat, I do not know. What more can I say? Yes, he has helped me. Yes, he is Father Frankie; you know that.'

Darabak paces. Staring from the window, Flower Child looks in shock at the man who killed her parents. She must kill him, but how? She had foolishly not brought the gun. Then she notices the other man in the corner looking very cagey like a rabid weasel. He is the same man she saw running in the hayfield and he had a gun, a strange looking thing.

'Have you seen the girl?' demands Darabak, carefully watching Remy. 'I don't want to hurt her.'

'No, I have not.'

'You're lying!' Darabak punches him square in the nose and it bursts with blood profusely.

'Why should I lie?' stammered Remy, rattled but maintaining his composure.

'Because, you're protecting her. Why are you so spiffed up and clean-shaven? Why? It's obvious; you're seeing her.'

'No, Darabak. Please, this abuse is unnecessary.'

'Abuse? Unnecessary? You'd like to think so, wouldn't you? Well I'll show you unnecessary abuse. Tie him up, Gus! He needs a little conditioning. You see, Remy Path, your life now is unnecessary. One of my spies has seen you with that old man and it may surprise you that the girl has been spotted too. Did you know we found their cozy little hideaway?'

Remy does not respond.

'Yes, up in the cliffs, all these years. We came across it as we were planning a lookout, in fact a whole series of lookouts. But unfortunately, it was abandoned except for a few supplies. We thought perhaps they might return, but it seems they've found another hole. For days I had one of our people watch you work from that location with a high-powered telescope. The old man seemed to appear and disappear out of the woods. We later combed the woods, found many tracks, a cow and a calf, but no lodging. Have you no idea where they live? One more chance.'

'For God's sake, no!' Suddenly, Remy leaps at Darabak with nothing else to lose, knocking him against the wall. Gus opens fire as Remy bolts out of the room.

'Get him!' screams Darabak.

The outside door smashes open and Remy dashes for the thicket as Gus opens fire again, his gun emitting a hiss and and what looks like a lightening rod from its muzzle. Darabak goes running after him. Poor Flower Child is in the open to their left, but they don't see her as they crash into the bush after Remy. Flower Child then circles around to the other side of the house. Taking a few deep breaths, she gathers some courage and continues around the house until she comes to the shed. Beyond the shed, she sees a vehicle. It must their car, she presumes. She approaches and looks at it; it is sleek and black, shaped like a bullet nose at each end. Without any idea how to drive it, she opens the door and sits behind the wheel. There is a small keyboard on the dash. She presses the enter button, and a whirring noise jolts the machine to life. She knows it is a fusion car, because she has seen pictures of them in many of the magazines Scratch had found for her from the old days before the Asteroid. Some of them had jets and could hover and fly in a limited way. She plays with the shift. First, it goes backwards, then forwards. Easy does it, she thinks. She manages to turn it around and proceed down the narrow lane to the old road as branches brushed the side panels and windows. She then turns in their general direction and increases the speed, testing the throttle. It is a beautiful feeling, but she puts that out of her mind. She drives down to the ruin on her farm and waits. She sees Remy sprinting down the side of the field. She gets out and yells at him. Seeing her he runs toward her. Now Darabak and Gus come into view. They scream as both Flower Child and Remy jump in the car and speed away down the hill on the old lane into the valley, escaping the laser gun flashing behind them in the darkening sky. The escape couldn't have gone better, but what are Remy and Flower Child to do now? Far down the river on the valley floor, they stop in a secluded wooded gully known to Flower Child and then look intently at each other. Though evening, it is dark in the forest, as what faint light remained could not penetrate the canopy of foliage and Flower Child had not turned on the headlights. Only with the ambient light of the blue dash could they see each other, but in a surreal aura. Spontaneously, she laughs with relief, and Remy too with tears in his eyes. All their pent up inhibitions fall away, as they seem to instantly bond in their precarious world. What prevailed is a sudden emotional need to hold each other. All their depraved loneliness melts into a love they had never thought possible. It is shocking how easy it is and how well they fit into it. Flower Child begins to kiss him on his face. Remy resists unsure whether to respond. But Flower Child assures him in her guileless way that it is all right, saying he is the only link to her past and that they had to be together to make babies! Scratch said so, she insists. He keeps apologising, and she expiates his unfounded guilt by stating that love must resurrect the goodness that went before and purge the bad. He relents finally and hugs and kisses her, having naturally found in her his emancipation. This spontaneity is something neither of them have experienced and the shock of their charged intimacy has them magnetized, doing what they could not express in words. As they fumble with the reclining seats having transformed their impassioned needs into unadulterated desire, the irony of events has no limit: only the gentle explorations and bursting of their innocence are enough to seal a conjugal will. In their modest raptures half-suppressed, nature's bequeathing is unduly given as divined in their stars.

And to the stars goes Cephren having witnessed his forbearers conjoining. He realises that in their isolation, such hurriedness may have accounted for the lack of a naturally evolving relationship with the attendant cadences of courtship. These are desperate times. Yet, nature is the ever-teacher. Cephren searches throughout his mental acuity and actually feels the pulling in her loins. He seeks some clarification for this phenomenon. This natural proclivity, he realises, is the integral beauty of her inchoate womanhood. He finds from the recesses of his mind a timeline or theme emerging within him. High in the atmosphere far away from those terrestrial hives of mortality he explores the possibilities. There he sees the universe in its munificent splendour teeming with life. Something occurs to him through this omniscience, but there are limits to what he can yet do. In Flower Child he sees the key to his needs. But what is it? It causes him some anxiety to recline in these dispositions. He knows there is something here that is eluding him. He must follow their lead; he must seek out the secrets that should deliver him in his quest. He plummets back down to earth.

Sipping a cup of hot chamomile tea, Chromolox sits in the Oliveto Café on the main promenade of Survivor's Walk. She has gourmandized two large cannoli and an apricot tart paid with her loose change, and does so, without being self-conscious. There are a number of passerbys and customers who recognise her. They would stop and look, not sure just how to react. Finally, a more brazen young man begins clapping at the next table, exclaiming, 'In the name of freedom, a hand to our leader!' More people begin to clap and soon the whole café is in an uproar. Chromolox tries to suppress the accolade, but finally slips out without finishing her tea.

She is at a loss to know what to do. She is hoping someone or something might point her in some direction. As least her being visible does attract attention. Mobius or one of Cleo's guerillas might know what to do. She has no place to stay in the Pyramid. Her possessions have been sent to Midland, where her father lives, her mother having emigrated to the Maritimes years before. She wonders what happened to her emop. She decides to place a call to Season Honey using her access code on the public monitor but it is denied. She goes to the Georgian Bank where she keeps her account and finds that her credit is inaccessible. She then inquires to a sympathetic accountant she had known who had been in some awe of her, to place a call to Season Honey. Season answers and they speak for a short while. Chromolox almost breaks down when she hears of Seymour's death, but renstrains herself in deference to the young account-ant. She hears that Strange had locked herself in her studio and wouldn't come out. Both Season and Reason are staying in the house because of the situation. They haven't heard a word from Treason and assume pessimistically she had escaped the country with the Chicagos. They claim Cephren had escaped, which she already knew, but that his dog, Blondy Boy, was with them. They suggest she come and stay with them, but Chromolox feels that she must find other alternatives for the time being.

Chromolox thanks the accountant who gives her a receipt for her transactions which is just to get a balance, but she notices on the back, six words: Go to Igi. Chromolox puts the paper in her pocket, thanks him and leaves the office. She knows the accountant must be a guerilla, but wonders how on earth he would have a message for her. She assumes Redman had figured she would need credit and would go to her bank. Mobius must have seen to its destination.

She decides to head for the maintenance department, which had numerous chambers and byways in the guts of the Pyramid. Afraid of being followed, she had to lose her tail, if she had one, which might be futile because of the monitor band on her wrist that could only be removed with a special code or wave frequency. Why would she then need a tail? She can't very well leave the Pyramid mid-winter on foot; she has no winter clothes, or credit, yet she has to get to the animal compound where Igi is the keeper. She feels trapped and destitute.

Chromolox quickly enters a garbage depot. Without thinking, she opens the chute door and jumps in. She knows where she is; the chute empties about ten meters below into large dumping bins ready to be transported to the pollution-free incineration complex. She doesn't even think whether or not the bin she would land in was empty or full. But she lands well in a bin half full of condo refuse, which is generally bagged, so not too hard. It is cold in the basement because the doors are open as a few garbage emops are coming through the west exit not far away. She runs there not knowing what she is looking for – perhaps a ride in a garbage transport. The emops are entering and leaving oblivious of this person standing there in the drafty cold. Something inhibits her asking for a ride. A wave of insecurity comes over her followed by nausea and the flushed stirrings of a fever. She looks outside at the grey and foreboding sky. The bitter drafts blow in dustings of snow that slowly turns to water on the hard rock floor. Again without thinking she runs in an almost suicidal rush outside the exit passage. An icy blast of snow and wind cut into her. The drifts are well formed right up to the edge of the exit where sculptured troughs were carved as the emops ascended, then just a swirling sea of white across the fields. Her exit is a shocking transition from the warm security of the Pyramid to the extreme cold surrounding it. The temperature must have been minus 25 Celsius and a wind-chill of at least minus forty. She thinks she can make a dash for the animal compound a kilometer away, but knows how reckless that would be dressed as she is, not to mention how sick she felt. The keeper, Igi, might have an extra winter coat and pants and even boots, but little good they could do her now. She runs headlong into drifts that stop her in her tracks. Up to her hips in snow is brutal in her simple runners and loose linens, which are useless, as the snow packs around her bare legs and the linens push up to her thighs. Panic sets in as she struggles one leg at a time through the deep snow. As the cold penetrates she can no longer feel her hands and legs. After what seems like eons, she makes it to the slope and sees the lights of the compound not half a kilometer away at the edge of the forest. She cannot feel her feet, legs, or hands and screams for help. Some dogs begin to bark as she reaches the trees. A figure steps from the building as she collapses in the snow. Hands lift her up and all she remembers is the warmth of a heater slowly permeating her frozen body.

Unfortunately, or fortunately as events would unfold, Chromolox does not recover from her frightful exposure as quickly as she might have under different circumstances. Her incarceration, general health and stress had weakened her usual hardy constitution. The cold entered her lungs and developed rapidly into pneumonia. Recovering from her near-death exposure, she glances at the interior of Igi's little wood-frame house. She feels sick to her stomach, is dizzy and her vision clouded. Attempting to speak, she is gently stopped by Igi, who puts his hand to her wrist and shows it to her. She realises that if she speaks, someone might be alerted to locate her, if they had not already done so when she escaped the Pyramid and called out in the snow. Igi gives her a written message that she reads with difficulty but understands that everything is taken care of. In her weakened state she reclines into her pillow giving herself up to whatever they had in mind. She sips some hot tea and blissfully passes out from shock and fatigue.

After dark, a door opens and Chromolox awakens to see the reassuring face of Mita Waterman putting a healing hand to her forehead. Chromolox can feel the emotional tears swelling from her own eyes. A man in white guerilla fatigues lifts her onto a stretcher and attaches two wires to her monitor band before turning a switch on. He then nods to Mita as he and another man lift Chromolox to the door and a waiting emop. Once inside and airborne, Mita speaks up.

'Chromolox, we may speak now; luckily, I was at the bunker, otherwise you might have been waiting much longer.'

'Mita, you have no idea what I've been through; but the wait was like a nightmare and I just woke up. Pinch me.'

'I don't envy your dream; welcome back to hell; are you alright?'

'No, I feel I'm burning up; but what's going on?'

'What isn't? But let's not worry; we must get you home. Being here is too risky. Redman and Vince have rigged up a device that neutralises the tag signal without sounding the alarm that would go off if there has been any tampering or removal of the band. But we don't have much time so we should not really talk now, besides you're feverish and probably have caught pneumonia or something. I'm injecting you with an antibiotic serum and herbal compound that will stabilize you until we get you home . . . '

'Home? They've taken my home, my condo!'

'Yes, we know. We're sending you back to Midland . . . '

'I don't want to go back to Midland!'

'Please, hear me out; this is what we've decided. First of all, they were probably monitoring you and may have picked up on your trail to Igi's. Igi will tell them that you got a ride with an employee who was picking up their dog. You will stay home with your father and recover under no pretences whatsoever. In other words you will lie low. We will then at some prearranged time remove your band and put it on a double – someone we have found in the ranks who lives nearby. Through the guerilla network, we will relay messages and meet from time to time . . . '

'What about this hair,' croaks Chromolox managing a laugh, deliriously. Her hair looks as though she had blown a fuse.

'Don't worry about your unique hair,' Mita smiles. 'The main thing is, you will be free to come and go. Emop restrictions were lifted last week.' Mita lifts her arms so Chromolox could see her wrists. There is no band. 'But, we must return to our respective quarters, as we don't want to blow our cover. All the Board now have duplicates, except Cephren and Seven, of course. Have you heard anything?' She has a very concerned look in her eyes.

'He escaped to Ottawa. That's all I know.'

'We do believe that he's still in Ottawa with Seven Moons, but know nothing more. He is remaining very incognito, even though he can communicate with various people. But I understand what he must be going through. I have a feeling, as does Olivia that he has gotten into Jimmy's Chip, but doesn't yet want to risk letting anybody know. He may need more time. We just can't imagine what he's into.'

'Oh Mita, what a travesty this is? What can we really do? We're trapped in our own country, relegated to oblivion.'

Her voice falters and head reels.

'Don't think about it, Chromolox. LeRoy, Bill, Vince, all of us meet regularly in Redman's bunker. We're coming up with a plan.'

'What of Cleo? I hear she's with the Yellow Tooths.'

'Yes, they're skirmishing with the Mississippis in West Tennessee. We believe there's a battle looming. Apparently, O'Reilly Al Khazzami has sent a large force of Mujahedin warriors to assist. The Chicagos are up in arms about it. There are talks now going on in Washington. I believe George is buying time but refuses to get the Americans involved. We are conjecturing that he wants to ruin Trinny Burnamthorpe's chances of being elected to the EF Chair. As you know, she has gained influence in many regions around the world with her biotech industries.'

'What then is this plan?'

'Well, we are hoping the Chicagos will leave Sunsetwind; and when they do, which they must, if she is going to get elected, we would activate our guerilla campaign which has turned out not to be so easy. You know Del Barker has begun recruiting for a new service, which many of our soldiers have disgruntledly accepted due to the alternative: treason and punishable by a traditional court martial. Moreover, many of our officers have severe financial problems because they have been stripped of their credit to coerce them. Del is gaining the undying emnity of many a Sunsetwinder, although he's promised a fifty percent increase in currency in his new Security. The Free Radicals are at this moment devaluing the land by mortgaging and converting it into equity funds invested with the Chicagos. It's highway robbery! Del claims everyone will be better off. We know it's a scam that will bankrupt us, and forever put us in their debt.'

'Welcome to the New World, Mita; one way or another, we shall never be the same.'

'Not without Seymour,' says Mita bowing her head, assuming Chromolox had heard about his death.

'Not without Seymour,' coughs Chromolox, sadly. 'Barker told me. We shall pay our respects in due course. That's a promise, Seymour.'

The barrage of laser fire and flashguns from the Mississippi guerillas lit up the cloudy night sky as if it was day. Cleo and her own detachment, an odds and sods bunch of Yellow Tooths and Mujahedin are dug in along the bank of an ancient lane and gully known once as the Hornet's Nest. It is on this very ground that they originally found themselves descending in their emops. Fanning out, the attempt was to dislodge the Mississippi forces from the area and send them retreating back into Mississippi through Corinth to the south. The great irony is the bizarre coincidence of fighting on sacred ground known to some as the American Civil war battle of Shiloh (meaning peace), where wholesale slaughter made its infamous etching in history.

As she is crawling through the muck to a better position, Cleo comes across an old time-worn memorial dedicated to a regiment on the union side. To add to the irony and confusion, some of her companies use traditional confederate and Union flags, and as well, the Mississippis use the same: Old Dixie and the Stars and Stripes that is also similar to the flag of present America, more or less neutral in the conflagration. The flags seem more to represent an iconographic nostalgia rather than cut and dry nationalism.

Laser fire quietly cuts and flashguns blast through the shrubbery and trees with an awesome destructive force. Swaths of whole trees and brush fly through the air taking everything in their path. The Yellow Tooths return fire courageously, but are vastly outnumbered and find themselves fighting a more conventional conflict not to their liking. Soon they realise their casualties are mounting far too quickly. Both Sunning Snake and Cleo unanimously agree to pull back. Strangely, the Mississippis also begin to pull back at the same time, which compels some of the warriors to defy orders and take up the chase. It is futile in the chaos of lightning flash gunfire and flying debris to muster and sustain order to that wild army, either in defeat or attack. Cleo and Sunning Snake can only smile and wonder what had made the Mississippis to high-tail the field. Surrounding them are the dead and dying, some limbless and burned in steaming unrecognisable masses. The brilliant colour of fresh blood looked surreal in the stacatto light-flashes all sound-tracked to earsplitting thunder. The futile horror of battle turns Cleo's stomach and changes her view of war forever.

This is a moment of truth for Cleo who for once has had her blood lust tempered. The grueling campaign and stubborn resistance though only three weeks old, wrought in her the need to seek an alternative solution. There must be a more fortuitous way to buy time for Cephren, she muses. Yet, at least she and her guerillas had succeeded in pushing the Mississippis out of Tennessee, with the exception of a section of land on the Mississippi river itself, which included Memphis. Her cautious review of their modest success is short-lived however; a frantic message comes over her emop monitor from Yellow Tooth City informing her that their people had just been surrounded by a massive flotilla of Chicago emops. The emops had dropped out of the atmosphere like a freak hail storm, and the defenses apparently fell apart almost instantly. The Mujahedin in their emops were hopelessly outnumbered and fell to the earth in horrible crashes one by one. Some tried to escape but were chopped down by massive odds. The only recourse was to take to the atmosphere and find sanctuary elsewhere. America, with its allies including Carolina then shut its borders. The situation is suddenly desperate. George Washington refuses to speak with her and Admiral McKee cannot be reached. Sunning Snake hides out in the Smokey Mountains with most of his warriors and planned to save Heyoka. But on reaching her home, they find the sacred buildings burnt to the ground. Only Never Waits is found unhurt, almost catatonic with grief sitting in the embers, repeating only that he had been paralysed and that the Chicagos had disappeared as quickly as they came. Even worse, it was learned that the Chicagos made a two pronged invasion of both the Kush and Yellow Tooth. Both Heyoka and Sam Burnamthorpe are obviously perceived to be the primary objects of these raids.

The world, though troubled again at the naked aggression of the Chicagos, cannot marshal the courage to take effective countermeasures. George Washington, to not appear weak, beefs up his rhetoric in admonishing the Chicagos, particularly Trinny Burnamthorpe, and draws the line on further incursions into sovereign states; but he is publicly rebuffed as her response is that they were only defending themselves and retrieving her son. The Yellow Tooths make an unconditional demand to have the Earth Federation enact legislation, or failing that set up an international force to bring down Chicago. No one has yet any idea whether Heyoka is dead or alive, because the Chicagos deny they have abducted or killed her.

Cleo is absolutely mortified that her war plans, having backfired, had caused the abduction, or possible death of Heyoka. Moreover, she feels she has been a pawn in a ploy, though perhaps honourably intended, to aggravate the Chicagos that has served to actually further tarnish their world influence. George Washington recognises that Trinny could easily take the Earth Chair with her influence and that he must stop her. And Cleo has become a convenient scapegoat for the covert American attempt to curb the Chicago's aggressions. In a very dejected state, she retreats to the Kush.

six Wild Turkey

To sit *down beside them*
And tell *the science fiction story*

                 –Jimmy Pidgeon

Old Scratch just knows something is wrong when Flower Child and Remy don't show up on time, and then don't show up at all. He puts his gun under his belt and goes up the cement exit shaft out the trap by the old log. Emerging, he looks to and fro keeping a keen ear and eye. They are nowhere in sight, so he heads straight for the fields up beyond their forested vale. He senses trouble. He had sensed trouble the day before when he had seen foreign footprints in the ground across a wet hole in a meadow nearby. He didn't think much about it at the time and didn't tell Flower Child; he assumed that some hunters or travelers had passed through. However, now he worries that Darabak may have made an unexpected visit to his ex-serf, Remy.

Once in the field Scratch looks towards the ruins up the hill and sees no one in sight. Flower Child might still be there, he thinks, because he had taught her never to expose herself on open ground. But again, intuition tells him she isn't there.

He walks carefully towards the red brick ruin, using old waterways and brush for cover. In fifteen minutes he reaches the ruin to find it empty. His heart pounds hard and he feels his temples pulsate. He starts up the road towards Remy's house and half way there hears the electric zaps of a flash-gun. Diving for cover he waits a moment to ascertain the direction of the firing. It definitely comes from Remy's. He rises and walks double-quick in that direction, ready to leap again into the bush for cover. Scratch stops when he reaches the edge of Remy's land and quietly enters the woods. He hears the unmistakable sound of someone crashing through the foliage and others in pursuit. Then he sees Remy running desperately away from Darabak and Gus. But where is Flower Child? Momentarily stymied as to what to do, whether to intercept Darabak and risk his life, or seek Flower Child, Scratch makes his choice and rises again to continue toward the house. He knows Remy has a good chance of outrunning Darabak and Gus. Once at the house, Scratch walks stealthily around it looking in the windows when he hears the sound of a car brushing through branches on the old lane at the opposite side. He runs to the lane and to the road, but too late; the car has vanished through the overgrowth ahead. What should he do? He ponders: go back to the house to see if Flower Child is there or follow the car? She could be held prisoner in the car. Frantically, he fol-lows the car.

Panting, he emerges from the road onto the tilled land at the one end of Barnett's farm. Running along the edge of the field, he sees the car go down the lane to the ruin a half-kilometer below. Then someone is stand-ing up on the wall waving and screaming. It is Flower Child. The nerve of the girl, he fumes. Scratch feels his pained heart and has to sit down on a rock for a rest. Relieved, he waits until the pain subsides. His heart has become an increasing problem in the last year, though he has not men-tioned it to Flower Child.

Scratch watches Remy run over to Flower Child and then scramble into the car to take off down the old road into the forest and valley. He smiles at their thriftiness, foolish and dangerous as it is; yet their escapade is the result of no fault of their own. Scratch then sees Darabak and Gus firing wildly in their direction as they made their escape. The sun is now setting and Remy and Flower Child would soon have the cover of darkness.

Scratch, hides in the bushes until Darabak and Gus, both cursing vituperatively, are well down the road in pursuit. He then jogs doggedly across the fields from whence he had originally come taking a shortcut to where the road came out in the valley. In the last light, Scratch discerns their car tracks heading north. The road, long disused is covered with dense grasses and weeds except for two tracks made by the occasional vehicle. He proceeds along the road until he notices their fresh tracks veering up a lane about three kilometers down the valley. Scratch then stops to listen for Darabak. There is not a sound forthcoming. Darabak may have taken the path across the river-stream that goes up to the other road that leads back to Sunset City over the mountain some twelve kilometers away. He hopes so, but waits a little longer to be sure – about the time it takes to walk there from Barnett's road – the way Darabak had gone – and then some more before following the car tracks.

Scratch knows it to be an old farm lane to another abandoned place. The road winds back and is almost completely overgrown. The faint light from the waxing moon radiates a silvery gloss through the brush. Arriving at the derelict homestead, he finds no vehicle in sight. The tracks lead from an overgrown pasture into a dark hollow. He knows the location well, but thinks them foolish leaving the tracks.

Now that he has discovered them and they were out of harm's way temporarily, he has to smile again at the guile of Flower Child appropriating their vehicle. She must have gone to Remy's when he didn't show, hidden herself, then took the car when Remy escaped with Darabak and Gus chasing after him. It was lucky, very lucky – even more so that she was able to start the car. Darabak probably deprogrammed the code not fearing theft. On the other hand, stung by his loss, he would be back with a small army to exact his retribution. Scratch knew they must act quickly: hide the car, which would be difficult, then hibernate in the bunker until Darabak cooled off.

As Scratch approaches the vehicle concealed in the dark grove, it occurs to him that Flower Child should be in the vicinity, or maybe they'd doubled back cross-country on foot. It is not until he is at the point of opening the door when he hears the unmistakable sound of Flower Child's sweet voice followed by Remy's deeper tone. Little utterances and quiet lapses intermingle with an obvious occurrence that deserved some latitude, given their predicament. But stunned with surprise and shock, Scratch stands immobilised. His thoughts are crushed twixt anger and forbearance. Resorting to the latter, he backs away to the trees nearby and sits down. He cannot bring himself to interrupt, though he somehow feels betrayed. A deep riveting sadness presses his old heart, but he knows that Flower Child, young Terrie Barnett, has obviously chosen her time. She is a woman and these are desperate times. She and Remy might never see each other again. Scratch realises there is a special bond between them and begins to feel guilty for his intrusion. Nevertheless, he just stays there all night watching over his young charges. He moves back farther out of sight at the first hint of dawn. And when he hears their voices emerge from the confines of their bridal suite, he retreats further still. Then with a huff and a puff he tramps in the bush making a racket that startles a wild turkey that he promptly shoots. Picking up the huge bird by its long legs, he walks by the hollow from the surrounding hillock hoping they would spot him, which they do and call out. Scratch turns and without saying a word walks down to them.

'Thank the good Lord . . . thank goodness . . . you're alive! My old heart was ready to give out, dear,' he puffs hugging Flower Child with one arm and hanging on to the turkey with the other, while casting stern eyes at Remy who looks as proud as a buck having had his first doe.

'Nice turkey,' chips Remy.

'Nice car,' intones Scratch a little sardonically. 'You two are quite a team.'

'Scratch, please forgive us!' exclaims Flower Child, realising how they have selfishly neglected to allay Scratch's evident dread. 'Forgive us for not coming home, please . . . if you knew what happened . . . we barely escaped!' she adds shamefully, as if it was an excuse for the apparent consummation.

'Forgive you for what, child? Stealing this car from Darabak and Gus under their noses?' he queries, backing up and dropping the turkey to the ground, knowing full well her culpability. 'You're all right, then?'

'Yes, but we should've come home to tell you what happened.'

'I understand, dear.'

'We should've at least returned to say we were okay,' she maintains, embarrassed.

'Why didn't you?' he asks gravely, laying it on a bit thick.

'Scratch,' speaks up Remy, 'Darabak surprised me and then almost killed me and would have if he caught me. Terrie and I spent the night together . . . in our new car. It's my fault.' They all looked at the shiny black car, the scene of their passion.

'Yes, the car,' he mutters, deferring from the obvious.

'You slept in this car. So what happened?' It is a pointed question.

'Nothing,' replies Flower Child, demurely. 'I mean, we had to...to do it, you know. I am to blame . . . '

'I take full responsibility,' declares Remy solemnly.

'For what?' asks Scratch with a twinkle in his eye.

'For . . . sleeping in the car.'

'Was it comfortable?' quizzes Scratch, scratching his head looking at the car and avoiding their eyes.

'No, not at all; well, sort of; it's just that . . . '

'We wanted to spend the night together!' blurts Flower Child. 'It just happened! We were . . . desperate.'

'Ohhh, now I get it,' replies Scratch, now poker-faced. 'You wanted to know whether it was comfortable.'

'No!' she contends.

'It's okay Terrie, he knows,' says Remy a little abashedly.

Scratch then changes his tune. He speaks now with great solemnity and asks if they believed they loved each other.

'Yes,' they both proclaim in unison.

'Well then, are you prepared to make that great commitment?'

'Yes.'

'For life?'

'Yes.' Remy and Flower Child hold one another.

'Well then, by the grace of God, and the authority vested in me as the only Holy Hermit in these parts, I pronounce that Flower Child, some-times known as Terrie Barnett, and Remy Path are man and wife. You may now kiss.'

They kiss and smile and kiss again.

'Enough,' says Scratch. 'Remy?'

'Yes.'

'You forgot one thing, the ring.'

'Ahh, maybe I could find one,' says Remy, optimistically.

'No, not good enough. Here, take this.'

Scratch removes a leather strap from his pocket. Attached to it is a sim-ple ring made of a luminous orange gold. He gives it to Remy who puts it on Flower Child's third finger on her left hand.

'It's beautiful,' she says beaming like dandelions.

'It was your mother's,' says Scratch, looking to the ground and his turkey. 'And your father's mother before that.'

'You mean, you saved it for me?' says Flower Child.

'I had always hoped this day would come. Yes.'

She puts her arms around the hermetic old man who had been her guardian all these years and tears come to their eyes.

'Darabak's car,' avers Scratch, shaking his head. 'Nice haul; quite the wedding gift!'

Another year comes and goes for the three of them, most of which had been spent inside the bunker. Darabak, true to his reputation, came back with a few dozen men and women to scourge the area for the elusive Scratch and his wards. He doesn't find a trace of them or the car, which had been driven away to another bunker that Scratch knew of. Long abandoned, this bunker was poorly made and leaked water making it uninhabitable. It had grown over with wild raspberries and they spent a week digging out the entrance and filling it back in before covering the car with an old plastic tarp. Meanwhile, back home, Darabak had uncovered every possible stone. He became inconsolable in anger and frustration at his failure to find them. Nobody dared speak to him and kept a distance. Finally, he seemed to make a tentative truce within himself and remained in Sunset City to brood. Scratch, Remy and Flower Child carefully ventured out one day to get the grain and supplies from Remy's house. It so happened that a spotter from the promontory across the valley saw them and reported to Darabak, who pistol-whipped the messenger so badly, the young man, who thought he would be rewarded a little more graciously was instead permanently scarred. However, something snapped in Darabak after his second rage and second unsuccessful search that precipitated oddly into the most uncharacteristic behaviour. Darabak was reputed to have cried pathetically seeking forgiveness from the ill-fated messenger and others for his obstreperous crimes. No one could comprehend this about-face attitude and believed he had gone insane. Some thought his health was the reason, knowing he suffered from stomach problems, possibly ulcers or cancer.

It was observed after those days, that he was a changed man who no longer vented his evil bile. He would talk openly of the crimes he had committed before and after the Asteroid. His long time lieutenant, Gus, became so disgusted with Darabak that with a small splinter group he settled near Great Blue Lake up the coast. This lot were never seen again. Much later, stories filtered through the country that they had been killed in a fight for control of some land. But back at Sunset City, there were problems. There had been some dismal crops, and most of the five hundred or so people who lived there now had branched out to farm on their own leaving Darabak alone with his few loyal concubines and serfs.

A family came by Flower Child's farm and claimed it for themselves. It was then necessary to reclaim it, which went without incident. There were many vacant farms around, and the family moved on informing Flower Child of the news concerning Darabak and Sunset City. This was good news indeed: a repentant Darabak? Yet it did not even send an iota of compassion Flower Child's way. Her compassion could only be expiated with a mercy killing. 'It'll be easier to shoot him,' she would say calmly.

They have a bumper harvest that year with more grain than they possibly needed. Many of the surrounding families look up to the peculiar integrity of Flower Child and her husband Remy, who use the black car to travel around and organise some basic services in the territory as well as meet other community people. In her own way Flower Child asserts herself as a dominant force and becomes a reassuring alternative to Darabak. Scratch remains as ever the stranger, keeping to himself.

So they thrive for another year living in the shadow of Darabak's empty shell of an oligarchy that had endured fourteen years. Still, there is peace. Darabak does not come their way and as such does not appear to care hearing about the young woman whom people call Flower Child. His apparent quietus is almost as if she and Scratch frightened him in some way, or at least made him feel a latent guilt.

That fall Scratch becomes gravely ill. It is believed he has some streptococcal malady that he just can't throw in spite of the antibiotics (which were likely ineffective) and it weakened his heart. One morning, he beckons Flower Child to his old mattress. Tears in his eyes, he reaches for her hand and says his heart is failing him and that he is about to die; but before he does, he must tell her something that had kept them alive. Holding his strong coarse hand, Flower Child stares disbelieving in the face of his impending death.

'Scratch, dear Scratch, you are sick, that's all. Do not speak of death. It is full of nothing. You are alive! We will roam the forests again. Do you remember the skeletons we found on my tenth birthday?'

'Please, Flower Child, I am dying!' he gasps with one more effort at being grumpy.

'You cannot die, Scratch,' she cries, worriedly.

'I will die, my little Flower Child. It is time. You will prosper here with Remy and some good people coming to these parts. Make a new world, Flower Child. I have seen the wind, girl; I have seen too many things. I must pass on very soon. Now let me tell you what you must know. These many years I have harboured the great secret your family entrusted to me.' He holds his heart.

'What secret?'

'Many times I wished to tell you, but I feared that if the bunker got into the wrong hands, specifically Darabak, all our hopes would founder. There is something extraordinary under this hillside . . . my heart fails me . . .' Intense pain now wreaks havoc in his chest. He looks up into her eyes for the last time and with tremendous effort whispers his last . . . 'Flower Child . . . the tunnel . . . find the tunnel . . . the panel . . . the ruin . . . the well . . .' and dies.

'Scratch? Scratch!' She shakes him as she had shaken Roughy when he passed away. There is no consoling her. Even after months had passed, she carries around her grief like an old, spent dowager. Death strikes home as the last leaves fall and the ancient earth closes its eyes once more before rolling over for winter. On a cold November day, she climbs to the ruins where her surrogate-parents, Roughy and Scratch, lay under the ground and thin blanket of snow. There, she watches the sun go down waving long red-purple streaks above her. The wind, the wind, she cries turning the ring on her finger. *Sunsetwind* it seems to murmur; *Sunsetwind*, it whispers through the hoary branches of the old maples nearby. The idea is sown in her mind like the unborn child in her womb.

Cephren too feels that moment of incarnation, not only the boy in her womb, but Sunsetwind in her spirit. He yearns to condole with her across the windy swirls of time, to tell her of her dream and how true it came to be. Cephren tries to convey this to her – he presses his consciousness to hers. Feel me, he urges, I am your descendant.

Again, the next day she sits on that broken wall and turns her ring on her finger. Overnight the weather has cleared to a warm Indian summer's day. The snow has melted and Flower Child has resolved to explore the possibilities of Scratch's last words. A tunnel. What tunnel? She did not know of any tunnel other than the one leading to the trap door in the forest. She surveys the ruins, stands up and walks through the rubble and old charred wood grown over with weeds. She wonders whether there may have been a tunnel from the house down to the bunker. But it is so far, at least a half a kilometer; and if there was why didn't Scratch ever tell her about it? She presumes there must be something in it that no one should know about. Or, he didn't want anybody but her to know of its existence in case of danger as a last resort, a final refuge. Yet, even so, she wonders, it doesn't explain why he had never mentioned it until he died. He did refer to the well! But what well? Perhaps he hadn't been sure if it was safe.

Flower Child pokes the ground in the ruins of the old basement. There is nothing but rubble. It is amazing what exposure to the elements could do after more than a decade. The freezing and thawing, rotting and growing of shrubs, grasses and various plants, people scavenging bricks and burrowing rodents laid waste a once stately home. One end of the basement attracts her attention. Sticking out of the rubble is a section of a round cement well-head. Using a dead branch, she begins to remove the bricks and dirt that covers it. Once done, she tries to lift the exposed cement insert lid. It is sealed in dirt. She bangs at it with a brick to try and break the natural seal. It works. She lifts the insert, straining slightly in the womb, which makes her rest fearing for the unborn of just three months. Rested, she peers down the black hole seeing nothing but ladder rungs formed into the well casing. It is too dark to see where they lead. She needs a torch, but decides to try and go down without one. The opening is narrow but wide enough to fit an average sized person. Flower Child is about to descend into the well when she hears something and stands up assuming it is Remy.

But two people, an older man and a middle-aged woman are standing over Scratch's grave. She doesn't immediately recognise them, so she quickly puts the insert lid back on the well cap. The woman turns, sees Flower Child and nudges the man who turns to see her standing beside the well.

'Hello,' says Flower Child, a little apprehensively.

'Hello,' says the woman. The man just turns to look again at the grave.

Flower Child comes out of the ruins and walks towards them. 'He was a great man, old Scratch,' she states proudly.

The man without looking up says in a deadpan voice, 'I knew him well before the Asteroid. I was passing through and came to pay respects, and I mean it.' He looks at her on the last word. Dark eyes bore into hers a dangerous disquiet within their steady gaze. An electric pause hangs in the air as sudden recognition rifles her response.

'Darabak,' she utters as calmly as she can, holding his eyes with a resolve of her own.

'Please call me Julius, Flower Child,' he says bemusedly. 'Or Terrie rather, your growing fame in these parts has earned my sincerest approbation, though I hardly expected you to gain such a following.'

Flower Child reaches quickly into her shoulder bag and pulls Scratch's gun and aims it at Darabak's face.

'Scratch taught you well,' he declares evenly, continuing to smile. 'Before you kill me – you know, I'm unarmed and have been these last few years – I want you to know that you have every right to do so, and my friend here, Dolly, would tell everyone how you murdered me in cold blood. She might even help you bury me, as I don't think you'd want my stench on your lovely property – please hear me out, Flower Child: I come in peace to do as I said, pay my respects. Father Frankie was the only friend I ever really had.'

'He was not your friend,' retorts Flower Child. 'And you will dig your own grave . . .'

'I like you, Terrie; you're tough and beautiful. I like that in a woman. I never would have hurt you, you know . . .'

'Shut up, Darabak. There is no atonement for you. Dolly move away from him; soon he will be a foregone nightmare.'

'You're not going to kill him?' implores Dolly.

'He means no one any harm. It was Gus who was the Trashie; Julius gave us life again, and our freedom. He clothed us, fed us, entertained us, protected us . . .'

'How about "killed us",' adds Flower Child. 'We were doing just fine before he came around. He killed my parents and most of the people who opposed him including the militia . . .'

'In self-defence!' Darabak suddenly exclaims, revealing the inner anger that caused so much fear.

'Is rape self-defence, Trashie?' she shoots back.

'Your mother offered herself to us probably to buy you time to get away, now that I think of it, but I wouldn't have hurt you! I declined your mother, but as for Gus there was no stopping him: I was even scared of him and only controlled him by letting him get away with it. I regret it! I shoulda killed the bastard! I wanted to find you and look after you, but Scratch found you first!'

'I found Scratch. No more talk! Walk over there past the ruin, now, or I'll kill you where you stand!'

Darabak turns and walks along side the ruin, before stopping to look down at the wellhead freshly uncovered.

'Odd place to have a well,' he remarks looking down, 'then again, at the time of the Asteroid people did all sorts of things to delay the inevitable. If you could've known what it was like for us, Terrie, trying to survive in 50-60 degree Celsius heat; millions of people going north just to get cool; starving and burning in the sulfuric acid fallout, filling malls and subways into vast mausoleums; cars abandoned; children orphaned, wailing; the suffering was incomprehensible. A well in the basement was the difference between life and death. After the heat then the cold, and no summer for years. If the heat didn't get you, the cold did. But I survived! Do you understand what that meant? To survive! Gus actually saved my life! The vermin that he was! He fed me human flesh! I had no will! Okay, I was bad! Bad! Father Frankie was my best friend! Did he tell you that? In the halfway prison, I was shunned by all because of my crimes, yes, there were crimes: I stole, I killed . . . those who deserved to die! But Father Frankie gave me friendship, no strings attached. When I figured out a couple years ago that it was he who was protecting you – I gave up my quest, and my fiefdom, for you – this mysterious Flower Child – who lived in the woods like a sprite from a fairy tale. I let you be and knew then the hate you must feel. I am sorry.' He stops and looks down at the well. 'You live in a bunker, don't you, Flower Child? That well is an entrance, isn't it?'

'Move on,' she commands, still pointing the gun at his head. Dolly, fearfully goes first. Once out in the field, Flower Child tells them to walk towards the north perimeter of the ploughed field. He walks and Dolly stumbles. At the north perimeter there is thick, ugly undergrowth. She tells him to stop and turn around.

'Whatever, you think I am,' he says with sorrow in his eyes, 'this is murder.'

'No it isn't,' she says plainly, 'this is an execution. You held our country in a virtual reign of terror for almost fifteen years. My husband, was basically your slave for most of that time . . . '

'Congratulations, by the way, I understand Scratch married you. I'm glad I saved Remy's life.'

'You almost killed him more than once! And was about to the day I stole your car. Your pathetic version of events does not move me in the slightest. You were the most evil Trashie to walk the earth. The likes of you will be given no quarter in our new province, Sunsetwind. We are committed to survival and the advancement of creation, to further gains made in the past, to rebuild a better world. This will be done over your corpse and everything evil that you represent.' Having said that she aims the gun at his head. Darabak stares mutely back, too stunned to speak. It is incredible how someone who represented so much terror and inspired acute fear could now, standing there alone, look so insipidly weak. Flower Child continues to point the gun, but something deep inside her will not let her pull the trigger. She begins to tremble, caught between what she is convinced she must do and that of her conscience regarding murder, however justified. She is about to lower the gun, tears streaming down her face, when out of nowhere, Remy comes running from the other side of the field calling out. In a matter of moments he understands what is transpiring and without a word gently takes the gun from Flower Child and shoots Darabak between the eyes just like that. He falls back, eyes staring madly to the open sky, his body twitching grotesquely, before expiring. Dolly falls to her knees and shrieks. Flower Child helps lift Dolly to her feet and tells her to walk back to her home and announce to everyone that Sunsetwind is free from tyranny; and that Darabak got what he deserved though without the benefit of a trial because they had no justice system, or jail for that matter, but that that would change as soon as possible. Remy drags the body into the bushes and leaves it for the scavengers.

'Murderers!' screams Dolly, as she backs up and runs off.

Flower Child stares after her unsure of her own feelings. Remy consoles her vowing Darabak's killing was necessary, reiterating that there was no institution yet in their world for law and order, but that they would pronounce Darabak's execution as a harbinger to the formation of a justice system.

Therefore, without so much as a twinge of remorse for the violent act Remy had just commited, Flower Child goes back to her well. She believes Darabak's killing was as natural as the body throwing a cold. The violent death of animals was immensely more difficult for her. His death had been something so firmly fixed in her mind, he really had been more like the specter of a dead man all those years and now she could wash her hands of him. Never mind, she thinks, forget about him. He is no more on her mind than a passing cloud or a dead fly. Remy like-mindedly, walks with her across the field, and giving her a hug he asks for the second time if she is okay. Responding affirmatively, she blithely kisses him without even mentioning the well and watches him go hesitantly back to his ploughing. Once back at the ruin with the deadly interlude over with, she collects herself by sitting near the graves of her parents and Scratch. Although, her parents have been avenged, Flower Child still feels empty and depressed.

After a time, she goes back to the well, lifts the insert lid, and steps carefully onto the ladder and climbs down inside the well to see if there really is a tunnel. The well is very deep, cool, and dark. The water can be seen down below and she can hear a slight trickle. Weird, she thinks: the well hasn't been used in years so why would the water level be that low? She presumes that there must be a leak in the casing or the spring had dwindled. She climbs down the ladder about seven meters to the water level. She sees where the water trickles out an overflow tile. Indeed there isn't any crack in the casing, only an old plastic pipe that drains the well to keep it at that level, yet the water is still three or four meters deep beneath the overflow and by the volume of the trickle, it refills at an excellent rate. Yet that shouldn't mean one would drain it to lower such a potential reservoir unless there is some special reason. She looks at the well casing. On the other side of the ladder, she notices a concrete seam outlining a square meter section that begins at her eye level and extends down to just above the drainpipe. It is certainly invisible from the top, but upon closer inspection it could be a possible entry. Flower Child holds the ladder tightly and pushes on the concrete section with her leg. It is firm and doesn't give. She has little leverage so she tries again from another angle. This time it moves inward. It is a door! She then pushes it all the way open. The hinges are large, stainless steel and swing easily. She peers into a black hole. 'Wow!' she exclaims, her voice muffled in the tunnel. She crawls in and feels stairs leading down. She is now able to stand while her eyes adjust slightly to the scant light, then searching with her hand for something to hold onto, she feels a switchbox like the one in the bunker. Farther down, it is so dark she can see nothing. Her heart pumps with anticipation and the vestige of shock from Darabak's execution. She flips the switch.

Reams of light penetrate Cephren's eyes, then the black passageway returns briefly. Her hand is still raised. There is a stuttering motion of light in the dark, like static on a screen. The stars come into view before blinking out into a blinding sun. Voices come from the distance that he strains to hear, being temporarily blinded. He feels the emotion of anger coursing through this light. His eyes finally open. There are three Native Americans standing cramped beside him in his emop foldout bed. His eyes focus onto none other than Seven Moons looking his usual implacable self, with a tall man whom he recognised as Jack Pine, the Governor-General of the Anishnabe, and a third man, of all people, Johnny Fish, the great hockey player. Cephren's anger at the interruption wanes and he breaks into a smile. 'Johnny,' he said weakly, 'have you decided to make a comeback? The Storm hasn't been the same without you!'

'I could ask the same of you, Chairman, sir! Are you all right? We pulled that wire off your finger.'

'Why, yes, I think so: thank you. How long have I been here?'

'Cephren, you don't know how good it is to see you, man,' Seven Moons remarks excitedly with a rare exultation. Seven is one of those people who doesn't smile much but seems to laugh all the time with his eyes.

Cephren sits up. He is dizzy and light headed. His body is tingling and numb. The feeling makes him tremor. 'Give me a minute; my body . . . has funny-bone all over. Wow, talk about dreaming . . . how long have I . . . '

'We just arrived, Cephren,' says Seven Moons. 'We found you grounded to your monitor. Today's the second of January. If it wasn't for Johnny finding you, we wouldn't be here. This is the Fish family's hunting grounds. He saw your emop from down there at Spirit Lake. You shone in the sun. A good beacon, man. We gotta leave. The Chicagos are everywhere. They have surveillance twenty-four hours a day. It wouldn't be long before they'd spot you and identify you. We gotta go to Ottawa. Only a crowd makes cover nowadays . . . '

'You mean to tell me, this is still January 2, 2396?'

The three men look at each other quizzically.

'May I officially welcome you unofficially to Anishnabe, Chairman Path,' says Jack Pine, a little more soberly.

'Thank you Jack, I'm sorry to have imposed on you like this; I've been trying to access this chip in my head; the time seemed much longer . . . years in fact...I up-linked this morning, I think. Have you heard any news? I took the liberty of hiding out . . . '

'You know we don't have much of a border policy, Cephren,' says Jack. 'We are flattered, though, with your decision to hide here. We want you to feel right at home. Those damned Chicagos – they're turning back the clock. We do not understand the world. Why does everyone sit and do nothing? Look at the Americans: they play old politics. George Washington sits on his butt.'

'Don't write him off yet,' warns Cephren shaking his head and standing up with Seven and Johnny assisting.

What are ya doin', Chairman?' inquires Johnny.

'He's surfing,' says Seven coolly, 'to get the mind off the Chicagos.'

'Hey, you should check out Gravitas in Ottawa,' quips Johnny, 'Some call it the House of Commons. They set up an anti-gravity beam and you can dance through the air with a light spectrum! Heard of it?'

'I think the Chairman has a different kind of Gravitas in mind, Johnny,' says Jack Pine. 'Listen, as your host, I'll let Seven Moons fly with you, and I'll go back alone. You will have some things to talk about. So, come on Johnny, let's go. See you in Ottawa, Chairman.'

'Thanks, Jack; see you Johnny.'

'Hey Mr. Chairman, you can count on me, anytime, man.'

They depart leaving Seven with Cephren. Cephren sits at the helm with Seven in the seat beside him. With a sigh he fires up the reactor.

It is well into February and for the past few days, Cleo stews in the throes of a severe depression. To make matters worse she is literally residing in a fog. The fog or dense cloud mass has settled into the upper Indus of the Kashmir Himalayas. O'Reilly had sent her there – Paradise Valley, he calls it for its beauty and isolation from the rest of the world. It had long ago been the seat of the Mughal Emperors. O'Reilly then lavishes her with gifts like the Emperor's golden houka, silks, Kasgars, colourful, finely woven pashm shawls (goat hair) and a priceless asli tush (wild goat hair) reputed to have belonged to a mountain girl who became an empress.

Cleo is situated in a crude stone cottage in a pine-covered valley. She has all the amenities to get by comfortably. But it is a self-driven isolation punctuated by fog and failure. Angrily inconsolable, she rejects O'Reilly, who suffers from his own impotency in the sweep of events. He has lost his charge, young Sam Path-Burnamthorpe and wallows in the dishonour. Their failure is a bitter pill they must swallow. Their professional judgment and personal power are not only impugned to disgrace, it seems, but their mutual sense of greatness is shattered.

Cleo has already sent Runaway to Ottawa to guard Cephren whose cover had been blown by the Gravitas incident with Anna Gram the actress. She wonders how he could be so stupid. She had received word from O'Reilly before Shiloh that Seven Moons had called to inquire whether Runaway could come to Ottawa, so she sent him, leaving Captain Dave to guard Sam. Cleo had mustered her will to plead with Cephren to come to the Kush, so that together they could hide away and devise a plan, but as usual, Cephren had other ideas. These always seemed so foolish! But she can't possibly know what he is thinking or what he knows vis a vis the $X13$, which undoubtedly influenced his decision that she desperately needs to know too. She doesn't push her views too adamantly, as is her nature, because she feels that maybe he doesn't fully trust her general security, and rightly so. Her forays into West Tennessee blew up in her face, and as well the Chicagos had made a big public windfall at her expense and even went so far to blame the disappearance of Heyoka on her! They maintained that Heyoka must have committed suicide by setting her old family lodge on fire. Yet not a human trace was found in the charred remains, and Heyoka's faithful guardian, Never Waits, insists she must have been abducted, having come across the destruction after returning from his errands.

O'Reilly, too, has taken a beating after the loss of a number of good men in the fighting. He is the kind of warlord who holds his formidable power, tenuous as it is, by retaining exclusive rights to pander technology and wealth through trade to local chieftains in return for their allegiance. He doesn't ask for much currency in exchange, only certain conditions based on new international laws, the crucible of which was the prohibition to bear arms unless a recognised national force, which in this case was O'Reilly's exclusive right to muster. Was it not for the wary loyalty of his many tribal leaders, he might have had a much bigger problem, especially when considering that most of them would never relinquish their arms. At least his leaders have never displayed them for fear of swift retribution. Fortunately, the Chicago's massive overkill did lessen some of the blame for his political mistakes, the main one not defending the Kush better. What really rankles him is how the Chicagos found out the exact location of Sam. It was a clean, precise operation backed up by thousands of emops that decimated a tenth of his force in about fifteen minutes. How could they have known that Sam was in the Llasa temple? Sam's whereabouts seemed so secure Captain Dave's presence was not needed. O'Reilly tried to convey the sense of all this to Cleo. He worries that her spirit has been broken because she has not shown him a single recrimination. He has purposely left her in one of his hide-away houses and showered her with gifts, but without response. He knows her well enough, and has faith that she would work it out in her own way. One thing for certain is that they had been betrayed and only one person comes to mind: George Washington. He is the only man who knows almost everything going on. O'Reilly perceives that George and his people including Admiral McKee and General Dennis, played Cleo in a plan of their own, not so much to probe

Chicago's defences without their involvement, or contravening the non-aggression pact with Chicago, but to manipulate public opinion against the Chicagos, which for the time being had served to do the opposite. Cleo was the perfect card and he the perfect fool to support it. There is great resentment in America at the Muhajedin presence in Tennessee even though the Yellow Tooths were pleased to have their help. And now the Americans would have nothing to do with Cleo. She tried numerous times to monitor them but was told by operators that all dialogues with foreign nationals were put on hold until the crisis had passed. What did all this mean? It must have been that America was in a state of emergency, but whose side were they on? And if they were on our side, thinks O'Reilly, why would George Washington betray us? O'Reilly believes there had been some kind of trade off: Sam for peace, or West Tennessee for Sam, or perhaps even Heyoka and Sam or else . . . America. Perhaps George felt that it was a small price to pay to ratchet down the tension. Notwithstanding, it has been three long days since O'Reilly had spoken to Cleo. He decides to visit her.

O'Reilly approaches the stone cottage on foot having landed his emop beside hers up the slope on level ground. The fog is showing signs of lifting. On his way above some of the highest mountains on earth, a wind had picked up from the north that would bring down a clear, cold front. He knocks and slowly opens the thick wooden door. Cleo is reclining on the large cotton-stuffed yak skin pallet engulfed in pashm shawls. She is propped by her elbow on one side looking beyond the window into the nebula of mist and trees.

'What the hell,' she mutters listlessly out loud, unaware of the presence of O'Reilly. The cool, intangible image of Heyoka sits front and center in her mind's eye. Cleo knows the epicenter of her vulnerability resides in the tragic disappearance of Heyoka. She reflects on those few days they had spent together, after that first extraordinary meeting that grew in stature in her mind during the days that followed like a somnambulist's fantasy. Heyoka had become to Cleo an intimate friend, even a sage, at least from her own perspective. She even felt the stirrings of possessiveness when others had encroached their space, including Never Waits, who was so unassuming as to seem almost invisible at times. Cleo wanted to know Heyoka more and be with her to the point of obsession, so overawed was she by her ethereal remonstrance and gentle foreboding. The impasse of her disappearance manifests itself in Cleo's mind isn't so much about the guilt and personal failure to Heyoka that Cleo fears, but that by her seemingly invasive and petty designs, she had destroyed Heyoka's immaculate world as Heyoka had even intimated she would.

One thing has clarified. Cleo's disposition has at least awakened in her a new frame of mind. Since there isn't any possibility of making overt action work, she believes now that covert action is the only option left open to her. She wracks her brains to think of a seam or crack to open in the Chicago armour from which to strike at their nascent hegemony over the western world. Their one great hope, America, it seems, has backed down and resigned itself to Chicago's superiority. Superiority! The very word makes her blood boil. No one is superior, she fumes, except perhaps Heyoka. They are all equal and are equal partners on spaceship earth. How dare they! Is it not treason at this juncture on the threshold of interstellar travel? And to think they would have given it all away – the X13, or whatever, in the name of freedom and creation! She holds onto that thought for a moment. She had hit upon something. A word. Come on! Yes! Treason! Treason Honey, the wily, little lovable bitch, her ace in the hole. Treason had been her best source of information on Chicago for the last couple of years. She had lived in Chicago with a geno named Babylon, who as it turned out earned a place in the court of Trinny Burnamthorpe. Oh, she was good. And no one knew, not even Chromolox. Even Cephren doesn't know, but probably had an intuition. Everybody including Treason's mom, Strange, still thought that she lived with the Neutrals, those people who lived between borders like gypsies, refusing to be enumerated or nationalised. And Treason had joined their ranks as a wayward adolescent coming to and fro with her Forager boyfriends, living in the wilds.

Then no one had heard from her for more than a year. She eventually told Cleo of her moving to Toronto to be with this geno, Babylon, a large Nubian black, whom she met in the Neutrals. Babylon had been a Breeder and chief of the Toronto district that territorially consisted of most of traditional Southern Ontario less the Neutrals and Sunsetwind. He was a "good" man who had taken on Treason as his "personal assistant". Treason had spoken of how they processed applicants for the Breeders. Pregnant women were blood tested for egg maturity. If a woman scored A she qualified and went through more rigorous testing. On the other hand, a man had to have a sperm count in the ninety-fifth percentile. Successful applicants then had to pass further physical examinations. The average successful applicant ratio was about one in a hundred. Once entered into the Hyper Genetic program, tremendous advantages in material lifestyle were offered as well as prestige. It was a free choice occupation and almost everybody tried to join at some time or other. Progeny were developed according to their abilities. The whole society was tiered on these various levels. It was in metaphorical terms one high-octane machine, fastest on the drag strip, but encumbered in the pit for all its technocentricity and elitism. But foremost, their society had devolved into a caste system, as well-oiled as it appeared.

Treason had ridden literally on the muscle-toned back of Babylon to the court of Trinny when he was appointed the head of the Genotech, a massive corporation that boasts the largest international geno service in the world. Cleo had Treason keep this cosmic hush hush and to cover her activities, had her become a guerilla with little formal indoctrination – Treason knew a lot about it already with her Foraging experience. As well, Cleo gave Treason exceptional leeway when it came to revealing the classified workings of Sunsetwind just to gain the Chicagos' confidence in her. Babylon loved Treason and Treason sort of loved anyone including Babylon of course. She travelled all over the world to attend World Symposiums as a private concubine, second to his formal mistress, a political mistress, who was his feminine peer and official escort. It is a perfect set

up. The only worry is whether Trinny had gotten to her. Trinny had discovered her origins, because Treason had been interrogated once on
account of it. Treason, true to her nature had played her cards with guile
and finesse. She had crossed over by giving the Chicagos everything she
knew about Sunsetwind and its closely guarded secrets. This disclosure is
no big deal to Cleo because Cephren and the Board had always stipulated
a policy of openness, which was common knowledge, and besides Treason
was not in a position to know much about those few inviolable things like
the X13. Not that it matters anymore anyway. Cleo remembers the last
debriefing before she assigned Treason to Cephren over the Christmas season. "She calls me her little spy," said Treason referring to Trinny. "Go on
home," she last told me; I'll wager you'll never get an erection out of
Cephren, but try. Get into his brain too; he's got something we need." Cleo
asked what that could be. "Oh," said Treason, "you know, that chip; but I
love Cephren, and know I could never do anything to hurt him. Trinny
says this chip should be hers. Babylon says their own B400 proves that
extraterrestrial life is here or was here. It describes the technology by which
the aliens can transport themselves in space, you know, like disappearing in
subspace . . . there's even stuff about aliens from places like Zeta Reticula,
Pentit Sines or something, who are not like us, like the Reticulans, who are
strange . . . like little dome heads with big shady eyes! Yeeuck! And they
have a hard time doing it, you know, so they crossbreed and clone; they
want to be more like us; Earth must be where all the action is. Am I ever
glad I don't have to do it with them, yeeuuck!' Cleo laughs to herself
remembering Treason's cute innocent face screwing up when she said that.

Collecting her thoughts, Cleo wonders how she could get in touch with
her. She remembers how Heyoka had reached Redman undetected on that
antiquated frequency through the old short-wave radio monitor hookup.
Did O'Reilly have one?

'Cleo?' he says softly behind her.

Speak of the devil, she thinks turning. He is leaning against the wall by
the door.

'How long have you been there?' she asks with a smile.

'Not long, ten-twenty seconds; I couldn't interrupt that beautiful contemplation. You seem better today – a smile even, for old Khazzami, who trembles at your sight.'

'You're not old, fool; come here, sit beside me; we must gather our wits, or what's left of them.'

He lies down beside her. She puts her arm around him. They kiss and pause, then kiss long and deep. Aroused, O'Reilly positions himself more comfortably. She responds by wrapping her wiry legs around him. They feign intercourse and laugh and kiss some more.

'I'll make you old yet, you Sufi jerk-off,' she teases.

'I'll die in your arms, bitch.'

'Not before you pump me Ali Baba . . . give him to me . . . I want him . . . I love you . . . mmm . . .'

They make long and feverous love on that yak pallet over and over until their bodies were limp and exhausted. Naked, they lie there spent in a post-coitus stupor.

'What the hell,' he says into her ear and dark hair.

'O'Reilly,' she responds in a little girl's voice.

'Mmm.'

'Who betrayed us?'

'I did.'

'What do you mean?' she asks severely.

'I didn't actually, but when conversing with George Washington, he told me about unumpentium – orange gold – and the possibility of getting to Cephren somehow. What better way than to appease with Sam's disclosure?'

'George would not have done that unless perhaps the Chicagos threatened to revoke their alliance or something.'

'But how else would the Chicagos know what George knew?' wonders O'Reilly.

'I don't know,' she says.

'Is it possible that Cephren spoke to Anna Gram. You know they've been seen together. She might have a bugged implant.'

'Or she could be a spy.'

'I doubt that; she's too much the pure stereotypical celebrity.'

'The Chicagos are threatened by Cephren,' states Cleo. 'They must know that the X13 is the motherlode of technological treasure and will do anything to get it.'

'What are you thinking, my wily tigress?'

'Why are you accountable, O'Reilly?'

'I agreed with George. I said basically we could work together to exert some leverage over Cephren to bring him to either of us.'

Cleo laughs and extricates herself from O'Reilly. Pacing around the room naked, she exclaims, 'Then I too am guilty. I was so angry with Cephren for holding out, I could have . . . he's the most stubborn person I know, O'Reilly. I realise now that he was right; we were all after him and looking for ways to round him up. Now I'm glad he's free, even if he is with Anna Gram. Cephren never ceases to amaze me. I must speak with him, but it's too risky; I will call Redman on the shortwave.'

'The shortwave?'

Cleo explains to him how Heyoka had communicated with Redman.

They search high and low for an old short-wave radio. In Kabul they locate an antique Soviet radio from the twentieth century collecting dust in a shop in the bazaar. The keeper gives it to O'Reilly when he sees who he is and O'Reilly returns the gesture with a free trip to Paris and a stay at the Ritz Nouveau, which really made his day.

Cleo rigs the radio to her monitor as Redman had explained to Heyoka. Redman had said at the time that transmissions must be minimized and sporadically timed so as not to stir suspicion. Only communicate if there is something that we can do, he had said, otherwise don't bother. What he meant, of course, was whether or not Cephren had come up with anything they could work with. That annoyed Cleo at the time. Redman has always angered her in fact. He is the only one who teases her and gets away with it, besides O'Reilly. Redman is the old guard who still treats her like a little girl and could never fully endorse her ability. Redman, as usual, would reprimand her for her haughtiness saying she was a Prima Donna who never got the discipline she needed as a child.

Cleo plugs in Redman's coordinates and presses the transmission signal. All kinds of static and haywire frequency notes emit. She adjusts the dials to a different band. A steadier signal is emitted. She waits. Nothing. She tries the earlier band. There is some kind of interference. The mountains are simply too much for that primitive signal. She would have to fly up above them and try again. She lifts off the mountain and ascends straight up until she is just over the peak. Hovering there in an auto pattern, she repeats the process. The frequency becomes clear of all the noise. She can hear the faint beeps at the other end. Redman's voice comes through faintly.

'Hello, who's this?'

'This is Ms. Little Chickadee,' she says. He used to call her that and she hated it, until now.

'Ah, my little chickadee. How are you, child?' he inquires mimicking W.C. Fields, as he did when she was a child.

Fine, fine,' her voice trembles. No matter how Redman incenses her, he is a pillar of strength.

'You don't sound so good.'

'Should I?' she replies.

'Do not fret, girl. It is to be expected. I believe Heyoka lives in a Bungalo near Windy City. In fact, it wouldn't surprise me if she turns Trinny's world quite Bungalo!'

'I really hope she's all right; but I need to know whether another certain strange young ward has been communicating at all, or whether I should attempt to round her up. She may have done some good foraging. Do I make myself clear, Mr. Grouch?'

'Let me think, dear . . . but what have you to gain by it? If you're saying what I think you're saying, there's been a fence jumping. Why don't you let the stray find her own way home? We should not jeopardize her appetite.'

'Because she's Bo Peep, silly, and must be returned to the flock; besides, I'm on a mission . . .'

'Then I suppose you have nothing to lose; but I think you'd best be patient until there is something . . . less risky; no point wasting time on lost strays. Have you heard the latest on our Knight in Shining Armour? It's just in.'

'No.'

'He has claimed publicly his intention to run for the Earth Chair.'

'What?'

'What a great idea, don't you think?'

'He must be out of his mind. They'll tear him to pieces.'

'On the contrary: what better protection. They tried to take him in Ottawa you know and he escaped to England. Go to him now; that's an order. We're networking something here. Can't talk. We're healthy. Take care.'

'Wait! Are you telling me a plan is in the works?'

'Come on, girl! Cheer up! Go to England. Remember the Alamo! Out.'

The Alamo, she ponders. What is that supposed to mean?

The line goes dead. Cleo sits for a moment disbelieving. 'What the hell!' she exclaims out loud. Cephren is running for the Earth Chair? As a lifetime member, he could nominate himself, but this is something, a real anomaly to his nature. He doesn't stand a chance though; most people hardly know who he is except George Washington and Trinny Bur-namthorpe and other heads of state, and they would be his rivals. At present it looks as though Trinny holds the majority with George a close second, and a half a dozen other candidates behind them.

And what about Treason? There has been no communication, which on one hand is characteristic of Treason, yet under the circumstances, Cleo would've thought she should have made some kind of advanced notice of her intentions. Perhaps she is in trouble, or worse, dead or simply treasonous. Then there is this 'networking' and 'Remember the Alamo'. After thinking about it, she believes it meant that Cephren could have made a breakthrough and they are working on it, all of them, Vince, Chromolox and Bill. They're up to something. Cleo takes control of her emop and flies up into orbit. She is on her way to old England. She then remembers Captain Dave who like Aladdin had hooked up with a Sultan's princess. She beeps him and he soon follows.

Jan. 25. 2396

Frustration, dear reader: for three weeks now I have been incarcerated for my own protection in the Leader of the Opposition Suite having just moved from the Prime Minister's Suite, a decadently luxurious hotel room in the old Parliament Block. It had been reserved for of all people, the famous actress Anna Gram, who frequented the casinos and recreation of the vast Parliament complex from time to time, which used to be of course the government of Canada. Now it is a Vegas North thanks to the Anishnabes, the original Vegas being no more than a deserted ghost town, and subsequently Ottawa has become one of the foremost world playgrounds for the elite. Vast indoor facilities were built over the past fifty years to accommodate the many needs of the exotic clientele.

Anishnabe has become one of the greatest credit holders in the world and could have printed money had they wanted to, but instead they hold onto a policy of foreign investment through the holding of foreign debt. In fact, Chicago is one of their big clients, and Seven Moons recently told me Anishnabe probably owned ten percent of the entire country due to Chicago's credit imbalance with them. The Earth Federation has strict guidelines concerning debt and it is surmised that Trinny wanted the Chair for that reason alone in

268   WITH AN OCEAN BLUE SKY

order to change the rules. Anishnabe fears the worst and are trading all they can to transfer their wealth from Chicago with foreign credits elsewhere. However, Chicago seems to find enjoyment in owing them credit and are not interested in trading their debt, when they really want the Anishnabes to use up their credit through more investment there, but the Anishnabes are hesitant to do so, especially now that Chicago invaded Sunsetwind and Cherokee.

So there I was in that Prime Minister's suite not being able to plug into my chip because of the security risks. I also felt out of place in the rooms where at one time long ago Danielle Perreault governed old Canada. She makes me feel Canadian, as we all are in terms of our forbearers, and guilty as such, for those lost hopes are so far from our grasp that even the notion of Canada seems antiquated to the point where only ghosts haunt these halls. Those lost hopes are our present lost hopes. And this circus of social entertainment has made me very cautious to proceed with my program. It is like I feel Danielle's taunting smile on my back, so I turn around to see if anybody is actually there. There is something uncanny about being here; this chip may have something to do with it. It's quite possible some of the things in this chip, (if I can ever find them,) were hatched from these very rooms. I look out from this vantage to the Ottawa river flowing massively beneath those steep banks and I say: be patient, Cephren!

I need more security. I need Runaway. With him at my door, I could work at complete ease with myself. Seven Moons, bless his good intentions, is trying to do that very thing and get me some security without alarming the press and people, but he is invasive in a quiet way. He is always busy, saying very little, yet implicit in understanding like a kind of telepathic sense. He knows what I need, but feels very responsible for my safety and although naturally cautious isn't about to leave me to my devices without some airtight security in place. He's right: the place could be crawling with spies. The Anishnabe are notorious for their lax security. It is a delicate situation. On one hand, I am safe here in the obscurity of a vast entertainment facility, but vulnerable to the slightest leak. I wish they would have left me where they found me back on Spirit Mountain, but I know I would have eventually been found by the Chicagos had I stayed out in the open. As it is, my Volcano emop has had to be temporarily "impounded" in Jack Pine's own carport at Rideau Hall. Jack is the Governor-General. If anybody sees the emop, word would get around. Such a machine would be just too amazing to go unnoticed, especially among the high rollers frequenting Parliament Hill. On the up side, Jack and Seven are best friends and I could trust Jack if Seven did.

Another nuisance is food service. I must rely on it, but Seven Moons has to order and receive it to protect my anonymity. Therefore, he has to be around whenever I need something. But a funny thing happened when Anna Gram showed up at Parliament and complained because she was declined her reserved Prime Minister's suite. So as she storms up to my door and knocks until I see her in the visual monitor standing there impatiently. Unsure at first who she is unaware of her presence in Ottawa, and Seven not around, I open the door anyway and she walks in, looks around, then turns to me and apologises. I realise who she is and turn into a vegetable. Then she asks, 'Haven't I met you somewhere?'

'Me? No,' I say self-consciously, 'Except on the screen; I'm actually a great fan of yours.'

'You are? You don't seem the type who lusts after me. But how do you rate this room when I had it reserved? No small feat, you know. Are you a wealthy geno?'

'No, but don't be disappointed; maybe we can trade rooms. I feel too many ghosts here.'

'I know what you mean; that's why I like it. Why would you trade? Who are you? And I'm not disappointed,' she adds warming to him.

She was everything that I had imagined her to be; but that face, that cool electric face made me nervous.

'I wouldn't mind trading. Where is your room?' I ask.

'Down the hall, round the corner at the other end – I'm in the Leader of the Opposition Suite. It's half decent. Are you married?'

'No.' I couldn't help smiling at her precociousness.

'Well, that's settled. I'll call the desk and make the arrangements.' She turns to go then stops at the door and turns back again. 'Thank you,' she says. 'Are you sure we've never met?'

'Yes,' I say.

'Do you have a name I can give the concierge?'

'Ah . . . Barnett . . . Terry Barnett.'

Then she leaves. Shortly afterwards, Seven comes in a little uncharacteristically hot under the collar. He asks why I would answer the door when I was told that could be a death wish. Then he said that everything Anna Gram does is always splashed across every entertainment bulletin in North America. But he simmered down and thought that maybe it was better that I had a less conspicuous room. So here I am in the Leader of the Opposition Suite!

All this exercise is so antithetical to what I'm doing at present. I have made tremendous inroads to the X13 and believe I'm on the brink of some fantastic breakthrough. As it is, I can rewrite the history of Flower Child! The experience in the X13 supersedes anything we have seen on earth. To think that during the five hours I was jacked in, I lived for years through Flower Child. I have to get back in, but these surroundings make it too risky; I need another Spirit Mountain. The past beckons mysteriously like a UFO. Jimmy Pidgeon must have been at the center of it, as well as Danielle Perreault. What did they know and how can they help us today if at all? I can't believe all this is in vain and that X13 is simply the stored virtual memory of Flower Child. She must lead me back to Pidgeon; it is his chip, probably given to him by the Reticulans. He too must have been implanted. They must be watching as they did when retrieving this thing before. But why haven't we seen them? Why are they so elusive? Isn't it about time they made themselves known to us? They are waiting for us, it seems, to grow up as a race. We are the contained or as Renée Antoinette decries 'the containers'! And Chicago will just prolong this human adolescence. I must find whatever information is needed to subdue them. Trinny cannot be elected to the Earth Chair! The thought occurred to me that perhaps I should run. Yes, what a strange idea, but just maybe if I go public, I stand a chance that by putting forth my candidacy, it wouldn't earn them any votes to assassinate me. Guaranteed *protection! I'll do as Vince said: 'Play the game!' Vince the Fox! And since I'm an EF life member, I don't need to be nominated by any governing body. I'm still a Sunsetwinder albeit ex-patriot. My present pathetic situation may even earn me a few votes. But I'm going to need more than a few. Everybody knows George Washington and Trinny Burnamthorpe are running neck and neck in the race. It's a long shot, but at least I have nothing to lose.*

There is a knock on the door. Cephren knows by the pattern that it is Seven Moons, who enters immediately after punching in the code key.

'Seven!' exclaims Cephren shutting down his monitor.

'Yeah, boss,' says Seven in his cool mellow voice.

'Any word on Runaway?'

'Nope, it's just too dangerous. Any and every call made from this country is monitored. Asking for Runaway Dumptruck is the same as targeting you. You're just going to have to trust me, sir.' Seven had been a little put off by Cephren's insistence on having Runaway, who was in the Kush. He had been informed by Seven via his contact in Washington. Before Cephren had been found by Johnny Fish, it was all over the news regarding Runaway's brave getaway with Sam Path, but it hadn't been known where they went. Nor did Cephren know that Seymour Psabo had been killed. Cephren has wanted to call O'Reilly on his scrambler, but held off on account of his hosts. The Anishnabe have undertaken a grave responsibility and Cephren isn't quite at the point where he could contravene their wishes; after all, he is their guest. There is no telling what Chicago would do if they found out he was there.

'Damn it, Seven, I trust you with my life. I just don't like this situation. It's driving me nuts. I need to get back into Jimmy's Chip! This place is claustrophobic.'

'I don't know what else to do, Cephren. It is imperative we minimize your movements. So far so good here, except Anna. Here's a note from her by the way.' He hands the sealed envelope to Cephren, which had Terry scrawled artistically across the front. Cephren opens it. It reads:

Dear Terry,

I never see you around. Thought you might like
some conversation. Meet me at the Senate Chamber for
supper on me – eightish. I'd be much obliged. Anna

'What does she say?' wonders Seven.

'She wants to meet me for supper in the Senate Chamber.'

'What a tragedy: an invite from Anna Gram and you have to turn it down.'

'I'm going.'

'What?'

'You heard me. I need to get out of this room.'

'Cephren, the Senate Chamber is one of best restaurants anywhere. Chef Mikael won the Nobel Culinary Prize two years ago. People would recognise you there not just as Anna Gram's dinner partner. You can't be serious.'

'I've made up my mind, Seven.'

'I don't understand,' he says, holding back in deference to his esteemed chairman. He assumes Cephren must have an ulterior motive. 'You're not telling me something.'

'Seven Moons, would you like to be my campaign manager?'

'Campaign manager?'

'Yes, I've decided to run for the Earth Chair.'

Seven doesn't utter a sound. He puts his hand through his rich, black hair. His cool, lidded eyes sparkle. His salesmanship and sharp reading of the other's motives computed through his thinking processes. He sees what Cephren sees and without a flinch says, 'So I gather, Cephren, you have come to the crossroads. When do we start?'

'I must formally nominate myself. The election capital is Paris this term. Seven years ago it was Singapore. Seven years from now it will be in Chicago, Windy City itself. If Trinny takes the Chair this year, there's a good chance she could take it next time too; that means fourteen years of

Trinny in the Earth Chair! Never! Seven, as my manager, you must contact the Earth Federation building in Paris and convey my intentions. Meanwhile, I shall write my nomination letter. Let no one know of my plans, except the Federation council, until I say so. I want to jump into the fray on my command. Got it?'

'Yes, sir. Anything else?'

'Anna Gram might just be the ticket to get splashed across the news. I will make this date and she won't regret it. Tomorrow, I'll make the nomination via my monitor. Then we will organise a world campaign. We can do this!'

'But what about the X13?' asks Seven.

'If I lived fourteen years in a few hours on Spirit Mountain – give me a few days of absolute privacy somewhere – perhaps in the Maritimes – look into it, discreetly – we'll get the ball rolling and *presto* disappear for awhile. We'll create such a furor, everyone will be blaming the Chicagos for dirty tricks at my disappearance! And when we show up again the world will be watching front and center! Perfect! We will be able to go anywhere with impunity according to the Earth Federation laws, even Chicago, most specifically Chicago! Seven, I can see it! Trinny Burnamthorpe is going to have kittens and the race of her life!'

'She won't stand a chance!'

'We'll be able to go home, too! Del Barker and his cronies will be so emasculated, their government will crumble in mockery and the Chicagos will be powerless to intervene, unless they seek to trash the Earth Federation. That would be a declaration of war to every law abiding country on this planet! She wouldn't dare!'

'I wouldn't be too sure,' ponders Seven Moons. 'There are many shady people who would kill for a fee.'

Cephren is pacing the suite now. Seven sits in the sofa chair weighing Cephren's comments. They speak of the Board and how they could get involved. They speak of Trinny who would attempt to scuttle the nomination, but concludes that if the same laws still applied, Cephren had every right to run as long as his nomination was submitted sixty days before Election day on April 2nd. But she would sue for his disfranchisement as a man without a country. They would have to look up the fine print to see if there was any requisite place of nomination, that is, the country of origin. And if so, he would have to cross into Sunsetwind to make his nomination, which might be risky, if the Free Radicals could arrest him. On the other hand, if there was no such requirement, Trinny might sue for his disfranchisement on trumped up criminal charges that he abducted a minor, his natural son, and swept him from the country and his mother. But that wouldn't hold in the international court, because Trinny maliciously usurped Sunsetwind from their autonomy on account of these so-called trumped up charges. Cephren hasn't heard the slightest news of Sunsetwind since the blackout and martial law, something unprecedented in Sunsetwind history for at least two hundred years since the days of David Path the Elder, the only child of Flower Child and Remy Path. But once his candidacy was formalised, he would go home after some campaign exposure. It is a necessary risk to legitimise his candidacy in the eyes of the world. People might think him a bit of a joke after the Chicago press had had their fun. They would debunk and discredit him with the usual doggerel! The irony stings.

He writes his formal nomination letter that day:

January 25. 2396

Dear Earth Council,

I submit to you this formal request that I, Cephren Path, Life Member, be nominated to run for the Earth Chair, April 2/2396. Being my due privilege as such and in the Earth Federation Charter of Rights under Section D – Candidacy: I hereby make known my intentions as required: I will run to submit to the world my necessary leadership in view of the crossroads facing

our human race at this time. In my possession is a much
coveted intelligence per se, and it reveals to me what
must be divulged to the whole world, something of
phenomenal import as we approach the twenty-fifth
century. It is too early to say at this point in time
what potential this may have, profound as it is, but we
should know before the election what I am not at liberty
to digress today because my work is still in progress.
In respect to my present difficulties, I hope you
will see fit to view with impartiality and
diplomacy my temporary demise.
Thank you for your patience.

Yours respectfully,
Cephren Path

Cephren approaches the Senate Chamber Restaurant up the old worn
stairs. A woman and a man in traditional native livery stand outside the
doors and greet him. They don't bat an eye as to his identity; in fact, all
the way over from the Executive Suites, not a single person paid the slightest attention. Seven Moons hangs back of course, but insists that Cephren
at least wear his Orbits (brand name sunglasses).

Looking at his watch as he waits in the quiet, low-lit restaurant, the
maitre draws near. The time is 8:02 p.m. – perhaps a little too punctual –
he looks around for Anna. She isn't there as far as he can see.

'Good evening,' says the maitre with a genuine smile. 'Please, your
name, sir?' He is an athletic Caucasian, blond and blue-eyed.

'Hello, is there a reservation in the name of Gram?'

'Gram. Anna Gram. Are you Mr. Barnett?'

'Yes.'

'Please follow me, sir. I am Gordon, your host this evening.'

Cephren follows the maitre to a private booth with a window looking out across river and beyond to Quebec. The interior decor is very elegant, but woodsy with old French Canadian murals and tapestries. The room is warm and soft in colours of Indian red and earth tones, green and grey with dashes of purple, which seems to work well. Antique lights made from old kerosene lamps and early pine furnishings give the place an authentic feel, remodeled as an art cuisine establishment.

'I'll wait for Ms. Gram, thank you,' says Cephren.

'As you please, sir,' says the maitre. 'Roberto will be your waiter this evening; ah, here he is. This is Mr. Barnett, Roberto.'

'Good evening, sir; is there anything I can get for you? A drink?'

'I'll have a glass of fresh-squeezed lime juice and some carbonated ice water, thanks.'

'Very good, sir.'

Cephren watches the maitre return to his post at the entrance. No sooner had he arrived, Anna Gram enters. She looks his way and smiles. She comes alone leaving the maitre still speaking to her. She turns around and says something to him as he motions to Roberto.

'Well, well,' she says approaching. 'Mr. Barnett does come out of his cell. I suppose appealing to your stomach was a success!' She holds out her hand and he takes it sitting. She then slides in across from him. In the candlelight, she is ravishing, as beautiful as on her films but better. The other day in the Prime Minister's suite she seemed frayed, which made him think that her beauty was more of an illusion. He is happy to be corrected on that. He marvels at her black antique fatigues that comfortably fit her sleek, medium build combined with a burgundy cashmere scarf and black gloves.

'Don't be modest, Anna; I'm not so big a fool as to turn down a movie star,' he says feeling a bit cocky.

'Well, honestly, I hadn't thought of that.' She laughs with a soft trill. 'No, I really just wanted to thank you for your kind gesture the other day, and you seemed a man of culture and . . . a loner, if I may say so.'

'You may; I am a little dispossessed as of late.'

Roberto the waiter stands before them. 'Yes, Ms. Gram, the usual, with a cherry?'

'Thank you, Roberto,' she says with that melodic voice that so captivated audiences. The waiter leaves. 'You were saying?'

'Nothing, really, I get the impression you're a bit of a loner as well.'

She looks down hesitating to answer and fidgets with the carved wooden napkin holder. Cephren looks casually at her to study her feelings. It seems he strikes a nerve. For a moment, there is sadness or mystery in her sharp brown-green eyes. Her profile, the line of her smooth, white jaw and cute Cinderella nose, with that subtle brow and forehead, as if taken from an ancient Grecian frieze festooned by thick, chestnut wavy hair tumbling about to her shoulders, is the immaculate Anna Gram mystique. He wonders naïvely if she is aware of the affect it had on men, at least this one. He has to check himself. 'I'm sorry, I didn't mean to imply it was a disease or something.'

She bursts out laughing again settling with her eyes on Cephren. They are shining with ardour and have a surprising depth. 'You really know how to rub me the right way. What do you do, Mr. Barnett?'

'Good question, as of late, I've been a treasure hunter, the computer chip kind.'

'Oh, and have you struck gold?'

'Gold, no, something better.'

'Really? Platinum, then.'

'No.'

'Is it a secret?' she asks tilting her head to the side and sitting forward in her seat.

'Yes and no.'

'Why don't you tell me the yes part, and we'll work on the no: I love secrets.'

'Well, it has to do with extraterrestrial life, old government bond chips.'

'Wow: now that's interesting. I read a book recently about the U.S. secret programs before the Asteroid and the evidence seems to be irrefutable that they worked with aliens for over a hundred years.'

'Yes, it's true. In the twenty-first century, even beginning in the twentieth for that matter, aliens were a standing joke in the western world. Many people suspected what some of the governments knew at the time, but as far as these governments were concerned 'ufology' was promulgated as utter nonsense and the mainstream media did all the rest by suppressing any inquiry to get to the truth; much like in the middle ages when for over a hundred years the church suppressed the fact that the earth was round: fear is the root of ignorance. At the time in the 20th and 21st centuries, I believe they probably had sufficient grounds to be fearful by keeping the lid on public awareness, otherwise they would've come clean with it; at least they should have. What began as a policy of derision to those who put their best foot forward regarding the hard facts concerning alien visitation: sightings, abductions, etc., eventually flew back into the government's face to the point that before World War 3, many wished to bring the government down on account of its hypocrisy, but they lost of course, everyone lost, on account of the war. No, I think the government must have had sufficient cause for concern regarding aliens; there was just too great of an evolutionary gap to bridge such disparate civilisations; I'm talking about hundreds of thousands of years in some cases. But what I'm interested in is where they are today, the aliens.'

'Wow, you know a lot about it. Have you heard of the X13? I was reading an article in Chicago last week that Sunsetwind is believed to be where this alien chip is hidden. It even suggested that the Chairman . . . Path, I think, had it implanted.'

Cephren smiles. 'Yes, I read something about that too; too bad about Sunsetwind, though. The Chicagos really stepped out of line . . .'

Roberto returns with the drinks. 'Fresh squeezed lime...and one Wild Turkey with a cherry. Enjoy and let me know when you are ready to order. I'll bring some bread with the first course.'

'Wild Turkey,' repeats Cephren thinking about old Scratch.

'Yes,' she says, 'bourbon straight up on ice with drop of juniper, and a cherry. Want a sip?'

'No thanks.'

'You know, I'm a Texan, born and raised, and proud of it. Hell, if Chicago ever did something like that to us, I'd join the army. I know the situation was more complicated, but still it was wrong; but people today, they just don't care; there's always some kind of rationalisation, in the name of freedom! Hell, live and let live. At least the Chicagos are sup-posed to pull out by the end of the month. Good riddance!'

'Who will you vote for in the Earth elections?'

'Oh, I don't know, probably George. He's reliable and cautious. I've met him a few times.'

'Mmm, he is cautious.'

'And you?'

'Oh, I want to see the new candidates. I heard a rumor that Chairman Path may run for the Earth Chair . . . '

'What a good idea!' she exclaims. 'He should run, but he'd have quite a time against Burnamthorpe and Washington. It would bolster his credibility; the poor guy really blew it. I mean, the world wasn't meant for people like him. They say he was just too nice. I met a woman in Chicago who said she knew him intimately. The guy has no balls, she said. He was so full of himself and his monitor he couldn't see a come-on for dog pooh, pardon me. Those were her exact words. I laughed at the time, but thought just the same, who would want that bimbo bitch anyway? She was a concubine of some powerful geno . . . Babylon, come to think of it.'

'Babylon. Can't say I've heard of him. Who was the woman?' queries Cephren, trying not to smile.

'What's so funny?' She smiles too, enjoying herself.

'Nothing, it's just amazing how some people can't take rejection.'

'Yeah, and I'm one of 'em!' she laughs again. 'But don't worry Terry; it takes two to tango, they used to say. Anyway, I never knew her first name; she said her mother was the artist, Strange Honey.'

Cephen visibly jolts.

'Do you know her?' asks Anna.

'No, no, just surprised.' He quickly regains his composure, though feeling a keen discomfort. First of all, what the hell was Treason doing back in Chicago and secondly, he is feeling guilty about this deception with Anna. He had been foolish to think that he could have supper with someone like Anna Gram and not develop some emotional rapport even in friendship, although from the look of it, she seemed open to more. He would have to come clean with her. She is young and volatile with a strong sense of righteousness. He likes her and doesn't want to hurt her; but what of the plan, the politics, the getaway, the X13? He hates politics. He decides to forge ahead, carefully.

'Are you into Piercemore?' she asks off the cuff taking a slow sip of her Wild Turkey and looking deeply into his eyes.

'Why do you ask?'

'You just seem the type.'

'Very much so: "Oh this child in me, no fame, no fortune, just the crusty certitude of a doughty recluse!"'

'Yes! yes! I like you!' Anna confesses excitedly. 'How about: "Let us take the train! You and me, into the virgin country, and starry scapes; to wring ourselves of pity and dare like school children!" Or, this: "You bastard! I can smell your lobster! How revolting!"'

They both laugh out loud.

'And this, she continues: "They danced to broken hearts, sick losers and paltry dreams, while he whispered into the nape of her lily soft neck, 'Hear me mother earth, your silent blast furnace beneath, we are your own, contained by volcanoes and ocean swells; hear our dire song and bequeath to us a molten eminence.'"'

She is good, really good. Her delivery is so eloquent, clear and body oozing the necessary chemistry. She envelopes one in her charms. Cephren sits mesmerised.

'What a great spirit, he was,' she says, 'like Shakespeare. Why were they both so mysterious? But Piercemore: no one knows anything about him. Strange for those times when everything was documented on video, books, news, journals – but all we have is a blank. This Max Light character is bullshit. You can't tell me Danielle's personal secretary, personal door mat, bureaucrat, was Piercemore!'

'Try explaining that to English and history professors. I personally believe Piercemore was Jimmy Pidgeon, a Canadian scientist working with cosmic top secret U.S. reverse engineering programs.'

'Really? I've never heard of him.'

'Well . . .'

The waiter, Roberto, is ready to take their order. Anna orders without looking at the menu. Cephren takes a moment, vacillating with prospects, as they are all so tempting. After the oyster hors d'oeuvres, he settles on the clear mushroom consommé with pumpkin ravioli, fire-brazed foie gras in cognac, wild vegetable moose-liver terrine, buttery lemon-steamed black bass, blueberry ice and the renowned spiced maplewood-roasted ground-hog filets. Anna has her Canard Erotique, otherwise the same meal. She orders the wine, a famous red California Shasta '79. Needless to say, they are having a fantastic evening.

Their conversation rolls on spontaneously as they both come to understand how they compliment each other. 'I'm so thrilled to have found you Mr. Barnett,' she says. And Cephren toasts her fame and fortune. She satirizes his compliment by affecting the complete starlet. Other guests in the restaurant even clapped at one point, which made her look around and wonder who they were clapping at, which is comic as she is sincere; but they clap again anyway.

When dessert arrives, she has drunk most of the wine, as Cephren has had only one and a half glasses. She falls silent, in a sort of visible fermentation. Cephren sits back and calmly watches to see what she will do. The silence is kinetic, even melancholic. They can sense each other's inner intensity. Her vanity relates to his sanity and vice versa. Both are tuned to each other, yet living in separate strata of being, though briefly touched by their common independence. But the melancholy remains: it is safer to keep afar the possibility of a replete love, rather than waste emotion on doomed yearning.

'Well, Terry, I'm an open book, as you can see. Sometimes I feel as if I have my legs spread for the world to see. I'm as free as a bird. I have simulated sex in every movie. I don't know what you really think of me, having been with many men that way. I'm really a prude at heart. I haven't had real sex, love sex, since . . . years. God, what am I saying? Why can't I shut up? I just wanted to have dinner with you, my treat. You intrigue me. No one ever has taken my suite, Danielle's suite. Just who are you that you're so important to them? The concierge said the Governor-General asked him to bump me for Terry Barnett. Well?'

She really puts it to him. Cephren figures he had it coming. Karma is karma: what goes around comes around. He thinks perhaps she's dipping into his pond, but needs some reassurance.

'At present, I'm Terry Barnett, Anna, treasure hunter for intelligence. I'm not at liberty to divulge the specific nature of my work. I do so much want to get it off my head, if you could only know, I wish, truly, I do. Maybe I'll tell you a science fiction story. Listen, we've had such a wonderful time. Why don't you let me get the check, on the Governor-General, but it doesn't matter; then let's go back to your suite . . . and watch one of those reruns . . . no, I'm sick of reruns. I've been cooped up so long. The *Reptoid* Series, *The Jane Smith Show*, even the age-oldies like *The Beverly Hillbillies*. Forget it. Why don't we just take a brisk walk along the canal to work off this wonderful meal?'

'Okay, then we can go back after, Terry.'

'Sounds fine to me, Anna.'

However Anna insists on picking up the check and they then exit the old building. In the bitter cold, they walk on the well-lit walkway down to the river. Anna puts her arm around Cephren's waist and snuggles in as he holds her tightly. The feel of her body so close to his excites him: he feels that tingling in his loins so long in disuse. It embarrasses him so he shuts the thought from his mind, reflecting: I shall not betray my sanctity! But another side insists by prodding him in the right places saying, I, too, am as free as a bird! Down at the enormous river moving darkly, silently, she turns into him and kisses him passionately. Cephren melts into the embrace, powerless to resist. Her mouth is soft and delicious. The image of caring Mita looms before him; it breaks the spell. They catch their breath.

'I can't do this,' he mutters.

Her body hardens.

'Why?' is all she says.

'I . . . just can't.'

She steps back disengaging herself. Her eyes are teary from cold and hurt. 'Don't be a bastard, Terry! What is it?'

'I'm a Sunsetwinder,' he divulges, looking over to the water.

'So?'

'My name's not Terry Barnett.'

At that moment a couple of emops come flying over the river. But the heat of the moment compels Cephren and Anna to ignore them.

'I can accept that,' she says.

'My real name is . . .'

The first emop casts them both in a blue gravity beam that jolts them off their feet from the walkway. Cephren manages to grab the railing to anchor himself. Anna is flailing about helplessly drawn to the emop. The other emop lands and a dozen fully armed commandos came running out towards Cephren who manages to pull his way out of the beam.

'Run!' she screams before going limp. Cephren jumps out sideways when the beam chases him into some trees. Behind them unbeknownst is Seven Moons who pulls out a flash handgun. He shoots the first two commandos who would have reached Cephren.

'This way!' yells Seven, who from behind a tree holds at bay the remaining commandos. The other emop lifts above the trees and tries to laser Seven. There is no way out for them. Suddenly another emop appears and lasers the hovering emop, though not crippling it as it breaks away and ascends. The commandos then scramble back into the other emop not before picking up their two casualties. The friendly emop then lands. Out runs Runaway Dumptruck with a flashgun towards Cephren who is covered in snow.

'Runaway!' exclaims Cephren, giving him an enthusiastic shoulder pat. 'Find Anna!' They both go down to the riverside walkway.

Seven is already there crouching over Anna who is inert on the ground. There is movement. She stirs and Seven and Runaway lift her to her feet. She teeters for a moment before recovering her composure.

'Oh!' she gasps, breathing deeply. 'Talk about a take!'

'Are you all right Anna?' queries Cephren, holding her shoulders.

'Yes, I think so. They dropped me from about two meters, the jerks. Who were those guys?'

'Chicagos. They won't be back,' assures Seven. 'It was a dash and grab thing. They couldn't get caught, but even if they did it would be denied. They weren't in standard Chicago fatigues. Most likely Trinny's special goons.'

'I'm out of here, it's freezing,' shivers Anna. 'And thanks, whoever you are.' She glances at Cephren, as she walks away.

'Wait, Anna,' demands Cephren. He runs over to her. 'I'm sorry. I had no idea this would happen.'

'Well, I should hope not.'

'Why don't we go back together; I want to make it up to you.'

She looks past him and sees the formidable Runaway and cool Seven standing there looking around awkwardly.

'Please, Terry, it's not that I don't understand; but I'd rather be alone now, you know, back to my fantasy. If I cry a little tonight, it won't be in spite of you.' She turns to leave.

'Anna,' he says holding her arm but letting go. She stops and turns around.

'Let's call it a night,' she conveys. 'But, you know, I don't know who you are or what you want. But hey, if you really want me, you have to come and get me.' She walks away silently in those black fatigues and runners, her figure silhouetted against the walkway lights.

Cephren watches her for a while, then turns to his compatriots. 'She's right, you know.'

'Wow!' remarks Runaway. 'Cephren, sir, I don't know what you've been doin', but I think I'm gonna cry.'

'She has presence,' understates Seven. 'Maybe we should consider her for our campaign, say in a running mate – just a thought, a purely objective thought. You'd win for sure.'

'Seriously?' asks Cephren.

'Why not?' reiterates Seven, taking his idea more seriously. 'No pulling punches, you know, to win that is.'

'What's this about?' wonders Runaway a little bewildered.

'Runaway,' says Cephren with a smile, 'I don't know how you found us, but you couldn't have come at a more auspicious moment. Tell him, Seven.'

'We're running for the Earth Chair, and thanks for your prompt response. Cephren, when you were eating supper, I got a message from Cleo that Runaway was on his way and to hone in on my beeper code. How did you get through orbit?'

'I came down at Hudson's Bay.'

'How's Sam?' inquires Cephren.

'He's good, sir; he's studying with the monks.'

'And Cleo?'

'She's fighting the Mississippis with the Yellow Tooth Cherokees.'

'Sounds like George Washington has gotten her to do his dirty work,' says Cephren.

'She's takin' her steam out on those freaks, sir, for Sunsetwind and poor Seymour.'

'What do you mean "poor Seymour"?' asks Cephren, earnestly.

'Seymour's dead, sir; he was killed after we escaped.'

'Seymour dead?'

'Yes sir.'

'How did you find out?'

'O'Reilly found out somehow.'

Cephren bows his head. There are many things happening that he just has no idea about. O'Reilly, Treason, and how did those geno commandos find him? And now Seymour dead? It's all too much.

'Let's go,' he says, 'I'm freezing.'

seven

The Mall

About the boy who traps a star in a box
And would not let it out –

—Jimmy Pidgeon

For Chromolox there is nothing more frustrating than being so sick it forces her to stay in bed. The pneumonia rockets her body temperature up to over forty Celsius for three days. She lies there half comatose on antibiotics, probiotics, willow bark tea spiked with morphine and homeopathic drops. The worst of it is the excruciating headache that accompanies the fever. Mita had made the original prescription, which mysteriously arrived that evening. In parting, she had said to stay there until someone got in touch, but Chromolox remembers nothing about those first days. And Chromolox's father was old and feeble and not altogether sound of mind. They had hardly spoken in years. Never very close, they had managed to keep relations tolerable. In fact, during her most delirious state, when she groaned and mouthed spontaneous prose more akin to avant-garde poetry, her father, Dax, had not shown so much interest in her since she was a child. He would sit there with a book in the corner of the dark room and tilt his frazzled head attuning his ear, both alert and somehow helpful. However, the day she gets up and opens the curtains to the winter sun, he retires once again to his remote Diaspora. Once recovered, she thanks him for his temporary return. He even smiles, though he has no idea why she is there or what seems to be going on in the world.

As the weeks go by and she has fully recovered, Chromolox goes shopping at the local market for much needed groceries, although a middle-aged woman who she does not know – nor Dax it seems – came by once a day with a few staples. The day before, she had introduced herself as Julia. She was so shy that she and Chromolox barely had a conversation. The one thing she said was that Dax never invested in the Trip-C implant program that Chromolox herself had set up years before when she was a junior executive in Health. The program was designed to create a fund to pay for those poor citizens who could not afford mental prosthetics for various aging ailments, hormonal, glandular and synaptic. Poor Dad, she thinks, too proud even in senility. But it isn't too late. She would look into some correctional remedy.

As she is walking down the snow-covered paths, the odd emop swoops by stirring up the frigid powder. The town is thriving. Many people scurry about. Commerce is booming. She feels low self-esteem as though she has been relegated as a Trashie. The new order seems to have been endorsed everywhere. In one sense it exemplifies how stable their economy had actually been. The Chicagos had rigged a masterful coup, but it could be reversed just as easily, which proved what a ridiculously futile thing it all had been and at the cost of life. Del Barker would answer for that she swears, as she shivers and pulls her jacket tighter. She knows she must find a survival suit and get out of this nightmare! But, for the time being she should defer responsibility to the others and wait.

At the market with four bags in each hand, she stops by the large viewing screen to catch the news. It bowls her over. Cephren Path is on the campaign trail for the Earth Chair! She lets out an ineluctable cheer. A few people turn their heads but don't seem to notice who she is. Ephemeral politics, she presumes, as if they couldn't care less. Besides, she has no reason to be proud, but Cephren! This must be what that cryptic message had meant! Del Barker must then be working on an ulcer! With diplomatic status during the campaign, Cephren would be immune to incarceration anywhere. Candidates are the exalted few. Only those individuals who are qualified as credible and influential in world affairs are eligible according to specific criteria. And Cephren had pulled an ace. He knew with his life membership as an EF founding state chairman and present circumstance, he could not be refused. She listens: his running mate is the actress Anna Gram! Incredible! What's this? She listens: if he was to be elected to the Earth Chair, he would attempt to make overtures to Chicago to do whatever they would consider workable in the best interests of all parties: greater economic linkage, access to new scientific data that would propel the world into the twenty-fifth century *and* into an association with a *galactic confederation!* Wow, he must have made a breakthrough, or he was trying to make some great play for attention! Trinny Burnamthorpe and George Washington, the other main contenders could be threatening to protest his candidacy. There is talk of an America-Chicago alliance, which might effectively undermine the Earth Federation. Del Barker has condemned Cephren's nomination as fraudulent and categorically denies him any entry into Sunsetwind, which had apparently caused a riot in the Pyramid! 'Hooray!' Chromolox cheers. A number of people watching too, followed her lead and call out encouragement. Then it's really happening! A riot in the Pyramid! But the news abruptly ends. Suddenly, Del Barker appears on the screen. He looks drawn and tired and very solemn. He speaks with a voice of doom.

'Good citizens of Sunsetwind, I am making this emergency announcement in the advent of anti-government riots that recently broke out here at our beloved capitol, the Pyramid. It is with great regret that I must inform you of the council's decision to reinstate martial law. Many of the instigators have been apprehended and charged with public mischief with the intention to overthrow the government. This, sorry to say, has forced your government to delay indefinitely the promised elections this spring. The world is frightfully teetering on the brink of chaos and corruption due to the persistent underminings of the former dictator Path, who has now shut out the one great hope of lasting democracy by his scurrilous bid for the Earth Chair. We, of the Western*

World all know what a sham this is. And we, of responsible government will continue to monitor and defy the brazen hypocrisy of Mr. Path. So do not fret or worry, everything is under control. We are linked to the most powerful nations in the world and will stop at nothing until this situation is corrected. Stand up and be proud! If need be, we shall fight for freedom, all or nothing! Support our cause and turn in anyone suspicious of subterfuge. This is a classic battle that will be fought in the streets if need be. How can you stand by and see your country kneel at the approach of serfdom? Don't let it happen. Freedom is within our grasp! Now may you forgive these trespasses on our lives. We will overcome! We must! We shall! Good day to you.'

There is silence after Barker finishes, the silence of disbelief. Then there comes on some banal bingo lottery commercial, thanks to Barker's new initiatives. Chromolox can't hold it in any more; this farce has reached critical mass. She begins to laugh hysterically like a dam burst releasing all her frustration. People are staring at her if she is completely mad. Barker's speech had to be the funniest thing she had ever heard. She couldn't laugh in his office, but she could sure laugh now. It was that tone of voice that had people quaking in their shoes, that myopic denizen of the material, that dinosaur. It is so ludicrous, Chromolox feels like standing up on one of the counters to applaud, but that wouldn't do, so she just laughs until someone asks if she is all right.

'Don't you know who I am?' she cries in stitches.

'Now that I think of it, you look like our old President Chromolox. What's so funny? This is a calamity.'

'What's so funny? You're so funny, all of you! Don't you see what a sham this is?'

'Riots are hardly a laughing matter, Ms. Chromolox.'

'Yes, yes, let me catch my breath, thank you.' She takes a moment to calm down. 'Okay, okay, I've had a good laugh, a release of much tension. Listen, if any of you could know what is really going on. First of all, I could be arrested for speaking out like this.' She raises her hand and shows them her tag. 'See this? They're worried about freedom you know, like it's a disease. Have any of you studied the twentieth century? Some? Good, no matter. Listen all of you before I go: at first I thought we had instigated the riots, but I realise they were likely fabricated by Barker to give them an excuse for martial law, or worse still: his new military exercising their muscles on an innocent crowd merely watching the international news. Heaven forbid! These Free Radicals usurped your government of fair representation with the support of the Chicagos.' At that moment two New Militia arrive and without a word escort Chromolox away. She speaks out taking no heed of her situation.

'These Free Radicals are Trashies! Call it Revenge of the Trashies. Now I must go. I am quarantined! And I've been ill. Be patient, Cephren will save this country, and the world, if we let him. Don't believe what they say about him; just vote for him. Now I will go peacefully.'

Chromolox is escorted home and left there with a warning.

Later that afternoon, Julia shows up at the old house, a ramshackle wood-frame that had somehow survived the Horror and subsequent centuries. It is situated on a road or track that now follows the shore of the Waubaushene inlet which opens up to Great Blue. The water in the bay is now frozen and numerous fishing huts dot the white expanse. Snow machines can be seen going to and fro, their quiet humming audible across the air.

Julia trudges into the front hall, takes off her snow boots and warms herself by the heat vents. Dax is sitting in the living area as usual minding the windows. He at least can still dress himself and bathe which is a blessing for Chromolox, who can't imagine having to take over that labour. She had asked Julia to take care of his needs in that department if and when the time arose. Julia sideswipes the issue by saying he is quite capable to help himself. Chromolox retreats knowing her own relationship with him: his selfishness in the past now paid dividends in that he disdained her help. She decides they are alike after all – Dax and Chromolox, singular proud Sunsetwinders. Looking at him there, she really wonders how he ever managed to love at all; her conception had been an accident as a result of a Summer Fête fling, and her deceased mother wouldn't have anything to do with him after he dumped her cold. Nevertheless, old age is an impediment to health, and she would take care of him. She calls the local health authority and sets up an appointment.

'So Julia,' says Chromolox, 'did you hear the news?'

'What news? The riots?' She gives Dax a cookie.

'Yes, and Cephren running for the Earth Chair.'

'That's old news. But they don't tell us a lot. I've heard they've shut down the international screens since the riots.' Julia sits down on the sofa and looks out to where Dax gazes to see if he was really looking at anything.

'Do you believe the riots were genuine?' inquires Chromolox looking at Julia to gauge her reaction.

'Why not? I mean it's not as if we approve of the government. Some people actually like Barker, though; the poor think he's gonna give 'em more money.'

'You don't strike me as being wealthy, Julia. Why don't you like him?'

'I like you, Ms. Chromolox. And I think Chairman Path is a good man. I'll vote for him, if they'll let us.'

'They have no choice if they want to remain in the Earth Federation,' comments Chromolox.

Julia looks shyly at Chromolox; her African features dominate the white. She is about fifty-five and is in excellent physical condition.

'What they have done to you and the Board isn't right, Ms. Chromolox. People know it too. But fightin' is wrong; we know that. That's why Mr. Barker won't have elections; he isn't a fool; he knows we can only resist through the democratic process.'

'I doubt that, Julia. And he's the worst fool I've ever known to come out of this country. We will resist: you have that right.'

'Well, maybe he is; I sure won't vote for him.'

'Does Dax ever speak of me?' asks Chromolox.

'Well, one time he said you were the cutest little girl acting like you were in charge. He says you never listened to a word of advice!'

'Really?' quips Chromolox, surprised, adding, 'Pride, yes, a family trait. Julia?'

'Yes?'

'Has anybody come around or called while I was sick?'

'Not here, but my boss said to me at work – I do shifts at the Linen Yard – he said that I could stay home with credit for three weeks back holidays! I told him I don't need back holidays, but I'll take it. That's why I can come here so much now. I used to come three days a week, sometimes four. I have family too.'

'Would you move in for a while, for me, and Dax?'

'Move in?'

'Yes, I'd like to visit some *friends*,' she mouths silently the last word.

'What about that?' Julia points to her wristband.

Chromolox replies abruptly, 'I'm going to enjoy some quality time with Dax.'

'I'd be honoured to help any way I can, Ms. Chromolox.'

'We'll just have to get domestic.'

They sit in silence. Chromolox is beside herself with frustration; she needs to be busy with something and can't stand sitting around idly. She must find a surrogate for her monitor band. Someone was supposed to take care of it. Why haven't they been in touch, she wonders? Had she been cut out of the loop on account of her 'public disgrace' with Season? Mita had not indicated any such notion.

'Are you sure nothing else out of the ordinary has come about around here, Julia?' queries Chromolox more forcefully.

'Now that I think about it: a package came for Dax the other day. I put it in his room. It was a birthday gift from his friend, Steve.'

'Steve?'

'I don't know. The return address was from Thornbury.'

'What is it, the gift?'

'Some kinda virtual game called *Safari Shoot*.'

'Show me. I didn't know Dax was into hunting.'

'Oh yes, he lives for his virtual games.'

'What d'yah know.'

Julia leads the way up the rickety wooden stairs to the bedrooms. In Dax's room on his desk is the antique computer Chromolox had used as a child. It is an IBM from the latter 21st century. The CD is on the desk. She turns the monitor on and inserts the disc. Strange she thinks, as she inserts the disc, as only antiquated systems required discs. At any rate, she follows the set up procedure and puts on the head mask and earphones. When the program has been entered an African vista appears. It is a perfectly simulated reality with sounds, smells and even the textured feel of the earth. She is driving across a bumpy savannah. The vehicle stops and she can get out to survey a vast plain and the surrounding rocky hills. She takes out a high-powered stun gun while a huge male lion appears from an outcropping of rocks. The mighty beast comes towards her slowly to observe and perhaps stalk a potential meal. She finds a perch of rocks from which to take good aim at the approaching animal. When the lion comes within twenty yards it attacks suddenly in a half dozen lightening leaps. She calmly raises the gun, takes careful aim and fires dropping the king of beasts at her feet with a thud. Then the strangest thing happens. A voice: 'Hi Chromolox,' it says; 'you may remove your band monitor now. You have two minutes from the time you disengage the game to reattach the band to Julia, who is your cover. Please do not discuss this with her. Then under cover of night, you will proceed on foot to the Indian graveyard.' Chromolox takes off the head mask and looks at the band. The sensor light is off and the band comes off easily. Julia is there with her wrist out. Chromolox looks at her. Julia smiles. The band is reconnected. In exactly two minutes, the sensor light comes on again.

'Fun game, Julia; I just stunned a lion.'

'Perhaps Dax should give it a shot.'

'As long as it doesn't give him a heart attack.'

'Gosh, Ms. Chromolox, you're right.'

That night Chromolox steals away. She feels exhilarated and free. The only Indian graveyard she knows of is the one that she explored as a child. It is situated near the top of the hill behind her home on a knoll of ground with a view of the inlet. One summer long ago when she was about four-teen, the Great Blue U. archaeology students conducted a dig there. One of those young students was Olivia Lee.

'Chromolox,' a voice calls quietly from the darkness of the woods by the clearing. A figure can be seen silhouetted against the white snow like a tree trunk.

'Olivia?' says Chromolox, hesitantly.

'Yes, it's me.' They walk toward each other and embrace. Olivia's light skin and dark braided hair and silvery survival suit are accentuated in the moonlight and the snow making her seem like an enchanting priestess.

'Oh, Olivia, if you could know how good it is to see you! Two months have been two years!'

'This time has been most difficult.'

'Ready to burn: do you have an emop?'

'Yes, my own Sport. Follow me.'

Chromolox follows Olivia back to another clearing, a small field that opens at one end to a large field. Her emop looks like an igloo in the snow. They scramble inside out of the cold. Olivia had left the reactor on at its lowest charge, just enough to keep the heat on and conductors alive. She quickly engages the reactor and gravity field ever so gently so that the craft lifts just a few feet above the ground.

'We must use the cover of the forest,' says Olivia tersely. 'If we ascend too quickly, we will surely be spotted by the New Militia. Many have joined because of the double credit. Barker is destroying our country. He has mortgaged our land to the Chicagos! Can you believe it? He really thinks our lives will improve. There's no reasoning with him; he's gotta go.'

Olivia sits back and looks confidently at Chromolox beside her. The Sport heads across the fields past an ancient post and beam barn and down the valley along the Huronia ridge. The route is plugged into the autopilot.

'What's going on, Olivia? What can I do?'

'You heard about the riots?'

'Yeah, a scam I bet.'

'When they opened up the International Screens around the country, and allowed the *Foreign Affair* to print again, under new editors, of course, people began to assemble and watch; the screens have always been popular, you know; well, after Cephren nominated himself to run for the Earth Chair, people were ecstatic. Soon, specifically in the Pyramid at the big screen on Survivor's Walk, many thousands would congregate during lunch as usual, you know, there are always a lot of people there. Anyway, Barker calls in his Praetorian Guards and viciously clears the area leaving many people wounded with lacerations and bruises, though thankfully no fatalities. There was no cause for his aggressive actions whatsoever. It was criminal: a malicious put-down of the people's right to watch the world news, let alone eat their lunch. Barker proclaims it a riot. People are now getting the picture loud and clear. Many of those who were ambivalent or non-committal to our old regime understand now the implications of the tragedy. Barker will never be elected, nor his party. He must do as he does – repress, in order to maintain his authority. The people don't want him, Chromolox; they want you, and Cephren, all of us. It's only a matter of time. The Chicagos won't dare invade again, not while the EF campaign has heated up. But if Trinny wins, which is very possible at this point, or even loses, she may still pounce again. We've got to get rid of Del Barker before the end of the elections. He surrounds himself with a kind of Praetorian Guard. The guy is a manic paranoid who gets worse daily with power-mad authority. He's convinced himself that the goals of his Great Vision can justify anything he does.'

'What would you have me do to get my job back, Olivia? Assassinate him?' asks Chromolox, jesting.

'Frankly, yes,' she retorts uncharacteristically.

'Are you serious, Olivia? I can hardly believe I'm hearing this. Does the Board condone this?'

'Absolutely, except Redman, of course: Vince and Mita are the strongest advocates. Your two months have changed everything, dear. We are desperate.'

Chromolox falls silent. The enormity of this resolution simply goes beyond her whole sense of being. 'Mita?' she says rhetorically to herself.

'Yes, Mita,' responds Olivia.

'And you, Olivia?' wonders Chromolox innocently.

'I'm not sure. To tell you plainly, I will support what you support, Chromolox; I trust your judgment.'

'Thank you, but what makes them so sure? Cutting out Del like a bad cancer growth isn't going to make the disease go into remission under some other screwball. Have you thought of that?'

Olivia refrains from answering as they near Clearview, the hub of Sunsetwind. She goes down into a forest clearing that opens to a trail which had been originally an old highway where portions were still clear of large trees. This road skirts south of Clearview toward the Neutrals of Orangeville. She then arcs up to the northwest under the Niagara escarpment and follows it to a forested valley near the Pyramid. They stop and settle into the deep snow in a forest glade of hemlock. She then shuts down all systems. 'That route we just took had been specially set up. It's one of five from different directions. We scramble our signals with Resonant Scanners which have been strategically placed by some of our loyal guerillas in order to facilitate our movements undetected.'

'Thank goodness for those Resonant Scanners, though it seems they got us into this mess in the first place.'

'A classic example of nuclear morality – one manipulates the fruit of the garden and presto – instant karma's gonna get you!' says Olivia with a smile. 'But with a lucky bounce this time.'

'Now that's the Olivia I know,' says Chromolox, 'but still, you've become quite a trooper!'

They laugh and exit.

'Where are we going?' wonders Chromolox.

'Redman's bunker.'

'I should have known. Isn't he watched?'

'Electronically, yes, but . . .'

'The Scanners.'

'Yup. All the tags have been manipulated.'

They trudge along making their own trail in the fresh snow, sometimes sinking up to their knees. Soon they converge with other fresh trails and finally arrive at Redman's bunker where all one can see is a warm-lit window and dense forest all around. At the door they are greeted by LeRoy MacGregor who smiles warmly, but without fanfare quietly letting them in.

The event is truly a joyous homecoming of sorts. Redman, LeRoy, Bill, Yani, Vince, Mita, Olivia and Gabriella all sit around Chromolox, in that order, back in Redman's workroom area by his office, which had been cleared of clutter to make way for a makeshift meeting table put together with assorted chairs and boxes to sit on. Though excitedly received, the underlying gravity of their desperation quickly precludes any celebration. The vacuum left by the missing Board members, Cephren, Cleo, Seven and especially Seymour hang in the room like a fog. Redman, however, cuts through the pensive mood with his somber warning.

'We will all be jailed or die, if we're caught,' he announces. 'Barker is mad, and madness appeases madness. He does this with particular finesse, and so too must we understand his every move.'

There is some heated discussion on whether or not his death would topple the government machine he had built. As Olivia had said, both Vince and Mita fervently believed his removal was imperative. Chromolox has never seen Mita so passionate.

'I've never hated anyone, but Del Barker,' she angrily volunteers to Chromolox.

Vince on the other hand betrays a seriousness she has never seen. Apparently, he is the most wanted by Barker and had been living like a refugee, spending nights in various places, but most recently at Mita's. Under the circumstances, Chromolox couldn't help but notice that Vince and Mita are not sitting together by accident and seem to thrive as a unit. Everyone, except perhaps Redman seems stressed out. Vince runs the networks and coordinates the guerillas with Mita's help. So it is safe to say, they are in charge. But the discussion is going nowhere and Chromolox has heard enough.

'Redman's right!' she exclaims above their voices. 'From the sounds of it, if we get caught, we'll die, mysteriously I suppose, to not attract attention. This won't do. As your past-President, if we are to survive, which is our duty to Sunsetwind, I submit the problem to, first: Gabriella, and then, to a vote.'

'The Board cannot vote officially without all present,' says Yani. 'I mean, if we're to play by the rules.'

'We have new rules, as an emergency. We must improvise. Gabriella?'

'Yes,' she replies indomitably, unfazed by the confusion.

'Is it within our mandate to murder Del Barker?'

'According to Sunsetwind law, of course not, but we haven't any mandate; then again neither did Flower Child when she purportedly killed Darabak.'

'Point taken; all right, so then is it within our right to execute Del Barker?'

'The prime directive of Sunsetwind gives no person or Board that right; only I have the right upon conviction, or our judges may send someone to their death, but only if the people wish it in a referendum.'

'Okay, given the circumstances what is your judgment?'

Gabriella, who has presided over the justice system sits pursing her lips for a moment. 'You know,' she says, 'we don't really have a law that he broke. The fact that a foreign power placed him in the position he holds lies so outside our experience as a nation that the closest we come to dealing with his corruption is unlawful seizure of property. Now, in terms of his abuses of power, we have always, at least since the last Election Act of 2271, had the Board's Power of Removal with the use of force if necessary. But if convicted of these crimes, he may spend his life in the Detention Facility, but certainly not execution. He'd have to kill someone himself for that and only if the people requested it, and there has never been a case where they have.'

'Chromolox, we've been through this exercise!' exclaims Vince, unable to control himself. 'What kind of charade is this? We're in no position to pretend we really care about him.'

'Let her finish,' declares Redman, soberly. 'Chromolox wasn't President for nothing.'

'The use of force if necessary, you said, Gabriella?' quizzes Chromolox.

'Yes, in which this is a case in point.'

'Good, so if someone dies as a result of such force, would the enforcer be liable to criminal charges?'

'Not if he or she were acting within their right as representative of the people.'

'Okay, so I propose we remove Del Barker by force. All in favour, let me see your hands.'

It is unanimous, including Redman.

'Okay, now that brings us to how we remove him. It was brought to my attention that I was the best choice to undertake this job. May I ask why?'

'He has put up walls, Chromolox,' declares Vince, impatiently. 'We think you're the only one who could gain access to him. He's never in public, you know.'

'Maybe, but maybe not, then what?'

Once again they debate heatedly.

'Please!' urges Chromolox. 'If this is all you have come up with, we've already lost. When I saw him after my incarceration in the Pyramid, I was scanned thoroughly.'

'Del Barker has a Trip-C,' speaks up Mita, more subdued.

'Do you mean to say we should be looking for Mr. Wall, or his daughter, the assassin, so-to-speak, of Impala?'

'Whatever gadget she had would still be scanned.'

'Not necessarily,' says Bill. 'Scans are designed not to affect implants. We believe the girl was completely innocent of Impala's death. She was given an implant that was made to create a distortion field around a specific implant. Only the Chicagos know exactly what Impala had, so they used someone who had the type that activated his. We haven't any idea what kind of Trip-C Del has. We'd have to get that information from the Chicagos, which is futile, and then we'd have to make one with the necessary combinations to distort it so that it would implode. These are deadly devices with some phenomenal technology. So, why aren't people being blown up all the time? They are very specifically tuned to exact harmonics. And there may well be some remote triggering effect.'

'So what you're saying is that we couldn't kill him that way,' says Chromolox.

'Yes.'

'Any other suggestions?'

None are forthcoming.

'What have you all been thinking?' she wonders incredulously. 'Now that we've got that out of our system, let's move on to some reality. I have to know what Cephren has come up with respect to Jimmy's Chip. What do we have? Redman?'

'You're a welcome addition here, Chromolox. I was beginning to wonder where the Sunsetwinders had gone, including myself. We've struggled at great risk to network our present circumstances – just the simple getting together has worn us down, yet I feel younger everyday. I don't think there's a tonic like fear. Old folks should get a dose of it from time to time. If you don't keep young, you die.'

They all laugh.

'But to answer your question,' he continues, 'Cephren's great breakthrough so far is his nomination for the Earth Chair. He's made some wild statements, the best being that if he was to be elected, he would bring us into a Galactic Confederation. We are very earnestly waiting for some concrete intelligence in this matter. Before Heyoka Yellow Tooth was abducted by the Chicagos, she told me over the short-wave she could possibly have something that might help us. We have reason to believe she's being held in the Bungalo. I have a feeling that Cephren knows something, but is hesitant to reveal it to us for fear of its getting into the wrong hands. I don't blame him, but I do wish he would let us in on it somehow.'

'What is this something,' asks Chromolox.

'Heyoka has a medallion of some sort,' says Mita.

'Orange gold,' claims Redman.

'That is the element we need,' Mita resumes. She looks tired and flushed as if she is fighting a germ. Vince picks up where she stops.

'If I could get this orange gold – unumpentium (element 115), I might be able to adapt it in the Volcano, because its reactor is the only one that might withstand the fusion charge of unumpentium and resultant anti-matter viscosity. However, I think the whole reactor would have to be refitted with an unumpentium alloy lining at the very least. The problem is logistics. Where can I work? How would I be able to forge a new reactor, and how on earth do we get the Volcano back to be refitted? For all I know the whole machine may have to be redesigned. Theoretically, I have the propulsion and structural dynamic ratios, but we really don't have any idea of the kind of power we are dealing with here, I mean element 115, when bombarded with protons it theoretically stabilises as element 116 releasing a perfectly clean anti-matter charge that we have only dreamt about. I need materials, a factory, people: it's an impossible task without more information. This is the sort of thing that takes years, not months. That's why we have been working on assassination, Chromolox. We can't seem to be able to do much else.'

'How about revolution?' quips Chromolox.

'We'd be squashed at the first hint,' says Yani.

They all become reflective. Chromolox feels let down. She was expecting more progress to have been made.

'What of Cleo, Redman?' she wonders.

'Cleopatra, my dear, would love to be let loose on Mr. Barker, but I'm afraid she'd get herself killed. Just as well she's out there. She called me the other day on the shortwave saying she was hooking up with Cephren. She alluded to something I'm not very clear on. She says we have a spy – though never intended to be a spy – in Chicago, who also doubles for them. I have a hunch, from what Cleo implied, that this spy may have sold us down the river, but has gained some rather good credentials. Have you any idea of whom she's speaking of?'

Chromolox sighs. She knows exactly whom she was speaking of, that talented little nosy sister of her dearest friend, Season. 'Treason Honey,' she utters beneath her breath.

'Who?' barks Redman.

'Treason Honey!' she says out loud. The room is silent. No doubt after the invasion everyone had been saturated with news of Chromolox's affair with her sister, and the well-founded suspicion that Treason had been implicated as a traitor in the invasion, because of her culpable disappearance and alleged homing point for Cephren's whereabouts.

'I know what you're thinking everyone,' she asserts self-consciously. 'But aside from my personal *peccadilloes*, I believe Treason, for whatever she's done or was set up to do, will redeem herself, especially if she knows that her stepfather, whom she dearly loved, was killed; we must reach her somehow. She may know what happened to Heyoka.'

'I think Cleo is handling Treason,' says Redman. 'And you don't know what we're thinking, Chromolox; and whatever it is, it's not about that…feel free, girl!' he remonstrates for her benefit.

'How is Cleo handling her?' asks LeRoy, ignoring the sentiments.

'She's always handled her, or thought she did; no one really handles her from what I understand. She's as wild as a coyote bitch in heat.'

'What is Cleo going to do?' queries Chromolox.

'Perhaps go to Chicago with Cephren under his diplomatic immunity,' proposes Redman.

'Then Treason would find him,' decides Chromolox, following his lead. 'She'd risk her life to see her Chairman. Over the Christmas season, Cleo assigned her to Cephren. From what I gather, she attempted to seduce him every night, but even Treason had met her Waterloo in that regard as a cunning seductress. You know Cephren.'

There is more laughter except from Mita, who looks pale and excuses herself.

'Well, then, there's little more we can do except wait for our moral master,' adds Vince, cynically referring to Cephren. 'What an extraordinary guy,' he goes on. 'I just don't understand him.'

'Meanwhile, Vince, let us plan a revolution,' insists Chromolox glaring at him. 'Our people need leadership. And a martyr or two. Any takers? Vince?'

'It's suicide,' he replies. 'Besides, you need me.'

'It's the only way,' she says looking around.

'What do I have to do?' asks Redman.

'Count me in,' says LeRoy.

'You got yourself a martyr, honey,' declares Gabriella.

'And me,' says Olivia, following the piper.

The Deerhills throw in their support.

'Now we're talking,' avers Chromolox. 'Vince and Mita will be needed elsewhere, but the rest of us are expendable, okay? No, Redman, you man the communications, and Bill or Yani, one of you must stay home to help Redman and Vince. Okay?'

'Yes,' they all agree.

'Good, now this is the plan: each of us will be given a district and all loyal guerillas within that district. Get the word out there: now is the time! To the towns and villages and farms! The guerillas will know what to do; they've been trained for this thanks to Cleo, and are probably just waiting for our orders! We must set a date . . . how about the 15th of March, the Ides of March? We'll call it Caesar's Revenge.'

Jan. 23. 96

Things have been moving at such a rip tide, it seems I haven't been able to sit down and collect my thoughts for days now. The decision to run for the Earth Chair has been the greatest boon to my flagging spirits, but the part of me that feels that I could be a major contender is reinforced by the rush to my senses that Anna Gram should indeed be my political running mate. The surprise of her life came when I revealed in her suite, after the sudden altercation with Trinny's commandos that my true identity was Cephren Path. She paced back and forth, I think pondering whether to reject or embrace me on the spot. She did neither. She simply apologised for being what she deemed 'flippant'.

'You must think me a tart,' she said.

I apologised for my duplicity, after which she then feigned to chastise me for not remaining incognito. It was her way of endearing me to her again.
I responded by saying it didn't really matter anymore; the Chicagos knew where I was and that I must leave that night. Seven Moons had found a potato transport that was returning empty to Prince Edward Island. The transport was big enough to move the Volcano too. We made arrangements to transport Seven's emop in a subsequent trip, hopefully to escape detection and concordantly spill a rumour that we were planning to head for Vancouver Island.

I am presently in my emop on the ocean floor in Oyster Bay near Sunnyside P.E.I. Runaway is here and will watch over me while I subsume myself yet further into Jimmy's Chip. I believe I understand the program now (if you can call it a program). One lets the mind go with it wherever it wants to take you and the program will decide what you need to hear according to your needs. And like an invitation it will lead you to what you require, one can only hope. I believe it responds to one's mental inclination if that inclination is not threatening or incompatible in any way. It really works like a merging of minds – its mind or technology is far beyond my own comprehension other than my intuitive feelings. For example, I have a hunch that once again inside, it will take me to exactly to where I left off before. Or in terms of future reference, if my hunch is correct, its source of information may be limitless, even taking me out into the galaxy. It very well could be God in a chip. I do not doubt it could take me anywhere, or discover, see and penetrate anything in the entire universe. There is an omniscience in this chip that exceeds the imagination. But at present, I must pursue my quest to save Sunsetwind.

Along that reasoning, I must further reflect on that last wonderful evening in Ottawa (notwithstanding a near catastrophe), I sincerely tried to keep emotionally clear of Anna, but her disarming humour seemed to frustrate every effort. I have tried to convince myself that my conscience is clear, but a resurgent guilt keeps prying me away. Is it my responsibility to Sunsetwind or humanity? I don't know. Is it the Mita mystery, or is it just a post-adolescent regret or even long-festering melancholy? Anna asked me when we spoke long into the night if there was another woman and I said no, but that I thought I was being loyal to someone who represented my homeland – an anchor of sorts, not that anyone was in any way pining for me emotionally. She reflected on that and our earlier intimacy and related her own experiences with men that generally fell flat because of her own peculiar needs, which were both occupational and emotional. I came to the conclusion that I had penetrated the real Anna, the rootless soul; she desperately sought someone willing to accept her as she was, all baggage included. We did seem to have a natural way with each other. I joked that she was just too hot to handle. She somehow complimented my retiring nature and I her intellectual rapport. I even think she found my lumbering appearance rather attractive. At fifty, soon to be fifty-one March 2nd, I have been told I can pass for forty or younger. She told me her age, which surprised me. I assumed she was twenty-nine for some reason, when in fact she had just turned thirty-eight. Needless to say, she appreciated my misassumption.

She insisted we go for a quick dance at Gravitas in the old House of Commons. Her instincts were superb. We received all kinds of adulation. She name-dropped me with such craft that I bathed in the limelight as I never had before. She also danced me so well that I didn't quite appear the complete ass. Our pictures were splashed across the news. One caption read: "Anna

Gram and Chairman Path? Who found whom? A match made in Heaven – the sultry actress and dispossessed statesman sizzle amidst rumors of his political rehabilitation. Is Path running for the Earth Chair?" Actually, Anna tipped off the concierge by saying: 'Do you think I'd make a good running mate?' The concierge replied, 'Perhaps, but I think you'd make a better goddess.' We shared a laugh. Later, in the Prime Minister's suite she kissed me again when we bid each other goodnight. Feeling relieved somehow, I held her closely and wanted to continue, but she kindly demurred, saying, 'Chastity is your ticket, darling. You have too much riding on this and I want to help you, not sink you with a sex scandal. I have to politicise myself, not submit to some sellout. I want to speak out on your behalf. I don't think we should work together too much.' I thought about that and for the time being agreed. I then stated that I would be leaving to attend some unfinished business, but that Seven Moons would be in touch with an agenda. I thanked her again and said we could probably meet in England within the next fortnight.

Now my thoughts turn to Sam. Poor kid is studying to be a Buddhist priest. Runaway said he was in good spirits, though. I wish I could speak to him, but that would be too risky right now. Later, when appropriate he could stay near me during the campaign. We will have a lot of fun, even if we lose.

I am excited about getting back into Jimmy's Chip. The tunnel has blown me away. I haven't told anyone, because I know if the information gets into the wrong head, we wouldn't have any chance of recovering what might be crucial to our plan. To think that during all these years, a tunnel existed under my very nose. I have walked across that field a thousand times. I sat and meditated by those ruins for as long as I can remember. I had always known they belonged to my ancestors, but had had no proof up to now that they were also Flower Child's aka Terrie Barnett. Blood runs thick; but this tunnel, does it go to the bunker? Redman might not be too exhilarated to know that he lived in Flower Child's bunker; it would become a national shrine, and he could be forced to move. I can't wait any longer. I'll sign off, dear reader, until next time.

The familiar spray of stars are bedazzling before him. He can even feel their awesome presence like a draft of fresh, cool air. Moving amidst them, as if in his own constellation, around and around, he slowly views the three dimensional vastness. Earth is nowhere in sight, but he sees the sun and where it fits in its own galaxy. He moves there brushing past the outer planets, three of which are lined up and come towards the now visible earth, hovering then to watch the ocean blue behemoth turn on its axis into the sun.

He focuses on the North American continent and descends to Great Blue Lake and that drumlinised till plain where Flower Child had just descended beneath the ground. He now sees her hand on the switch in the faint light emitting from above the hole in the well casing. He smells the cool, pungent air. She lowers the handle on the switch. There is a slight delay before a series of bulbs flicker, then hold their charge steadily extending down the passage into the distance as far as she can see. With eyes wide open and bursting curiosity, she follows the moderately down-sloping grade for more than three hundred meters (a thousand feet) and comes to a series of steel doors. They are locked. She looks high and low for a key, but finds none. Instinctively backtracking she slides her hand along a deep cement groove between the ceiling slab and wall containing strapped polyethylene pipes and wires. Almost all the way back to the entrance about three bulbs down from the switch, a set of keys are stuffed back in a recessed crack. Whoever had put them there had been very thorough by inserting a shallow steel casing so in case the cement settled from stress, the keys would not be lost.

Back at the door, she tries the keys. The second one works and the door opens easily. Behind it is a huge room, full of supplies of all kinds. There are power tools, small fusion generators, assorted parts, hardware, glass, lumber, appliances, utensils, paints and thousands of miscellaneous items. Wow, is all she can utter. She goes to the next door. It opens into a food supply room. It is dry and cool, about two degrees Celsius. There are tons of boxes full of cans of vegetables, fruit and stew, boxes of dry foods such as vegetables, pasta and beans, vacuum-sealed plastic bags full of many kinds of flour and whole grains, spices, dried dairy products, vitamins and even a corner full of medical supplies. It is a survival cache that could last a lifetime for many people. Stupefied, she goes to the next door. In it are about a hundred burlap bags of seed grain piled to the ceiling. Beyond it in an unlocked adjacent room are thousands of new and used clothing articles, from children's sizes to large, casual and formal, winter and summer. Also on deep shelves piled to the ceiling are hundreds of pairs of footwear: boots, shoes, runners, and rubbers of all sizes. She always had wondered where Scratch found new boots for her; she assumed he had scavenged abandoned homes and stores in the towns. But they had been long emptied of their goods and most in disrepair by abandonment. She wonders why Scratch never told her about this place sooner. She opens the next door and finds out why. The room was a munitions depot of old guns, new guns, flash guns, stun guns, mortars, missiles, tons of ammunition, special gear, fatigues and bombs. Scratch had obviously been afraid that the Trashies would find it. They could have fielded a small army, a malevolent army. She moves unhesitatingly to the next door that opens to a utility room. There is a generator mounted on a cement platform with a wooden surface. It glows a bluish light from its force field. It is no more than half a meter high and three quarters wide. Cables come out of it and snake out through the walls to the various rooms. Another smaller door exits ninety degrees from the direction of the previous doors that had followed in a straight line. She opens this door which leads down a passage at a steeper angle and comes to another tunnel leading uphill at another right angle. At the angle, there is a big door but none of her keys work, so she walks up the tunnel and comes to yet another door. The last key opens it into the smallest room yet. Here there are many personal articles: papers, books, magazines, all from long before the Asteroid. There are photos in a wooden box, some very peculiar ones that catch her eye immediately. The first one she picks up is of a middle-aged man standing with one of those creatures she had met in the woods that horrible night long ago. The eerily beautiful creature is only as tall as the man's chest and holds her hand up, as if she was waving. She has dark hair with large blue yet sadly foreboding eyes garlanded with that wispy hair. Flower Child shudders and puts the picture down. An old computer resting on the simple wooden desk made from bricks and boards catches her eye. She pulls another box up to sit on and scrutinizes the keyboard. It reads *Compact Custom* on the bottom of the screen. Noticing that the unit is wired into the wall switch, she presses the power button. The screen comes to life after a series of beeps and shows a view of the night sky cosmos. Never having operated a machine like this, Flower Child has no idea what to do. She presses the enter button and a series of codexed symbols appear. She figures out that an arrow could be moved with a round thing, so she moves it to the first symbol. Nothing happens so she presses the enter button again and the screen brings up an old man sitting comfortably in an armchair. It is the same man as in the photo, though older. The man, wearing a rumpled navy tweed jacket and old cottons with leather ankle boots is about eighty she presumes. His hair is white and thinning. He has about five day whiskers and smiles pleasantly. His blue eyes sparkle and look at her as if they even recognise her.

'Hello,' he says. 'Jim Pidgeon's the name; *Don't Spite Him* is the game. And if you want to be good, you must enter the wood.' He then disappears and the night sky returns. Poor Flower Child tries every symbol with the same results. She is unable to figure out what this odd character means. So after a time she shuts it off and with a sigh turns and rummages through some of the other things. She is overjoyed that she has found this little treasure trove, especially the thousands of books. It instantly becomes her secret garden and no one would know about it, except Remy. The munitions worry her, so like Scratch she too would keep them a secret.

Hours later, she exits the room and goes back to the last locked door. She can't find the key after looking everywhere and assumes it must be on the other side. There had to be a secret passage leading from their living space to connect with the tunnel. Finally, she goes all the way back to the well, shuts the switch, closes the door, climbs up the ladder, looks around to see if anyone is about, then gets out and strains to replace the insert cap. Succeeding, she covers the well with debris as it was before.

No, no Flower Child, go back! urges Cephren, I must get into that program! That's what I've been looking for! But she walks back down across the field into the maple wood to the bunker. Remy would be home by now, she muses thinking longingly of him. She wants love to be the standard of their new world. It is within her grasp to mold a society with the supplies and knowledge from the tunnel beneath. She wants Remy to round up all the able-bodied men and women for miles around and meet with her. She would direct a campaign to create a country with law and order. Borders would be devised, a system of rule established. She would assume the role of overseer until a fair system of power was achieved. She would back this fledgling country with a militia armed with her own arsenal. She isn't sure just yet how she could accomplish that without giving up the secret. Maybe Remy would know. He could remove the necessary supplies when needed. The country she envisions, Sunsetwind, would one day encompass Great Blue Lake.

She goes to the trap by the old log and climbs down into the bunker. Remy is napping on the ratty mattress with a tattered Time magazine on the floor. DOOMSDAY! is boldly written across the cover – the world in chaos and panic the final days before impact. She had read it a hundred times, people scrambling for supplies, going underground in the vast government bunkers and corporate research facilities wherever they were located, masses of people moving away from coastal areas, the sick and starving left in their misery, governments collapsing, anarchy in the west, armies rudderless, each hopeless under ineffective leadership, survival of the fittest. It goes on and on.

Humanity had reached an apogee of mismanagement, foreclosed to nature to sort it out.

Flower Child sits beside Remy and puts her hand on his hip. He reaches for her and they curled up together with his arm around her.

'Where have you been?' he murmurs.

'At the ruin,' she says snuggling in.

'I made some pancakes, if you're hungry.'

'Mmm, later.'

Cephren meanwhile, is impatient. He manages to remove himself from her proximity. He must get away, as doesn't want to be there. He rises up above the bunker and goes back to the ruin. Easy as pie, he thinks. Why couldn't I do this before? Experience, echoes the response. But even with experience he can't penetrate the darkness beneath in the tunnel. He can only envision the computer and Jimmy Pidgeon. *Don't spite Him* is the game. A game called *Don't Spite Him?* What kind of game is that? he wonders. If you want to be good, you must enter the wood? What wood? Another anagram like *atom deeds fit* derived from the 'maplewood' line in his enigmatic poem? Cephren attempts to make words using the letters in *Don't Spite Him.* After many tries, the best he can come up with is The Midpoints. *The Midpoints.* Nothing happens when he processes it. The midpoints between what? The one thing that comes to his mind is an astrological term – the midpoints on a composite chart. Could it be the natal midpoints between none other Jimmy Pidgeon and Danielle Perreault? He quickly computes the birth information that becomes instantly accessible through the X13. Jimmy – born November 23, 1980, 12:32 AM EST, North York General, Toronto, Ontario. Danielle – born April 12, 1981, 12:28 PM EST, Hôpital Ste.Thérèse, Montreal, Quebec. Cephren works out the degree midpoints between each sun position and for all the planets. The numbers roll off his mind like water: 11-10-24-26-25-04-06-27-23-23-22.

For a split second, Cephren thinks he is back on Survivor's Walk during lunchtime, but as soon as his eyes focus on the apparel of the busy crowd, the unfamiliar thoroughfare, the generally antique ambience including ghetto blasters and lottery stands, he knows he is somewhere in the distant past. He observes after a while of adjustment the shocking reality of what he was witnessing: a teenage girl in a black leather jacket, a short black dress and light pink hose, ambling along without a care, stopping every so often to look into a store front. His heart begins to pound uncharacteristically. He looks at his own feet and hands; they too are unfamiliar. He tries to separate himself from the stranger standing in his place. The program won't give an inch; it wants Cephren right where he is. He can thrust up away only as high as the vented ceiling but powerless as he springs back down into this new body much like the retraction of a bungee cord. But like radar he can also pick up on the adolescent girl in the black leathers. He can even see what she is looking at, lingerie and evening wear – satins and silk, high fashion prices. Then he sees a few CDs in a music store: one by a raunchy female grunge band, and another by someone singing the chants of a medieval German Abbess, and of course, her favourite, Jim Morrison and the Doors. She slips both CDs inside her leather jacket leaving one out to buy. As she goes through the exit turnstile with another unassuming customer, the electronic buzzer blares away. The other customer who goes through turns in surprise to confront the floor manager who beckons immediately to him, as Danielle has already disappeared into the crowd to quickly hide the discs in a leafy tropical garden arrangement, and turn back innocently to the music store to wonder whether the buzzer had gone off for her. The manager looks at her and seems to stand mesmerized by her jet-black hair, lily-white skin and dark green eyes, before apologizing profusely for any inconvenience they may have caused.

Jimmy, who stands bemusedly watching all of this with his hands in his pockets, suddenly turns away as she walks close by not giving him the slightest notice of recognition although she attended the same school and had actually met him briefly through his best friend's brother, Jerome or J, a dropout, four years his senior. Jerome, according to Ricky (Roderich), the brother, had been quite taken by this French-Canadian girl. Jerome had nick-named her "Snow White" and sometimes "Morticia" but let it be known that she was his "bitch". Jerome and Ricky Fleming are black, but that's where the similarity stops. Ricky is an Honours student and Jerome the leader of the Jam, a gang. Their clubhouse was sometimes the utility storage room of that same North York mall, by an arrangement with the night janitor, Mosh, a Jam Honouree, whereby they could use the facility that had an inside and outside door by the garbage ramp. No one ever comes in without Mosh's knowing about it as he had the only key, except for the supervisor and manager. But Mosh keeps all supplies topped up in the maintenance room and when stocks were refilled, the supervisor had his inspection with fair warning from Mosh to the Jam. It is common knowledge that Jerome alone wants personally to introduce Snow White to the clubhouse. The only amenities are a hotplate, mattress and ghetto-blaster of course. But it is Jimmy who feels weak at the knees within view-ing distance of Danielle because of an overwhelming infatuation.

James Terrence Pidgeon has lived his entire life in the West Hill subdi-vision, "the Bricks". From the earliest age he remembers the bleak, treeless landscape where new homes pop up by the hundreds. Out back from his basement bedroom window what had been once a desolate lot becomes the newest subdivision. In his mind, life is a series of subdivisions and emerging squares. Eventually little trees become bigger and the squares flesh out bit by bit, but the sterile environment cannot keep him down. His sanctuary is his mind and what his mind can plot on a hard drive. He has an irrepressible desire to know the physical engineering of nature, complimented by a wayward imagination. Even at a young age his inter-ests focus onto the supreme challenge of understanding the universe. Phe-nomena such as light and gravity are the superpowers giving the essence of life. Jimmy is fascinated with the idea of harnessing these basic phenom-ena into practical uses, specifically to engineer vehicles to travel in space. It has always been a dream of his to supercede our terrestrial bounds, as if possessed with the thought that decoding the secrets of nature were within his grasp. But there is more to him: he had a flair for words and numbers and would work them into beautiful patterns dabbling with poetry and quantum formulae just to fill his time. Music and visual art even found a place in his scheme of things, but when it came to school and an organised regimen, he faltered miserably. His boredom arose not from the lack of stimulus but from too much wishful thinking and distraction. Jimmy was a clean-cut dreamer. His dreams were partly the product of the cinematic vision of late twentieth century Hollywood. Any adolescent growing up in the 1990s was inundated with that accessible fantasy, as well as the ever-growing intimacy with new technically graphic interpretations of human events, be it contemporary, historical, or futuristic. Violence, sex and morality (or lack thereof) were all wrapped tightly in a package designed to deliver with uncanny effect. The reality of life, however, rendered these impressions into an over-stimulated juvenile mind a confusion so demoralising, many kids of his generation were like empty vessels adrift in a sea of sensationalism unable to find their moorings. And stereotypically, Jimmy ate it all up like candy living through the easy mediums of video and music. There was nothing unique or rebellious about his accommodation to the commercial venues. The big difference between Jimmy and most of the others was that he never stopped believing in the big pie in the sky, as he was an inveterate optimist; he just wanted to prove it for himself. Unfortunately, this kind of optimism was a terrible thing when one discovered that all he or she had dreamed of as a kid was insignificant and underestimated, and that most of their ideas had already been sold and marketed to the economic grist mill before they were even born. Jimmy was sold the moment he first heard Nirvana, Pearl Jam, Fried Pumpkin or whatever and also some of the 'big' movies that highlighted the nineties: Titanic, JFK or Independence Day. The great thing about Jimmy was that success was being true to your beliefs and an incidental fame was simply a thorny reward for your pains. Therefore, to the end of his life, after all he had accomplished, he remained incredibly anonymous, believing that fame and adulation were a disease like cancer and to be preempted at every opportunity. This was the essence of Jimmy: he sold himself to the elusive dream, but never the illusion; yet ironically the illusion of his dream sufficed to sustain his oft-challenged humanity. This began that day in the mall and would continue until the end of his life.

Watching Danielle walk pass that day, Jimmy, the quintessential mall rat with a free pass anytime into the 'club', turns away from his bliss, not able to bear his crush for Danielle as she comes by. This shyness is symptomatic of his curious nature. It is an incorrigible deprecation; he would separate himself from the person or object that he thought he desired, almost like a martyring to some fidelity of self-preservation. Is he worthy, or is she worthy? He will be the equilibrium – the template of desire and sacrifice. The result doesn't matter; his reaction is compulsive and feeds his fire. This is his poetic soul.

Danielle on the other hand is the absolute opposite. What she likes, she takes; it is just that easy. There is no moralising or thought processing; it just happens that way. She has learned from a very young age the value of great expectations: zilch. You simply do: you survive. And Danielle is very smart. She emits a kind of anti-popular persona who yet seems popular, Jimmy can't help but notice. Though everybody knows her and talks about her. She can cast a spell over people and remain distant, yet personal. And she must obviously be the mall rat extraordinaire, if her shoplifting was any indication. What does she really think? Jimmy is traumatised by her uncanny coolness: in fact, her intelligence is as profound as Jimmy's, the difference being that her depth is so obscure no one can plummet it, and she is a genius in evading any scrutiny of her feelings. Jimmy couldn't have known this of course, so he is at a disadvantage. As far as she is concerned, all boys with few exceptions are interested in her, so she has the advantage: a kind of preemptive strike. Even Jerome embarrassed himself the day he approached both Jimmy and Ricky with Danielle to boast to her that Ricky, his brother, was an Honours student too. Danielle laughs, moves away from Jerome and puts her arm around

Ricky to mock lightly in her Quebec accent, 'It is difficult being smart, don't you think Ricky? Everyone thinks you have it all together, when you really don't.' Ricky is struck dumb by her attention, which proves her point, and makes them all laugh including Ricky; but it is Jimmy that has the temerity to say: 'Hey, I'm not all that together, and I get Bs.' She stares at him for a moment. Jimmy can feel the casual intensity in her eyes. Danielle then ignores him and Jimmy just smiles back, already smitten having just met her. However, she more than noticed those sparkling blue eyes, plain complexion on a well-chiseled face, his medium build, messy brown hair, Jimmy Hendrix t-shirt and features that seem almost to go over like a hippy redux a quarter century out of date. He presumes mistakenly she is too caught up in herself, but for Jimmy that moment in time was to be cherished as long as he lived. He sees her as his secret dark angel – an exquisite natural beauty: delicately white complexioned, dark green-eyed, dark red-lipped with long, rich, black hair with a mini braid on the left side. But what really gets to him is her persona: it appears to him that she is not just foreign even for a Quebecois, but oddly so. He sees something in her that defies his usual keen analysis. She has that aura of devil-may-care inscrutability. Pervading Jimmy is a sickening premonition that he is about to suffer terribly on account of that one mutual look. He loved her instantly, shockingly. He excuses himself in a dismissive manner and for the rest of that day avoids her like the plague. He runs home utterly destroyed and writes that desperate first poem which would become the opening stanza of a long rhapsodic literary process: the juvenile induction to one of the most indispensable quotients of the human condition. It reads:

Plutonium Sucks

Forsake me, babe.
Save yourself a headache,
Just dump me without the psychology:
And the haunted choirboy treatment

I'll be your underworld demon
Emerging in the senses
Like chemotherapy:
Toxic and pale green.
You can cut out my tumor with your switchblade,
Precisely please, it's yours –
Then cure me of you
So I, in dear hell
Will post the hours for centuries,
Puzzling in your drug
And microwave eyes
Paranoid of your cool white hand,
And your ghostly halo –
We are mutated into a new isotope
Irradiating, irradiating . . .

As it turns out, Danielle soon tires of Jerome, who takes her back to the clubhouse one day and overplays his palace thing (which it actually was for a mall rat), but she turns cold when he does his schmooze thing, kissing her so oppressively he almost suffocates her in his anxiety. Turning beet-red, then laughing at him, she tells him he reminds her of a Wally Cleaver on crack.

'Okay Morticia,' he says tediously, 'let's turn the page of the script.' Jerome doesn't stand a chance, especially if he needed a script, even with the hash or the cocaine. She is so cool the drugs (which she freely indulges) has only a galvanizing effect, quite in contrast to Jerome. He puts his arm around her and he apologises about his "nerd" brother Ricky. Danielle then asks Jerome what he knows about Ricky's friend Jimmy. Jerome hesitates, then laughs saying, 'You mean Wonder Bread,' and how he only tolerated him for something to laugh at like his own brownie brother.

'Then why do they call you the Jerk?' she quizzes, amused.

'I think maybe you should find out, Snow White.'

He then takes her forearm and gently directs her hand onto the lump in his pants. She doesn't immediately remove it, but neither does she entice it.

'So you are named after your cock, no?' she teases.

'Just the Jerk, like hot pork, baby.'

'Like a pig?' she teases removing herself.

'Yeah,' he intones, holding her tightly. 'You gotta try jerk food?' He gently pushes her back on the mattress.

'No,' she replies, slithering with agility out from under his stoned body to kneel beside him as he still held her. 'I don't eat pork.'

'Hey, baby, don't worry; I'm cool. There's always chicken.' He pulls her back to him restraining her. She reaches down and gives him a gentle squeeze of his balls. He relents slightly. Then she squeezes them as tightly as her strength can manage. The shock from pleasure to excruciating pain releases his grip instantly and she quickly leaves him lying there on the mattress a dithering mess.

Back in the mall, as she is coursing by, Jimmy turns away mortified she might see him. After a moment, he looks expecting to see her fading into a blank crowd like Eurydice, but just about jumps out of his skin when he realises she is standing there beside him with a cute smirk on her face. Her eyes seem even more electric than before. All he can do is smile stupidly, which she doesn't acknowledge.

'You English,' she says in a deadpan Quebecois accent, 'are too waspy. You either pretend to be something you're not, or you're nothing at all.'

Jimmy's first reaction is absolute panic. Not a word comes to his lips. He gazes mutely for those few moments – their eyes lock like two species viewing each other for the first time. As she is about to turn and leave, Jimmy surprises himself and speaks up: 'Maybe there's nothing I need to pretend about; besides, I didn't want to attract attention to you.'

'Attention? Pourquoi?' she wonders, smirking but staying.

'I saw what you did back there,' he says, referring to her shoplifting.

'Oh, and are you going to tell?' She is amused.

'Of course not, but I wonder why you do it, nevertheless.'

She looks around, back at Jimmy, who continues to stare at her, his blue eyes revealing powerful feelings. This surprises her. Feelings are something very private to her and it is written all over his face, but she does not really want to know what it is she sees in him. Feelings are a threat and too personal for comfort; yet she knows she likes him; she liked him the first time she had met him.

'What is your name again?' she asks.

'Jimmy Pidgeon,' he replies.

'Danielle Perreault,' she says holding out her hand.

Their hands feel good together, almost erotic. She suggests they go down to the lower level where all the food vendors are located. Jimmy shrugs and agrees. On the way, they walk down the esplanade; Danielle stops at numerous window displays. One particularly enthralling to her is a pseudo-ancient Egyptian fashion display. She keeps staring at one dress and jacket with sleek earth-tones. Jimmy imagines her dressed like that and fantasizes about buying her the outfit, but at $1399 dollars she'd have to steal it.

Sitting at a table among the claustrophobic subterranean fast food vendors, it becomes apparent after less than half an hour together that there is something exceedingly profound about their budding friendship. She sits and listens to him sincerely affected by his gentle speech and intelligent wit. She caves in to his beliefs about pyramid dating and the ancient Egyptians inheriting a legacy of knowledge from a civilisation far more remote in antiquity.

'New geological dating methods have indisputably put the building of the Giza pyramids to between 12 and 15 thousand B.C.,' he tells her.

'We must then live in a stupid time,' she comments lighting up another Lucky Strike, which she does with devoted frequency.

'Oh yes, they were tuned into the stars like we can't imagine. I really believe an alien race subsisted here because they couldn't return, or came here to colonize, or experiment.'

'It wouldn't surprise me,' she says. 'I saw a UFO above Montreal about five years ago. It was in the Gazette; many saw it including a scientist, but nobody pays any attention. People are not ready to accept them. But they're here, the aliens. And for anybody who actually sees them, they're real; and for the rest, we're lunatics. The governments are liars. I hate government. They make the people think they're stupid.'

'Why don't they want to meet us and help us?' asks Jimmy.

'Because as a race we are too primitive,' she states point blank. 'I would not want them to meet us. Well maybe Hendrix.' She smiles looking at Jimmy's shirt, then changes the subject as if it doesn't agree with her.

The conversation turns to politics. She announces she is a Separatist and claims separation isn't about sovereignty, it is about regionalism. She goes on to say that the whole world will become regional again, all working towards a universal understanding. It would be the only way to manage so many people. Jimmy concedes that regional politics would be more hands-on with local problems, but that federalism is no accident and that people need overall leadership. He explains that society isn't advanced enough to do it otherwise. They amicably disagreed with certain issues, but seem to thrive on their differences. She becomes quite passionate in political debate and swears that if she ever became Prime Minister (which she said was very unlikely), she would change the Constitution so that all regions could be free. From what? wonders Jimmy.

Conversation leads from one subject to another with no exhaustion in sight. It comes around to science, anti-matter and gravity propulsion. Jimmy's knowledge appears to be refreshing to Danielle, as she picks up on it openly. They are mutually impressed and even shy to look at each other too long because the feeling is so strong between them it almost hurts to look. And life is difficult for teenagers, so it isn't cool to act as if it was amazing. That's why she steals, she admits.

'I want people to think I'm good, when I love being bad; it's more fun,' she declares looking more sultry than ever, putting on her most cool vibes.

'You should come to my house sometime, Danielle; I'll show you my ufology collection. I have every magazine and book about it from Roswell up to the present time. I'll even show you my experiment.'

'Okay,' she says, without much interest.

They talk for an hour until the mall shuts down for the night. Jimmy walks with her over to Yonge St. and then to the street where her high-rise apartment is situated. They stand there in the clear, cool April evening. Danielle explains her circumstances in that she is only going to be there until the end of the school year. Her stepfather is a computer technician whose principal employer has been the federal government and they move around a lot. They were going to move to Calgary in June. The only reason she was in Toronto that year is because Ray, her stepfather, also did freelance work for companies, setting up new programs and software.

They say goodbye outside the apartment. She smiles, but doesn't seem in the least interested in a kiss. The fact is, it doesn't even occur to her, as she is buoyant with good feelings. Jimmy suggests that they do something on the weekend and she turns and says, 'Okay,' in that distant way before disappearing inside.

The following day after a sleepless night, Jimmy is perturbed that he hadn't seen Danielle at school. Although she is in a grade beneath him (he is in twelve), he had become aware over the last months when to best spot her during school hours. He doesn't even have her telephone number, so he feels a little on the outside fearing that she wasn't interested in him anymore. It is silly, but being for the most part a loner and not a people person like herself, as she has a visible persona, he feels the need to have at least her loyalty in this regard. Unbeknownst to him, Danielle had stayed home that day to finish a few essays, which were due. It isn't that she had to miss school, but she somewhat uncharacteristically couldn't face him in school, partly for Jimmy's own good, as she doesn't want Jerome to know that they are suddenly fast friends. But that is just an excuse; the truth of the matter is that she deems her own nature to be aberrant and unsuited to Jimmy's innocent charm; but significantly, in her own sleepless slumbers she can't get him out of her mind. It doesn't even occur to her that it might be infatuation or even love. Her natural response is just too uncom-fortable to face. Yet most of that day, his free and easy intellectual curios-ity and boyish charm had captivated her. It is Friday and she thinks that if she doesn't see him until Monday, maybe by then it would all go away and she could pick up her life as it had been before. Unfortunately, or fortu-nately as time would reveal, her life had been irrevocably changed forever.

So poor Jimmy, puzzled and hurt, as he had succinctly put down in his poem *Plutonium Sucks*, gets the sinking feeling she was opting out of their new friendship. And to make matters worse, Ricky, his best friend, tells him after their first class that Jerome is really pissed off. Mosh had men-tioned to Jerome that Snow White left the mall at closing with Jimmy and that in his words: ' . . . They were connected.' Ricky advises Jimmy to lie low and avoid the mall for a while until things cooled down or at least until he could somehow get through to his brother. 'But you know the Jerk,' he says, 'when the goin' gets bad, he gets worse.' Jimmy, however, doesn't seem very concerned; he had always had a way with the Jerk that disarmed him. Jerome referred to him not only as Wonder Bread but his Honky Nigger.

But the very next day, suffering with anxiety over Danielle, Jimmy can't stay home or concentrate on anything. He sets out for the mall ready to die under the switch-blade of Jerome. He has a fatalistic streak that emerges from time to time that one day would gain him some notoriety among the ruling elite.

He wanders around the mall looking for any sign of Danielle, but finding none he thinks he might just sneak down to the clubhouse to see if she was in any kind of trouble. Still nothing happening, he sits down in the same seats where he and she had had their magical afternoon. It makes him bitterly depressed. Lost in his reverie, he fails to notice Jerome and his friend Briar come up from behind. Dressed in their baggy coats, pants and runners, they each take an arm and playfully lead Jimmy away to the clubhouse. Jimmy smiles along too in haphazard damnation. He knows Jerome too well to actually fear him, but had never really been on the receiving end of his wrath. But someone has to pay for Jerome's humiliation.

It so happens that Ricky having called Jimmy's home, finds out that he is not there. This compels him to race for the mall and locate him before Jerome. Although Jerome does not live at home with his brother, Ricky had seen him earlier in his derelict flat. Jerome kicked him out, angered by Ricky's defence of Jimmy. 'Jimmy's a man, brother,' Jerome said, 'and a man must rise to his station. He just rose to the wrong station. Nobody fucks with me, man! Snow White is my bitch! We just had a little misunderstanding.'

When Ricky finally catches up with Jimmy, it is too late; he sees his brother escorting him across the long level to the clubhouse. Frantically, he runs back upstairs looking for security, but instead is surprised to find Danielle. He goes to her and blathers Jimmy's predicament. Without emotion she turns and heads down the escalator to the eating level. Ricky walks along explaining that they should call security. She wouldn't even dignify a response and keeps walking. Looking around, they enter the maintenance area and go to the storeroom. She knocks. Danielle hadn't even planned to go to the mall that day, but her own restlessness compelled her to do a little shoplifting to see if that might lighten her spirits. But she can only think of Jimmy. She had never met anybody like him in her short varied life, nor would she again, she thought. She just seemed incapable of carrying on with these feelings. And now this: what could be more perfect? she muses behind that door. If this isn't a way out, what is? She would save his butt then quietly dismiss him making him think he is unworthy, or some such idea.

The door opens. It is Briar, Jerome's cohort.

Hey J.,' he says, 'guess who's come to the party?'

Jerome comes to the door.

'Snow White!' he says, letting her in. 'Now that makes my day. We're just about to blow some sparkle, baby, just in time.'

Danielle sees Jimmy sitting on a box with that smile on his face. Her heart races, but no one would know.

'Sorry J.,' she says to him brightly, thinking about the other day but meaning otherwise. Then she adds, 'Hi Jimmy, you okay?'

Jimmy says nothing for a moment but quickly recovers, 'Yeah, how 'bout you?'

'Hey, Snow White,' interrupts Jerome, 'what's this bullshit? You gonna stiff my party with Wonder Bread here?'

'You're going to have to do a rain check on your party, Jerk.'

'I don't think so, baby,' snaps Jerome flicking out his knife and moving it in front of her face. 'The party's on me . . . '

'Jerome, take it easy, man,' says Ricky putting himself close to the knife. 'We're all friends here; Danielle and Jimmy 'r cool, okay?'

'Fuck you, nigger; we need some entertainment. You can have some action if you're good.' Jerome with the knife runs the flat side down between her breasts over her blouse beneath her open jacket.

'Easy Jerome, you have nothing to gain by this,' exclaims Jimmy, coming over beside Danielle. 'You think you're the only one who's ever been dumped?'

Danielle turns to look at Jimmy with a funny look on her face.

'Shut up!' yells Jerome, pointing his knife at Jimmy's face. 'Keep outta my face!'

'Jerome,' says Danielle, unflinching, 'what do you want?'

'Okay baby, I think you know what I want. I want you.'

'I can't believe I'm hearing this,' she says, looking at Briar. 'You are so juvenile, Jerome; I mean, would you please get off this gangsta shit?' She looks about in exasperation.

'I'll cut that pretty face, baby, if you don't apologise: on your knees now!'

'For what? And that's supposed to change my mind about you?' she asks.

'You know what I'm talkin' about, Snow White.'

'Why are you being such an asshole, Jerome?' demands Ricky.

'Fuck off brother. I got my pride. This is a matter of pride.'

'Jerome, let us go,' demands Jimmy, calmly. 'Well forget about the whole thing.'

'I'll deal with you in good time, Wonder Bread.'

'Like hell,' says Danielle to Jerome, before turning to Jimmy. 'Do you know what they're going to do with him?'

'Shut up, bitch! Now get down on three!' orders Jerome.

'You call yourself a big man? You're a joke!'

He grabs her by the hair and pulls her toward him.

'One!'

'My father was a Hell's Angel,' she mentions as calmly as she can, 'and they will come for you. Do you know what they are going to do to you?'

He throws her down on the mattress.

'Two!'

'They'll skin you alive in a vat of paint-remover . . .'

Incensed, he raises his hand to strike her, when both Jimmy and Briar make a lunge for his arm. In the scuffle, Briar removes the knife from his hand.

'J, easy,' mutters Briar, 'this bitch ain't no fool, man. We don't need this.'

Jerome is shaking all over, as Briar holds him back.

'Get out,' yells Briar, 'all of you, now!'

They all exit.

'I've never seen him so ticked,' says Ricky. 'It's the dope.'

Danielle twists her finger to her head. 'Psycho. I never knew he could flip out like that! He won't change; he'll get worse. I know the type.'

Jimmy looks over at her; but she doesn't look back.

'Come on,' she says on a lighter note, 'Let's get something to eat.'

They leave the mall and at Danielle's request choose an East Indian buffet. After, they go to a friend's house in Willowdale, whose parents are away for the weekend. A classmate of Danielle's who Jimmy and Ricky know, but are not impressed, is nevertheless ingratiating as he is another of Danielle's innamoratos. Some others arrive as the evening deepens. Danielle then secures a ride downtown to a reputed burlesque art show that someone claims to know is happening in a warehouse off King Street West.

That day and night are of the more memorable times in Jimmy's youth. From near catastrophe with mad Jerome to Danielle's brave intervention, not to mention Ricky's providential interloping, then Briar's fortuitous sense of fair play, they are freed from a random mugging or worse. Both Ricky and Jimmy had afterwards applauded Danielle's cool demeanour throughout the whole ordeal and the temerity of her counter-threats, which seemed so convincing. She simply shrugged them off not saying anything to arouse curiosity as to how she came up with the Hell's Angels story. They had then stuffed themselves with Tandoori chicken, curries, daita, dal and basmati. Preoccupied with her supper, Danielle doesn't pay much attention to Ricky's boyish panegyrics.

'Holy shit!' says Ricky. 'You hit the jackpot with that line. Briar figured dealing with Jerome was a better hedge than being skinned in paint stripper!'

Jimmy is more cautious and believes Danielle has exposed herself somehow and senses a deeper connotation to the whole episode. He knows she lived with her step-dad and real mom, but is curious about her origins to which any query is met with an immediate portcullis. Nevertheless, he lets her know his gratitude in a half-witted admonishing of her foolishness and she responds in her usual apathetic cynicism, indicating that she would do it for anybody.

'As a friend, I could do no less – *et rien de plus*.'

The arty warehouse party turns out to be a freak show. Jimmy and Ricky have never seen anything like it. Danielle, on the other hand fits in quite well and disappears for periods of time to emerge as if from some secret back space with a certain air of detachment. She basically ignores Jimmy and Ricky who slink around trying to appear innocuous. They stick out like typical suburban kids among the neo-punk demographics.

On the stage a mad speaker swivels around on a steel contraption. He looks like a day-glo Rasputin ranting like a street corner communist. Then the bands: *Bonked Mannequin*, and *Rat Soup*. The lead singer screeches go-go tunes to heavy metal. She wears a neon tiara on a literal rats nest coiffure with a little mounted cage and a brown mouse poking its head out of a hole in her hair. There are even uptown people dressed for the occasion in their black tie suits and high fashion evening dresses.

Danielle dances much of the time. Jimmy sips on a beer but won't indulge in the more exotic libations. Ricky acts a bit wildly having stoned himself on somebody's science lab cannabis. Everyone goes mad when the infamous *Cheeseburgers* take the stage by storm with their metal lullabies and ten-foot dildo balloon. The all-ladies band is dressed prissily but keep flashing their porno underwear in sync with the beat. Ricky is dancing with everybody including Danielle.

Insane! thinks poor Jimmy hanging back from the fiasco. In a wave of melancholy, he gains a deeper understanding of Danielle. If the party symbolised life, Danielle would always be front and center, dancing; and he would be back in the rear watching, thinking. His post-adolescent dream of Danielle by his side is an illusion. She would never stand by him. She would never be there for him. She would always be out there somewhere riding the crest of the happening – living the moment, whereas he lived for all time, something obscure, yet promising. But he knows he loves her and would do anything for her. He needs to penetrate her secret world and scale its formidable ramparts.

But Danielle is not unmindful of Jimmy and believes she knows him better than he knows himself. She notices him standing and looking only at her like a spot light, shining down from his blaze of light. She hasn't quite figured him out, nor would she ever, but she suffers through him a kind of catalyst to her very life force. Since she has known him a reluctant happiness has pervaded her soul; it was unasked for, even denied, but useless to resist. She can feel it extend from her toes through her loins to the top of her head like a vortex of light connecting to the very stars. Dancing and carrying on, she glances at him hovering on the outside, contemplating in that ridiculous intensity. She detests her old self, yet rejects the new. She knows in her heart of hearts that her love would bequeath his banishment, though she feels the immediate need to give herself, all of herself, body and soul to him. It scares her, because she doesn't want to hurt him in spite of her love, knowing she should never be with him. Yet meeting him is the catalyst that impels her to seek new ideals, something she has wanted to do for some time now. It is so simple, she thinks, though not quite ready to acknowledge change. The past scars are festering wounds.

Early that morning the three of them take the subway back to North York. They sit together leaning on one another, Jimmy and Danielle more fluidly. Ricky is just tired and wants to get home. Once they reach their stop, Ricky saunters off in his direction and Danielle and Jimmy are ready to go in theirs. They speak of nothing really, empty words to fill in the void left by the excitement. But saying goodbye Danielle hugs him and he reciprocates. They look into each other's eyes under the streetlights not so inclined to suppress their desires. And so induced in that split second of perfection they kiss deeply, sensually, like they have never kissed before. She frenchs him passionately: her tongue probing thirstily haven given up on her reticence to dismiss him. The sensation of the moment lingers timelessly until they stop nose to nose breathing in unison. Finally parting with nervous trepidation, he says he should walk her home. Holding each other without speaking a word, they are one person walking, before letting go at the apartment building. She says, 'Stay here, tonight. It's too far to walk home now.'

'Okay.'

Later in the apartment, she gets a blanket for him on the couch. She whispers that her parents are asleep, but wouldn't mind. She sits down beside him and puts her head against him. They fall back on the sofa and kiss again. Aroused again, they hungrily explore their passion. She removes her blouse and bra and he his shirt. Their body warmth kindles a feverous dilemma. It is no use: her warm white breasts and rosy nipples firming under his gentle caressing drive her beyond restraint. She reaches down and runs her fingers over his hard organ. Adeptly, she must have him out and caresses him playfully. The sensations are too much to bear; he removes his pants, and she hers. In the partial glow from the city night, she lies beneath him as he raises himself over her body. Their synergy has fused like a nebula. She opens her thighs without hesitation, and suspended in amazement, he holds back as she softly rubs him against her little black mound by arching her hips. Once accommodated they desperately cling to each other as powerful spasms catapult into a shocking ecstasy neither knew possible. Restrained from any verbal elicitation, due to the proximity of her parents, they twist and squirm frantically as they climax. Not until the hint of day does Danielle, half asleep, let him go. At her behest, Jimmy stirs from half-sleep and dresses to steal away. Feeling euphoric, spent and guilty, they want to avoid the awkwardness of breakfast with her parents. Kissing her good bye, he lets himself out.

In the weeks that follow right up to the end of the school year, their relationship for all appearances does not change a bit. Danielle is hardly one to display any form of public affection, nor is Jimmy. Yet, whenever alone together all pretensions fall away, as they literally devour each other. Ricky doesn't even have any idea what is really going on: Danielle is so aloof and Jimmy is just Jimmy – his usual affable self. Ricky sometimes advises that he should make a move on her; she just needs to be motivated. But Jimmy smiles and says he likes it the way it is, friendly with no expectations. His secrecy and modesty in this matter and for all purposes, Danielle's, are to remain the pattern the remainder of their lives. In no way is their affection for each other impugned upon as reckless temptation. They are following the yellow brick road one day at a time, but no Dorothy and her pals here: this is a road to the 21st century and a world to be stood on its ear.

For Jimmy, the first blow comes when Danielle announces to both

Ricky and him that she would be leaving at the end of June. Jimmy doesn't say much, though it dawns on him suddenly that she would be leaving his life – maybe for good, and he just can't see it that way. Danielle feels it too, but insists that she is leaving. Her announcement is really a reminder, the kind that says I'm not the writing type; I'm not the pining type; I'm not the romantic type; I'm the kind that reality bites and I've been bitten hard; accept it and be happy, because I will, in spite of this happiness we've had. She hardly glances at him.

However, in spite of her cool attitude, she plans a special day the next weekend. She convinces him to swallow a tab of Bazooka Joe blotter acid that he initially refuses but relents as she just blithely took hers. He is vulnerable and senses he has little choice if he wants to be with her. The day is hot and sunny and they take the bus to the zoo. On the way things become quite strange. They have a hard time looking at each other even at the most sober of times, their intensity is so great, but on the magic bus they would exchange long looks and break out laughing uncontrollably. People appear to be very odd which exacerbated their hyper mirth, compelling them to hysterics. By the time they reach the zoo, it becomes so ludicrous, the bus driver must tell them to join the zoo. Jimmy tells him with a straight face that the bus is a zoo of its own. Danielle then says sincerely that she is extraterrestrial. The bus driver shoos them away.

In the zoo things become outrageous. Visiting the monkeys causes such a stir on account of the monkey's sensing something out of the ordinary – especially in Danielle – some staff are summoned to move people along fearing a general uprising. Undeterred, the cacophony raised by the monkeys stirs the gorillas from their afternoon torpor, who begin thumping the glass partition so hard – again at Danielle – the gathering crowds begin to panic as mothers and fathers grab their children to race for the exit. Spontaneously, Jimmy and Danielle direct traffic so mellifluously the bewildered staff join them before Jimmy and Danielle jump into the throng and exit the building. Outside, they have to rest their tired diaphragms from so much laughing. Even outside when they come upon a seemingly friendly rhinoceros, they start up again but are pained to laugh as before for their spent energy. Now subdued, they gaze into the sad eyes of the rhino. For a moment before their eyes the animal transformed its unique DNA into a microcosm of all living matter appearing as a virtual bingo spin in which they are all unique mixes of the same basic ingredients and Jimmy and Danielle intuit their own bizarre equation. The rhino continues to look at them with those sad, absurd eyes as if to say: 'It must be nice.' Danielle says, 'And so it is: we must anoint the solemnities, my friend.'

They take a nature trail and find a remote piece of grassy turf surrounded by bushes near the wolves compound. Cryptically reflective, they make love in the hot sun relieved to be away from the genetic insanity. What began as a naturally glib conjoining becomes a deep, pensive copulation hanging on for nearly an hour. Exhausted and numb with the Bazooka Joe still coursing irreverently through them, they lie for another hour in a mindless stupor. Danielle finally sits up looking surreal in a kind of smiling melancholy, her long hair tousled about her face and naked body glowing in the sun, nipples like neon cherries, with Jimmy mesmerized, looking through her. She begins to tell him what only she knows in the entire world. It is a dark secret, and only he can know. She swears him to secrecy, because her life depends on it, saying enigmatically, 'The animals know about me, the animals know.'

'Know what?' asks Jimmy lethargically.

With a sudden pause and recognition of the moment, she seems to change her mind. Jimmy can tell by the altered incantation of her voice, but does not contend or question what she was about to say or not. Then she begins again, as if to wave off her indiscretion on some other tack. She reveals that three years earlier at the age of fourteen living with her mother who had been a heroin addict at the time, her father was a drug-crazed Hell's Angel who was known for being a little psychotic and had killed people before. The father came and went disappearing for months at a time. It so happened that one day he had become seriously indebted to a bald, fat, middle-aged "slime ball mafioso" she said, who supplied his father and mother's drugs. Her father in a careless drug-drenched bender put her young self on his bike and drove to this man's country house. She was left there for the entire weekend. Her mother meanwhile was so doped up she didn't know what was going on. Danielle speaks matter-of-factly about being subjected to the obsequious perversions of this "human jellyfish", as she described him. She had been told that she must save her mother and father's life by doing whatever was asked of her. She subsequently had her virginity taken and was sodomized. Danielle describes carrying out her supposed duty with such fear and zeal, Jimmy has to wonder whether she had lost her mind. When she was finally dropped off at home, she found her parents screaming at each other. Danielle had arrived so wasted and shell-shocked, the mother knew what had happened and in a fit of drugged rage went searching for a handgun to kill her husband. The father too began looking for the gun and beat the mother senseless when he couldn't find it. Danielle had previously hidden the gun herself because she was afraid her mother or father might use it. She then retrieved it and confronted her father who advanced aggressively towards her to take it. Danielle claims she didn't really mean to shoot him, but as if on autopilot shot him point blank in the head killing him instantly. The mother, almost beaten to death was unconscious at the time. After a while the mother revived and seeing the father dead called her boyfriend who was sworn to secrecy. He apparently disposed of the body and gun in the St. Lawrence River. About a year later, that fellow was killed in the bike wars, leaving only Danielle and her mother the keepers of their secret. They moved away. Her mother straightened out and met her step-dad. When the body and gun were eventually found it was assumed the father had been yet another victim of gang warfare.

After telling Jimmy this horrific episode in her life, she sits there impassively cross-legged and plays with strands of grass. She looks up at him with eyes so haunted, exacerbated, by the drug, that Jimmy thinks he is seeing her for the first time. Trying to comfort her, she resists his sympathy.

He tells her how much he loves her, but she does not respond. Getting dressed, she explains that her life is not all that he might imagine in spite of the fact she had been abused. She goes on to say that her ordeals are really insignificant.

'As compared to what?' presses Jimmy.

But she does not elaborate. He then wonders aloud whether she is religious.

She laughs. 'Religion is not so good as Bazooka Joe, eh?' she quips, draping herself over his sun warmed body.

Danielle leaves for Montreal the next day wanting to spend some time with her grandmother. He tries in vain to reach her, but somehow understands why he can't. Still reeling from her revelations, it was to be a summer of suffering, and he wonders after a time if he would ever see her again. He knows she was running, not from him, but herself. He wants to tell her again that it wasn't her fault and he would love her forever, but he just suffers, quietly, desperately. Almost a year would pass before she would come into his life again, suddenly, unexpectedly.

eight Uncle Sam

But Mommy steps into the Stone Age
As an Avenging Angel

> –Jimmy Pidgeon

S ince the day he was brought back to Chicago, Sam would not speak. His mother attributes it to the shock of his abduction and subsequent indoctrination in Tibetan-Buddhism. Sam has thought actually that the monks were very funny and treated him much like a god. They called him Uncle Sam. Now, back in the Bungalo, he considers the best part of his life to be over, and he would never be allowed to return to either his father or the Kush or even Sunsetwind. It had been two weeks of a vow of silence in commemoration of his short-lived holy time.

Sam has the run of his mother's sprawling estate on the Lake Michigan waterfront north of Windy City. Guards and electronic surveillance systemically surround the hundred-hectare property. Emops circle high and low twenty-four hours a day – a superfluous testament to the 21st century adage: peace or death. The Bungalo is both an arsenal and a fortress, as well as home. When playing in the snow one day, he discovers to his delight someone whom he had never seen there before. Crawling in the bushes around the walls and gardens of the commando wing, while pretending to carry out a clandestine mission for Cleo and the guerillas, he passes a basement window and sees a young woman waving and smiling at him. Suspecting he has been discovered, he quickly moved on thinking he was lucky not to have been caught. On second thought he decides to go back and spy on the woman. He pokes his head ever so slightly above the windowsill and there she stands waving and smiling again! He pulls back in fear, but decides to look again anyway. She had come to the window and opens the slider of the casement to its limit about thirty centimeters (a foot).

'Hello,' she says softly. 'Are you playing guerilla war?'

Remembering his vow, Sam resists answering. Yet, he likes her and thinks that perhaps he should make an exception as she is kind of strange and pretty too with those large eyes, not that that inspired him in any way.

'You're not allowed to speak,' she says reading his mind and liking him too; she saw the Path in him and their fine disposition. 'I understand how things are around here. You know, I am also a guest of my sister Trinny, but am not allowed to leave, a bit like you, I think . . . '

'You're my mom's sister?' Sam can't help but blurt out.

'Not really,' she says. 'I'm Heyoka Yellow Tooth from Yellow Tooth and you must be Sam, Cephren's son.'

'Do you know my dad?' he demands warily.

'Not in person, but I know he's been wronged.'

'What are you doing here?' he asks.

'They took me from my home,' she professes.

'Is my mom bad?' he asks, bridging the implication.

'I don't think so, Sam; she just wants things to be right according to her view of the world. Unfortunately, some of us get in the way of what is deemed to be progress. Do not think your mom is bad. She is simply maladjusted.'

'I better go,' he says, though staying put.

'Come back again, Sam, and don't be sad.'

'My mother's in Washington,' he volunteers.

'Maybe she's on the monitor; would you like to watch?'

He doesn't answer.

'Don't worry, I won't harm you,' she says reassuringly.

'I know I am not allowed to go in there,' he says. 'We might both get in trouble.'

'We can take our chances,' she offers, smiling.

'I'll let you out, if you want,' he announces suddenly.

'Oh, that'd be no good,' she declares. 'We'd both get caught and then you might really get in trouble.'

'What if the door's locked?' he asks.

'You're right, maybe you can climb in the window, if I could get this screen off.'

Heyoka removes the screen with little difficulty. The window is just wide enough for Sam to squeeze in. Once inside, having taken off his snowsuit and boots, he sits in the chair beside Heyoka who turns on the monitor and sits near him on the edge of the single bed. She is dressed in a loose red jumpsuit. One monitor channel specifically follows the EF election. The show at present is a debate among prominent proponents of each North American candidate. Babylon represents Trinny, General Dennis for George Washington and Anna Gram for Cephren Path.

'So,' the media anchor announces, 'moving on to our next issue which has become an increasingly heated focal point of this election, since Cephren Path has proclaimed his candidacy, the seemingly outlandish promise that if he was elected, we as a race on earth could join a galactic confederation. First, I'll direct this question to you Ms. Gram: are we really to take Mr. Path seriously? Isn't this really an extravagant bid to gain attention? And, if not, we all want to know what Mr. Path knows and to the best of your knowledge, has there been some contact with an extraterrestrial race? If so, who are these beings and why have they not made contact before?'

Anna smiles into the camera. Her endorsement of Cephren's candidacy, given her high profile in the entertainment world and photographic charisma, had come as a great shock to both George Washington and Trinny Burnamthorpe. Various media venues have tried to debunk and discredit both her and Cephren, but public opinion seems to be in favour of their unique teamwork, she being the star and he being the underdog trying to regain his former stature. His campaign had propelled him now front and center in the bid for the Earth Chair. And his seemingly preposterous proclamation is considered to be very creative, though perhaps a little silly. But it doesn't really matter whether people take him seriously, he has captured their imaginations with the dangling bait of some great information.

'Well, yes on the first question; he is serious, and no on the second, although it may appear to be extravagant. And yes, there has been contact,' she states confidently, 'although due to the sensitive nature of this kind of phenomenon, in regard to how well people accept this information, Cephren has chosen not to reveal, as we are all aware, the details just yet. There are forces here on earth whom would kill for this intelligence to bolster their own space programs and prestige. And Cephren feels they, the predators, are not so interested in the well-being of earth itself, but merely their own power and control of space. We, the keepers of this intelligence seek only to enhance the well-being of all citizens and not to irresponsibly trade off our integrity for technology.' She looks over at Babylon who returns the smile, but it is General Dennis who responds.

'And who are these beings? Little green men?' he asks, chuckling to himself facetiously.

'General Dennis would like to keep everyone in the dark about the Greys, beings from the Reticula star system, or even the Pentit Sinesians, beings much like us, and many other advanced species out there,' Anna counters. 'The Greys are not green from what I understand, but are quite small and greyish with a translucent quality to their skin. They have been coming to earth for many hundreds of years, possibly thousands, as General Dennis, I'm sure, is fully aware, as many of the earlier secret U.S. files on the subject have been made available with the B400 chip. The old world's hidden agenda regarding these beings was – and to be fair to

General Dennis – a mutual agreement with these aliens to keep their presence secret, because of the vast differences in development between our
races and our own inability to rationally accept their superiority. Their
advances technologically are literally off the map of our own comprehension, and might provoke through fear a sudden breakdown of our relatively limited psychological mainframe and more importantly the
potential chaos that would threaten our antiquated institutions, cultural
and otherwise – in other words, a security nightmare. I might add General
Dennis is in an acute state of denial with all this alien business, as this is
his job. It is hard to admit to ourselves that we are not the center of the
universe, as our predilection to ethnocentricity subscribes. The fact of the
matter is technological advancement is not necessarily a yardstick for superiority of any kind. I believe most of the aliens actually cherish all nature,
but particularly ours, at least those who are attempting to wean themselves
of their terrestrial confines. Their belief is one of mutual consideration for
all forces of creation, not just for who's in charge, although we would like
to have the ability to remain autonomous and develop unilaterally as a
race. It should be observed, if there is a threat galactic-wise this confederation would serve to protect us. There are numerous races like the Eridanis,
a race very similar in appearance to our own though thousands of years
more evolved, who would welcome us wholeheartedly when we are ready.'

'I have never heard so much bullshit in my entire life!' exclaims General Dennis. 'This whole alien thing is a political device to rehabilitate a
man who could not even look after his own country! And even if it was
remotely true, what gives him the right to sign us up with a galactic con-
federacy over, say, George Washington? Path denigrates our intelligence,
thus our leadership. It's a cheap trick! You would have us believe Mr.
Path, because of some damned wacko computer chip being privy to something alien? Mark my words: the man's bonzo. He's not fit to run for the
village idiot!'

'Excuse me!' rebuts Anna, flashing her passionate eyes to the camera.
'We stand for truth! Not some hard-bitten scorn that would have us back

in the dark ages! Here, you character-assassinate Cephren Path, when your own candidate presumes to equate himself with his namesake, our forefather. Would the original George Washington stand for such blarney? What kind of institutional claptrap is that, in our modern age, General?'

'How dare you insult the most hallowed name of our country? Is this what you propose to do, knock the great institutions that have preserved us for all these centuries? For the love of God, shame on you! Look at the facts: Chairman Washington has successfully steered us through a turbulent time, laying the foundations for peace and prosperity into the 25th century.'

'Have you any comments, Babylon?' quizzes the media anchor.

'I do, indeed,' he says in his best cool voice. Babylon smiles well. He commands respect, and for his fifty odd years appeared still a young man. He has a shiny shaved head, a virile athletic constitution and handsome to boot. 'I believe Ms. Gram has just delivered her well-crafted script with her usual impeccable skill, yet I can't help but hear Cephren Path's thinly disguised penmanship behind this lecture on the perils of 'man meets alien'. We must applaud his sagacity of choice for a mouthpiece. All this talk about aliens goes on and on, but let's get down to earth. I've been saying for some time and I'll say it again; we think the scenario is fantastic, if it's true. But we need proof, and if proof is forthcoming, we want the people of this earth to be reassured that Trinny Burnamthorpe as leader is the most responsible person to contend with such an important issue. No more smoke screens. We have the most extensive space program on this earth. Cephren Path is just not capable of looking after earth's best interests. We believe this whole alien thing is just a very smart ploy to put himself and his tribe back on the map. He failed in Sunsetwind and he would fail again with the Earth Federation. Even you, Anna, haven't any idea what he's really up to because you all share the burden of proof, which you can't deliver. You have nothing without proof. Even your mandate is dubious. You make a mockery of these proceedings. Enough is enough. We have important issues to deal with. My advice to you is get out before you lose all your credibility, which must be now at a lifetime low. I have to say, though, for entertainment value, you are a very special lady. And we all know what that means.'

'I will not stoop to dignify your remarks, Babylon! I hardly think a breeder has any place in politics! Don't think we all don't know how well you *stand* in Ms. Burnamthorpe's esteem.'

Babylon continues to smile. The crowd laughs. The media anchor intervenes. 'The question, then begs, Ms. Gram, when is the proof forthcoming? As you can see, people need to know in order to bolster this credibility gap. Most people are scratching their heads. I think they want to believe you, but . . . '

'Well, I know it's been difficult, but we are working on that right now. The fact that Cephren can't go home and use his own base to announce this has caused us some security concerns, which all of you are aware of. Twice, he has been attacked by geno commandos. I suppose, Babylon, you wouldn't know anything about that?'

'Proof, Ms. Gram, proof!' he reiterates, continuing to smile.

'I think everybody knows Chicago invaded Sunsetwind, and the Yellow Tooths, abducting or killing their spiritual leader, Heyoka . . . and many other incidents.' She looks directly at Babylon, then General Dennis. 'You people don't respect law and order, and you expect to win this election? Only a fool would vote for Trinny Burnamthorpe or Washington! Yes, we have security concerns. We also predict that if Trinny doesn't win the Earth Chair, she'll simply opt out of the Federation and help destroy the many achievements and advances it has made for our race. What kind of leader would she make, having no respect for the very Earth Federation she seeks to covet? The aliens, I should add, would not want our membership in the galaxy if we are seen to have regressed to old, selfish tribalism . . . '

Heyoka shuts the monitor off.

'Why did you do that?' asks Sam.

'Well, we are, you know – selfish old tribalisms. I am ashamed. I am ashamed to be human. We are the worst animal, the most perverted. Your father is the least perverted. He must win!' Heyoka's strange eyes sparkle. She takes Sam's hand and holds it. She looks into his hazel blue eyes and sees some of his pain. 'What can we do to help him, Sam?'

'We can spy on my mother,' he offers seriously, so much so it would have made anybody laugh except Heyoka.

'Spy? I think you are the spy, Sam. You must find a way to get your corn home. In ancient Cherokee culture, the dog ran with some corn spilling from his mouth, which became the milky way. Your Indian name will be Where-The-Dog-Ran. Can you use the monitor?'

'I'm not allowed, except for a closed one like yours.'

Heyoka then goes into some kind of trance. She lets go of Sam's hand as her body begins to shake. Her gangly hips start to rock and her chest palpitates. Her seizure stops as suddenly as it began. On her face there is a thin sheen of moistness that flushes her cheeks. Her eyes roll in her down-cast head.

'Are you okay?' says Sam taken aback.

'Yes, Sam, do not be afraid; it is just me. I am known for this. I see things.'

'Did you see something?'

'Yes. I have seen what must be done, Sam.'

'What is that?'

'There is someone coming soon. A woman. You must trust her. She is our only hope. You must give her this.'

Heyoka pulls from her necklace beneath her sweater an orange-gold medallion with odd hieroglyphics. She reaches behind her and unclasps the necklace. Then taking Sam's hand, she carefully places it in his palm.

'Hide this very carefully, Sam. It is a very special stone very sacred to my people given to them from the Sky People. I entrust it to you. Now you must go and give it to this woman. I cannot tell you who she is, but I know she will know you and you may know her. You must tell her to give it to Redman of Sunsetwind. Tell her she must do it. There will be a war if Redman does not get it. This war can be averted.'

'How do you know all this?' queries Sam, sceptically.

'Why did the monks call you Uncle Sam?'

'How did you know that?' Sam's eyes open wide.

Heyoka pauses, then looks at him directly. 'Uncle Sam,' she begins slowly, 'I will tell you the most guarded secret about me. Only my mother, her mother before that and back many generations have known this. No man has known, as it was wished by the first mother. But I think that I will never have a child, so I will tell you. The first mother lived before the Asteroid. The Sky People gave her a child. The girl child then had a child who became Yellow Tooth Kentuckee's wife. For every generation every child born was a girl. I am the end of the line. The Sky People did not speak. They had talking minds. I have some of these powers. It is a true story. Your father has been trying to reach the Sky People. They will help us. Now go and find this woman, Uncle Sam.'

'Where do the Sky People come from, Heyoka?' asks Sam.

'I do not know; but they would welcome our friendship if they believed that we had advanced from our self-destructing ways.'

'I will help my dad,' asserts Sam, going to the window.

Heyoka helps him out of the window. Sam crawls away feeling wise and strong. She has had a very positive effect on him. He knows it is okay to love his mother in spite of her 'maladjustment'. And now he is Where-The-Dog-Ran, not to mention Uncle Sam.

Three days later Sam has the surprise of his life. As he wanders through the huge Bolivian styled kitchen and the pantry and back vestibule then into the Great Room looking out to the snow-laden gardens and lawns rolling down to the lake, he notices there is no one about. He goes to the next room, the ballroom and opens the door. Surprise! There are a hundred people beaming at him and calling out his name. His mom, Trinny, comes to him first and plants a kiss on his cheek. 'Happy Birthday, Sam!'

Indeed, it is his eleventh birthday. He had thought about it that morning in his room. He hadn't said anything to anybody as an exercise in the game. It seems he was duly rewarded for his forbearance. Much of his time is spent plotting out the world plan. There has been a bit of preparation to make ready for the galactic neighbours. He really isn't at all sure what to believe, but whatever it is must be important. He had hidden the alien medallion in his room under a corner of the wall-to-wall rug that he knew to be loose. He then put a box of toys over it. Despite the surprise of the party, he can't stop thinking about it. The subterfuge gives him power to know that the medallion is the potential lynch-pin that would hold together the Earth Federation; and here are all the top Chicagos smiling at him: Babylon, Judy World, Hallelujah, Bob Fix, Tomasina, Super Mario, etc. including his mom, Trinny; they are all looking at a spy, the perfect spy, the Tiny Tim with whom everyone sympathised.

Other children are invited, though Sam has a tough time relating to any of them. One child, one of Babylon's many, a girl of Sam's age keeps goad-ing him to play with her. She makes up this game called Asteroid in which the winner is whoever stockpiles the most food from the tables and gets to live, and the loser dies of course. Intrigued, Sam makes his stash under the main table laid out with heaps of food such as shrimp, tortilla chips, pâté, guacamole, spiced meats, cheeses, breads, antipastos, etc., while the adults mill about eating, drinking and babbling. The novelty of his party turned out to be its social casualness that serves to break the strain of election fever. Sam, while hoarding mounds of food, can't help but overhear some inter-esting snippets. He hears Super Mario, the Head of Communications say to someone, 'We have the election in the bag; we've wired every candidate from here to Singapore. We'll pre-empt every speech and policy directive like poking holes in a water balloon.' Sam even hears his mother say, 'Our worst nightmare is that damned bitch Anna Gram; she's everything that Cephren's not. We've got to neutralize her; Bob, come up with something fast.' Next, the girl sticks her afro head under the table to say time is up, and that he lost by a mile. 'You're dead, Sam!'

Later, after the clown show, Sam wanders into the kitchen. There are numerous people helping out and suddenly he just about jumps out of his socks upon seeing Treason Honey extracting marshmallows from the pantry cupboard. They are to have a marshmallow roast outside. A big fire had been prepared and blazed in the yard. Some of the kids were already dressed and playing outside in the snow. Sam almost blows his cover when he stares at her, and she turns to see him. She looks back though feigning not to recognise him immediately. Sam had no idea that his dad's personal bodyguard at Christmas would be at his birthday party. Her presence is fortuitous because it meant that she must be a spy too, remembering Heyoka's premonition. He suddenly realises that it is Treason who must take the medallion to Redman of Sunsetwind. Treason continues to pile marshmallows in a big bowl. She winks at him and says, 'Having fun, Sam?'

'Yes,' he says staring.

'Why don't you get your snow stuff on and go outside?'

'Okay,' he says numbly, and leaves. After exiting the kitchen, Sam takes the back hall behind the kitchen and rushes to his bedroom. He quickly retrieves the medallion and puts it in his pocket, then proceeds to the boot room to put on his snow gear.

Outside, all the children, about thirty of them, run about throwing snow and kicking a soccer ball. Little groups wanders off here and there excitedly. A number of adults including Treason are outside with the children. They too, mill around to keep the kids in line. Sam hangs about the fire and roasts a few marshmallows. He watches as Treason helps the younger ones put the marshmallows on their sticks. Treason would look up and watch Sam glancing at her. She would smile back with that cheery face that he had come to know that fateful time in the Kawarthas. Sam needs to speak with her, but he isn't sure how for fear of attracting attention. He assumes she is on a spy mission and doesn't want to blow her cover, and for that matter his own, if she was his father's enemy. He had once seen a spy movie where they used a password. He thinks maybe if he says something to attract her attention, she might understand; besides it would likely be that she wanted to speak with him. He goes over to her with his stick and gives it to her. She looks up and says, 'How are you Sam?'

'I have to go to the bathroom,' he says.

'Is that why you want me to hold your marshmallow stick?'

'No, I have to go to the *bathroom*,' he intones more forcefully.

'Okay, go on,' she says smiling and taking another stick to skewer a marshmallow. Sam turns and walks back to the house.

In the bathroom across from his bedroom, Sam waits. It appears she isn't coming and he dejectedly puts his hand on the doorknob to leave when the knob turns against his hand and Treason quickly enters. Without a word she hugs him and says they must whisper and go back outside quickly so as not to arouse suspicion. She explains she is lucky to be there, as she is not at all that important, but that Babylon asked her to help with the children.

'Why are you here at all?' he whispers.

'I escaped capture New Year's Eve and literally crawled in the snow to get away under cover of night. I made it to the Neutrals where I found some Forager friends. Then I made it to Toronto and linked up with Babylon's network. Babylon is an old friend who is now very important.'

'But he's an enemy.'

'I'll tell you something if you can keep a big secret?'

'Yes.'

'Promise?'

'I promise,' he avows soberly.

'I'm a spy, Sam.'

'So am I.'

'You're a Sunsetwinder too, aren't you?'

'Yes, but how do you get away with it, Treason?'

'I'm a double agent,' she admits. 'I also spy for Chicago.'

'Why?'

'I wouldn't be here if I didn't.'

'Did you betray dad?'

'Never Sam. I had no idea what happened to us. I know now that the Free Radical party had a mole in the communications room in the Pyramid. They jammed the defences for a few minutes while the Chicagos got in. In retrospect, however, it was better that way; otherwise many of us may have died defending our country.'

'Treason, I have a mission for you,' declares Sam sincerely.

'What can I do, sir?' she answers obediently with a smile.

'Did you know Heyoka Yellow Tooth is locked in a room in the basement here?'

'No, are you sure?'

'I climbed in her window and spoke to her myself.'

'Oh, I'm so relieved she's alive.'

'She gave me something to give to you.'

'To me?'

'Yes, she has powers and said that a woman will come whom I'll know. She gave me this.' Sam pulled the medallion from his pocket and shows it to Treason. 'You must give this to Redman in Sunsetwind.'

'What is it?'

'She said it's an element given to her from the Sky People that will help prevent a war.'

'The Sky People?'

'Oh yes.'

'What's so special about it?' asks Treason.

'I don't know; why is my mom keeping Heyoka here?'

'Because your Aunt Cleopatra was trying to start a war against your mom with the help of the Yellow Tooth Cherokees and Heyoka was their leader.'

'Is my mom wrong?'

'I think your mom does the things she does because one thing leads to another when you are responsible for a huge power such as the Chicagos. Chicago is the most powerful country in the world. She wants to keep it that way.'

'Why did she invade Sunsetwind?'

'Technology. Sunsetwind has the best technology, although they act like they don't.'

'What do you mean?'

'Your dad has a chip implanted in his head. And your mom thinks he's going to use it against her.'

'What's in this chip?'

'I don't know, but it ain't a potato.'

Sam laughs before becoming taciturn again.

'Will you do it?' he wonders.

'Why does Heyoka want Redman to have this?' she asks.

'Maybe because he'll know what to do with it,' he suggests.

'I'll do it,' she announces taking the medallion and putting it in the pocket of her designer survival suit. 'Sam, you're a hero.'

'Also get word to dad that I'm all right but that they're going to "neutralize" Anna somehow, because she's too dangerous for the Chicagos and must be neutralized. I heard my mother say that and other stuff to Bob Fix.

'Boy, you're good, Sam. We make a great team.'

Trinny Burnamthorpe sits at the head of the long, butterscotch marble table. Her Senior Chiefs surround her. Her hair is tied at the back severely. Her lusterless blue eyes and sharkish mouth betray her stylish apparel. She is too busy for the political smile at home. There is always too much to do and too many appointments to keep. That very evening she is to begin a road trip around the world, spending time in New Zealand, Australia, Indonesia, China, Japan, India, Europe, Africa and home for another North American tour, then South America, North America, Europe and back around the world again. For all her autocratic rule she is a tireless leader who usually measures up to her people's expectations. She is also a great admirer of the legendary Flower Child, who is purported to be her ancestor, and hence has strong feelings about Sunsetwind, and needless to say, her own bitterness over her marriage. Trinny as well is a great admirer of Danielle Perreault, though unaware of her ancestral connection to her. Of men, she prefers African black-white crosses, like Babylon and Impala. She feels they have a more potent gene pool, and if mixed with certain others, her race agenda has great possibilities. Trinny's peculiar racism stems from her overwhelming superiority in human resource management. This had nothing to do with belief in superiority of one race over another. Her religion teaches her this and she exploits it. She openly flaunts the old Christian card in the election and according to the polls, most of the Christianized world approves of her candidacy. However, the Christian-ized world isn't what it used to be. Its centers have migrated from its origi-nal roots in Caucasian regions to poor, developing countries in South America and Africa whose populations are the largest on earth, displacing Asia from earlier centuries before the Asteroid. The Chicagos' power is supported directly from this relationship with these countries. Their Christianized paganism suits the Chicagos' designs perfectly. The rest of world, on the other hand, are divided among many economic and reli-gious beliefs. If Trinny could even take thirty percent of their vote she would win the election. Her success seemed a shoe-in until Anna Gram showed up. Anna Gram, a Texan raised as a Christian, had a Mexican mother who came from a wealthy family that had considerable holdings throughout Latin America. After much talk and debate Trinny is ready to terminate the meeting.

'It has come to my attention,' concludes Trinny, 'that our well thought out plan for domination of the Earth vote has begun to erode. Cephren Path and Anna Gram are gaining momentum every day. We have come to a bridge burning, my friends. We either take action against them, or lose the election. My Washington trip was a complete failure. People are looking to capitalize on the entertainment value of both my own and Cephren's per-sonal history, thus lowering me to his level of political mediocracy. He carries a sympathy vote too, which irks me to no end. If he had been captured, as was planned, none of this would have happened!

'Furthermore, I had some very frank talks with George Washington the other day; he thinks my proposal that we join forces under a joint leadership would undermine the democratic process. I tried to explain to him, that the elective process would remain inviolable, but to no avail. He wants the goods we have to offer through close economic ties, but is unwilling to pay the price! I mean, as we produce an accessible and affordable product, like the new Virtual Class monitor, or our old faithful, the Trip-c implant, or even our Technohuman Services which all countries seem to condemn, yet are found to be indispensable, they want to share them from Biogenetics to Hardware Leasing. What really bothers me is an ignorant voting public! Can't they see that our security and standard of living are their very own? It seems this New World Tribalism that Cephren and Anna Gram have concocted about us is putting the fear of God into them! What a joke! That atheist lout of an ex-husband turning religion against me! He'll paint me Macbeth, he will! The cunning bastard!'

'Wouldn't that be Lady Macbeth, Trinny?' smiles Babylon.

Trinny bursts out laughing, the others following her lead.

'Ever the gentleman, Baby,' she says putting her hand on his. 'So Bob, what do we have in mind? Fill us in.' Her sudden about-faces are a well-known personality trait.

'I think we should go with the East African option. They are friendly to us now because of our aid program in spite of our old friend Impala having met his demise. Poor fellow, he really thought he had it made; our success with the trip-c system has virtually landed much of the world into our laps. I have arranged . . . '

'Spare me the details," interrupts Trinny, 'when will it happen?'

'It was not intended for effect,' said Bob Fix, 'but March 15th works best. Our unwitting Wall family is on a holiday at the time.'

'On the contrary, how appropriate! The Ides of March. Lady Caesar falls to a school girl. Beware the Ides of March!'

They all laugh again. Then she dismisses them.

'Carry on everyone. Be vigilant. See you in a few weeks.' All but Baby-lon exit, as he is her personal advisor during the election.

'Trinny,' he says, when they are alone, 'if you think someone else would do a better job, I'm prepared to drop out. I don't like this policy of elimi-nating the competition. We have nothing to fear from anyone.'

'Tush, it's not a question of fear, rather efficiency. I won't hear of it, Babylon; besides no one relaxes me like you. Come here, massage my neck, please.'

He stands up and dutifully massages her neck. She moans under the kneading of his large, strong hands, which then move lower down to her breasts. He kisses the nape of her neck.

'Enough,' she commands, pulling away. He sits down again.

'What of your young vixen Sunsetwinder, Baby? She seemed to enjoy herself the other day with the children.'

'She has asked me to let her go home,' he says in that deep assuring voice. 'I told her there's no point; the country's effectively shut down. Barker has really turned into a paranoid by postponing elections.'

'Should we remind him that *we're* running an election?' she asks still half melted from his brief massage.

'I don't believe people will think we have anything to do with his megalomania. For the time being, it can't hurt our cause. We went in, set things straight, then got out. Down the road, we shall set him straight, if need be. Perhaps we could put Treason's talents to good use. Barker could use a little encouragement, a little relaxation.'

'Perhaps, I'll think about it. But we should never really trust a Sun-setwinder,' she insists.

'We've learned some good stuff from her and she was duly rewarded. Yet she declined my offer to enter the program.'

'Why?'

'Once a Sunsetwinder, always a Sunsetwinder,' he presumes.

'Why would she want to go back to a country that's all bottled up?' she queries more alertly.

'She claims family concerns.'

'Does she know about her step-father?'

'I haven't told her,' he replies. 'I think I would have heard from her if she had; she was fond of him.'

'Well, let her go then as long as she's not taking anything with her – intelligence and the like, not that she's any real threat to us. We haven't any use for her anymore, unless you do, dear.'

'No,' he says sighing, 'she was enjoyable, but without a scintilla of depth. She's like an nimble lemur.'

'And how would you know, darling?'

'I've seen them do it. In trees, while eating, preening . . . '

Trinny breaks out laughing in her characteristic twitter. 'Is this criteria for your program, dear? Why don't you pretend you're a nimble lemur? I'm curious.'

'I didn't think you were game.'

'Perhaps I am. A daily dose of your goop keeps me focused.'

'Well, focus on this.'

She maneuvers herself onto the table. Babylon slowly lifts her long dress from behind . . .

'On second thought, be my gorilla,' she gasps.

In spite of her optimism, things have not been going well for Trinny Burnamthorpe. According to the polls, Cephren had split the vote between the main contenders, Trinny and George Washington. When her unbridled ambition flounders, she simply steps out of bounds either to skirt the issue or destroy it. Chicago has nothing to lose economically and the new political reality seems to follow the economics in terms of power and control. Market forces in the more heavily populated regions like South America are dictating tremendous exchange between these regions. Yet with the advent of Anna Gram into the fray, Trinny's political hegemony is beginning to wane. In her own mind, she has ignored this due to pride alone and then enters the stage of unaccountability like so many directives in her repetoire. But one thing has uncharacteristically stymied her usual perfunctory manner: Heyoka. Trinny keeps Heyoka a secret unto herself. A special team had abducted her – the same team that had failed with Cephren in Ottawa – and they were bred to their profession thus posing little risk of their allegiance. So over the weeks her usual condition of denial has evaded Trinny, partly because Heyoka is alive and well in her care; but also because she has become a friend of sorts. Trinny, for some inexplicable reason believes Heyoka felt some fealty toward her and sees Heyoka as a potential convert to the Chicago cause, and that of global leadership. Trinny has even felt comfortable enough in Heyoka's presence to open up that hardened heart of hers. She would never admit it to herself, but Heyoka has become her personal psychologist.

Before leaving on her world tour the same evening that Trinny and Babylon had used the council marble top as their lustful prop, she goes first to see Sam, then to Heyoka. When she opens Sam's door, he is speaking to Tutti the little Japanese android toy she had given him for his birthday. Conversation is limited with Tutti, yet the novelty has not worn off as it could memorise up to about two thousand words and repeat them, before resetting the program. Sam stops talking and smiles at his mom. She had noticed since his birthday that his disposition is much improved. Part of her is pleased, but another part is a little surprised. He had never seemed that content; he had always been a rather sullen boy. She wonders what had come over him and even thought perhaps he might be up to no good. As a child he had seemed happiest when he had succeeded in some deception. At any rate, there is little trouble he could get into while she is gone. The thought had occurred to her to take him, but his presence would only interfere, especially with

Babylon around. So she gives him a kiss and departs leaving him with his synthetic Japanese friend, though she wonders about the android when it calls out strangely as she departs, 'Where-the-Dog-Ran, show me your star!'

Downstairs in the restricted basement wing, Trinny comes upon her elite Commandos made up of a dozen men and women. Some are lounging in the living area watching movies, others in the kitchen and the rest on duty. She gives them some last minute instructions, one of which was to watch her son more closely and she warns that under no circumstances is he to know about Heyoka. She then speaks to her special staff, who cook, clean and provide for her expansive Bungalo. Finally, she heads down the hall and arrives at Heyoka's room. She waves her hand over the code key, knocks then enters. Heyoka is in the bathroom. Trinny waits. The room is neatly kept. Her supper tray is on the table; the monitor is on without sound, the bed made and the desk lamp on, casting the monotone room in a dusky light.

Heyoka enters and smiles at Trinny. Her ethereal qualities are pronounced in the warm light. Her eyes look dark and reflective.

'I'm going away for a while,' explains Trinny. 'If there's anything you need like a book or some type of food, anything, a man even, just let them know. Okay?'

'Have you heard from my people?' Heyoka inquires.

'I believe they think you are dead, Heyoka. I am sorry about this. Please forgive me my ruthlessness in these matters. I can be a vociferous bitch. It is this personal sacrifice that I make that gives much of the world its prosperity. Can you not see how it is for me? You, of all people?'

'I see you very clearly, Trinny. You have sold yourself to man. It's like that folk song that says freedom's just another word for nothing else to lose. But you have everything to lose. Your freedom is my prison.'

Trinny sighs and falls back on the sofa. She puts her hands to her head and turns her head back and forth. She begins to cry. Terrible sobs emanate from deep within her. Heyoka goes to her sympathetically and puts her hand on her shoulder. Trinny collects herself saying, 'I'm sorry, I'm sorry', over and over. Heyoka sits quietly with downcast eyes and removes her hand.

'It's all true, isn't it?' questions Trinny still teary-eyed. 'It's true that there are aliens out there, watching us. I know Cephren, and there's one thing he isn't, though I wouldn't say it to anybody else; he's not a liar. He wouldn't say the things he does if he didn't know there was some truth. Have you any idea who these beings are, Heyoka?'

'I have heard many things,' she says, calmly. 'My own family claims a certain privilege; some ancestors lived near the bases out west and saw the machines fly without wings long before the people had the knowledge. Like the earth that has many kinds of life, so too does the night sky as my people say Where-the-Dog-Ran has left his corn for all to eat across the heavens. Nature is prolific, everywhere.'

'My son's android just said those very words!' utters Trinny.

'Which ones?'

'Where-The-Dog-Ran. Have you spoken with him?'

'Yes, it was supposed to be our secret, because he didn't want to get in trouble. He came to my window one day while he was playing outside. We spoke a little and I gave him an Indian name, Where-The-Dog-Ran. I hope it is all right . . .'

'When did this happen?' Trinny demands angrily.

'Five or six days ago,' she says, sincerely.

'And Treason wants to go home,' says Trinny under her breath. 'What did you tell him?' insists Trinny.

'Do not be angry, Trinny. Your son means no harm.'

Trinny looks at Heyoka with an intense scrutiny. 'Answer my question!' she hisses venomously.

'I told him that you were struggling with terrible responsibilities and not to be angry with you. I said you were my sister in that we come from the minds that created the Sacred Stones, one of whom was your ancestor Elias, a man of great integrity and power.'

Trinny seethes underneath. She knows something had transpired between them. She notices that Heyoka's necklace is missing.

'Where's your necklace?' she snaps.

'I gave it to your son,' she replies.

'Why?'

'To remember me . . .'

'I don't buy it; what's the significance of your necklace? It was gold wasn't it?'

'Yes, and very sacred to my people.'

Trinny flashes out her pocket monitor and punches in a code. 'Babylon? Don't let Treason go,' she shouts into it.

'She's already gone?' she screams.

Trinny is livid.

'On the Toronto shuttle? Fuck! I know I said she could go!'

There is an electric silence.

'She knows Heyoka is here and probably has her necklace to prove it,' she asserts.

Again, there is silence.

'So now you know! And soon the world! Call back that shuttle!' she screams.

She listens and fumes.

'I don't know what kind of necklace! It had a gold medallion that she claims is sacred to the Yellow Tooths. I saw it when she first arrived. I remember it had an bright orange gold colour.'

Trinny's face turns crimson.

'What! Washington told you he had thought there might be some truth to it? Why wasn't I informed?'

Babylon says no one was allowed to see her and assumed she had been searched.

'You didn't know she had it?'

She puts the pocket monitor back in her inside pocket. 'Well Heyoka, I have to hand it to you. You just smuggled out of Chicago, my home in fact, the very substance we have been trying to procure – unumpentium (element 115). That was an alien element, wasn't it?'

'It didn't matter to me whether it was alien.'

'I'm not asking you whether it did!'

'Who is Treason?' quizzes Heyoka as placid as still water.

'A precocious slut,' spits Trinny leaving the room, 'with the mark of death.'

'Be careful,' warns Heyoka.

For many months over the sultry Toronto summer, then through the pensive autumn to disconsolate winter, Jimmy Pidgeon endures terrible angst as a result of Danielle exiting his life and no way to reach her. He keeps his spirits alive by converting this suffering into a compulsive drive to discover the secrets of universal life. This daunting task seems not to be so out of reach for his vibrant cerebral energy and transfers easily into obsessive workaholism. Roderich Fleming, his loyal friend would often be the sounding board for Jimmy's bursting expostulations. Even Cephren riding the back of the X13 finds himself in the enviable position of not only experiencing the resolve of a great mind but witnessing it relative to his own timeline and general knowledge of the future. What is interesting is how Jimmy juxtaposes the laws of science relative to those in his own time and just how far beyond that paradigm he soared into Cephren's.

Jimmy would muse about elementary formulations of the engineering of a fusion anti-matter reactor to fuel electromagnetic propulsion. He speaks of certain chemical and physical reactions to elements irradiated with both high and low atomic weights. As well, other interests capture his fancy such as the theory of earth crust displacement (ECD) as the major reason for precessional climactic shift. Ricky takes it all in blithely: he has always marveled at Jimmy's electromagnetic experiments like the one that twisted metal and suspended objects in the air by generating force fields like magic; but he appears to be most curious about the earth's crust, the other things being beyond his sphere of understanding. Urged on by Ricky's friendly probing, Jimmy would run on a long complaint against the standing orthodoxy of prevalent notions on these subjects. He would refute their intractability on point after point citing that there is no great mystery and ramble off facts so that the answers to the questions of scientific truth would seem to be as plain as day.

'Even Einstein knew,' says Jimmy pacing his basement pad with his hands waving about, 'that the earth's crust must realign itself when the asymmetrically deposited masses of the polar regions produce centrifugal momentum that will, with the gradually inclining poles due to the precessional movement of the earth's ecliptic in relation to the galactic constellations, reach a certain point when something's got to give. Hence, the earth's crust will move over the earth's body or mantle and displace the polar regions slightly toward the equator, thus melting the existing poles and creating new ones. That is why in mythology we have the great cataclysms of the end of the world, the floods and tidal waves, earthquakes and volcanoes. This happened suddenly every 12000 to 25000 years or so depending on the polar mass and its particular climactic effect, whether it's situated on a land mass or ocean. Take Antarctica for example: there's your lost continent of Atlantis – staring at us all these years – an ancient civilisation buried under two miles of ice. And the next crust displacement, according to some of the ancient civilisations like the Maya, will happen in the near future.'

'You mean, the ice caps are going to melt?' wonders Ricky a little uncomfortably.

'Naw, not exactly overnight, but perhaps in a generation or two; it depends how far the earth's crust will displace and how fast. Remember, during the last cataclysm between 9000 and 10000 BC, thousands of animals like mastodons were frozen seemingly overnight. You know, they've found giant fruit trees, fruit intact, within the permafrost of the Arctic Circle frozen solid!'

'Really?' says Ricky.

'It's a fact,' adds Jimmy. 'So we have dramatic climactic change as symptomatic to the real cause: crust displacement. Now you throw in a little global warming which may delay it.'

'So what can we do about it, vote Green?'

'Nature doesn't vote.'

'So build bunkers.'

They have a laugh talking about it but in the year 2012 they wouldn't be laughing when the worst year for earthquakes, volcanic eruptions and global bituminous fallout known in the present cycle of recorded civilisation would cause the western world to shift its geopolitical position dramatically from global maintenance to one of unconditional survival. The poles actually shifted so that North America moved farther south in latitude and Antarctica moved north by way of the Pacific a few degrees. Then in the following decades severe water shortages in the United States brought Canadian resources to the rescue that presaged Danielle Perreault's political star.

And where is Danielle at that moment in time as Jimmy and Ricky discuss doomsday? Cephren knows exactly where she is: giving birth to a baby girl in the nun's quarters of a hospital in Ste. Thérèse, a northern suburb of Montreal, under a false name in the care of Sister Anne-Marie du Plessis, an old and dear friend of Danielle's maternal grandmother. Andromeda Pidgeon is born February 13 on a bitterly cold, grey day. The birth is difficult but invariably successful. Danielle, finally in a fit of excruciating pain pushes her out. And after a brief convalescence with the nuns, she goes back to her grandmother's house to recover. Disdaining breastfeeding, she puts the baby on a bottle against her grandmother's beseeching.

The months go by and one fine spring day, Jimmy receives some great news. He had been accepted into MIT on a special scholarship. And to make matters go even more orbital, as he was considering some of his course options, he picks up the ringing telephone to hear Danielle's voice at the other end. She has to repeat his name twice before he responds his shock is so great. She speaks calmly and eloquently asking him of Ricky and school. She makes no mention of her recent event. And Jimmy makes no inquiry as to her absence and lack of communication. Briefly, she says she wants to see him, as she is now going out west to join her parents. She insists they rendezvous in a park near Jimmy's house. He thinks this peculiar, but is not about to oppose her.

Jimmy is beside himself. He doesn't know what to feel. Part of him is amazed that she wants to see him. The other part rebels because only more personal trauma could come of this, as she is just passing through seemingly with some urgency. But his love for her prevails and he longs to see her.

Jimmy sits on the park bench in nervous anticipation. He wants to tell her about his plans: the working of his ideas into viable new technologies, as well as his writing in which he avidly engages himself to find expression in his lonely life. There is so much to do and he knows exactly what he wants. He dreams that they could team up and start their own company to promote his inventions. She could sell them and he could create them. They could experience together sublime happiness. Unfortunately, Jimmy's idea of a life plan would never materialize. Nothing could have prepared him for the sight and shock of an old decrepit barge of an Oldsmobile, two tone blue with the Quebec license plate motto *Je me souviens* pulling up to the curb, Danielle stepping out to open up the rear door to remove a baby from a car seat.

Jimmy does what he does best and ignores the shock to hug both Danielle and the baby. Danielle is tearful which seems out of character and rubs off on Jimmy too. They all sit down on the bench. The baby is hungry and Danielle gives her a bottle.

'Where did she come from,' he utters in disbelief.

'Meet Andromeda Pidgeon,' she says. 'I call her Andie.'

'Who…is she…'

'Yes,' she replies definitively.

Jimmy, without considering for a moment the implications of this phenomenal revelation, is speechless. His instant fealty towards this little bundle and great passion for Danielle eclipses any thought of the looming responsibility he might share. And after ten minutes of familial joy, the boom comes down. Danielle begins by saying she had known she was pregnant after she returned to Montreal late spring the year before. She had stayed with her grandmother making her promise not to tell her parents. Her grandmother introduced Danielle to Sister Anne-Marie who helped her through the pregnancy. She had told her parents that she would come out west the next year, but wanted to spend the year with her grandmother as she was getting old. Danielle quit school and lived quietly until the baby was born. She tells Jimmy that she put a false name on the birth document naming the mother as Lisa Bouchard, but that he was named as the father. Danielle tells him that she is giving up Andie to Jimmy, and that he must be the primary guardian, explaining that she loved her but couldn't possibly raise her. She doesn't feel she is capable, nor patient enough to be a good mother.

'This is my gift to you, Jimmy! This is my true love, and all I can give you! I had this baby for you! I am not worthy of you! I cannot give myself to you! I have to lead my life without you! Don't stop me; it'll just make it worse, please Jimmy. Perhaps in time, we can be together.'

'Danielle, what about me?' he declares stunned, feeling as if a boulder landed on his chest. 'I haven't any means to look after her!'

'You have a nice family. I know you can do it!'

'How can you do this to me?' he cries.

'You must! I have no choice! Jimmy, please!'

'I'm moving to the States for four years. How can I?'

'Ask your parents; they would understand.'

'They'll flip if I bring her home,' he says resignedly. 'I just don't understand. Why don't you have a choice?'

'I can't explain; I wish I could; I just can't!'

She does not back down; she is crazy it seems. The situation is de facto. Danielle Perreault has given birth to their baby, and now she has gift wrapped it and given it away. She stands up and leaves Jimmy with a bag full of clothes, diapers, a car seat, a supply of formula, and of course Andie Pidgeon. She then kisses him goodbye saying she loves him and Andie who smiles, then walks to her grandmother's car and drives away waving and crying.

Jimmy sits there with Andie too shocked to speak. A young mother comes by with her baby and stops to speak endearingly to Andie who keeps smiling. Jimmy, slowly, paying little attention to the mother, puts Andie in the car seat, grabs the bag and walks home, his shock soon transforming to anger: how could she be so callous, so calculating? He just can't believe Danielle could do that; there had to be some extraordinary circumstance compelling her to do so.

Jimmy explains the situation to his equally stunned parents about everything but the true identity of Danielle, believing that perhaps she had a criminal record and didn't want to taint the family with it. Once the initial shock wears off, Jimmy's parents actually become quite sympathetic, and naturally warm to Andie as their granddaughter. Mrs. Pidgeon decides then and there to take it upon herself to raise the little girl, while Jimmy completed his undergraduate studies in the States. Meanwhile, Danielle completes her high school in Calgary and takes a three year economics undergraduate degree at the University of British Columbia in Vancouver.

Over the years, Danielle often writes and calls using the name Lisa Bouchard. At first, Jimmy would have little to say to her; but when she tells him he is the only man she would ever sleep with, he maintains wary communications in the vain hope that there might be some kind of reconciliation. She would often show contrition over the phone at her own selfish nature that always has an effect on Jimmy. He realises that she is not quite right psychologically and must suffer terribly in her own way. He cannot understand why she doesn't let him into her life, when she had supposedly revealed to him everything there was to know about her. Her early adolescent experiences were too awful to bring up and she would never acknowledge the slightest intimation to them. Her reticence compels Jimmy to think that perhaps there is more than she divulged.

When Andie turns four, Jimmy decides to move to Vancouver to be near Danielle. They had recently spoken, and Danielle in one of her rare emotional breakdowns, revealing a small chink in her armour, had admitted to Jimmy that she missed him and Andie desperately. She called to say she was moving and had been accepted into law school. Jimmy suggested that maybe he and Andie should come out and stay for a while, though uncertain what to do. He thought that with his credentials and top honours in Astrophysical engineering, he might find some work out there. She actually alighted onto the idea and exclaimed excitedly, 'Maybe we could really be a family!'

So Jimmy makes the move to Kitsilano in West Vancouver. At first, Danielle is absolutely thrilled. She would spend days with them at a time. They make love again passionately. She swears that she was true those past few years and claims that if it hadn't been for him, she would have entered the convent with Sister Anne-Marie of Ste. Thérèse. She does not move in with them, however, and insists Andie call her Danielle. Nevertheless, there is a blissful familial sharing. Danielle takes Andie for rides on her bike in the cubby. After a long grueling day of classes and study, she would often come over to kiss Andie goodnight and then rush off. There is indeed heaven on earth. Jimmy finds part-time work as a lab technician and soon becomes indispensable to the Physics department for his knowledge and gift for innovation that simply astounds the seasoned professors. Life is all just too perfect.

Then the boom falls yet again. Danielle calls one rainy night in March. She has been unusually busy and hasn't been over for a while.

'Jimmy,' she says, 'I'm having an affair.'

Jimmy won't say anything for there aren't any words to say. His mouth goes dry and his heart hurts with sickening anguish.

'I . . . I can't believe this,' he finally says with a breaking voice.

'Jimmy, take Andie and go home,' she demands without conviction. 'I have to do this. Please!' she begs.

'I don't believe you, Danielle!' retorts Jimmy, his pain blistering into spleen. 'Who is this guy?'

'It doesn't matter, Jimmy; you're the only one I love, and Andie. Please!' she pleads again. 'You know me! Do this for me!'

'Why? Why?'

'I just need to be alone,' she utters resolutely.

'I just don't believe you,' avers Jimmy, charged. 'You're acting crazy again.'

'You know what I'm capable of,' she says cryptically. 'There are things...'

'What things?'

'Psychological things.'

'We'll get help.'

'There is no help. I cannot say more; just believe in me!'

'I love you, Danielle; we love you. Don't do this!'

'I've already done it.'

'You have? You've slept with some guy?'

'Yes,' she replies unconvincingly.

'Why, Danielle?'

'Good bye, Jimmy.' She hangs up. This time just about kills him. Had it not been for Andie, there's no saying what a loss it would have been for humanity. Jimmy and Andie stay on until early May. The rain pours almost every day for six weeks. At first, he would go to her apartment with Andie, but she is never there. Next he would go to the law school, but could not bring himself to make a scene when he sees her with an older man with a moustache. They certainly do not seem like lovers. Jimmy tortures himself over and over. Finally, one day after calling her and she disconnects it, he goes to her place and finds her at home. He waits thinking what he might do. He needs proof that she is having an affair, and if it is true, he would give up and leave forever.

About ten thirty at night, Jimmy is standing in the rain under a tree. Then a car pulls up and parks on the street of upscale row houses some divided into apartments. A man emerges. It is the man with the moustache. He walks up to Danielle's house and enters. Jimmy goes around to the fire escape at the back of her upstairs apartment and climbs up onto a flat veranda roof where he can look into her apartment. He can see them holding each other in the kitchen. She leads the man into the bedroom.

Jimmy walks home in the pouring rain, his tears falling from the sky. He swears he will never see her again. Within a week he and Andie are on their way home. It would be almost two decades before they would see Danielle again. Time does heal Jimmy's bitter smart and in spite of this separation, he cannot stop loving this seemingly heartless woman. But more poignantly, this situation is a case not so much as healing, but revealing.

The day Danielle actually came back into their lives, she showed up unannounced at Jimmy's brick farmhouse on Andie's 21st birthday seventeen years later. The surprise was a reserved but welcome reunion, without either admonishment or blandishments of love; there were regrets, though a general communion of forgiveness. Prior to that there had been phone calls, gifts, emails still swearing her undying fidelity to Jimmy, but her strange aversion to their love and Jimmy's enmity toward her had held fast until that day. She explained that she was entering into politics and needed their support and blessing, wanting to rekindle her attachment to them on terms that would benefit them both without upsetting their secret arrangement regarding Andie. She again confessed that she had never been unfaithful and disclosed that years before on that fateful night in Vancouver, she had seen Jimmy standing outside in the rain and knew that Max was coming over to work on business. She had let the ruse do its work feeling that otherwise Jimmy would not leave. She admitted it was cruel and she hated herself for it. Jimmy, nonetheless, was disbelieving of her purported honesty, although conceded eventually to a professional relationship in view of her avowed repentance and meteoric success in the world, but specifically because of Andie. However, it would not be until Danielle became Prime Minister that they once again resumed intimate relations.

In spite of her apparent duplicity in Vancouver, Danielle has now for a long time cleaned up her peculiar lifestyle. She is now a much-altered person, who not only had long before stopped smoking and taking drugs, but obtained a law degree, and entered the resource business with Max Light (the man with the moustache) a well-to-do entrepreneur, becoming involved in mining and water. Platinum, gold and lithium are their elements, as their related uses propelled exponentially in the years to come. Water was fast becoming a sleeping political giant so she delegated their interests by creating a company that specialised in environmentally sound water resource planning, specifically promoting public exposure and in effect a certain notorious self-serving prominence using the funds from other mineral ventures. Later, in another amazing twist as if on some mysterious cue to destiny she began new television show called Deep Politics, which earned her a growing international reputation for exposing the hidden agendas of government, especially in the United States. Being across the border insulated her from the U.S. network control and the satellites beamed her into every household in the western world. Her most brazen accusation was when she expostulated to the world the touchy subjects of the supposed recovery of alien technology and the secret study and development of this technology underscored by interviews with credible people including one who had been a member of the National Security Council. Through back channels the U.S. government bore down on the then Prime Minister to shut her up labeling her a "lunatic". Their efforts backfired and because of other concurrent lobbying within the states, congressional hearings were initiated only to be stymied by a last ditch pitch by the executive branch, of which troubles actually carried into the next election that they lost. The next President had been elected on the platform of an "open book" with the mandate to clean out the drawers so-to-speak of the vast secret world, but later backed down declaring there was nothing to clean out. Few people believed in his sincerity, indeed the entire government, which instigated the Righteous movement that one day would contribute to the causes of the Third World War almost sixty years later. The buzz: which government held the real power? The secret one or the elected one? Was democracy an elaborate façade? Danielle in her inimitable way kept picking at the seams to the glee of the Western world, speculating as to what monstrous secrets were being kept from an unassuming electorate.

Danielle then began her political career on the crest of that notoriety as leader of a new party that she named the Conservative Democratic Party or CD's, tailor-made to her particular views. She won an overwhelming landslide in the elections of '23, '28, a slim majority in '31, and lost in '36, but won again resoundingly in '40 and '44, which was her last election. She was assassinated on Sept. 20, 2047 at 4:07 p.m. by an apparent bomb set off in her Gatineau summer residence. That tragedy would become one of the most infamous mysteries of the 21st century; no one ever claimed responsibility, and it was never determined if it actually was a bomb that pulverized the house, as there was no trace found of any known residue. It was blamed, however, on Danielle's personal secretary, the man with the moustache, Max Light, who promptly committed suicide and took to the grave their secrets, leaving for posterity a series of micro discs bearing the name James Piercemore. The rest, of course, is history, and hence the enigma.

Danielle, at fifty-one, is at the end of her second successive term as Prime Minister of Canada and ready for a third. Jimmy Pidgeon heads the new Astro-Physics Propulsion Lab of York University. Both remain unmarried and seem determined to remain so, although apparently no one special with Danielle, and few with Jimmy as it turned out, enter into each other's lives. Andie, now a thirty-four year old woman, works in a bio-genetics firm and lives with a man named Robert Barnett. She is the very image of her mother, but with the personality of her father. Naturally, she knew who her mother was and had met with her on many occasions during the course of her adult life, but had always disdained the truth believing the ruse of Lisa Bouchard less complicated. From her earliest memories, the subject of her mother's identity was both her and Jimmy's family secret. Public disclosure could only betray her tenuous hold on either of them. And she loved her father dearly.

On a cool, cloudy May day in 2031 Jimmy picks up the phone to hear Danielle's voice, which had mellowed over the years, but sounded that lovable coolness. She informs him she will be in Toronto and thought she would make a quick visit to his country home north of Toronto. He agrees of course, having not seen her for a couple of weeks. She had spoken at the Empire Club about new initiatives in space technology and among other things was very warmly received. Her strong decentralist views had been perfect for the times, but surprisingly when it comes to certain business initiatives, she somewhat anomalously sought control and got her way by imposing restrictions that seemed to curtail competitors. She qualifies this publicly by saying that national resources must benefit all, and only the government has the legislative power to protect some of the patents of the new technology from being exploited. Ostensibly, Jimmy Pidgeon had developed most of this technology, but due to Danielle's paranoia regarding her past, she had Jimmy create a pseudonym with which to safeguard any relationship or connection between herself and Jimmy Pidgeon. The pseudonym, Piercemore, on the other hand became a classified government code word for patents. It was assumed by those in the know (lawyers and technocrats) that Piercemore was simply a "project name" not representing anyone in particular. It wasn't of course, until Light's suicide when the contents of the micro discs found on him were revealed and subsequently published, confirming a real person existed behind the Piercemore name. This ploy created a huge windfall economically for Canada, to the point where Canada was looked upon by the world as a great power even eclipsing America in some areas of prestige and global leadership, which in fact suited the Americans just fine, up to a point. Perreault, particularly, symbolised this distinction.

Tensions arise however over a water deal, a colossal water project that required Canadian approval according to an International Ecological Pact signed by Perreault and the President in her first term. The Americans wished to redirect a significant portion of the Hudson's Bay watershed south into the Dakotas as well as Lake Superior to water the plains that were gradually becoming desert, specifically in the south due to the crust displacement which was estimated to be catastrophic to American agriculture if nothing was done very quickly.

The earth crust displacement of 2012, though mild in terms of what could have happened – certainly falling far short of the many doomsday scenarios – did activate numerous major earthquakes that were thought to be dormant. Notwithstanding the terrible loss of life, the political and economic repercussions were apocalyptic. Due to the circumstances, the dominant powers of the world were not so ready to give as to protect and preserve what they had. The new attitude was survival of the fittest. Nature's will had been vented and religious leaders proselytized it as a moral reckoning, which served to justify protectionism. The doomed victims around the world were unduly recognised as those whom paid the ultimate price.

In any event, the great water aquifers of the south central plains were basically empty and net production of farm produce was down anywhere from fifty to one hundred percent. Even in some of the traditionally fertile areas of the green belt, such as southern Illinois and Indiana, drought was commonplace and a new norm. But Perreault was holding out. She knew there would be terrible ecological devastation for that vast environmentally sensitive region of the Hudson's Bay watershed. She also knew that to turn the Americans down would be politically irresponsible for future generations. Canada must come to their rescue in this time of need, but way down the road, she knew nature would have her way and dry up America. This could not to be helped. Her decision came as an historic demarcation in U.S.-Canadian relations. As much water as possible would be redirected with a mutually agreeable criteria for ecological damage and emptied into the Missouri to be siphoned off in a vast underground refilling system which would refill the dry aquifers. However, Danielle had made negotiations particularly difficult. When all the details had been worked out by the experts, and a package had been prepared for both the President and Prime Minister, a high level meeting was held in Ottawa in which at a certain point, Perreault dismissed all her advisors and asked the President to do the same in order for them to be alone.

'Now, John,' said Danielle, 'I want to tell you in person of our commitment to go ahead with this project. Everything has been worked out, the cost, the engineering, the ecology etc. It is lucrative for us and of great benefit to you. I will sign this agreement this afternoon, but ask for one small thing. It is personal. I have someone in our employ, on the government payroll code-named James Piercemore. He has invented many technologies used today. Our new Hometech patents for fusion reactors are now being utilised worldwide, as well as jet fusion engines and automobile reactors, and I know you compete with us in these fields. Now, over the years, we have tracked and engaged a few UFOs over our skies. You know and I know that they're not yours nor anyone else's on this earth for that matter. I want you to secure a place for Piercemore in your alien skunkworks or whatever you call it. I must insist, or the deal is off.'

The President, a little taken aback with her forceful request was nonplussed to say the least. He looked at the carpet and around for the advisor who wasn't there.

'Ms. Perreault,' he said finally, 'you obviously have been misinformed. I haven't any idea what you are talking about. I know about UFO's and we do have some information on them. Yes, contrary to general public knowledge, I admit they exist; I'll say that, but unless I'm misinformed, I know no more. I can't believe you are holding me and America hostage to this whim! Are you out of your mind? This is blackmail!'

'Not at all, John. I'll call the press and delay the deal on some technicality. I don't think you can afford to do that. The American people need action now, and you know it; at least you will, come election time.'

'Why are you doing this? I can only call your bluff. I haven't any idea what you're talking about.'

Danielle got up to terminate the meeting. She walks to the door.

'Wait, Danielle,' he said nervously, 'let me at least speak to some of my people. Maybe there's something going on that I don't know about. You know how it is these days; I'm just a public official. Everything's on a need-to-know basis. I'm fed information just like anybody else.'

'Okay, I want your personal assurance in writing, and if you don't come through, I'll blow the whole alien thing wide open; let the chips fall where they may.'

The famous Water Document was signed that very afternoon.

Two weeks later Danielle spoke in Toronto at the Empire Club, then afterwards from the hotel was whisked away undercover of night by Max Light into the country to Jimmy's farm house.

Jimmy opens the door and waves to Max, who drives back to the hotel. Danielle gives Jimmy a big hug and kiss, which he returns with his usual reserve.

'Oh Jimmy,' she smiles in a happy mood, 'do I have news for you! Our juvenile dreams have come true!'

Jimmy has no idea what she is talking about.

They hold each other; Jimmy doesn't smile so much, but acknowledges her happiness nevertheless. He had taken a long time to forgive her games out west almost thirty years before. She had used him like a dishrag and Jimmy let her know it. Then there was Max. Jimmy had in fact become friends with affable Max. Max, a plain, clean complexioned man had been that unwitting pawn that rainy night in Vancouver long ago. Her regret was sincere, but Max was indispensable to her, and vice-versa. They had a professional relationship that proved to be impervious to the slings and arrows of political tides. Max was the type of man who looked, acted, and spoke like an Anubis guarding the secret vault. He had never in his entire life raised his voice in objection to either Jimmy or Danielle, nor succumbed to the swings of despondency. He was almost inhuman in his ability to serve his platonic mistress like a eunuch. The media called him rather callously Friday or The Sphinx. It was all the rage for years whether they led mutually private lives, to their unequivocal denials.

Jimmy still saw in Danielle the muse and apparition of his fantasies, because she never stayed around long enough to come down to earth. Her rendezvous' with him were always classified and thoroughly arranged through Max. She rather shamelessly used Max as the liaison under that pseudonym James Piercemore. And to further insulate her potential liability, she had all Jimmy's birth records classified. He did in fact use his name at university and life in general, credit cards and the like, but any trace to the government, hospital at birth, or Revenue Canada would turn up classified. When he traveled, he carried a passport under his name James T. Pidgeon, but again with no public record with Internal Affairs, External Affairs or any other government branch. Only Danielle, Max and a computer program knew the truth, and the program was erased as soon as it had completed an assignment. Max was indispensable. Their power was absolute.

The first thing Jimmy and Danielle usually do when they haven't seen each other in a while was to make love. She would unleash herself without restraint giving completely over to the flesh. Jimmy would return her passions, but in a more cerebral manner. He would watch her and himself with a detachment that made her even more ravenous. And the older they get the better it becomes. Both now over fifty, Danielle just so, had them aged like the rarest Beaujolais, wise and mellowed with a long lingering aftertaste.

'We are a strange mix,' remarks Jimmy languishing in bed.

'How so? Literally?' she murmurs, watching him with her steel blue eyes.

'What a cocktail,' he continues. 'Can we keep up this charade forever?'

'I like your play on words,' she purrs giving him a pull.

'Danielle, I'm serious; what will become of us when we retire?'

'Retire? I'll never retire.'

'Doesn't sound right, does it?' He caresses her soft, white shoulder. He

loves her body, which had barely changed in over thirty years. 'Nevertheless, it would be nice to enjoy our grandchildren.'

'What?' she perks up. 'Is Andie pregnant?'

'I meant to tell you earlier.'

'But she's not married.'

'Now that's an oxymoron, Danielle, hearing that from you.'

She doesn't pursue it and falls back into her impervious reverie. 'I have
a surprise for you,' she declares suddenly.

'What, a new high in Hometech revenues?' he asks sarcastically.

'Actually, no, but since you ask, yes. And we forecast conservatively, no
pun intended, that revenues in the next five years will top over a trillion
dollars. In the coming election I plan to propose lowering income tax levels to almost nil; that's what they were one hundred years ago during the
Great Depression.'

'Very good. Do you then plan on revoking your ludicrous Health For
Yourself Program?'

'No way. It's the best compromise, babe. Doctors need some autonomy.
Lower income people can qualify for the best assistance. Listen, you
dummy!' She nuzzles into his hairy chest, then raises herself on top of
him nose to nose. 'Do you remember when we met?'

'Yes.'

'Don't you remember what we talked about and you said: no way,
they'd never do it?'

'Yeah, alien technology. The Americans have it all for themselves; so
what else is new?'

'I got you a new job, babe.'

'Doing what? And shouldn't you ask me first?'

'No, of course not. I own James Piercemore.'

'But I am James Piercemore and you don't own me,' he retorts.

'I mean the cover silly.'

Jimmy stares back at her nose to nose. Her eyes are teasing. 'Well?' he
presses.

'A man from the State Department called me this week – a Mr. Smith – very cordial. He asked me to set up an appointment with Mr. Piercemore. I said Mr. Piercemore could be found at York University at your email, which I gave. They'll be checking you out for a while. They won't come up with much. They won't know whether to call you Pidgeon or Piercemore. It doesn't matter; both of you are classified.'

'Very funny, Danielle. Do you have any idea what you're getting me into?'

'Not really,' she murmurs moving on him, 'but it feels right and I know we shall benefit immensely from the experience, don't you think? I mean we'll be privy to the vault.'

'Ever the thief,' sighs Jimmy, positioning himself more comfortably.

'To give to the world, my friend!' she whispers seductively into his ear.

'It'll be the end of us, Danielle.'

'I feel divine,' she utters passionately.

'Sometimes I just don't know who you really are,' declares Jimmy.

'Snow White . . . and horny.'

A week later, Jimmy's secretary comes into his office one afternoon at the university. She tells him that she must leave early that day for a dentist appointment, but mentions that a Mr. Smith called while he was in the lab. The man claimed to have spoken to Cal Emory, the President of Hometech, the public government company that Jimmy's inventions were patented under, and that Cal had put him in touch with Jimmy. Mr. Smith would come by that afternoon. Jimmy doesn't think about it much as there are always people coming and going with connections to Hometech.

Hometech was of course Danielle's brainchild, with Jimmy being the progenitor of its patents. Roderich Fleming was the first President before he entered politics and then the Energy Minister. Ricky knows Jimmy had an integral hand in the technology, but when he came across the name Piercemore as Energy Minister, he was at a loss to know who was really behind the patents, though presumed Jimmy had to be. And since Piercemore was classified even for Ricky because of Danielle's paranoia regarding her past, Ricky really doesn't take issue with it assuming it had something to do with Danielle's terrible secret as a mother who gave away her child. To satisfy his curiosity, he once solemnly addressed Jimmy about that, and Jimmy simply replied that Danielle had her personal issues and that we must support them.

At the time, Jimmy worked with Dr. Ramsay Jones in atomic engineering research. Ramsay was really a front man who unwittingly covered for Jimmy under Danielle's machinations. And Doc, as they called Ramsay, won the Nobel prize for physics, having taken credit for Jimmy's breakthroughs in harmonics and electromagnetic fusion reactors. It must be said, however, that the fusion patents had popped up almost simultaneously all over the West under slightly altered prescriptions after the first breakthrough, which occurred under Doc's supervision. Humble Jimmy, a lab technician at the time, who hadn't even pursued a doctorate, was of course the genius behind the breakthrough. Dr. Ramsay Jones, being the patronizing man that he was and politically adept given his public position as Head of the Physics Dept. and Chairman of the government-funded Atomic Research Council, had sold out to many prospective companies, which subsequently got him into trouble. He had become immensely wealthy slithering through the grey areas of vested interests and personal greed. And when Jimmy, pugnacious as he was at times, confronted him about his shabby attitude regarding this technology, Doc had sent him up to the York Board of Trustees to be reprimanded and threatened with termination of employment. Jimmy, however, stood his ground and presented evidence that supported his having been the brains behind Doc. The result was that Doc was retired with fanfare and Jimmy given absolute control over the the new propulsion lab at a country location, thanks to Danielle, which was a special government-funded facility for

Electromagnetic Engineering research. Jimmy was forty-six at the time and Danielle was in her first term of office.

When Danielle was elected Prime Minister, she recognised a good thing in Jimmy's natural humility and his reclusive ways. No one she knew worked so tirelessly and was so dedicated to the lab, not to mention his writing and other interests.

At work Jimmy was the source, switch, and conduit to Hometech. Even the Americans were interested and used many of the patents, which proved to be worthy. The Americans, however, had something far greater, kept from public view and mainstream science. Indeed, mainstream science was catching up, but had a long way to go. The Americans could sit on their information for a long time. Danielle knew it, but until the Water Document, she was in no position to barter. Ever since Jimmy's interest in alien technology, at least what he had discovered for himself through various sources, he now believed was safe-guarded in highly classified agendas. He was unsure how authentic this information was but if any indication as such was forthcoming, anyone who stuck their neck out to reveal it soon found themselves helplessly outcast, discredited, even vilified and driven to penury. The likes of Bob Lazar, for instance, back in the late 1980's had blown open to the unbelieving public some of what was going on in Dreamland (Area 51) in Nevada. And that was just a pinprick. Lazar had been a credible source, having held a Naval Intelligence W4 tax form confirmed by other employees who knew him at Los Alamos National Laboratories, one of his previous employers. Stanton Freidman, a nuclear physicist, who had worked on government projects, was another good source who exposed the existence of MJ-12, a highly classified group of public and private individuals who presided over all alien intelligence. Nevertheless, for all the discrediting and debunking by the government and media reserved for anyone remotely interested in bringing this information to public light, Danielle would do her utmost to protect Jimmy's interest, which she considered to be her own. For Jimmy, any knowledge furthering humanity's desire to travel in space and communicate with other species from other star systems was of paramount interest. The technology was possible, he insisted. He just needed some special minerals that probably could not be synthetically manufactured here on earth. He was speaking, of course, of the mythical unumpetium (element 115) that had been produced by aliens, or procured on some other planet.

Danielle told Jimmy and she had it in writing from President Arnold that, 'Piercemore will have my personal guarantee of safety, and it would indeed be a pleasure to introduce our brilliant Canadian friend to some of our discoveries.' Jimmy was almost stunned over Danielle's amazing verve.

'Why do you think I became Prime Minister, you fool?' she had said.

'I would hope to manage the country, Danielle,' he replied, sincerely.

'Of course, that goes without saying, but I'm still corrupt for you,' she half-joked.

'If anything's corrupt, it's this whole Piercemore charade,' he said.

'You're probably right; he's a billionaire by now, and unfortunately, Revenue Canada may audit him and we'll have to give it all to charity. Do you have any preferences?'

'How about World Literacy?'

'Oh Jimmy, you're such a bore.'

'Me? Well then how about a Canadian aerospace program; we'll call it the New Arrow.'

'Too contentious. The Americans enjoy their superiority in that sphere and plan to keep it.'

'What did you have in mind?' he asked feeling her soft under-regions.

'Mmm, I thought maybe you could build a secret space craft and we could elope together.'

'And I thought I was the dreamer.' He pauses from caressing.

'Don't stop . . . yes, yes, I would marry you, then.'

Jimmy sits in his study thinking about these matters. He hadn't had a good night's sleep since that night with Danielle . . . not that he did then, either. Life was like a bowling ball, he thought: just when you thought you'd strike, the ball would miraculously miss. What was he getting into?

The floor receptionist shows Mr. Smith into Mr. Pidgeon's office. Mr. Smith is a man about forty, balding, but in very good shape, with a firm jaw and not an ounce of fat. His brown eyes had both a severity and angst in their lightness. Jimmy shakes his hand and invites him to have a seat.

'What can I do for you, Mr. Smith?' says Jimmy relaxing in his chair.

'Is this a secure room, Mr. Pidgeon?'

'Secure? I have nothing to fear. Why?'

'Don't you worry about people stealing your technology?'

'Not at all, in fact, we willingly impart it through Hometech; that's my job.'

'Yes, naturally, I didn't think of it that way.'

'And I didn't think Hometech has any business questioning my integrity; I am Hometech. What's all this about?' asks Jimmy, humoured.

'I'm not from Hometech, Mr. Pidgeon . . . '

'My apologies, then where, may I ask?'

'If you'll let me explain, I was ordered by the highest authority of the U.S. government, with your government's permission, to brief you on what's required of you to join our reverse engineering program – so classified you must take an oath binding for life.'

'Ah, yes, Mr. Smith,' says Jimmy amused. 'I was told you'd be in touch. This is interesting. Please proceed.'

'Goddammit, Mr. Pidgeon, if I may say so, you have to be one of the most elusive persons I have ever dealt with. We pride ourselves on secrecy and accurate intelligence and we have absolutely no record of your birth or citizenship. And I understand that maybe you're working under an alias, James Piercemore, which is even more obscure. We can't find anything under him either, and believe me, we are very thorough. Who are you, anyway?'

'You're looking at him; don't mind all that hocus pocus: the Prime Minister is paranoid. But I'd like to know who you are, Mr. Smith.'

Mr. Smith looks at Jimmy, hesitating for a moment. 'Yes, of course. My real name is Lieutenant-Colonel Jeb Wickling, Naval Intelligence Special Services – Research.'

'Glad to meet you, Jeb,' says Jimmy standing up. 'Jimmy Pidgeon. Born and raised.'

'What about Piercemore?' queries Wickling standing too.

'That's just a lot of cloak and dagger baloney. I'm just a scientist. Come on, Mr. Smith, I'll give you a tour of our own skunkworks.'

Jimmy shows Mr. Smith to the laboratories and engineering facility that of course had its own security clearance.

'Are you prepared to leave this cozy enclave?' asks the Lieutenant-Colonel as they walk back up to the offices.

'That depends on what I'm getting into, Mr. Smith.'

'If I were you, Mr. Pidgeon, and I speak from the bottom of my heart, you don't want to go to Nevada.'

'Why? Sounds challenging. Isn't that why I'm going?'

'Challenging isn't the word for it. Once you're in, you're never out until you're dead. The security is without doubt . . . paranoid. It has to be. I think you have a good life here. You still have the option not to go.'

They arrive back at Jimmy's office, but remain standing.

Jimmy goes to the window and looks out to see a few of the graduate students go home, then turns around.

'This may sound corny, Jeb, but I really want to go. I don't see it as an opportunity, so much as an avenue of fate. My understanding, and correct me if I'm wrong, is that your government has for over eighty years – that's pushing a century – had knowledge of extraterrestrial life, interacted with them, gleaned technology from them, while keeping the rest of the world still watching the sun come up over the dark ages . . . '

'Jim, please, no need to extrapolate. We all have a big problem with that very thinking; however, we have an even bigger security problem here on earth. We believe that by releasing advanced technologies to the public and the world, our fears would be one hundred fold . . . '

'Perhaps, but the public knowledge of aliens shouldn't pose such a threat; in fact, it may enlighten people . . . I'm thinking of murderous fundamentalists who want to turn back the clock on progress – a kind of wake-up call.'

'Progress? Our track record for progress is debatable, and the fundamentalists you speak of may just get more support to fuel their insanity. Furthermore, you speak confidently of aliens, Jim, as if they are a manageable entity. But we, those of us in the know, are still in the dark, because they want us there.'

'Come on, Jeb; they're certainly not the stereotypical Hollywood monsters; they are advanced both spiritually and technologically. We haven't been threatened by them, have we?'

'No, but you cannot know what the hell we're dealing with out there! Believe me, it's not that simple. These beings are so far beyond our way of thinking, breathing, mating, and doing. I'm talking about thousands, tens of thousands of years, and some hundreds of thousands, even millions of years. If we assert ourselves into the galaxy without their help, we'd be swallowed up like a frog eating a fly, or snake a mouse. We are primitive in comparison! And, sir, frankly it scares the hell out of me and everybody. Oh yes, there are good people out there, if you want to call them that, some like us, but there are others not so far away, who are our worst nightmare. Our status in this vicinity of the galaxy is tenuous as it is! We are containers. We are being closely monitored like a bio-lab beaker. When we decide to go blasting off with our own fusion-powered gravity propulsion spacecraft thinking we're like Columbus, well, are we in for a surprise! Almost every viable solar system out there has life in varying degrees, like a primeval swamp!'

'The way you sound, it's like: what's the point?' Jimmy sits back behind his desk.

'Exactly,' says the officer. 'It's like staying home on the farm, rather than venturing out to some urban ghetto and getting mugged because you look like a tourist.'

'Are you saying we'd be mugged out there?'

'Worse. They see life very differently. There's no commerce, little individuality, no freedom like we see it. Some of these races don't even speak! They use the environment, manipulate it, for one thing only: to enhance their species and all species as they see fit. They're not cannibals, or murderers like some sci-fi bogymen. They are survivors. There are some species so advanced, they literally play God with species such as ours, not to hurt us, just to hasten or inhibit our development as they see fit with their own genetic manipulation. For example, we know for a fact, that over thirty thousand years ago, a relatively evolved race of people here on earth were genetically enhanced by alien intervention. These people originated on what today is Antarctica, which at one time was higher in latitude towards the equator and had a temperate climate on the northern half. As far-fetched as it might seem, they were the ones who built the Pyramids. I have actually seen digital video of their construction taken in 10792 BC!'

'Really? Incredible . . . what happened to them?'

'Once their continent was lost in the cataclysm – the great flood – apparently caused by a major precessional correction, which we experienced to a far lesser degree in the 2012, the survivors were spread too thin and over thousands of years they completely vanished like an extinct species, swallowed in the overwhelming genetic morass of human evolution. All we have are the legends and legacies.'

'So I gather, the alien experiment was a failure.'

'Not totally. Who are we after all?'

'The curse of the mummy?'

Mr. Smith laughs a few syllables: 'In a metaphor, yes.'

'I'm sold, Jeb; I couldn't live with myself, if I turned this one down.'

'Just remember what I said, Mr. Pidgeon; once you've become radioactive – a term we use – it's a one-way street. Everyone is expendable, even the President.'

'I understand,' accedes Jimmy.

'I really hope so.'

'When do I start?'

'I suggest you resign at the end of this term. Pack your bags and fly to Las Vegas and call this number. Think it over Mr. Pidgeon. I envy you, your choice.' With that, Mr.Smith gives Jimmy a card with a number of an employment office, then quickly departs.

A man in his sixties, dressed in a green jumpsuit stands in an alley looking out at Survivor's Walk. He carefully scrutinizes the lifts. Mobius can't help but notice there is some unusual activity going to and fro from the executive levels of the Pyramid. His watchful network, however, could not report any clue as to what it was all about. It was apparent though that tensions are high, not only at the executive levels, but with the populace as a whole, as if everyone had finally awakened from a bad dream to discover that their cozy world was no more and had in fact been usurped. Inflation and the cost of living have risen dramatically because of the deflated credit of the regime. The agricultural sector, the supporting pillar of the Sunsetwind economy, had been dealt a serious blow the previous week when Del Barker and his Board passed a new law stating that all lease holders of land were now liable to a new assessment. The outrage that this incurred had yet to spill over, but when the shock subsided, LeRoy MacGregor had secretly organised an assault on the government's plans.

There had been rumors that Del Barker himself had become incensed, not at the landholders, but at the Chicagos. So far, and it was already March, the assumed windfall of the raised currency in mortgaging Sunsetwind through foreign investment had turned out to be a disaster – hence the assessment – and Barker was fighting mad that the Chicagos hadn't lived up to their bargain. The billions raised, according to some highly placed sources, had been lost like water through the cracks of an old floor. The money was used to buy up equities in a new fangled currency exchange that Chicago had begun with the Americans. The Americans, however, dragged their feet and finally opted out saying their economy was not stable enough to risk new capital. The Chicagos hadn't even put up any of their own money. It was Sunsetwind that underwrote the whole scam at the Chicago's prompting. In the end the Chicago Head of Finance, Tomasina, had to say the money had been used as payment for the invasion. As a result, it was claimed that what the Chicagos had previously owed Sunsetwind, had been paid in full with Sunsetwind money as a trade off!'

Consequently, Del Barker had effectively sold Sunsetwind down the river. The terrible irony was that the original system he had trashed in an attempt to "revitalise" the little province, was now an archaic form of capitalism and their only hope for survival. At least by feeding themselves, Sunsetwind could create more wealth with a healthy perspective. Even their technological superiority was now in limbo because the Chicagos had muscled in on many of Sunsetwind's little markets which had up to then sustained them. Costs of production had risen more than one hundred percent due to inflation. In short, in a matter of months, Del Barker had turned Sunsetwind from a thriving autonomous province into a crippled sub-state. Previously, its economy was small, but stable. It seemed incredible that the economy could deteriorate so quickly.

Treason doesn't know about the state of affairs when she returns via Toronto to stay with her Forager friends. Although her friends had warned her not to go into Sunsetwind, she explained that she had to go to see her mom and Seymour, whom she had yet to hear was deceased. But also her precious little cargo intrigues her. It is the sort of thing that really excites her and makes her feel powerful and useful. To think that she was chosen to bring some strange medallion to the great Redman, whom she had met only once as a child, is indeed the challenge of a lifetime, apart from partying with the Chicago elite. She hasn't the faintest twinge of remorse for her double standards. Wasn't that what she was supposed to do? No one but she could have accomplished what she did. That is her gift. Sam, by way of the mysterious Heyoka, knew instinctively she was the one to deliver it and that she would do it willingly.

Once she arrived back in the Neutrals, the Foragers there again beseeched her not to enter Sunsetwind, but stay with them until things cooled down. They suspect that after the EF election, if Cephren was to be elected, a great deal of pressure would come to bear on Del Barker to step down and allow an election. They, however, don't know the man and his zeal. Treason doesn't seem to care one way or another; Sunsetwind is her country and she is going home. She is oblivious to political partisanship. And what could they possibly want from her? As far as the new regime is concerned, she is nobody, or so she thinks.

The day she shows up at her mother's door seems to be the best day of her life. With eager anticipation, she rushes in to find the house empty and cold. Without thinking anything out of the ordinary, she browses around looking at the familiar mementos which gave her a sense of being home. When she reaches the studio, she calls out to her mom and hears a venomous screech in reply.

'Treason!' Strange stomps out of the studio covered in dust from working on a marble statue. She stares with that scowl Treason knows so well, but now cringes from in shock.

'Do you have any idea what you've done?' demands Strange in voice ready to kill.

'Mom? What's wrong? Why aren't you glad to see me?'

'You're not my daughter any more! Treason how could you?' Strange is an identical but older replica of Treason.

'Mom!' cries Treason. 'What have I done?'

'Don't you play games with me, you little bitch!'

Treason begins to break down. 'I want to help,' she says, ashamed of something she isn't sure of.

Strange turns and goes back in her studio and slams the door. 'Good riddance!' she screams.

Treason stops crying. A thought occurs to her: her mom has gone completely bonkers. She musters some courage.

'Has Seymour left you?' she asks in a faltering voice to the door.

The door swings open. Strange stands there cynically with hate in her eyes that blister through Treason.

'Do you want to know what's left of Seymour?' she declares in a low blood-curdling voice.

'What's wrong, mommy?' whimpers Treason fearfully.

'What's wrong, mommy?' Strange mimics.

'Why are you doing this?' she wails.

Strange grabs her by the wrist and pulls her into the studio up to the work in progress.

'Look!' she yells. 'Here's what's left of Seymour!'

Treason stares at the unmistakable appearance of Seymour being shaped out of a giant chunk of carnation red marble.

'Where's Seymour?' sniffles Treason diminutively.

'Are you telling me you don't know?' mocks Strange in exasperation.

'I escaped, mom. I've been in Chicago, spying for Sunsetwind!'

'So I understand!'

'I was spying for Sunsetwind! I had to do things!'

'Well, indeed! And it cost Seymour his life!' Strange begins to cry against the door jam. 'You can't know how much I loved that man. You have destroyed Sunsetwind, Treason. My own flesh and blood . . . and Seymour . . . I never had a chance to say . . . to say to him I was sorry . . . you ruined everything!' She sobs.

Treason, crying, goes to her. They hug.

'Seymour's dead, isn't he?' weeps Treason.

'He was butchered by the Chicagos!'

'How? Why?'

'Trying to save Sam from getting caught while escaping with Runaway . . . it all happened so fast. It was horrible! Horrible!'

'I'm so sorry, mom! I'm so sorry! I didn't know! I did only what I thought was best for Sunsetwind. You must believe me! I never had anything to do with that invasion! How could anybody think that! Cleo knew about my spying! She told me to!'

'How do I know if you're telling me the truth?' quizzes Strange, coming to her senses and letting go of Treason. 'I heard that you were under suspicion, because no one knew your whereabouts and there was some rumor you were working with Trinny herself and Babylon, her special advisor.'

'He was my lover, mom,' she concedes wiping away her tears.

'Your lover?'

'Yes, since I was nineteen, when I went to Toronto with Mike. Remember Mike, the Forager?'

'And when Cleo found out she engaged you to pursue the relationship?'

'Yes.'

'And you spied on the Chicagos?'

'How do you think we knew as much as we did about their inner workings these past few years?'

'Oh Treason,' gushes Strange, 'I'm so sorry; you're a heroine! I've hurt you; please forgive me. Things are so crazy around here. Del Barker is destroying Sunsetwind and he's too stupid and power mad to see it!'

'I heard about the mortgaging of the land to the Chicagos. There was nothing I could do. But I finally got a break.' Treason pulls the necklace chain out from under her survival suit and shows her mom the alien medallion.

'What is it?' wonders Strange taking a closer look and turning it about with her dusty fingers.

'I don't know exactly. Sam gave it to me and told me to get it to Redman with the greatest urgency.'

'It's so heavy!'

'Tell me about it. My neck is sore.'

'How is Sam? We heard what happened to him.'

'He's fine. He's a Sunsetwinder all the way now.'

'Where did he get this?'

'Would you believe Heyoka?'

'Heyoka Yellow Tooth? She's alive?'

'And incarcerated in the Bungalow.'

'Trinny's Bungalow.'

'That's right. I got in to help with some of Babylon's children and Sam's birthday party. Trinny put on a bash for him.'

'Thank you, Trinny.'

'Somehow he met with Heyoka and she told him to get this to Redman.'

'Does Trinny know? How did you get away?'

'I just left. Babylon let me go.'

'Just like that?'

'I'm good, mom,' she boasts with a sexy smile.

'Seymour would be proud of you.'

'Not until I avenge his death!' The pout was back, appropriately.

Redman gets the message from Mobius. His old, wiry frame sits coiled like a spent spring. He sighs and sighs again. He is at a loss to understand the implications of what he had just heard. Being escorted down through the maintenance section to the very gaol of sorts that Chromolox had once occupied a month before, are both Strange and Treason Honey. Strange had screamed obscenities at her captors, Barker's well-paid Praetorians, doing obediently what they were told. Furthermore, Mobius, that cunning janitor, managed to find out that the Chicagos were demanding the return of their agent, Treason Honey. This, Redman thinks he understands. But on second thought, he wonders why they would publicise it. Why purposely dash her cover? He peruses the labyrinthine psychology of espionage. It isn't really his cup of tea; but, he eventually concludes that the Chicagos had just signed Treason's death warrant. Del Barker would make an example of a traitor to bolster his own discredited patriotism. Redman agonises over these consequences. His old synapses snap and crackle.

There must be something she knows that is dangerous to the Chicagos! Could it be that Treason was true after all? And now she would be the lamb led to slaughter? But what of Strange? She must have been helping her. But he had heard that she was ready to strangle her if she saw her. He must communicate with them. He prepares a message.

nine God Is a Transvestite

That compels the boy to let it out
And behold the pie in the sky

                                        –Jimmy Pidgeon

Incarcerated in the same windowless room where Chromolox had stayed, both Treason and her mother Strange, sit glumly on the cot. Another cot is folded in the corner, but they make no attempt to dignify their surroundings. Written on the wall in large letters by the toilet says it all: Have no fear, the comforts here.

Earlier that evening, after their emotional reunion and suspecting nothing, they had sat down to eat spaghetti when Praetorian emops descended, and out stormed the stone-faced occupants to invade once again their old, quaint house. It had been a strenuous ordeal. Strange threatened them with a knife yelling that they were cowards, but they ignored her and she had to be physically restrained in electronic cuffs which semi-paralysed her hands and arms turning them into pins and needles. Treason on the other hand, had already begun playing into their hands offering her natural warmth and camaraderie as a guerilla. She asked one of the women why she had turned her back on old Sunsetwind. The woman replied that she needed the credit, and then promptly removed the medallion from Treason's neck. They were bundled off to the Pyramid without further explanation other than the government had evidence they were involved in an espionage operation with the Chicagos, and under martial law their lives could well be in jeopardy.

They feel betrayed sitting there, but know that Treason's circumstances are less than ideal. Treason says she will take the fall to save her mother if need be, but now that Strange knows the truth about her daughter, is not about to abandon her to her fate. She swears she will go down with her if necessary, to prove her point. Any judicial process, if there is one at all, would not be simple. Both Treason and Strange have every intention to fight Barker to the bitter end.

Del Barker had received a threatening message from Bob Fix, Chief of Chicago Security (the Genos), saying that the Sunsetwind guerilla, Treason Honey was in possession of a stolen medallion belonging to the Yellow Tooth Cherokees and if they didn't give it back, they, the Chicagos, would come and retrieve it. Del assumes that Treason had been spying for the Chicagos and then ran afoul of them; he was certainly not aware of her spying for Sunsetwind. And if she was not spying for the Chicagos, who is she spying for? The old regime is no more, unless she knows something that he should know. On the other hand, he believes Treason might well be a great source of knowledge about the inner workings of the Chicagos. And, he is very curious just what this medallion is all about, thinking possibly that he might be holding an ace.

Del sits in his suite in the apex nursing a scotch. Treason is escorted in by two Praetorians. He has them stand by outside, while holding the medallion in his hand and turning it in his fingers.

'It has a good feel to it, don't you think, Treason?'

'It's downright shabby of you, Barker, to pollute these sacred premises with your corruption.'

'Is this your idea of repentance, Treason? From what I understand, the Chicagos held you in some exalted favor, before you stole this. But I shall not stoop to your lowly, sluttish ways. Let's get down to business: I will incarcerate you and your mother indefinitely, if you don't explain the importance of this medallion and why the Chicagos want me to surrender it. Furthermore, why did you take it, and why didn't the Chicagos simply abduct you when you got back here, if they want this so badly?'

'You are one snide bastard, and I'm one well-trained guerilla; and I have no reason to repent, Del. But I'll tell you if you harm my mother you may do well to remember who your enemies are: Sunsetwinders. You are an uncommon slug who has destroyed the most beautiful country in the world. I will not speak to you of loyalties. My sacrifices are privileged information, including that of the medallion.'

Del laughs quickly, a tenor staccato, and downs the remainder of his scotch.

'I must say, Treason, I can understand why Babylon must have had a hard-on for you. I've heard that you were his favourite bitch. That might not go over well with the average Sunsetwinder. I think you should reconsider: if you haven't anything for me, what use are you to us? Personally, I believe you may have even been faithful to Sunsetwind, albeit a dubious sacrifice; after all you came back. The Chicagos obviously think so. Did Cleo put you up to it? What are you up to?'

Treason says nothing.

'Yes, I think so,' he says scrutinizing her. 'Yes, and I think you would make a good scapegoat for all the suffering our poor country has endured at the hands of the Chicagos. You know they bankrupted us. It was very clever of them; I give them full marks for the ruse. Nevertheless, sometimes the price for power is steep, and I have the power. I've got the power! Are you listening, dear? You could share this power with me. I'm looking for a woman like you, someone I shouldn't trust too much, because a man of my position shouldn't trust anyone, and that's comforting, you know. The world's a rat's nest, so as far as my needs are concerned: easy come, easy go.'

'Are you bored with your little girls?' she asks, remembering people speaking of his peccadilloes.

Del feigns a wince.

'Oooh, very good, I like moxy in a woman. Would you like a drink?'

She doesn't hesitate. 'Please.'

'Scotch, brandy, juice?'

'Brandy.'

He pours her a tumbler of brandy and hands it to her. Treason takes a good sip. She already knows what she must do.

'So tell me about this medallion, dear.'

'Well, it belonged to Heyoka. She's alive, you know, held prisoner like me. She said this would be proof of her being alive, at least her being abducted by the Chicagos. Any Yellow Tooth would corroborate that; it's sacred to them.'

'Indeed, and the Chicagos don't want that to get out, do they? She's a dark secret, isn't she?" he persists aggressively.

'I suppose, but soon an open one.'

'You suppose. I know so. News of that kind might just dismay the electorate against our good friend Trinny.'

'Maybe,' she says disdainfully, feeling very confidant. She gives him her best angle.

'I could like you, Treason. You're so very good at this sort of thing. What would your mother think? Maybe, I shall have a try at her too. What do you say?'

'Go ahead.'

He laughs. 'Come here,' he demands. 'Sit beside me.'

She obeys reluctantly and faces him on the sofa. She notices a protuberance in his pants.

'I'll guarantee you and your mother's protection,' he says putting his hand on Treason's knee.

'Really? Why?' she asks with a cynical smile.

'You're a little trickster. A crystal blue-eyed mulatto with a smart mouth.' He slides his hand down her thigh.

Treason stands up abruptly and walks around the sofa.

'I didn't give you permission to stand up,' he declares.

'Let's get something straight, Del: even Babylon didn't order me around. I won't be anybody's sperm depository, least of all yours. I might reconsider if you let my mother go, now, and you release me to do as I please. And one more thing: you give me back my medallion. Heyoka gave it to *me!*'

'You drive a hard bargain, dear,' he says, sitting back and smiling like a wolf.

'If you want me, that's the deal.' She stands there with her legs parted and hands on her hips.

He salaciously looks her up and down.

'On one condition,' he stipulates. 'No, two.'

'What's that?'

'We must sell that medallion back to the Chicagos to buy our silence about Heyoka for the very same amount they stole from us to "pay" for the invasion. We must pay back our mortgage, don't you think? Wouldn't that make everyone happy? A few billion dollars in credit? Eh?'

Treason can hardly believe she had gotten herself into this mess. She could save Sunsetwind by selling the medallion back to the Chicagos and at the same time forfeit Sunsetwind to Barker's success and dash the hopes of Heyoka, Cephren and Redman. A two-faced toss-up: damned if she does or doesn't. She knows she must prevent the Chicagos from getting that medallion at all costs even if it meant letting Sunsetwind remain bankrupt. She thinks she must somehow do more: keep the medallion, pay the mortgage and dump Barker. If she could only get to Redman!

'If I may keep it,' she states firmly, 'until an agreement has been reached with the Chicagos. It has sentimental value to me.'

'Oh, really, she has feelings – how cute,' he gibes sarcastically. 'But do you really think the Chicagos would pay us?'

'They might if we play them right or they want that badly enough, which it appears they do; but I wouldn't trust them.'

'Trust is a ploy, my little mink. And what would you propose?'

'That's for me to know and you to find out,' she taunts him flippantly, letting the 'mink' epithet go.

Del Barker rises and goes to her. He holds her face and deep kisses her. She breaks away and slaps him hard.

'Do we have a deal?' she exclaims bitterly, wiping her mouth.

'You little bitch!' He recoils from her slap, nursing his cheek. Recovering, he then smiles again, saying more gently, 'The fruits of victory, my dear, shall we celebrate tonight? I think we can compromise on that, so long as you wear our little wristband tag, so we can keep an eye on you. And I do have one more condition: you may wear the medallion only if you are with me, otherwise it will remain in my possession. We can't have such a valuable object put at risk can we dear?'

'No, I suppose not. Thank you,' she says, looking down with her best humility.

'But tell me something, Treason: how is it the Chicagos let you go so easily, or at least never caught up with you, once you left the country?'

'Well, Mr. Barker, I think you already know the answer to that,' she says putting her hand onto the erection in his pants. 'I'm the best there is, dear.'

He attempts to kiss her again and gropes for her breasts.

'Oh no, my mother is not on her way home yet.'

Del beeps his monitor and eagerly dispatches the order. He then pulls her down on the sofa. She reaches the table and gingerly grabs the medallion to stuff in her pocket; but he takes her wrist and reclaims the medallion. Then he puts it around her delicate neck. Following this gesture she gives in to the gut wrenching night that lay ahead. Her nausea is suppressed, however, when she sees the possibilities arise with his lecherous needs. He would be sowing the seeds of his annihilation, and that is the only way she could stomach him.

The moment Strange is dropped off at her home that night, the first thing she does is cry when she surmises what her daughter must be doing to save her skin, not knowing even, the full extent of the situation. She goes straight to her monitor and punched in a code to order a pizza from Lindsay, the nearest town. When the pizza comes, she tells the pizzaman that she must see Redman. But Redman has already received his intelligence and is at that very moment arranging to have Strange picked up and dropped off via the secret way. The pizzaman guerilla tells her that someone would be there shortly.

Not twenty minutes later, another guerilla trudges through the crusty snow and knocks. He bids her follow him and they walk to the lake where an old emop is parked on the frozen bay. They get in and take off through the trees heading to the prearranged route, which had been jammed with the scanner to escape any detection of their movements.

In about an hour they arrive near Redman's bunker. She is whisked inside and back to the workroom. The Board eagerly anticipate her arrival. There is a high degree of anxiety, because no one has a clue as to what is going on. Strange is seated opposite Chromolox who is at the head of the table. Strange hasn't seen her since New Year's and feels a little uncomfortable with her having been the lover of her daughter, Season. But pleasantries are availed, and Chromolox gets down to business. It is Redman, however, who speaks, sitting innocuously to the side.

'Glad to see you, Strange,' says Redman. 'And to hear of your release. Could you enlighten us as to what the hell is going on?'

'Treason came home this afternoon. You know that she was living with Babylon in Chicago . . . '

'Well, we heard . . . to our dismay,' interrupts Chromolox. 'But refrained judgment for the time being, not knowing her . . . politics, as you know, hence the rumors . . . ' She, too, is a little uncomfortable, but gracious.

'My daughter is innocent,' quickly replies Strange. 'I almost beat her when she arrived, but once she explained herself, and the medallion, I was convinced of her sincerity.'

'What medallion?' queries Vince.

'She was given the medallion from Sam who apparently was given it by Heyoka Yellow Tooth herself.'

'I knew it!' exclaims Chromolox, as the others nod their affirmations.

'Heyoka,' continues Strange, 'is incarcerated in a basement wing of the Bungalo. Sam actually spoke with her from outside by happenstance playing near her window. She gave him the medallion claiming it was alien and said to give it to someone he would know from here. She had had a premonition (apparently a natural ability of hers). As it turned out, this person, presumed Sam, was Treason. Sam told Treason to get it to Redman, pronto; also to say the Chicagos were going to neutralise Anna Gram. Treason immediately asked permission to come home, but unluckily for us, we believe they found out about Sam and Heyoka and the missing medallion, though fortuitously too late to stop her. With the aid of her Forager buddies, Treason slipped through their fingers until she arrived home at which time, I believe, the Chicagos were hesitant to cross into Sunsetwind and further exacerbate public opinion during the election. And we all know how Del Barker has made recent public recriminations against the Chicagos, not to mention his bolstered defences. You know, to clear the record, Treason swears there was a mole in our ranks – a Free Radical – who shut down our perimeter during the blizzard. Anyway, to make a long story short, Del must have been tipped off and now has the medallion and is probably negotiating with the Chicagos in some tradeoff. And, the fact that I was released, means Treason has no doubt been taken as a pawn of sorts, which she must have agreed to on the condition that I was released and we all know what else. The poor girl is being used like a dishrag. Our little noble heart has been so abused by these powers arrayed against us . . . '

'Therefore,' addresses Chromolox, ignoring the sentiment, 'Barker will hopefully sell the medallion back to the Chicagos to regain some lost credit. But does he know that this medallion is alien?'

'Treason would never tell him, but the Chicagos could well have,' allows Strange.

'I doubt it,' differs Vince. 'Why would they inflate the value of it if they knew they might be forced into a trade off, let alone the technological benefit?'

'What is the medallion made of?' asks Mita, quietly.

'It's heavy,' answers Strange. 'Heavier than plutonium; it has an orange glow to it with bizarre hieroglyphics front and back.'

'Unumpentium,' utter both Bill and Vince in unison.

'How can we get it?' poses Chromolox to them all.

There is a heated discussion.

'Quiet, please,' Redman speaks out. 'This isn't a schoolhouse! There is only one thing to do: get the medallion, but not before Barker has banked a hefty fee for it . . . '

Voices rear up again.

'Let me finish!' he retorts. 'Have you no respect for your elders? Heyoka wanted me to have the piece, so give me my say! Now, in order to do this we have to rely on Treason getting the medallion to us, possibly through Mobius. Now, we don't know whether she will have any autonomy, which I doubt, unless – pardon me, Strange – your daughter's talents exceed our expectations; and if they do and she has access to the medallion, we must get it and make a duplicate, a fake, and return it on time so the Chicagos will honour the presumed tradeoff. Do I make any sense?'

Everyone nods in agreement. Strange, however, isn't so excited. 'What about my daughter?' she asked worriedly.

'We will try to get her out,' avers Chromolox. 'We all know the sacrifice she has made. We are all prepared to make the same sacrifice if need be. We are at war.'

They go about their preparations. Redman retires and beckons Strange to come with him.

'Leave the nuts and bolts to the Board,' he says. 'Would you like a cognac?'

They relax in his living area with their cognacs and stare out into the dark forest through his window. The drinks have their effect and the warmth suffuses their weary minds.

'I have to say, Strange, like you, I had my doubts about Treason. I think everybody has, but no one had taken the time to appreciate what she has done. Bless her sweet soul. I shudder to think what strength she has summoned to get through this one. She will be all right, Strange, and if it's any consolation, she will be remembered long after these heady days – a true heroine.'

'Redman, what is this unumpentium?' she asks ignoring his eulogistic tone.

'Atomic Element 115: it is probably the heaviest known naturally-occurring element in the universe.'

'What good can it do for us?'

'Well, if we can substitute it for our own fuel, we may be able to paralyse both the Free Radical hold on our people *and* the Chicagos by a much more powerful electromagnetic pulse (EMP) rendering their emops, beam weapons, stun guns and communications useless.'

'That I would have to see to believe. What about our own reactors? How could this EMP not affect us, even if we were successful in creating it? And couldn't they resort to conventional munitions?'

'Those of us on the ground could do nothing. But our emops would be resistant because they'd be insulated with a finer gravity frequency developed through the element. And to answer the last question, they'd be in such a state of chaos, no organised effort could suddenly take charge without communications. Then we'd pounce on them with every weapon we could drum up!'

'I suppose.'

'But we have a problem.'

'What's that?'

'There's only one emop capable of using unumpentium: the Volcano, and we're not even sure about that; we may have to make modifications. Vince thinks it can be done. I hope he's right.'

Chromolox enters the room.

'Strange,' she says, 'We have a job for you. First, we need you to help us mint a medallion. Bill, our 'medieval alchemist', will be mixing up a mineral broth to come up with a comparable alloy, and you can best adjudge its approximate weight and colour, and then Vince would cut with the laser a die-cast with which you could also decide an approximate size and etch the hieroglyphics. In fact we would like you with your formidable expertise to do that yourself; and lastly, we wonder whether you might be our best bet to deliver the merchandise on the pretense that you were worried about your daughter, or something. You could then make the switch and hope for the best. What do you think?'

'Now we're talking,' says Strange, jumping to her feet. 'But I'd think I might raise suspicions. I'll do the medallion of course, but you'd better think up a better plan to get it to her.'

'I thought maybe we could rely on you,' says Chromolox, smiling.

They depart, leaving Redman musing to himself. He wonders what Cephren had come up with and why he hasn't communicated with him, as Cleo had done before. Redman senses that something very much out of the ordinary has compelled Cephren to hold his peace regarding Jimmy's Chip. Nevertheless, he is sure Cephren must be doing the right thing. On the foreign news that day, although censored, he had heard that Del Barker had denied Cephren access to Sunsetwind during the election. This contravenes Earth Federation Law and would show clearly to the world the true nature of the revolution. Barker is an ass, as well as Burnamthorpe, although she hasn't yet barred Cephren from going to Chicago. She knows better. Redman hopes he doesn't go; it wouldn't serve any use. Cleopatra on the other hand . . . it gives him an idea: the world must know that Heyoka is imprisoned in Chicago and Cephren with Cleo's protection could be the very person to push the right buttons on a diplomatically immunized visit. But they must be very careful; Anna Gram has to stay out of harm's way; Trinny is obviously very threatened by her influence. Then this present situation with Treason has to wash, and

Chicago must swallow the bait. For once, Redman hopes Barker will succeed where before he had failed: at least to recover the lost credit. The only problem is that if he is successful, he might then have the support to win an election. Redman feels old then, very old; the world was spinning on in ways he had never imagined. And he is right.

The weather is hot and humid the day Jimmy prepares to depart for Las Vegas. He is making last minute preparations with his daughter, Andie, who is five months pregnant. There has been so much to do: resigning from the university and the send-off party. He jokes that he is going into the gambling business, not to mention some freelance aerospace contracts, and a change of scenery to boot, moving Andie and her husband Rob into his Clearview farmhouse after giving it to them, and many other tasks that add up to his presumed anonymity.

He had spoken to Danielle the night before his departure and discussed how best to communicate once he "ceased" to exist. She suggested that he simply call her special link with a secure phone when he had the chance. The week before, he and Danielle had spent the night together in Andie's old house in Aurora which had yet to be sold. And after their usual all consuming love-fix, they hold each other sympathetically. Danielle really needed Jimmy now, probably more than he needed her. It is ironic how their relationship had evolved from her early narcissism and his dependency, to her dependency and his scientific narcissism. Perhaps it had always been that way like a merry-go-round. That night, however, Danielle was having her doubts. She doesn't want him to leave. He feels that there is something she fears, but typically won't reveal her vulnerabilities.

'Don't go,' she says, holding him nervously. Her face is an impenetrable mask.

'I want to go,' he says, caressing her shoulder and breast.

'Then, send me your literary documents,' she demands.

'You know I send them all to you.'

'Your new ones.'

'Of course, if and when I finish any.'

'Is the sky blue?' Her mood lightens.

'Like your ocean eyes, Danielle; but I insist that I should try and get some of them published. All my life I have been reluctant to get my stuff out there because of my professional circumstances, but Piercemore could easily fill in my shoes.'

'No way, Jimmy,' she frowns, removing herself from his caresses. 'It's too risky; Piercemore is classified and will remain that way over my dead body! No, you cannot publish; your work is too close to me . . .'

'But Danielle, maybe I could use another pseudonym; how about Bert Priddee? Or maybe Russ Rumford, something low key.'

Danielle laughs.

'What's so funny? I'm serious,' he says.

'And so am I.'

She continues to laugh in a mocking tone.

'Give me a break, for God's sake, Danielle,' utters Jimmy angrily. 'What do you have to fear, after all these years? People accept you as you are, like some beautiful freak of nature. My attempts at literature can in no way impinge on your precious sanctity. This is my life!'

'How dare you call me a freak!' Laughter quickly turns into bitter recrimination. 'You sit in your cozy little world, a world need I remind you, that I have made for you! And all I ask is that you consider my feelings a little bit. I am living a life that no one, I mean no one, can possibly understand, except maybe Max, but he's a trained automaton . . .'

'Okay, okay Danielle, I'm just frustrated; soon I'll be the invisible man; I just want a little support and a promise that you'll consider my feelings too. And I think you are being unduly rigid, not just with me, but with yourself.'

Danielle says nothing and looks away.

'Danielle, when we have these conversations, I can't help but get the feeling that you're holding out on something with me. I can't help it. I think it stems from your youth. Please help me out here, Danielle; I know you too well.'

Danielle gets up from her defiant sitting position and paces naked at the bedside. Jimmy has touched a nerve. She fumes there momentarily before facing him, her eyes burning and her long, dark slightly silvery hair tumbling about her shoulders.

'You don't know me, Jimmy,' she begins. 'You think you do, but you don't. Yes, I'm the Prime Minister; yes, maybe I'm your beautiful freak; yes, I love you more than you could know; but I'm . . . different from you . . .' She pauses, seeming not to know how to explain. 'What we're doing is dangerous, but possibly a way out.'

'A way out? What are you trying to say, Danielle?' probes Jimmy.

'I'm trying to say . . . please believe in me . . . sympathise! Believe the loving Danielle, the one that wishes she could be your wife. Oh, Jimmy, you're so wonderful. I'm sorry; I'm so sorry.' She lies down beside him again pensive as before.

'What are you sorry about? And don't tell me about the Vancouver thing, or your dumping of Andie as a baby, or your callous treatment of me; I know those unfortunate situations were symptoms of something far deeper in you. What do you really mean when you say you are sorry, Danielle?'

'Don't Jimmy,' she says, calmly. 'Let's just consider what we have: extraordinary lives, and family.'

Jimmy sighs. There is no way to get to her.

'It's okay, we'll make it, someday,' he remarks, finally.

Danielle indeed hoards all of his literary work, and up to then his scientific work. And although fanatical, she is somewhat justified in dreading someone getting hold of it and rooting out her secret life, but obviously there is more to it than that and only Danielle knew what that was. Certainly Jimmy cannot root out what lurks in her heart of hearts, and the awesome paranoia that perhaps he doesn't even want to know about. Nevertheless, his literary endeavours, however obscure, act as a counter-weight to the sometimes tangential spirit of astrophysical formulae. He finds he cannot be happy without one or the other, nor productive. Considering himself as an electromagnetic-engineer first and foremost, the mathematical and literary voyeurism served only to evince meaning like philosophical building blocks. He grudgingly, though willingly, gives her his literary creations as if it is her given right and what she does with them could only serve an even greater sacrifice that seems to spur on some form of glorification of his purpose. He begins to see themselves as partners in a metaphorical ballet of martyrs sparring with each other in choreographic duals.

'What makes you think I'm so wonderful?' he asks referring to her previous exposition.

'You tell me; you're the writer,' she contends.

'You have a way of turning things upside down.'

'Well then, what does Piercemore think?' she teases.

'To hell with secrecy,' he proclaims, automatically. 'Good writing, like new science, is truly of the mind and the mind, per se, has little agenda for secrecy. Therefore, it makes me feel free, really free, even of you.' He kisses her ear.

'Am I then your gaoler?' She purrs pleasurably.

'Rather a haughty muse whereby you stand between me and womankind.'

'Oh Piercemore, the egoist,' she whispers. 'So what does Pidgeon think?'

'Beware of modesty in a beautiful woman.'

'No, really.'

'My occupational hazards seem to be unwittingly preoccupied with social power and secret authority – the man behind the woman.' He positions himself upon her.

'What do you mean?' she says, wrapping her legs around him.

'Actually, on top of the woman.'

'Fuck me, you bastard,' she murmurs.

Later, they speak of intelligence and whether he should bring some of the new technology home. Jimmy shrugs and says he could keep it in his head. He has a mind that could pull information like a computer. He once claimed that under certain conditions his brain had radar; he could sense equations and complex formulae. He could hear pins drop in other parts of the house or trains go by ten miles away. Danielle adores that part of him – the unfathomable. She too is very deep but with dark secrets that no one even knew she had, yet Jimmy is deeper still and penetrates her whole being with his illumination. She tells him that the happiest day of her life was when he forgave her after their long separation since Vancouver. There is still some latent bitterness from that memory which seemed etched in his bones, but more than a twinge of guilt presses at his conscience as he believes that she spoke the truth when she said she had been faithful to him all those years like "a pious nun", whereas he hadn't by any measure. He rationalises it by negating the bitterness with the guilt.

Andie is the one who had had the most difficult time with the family dynamics. She refused to speak of her mother, or to her, until she was an adult, at which time her curiosity got the better of her when her mother became so famous. Over time she gave her the benefit of the doubt, but only when Danielle appeared genuinely grieved and showed her heartfelt, although peculiar love, did she somewhat forgive her. Danielle tried to explain to her what had happened in her life but as usual could not. It was not enough. But somehow, Andie loves her. She wants so much to tell everybody whose daughter she is, but holds her tongue for her father's sake. Only her common-law mate, Rob Barnett, was told the truth though it doesn't take much of a look to see they were mother and daughter when they were standing side by side, hence their strict ritual of being together only under their own roofs. And Rob was told in no uncertain terms by Danielle, that if he revealed the truth it would be denied and unsupported by official fact; furthermore, it would ruin their family life, sporadic and unusual as it was. Barnett is a kind, patient and understanding man who loves Andie deeply and respected their wishes.

❦

When Jimmy arrives in Las Vegas and steps out of the terminal, the heat just about knocks him over. From late spring throughout the summer, Vegas appears like a ghost town. The pseudo-sphinx and black shiny pyramid can be seen across the tarmac in blurry waves of torrid air. No one is about.

People are there all right, but air-conditioned inside. In the last twenty years since the EDC of 2012, the southwest had become much hotter. Temperatures close to 50 degrees Celsius (120 degrees Fahrenheit) are average at that time of year. Some days it rises to 55 degrees, even 60 Celsius. The dry heat that blows out of the desert is like opening the door of a blast furnace. Jimmy puts his hand out to shield his mouth that became instantly parched. He hails a cab, empties the cart of his trunk and bags and proceeds to the Rattlesnake Motel, a dingy and innocuous location on the outskirts.

Lying in his air-conditioned room, he meditates on these last hours of freedom. He knows that once he becomes 'radioactive', there would always be the risk of security leaks. He understands why, because according to Mr. Smith, a relatively primitive humanity could not bridge the emotional, technological and psychological differences in the evolutionary ladder between humans and the extraterrestrials who visited there; nevertheless, Jimmy believed that humanity for good or ill must sooner or later be apprised of the situation, in spite of the need to secure the technology to prevent any conflagration from terrorists using the destructive potential from it. The present secretive shadow government was a looming monster that could, down the road, cause more havoc than by revealing its existence now. But he is prepared to put aside his personal feelings and go along with the program to see if he could be of any help. Yet, the nagging doubts persist. He is a free thinker, and there is not a free ingredient in this situation, the security being so paranoid.

The drone of the old air-conditioner lulls him to sleep. He has a dream and when he awakes writes it down:

> Marooned
> Some fools think we are fiction
> Breathing our hyped air in hyped rooms
> Winking at civilisation and its doom.
>
> Now I sit upon my rock with my broken machine
> Eating raw crustacea while keeping an eye on the dog star
> Looking to the impossible horizon – I, the great civiliser,
>
> Propound into my beard the malevolence of ages
> And into my woman the love of the gods
> Who still show themselves in the constellations.
>
> Sailors we are, Quetzalcoatls
> Plumed and awesome with long women
> Stirring enmity among the savages.
>
> And the Atlanteans are no more – their lands forsaken
> To the ravages of ice and their buried monuments
> Lost to electromagnetic winds of the precessional arc.
>
> Our secrets are no more – blown away like volcanic ash
> Spread as foam on the sea swelling to the heights of stars.
> They would come again within us – a chosen few.

Jimmy folds the paper and puts it into his pocket. Then he opens his wallet and takes out a number to call. The message is a recording, saying the Leghorn Resources offices are no longer recruiting, but you can leave your name and number on a waiting list. Jimmy leaves his name and number. Then looking up Leghorn Resources in the telephone book, he finds nothing, as expected.

He spends the evening fretting about his room watching TV and eating pizza. Sleepless, when no call seems forthcoming, he heads out into the cooler night air and stargazes. They kind of twinkle back at him, enticing with their mysteries. The sky is vast and alive with all that unrealisable light, a veritable swamp of life, as Mr. Smith had indicated. Restless, Jimmy calls a cab and tours the infamous Vegas strip. It is a constellation of its own. The Elvis is the newest hotspot and Jimmy checks it out. Drinking lime and soda, he walks about each gaming area dropping a hundred dollars. Settling into black jacks, he finds it amusing when he makes his money back and a somewhat inebriated woman latches herself onto him. Embarrassed, he helps her to the lounge and deposits her on a couch. He then tries the slot machines and wins thirty dollars in change. Up thirty bucks, he decides to try his hand at craps. On a roll, he turns up seven three times and doubles his money. Now tired, he considers getting out while ahead, modest as it is, but the bug bites too hard and he has to itch some more. He tries the poker tables and loses some, then gains some. Another woman, sensing a man of quality, smiles and asks him if he is having a good time. Jimmy returns the smile and says he hasn't had so much fun in years.

'Care to take a breather and count your pennies?' she suggests, flashing her brown eyes.

'Why not?' he says collecting his chips.

He cashes them in and realises he has just over three hundred dollars. 'I've tripled my money,' he says.

She suggests they go to the lounge and catch the schmoozer, Hassad D'Angelo, accompanied by an elegant pianist in a gold evening dress.

Jimmy has another lime and soda and the woman, a Singapore Sling. 'First time to Vegas?' she asks.

'Yes.'

'On business?'

'No.'

'What then, just fun and games?' she presses.

Jimmy isn't really listening to her. He is too humoured by the whole scene. At the next table sit three elderly women on some kind of reunion. A young man sits with them and they are ogling over his schoolboy looks. Young and old commune there on every kind of life trip. And cascading through them all presently is Hassad and his mellowtron voice, suave and warm, like a balm. At the piano, lithe fingers move up the keys in perfect compliment.

Ignoring her question, Jimmy asks: 'Do you come here often?'

'I work here.'

'Doing what?'

'I'm a hostess. I make people feel comfortable. The name's Cora Little Feather.' She holds out her hand.

Jimmy looks at her. As a brunette, she could have had some Native American blood, but it doesn't show. She is petite and cute.

'Jimmy,' he returns, taking her hand.

'I'm not a friendly, if that's what you're thinking,' she says.

Jimmy presumes friendly is synonymous with prostitute.

'It never occurred to me, Cora,' he says smiling. 'I was wondering about your name; you don't look native North American.'

'I'm married to a Navajo,' she says, matter-of-factly.

'I didn't realise . . . '

'No apologies: how could you know? Besides, we are separated, but remain friendly.'

They both laugh.

'But not too friendly.'

They laugh again.

'You never answered my question,' she reminds him.

'I'm sorry. What?'

'Are you here for the fun and games?'

'But, of course.'

'You're Canadian, aren't you?'

'Yes, and for a hostess, aren't you asking too many questions?'

She laughs delightfully.

'I'm a bit of a tease. I work for Leghorn, Jimmy. We have to be very careful these days. There is so much pressure on our security from wannabes and ufologists and even scientists, senators and congressmen.'

'You really fooled me, Cora . . . '

'I did too, didn't I?'

'About being a tease.'

'Oh,' she laughs. 'You know,' she declares, 'I'm really a farm girl who grew up in Kansas, but my life has taken a few interesting spins . . . '

'Putting it mildly, I'd say. The yellow brick road to the stars.'

'Indeed, and from what I understand you are my most curious freshman yet. My superior, who you will meet tomorrow, told me the President ordered your indoctrination. Now . . . '

'Indoctrination?' queries Jimmy raising his eyebrows.

'Don't ask me what, Jimmy; that's not my job. I know about nothing other than being your liaison. Where you go and what you do is classified. I'm here only to acquaint you to the system so-to-speak. Anytime you're in town, Leghorn is here to help you, if need be. It may not always be me, unless you put in a special request.' She smiles again.

'So where do we go from here?' asks Jimmy.

'I will escort you back to your motel and spend the night with you . . . '

'What? I mean, why?'

Cora laughs.

'I'm teasing, silly. But yes, I will go back with you and spend a little time in your room to throw off any scent. Know what I mean?'

'No.' Jimmy is curious.

'Fun and games, remember? We don't want any nosy people thinking we're working for the government, now do we?'

'Okay, then what?'

'In the morning, you will drive out to Nellis Air Force Base just north of town. They will deliver you to Dreamland.'

'I don't have a car.'

'There's one parked in front of your motel room.'

She opens her purse and gives him the keys under the table and some ID.

They finish their drinks and walk out to the valet. Soon another car is brought around, a '31 Crazy Horse, one of the new prototypes on the market, fusion charged and able to go ten thousand miles before refueling. They drive to the motel.

Once inside, they both sit on the double bed with their feet extended and watch a late night movie. Cora leans onto Jimmy, who was falling asleep. Then she gets up, turns the TV off and leaves.

The next morning, Jimmy takes off early. On the way, he stops at a Griddle King for a few flapjacks. Feeling good and adventurous, he thinks about Cora and how comfortable she made him feel. Not half an hour out of town, the outside gates of Nellis are upon him. Lowering his window, the security guards phone in, checks his ID, which Cora had given him, and waves him through to a specific parking lot. There, a Major who helps him with his bags into an old, gas motorized carrier wagon meets him. He is immediately driven out onto the tarmac near a series of hangars. A small, new Air Force Transport is running and ready, and as soon as he is aboard with his bags secure, they taxi down the runway. The fusion-powered jet rotors whine quietly and in a minute they are airborne. All the window shades are secured shut. Jimmy thinks he could be flying to Hawaii for all he could tell.

The flight is short and inside an hour Jimmy sits in a closed waiting room at Groom Lake, deep in the heart of the arid mountains of Dreamland (Area 51). There is another man in the waiting room besides the Major, who had yet to speak. The Major is young, early thirties, dressed in desert fatigues, and the other was quite a bit older. Jimmy thinks that hopefully there are some more socially engaging fellows around. Perhaps these guys are there simply to decorate the old, windowless room like a neo-Rockwell montage.

'So what's on the menu today, gents?' asks Jimmy, lightly.

The older guy turns to him and leers limpidly. 'Hell, if I know.'

The Major shrugs, smiling.

'First time, Major?' asks Jimmy.

'No,' he replies.

'So, is the food any good?'

'Food is food,' he states.

'You mean like chlorophyll burgers,' quips Jimmy.

The Major continues to smile and shakes his head. He has intense brown eyes.

'Yeah,' he growls straight faced, 'with A1 sauce.'

It's Jimmy's turn to laugh. The older fellow turns away smiling. The Major looks down at his feet.

'That's pretty funny, Major; how long have you been here?' quizzes Jimmy.

'Nine months.'

'Nine months, eh; ready to hatch.' Jimmy can't help himself with banality, but adds, 'See anything weird?'

'What do mean by weird?'

'You know, people walking through walls and such.'

'What's so weird about that?' counters the Major suppressing his mirth.

'Nothing, just asking,' smiles Jimmy.

'Have you been experienced?' spars the Major.

'No,' says Jimmy, 'You mean, abducted.'

A morbid smile comes over the Major. 'No, but welcome to the real world, sir,' he says. 'Now Vegas: that's weird.'

Jimmy looks at the other man. 'Are you experienced?'

The man nods. 'Ten years, genetics.'

'Really? And may I ask why you are here waiting, or rather, why are we here, waiting?'

'I was told I could get a ride back to Nellis. And I assume you are waiting for Colonel Blaine,' says the older man.

'Colonel Blaine. Who's Colonel Blaine?'

'He runs the program. What's your field?' asked the man.

'Poetry.'

They all laugh again.

'Good luck. It ought to be inspiring,' says the man.

'Thanks.'

Some security personnel arrive and escort the man away. Jimmy keeps turning "Good luck" over in his mind. Did it have some hidden meaning?

'What did he mean by "Good luck"?' Jimmy asks the Major.

'Dunno, maybe he meant it.'

'Who is he?' probes Jimmy.

'Doc Williams, he's chairman of the Naval Research Committee, National Foundation of Science and the Institute of Defensive Analysis.'

'Not what you'd call a slouch; he must know his stuff.'

'He's one classified dude.'

'You mean the rubber stamp man.'

'Naturally.'

'Tell me Major, how do you rationalise the program, when mainstream science – the world out there – is left in the dark? Anybody that's smart and knows what's going on who opens his mouth is considered a nutcase. The mainstream media are the worst debunkers. How do you do it?' queries Jimmy.

'We don't do much. I think it's human nature to debunk what can't be verified officially. I don't have a problem with it because it's strictly in the interests of national security.'

'Are you here with me now to befriend me or assess me?'

'Yes and no,' he says sincerely.

'Where's the Colonel?'

'Colonel Blaine would like us to get acquainted.'

'I see, so what do we do now?'

'We're waiting for the chaplain.'

'Ah, the oath.'

No sooner than those words are spoken, Colonel Blaine and a morose looking chaplain enter the room. The Major stands up and Jimmy follows a little slower. They shake hands all around. Then the chaplain without hesitation holds out a bible on which Jimmy has to place his hand.

'Standard procedure,' says the Colonel gruffly, without aplomb in a voice that resonates a strict authority.

'Repeat after me,' the chaplain says. 'I do solemnly swear . . . in the eyes of God . . . and in allegiance to the United States of America . . . I will serve, obey and protect . . . those vested interests thereof . . . duly franchised in national security . . . and other such matters when called upon to do so . . . I will carry out my duty . . . faithfully, assuredly, without question . . . in the cause of the freedoms defended in our constitution . . . to the end of my life and beyond . . . so help me God.'

Then they have him sign some papers.

Afterwards, the Major and Colonel Blaine escort Jimmy through various old passageways. The building seemed to be vintage nineteen-fifties Air Force architecture. Jimmy is led into a briefing room in which a micro video projector and large screen are built into the wall. Colonel Blaine reintroduces Major Good who sits down and asks Jimmy to do the same. Colonel Blaine then exits.

'So what was all that about back there in that waiting room?' Jimmy asks the Major. 'And I liked that "for life and beyond".'

'We have our ways, Mr. Pidgeon. I hope you realise that with that oath, you are bound to us, and we to you. It is reciprocal. I sit with you for twenty minutes to gauge your temperament, to better experience you, if you will. Now what you're about to hear and see will re-educate you. You will then receive many volumes of literature, which you may keep in your

quarters for your perusal for as long as you remain here. Today, I will sum-
marise for you the situation, the bottom line, etc.

'What you are about to hear, will change your view of the earth, the
sky, the universe, everything that you hold dear and sacred. From the outset, I want you to know that we wish it could be otherwise, but we are
powerless to do anything about it. The best minds in America for almost
one hundred years now have helped direct, mould and streamline our program here today. We are very grateful to have you aboard with your know-
how in your field. I understand you were recommended by your Prime
Minister, Ms. Perreault.'

'Yeah, she got me into this.'

'Do I detect regret?'

'None, just a personal joke; Danielle and I go back a ways.'

'Fascinating woman.'

'She's unique.'

'Yes, well, now that you're here, let me begin by asking you a question.'

'Okay.'

'How would you feel about revealing to someone, say an old friend or
wife or lover, something about what you know here, if there was a chance
you could do some good in it, say save their lives in the advent of something destructive coming their way?'

'That's loaded, Major. I'd have to say I'd hold my peace. I couldn't
begin to describe how difficult that might be. However, what difference
would state secrets make after a cataclysm?'

'How true, yes; but remember, we can be more effective working as a
team. If a member of that team, goes awol, we don't have a team and we
lose our integrity.'

'Integrity? Life may have just been wiped out.'

'This is survival of the fittest. Living on earth is a precarious thing. It
is our job to see that we survive. It used to be the threat of nuclear holo-
caust, and still could be, among other terrorisms. However, we are preoccupied with the threat of being swept away as a race with our own right

to self-determination; and believe me, this is a very serious problem. That is why security is so important, not just to protect mainstream society, but as a built-in insurance plan that underwrites the problem of extraterrestrial interference.'

'I have presumed as much,' comments Jimmy.

'There's nothing wrong with a little presumption, Mr. Pidgeon; in fact, part of the program is geared to enlighten the mainstream eventually. We hope that the mainstream will come by it themselves, psychologically and technologically speaking. It would make it a lot easier for us. However, presumption can in no way compete with being consumed by it. The reality, even for hardened veterans like Colonel Blaine is almost unbearable.'

'How so?'

'Let me backtrack a little here, Mr. Pidgeon. Since antiquity people have observed strange and unusual objects in the skies above earth. Many ancient texts allude to this, some explicitly. However, UFOs are considered to be a modern phenomenon. For almost the last one hundred years there have been thousands of credible sightings and even numerous encounters around the globe by both civilians and the military who have happened to actually see UFOs and their occupants. Many encounters have been written about. Some are true and others fiction. It was difficult for the credible witnesses to be lumped together with all the dissemblers. Thus, for decades, secret authorities (those responsible officials in the loop) had a relatively easy time dealing with attempts by individuals to get the government to open up to the public these ultimate facts of life. But no such luck. All ufology was discredited and debunked to preserve national security concerns. It was a cruel fact of twentieth and now twenty-first century life: people are made to feel victimized by being told they are nutcases and worse. Mainstream culture will not permit the reality of ufology into its "responsible" ranks, as long as the government won't volunteer any enlightenment on the subject. Like the medieval church, we have been compelled to be the truth police, and no one could get away with the truth if it threatened national security. And ironically, ufology has taken on religious dimensions – believers and non-believers.'

'Well,' says Jimmy, 'It's pretty obvious to many people who have informed themselves through the many books and documentaries on the subject.'

'Yes, but the uninformed majority has a difficult time with the reality; furthermore, as a society there may be great dissension and polarisation on all kinds of cultural and religious fronts on how best to deal with and control extraterrestrial interference in our affairs. In simple terms, humanity for the most part is not equipped emotionally to comprehend the awesome intelligence of these beings; it would always boil down to a threat and some extreme defensive reaction which might lead to chaos and global catastrophe.'

'I get the point,' affirms Jimmy. 'We're basically undeveloped on the evolutionary front and complete openness on your part will bring out the primitive beast in us all.' Jimmy growls and shakes his head. They both have another laugh.

'You have an interesting way of putting it, Mr. Pidgeon. Now, I'm going to give you a very general briefing. All the details are in the bible.' He points to the huge volumes piled on a table. 'The bible, of course – not the real bible – is a euphemism for everything we know about aliens, or the proverbial truth as we know it compiled in these volumes stemming from the gleanings and experience of extraterrestrial knowledge and their agendas. It covers everything from the natural sciences, alien history, species, technology, biology, astronomy to even politics and especially where we fit in the swamp, i.e., the universe.

'The present state of our evolution as a species began for us approximately four hundred thousand years ago, although we are told we have been subjected to alien influence far deeper into our past, back millions of years, in fact. What I'm driving at is that we wouldn't be who we are today if it hadn't been for an infusion of alien DNA into our remote ancestors by various races of beings, the most predominant of which were the

Neteru. The Neteru lived in the Orion constellation and numerous star systems within that vicinity like Sirius, for example, but their progenitors apparently evolved in another galaxy. The Neteru were humanoid like us but were obviously hundreds of thousands of years more advanced . . . '

'It's like we were some kind of giant experimental biosphere.'

'Yes, but at least thirty thousand years ago the Neteru as a race were dispersed or absorbed by another race we call the Reptoids, who were less refined, but extremely intelligent. Some of the surviving Neteru were forced to travel the galaxy and find refuge here and there, dropping themselves off onto these wild under-evolved planets like missionaries with not much more than the clothes on their back, and to integrate into a small sector of the population to promote bigger and better things in a hurry, relatively speaking. Their ships were apparently lost or scuttled into deep unchartered space. At any rate, we were lucky enough to have them come here, poor devils. One of the criteria, though, was to have an isolated, moderately sized archipelago or continent on which there was some homogeneity among the people. They didn't want to land into a frying pan, after all, with warring tribes, however inevitable. The continent they chose was Antarctica. Back then of course, it was called Atlantis, and it wasn't on the south pole. Before the catastrophic earth crust displacement of February 2, 9481 BC, Atlantis was situated almost thirty degrees farther north in latitude towards the equator. Part of the continent was glacial, but the northern part was warm and temperate. It was here the Neteru took root. Eventually, they had completely intermixed with the original inhabitants and over thousands of years turned a primitive people into an intelligent race who learned to navigate the seas, build lofty structures, understand the stars and the precessional path of the sun and earth. They developed agriculture and even had solar power and generated electricity as can be discerned from some of their ruins. This was a unique step as they completely bypassed the use of fossil fuels. It's a standing joke among a few of us that fossil fuels kept us in the anal stage. The Neteru had blended into the fabric of their adopted race, but left an indelible design. They had served their purpose well having been left alone by their own extraterrestrial progenitors, who in all probability never intended to go back to these backward planets to protect their colonists from absorption by the Reptoids. Let's face it: there wasn't much else they could do with us, anyway. They realised that we would have to develop on our own to attain the starry heights of their own civilisation. You cannot supercharge a two-stroke engine.

'Then there was the deluge. You remember 2012, Mr. Pidgeon. That proved beyond any doubt among the sceptics, that earth crust displacement (ECD) was indeed a naturally occurring phenomenon. But what is now established fact, that evolution has many hazards in its path, including recurring cataclysm, has come to a new meaning. And the hundred million killed worldwide in 2012 was just a blip on the human journey as compared to what happened in 9481 B.C. The 2012 ECD was only a two on a scale of ten as compared to a nine in 9481. The survivors of Atlantis migrated to North and South America, Africa and Asia. Cultures sprang up in specific regions, but the gains made were soon lost. The legacies, however, have stood the test of time. Tihuanaco, Teotihuacan, the Giza Pyramids and many of the ancient stone works, which we previously believed to have been built more recently were actually the superior work of the descendants of the Atlanteans. It is apparent now that the primitive morass of humanity swallowed any enlightenment attained long ago on that mysterious archipelago, Antarctica, begun by the Neteru. The Neteru then faded into obscurity and the Reptoids discovered earth as their own container. Earth was considered too unstable and barbaric and used as a DNA resource farm. We had too long a way to go to achieve the kind of harmonizing needed to be welcomed into the universe by the advanced races; and earth was and indeed still is looked down upon as a pitiful and dangerous place.

'Meanwhile, in another sector of the immediate universe, a very different species had evolved. The Reticulans or Greys as popular sci-fi describes them (and they are real), appeared on the scene. But unfortunately, the

Greys have been absorbed – I'll elaborate on that in a minute – into a vast empirical-like dominion controlled by – yes – the Reptoids. The Reptoids are actually reptilian in origin, but humanoid in stature having introduced human-type DNA into their species, probably thanks to the Neteru originally. As frightening as that is, they are rather defensive in nature and not prone to take offensive action unless circumstances warrant it. Yet, they are highly developed and view technological and genetic progress as their spiritual directive. They have a way of absorbing cultures and life-giving planets into their folds genetically. The Greys are really their minions and for the most part obedient to their masters. They are a passive-aggressive species who won't come out of the skies like in a pack of killer bees and annihilate the race, but they will ultimately, very gradually seek to modify and assimilate our DNA with theirs. The Greys have already begun this, being integrated with the Reptoids themselves. And over a long period of time, and believe me, time is on their side (they live far longer than we do; in fact, that is one of our inherent weaknesses), they will become us, and we them. As we see it, tally one more conquest for the Reptoids.'

'So what are we doing about it?' wonders Jimmy, perturbed.

'We can't stop them. We're hog-tied in lesser evolution. We don't have the ability to stop their experiments, their invading of our space, or anything. We have only one alternative at present.'

'What?'

'To compromise, to buy time in order to catch up. Once we can fly into space and maybe solicit help from some of our human-like neighbours such as the Eridanis or Normals as they're sometimes called because they are most like us in appearance, or even the Neteru if they still exist, maybe we can hold our own. There are many other races too, but we have already been contained by the Greys, not that we're going anywhere. There are also some strange species like the Little People, these tiny beings who were named after those of Gulliver's Travels, you know the fiction by Swift.'

'All so incredible,' utters Jimmy. 'But, why would the Greys let us break out into space if we could, when they contain us?'

'You don't understand the Greys. They don't think like us. They are so advanced in technology, they wish even to help us, to a point. They see us as inevitably wanting to be like them as an inescapable fact of life. They want to enhance our race for the benefit of all. We have much to offer them in our life form and vice-versa.'

'So where do the Neteru fit in now?' queries Jimmy.

'We don't really know; as I said we don't know whether they still exist, except in our recessive or mitochondrial DNA. We now know that we all contain 37 genes of this distinctively circular DNA that are totally foreign to the original human genome that may have been introduced not only by cross-breeding, but by infection. Some of the Greys have said they wish only for our right to self-determination, eventually.'

'And the Reptoids?'

'It's in their best interest to agree to our self-determination, but they still control the skies.'

'So is this the compromise? A silent auction? A trade off between DNA and technology? Sounds like we're the proverbial bug between a rock and a hard place.'

'Yes, they have warned us that our keeping their presence officially secret is by far the least risky. They have spoken of other planets in other solar systems where this was not adhered to and all hell broke loose precipitating global war between those who wanted to destroy the "invaders" and those who deemed their presence to be beneficial. It spells chaos where every social institution is in upheaval and lunatics wrest control. We cannot afford that. With all of our world problems it would spell disaster. Also, they wished to have a couple of bases here on earth. There's El Cayul in Puerto Rico and X13 near here and one in Antarctica called Atlantis with an undersea entrance that comes up under the ice where the city of Atlantis used to be, and other ones in the oceans and one in Australia. In Atlantis, some of the massive stone buildings are relatively intact including the Pyramids. Yes, they had Pyramids too. The Colonel has seen them.'

The Major then stands up and pours some ice water from a pitcher into two glasses and handed one to Jimmy. Sitting down, he pulls a remote receiver from his pocket and directed it at the large screen. A video begins by depicting some of the history of the U.S. involvement with EBE's (extraterrestrial biological entities). It covers the Roswell crash in 1947, and many other situations up to the present time. It shows some of the Greys, their vehicles, motherships, their magic and how they manipulate gravity waves to do almost anything including dematerialisation. The reality is spellbinding. Jimmy can hardly wait to get started. He feels that if humans had the technology, they could emulate or recreate it to suit their own design and advantage.

'Major,' asks Jimmy, 'How is it that after all these years we haven't been able to use this technology more to our advantage? This stuff makes our mainstream space program seem like a waste of time.'

'Oh, but we have: we just don't know how to build a space vehicle yet that can use this technology. We're a little like those early Phoenicians, who upon first sighting the Atlantic ocean, knew that they would have to come up with something better to sail with, because they had no idea where they were going; or think of Columbus building a fusion submarine. The Greys have given us some of this technology, but that's as far as it goes. We must figure out the rest. The vehicles in our possession are reconnaissance only and we barely fit into them. The Greys are tiny, at least most of them. They use colossal motherships for interstellar travel and the little ones for global.'

'We obviously don't have the resources to build a mothership,' says Jimmy, 'and it might blow our cover even if we did.'

'Precisely. A bit of an oxymoron, isn't it?'

'Perhaps I could design something smaller, something to comfortably fit three or four people, like a discoid RV.'

'We still don't have the resources. The Greys have given us unumpentium, a high grade alien element 115, but we don't have the technological infrastructure. We also need other alien metallurgy to make the alloys necessary to withstand the dynamics of artificial gravity, let alone interstellar travel. The shell moulds are a problem too, bismuth-beryllium-titanium alloys in composite shell structures. We don't know how to make a one-piece craft without any rivets, bolts, or welds. Through physical and chemical manipulation of their alloys they can render hatch seams invisible and hulls transparent, as clear as windows. And there are inner and outer shells, no wiring, and reactors that look like exotic vases and others with rotating rings cycling water. We've known about this stuff for decades, yet we can't reproduce it. It is very frustrating. Actually, as you may be aware, over the past eighty years we have developed reams of new technology from them such as: fiber optics, laser beams, chip circuitry, alloys, night vision and countless spin-offs; but you see, we have to come by the big breakthroughs ourselves. We're only fortunate enough to know where it's all going, but it might take hundreds of years to get there. By then the Reptoids could well have made their irreparable absorption.'

'Not while I'm alive,' predicts Jimmy, confidently.

'What do you have in mind?'

'Introduce me to some of your *friendly* Greys,' he intones, remembering Cora Little Feather, though not insinuating the connotation.

'That's up to the Colonel. But first things first: I'll give you a tour of our facilities here which aren't much on the surface, pretty shabby in fact, which we like for appearances, but beneath the ground, it's another world; we can take the tube to S4 where you will live and work, but as I've said, only Colonel Blaine and MJ-12 can give you clearance for X13.'

'What's this tube?'

'An electromagnetic underground shuttle tube: it's very fast and safe. It crosses a half a dozen states. We could be at Cheyenne Mountain in an hour.'

'Impressive.'

'You ain't seen nothin' yet, Mr. Pidgeon.'

'I have to say, you are very accommodating.'

'Believe me Jim, you've been given special consideration, against the Colonel's instincts mind you; but his superiors have over-ruled him. We expect big things from you, though you don't seem the type to get too worked up about it. Most newcomers around here are treated as if they just arrived at boot camp, and certainly under no circumstances are given the run of the place. The Colonel has held his ground regarding some of the deeper aspects of the program. You will have to prove yourself in your specialty before the highest clearance would be forthcoming.'

'What is your specialty, Major?' inquires Jimmy.

'You are my specialty, Jim,' he says, gravely.

True to the Major's word, it would be almost ten years before Jimmy obtained the cosmic clearance to have the run of the program. This entailed access to X13 and the alien personnel, which upon first meeting, Jimmy could never have imagined in his entire life. What a shock it was to experience their reality. For years he had patiently waited and hoped that day would come, meanwhile doing his utmost to utilise his talents with alien technology. It had proven to be a more formidable task than he anticipated. Major Good, who had been promoted to Colonel, became a close friend, but General Blaine (also promoted) remained distant.

From those first days to the present, Jimmy became their most brilliant technician. He became an expert on all aspects of the program. He even contributed a whole new volume to the bible. His biggest hindrance was resources, as Colonel Good had forewarned. Jimmy, however, prepared for that day when the resources might become available. He designed a saucer-shaped craft to human specifications. The round shape was better suited for manoeuvrability in gravity propulsion. His electrical conduits were all designed to be inlaid in the inner hull like a massive, living, breathing computer chip. He named his craft the Meteor. The whole design centered around the anti-matter reactor in the core tube in the lower middle of the craft. The reactor was fueled by unumpentium, and when bombarded with a proton stimulator it became unumsextium, which actually gave off zero radiation, becoming absolutely stable. The charge fired up the core from the reactor converted through a super generator that was specially designed to emit the kind of power akin to the energy of an electrical storm. This power was directed into three amplifiers that taken together powered, propelled and directed anti-gravity beams to pick up objects and could even disrupt atomic structure by suspending the charge that held solid matter together such as rock, actually making it permeable. In theory, according to his understanding of the alien vehicles in their possession, his design was sound. As long as the charge could be conducted around an obloid ship, the artificial gravity generated in the ship was out of phase with the naturally occurring gravity of the earth, therefore the craft could 'surf' on the atmosphere with no resistance to the air. But there was still trouble concerning a blow-mould without imperfections, and most certainly the electric system that was as intricate as flesh with capillaries. But he thought he had a way around it. They would make the fiber conduit system first and install it in the mould before blow-melting the hull alloys. The reactor would be positioned in the core mould with the starter conduits. The gravity amplifiers would connect the whole conduit system to a panel mount in the main console.

They attempted to make such a craft with inferior alloys, just to experiment if it could be done. After many failures, they managed to succeed, the problem being the correct heat intensity and timing. It had to be cooled almost instantly for the mould to hold in such a thin epidermis – not two centimeters thick on the outside and one in the inside secured by internal struts for support. And once cooled, they had to chip away the special ceramic mould and presto: the prototype shell of the Meteor. Yet, the real problem eluded them. They soon realised that they hadn't discovered the seemingly magic formula to emulate the fantastic alien alloys. The combinations were infinite: whether to ionize or de-ionize, or what temperature elements such as bismuth, or titanium must harmonize with the other ingredients like cobalt, boron, chromium and beryllium to make it durable and solid enough to withstand the kind of atmospheric gravity force bearing in on the hull, even intense pressures deep within the ocean, if the anti-gravity force-field failed.

❧

Over the years, Jimmy earned tremendous respect, and was given free access to come and go from Dreamland as he pleased. Working underground in the vast complex was stressful, and he frequented Vegas every other weekend, having developed a good friendship with Cora. He spent two to three weeks every three months or so in Canada with Andromeda and her family. Rob and Andie had two sons with whom he had naturally forged very close bonds. The family didn't have any idea what he was really doing in Vegas, but understood it was classified. On a number of occasions they met him there and went on trips to the Grand Canyon and skied in California, British Columbia, Utah and Colorado. During the years 2036 to '40, when Danielle was in opposition having lost to the Liberals over economic policies and tough welfare programs, she found she was taking more time to enjoy herself. So Danielle made sure her busy schedule never interfered, if possible, with Jimmy's vacations or even her family once in a while. She would show up at the same ski resort or cottage area.

Jimmy revealed to her almost everything he knew about the alien problem, technically breaking his oath, but trusting in her the responsibility of her office and her obvious influence in respect to the situation. Danielle took it all in cavalierly, but remained oddly ever-impenetrable underneath that cool exterior with regard to his revelations. Jimmy thought that she would have been at least astounded at some of his reports, not to mention the implications. Yet the more he talked, the greater a wall seemed to come between them.

Then one summer while camping for a few days in Northern Ontario, they sit together around the fire after Jimmy had expressed his disappointment concerning her lack of passion about the aliens. She contemplates for a while. The shadows of the fire look like thoughts prancing on her face. Jimmy couldn't have known, but the first stirrings of what would bring about her demise in six years began as a romantic attempt to reconcile with her apparent disinterest.

'You know, Jimmy,' she says, 'I have a feeling the political process could possibly handle some of the revelations coming out of Dreamland. Home-tech is coming out with a new reactor developed from your own theories on anti-matter. I'd bet on it, that within a generation, we'll have our own gravity propulsion system, however crude, but nevertheless airborne. Isn't that what they want? The mainstream catching up? This is what justifies my thinking.'

'They don't have a problem with that, Danielle; it's the can of worms that comes with it. For instance, revealing we are containers, we'd have every fanatic fundamentalist flying kamikaze into Dreamland. God is Great or Praise be the Lord!'

'Then it seems to me nothing's changed in twenty-five thousand years or whatever. Do we throw up our hands and say: so what? Who gives a damn? Well, I do. Politically, we can assert our sovereignty, can we not?'

'We're surrounded by lizards, babe. And no one's questioning our sovereignty.'

'Hell, they're not crocodiles!' exclaims Danielle. 'They sound down-right effeminate, even civilised. I say to hell with the secret world. If I get elected again, I'm going to stir the pot. I want to feel it out.'

'You'll be denounced as a lunatic, deposed or worse.'

'What else is new?'

'A few grey hairs?'

Danielle's beautiful long hair has held its black colour naturally for a long time. In her mid-fifties, it finally began to grey. All her political life she wore it tied up at the back in a French manner. The grey, though, only enhanced her natural beauty.

'Are you punning?' She looks at him teasingly.

'Oh yes,' he laughs 'the Greys are coming! The Greys are coming!'

'When, may I ask?'

'Arcana imperii.'

'Enlighten me please.'

'State secrets.'

'You rascal!' She shoves him over. 'No more sex!'

'Has it come to this? Sex for secrets?' he jives.

They play like children under the stars. There is no love diminished here. Then they jump in the lake skinny before crawling into their tent to make love and sleep like tired children.

So finally in 2041, the year after Danielle is elected Prime Minister for the fourth term, Jimmy gets his wish to participate in the X13 program. It is really Colonel Good who gained access for him, as the General, as a rule, restricted everyone except key personnel who are directly involved with necessary work such as communications, genetics and translations. Even Colonel Good had rare access before he was promoted. But General Blaine was soon retiring and Colonel Good had been groomed to assume command.

One day after he got back from Vegas, the Colonel comes into Jimmy's cozy quarters, which has a kitchenette, living area and bedroom. He says that the General would like to meet with him, so they head down the corridor to the military wing and the General's quarters.

The General beckons them in with his usual steely-faced demeanour that everyone accepted as a natural condition due to the responsibility of the man who knew everything and would be held responsible if the aliens got out of hand. He is of medium height, with a full head of white hair cropped short around a square head. His eyes are deep set and he rarely smiles. Telling them to sit down around his kitchen table, the General, a non-drinker, (a requisite for the job) brings out a jug of iced mineral water and three glasses.

'Help yourselves, gentlemen,' he grumbles, pouring one for himself. 'Mr. Pidgeon, I asked you to come here today with the Colonel, because of your outstanding contribution to our program. Over the last ten years, we have made gains that otherwise might have taken, hell, a hundred years. I wish to extend to you on behalf of the MJ-12 our highest commendations. Unfortunately, due to the sensitive nature of our work, we cannot award you the public honour you so richly deserve.'

Jimmy expresses his thanks to the colonel and by extension, to MJ-12, the executive council of twelve carefully chosen people originally set up the previous century by President Truman to deal with the Roswell incident (a UFO crash retrieval operation near Corona, New Mexico) and other UFO activity. Initially, Jimmy had heard that this event had so shocked the President that he was reputed to have said, "I suppose this means I am a lunatic for believing in little green men!"

'As a retiring member of MJ-12,' the General proceeds gruffly, 'I have recommended that Colonel Good assume command here and take my place on the council. Furthermore, the council is losing another member, a scientist, Dr. Williams, who has had a stroke. Again it was my recommendation that you, Mr. Pidgeon, fill that spot. This is unprecedented, as you are the first non-American chosen to the council. Congratulations. Now, let's get down to business.'

'To begin, I'd like to tell a little story, a true one.' The General reveals the flicker of a smile. 'My father, also a General, had the responsibility of maintaining the program. He lost a leg in what we now call the Dulce War. It was a small and tragic war. Not two hundred died, most of which were Greys, the rest our best Special Forces. It took place in the underground facility there in 1980. My father claimed it began as an accident or misunderstanding. The aliens had altered the atmosphere and incorporated a security frequency wave of some kind in their housing facility. A security officer who pulled his gun when he thought he was being threatened – there had been a communication problem back then – and fired it by accident and the alien security shield sent the bullets back killing the officer with a bullet to the head. Thinking they were being attacked, the Special Forces were called in to secure the area. My father lost his leg when a blaze gun back-fired from the shield. At any rate, the shield was destroyed and many aliens died. Some of them escaped and took off in their gravity vehicles. MJ-12 almost gave up the ghost after that. They didn't know whether there would be a massive retaliation or not. They were divided as to inform the public of what could occur. Thank God nothing came of it. I tell you it sure scared the heck out of that peanut farmer, Jimmy Carter. The point is you must never let that kind of thing happen. The program has been successfully directed for ninety-four years now; you must continue for another ninety-four, if need be, or until we are capable of protecting ourselves from these goddamned little alien fuckers. Don't buy the popular view that they're a bunch a fuckin' people-lovin' pansies – peace on earth bullshit! As a race, they are predators, super-predators who respect only the quality of their possession, like successful slave-traders. Good slave-traders never whipped or starved their people into submission, hell no; they treated them like valuables with tender loving care, so they could make more money on the auction block! But the Reptoids and Reticulans don't use money. Nor do they buy and sell; they just control life on earth and no one knows about it, except us. So don't be fooled by them and watch the females, they're the horniest little she-devils since Sodom and Gomorrah. Once they look you in the eye, you're halfway fucked. They will read you like a book and have you brainwashed for breakfast. Mark my words: be tough, mentally tough. Let there be more than the obvious distinction between us and them. We haven't any choice about their being here; the least we can do is to make it as restricted as possible under the circumstances. We know their motives and they know ours. Defeat is when we have lost the distinction. Be vigilant!

'The technology is one thing, but our right to self-determination is another. Our mutual agreement is not written in stone, although we honour it as they do most of the time. The problem is their race is so vast and varied and the galaxy is filled with such a plethora of life, it's a miracle our containment hasn't been blown. We have to date records of no less than one hundred and fifty-eight alien species within our vicinity of the universe that we know of – say within 20,000 light years, and we are in the lower percentile of these civilisations. The fucking Reptoids have over the last twenty thousand years pretty much cast their shadow over us all. Within a few thousand years, humanity as we know it may be no more. They think us ignorant to want to maintain our evolution as it stands.

They say we are a fragile species who must evolve to survive. We're not arguing that; it's just that we want to do it ourselves. They all smile at our naïvety, but not at our bombs. Any questions?'

'Are there not a few Reptoids or Greys who sympathise with us?' queries Jimmy. 'Let's face it; they've been cross-breeding all these years; where are the hybrids?'

'Most are taken away to Zeta Reticula or who knows where. Some remain. Make no distinction about the half-wits, they're neither Grey nor human; but guess who mommy and daddy are? The Greys and half-wits: does that answer your question? Besides, they breed full blood humans too. But that's another monster.'

'Yes, and so hasn't there been a human influence? Perhaps we can turn some of them to our way of thinking, like control the monster.'

'Colonel,' remarks the General smugly, 'enlighten Mr. Pidgeon.'

'Jimmy,' speaks Colonel Good, 'The thought processes are so foreign to us. To communicate telepathically, there is something lost in their individuality. Think of a hive of ants: they segregate themselves naturally according to rank and file. There are leaders and workers. No one earns brownie points and gets a promotion. You are what you are. There's no need for politics and elections and all the fundamentals in a democratic society that we take for granted . . . '

'Still, we should not judge every Grey as a non-thinking entity. There may be a way to communicate with some of them, maybe even one, to know more . . . '

'Mr. Pidgeon, with all due respect,' contends the General, 'If they read each other's minds like we chit chat, that entity would be considered undesirable and shunted off to some distant star to mine rocks or something. Believe me, we have tried everything over the years. There are no bleeding-heart aliens. Maybe, the Neteru were, but they're gone and we can't go looking for them, at least not until we can get a ship out there. But don't take my word for it: give it your best. Perhaps there's something there we don't know yet. Hell, the little fuckers sure know how to make spacecraft!'

The General actually laughed. Jimmy and the Colonel looked at each other not at all sure what was so funny.

'What of the Eridanis or Itibians?' asks Jimmy. 'They're like us.'

'They won't interfere with the Reptoids and unfortunately the Reptoids are here to stay. And neither you nor I or Superman can change that,' exhorts the General.

'I might add,' remarks the Colonel, 'There are some tenuous links with the Normals. They do come here. Call it moral support.'

'Well,' says the General regaining his former composure, 'Let's go and see what they're up to today, shall we?' He stands up and they head off to the shuttle tube. Area 13 or X13 is about a five-minute tube ride to the northwest. There are no visible surface buildings there. Everything has to be shuttled in. The Greys, however, could dematerialise solid rock and make an exit. This is one of the magic features of alien technology. They would literally alter the atomic structure of solid substances and osmotically permeate them either physically themselves or in their machines, by directing an anti-photon beam through one of the craft's amplifiers on a disruptor mode, meaning they would neutralise the electron charge that held substances together. Certain minerals are risky, but in terms of rock, sedimentary is easily manipulated into suspended dust and back again into rock. Jimmy had implemented his own type of magic in the Meteor, but is a long way from trying it out.

Once at X13, or Xanadu, as it was referred to by the security personnel, they disembark. Two special military police dressed in black overalls holding stun guns salute the General. They stand aside and Jimmy gives them a smile and half salute. They then enter a large steel door. There is an absence of any directions in English. Only symbols are written along corridors and doors. Everything is made out of steel and feels quite sterile, though warm. There is a slight ammonia and sulphur smell in the air, due to some of their synthetic physiology – developed apparently to enhance bio-electric stimulae derived from proteins containing 3-thienylalanine replacing the natural amino acid alanine. They arrive at an elevator, step in and the General presses a symbol on the console. The door shuts and with a whoosh they ascend in the elevator tube which actually emerges beneath the complex.

When the door opens, standing there are two Greys and a third who looks like a half grey-human – a hybrid. Undoubtedly female, she has dark brown, wispy hair that has body though it appears full of static. Her eyes are huge, pale blue orbs surrounding large pupils, set in a little chiseled face with a small nose and mouth. Jimmy is reminded of a character out of the Sailor Moon repeats, which he had watched with his grandchildren back home. She is dressed in a one-piece suit made out of a shiny synthetic substance. She can't have been 160 centimeters tall (five feet) with long arms and hands with a skinny body. Her skin colour seems almost to shimmer from opaque to white; Jimmy knows the hybrids have some red blood cells, but mixed with the Reticulan clear blood, it turns a watery pinkish colour, hence the opaque, or pearl-skins they were sometimes called. She is extraordinarily beautiful if one can appreciate the alien genes, and her watery-eyed scrutiny of him sends some kind of warm message that has an uncanny familiarity. He breaks away from her stare and turns to the others. The full-blooded Greys standing forward from her are indeed shocking too. They too scrutinise Jimmy with their large, dark, wrap-around eyes and over-sized, hairless craniums. Everything that is skinny and long in the female is exaggerated in the males. Jimmy finds the hybrids are much easier to look at; the full bloods definitely are much cooler like the chill of winter, yet the environment there is actually hot and humid. Maybe that's why they brought her along, he wonders. The full bloods communicated only through telepathy, which at first, as Jimmy finds out, is a frightening invasion of one's own sense of sanctity. They could plant and pull one's thoughts with impunity.

The General shakes the first Grey's long four-fingered hand. Jimmy can sense the Grey's mind communicating his greeting. When the Grey shakes Jimmy's hand, the thought is firmly planted in his head. *Welcome to X13*, he says. The Grey lets go. His skin is cool and dry to the touch like a reptile. Then they are led down the steel corridor to a large room where numerous other Greys are busy about a large console with many lights and hieroglyphs. Most of the Greys there ignore them. The senior Grey keeps looking at Jimmy who can feel his mind being drawn into the Grey's. It is as if his brain is being sucked by an invisible vacuum cleaner. The sensation is eerie at best and Jimmy seems to stop it by ignoring the Grey completely. The General notices and says, 'Don't mind the probes, Jimmy; they do it to newcomers. My brains have been so scoured, I recommended my own retirement.'

'Do they have names?' asks Jimmy, resisting the probe.

'Their names for everything are unintelligible to us, so we make up our own. The one that's scouring you we call Big Cheese, the other, Bart, and then Lilly; she asks that we pronounce it like the French would: Leelee. 'Speak Lilly,' he demands, 'Meet Jimmy Pidgeon.'

Lilly says, 'Hello Jimmy,' in this high diminutive voice that sounds like she's high on helium. It seems uncanny that she can actually speak. Jimmy wants so much to speak with her.

'Hi Lilly, how are you?'

She doesn't respond vocally but sends a message: *I cannot speak right now. Big Cheese is controlling the scene and the General is a jerk.*

Jimmy looks at Big Cheese, then at the General. 'What the hell are they doing, General?' he asks.

'This is where they monitor, record and assess their activities twenty-four hours a day, all year. This is the main base on earth. Everything the Greys do is controlled from here. We simply monitor their activities. We know exactly what they're doing most of the time. It's part of the program.'

Big Cheese then puts a thought directly into Jimmy's mind: *We co-exist, Jimmy; our species need yours to help survive and vice-versa.*

Jimmy looks right at him and says: 'If we are so important, why then do you wish to remain anonymous?'

Big Cheese replies: *We do it for your own protection. The Reptoids, our supe-*

riors would like to dominate you genetically. We persuade them, this would not be in their best interests.

'And what are their best interests?'

Their best interests are for the greater good in creation. Creation is our modus: to further the cause of creation, all things being equal.

'But we are created, and living as best as can be; why interfere?'

We are all interdependent, all species in the universe. Then he shifts his attention to the General.

The General listens, then speaks: 'Yes, Mr. Pidgeon is one of our most intelligent.'

Big Cheese continues to communicate with him.

'What you decide to do mutually is within our mandate, so long as Colonel Good is kept apprised,' says General Blaine to Big Cheese.

Big Cheese then turns to Colonel Good.

'That's up to Mr. Pidgeon,' the Colonel finally says.

Big Cheese looks at Jimmy. Your people say it is up to you whether you would like to fly with us.

'I thought you'd never ask, as long as Lilly comes,' Jimmy adds as an after-thought. These Greys with the big craniums sticking thoughts into his mind is just too weird. But it isn't that that makes him feel uncomfortable. These four to five foot luminescent beings, for all their candour, are not completely honest with him and he knows that they know what he knows.

'Have you gone with them before, Colonel?' asks Jimmy.

'No, I haven't; they are very selective, but don't worry, others have and came back without incident.'

'General?'

'Go for it, Mr. Pidgeon; get a load of the future. Quiz them; see if your work is on line. I want you to be the liaison. That's why you're here. Our last man Dr. Williams lost his nerve. Just relax and pretend its Halloween!'

'I thought he had a stroke,' recalls Jimmy.

'In a manner of speaking; he kinda blew a fuse. You have to keep the telepathy to a minimum. Our brain waves only come with a 20 amp fuse. These guys run with an open circuit if you know what I mean. Use Lilly; she's great in more ways than one, from what I understand.'

'General,' whispers Jimmy, shocked at the General's implication, 'She's right here! Shouldn't you be a little more considerate of her feelings?'

'Jimmy, they don't have morals like we do. When they talk about creation; they really mean procreation. You'll see soon enough; hell, she takes it as a compliment.'

Big Cheese then leads them into another elevator tube. They go up to another level. Jimmy sees more loose, black-jumper security men. They all greet the General and Colonel warmly. Then through another door, the level stretches on as far as the eye can see. In every room are glass tanks with growing fetuses and many Greys about tending to their various duties. Jimmy and his entourage are completely ignored, such is the power of Big Cheese. It appears he really is in control.

They enter a large room and Big Cheese begins probing Jimmy again. The feeling is indeed strenuous to have to compute his thoughts: *We breed many children*, he said, *as you can see. We do love our children and raise them to be our replacements one day. When they are born, they will be taken to one of our star systems to mature. Then they will return. Have no fear, we will not invade you, as they would have it in Hollywood!* Jimmy laughs freely at his jab at humour.

'Where do you get your human sperm and eggs?' quizzes Jimmy, staring at the vats of amniotic fluid and dozens of fetuses in each vat. They all looked like miniature replicas of Lilly.

We have a selective supply coming in from your populations as a requisite of our agreement. The Program, you know. We regret it has created problems for you.

Jimmy thinks how the alien abduction phenomenon had created a whole new field of psychiatry over the last seventy years in the attempt to fit the symptoms of those afflicted into a pathology. The thousands of cases underlined their importance, but for a generation the implications have been resisted vehemently as a legitimate problem by the medical establishment. However, of note is that patients in most cases had no pre-disposition or personality similarities to indicate any common disorder or pattern of affliction, but nevertheless, few psychiatrists can accept that the abductions are in fact real. Most professionals believe, in the face of mounting evidence – some of it supported by credible witnesses and even medical proof – that such an awesome phenomenon just couldn't be pos-sible and must obviously be a mass psychosis, which it inevitably has become, especially in view of memory erasing by the aliens.

'Amazing,' is all Jimmy can say. The umbilical chords are all attached to these placentas that are attached to the upper surface of the tank that must have been some kind of organic nutrient compound feeding the fetuses.

They leave the vats and visit the alien quarters and storage facilities. Everything is sterile and inhospitable, though humid and warm. There isn't any entertainment center for relaxation. The only thing that remotely seems like a break in a monotonous routine, are the absorption baths. Some of the aliens had to submerge themselves in these steamy baths of greenish water made of a chlorophyll concentrate. It is explained by Bart that this is the best way for them to absorb nutrients that rejuvenate their health; it is therapy to offset our somewhat inhospitable environment for their life form. Since they had biologically evolved beyond the mastication of food in the orifice of the mouth and the excretion of waste out the anal canal, they now retain and secreted a fluid only. But it is also difficult because many of them who could still masticate had flawed intestinal tracts that can not produce certain digestive enzymes, in which case they extract some of these and other hormones from animals. Hence, there are many surgically precise cattle and horse mutilations over the decades that the public could never understand – cored out anal regions and genitals, hearts, glands around the mouth, and draining of blood etc. It is a vulner-ability: they need to retreat from their advanced state of genetic evolution. Jimmy realizes that without the introduction of new DNA they would eventually become extinct, having evolved beyond sustainable life.

Lastly, they are escorted to their space vehicle facility where a few black fatigued security personnel are posted. The metal encapsulated area is at least thirty meters high and a hundred meters long and wide and housed some small discoid metallic craft. The exit appears to be at one end where there isn't any metal, just exposed rock. The General and the Colonel decide to head back then, leaving Jimmy with his new friends.

Jimmy is escorted by Lilly to a craft near the presumed exit. A hatch is open with a ramp leading in. The design is simple, similar to some of the types they have experimented with down at S-4. In the stark interior the round consoles have no sharp edges. There are small seats with little padding, and a sofa chair not even secured, which was obviously brought in to make a human passenger comfortable.

Jimmy sits down in the sofa chair by the console and Lilly where they both quietly look at the large screens around the control room, which take up most of the craft's rounded interior. The strange lighting source emanates uniformly from the interior walls. Sensors and glyphs adorn the console. Remarkable as it is, some of their ships could be flown telepathically with their enhanced synthetic synaptic receivers. Jimmy is astounded by their magic. He had read about it, but certainly there hadn't been a manual, nor would there be. The Greys defy nature, but would not assist the program.

Big Cheese and Bart come aboard and sit down. The ramp shuts and seals behind them so perfectly Jimmy cannot detect the seam. The screens light up and they can see the interior of the underground cavity. Jimmy watches stupefied as a beam of light shoots out at the rock, before they rise up and go straight through it – *poof* and they are flying up and away into the clouds, then blue sky, then dark space and orbit in a matter of seconds, but they keep going. Their trajectory must have been almost vertical but Jimmy sits in his unsecured chair as if he reclines in his living room. He has never experienced gravity propulsion when the ship is the center of gravity; it doesn't matter whether they are flying upside down, it always feels right side up, just like on planet earth.

Transfixed, Jimmy observes earth recede behind them to a tiny speck and completely disappear. In front, he can see Mars approach. They enter orbit and come out on the dark side where a huge cylindrical ship at least a kilometer in length is positioned. Within a minute they are docked inside. Stepping out, Jimmy notices a number of humans, Greys, hybrids and an obvious Reptoid about the receiving area. The humans greet Jimmy politely. The Reptoid even shakes his hand. He is of medium height with smooth, yellow-green skin that has a waxy sheen to it. He is pleasantly mannered, yet frightening to look at. He has humanoid facial features, almost handsome but with vertical pupils! He then walks off with Big Cheese and Bart.

Jimmy is in a daze as to how fast and efficiently their craft had transported them. Standing there, he feels Lilly tug at his shirt and lead him away. In shock, his brain cannot get over the brevity of the trip and his new surroundings.

He understands that they super-charge their reactor to produce anti-matter which is converted into an intense harmonic of electromagnetic power, and once amplified and released is aimed as a gravity wave, which propagates itself in space by opening a fissure in the time-space continuum and then pulls them to their targeted destination. Obviously it makes Jimmy appreciate how much work he had yet to do. The thought occurs to him that a lesser harmonic in the anti-matter charge spectrum could make it possible to gravity propel cars and aircraft, or any vehicle in a limited way, as long as the conduction was uniform as a spheroid.

Jimmy is taken to a featureless room and told to sit down on a padded bench. Lilly sits with him like a dutiful caretaker. She seems to act in a way that she knows what they were going to do with him, perhaps for his benefit.

'What's going, Lilly?' he asks, worriedly.

'That Reptoid you met and Big Cheese communicated,' she says, with that euphonious voice. 'They wish to give you something very special.'

'Me? Why?'

'They are intrigued by you. When they read you, they see many images and a unique reflection of themselves which perhaps is a lost character trait, though not necessarily primitive. You call it poetry or soul; they call it ego. The Reptoids believe ego is a weak link in their species in the sense of personal expression.'

'You know, I don't think ego is such a good idea for them. Who's to know what they'll do with a little ego.'

Lilly laughs. Her eyes light up. She puts her long sinewy hand on Jimmy's. 'Don't worry; they believe in God, in that the universe is a vessel in which we all transcend; but there is nothing really holy in it; it just is and always will be.' She smiles at Jimmy's stricken face.

'That's what worries me,' he says. 'At least we have conjured a loving God who represents everything that is supposedly good.'

Lilly cocks her head like a cute puppy. 'You mean like a friendly old man or woman, with an unholy temper, and who uses some real perverts to do their dirty work.'

She laughs again.

'Yeah, sort of.'

'They are amused at your primitive concepts,' she continues. 'They find it hypocritical that your God is so one-dimensional, so human, full of rules and limitations. You see, nature destroys and rebuilds incessantly. Good and bad must be interchanged for survival; in other words: life is sacrifice and preservation.'

'Then what is God to you, if not a moral one?'

'God is a transvestite, a shape-shifter, Wiley Coyote, or perhaps a road-runner.' She laughs in a high-octane twitter at her own joke. 'The universe doesn't have any moral destiny,' she adds, 'The cosmos is a chaotic process where galaxies collide and planets crash. There is beauty everywhere: rebirth, love and even the moral destiny of humankind. I like it, but many are sick in mind and body. One crosses out the other. We try to show you your corruption and if you fail, like gods we will remonstrate.' Lilly now comes across like a school matron, teasing, and reassuringly all too human.

'You try to teach us, you mean,' infers Jimmy.

'They just don't want your pollution to escape.'

'And I might help humankind escape? Is that it?'

'That is why they are giving you something.'

'What may I ask?' Jimmy keeps thinking: lobotomy. Why would they give him something to aid human progress in space, if they wanted to contain human "pollution"?

'An implant. It is a unique organic mineral encapsulated in an unumpentium alloy. It is very rare like the rarest of diamonds but much rarer. It is only found on certain planets in a hot system, a star system which burns too hot and too soon for life to develop. On a planet distant enough, under certain terrific pressures and the right minerals like unumpentium, this organic compound generates and reproduces in tiny quantities beneath the surface of the planet. They have found that it is a substance that once fed information, retains it encoded in its strange synaptic microplasma which can be easily processed by the natural synaptic rhythms of our brains. They are going to implant this device loaded with information pertinent to your skills . . . '

'Did they do this to Dr. Williams?' queries Jimmy alarmed.

She hesitates.

'No, he really did burn out.'

'What happened to him?'

'Synaptic overload.'

'What does he do now?'

'He retired to the country, in Maryland. He gardens, I hear.'

'Lucky him.'

'Lucky you,' she avers. 'In this device, our known universe is charted with navigational coordinates and anomalies. There are very few of them in existence. They are very old. With this they predict great success for you as a human.'

'Success? For whom?'

'For you of course. It is a gift of appreciation!'

'But why? They don't know me.'

'I don't know; but I think they see you as a threat to their containment.'

'How?' asks Jimmy, incredulously.

'You have succeeded where others failed.'

'Then why don't they kill me if I'm a threat?'

'They would never kill someone of your intelligence. Their way would be to enlighten you further, in order for you to help humans understand what they are all about.'

'It's overwhelming,' he says looking down and shaking his head.

'Not with this gift.'

'So what is it called?'

But before she can answer, the Reptoid enters with Big Cheese and Bart. Bart is carrying a metal rod device that Jimmy already knew to be the notorious magic wand that had a neuron disruptor charge in it and when activated rendered the recipient of the charge numbed, but still relatively coherent.

Big Cheese telepathises only to relax and Jimmy is instantly stunned. He senses his brain going into some kind of hyper state but feels nothing. The next thing he knows, he is lying on the table face down and can sense something tickling inside the back of his head. This is not happening, he ponders.

The image flickers and shuts down. Stars appear, then streak in blinding flashes. He can hear a familiar voice and feel a hand on his shoulder. 'Cephren, sir, Chairman, wake up!' He can't place it then the name comes to him. Cephren knows who he is, as he recognises Runaway's voice. He opens his eyes to the familiar surroundings of the Volcano.

'Incredible . . . incredible . . . so explicit,' mumbles Cephren, finding his voice.

'Sir, Seven just called from the beach; there are unidentified emops flying about over the bay. They're monitoring the bottom. We gotta move. It must be those commandos again.'

'How did they find us?'

'They must've found Seven and knew we'd be nearby.'

'They followed the transports,' says Cephren, coming to his senses disengaging the auxiliary ground. He stands up and stretches his large frame. 'How long have I been down?' he asks as he moves to the main console.

'Eight hours.'

'Is that all? Incredible.'

'We gotta move, sir.'

Cephren, after visiting the washroom, sits down again. He fires up the reactor to a high mode and inches along the murky bottom out of the disturbed silt clouding around them. Suddenly, lights loom in front of them and block their passage.

'Emop!' exclaims Runaway.

Cephren reverses the pulse inhibitors and flies back into the cloud of silt. Then he lifts off like a rocket straight up missing yet another emop by a few feet on the surface. Startling it, Cephren gave themselves a few moments to gain some distance. But another hovering emop directs a disruptor beam attempting to immobilise them. Runaway, however, slams his hand on the particle shield sensor in the nick of time.

'Dive!' yells Runaway.

But Cephren has already made his move. They hit the water at great speed but slip in like a bullet and head out to open water as quickly as the Volcano could go underwater at about a thousand kilometers per hour.

'I didn't know they could go underwater so well,' says Cephren.

'Most likely a recent refitting,' assumes Runaway.

'After downloading Sunsetwind.'

'That's for sure,' remarks Runaway.

'We're not shaking them,' says Cephren. 'They're above us and behind us. But we're safe in the water from their disruptors.'

They head east and north to get around Cape Breton. In a few hours they approach the Grand Banks where they descend to two hundred meters. The emop behind them levels at a hundred meters, seeming to fear deeper submersion.

'Where do we go from here?' asks Runaway, looking about in the dark gloom of the North Atlantic.

'We can't go up and they can't come down. I think we'll just carry on. I have an idea.'

'What's that?'

At that moment a submarine appears for a second. They narrowly miss it. The Americans have a massive undersea base in the mid-Atlantic built in the mid 21st century. It had been used by the Chicagos since one of their recent treaties. Although fast, the subs were no match for the Volcano. 'A sub. That was close. You watch the monitor, Runaway.'

'Is George in on this too?' inquires Runaway.

'Not by design. I think he considers our friendship a good excuse to bring me in for my own good.'

'You're doing the right thing, sir, if you don't mind me saying so. If you want the Earth Chair, you've got to be in charge.'

'That's the plan.' Cephren drops another two hundred meters over the Grand Bank.

'So what is the plan?' presses Runaway.

'We're going to Antarctica, or Atlantis rather.'

'Atlantis?'

'Yes. There's an undersea entrance that comes out above ground from under the ice.'

'I don't get it.'

'Three hundred or so years ago, the Americans conducted a highly classified operation by excavating a huge cavity under the ice to study the ruins of Atlantis. I have the exact coordinates of the entrance. We will simply disappear. They will presume we're dead again.'

'Are you serious? Atlantis? Why didn't they tell anybody?'

'Because it was also an alien base, and I'm dead serious.'

'Mother of God!'

'That's about it and nobody's been through it since the big Asteroid.'

'Could the aliens still be there?'

'That I don't know; but I aim to find out.'

ten Blue Phoenix

Then sing magically with the silver birds
                                        –Jimmy Pidgeon

For a few days they have been followed deep beneath the ocean blue, as they carry on towards their destination. Cephren marvels at the Chicago tenacity. He thinks he could contact help if he emerged long enough to get a signal to O'Reilly, but by then the Chicagos could get a hundred more emops. He had presumed Seven Moons had stayed behind; there was no point in risking his life under the circumstances. Cephren knows Seven would have figured that nothing on earth could catch the Volcano underwater.

He submerges to a thousand meters and stops to play dead, but the Chicagos stop too and wait patiently for him to come alive again. They presume he would come up eventually, at least for air. The Volcano's oxygen supply, however, thanks to George Washington's Ecosphere Inc., was good for at least a year. The Chicagos may know that so they would be calling on back-up to force him to the surface. One of the Chicago emops emitted some ultrasonic beams attempting to disrupt their antimatter charge. After a few moments of terror with the chance of implosion, Runaway easily disarms them with the defensive shields, though the intimidation works and the Chicagos were successful in rousing their prey.

After a long week of cat and mouse, Cephren and Runaway finally arrive at that mysterious archipelago, Antarctica, alias Atlantis, rising in colossal, white splendour from the cold, blue sea. They skirt underneath the massive ice flows. Cephren has explained that there is an undersea tunnel at 61 degrees 12 minutes west and 76 degrees 47 minutes south, but the ice flows are proving to be more difficult than they thought. They have to go out of their way almost fifty kilometers to get around some shallow ocean and deep ice flows. An extraordinary thing happens as they think they are finally free of the obstacles of ice. Far to their left, they see a speeding flash of light. It moves so fast they think it must be their imagination. They rule out the Chicagos and conclude it could only have been some freakish natural anomaly or an actual UFO. So they carry on, and after a day of playing labyrinth with more ice obstacles, they find a deep trench that leads them far under the ice shelf. Antarctica is actually made up of numerous islands and a major landmass towards the Australian side, and as they approach their desired location, they can't help but think by observing the undersea topography and the mountainous islands that it must have been an absolutely stunning country at one time. The city of Atlantis had allegedly been surrounded by mountains and yet situated on a coastal plain, so it should be assumed that they would be able to get close to it by water in the deep channels. The undersea passage that they travel begins to narrow and the ice above looms closer. When it seems they are coming to a dead end, a large black hole appears in front. Just beyond, the ice and sea bottom converge to seal the passage shut. They enter the hole, which has a diameter of about twenty meters. It narrows slightly once inside. Heading down at about a thirty-degree angle for at least a thousand meters, they level and go along slowly for an excruciatingly long ten minutes. Cephren particularly, is anxious not just by the phenomenal implications of the undersea passage, but the veracity of his information.

Soon the passage begins to climb and almost two thousand meters farther the water ends as the passage opens. Air borne, they emerge into a vast, interior cavity of ice. It is pitch black, so they light it up with their high beams and behold truly one of the most beautiful sights on earth, even though they were over a mile beneath the ice. For here was the epi-center of a lost civilisation. The ceiling of the ice dome is at least a hun-dred meters high and extends for over a kilometer in every direction. A series of broken pyramids and temples grace the central area. Massive walls of precisely cut stone appear to be part of a canal system surrounding the ruins as water from melted ice fills them and runs off under the ice in lit-tle cracks that presumably find their way to the sea. The ruins of many buildings lie in piles of rubble due to the millenniums the ice have done its thorough excavation. It looks as though there had been an attempt to rebuild many of the central buildings. The pyramids had been remarkably preserved, and about their bases sheets of shiny metal lie scattered about. Hovering above these wonders, Cephren notes that Atlantis had been adorned by orichalcum, a bright, fiery metal on its walls. What a tragedy, he reflects, that such a place came to an end and was lost to the world all this time; but he understands the tenuous links of survival as experienced through Flower Child in the post-asteroid world. To have the sun sud-denly change its course in the sky must have signaled literally the end of the world – the day the sky fell – the ear-shattering rumblings and rip-pling earth as its crust shifted on the mantle, the frightened people, rich and poor, young and old, with nowhere to run as the oceans spilled across the land in towering tidal waves sweeping everything away.

They fly slowly around the periphery of the dome. At one end, a com-plex had been built. There is even an old U.S. flag that still hung in tatters. They decide to land and exit their craft to walk about. Once outside, it is cold but surprisingly temperate considering the vast ice around them – a little like a colossal igloo. They look about and realise that the place had been abandoned rapidly because assorted items such as excavators and boxes of supplies are scattered around. Cephren assumes the aliens had deserted it too; there certainly isn't any trace of them. Inside the building, in spite of the mold and dampness, they turn on an old generator that actually fires up without trouble. Lights turn on proffering the place a little life again. They rummage through many of the rooms. Old videos, electronic paraphernalia, papers, and assorted junk decorates that bleak outpost. Against the back of the building by the wall of ice, an elevator shaft ascends apparently to the surface, but the shifting ice has blocked the passage. There couldn't have been a more inaccessible place on earth. It scares Cephren to think that if something went wrong with the Volcano, they were doomed and no one would ever find them, as no one knew where they were. Besides, the Volcano is the only vehicle that could possibly get there in a hurry. Still, he feels it would be prudent to go back to the entrance and make sure they hadn't been followed, though that seemed quite unlikely.

They take the liberty of walking among the ruins. In a little area between two temples built of massive 300 ton blocks and delicate engraving depicting astral images, agrarian labour, sumptuous feasts, cultural iconography such as a shining object in the sky and sailing fleets, are two statues that have been raised and repaired. On the base chiseled into the hard stone were hieroglyphics, yet more etymological in appearance than pictorials – in other words, a simple alphabetical language. Upon closer scrutiny, Cephren sees a little plate more recently lagged to the stone. On the one statue it reads Osiris and on the other, Isis. Incredible, wonders Cephren: these two must have been the original Neteru who came as missionaries or refugees so long ago. It was they who rose to the pinnacle of the great pantheon of Egyptian mythology as its highest stars, and became the prototypes of martyrdom in later religions, specifically Christianity.

The statues, both naked adaptations, are presumed to be likenesses of the original persons: Osiris is noble in appearance and sculpted perfectly in the image of godly man. Isis is still beautiful over the ages with a calm face but brilliant eyes that show her courage and intelligence. Their bodies are well proportioned and unmistakably carved to signify erotic renditions. Cephren ponders their influence: they were gods who changed remarkably the world – extraterrestrials thrown into a virtual zoo, seeking to enlighten a primitive race. It was a generous dream, though doomed to fail. The

Neteru had to have been an extraordinary advanced species. Could they still be with us in the universe? Cephren knows that he must find out. Perhaps, he should get back into Jimmy's Chip. He would be safe in Atlantis. And after a few days, the Chicagos would give up; they would have no idea where Cephren could be under thousands of square miles of ice. With a smile, his mind is made up. There is no more appropriate place anywhere to seek the Neteru.

~⁹)

Treason Honey pushes herself off the edge of the Heights, a steep pitch at Osprey Heights. She flies down in fast arcing turns feeling the wonder of motion on the snow and freefall gravity. It is a great thrill to feel the cold air rushing at her body and the freedom of the sport after the past week of depraved activity as the new mistress of Sunsetwind. Her timing as usual is perfect; she doesn't even try – things just come her way, such as Heyoka's medallion, but with one rather painful exception. Already, the people have cautiously begun to comment disparagingly of her lurid ascendancy to Del Barker's bedroom. She knows that she is vilified and as well a prime patsy as the scapegoat for Del Barker should he have to use her to protect himself. Her name even says it all: Treason. But her worries dissolve in the fresh air and fabulous ski run. At the bottom of the hill she engages her fusion-powered boots and swooshes back to the top as adeptly as she went down. Two Praetorians follow at a distance, with others stationed at the top and bottom.

True to his word, Del Barker had let Treason wear the medallion within his presence, usually in bed, unaware of its true worth. He especially doesn't mind when she betokened it to fulfill his sexual needs. Barker sees it as a convenient floater – a cheap tithe for her obedience. They had been negotiating a reasonable settlement with Bob Fix, who was assigned to the problem. Fix had tentatively agreed to the terms, but had been procrastinating on Trinny's account who so seethed at the process that one could feel her anger exuding from Fix's pallid skin. The price amounted to the repayment of Sunsetwind's expensive mortgage plus the redemption of lost markets. The Chicagos, however, are loath to sign the agreement, but for one small detail: they want Treason back, or she must be publicly indicted for what else? Treason.

At first Del could live with that; but by the week's end, he had grown uncommonly fond of his new possession. Her athletic guile literally drove him mad with the kind of lust and gratification that she amply supplied. He is all but hooked, lined and sinkered. So when he refuses to agree to their last demand, the Chicagos threaten to reinvade and depose him, to which he laughs and says this time there isn't a mole working his defences. The Chicagos flinch knowing that a second invasion would be seen as ridiculously puerile, particularly when they had been flouting Sunsetwind's great new initiatives. Treason is safe for the moment.

Feeling chilled after a dozen runs in quick succession, Treason heads into the ancient log building at the top of the Ski Way. Tradition had it that the building had been constructed over four hundred years before when the original ski area with chairlifts had existed prior to being abandoned after the Asteroid and reclaimed by the forest. Treason cups her hands around a hot chocolate. Two Praetorian guards, a woman and a man sit nearby. She gets up to go to the washroom and the woman follows her. On the toilet, she begins to unroll some toilet paper to let the Praetorian woman outside know she is doing what she is supposed to be doing. Quickly, she reaches into her underwear, removes the taped sanitary pad, undoes the tape and extracts the medallion. Then behind the water reservoir at the bottom left, she feels for some tape stuck there. Finding the tape she removes it, sticks the medallion to the tape and returns it to its position behind the tank. She then flushes, exits and washes under the watchful eye of the steely-faced woman before going back to her hot chocolate.

Fait accompli, she sighs with a smile. The strain had been titanic, even for her. She was never out of either Barker's or the guard's sight and always wore the wrist monitor. If it hadn't been for her mom's note in the thick Calaloo soup, she would have been stymied. She had been sick at heart suppressing nausea at Del's salacious appetites. And the tag on her wrist inhibited any use of a monitor or word to a friendly face even if left alone. And to top it off, an exchange time with the Chicagos to swap the medallion for the credit had been designated that Sunday at 3 p.m. the next day in a place called Orangeville. It is a large Neutral town known for its licentious and lawless ways, which she is no stranger to, having caroused there during her unruly adolescence. Since the note came Thursday, she had had to act fast. The note had simply said:

> Hope you are still kicking, babe.
> Time to play fun and games.
> This is a long shot, so don't worry.
> We really sympathise with you.
> Hang tough. We have a replica.
> Get access to you know what.
> Pick a location by soup eaten:
> One. Today, La Petite Vache -
> return soup mostly full.
> Two. Tomorrow, Osprey Heights
> log cabin at top – soup empty.
> Use bathrooms – go to left toilet
> behind reservoir – exchange –
> then flush this note.
> await orders will rescue
> love mom

That's all there was: it literally made her frantic with fear as she assumed it required her to steal the medallion under Barker's nose and replace it with a fake. How was she to do that? But at least the thought raised her spirits. As quick as lightening her fertile mind came up with a plan. She would send back the soup mostly full asking for another bowl of something different, which she would finish, hopefully letting them know she would go first to Restaurant La Petite Vache, pick up the fake, then replace the fake with the real one somehow while she was allowed to wear the real medallion in Del's presence. Finally she would persuade him to let her go skiing where she would drop the real one off. It was a long shot, the whole masquerade being contingent upon Del not noticing a fake which meant it had to be an almost perfect replica, and of course above all, exchanging them in his midst. This would be difficult because as of late he would only allow her to wear it during sex; he seemed to get some peculiar pleasure from it. She realised then that her mother would have been given the nerve-racking job of designing the replica having been the only person among the Board to have seen it. It was very risky business, and failure meant the end of herself and Sunsetwind. With terse will power she forced that scenario from her mind.

The second bowl of soup arrived and she ate all of it, hungrily. Later, when Del returned she persuaded him to take her to La Petite Vache for supper. It was a strenuous ordeal, as Del rarely went out. She lost her appetite in the persuading, but succeeded in her mission. She had been increasingly alarmed at his burgeoning perverted needs. The things he made her do were depraved, making it more difficult for her to keep up her mask of complicity in his indulgences. However, there was nothing she wouldn't try now; her life depended on it.

That evening in the restaurant, she excused herself from the table. Everyone in the place seemed to watch as she sauntered casually across the floor in a vampy dress to the ladies room. She could feel their hatred boring into her from all sides; it made her smile all the more, to appear to be the perfect cover. There was a side to her that found some morbid fascination in that agonising deception. She went to the designated toilet and to her undying relief found the fake medallion taped to the back of the water tank. 'Thank you, mom,' she mouthed. One quick look bespoke the Board's serendipity – moreover, the fake was not a bad replica, if a hair lighter in weight. She then taped it inside a sanitary napkin, which she replaced in her underwear and returned to the table.

Back in the Loft she put the replica inside her pillow on their bed when he was in the bathroom. After, Del came out and undressed without talking. He was in one of his dark moods, but he went to the safe, decoded it, removed the medallion, ordered her to take her clothes off, which he hadn't noticed were already off, and put it around her neck before pushing her down to her knees. She then exerted an extra special effort that night to so sate him that he might nod off before putting the medallion back in the safe. It was all too easy: after a long and laborious session of intercourse, she curled up with her pillow while he lay back wasted. She then adeptly unclasped the real medallion and quietly replaced the necklace with the fake putting the real one in the pillow. But then Del fell asleep. What was she to do? She didn't want him to see it in the bright morning light and possibly discern its flaws, nor did she want to wake and remind him to put it back which would be an uncharacteristic behavioural move on her part. She decided to try and arouse him for some more sex. It worked, but then he said he was too tired as she dangled the medallion over his face indirectly prodding him to return it to the safe before climbing back in bed, which he did.

The next morning, Treason surprised him with a special wake up kiss bringing him close to climax before blithely ceasing her action to suddenly ask him if it would be all right to go skiing that day at the Heights. He agreed wholeheartedly.

The situation had been a marvel how he could be bought. Del saw it as a harmless gesture of romantic indulgence. Treason read every weakness in him as if he were poked full of holes. She even pondered that she could be Ms. Sunsetwind if she had wanted it. She thought Del had fallen unwittingly in love with her. But she knew it would all come crashing down the minute Chicago found out that they had been snookered. She foresaw their reaction as a call to arms and to hell with the EF elections. Her life would be held forfeit, unless she came up with the real medallion. But this was war and the chips would fall where they may. She was prepared to die.

After a couple of more hours of skiing, Treason flies back to the Pyramid with her escort. She has a hot bath and meditates on the possibility of escape before the "exchange" would take place on Sunday. It occurs to Treason that the Chicagos appear to be sincere in their motive to contain the problem she had caused them by taking the medallion, but for the life of her she can't quite believe they would actually give back Sunsetwind's credit. Nevertheless, the deposit, to be made to the Nottawasaga Bank Line, would be made and cleared before the medallion changed hands. Treason knows that the Paths originally held the people's credit in trust and that now Del Barker would be the sole beneficiary of this vast sum. It is supposed by all good Sunsetwinders that their standard of living would immediately rise and the national debt be balanced. It appears, however, that Del wants to be like Santa Claus and would start giving credit away where he and only he decides. Treason recalls the other night, Del saying, 'If you think the Paths were wealthy, give me five days; I'll show you success, darling. Sunsetwind will be looked after; that's my mandate, but just remember who's the boss. I'm due for a raise.'

Del Barker returns to the apex from an extended visit to the Logistics sector of the Pyramid. It seems his mood is somber as if he had been embroiled in some think-tank. Treason acts aloof, though keenly gauging the situation. He refuses to greet her with his usual smile and sexual leer. Keeping to himself, he broods at his desk and monitor.

Treason's intuition tells her that he had become aware of something new. It is less than twenty-four hours before the exchange with the Chicagos was to take place. With his brooding, she can see that this duration was going to be really strained. It is already taut. Pure adrenalin is the symptom, and sex had to be the therapy. The bath has relaxed her sufficiently to think clearly, now that she had succeeded in getting the medallion to the guerillas, thanks to their incredible foresight. They acted with the same alacrity that she had mustered. Her mother must have informed Redman and the Board, who then immediately implemented a plan of action. What a success, she gloats, as if realising it for the first time. But only escape emerges to the forefront of her thoughts, and she doesn't have a plan. Yet, she knows she has to find out what is eating Del.

'You seem tense this evening, Del,' she says rather unctuously, so not to reveal her gloating. And he is used to her sassy cynicism. She then walks behind him to massage his neck and shoulders. 'Let me draw it out of you. There, release the pressures of office . . . ' She can feel him giving in.

'I have a problem,' he states with his eyes closed.

'Oh?' she quips.

'I was speaking to some of my people. They claim the Chicagos would be crazy to refund Sunsetwind. It got me thinking again. What would it matter to them if we had some dumb medallion? Even if we went public with it, they would just deny this evidence of their abducting Heyoka. Denial is a lot cheaper than paying us an exorbitant sum for a hush up, and what's to say they would trust us with our silence after the exchange? What guarantees do they have? No, there's something wrong with this. They're up to something. I took the liberty to find out more about this medallion. Did you know that Yellow Tooth legend has it that this medallion . . . ' He pauses looking as if a new thought has suddenly presented itself to him. 'That's it,' he continues, 'They've set us up. It must be a fake!'

'A fake? Maybe you're right,' she supposes, still working his shoulders. 'But . . . ' She hesitates. She isn't sure whether she should point out to him that it seems like a lot of trouble for the Chicagos to go to over a fake medallion, not to mention the exchange amount; on the other hand, she doesn't want Barker to think that the medallion is fake and then scuttle the deal no matter how tenuous the possibility of the Chicagos actually paying. It would be a miracle if everything goes according to plan.

'Well, what then?' exhorts Barker, impatiently.

'Oh, I don't know; it seems ridiculous to think the Chicagos would go to all this trouble over a fake.'

'Well then, if it's not the medallion, what is it they want, my little squirrel?'

She hates his names.

'It has to be the medallion, Del,' she says softly.

'Maybe it's you they really want,' he declares matter-of-factly.

'Me? Why do they want me?'

'Because you're their top spy and know too much.'

'Know too much? No way, Del. I'm good but not that good.'

'Then why do they insist I either hand you over or execute you for treason?'

'Because they want to execute me, silly; wouldn't it be convenient for them if you did?' She tries to be as calm as a body of water just before the storm. It seems to work.

He sits there brooding for a moment.

'So what did you find out about the medallion?' she asks gingerly.

'Not a hell of a lot,' he begins irritably, 'This medallion was given to them by the Sky People. Now what the hell is that supposed to mean? Who are the Sky People?' His growing agitation is apparent.

'Sounds like: you know, Indian legends,' she replies. 'They're all metaphorical. Stories down the centuries become . . . animated. They take on mythical meanings.'

'Then this isn't just any medallion,' he proposes, 'This is a national treasure to the Yellow Tooths. Maybe it is Heyoka's, but I think the Chicagos want it back for some reason we don't know of. That's why they're paying through their teeth.'

Del suddenly stands up. Treason backs up. He turns around.

'You know, don't you, Treason?' he asks soberly.

'I know what you know, Del,' she says holding her ground stoically.

'The Chicagos sent you here with this to make it appear that we stole it and that maybe we have Heyoka.'

'Why would they do that? It's costing them billions of credits.'

'They're not going to pay, are they?' He moves closer to her. 'Are they?'

'Believe me, Del, I wonder about that too; but I have nothing to do with it. The question is: what do you propose to do about it?'

'I'll tell you what I propose, my little squirrel. I propose to hand you back to them, on a platter. You're just too good to be true, honey buns. I'm going to send you back where you belong, like a spent whore.'

Treason has had enough. His invectives are no longer worth swallowing.

'They will execute me, fuck head! I stole that medallion! For Sunsetwind!'

'Nothing personal; you're just a too perfect scapegoat for some of our . . . miscalculations, besides I thought Heyoka gave it to you.'

'I absconded with it from the Chicagos,' she exclaims heatedly.

'Well, perhaps you've been set up too. Too bad. I just get a bad feeling about this. I'll let them do the dirty work.'

'Believe me, I'm not one to disagree with my life on the line, but if you wash your hands of me, you're a dead man,' she utters desperately.

'That's why I like you, dear, and don't think it doesn't come without sentiment. Be grateful, if I did believe you, you wouldn't be here right now. True statesmanship comes from knowing your enemies, intimately, as friends, even lovers.'

He then leads her to the sofa and forces her to lean over it as he proceeds to mount her viciously. When it is over, he goes back to his monitor as if nothing had happened. She curls up on the couch and cries. It is all too much, and she has no way out.

Later, after a supper of Osso Bucco and rice with a Leonardo red, Treason is seething with revenge. Del is being very distant and cool. Even when she calls him a cocksucker by trying to arouse an emotive response to somehow find a way to neutralise him, he ignores her diatribes. She then tries locking herself in the bathroom but to no avail. Sitting there desperately, she writes a note on a piece of toilet paper saying: *He's sending me back to Chicago 3 p.m. Sunday, from Orangeville. Get me out of here!* Then letting herself out, she sticks it under her plate before they take the trays away. It is a gamble, but she has nothing to lose.

In bed that night, he demands that she fondle him while he reads his reports. She refuses, citing facetiously that his supposed religious proclivities do not accord with such behaviour. He actually laughs, saying he knows what she is up to.

'And what might that be?' she asks, turning away.

'You want out, that's all; so forget it.'

'Why don't you wait and see if they'll deposit the credit before you hand me over. That would redeem my sincerity, would it not?'

He doesn't answer.

'If they don't pay,' she continues, 'Then call their bluff and blow the whistle on Heyoka; maybe you don't have what it takes . . . '

'Just shut up!'

'I will if you reconsider my worth!'

'Your worth? Your worth's your tail, honey buns.'

'Fuck you, jerk off!'

'Now we're talking.' He grabs her aggressively.

'No way, asshole.' She fights her way out of bed. 'Have them take me back to the cell!'

Del is fuming. He goes to her and slaps her hard across the face. In a fit of blind rage, Treason instinctively karate kicks him square to the groin with a sharp whack. Hitting the floor in agony, breathless in a catatonic gasp, he reaches for his beeper but not before she kicks him in the head so hard it knocks him senseless. This conflagration happens so fast that her intuition to escape overrules the need to finish him off. He is lucky, for she is fully capable of killing him. Regaining her composure, she quietly dresses in her survival suit and steps outside onto the balcony. The bitter wind bites into her face. It soothes her hot-blooded spirit and she jumps down to the next level where the apex garage is situated. The door is locked, and she tries to smash the window, but it won't break. The beeper. She needs it to get into the garage from the outside. She looks back up to the Loft and stares at the flashing beacon on the point of the apex realising she must climb back up the balcony using the little cut grooves between the slabs of granite for grips. A few hair-raising minutes later she is back inside and picks up the beeper and notices that Del is stirring. She gives him another drop kick, this time to the neck, almost killing him. She believes she had, but is unconcerned and hurries back down to the garage level where she presses the code key as she had seen Del do. To her relief, the bay door opens. She knows she has just seconds as they would see the signal in the communications room and raise an alarm if Del didn't verify his departure. Once inside, she climbs into none other than Cephren's old Experimentor, which had been confiscated from her mother's on New Year's Day after the invasion. She knows the machine well enough and starts it up and flies into the black night as fast as the emop would go. Treason can hardly contain herself, the events happened so quickly; she is free, almost. But no sooner has the thought passed than, one blip, eight, then fourteen are converging onto her position. She heads for the Neutrals. What worries her is not that she couldn't escape from the emops but that she is a living breathing homing device with her damned wrist tag. To forcibly remove it would detonate, killing her and anybody within her proximity. She would have to have it removed by a specialist or one of the Board who had access to a scanner as her mom had mentioned, then high-tail it to drop it somewhere inaccessible, making it appear she was likely dead. What a nightmare that won't end! Maybe someone could rendezvous with her. Her mind races as she crosses into the Neutrals at a great speed. They follow her in! She keeps going until she crosses over into Chicago territory north of Toronto; she would have a few minutes before they could scramble for her, as their response was slow in that area. The Praetorians certainly wouldn't follow her there. Then she could loop around to the Neutrals in the east near Kawartha. The emops behind her fall back, assuming she had sought asylum in Chicago as she had been considered a traitor. She is free.

Cleopatra descends from the thick cloud cover to the coast of Devonshire in the English southwest. The sea is raucous and severe whitecaps crash onto the rugged rocks. She has been given coordinates that by the look of the bleak hills and valleys, are a stretch of remote coastal countryside. The town of Dartmouth can be seen east about ten kilometres away in a verdure valley. She sets down on a wind blown field near a picturesque cottage with wild gardens and scrubby trees. There are no other emops about. But the place would no doubt be secure. Cattle are scattered down the lee side of the vale and sheep can be seen in the fields beyond. A man comes up to her emop waving merrily. It is King Willy Five himself. He is tall and thin and appears to bow in the wind. His long face smiles from ear to ear. Cropped dark hair stands on end. He hollers, 'Just in time for a spot of tea! Dearest Cleopatra!' He gives her a hug as she exits and they scamper into the cottage out of the wind and spitting rain.

'Welcome to Bramble Cottage,' he declares, shutting the door and the weather, 'The seat of the British Empire!'

Cleo smiles and looks about the ancient cottage smelling of sweet smoked fire and some baking treats.

'Honey-scones with double cream,' he says taking her leather jacket. 'I made them myself. As well there are some pakoras made by my cook.'

'Mmmm,' she says. 'It's good to be here, Will.'

'Go to the hearth, Cleo; warm yourself. He's in there. I'll bring the tea. English or spiced?'

'Spiced, thanks,' she says heading inside.

The decorum is quaint and comfortable with many framed photos of the past, some hundreds of years old. King Willy Five's family is the longest surviving family – the house of Twist – of any Royal line since the Asteroid. King Willy's ancestors wrested control of the country from the anarchists of the post-Asteroid generations. Willy Five, as he liked to be called, had handed over the reigns of government to the New Parliament after its rehabilitation and the refurbishment of the ancient buildings in London along the Thames. The Twists are derived of sturdy East Indian stock but have collateral links to the lineage of pre-Asteroid royalty. It is a dubious link, illegitimate at best, but fully sanctified by the test of time and their propitious thrift in matters of commerce, power and justice. For generations they have been revered by the English people, because they represent some inexplicable common-sense approach to rule that previously ran askew with the old class of English speaking people for its cultural quiddities. Gone are the pomp and tradition of Anglo-Saxon supremacy; yet what remains is the perpetual enigma of English wit in a post-apocalyptic world. The Island Race are above all survivors whose great dominions of the past now coalesce into a people truly idealised in principles of equality. The old class system had outlived itself and finally eroded in the bituminous black rains of the early Horror.

Cleo draws near the hearth, and sees someone sitting in a large comfortable chair facing it.

'Cephren?'

Cephren stands up and looks at her. He is smiling, but his happy-sad expression is a notch more sad, and to him she seems older, but no less vibrant in looks, just wiser. She goes to him and they embrace. It is like a homecoming of sorts on a windy bluff in Devon.

They sit in their comfortable ambiance sipping tea and devouring honey scones. Little is said at first, as Willy Five comes playing with his cat. So much has transpired since they had last seen each other that they need the respite of their easy familiarity before putting their predicament into perspective. So much needs to be said, but they just aren't quite ready to reacquaint themselves with the dirge of that responsibility. In due time is the unspoken agenda. They do, however, lament on Sam's abduction, although rather than pointing blame, it becomes just one more calamity on a long list.

Cephren observes the strain in his sister and the superhuman efforts she had been making with little headway on behalf of Sunsetwind. He asks of her health, to which she admits mental exhaustion; but now she is rejuvenated after a week of rest in the Kush. He also asks of communications with Redman and the state of affairs at home. He visibly winces hearing about Del Barker's deals and perversions. The mortgaging of Sunsetwind particularly rankles him. He knows Redman and the Board need some word from him, anything to bolster their spirits from their plight and he wants to oblige, but refrains to minimize exposure in the hope that his present course of action would suffice. It is simply too dangerous for him, just yet, to chance any communication with Sunsetwind. And Redman had a way of getting things out of him. Besides, the last few weeks touring the capitals of Europe and speaking out against the new tyranny must have sent home some positive signals, at least to let them know his strength at present is empowered through the political process.

Cleo, on the other hand, senses a tremendous weight bearing on Cephren, something unusual. She knows him well enough that when an all-consuming endeavour absorbs him, he would internalise it as if harbouring its potent secret to spare others his perturbation. She wants to believe in him wholeheartedly, but his strategy is a huge gamble. However, she is at a loss to come up with a better alternative.

'How is O'Reilly?' he asks, politely interrupting her thoughts.

'Sorry that he let us down,' she replies.

'It's going around,' he comments.

'Indeed, we all feel very sorry,' quips Will in an affected Indian cockney, 'Sorry the fat lady sang.'

They laugh together.

'She won't be singing for long,' says Cephren.

'So tell me,' stipulates Cleo looking at the fire, 'Is Jimmy's Chip worth its salt?'

'It's one hot potato, Cleo; that's all I'd like to say.'

'If you'd prefer to be alone . . . ' says Will, seriously.

'No, no, Will,' says Cephren. 'We're all on a need-to-know agenda here. It's a question of timing and security. As I've been proclaiming publicly, I must win the mandate. With the implant technology available and its ulterior tapping of those users by the Chicagos, I can't compromise with any breach of intelligence, as safe as it may appear to be, even within this premises. The magnitude of the X13, I fear, far, I mean, far outweighs even the hint of what importance I as its carrier might bear. I see myself as a tortoise that must unremittingly strive to reach its destination. Cleo, I want so much to download this. And that's a joke, because that might take centuries! I think you know me well enough to support me now more than ever before. The resurrection of Sunsetwind is dwarfed by the implications of this thing in my head. Holy Hell! I can't begin to express it. But inevitably, the regaining of Sunsetwind and the resolve of Earth Federation politics are inextricably connected. We must proceed, first politically, and then when we win the EF election, we shall carefully bring the planet in line with the new reality. I can say no more. I'm sorry to sound so damned melodramatic like it's the end of the world: hell, we've seen enough of the end of the world; it's just that it's all so genuine.'

'Give me an example or something, Cephren,' contends Cleo. 'I can't stand this tension; what must I do? I feel left out, though I respect your judgment on this; just give me something I can chew on.'

'That would be most appetizing, I must say,' quips King Willy Five, still fidgeting with the fat tabby.

They all laugh because Will is just too disarming to resist his wiles.

Cephren sighs and puts down his empty tea cup. He begins to pace in front of the hearth.

'I'll tell you something unrelated that symbolises the gravity of my meaning. Do you remember your history, Cleo and Will – the assassination of Danielle Perreault?'

'Yes,' they both say.

'It is believed she was blown up by terrorists; some thought Quebecois nationalists for not being granted their absolute sovereignty. Others thought foreign mercenaries who killed her for political reasons because of her efforts to corner the water market. Some even thought it was a revenge killing by her mysterious lover 'James Piercemore' whom she supposedly dumped; because after her death his works were conveniently released,

thus implicating him as it was supposed she had curtailed their publication. This was, of course, presumed to have been carried out by her personal secretary Max Light, who also conveniently committed suicide.
Some even speculated that he was the other lover. Piercemore became the
convenient scapegoat; but of course, there was no known person on record
ever having been Piercemore. He was a non-entity, a name, with nobody
to fill his shoes, or if one did, you could pick somebody and put him in
Piercemore's shoes. Certainly, many theories abounded. Reams were written about it, but nothing conclusive was ever positively uncovered. It was
the old enigma wrapped in a mystery dunked in the deep, sort of charade:
shades of the Secret Age. Well, I'll tell you, I have discovered, vis a vis
Jimmy's Chip that there was once a code name called Blue Phoenix
designed for the removal of a person, or persons no matter what their
power or position, to protect something vital to not only national security,
but Earth Security. It was considered so necessary, that the full extent of
the force of this code unleashed was comparable to the kind of resolve that
earned Masada its name, you know, the Jews who committed mass suicide
rather than submit to the Romans; such was their intent. This was serious
stuff! I know for a fact that Piercemore was Jimmy Pidgeon and the one
directly responsible for the creation of Blue Phoenix; moreover as such he
was indirectly part of the decision to eliminate Perreault, but I should add,
went AWOL to prevent it. Blue Phoenix was a code word used by the old
NSA and by extension the aliens themselves – and herein is the crux of
the matter – to implement counter-measures dealing with an emergency of
great magnitude which amounted to a credible attempt by any authority to
expose alien involvement on earth. Perreault was courageously about to
reveal to the world what was known about extraterrestrials, defying
great pressure from certain powers that she was well aware of. Her death,
as we know, was one of the great tragedies spawned on a yearning world.
Everyone loved her and mourned her like a pan-world Evita: Canadians,
Americans, Europeans, Asians. Yet her obvious martyrdom was deemed
irrevocable; it had to be. Now do I have to invoke one's imagination to

presume the dreadful reasons behind her assassination? Blue Phoenix had to be the authorities' worst nightmare, and it may well be ours. We must do as I say, or all is lost. The Chicagos cannot be allowed to win the EF election, nor can they be allowed to get me, and the X13. Please believe me; Blue Phoenix is just the tip of the iceberg. I also know now that World War 3 was a direct result of Blue Phoenix. The notorious Colonel Blaine, the descendant of a fine line of great air force men, was not exactly the monster history has painted him; his sacrifice was unduly rewarded by our continued freedom. I know that World War 3 was Masada on a global scale. Need I extrapolate any further?'

'Freedom from what?' urges Cleo. 'Romans?'

'Need I say it, Cleo? Aliens, rather alien integration: in other words, goodbye humanity as we know it. They would rather commit mass suicide than be subjected.'

'Point taken,' says King Willy quickly. 'Thank God for Colonel Blaine and pity his reincarnate.'

But levity doesn't lessen the solemnity of Cephren's revelations as over two hundred million innocent people died in that war.

Cleo stands and hugs Cephren again. She queries no more for the time being. Her thoughts refuse to register the unthinkable and are fast coming to the present logistical nightmare of security on the campaign trail. For the remainder of the day and evening, they enjoy each other's company. Cephren speaks of his adventures in Ottawa and Antarctica, and naturally of the redoubtable Anna Gram. Cleo quizzes him at length about the wisdom of her being his political running mate. Cephren notes a twinge of jealousy in her inquisitional direction. He knows that Cleo sees herself beside Cephren as his cohort on the campaign trail. This Anna Gram is quite literally just as her name sounded to Cleo, an anagram. After a time of reflection, she can't help herself. She needs to do a thorough background check.

'You barely know her, Cephren; she's a diva, not a credible running mate. No one will take you seriously.'

'On the contrary, the political winds are so full of jabberwocky, no one gets away with full marks in sincerity. In fact, I perceive the winds to be in our favour. My position is that of a disinherited benevolent despot – as I'm told – and with Anna's consensual dynamics, we have a team. Already the public is chomping at the bit to devour us. I think they will masticate with delight and give us rave reviews. We mean change for the better. We stand for justice, something that has been perverted as of late; and above all my belief is that we may indeed become the first authority to bring us into the Galactic Confederation, one of hundreds of intelligent species, in our own right, and certainly not just as containers anymore.'

'What are you talking about?' snaps Cleo a little disconcertedly.

'I'm talking about advancing into the universe, Cleo; we now have the means to create the technology to do so. We are teetering on the brink of interstellar travel. But in a way, which as I've said I cannot divulge, but implied, we must earn exit visas. We will not be welcome if we rampage like Cortez on a deadly mission destroying what we don't understand. I know that's not our nature, but it's funny how history repeats itself with the unknown. And we won't be dealing with sacrifices to the sungods, but DNA enmeshment to appease the gods. We are the sacrifice. It's a frightful swamp, Cleo; earth is a giant Petri dish containing extra ripe organic DNA, necessary for their survival.'

'I can't make head or tails of what you're talking about,' sighs Cleo. 'I'll do what you want. Maybe this Anna Gram holds the key to your success. Still, I want to check her out.'

'Seven thinks she's the ticket. But do what you have to do.'

'I will. Where is he?'

'He's arriving tomorrow with Anna from an appearance in Washington.'

'Washington,' she says disdainfully, but drops it. 'Well, what can I do that would best serve the cause, Cephren?'

'Set up a security net with Runaway – he's gone to fetch some supplies – and Captain Dave – he's coming, right?'

'Yes.'

'Confer with Seven, who is our Campaign Manager, and work out the security for the itinerary. Set up a security web around us. Our own security takes absolute precedence over all other security including that of our hosts. No offense, Will.'

'None taken, my friend,' says Will with his feet up. 'Double protection is better than single. But if I may make a suggestion, I think you should travel separately. The two of you would make a sensational target.'

'I suppose so,' agrees Cephren gloomily.

'I look forward to meeting Ms. Gram,' adds King Willy.

'This should be interesting,' says Cleo, teasing.

'I don't like the tone of your voice, Cleo,' says Cephren, admonishingly.

'Well, I'm just very curious, Cephren.'

'I told you, our relationship is strictly political.'

'Political. And there's nothing remotely tantalizing?' she wonders matter-of-factly.

'Precisely.'

'I know you better than that, Cephren.'

'Nothing's happened between us. We have repartee.'

'Oh, so there is something between you. Oral syntax.'

'Cleo, we have an understanding – an interesting dichotomy that holds promise. We are good friends.'

'You've already fallen for her, but is it Anna or Piercemore's Renée Antoinette?'

'Give me a break, Cleo! Anna's wonderful, full of life and integrity with a kind of sorrowful vulnerability.'

'Go on.'

'I know it seems an unlikely match, but we have faith in each other. We're both idealists.'

'She has no idea what she's getting herself into.'

'Exactly, and aren't you a little surprised at my course of action? Before all of this, would you have believed this?'

'You got me there.'

'She'll win this election for us, Cleo.'

'I really hope so.'

'I know you'll like her.'

'I wish you could've met Heyoka,' she says.

'Heyoka Yellow Tooth. I heard what happened,' recalls Cephren.

'The Chicagos must have her,' interjects King Willy enjoying himself with these siblings.

'You'd fall in love with her,' she states assuredly to Cephren.

'Spare me the matchmaking, please, Cleo. Besides, I had heard she was a little odd, or childlike.'

'A child going on thirty, but ninety in wisdom. I have never met someone so . . . strange, yet beautiful. Barring the age difference, you would like her, like me, albeit platonically, but you, I think, all the way. She spoke of aliens and Jimmy Pidgeon. Mark my words, if she survived . . . I feel so awful. She believed in me.'

'She spoke of Jimmy Pidgeon?' asks Cephren excitedly.

'Yes, she told a story about how a native man had been taken aboard a space craft and introduced to a man named Jimmy by a hybrid female Grey.'

'Did she say what took place during this meeting?'

'Only that the native man was given what was to become the Sacred Stone, a medallion of orange gold. Heyoka showed me this very same medallion which she kept around her neck.'

'Unumpentium,' says Cephren, thinking aloud. 'Heyoka has the unumpentium, which the Chicagos now have. We are doomed if they have already implemented their technology with it. My greatest fear is the Chicagos blasting into space with their new-found gravitonics. I fear earth will be hermetically sealed for another couple of centuries. As it is, we are the pariahs of our vicinity . . . '

'Not exactly,' interrupts Cleo, not fully comprehending the cosmic bent of Cephren's foreboding. 'At least there may be a chance the Chicagos haven't any idea what the medallion is. Heyoka kept it beneath her shirt or dress.'

'They must surely know; why would they have taken her then?' asks Cephren.

'Because of my success in pushing the Mississippis out of Tennessee. It was a gesture of retaliation,' said Cleo.

'But still, they must know what orange gold is,' assumes Cephren.

'We cannot assume anything, Cephren!' cries Cleo.

'Heyoka has special powers. She would not let the medallion get into their hands; we must have a little faith in her, I think.'

Cleo holds back her emotions, but Cephren can see what a superhuman effort it takes. He doesn't press any more. He knows Cleo has suffered greatly on account of it. It can serve no purpose to allude to her unwitting part in Heyoka's capture. Cleo's impulsiveness is a valuable strength and to criticise it could only hurt their chances for success. Besides, Heyoka, by the sounds of it, is too intelligent to fall prey to the Chicagos without some kind of ulterior motive. It is unlikely she was dead as presumed by some; rather, her capture could prove a boon to their own cause.

'Cleo,' says Cephren, 'You have done your utmost to right the wrong. I have absolute faith in you; and if you believe Heyoka is as powerful as you say she is, we must believe in our salvation and continue on our path to freedom. Nothing will stop us, and you are our vanguard.'

Cleo looks at him faithfully. Two tears drop from her eyes. She then leaves the room abruptly and walks out into the sea breezes. She couldn't have known that at that very moment, Uncle Sam had just met the wonderful Heyoka, and that soon Cleo would be refueled with a personal mission, veritably to light up her sky.

It is well after midnight when Anna Gram arrives with Seven in his emop with an Anishnabe escort, courtesy of Governor-General Jack Pine who, declining refreshments, heads back immediately to Ottawa.

Anna Gram had been in Washington all day involved with interviews, a panel discussion and a speech to Congress. Dead tired and after a brief attempt at pleasantries, she excuses herself to go to bedroom. Cleo and Cephren watch the monitor to pick up the American news. There are various clips about Anna and reactions to her speech. By far, her treatment of General Dennis and Babylon is the most intriguing. Public sentiment stands firmly behind her in spite of her condescending remarks. What really impresses Cleo and drives home the true effect of Anna's charisma is the sincerity she emanates. Cleo knows quite well that had she done what Anna did in that crossfire debate, she would have been lampooned maliciously. Either it was her acting ability, or an inlaid character trait that seemed to insist sympathy from others, or both; but she definitely attracts people's attention. It doesn't seem to matter what she says; people just fall for her. She is a plain-speaking Texan in the mould of a demigoddess. Her over-riding sense of purpose and urgency is truly compelling. Cleo, as a person can't have been more different, and she keeps fighting the impulse to believe that Anna has come by her talents innocently. When Cleo finally shakes Anna's hand and makes eye contact, she detects something in those tired yet friendly eyes that is a little too mercenary, or feigned. Cleo ruminates on Anna's whereabouts the previous weeks, since Cephren had met her in Ottawa. She had gone back to Texas, then on to Paris to meet Cephren at the opening of the campaign, toured Europe with Cephren, then went back to Texas again, then America, and now here. Her sudden political allegiance with Cephren has pushed him front and center. It is truly a miracle. She realises that at the present rate Cephren would indeed be a shoe-in for the Earth Chair. But what worries her, is that his very success with her ticket would drive a serious wedge between Chicago and much of the Western world. Cleo ponders the implications: she appreciates the fact that the Chicagos would be alienated, but it might make them very prickly and stubborn regarding the return of Sunsetwind to the Paths; after all it was in their own backyard.

Accessing her extensive resources on her monitor, she finds that Anna had spent her early acting days in Baltimore before moving to Berlin, then Paris where she earned some notoriety as a low-budget sex diva, then

Hollywood, where she attained her superstardom. Everything seemed to be hunky dory. Her life is laid out like a plaid tablecloth for a Panhandler's lunch: lots of bread and butter, iceberg salads, hot beef, frijoles and Tabasco with a few gallons of beer. She goes over Anna's biographical history again. Anna was a busy girl. No wonder there was little time for real romance. But something catches her eye: Anna had spent nearly six years in Baltimore during her twenties at the Oxford Repertory Theater doing Shakespeare and other classics. On the list of patrons at the time, when she dug deeper, was one George Washington, Bio-Chemist, creator and CEO of Ecosphere, a company that developed high-tech artificial environments for emops and space vehicles. His systems became the standard worldwide and made him exceedingly wealthy. But the question remains: did George Washington know Anna Gram personally, and if so, are they still friends? Certainly, Anna has met many important personages over the years; it is to be expected; yet what if she had a special relationship with George Washington? Could it not be possible she is his casual spy, or better still, a very active one?

Cleo keeps it to herself. George, after all, isn't the enemy by any yardstick. And if Anna is such a godsend for Cephren, maybe she had George's blessing in spite of the fact that it hurt his own bid for re-election. He may have unwittingly destroyed his own chances by engaging her to go to Ottawa, as was her want from time to time to honestly enjoy herself, and just possibly run into Cephren, the sole purpose at the time being simply to get any information on the X13, the cursed X13. She wishes Clem Reesor had been sacrificed at one of his stupid religious conventions, and then none of this would have happened. At any rate, Cleo gives Anna a nearly clean bill of health for the time being.

In the morning, the wind has calmed and the sun even breaks through. The weather is mild and almost spring-like. It is incredible how the warm, ocean currents kept such a northern land temperate. The British Isles hadn't gained nor lost their capricious climate due to the ECD almost four hundred years before.

Cephren has been up early and has gone for a stroll on the bluffs overlooking the ocean. In spite of his success to date on the campaign trail, he is not having an easy time. He bore a terrible burden of knowledge that literally has him reeling from moment to moment. Since the last immersion into Jimmy's Chip beneath the ice in Antarctica among the ruins of Atlantis, and the subsequent shock of his first meeting with the two aliens, Eridanis to be precise, who had suddenly appeared in the Atlantis base, his mind would not rest. Every time he looks into a mirror to shave, the person he sees is almost a stranger. He wonders to himself: what is this combination of matter that is me? He feels as though the reality of cosmic existence has so dwarfed his sense of self and purpose that he cannot summon the strength to carry on his task. And what else is new in the spittoon of humanity? he muses. Not much. A genetic soup, the main ingredient being a potpourri of unlikely proportions unless steps were taken to guarantee self-determination. Those steps require supreme leadership and discipline for an unruly race. In many ways earth civilisation is nowhere near ready. En masse it either is too prone to kill what it does not understand or too ready to deify higher beings rather than humbly learn from them. And the criteria for membership requires at least some compromise with galactic members. Cephren also realises that humankind's own sense of commerce and fiscal economy held little merit in the cosmic scheme of things. But there is the possibility of the sharing of resources: mineral, geomagnetic, and undoubtedly human. How does one bridge, hundreds, thousands, indeed hundreds of thousands of years of emotional and technical development? You don't, he assumes. But if we are to progress into space, we must find a way to co-exist. The leaps and bounds would have to be carefully administered. To over-reach these leaps and bounds would surely fail and cause terrible havoc for all. The huge shadowy presence of the Reptoids is a daunting specter. They would not hesitate to quash an upstart race. Such a scenario would be the ultimate disaster to see wonderful humanity reduced to an expendable resource. Cephren believes that humanity must step carefully, modestly and intelligently to win the respect of its neighbours. Human power is alien power and vice-versa. Solar energy is the common-denominator for life in the universe. All the variant syntheses of terrestrial life, he realises, consist almost entirely of multifarious concoctions of phosphorous, sulphur, carbon, oxygen, nitrogen and hydrogen. 'We all need light,' he muses, 'If only we can curtail our egocentric need to possess and impose our will onto others. This is the key.'

He sits on a stone and rummages through these thoughts. He knows that if there isn't a strong terrestrial unifying ideology, at least among the superpowers, their venture into space would fail. He would have to get that across. For the next three weeks, his entourage would be touring Eastern Europe, Russia, etc., then proceed to the Middle East, the Kush, the Far East, Australia, New Zealand, and finally South America, before doing North America, ending up in Washington.

Cephren mulls over his core theme: unity, but in the sense of a global community, like the universal community, each culture and region free and autonomous. Cephren feels the only way to succeed is to have an Earth Federation powerful enough to enforce democratically such a benevolent community. What of Chicago? America? Would they submit in the interests of expansion in space? To what kind of carrot would they kowtow? Would they demand territorial rights? If so, they would fail. It is a seemingly impossible dilemma.

'A penny for your thoughts,' angles Anna Gram coming up suddenly from behind him and putting her hand on his shoulder.

Cephren looks ahead, unruffled, so deep is his concentration. Clearing his head, he looks up to side to see her smiling there that same smile he'd seen so many times before, on monitors, screens, and news flashes. It is as if she isn't real and her very presence is a hologram. She is, however, warm and comforting company.

'Anna,' he says, trying to sound energetic, 'I'd even pay a hundred to unload my own thoughts. Since Paris, I have been finding it increasingly difficult to think clearly at all. I'm afraid my thoughts wouldn't make much sense, at present.'

They had met over two weeks before in Paris for the campaign inception. That time had been difficult for them, because not only were they neophytes in the political game, but tense with themselves on account of the promise they made not to get romantically close, whereas by virtue of the pressures, they were really leaning on each other. It culminated after a state dinner at the Elysée, when they were left alone in adjoining rooms of a double suite, and had to put their heads together to get their campaign off to a good start. They could both feel the desperate need to release their pent up emotions, but did their utmost to keep their intimacies strictly political.

'I don't believe it for a minute, Cephren,' she utters warmly, while sitting down beside him and giving a little nudge with her bottom to move him over on the rock. 'So, you watched my performance in Washington yesterday?'

'A true Texan,' he smiles, speaking with a swagger, 'The way you lassooed your opponents. You're gonna win me this election, little sister.'

'Well, pilgrim, only for you, and Sunsetwind, and Terry Barnett.'

They have a laugh and watch the grey-blue sea.

'But I have a problem, Cephren . . . perhaps two,' she adds after a few moments.

'Shoot me,' he jokes.

'I'll shoot you if you don't give me some answers, luv. As you know, I'm taking a lot of heat about this alien thing; I need to give people more. In Washington I pulled it off by pure craft alone, but the honeymoon's over. The tide will turn against us unless we follow through with some credible evidence to support your pledges. To most people they're outrageous – galactic confederations – I mean, I love it, but we gotta come down to earth if we wish to sustain the thrust of our success so far. This ain't a Star Tripper episode.'

'No, more of the Igor Sputnik Spoof Show.'

'Cephren! I'm serious!'

'What's the other problem?'

'A touchy one.'

'Yes?'

'Your sister. I find that she is treating me rather coolly. I know it's her job, but I am on your side. This morning just now before I came outside, she asked me some personal questions to which I took some offense. I didn't want to ruffle her feathers, so I politely responded. However, she persisted and almost insinuated by her tone that I'm a spy for either the Americans or Chicagos or even the Texans! I kept repeating that I'm an actress and do what actresses do: act professionally, but that this present occupation was an opportunity I couldn't resist, to do some real good. It obviously isn't enough for her.' She shakes her head. 'I don't need to have your sister hang a sword over my head.'

'I'll speak to her, Anna. She's taken much of the blame for the demise of Sunsetwind upon her shoulders. But, she's good, really good.'

'I don't doubt it; thank you. Now what about the aliens?'

'The aliens. Yes, well, I suppose I must at least outline the situation. There is so much to say, I really don't know where to begin. You are right, though, we must dole out enough information to keep the people interested. But please, Anna, if I reveal our past subservience to the aliens, I could destroy our chances period. The Reticulans, you know, or the Greys, are not in absolute control anymore, neither are the Eridanis, an alien human-like race. They are very hands-off and will not under any circumstances interfere with our natural evolution, which in itself isn't so natural anymore, due to their presence here . . . but what is?'

'They're here? Now?'

'The Greys, yes, and even the Eridanis, rather the Jah, as they call themselves. They're here all right. It seems the Greys are quite concerned about our welfare and would not hesitate to contain us if we begin to explore space. You see their masters, the Reptoids, are probably the most powerful life force in our immediate universe and do not want to destabilise the status quo. They consider us extremely hazardous.'

'You mean there are Reptoids like the sci-fi show?'

'They're not so reptilian as portrayed by the show. The Reptoids are human looking in that they have hands and feet, nose, eyes and ears but no tail! They are highly intelligent and wear clothes, read history, raise children and do most everything we do, but they are stronger physically, live almost ten times longer, are cold-blooded, in other words are highly adaptable to both hot and cold climates, although the cold slows them down unless they are artificially warmed with thermal gear. But make no bones about it; they are in control and would curtail us if we go out into space with the wrong attitude. Their minions, the Greys, are their eyes and ears.'

'This is hard to take, Cephren, no one's going to want to hear this! We are like planet zoo! If we're nice, they'll let us out into the jungle where we'll be slaughtered because we don't know how to survive in the wild?'

'That's about it.'

'So what's the point of bringing it up at all?'

'I thought it a good platform to win the election, and hopefully make humanity humble themselves to the reality of life in the universe; it *is* a jungle out there. And we must get our act together *here*, before we venture out *there*. And out there is the future. And if humanity wants to be a part of it, let us begin here.'

'Should we go public with this, Cephren?'

Cephren has never seen her so serious.

'I don't think we should unless we can get the Greys to make some kind of cameo appearance. But we don't want panic and the whole plan to backfire in our faces.'

'How do we do it, then?'

'That's the big enchilada.'

'So we're back where we started.'

'Not quite, we've got a handsome lead in the polls. We can still win this thing on terrestrial issues alone. The big enchilada is contingent upon getting Sunsetwind back.'

'How so?' she asks.

'It just is; I can't elaborate.'

The awesome magnitude of Jimmy's Chip flashes through Cephren's mind. Poor Anna. What he said only scratches the surface. It is a terrible responsibility to wean the earth. Yet, he feels confident an actress is probably the most qualified to help do it. Her motives are personal, he presumes, at least connected with him as a comfortable prospect for a new life and doing something of great importance. His motives are fast becoming unconditional in regards to his political choices. There is a point where responsibility and reality clash and he is fast approaching it. What will it be: responsibility or reality, in other words, to Sunsetwind or the universe, or both. He suddenly has a real need to speak to Redman, but knows it is too soon. Cleo had reported that everything is on course back home. The Chicagos have gone home; the Board has taken control of the underground; Barker has become the most detested man, and then there is the mystery of Treason. She had escaped from the Chicagos during the invasion and somehow ended up in Chicago with Babylon. He found that out from Anna, and when Cleo informed him of Treason's double game, he hoped she hadn't dug herself in too deeply.

'Cephren?' asks Anna getting his attention.

'Sorry, just thinking.'

'Perhaps, my doing this wasn't such a good idea. I have to admit, my reasons were a little on the vain side; I kinda wanted to really mean something . . . yet, now . . . I feel I'm a little out of my depth. Maybe we should reconsider . . . a more consensual approach. I hesitate to tell you, Cephren . . . but I think I've fallen in love with you. It grates on me, that's all. We're so near, yet so far.' Her brown eyes look longingly at him. It is impossible for Cephren not to be drawn in.

'Anna . . . I'm . . . I don't know what to say. Your honesty is so powerful. I'm so afraid of not measuring up. I . . . I fear if we do as you convey, we may lose our . . . '

'Integrity? Hogwash!' She puts her arm around him and touches his leg with hers. Cephren cautiously puts his hand on her knee. She separates her legs slightly and with her other hand puts it on his, moving it down her thigh, closing her other leg on his hand. 'Gotcha,' she purrs.

'Anna, you don't want to drop out, do you?' he asks nervously.

'Not if you think we can be a little cozier. Cephren, I don't want to upset you by causing you to think I'm trying to entrap you.'

'Well, I kind of like the arrangement the way it is. Anna, love is an aphrodisiac. My head has an alien device in it that not only consists of hundreds of light years of astral navigation, but history, both human and otherwise, mountains of technological data, human personalities and their art, and countless other unrelated things. Since we met in Ottawa, I have been exposed to things that cry out to be told, but for reasons that I've explained . . . '

'You cannot love me,' she says taking her arm away, and removing his hand.

'Anna, I do love you for who you are; it would be dishonest of me to love you in body in lieu of the love I bear your being. I can only be true to my instincts. But if you need me physically to stay on, maybe we can mutually find a way to subsist as long as we run this campaign together. I want you to stay with me, Anna; I can't do this without you. Don't let our emotional pride hurt our chances.'

Anna says nothing. She looks out to sea and breathes some heavy sighs.

'Anna,' he says, 'I'm sorry, if I've hurt you. I feel hurt myself. Why don't we let things unfold naturally.'

After a moment or more of silence Anna stands up continuing to face the sea. 'Okay,' she says finally, 'Okay, you have me the way you want me. I'll do this, but keep Cleo away from me. You know, I really am something.' Her voice falters and tears begin to form in her eyes. 'I live my life so well, I become all the parts of my career wrapped in one – a damned fine martyr to love, but at least in the movies I get my sex. Sex. But look at me!' Her tears roll freely.

Cephren stands up and holds her. She doesn't resist.

'When this is all over . . . ' he begins to say.

'Oh, Cephren, it's like in the movies; it's now or never.' She separates herself and walks back toward Bramble Cottage. 'Come on,' she calls out, 'We have work to do.'

Cephren follows mutely.

They stick to their plan of their world tour. Cephren will reveal his terrestrial agenda only if he is to be elected. He keeps the alien theme to a minimum, getting around direct questions by citing security reasons. But he is more than preoccupied with the growing demands of the global village. Economic and political restraints severely curtail greater freedom and prosperity in many disparate regions, and their voices are among the shrill for change. Traditional governments naturally defer to Cephren's libertarian ideas but secretly wish he would not advertise them. It is true that many governments of the more disparate regions support Trinny Burnamthorpe's bid for power because she appears to have their best interest at hand. But the people have a right to vote in many countries, and would decide themselves; yet powers like O'Reilly's Kush know that nothing would change with a new Earth Chairman. The Earth Federation mandate hasn't yet become so powerful that it could make all of the changes that Cephren desires to meet the galactic criteria. Ironically, Trinny and the Chicagos are powerful enough that if they take power, they could effect the necessary changes more easily.

Touring the east gives Cephren some respite from the pressures of the West and Jimmy's Chip. But he knows that once they get to Washington public scrutiny may become intolerable, unless he reveals what he had learned from the X13. Anna too, enjoys the relative calm of their campaign. She canvases different cities and countries and meets up with

Cephren only three times – in the Kush, Sydney and Mexico City. In each place, she threatens to walk out, but hangs on with the anticipation that she and Cephren still had some fantastic symmetry and just needed the victory they could taste in their mouths when they could take up again the romantic song and dance privately. Cephren resists but relents partly because it seems the only way Anna can go on. In some ways he finds their relationship as big a strain as the campaign; needless to say their kissing actually is the most effective relaxant. It is impossible to deny. Cephren even assumes that when it is all over, he would have to do the honourable thing by proposing marriage to her, yet the thought keeps being overshadowed by other more pressing concerns.

Cleo stays with Cephren and assigns Captain Dave to Anna. With a monitor band, the same as she supplied most of her guerillas back home, both Anna and Captain Dave are connected to a specific frequency circuit that warns them up to a kilometer away from any threatening frequency including activated stun guns, gravity beams, microwaves, electronic bomb devices and active metal detection. Only when an area is secure would they leave the protection of their emops. Likewise Cephren, Runaway and Cleo would do thorough scans before disembarking.

Rested and ready for a grilling, they arrive in Washington after a visit to Anna's ranch in the Texas panhandle, where they celebrated on March 2nd Cephren's 52nd birthday. But nothing could have prepared them for the crisis hat crashed upon them out of the blue as a result of Chicago's keen desire to retrieve Heyoka's sacred medallion. No one knows what is going on until breaking news flashes across the monitor that Trinny Burnamthorpe had just announced that she was dropping out of the EF election as a candidate, condemning the Earth Federation as hopelessly corrupt. It is then learned through America's own intelligence that Chicago is mounting yet another invasion of none other than little Sunsetwind. All semblance of a civilised world tumbles like Humpty Dumpty. Cephren knows his time has come. His mind flashes Blue Phoenix and he knows what has to be done.

'What the hell!' declares Cleo to George Washington.

George looks down at his brown synthetic runners with that same look of exasperation he had the last time she stood in his Oval Office. 'It's now or never! If they get the medallion we're screwed! Pardon me.'

'Shall I forfeit the election?' he exclaims facetiously, 'Then fight a war?'

'Not a bad idea,' Cleo says, toning her invective. 'A united front might deter them long enough . . .'

'What do you think, Cephren?' asks George walking to the window.

'As a friend, George, politics aside a contending candidate, you know what has to be done. They've finally done what they have been intimating all along: world domination. The consequences of their actions may destroy the Earth Federation, and if they get the unumpentium, nothing short of world domination will stop them. George, you must fight, for democracy, for freedom, for our survival as a race. Looks to me as if we have another Blue Phoenix on our hands.'

Cephren had explained what he knew about Blue Phoenix, and the President seemed genuinely convinced when General Dennis verified that in the archives there had been references to it; but the information was lacking due to the loss of other chips which obviously contained key components of that ultra sensitive intelligence. During the Secret Age, information had been so encoded and compartmentalised that there were probably only a handful of people who had access to the big picture, and it was frightening.

George paces and broods. General Dennis and Admiral McKee sit implacably on the sofa. Anna Gram sits in the chair by the sofa looking about the room quite seriously.

'Blue Phoenix, Blue Phoenix,' President Washington mutters to himself under his breath. 'It seems unbelievable we must invoke a paranoid plan that died with the old United States. Are we no better off?'

'That may bring about a new United States,' interjects Anna, positively. 'The South will rally, and the West.'

'Wouldn't that be something,' continues George, thinking.

'And Canada,' adds Cephren.

'And Canada,' confirms George.

There follows a lengthy silence.

Cleo breaks it: 'Trinny Burnamthorpe is a coward. She will capitulate if we make a show of force and resolve. I know her. All we need is something to bring her to her knees and beg for forgiveness when she sees that her position is hopeless.'

'And what might we have that they don't have?' queries General Dennis, sceptically.

'The unumpentium, of course,' she answers.

'Where is it?' he presses.

'Where else? Sunsetwind.'

'Cephren?' asks George.

'Before we share our intelligence, George,' says Cephren, 'We need your commitment. But suffice to say, it's rather obvious that the Chicagos are feeling a little deprived of their treasure, at least Heyoka's, hence their imminent reinvasion. We can thank Cleo and one of her guerilla agents for their propitious actions.'

'And thanks are extended,' confers George. 'But we haven't any guarantees we can pull this off. What exactly are you getting at?'

'First your commitment to whatever it takes.'

'You've got it.'

'Okay Cleo, tell him,' directs Cephren.

'Don't you think he should submit his resignation to election headquarters, Cephren?' asked Cleo a little impetuously. It was a strict EF regulation that no candidate could wage war during the election unless it was self-defence. With George Washington's withdrawal, Cephren could easily win the Earth Chair.

'If we can't begin to trust again, Cleo, this is all for naught. Don't you agree, George?' asks Cephren.

'No more procrastinating: General Dennis, prepare my resignation as a candidate in the election,' states George Washington. 'Cite it for reasons of national security.'

'Yes, sir.' The General exits.

'Admiral McKee, summon the war council, and get a message to Burnamthorpe, that if she so much as makes one offensive move toward Sunsetwind or anywhere, we are in a state of war. Furthermore, she must immediately release Heyoka Yellow Tooth, or we are at war. You have your orders.'

'Yes, sir,' he says, and exits with a smile, nodding to Cleo.

'We've been doing our damnedest to avoid this, but she has gone too far,' declares the President. 'The time has come to draw a line and back your true friends. I realise that the world cannot do without Sunsetwind. By the grace of God, you are the chosen one to lead the Earth, Cephren . . . '

'Or rather the X13,' proffers Cephren.

'It's all God to me,' remarks George, 'With a small 'g'. You were right and we were wrong.'

'I'm sorry it has had to come to this,' considers Cephren.

'We have been blinded by our desire to control, like Trinny. I pray she sees our point of view. So tell me what you know, Cleo,' demands George, sitting back in his chair, giving her his undivided attention. His kind eyes, good looks and close-cropped grey afro convey the essence of equanimity.

'I spoke with the Board last night,' begins Cleo. 'It was revealed to me that they were in possession of the unumpentium medallion that was Heyoka's. Apparently little Sam Path was given it by her at the Bungalow. He then gave it to our agent who happened to be invited there as a chaperone for some of the many children attending Sam's birthday party put on by his mother. Our agent then bolted the country and somehow made it back to Sunsetwind where she was promptly arrested to be kept as one of Barker's concubines. She managed secretly to exchange the medallion with a fake one made by the underground Board. A fantastic piece of work, I must say.'

'Sunsetwinders never cease to amaze,' praises George.

'Barker hadn't a clue as to its real value,' continues Cleo, 'But understood that the Chicagos wanted it back desperately, because he presumed they didn't want proof publicised that they held Heyoka, or so it seemed. As it turned out, Barker got wise and felt there was something more to it than he knew. So he was prepared to hand our agent back to the Chicagos with the medallion in return for financial compensation to the tune of several billions. Barker had originally sold out Sunsetwind in some hair-brained scam the Chicagos had concocted. Well, to make a long story short, on the day of the exchange, the Chicagos again scammed Sunsetwind by wiring worthless credits from their own defunct scam, and Barker unwittingly handed over the fake without the agent who escaped fearing for her life, thank goodness. That's about it. We have the medallion and it is undergoing experimentation. Redman told me that they have made a crude device with an old fusion reactor that could set off an electromagnetic pulse that could cripple any defense system known to us. If we could get this device and set it off over Windy City, we could paralyse their response and raid the Bungalo to free Heyoka and Sam . . . '

'Cleo, let us leap one hurdle at a time,' intervenes Cephren. 'We haven't any idea how we will get the device. Barker has locked up Sunsetwind like the Kremlin under Stalin. We have to free Sunsetwind before we do anything . . . '

'Which means we would have to invade Sunsetwind before the Chicagos,' foresees George.

'Or,' suggests Anna Gram, 'Become allies with Barker, as detestable as it may sound, to repulse the Chicagos.'

'It depends on Barker,' says George. 'He may demand to know why we would do that and fear our intervention as a grab for Sunsetwind, especially now that the Paths are with us. At least the news has said as much . . . '

'I suppose, he'll figure it out when he hears you've dropped out of the election,' asserts Cephren.

'Therefore,' concludes George, 'If we were to join with Barker, would we have to make a deal with him concerning the unumpentium?'

'Why?' exclaims Cleo. 'Would not Barker be grateful just to hang on to power in an alliance?'

'From what I understand of the man, he is one idiot with an inflated ego the size of a Zeppelin balloon,' comments Anna.

'He may insist then on a piece of the action,' says Cephren. 'If he gets wind of this unumpentium and figures out that he had it under his nose and lost it . . . '

There a ponderous silence befalls. It is a dilemma. To become allies with Sunsetwind they might have to share the unumpentium with Barker. The question is: what would Barker do with it? Yet if they didn't share it, Barker would still have no choice but to agree to their terms if he wanted to defeat the Chicagos, unless he was such an utter fool as to throw it all away and they could depose him.

'Why do we need Barker's approval for anything?' wonders Anna, 'Or with the condition that the unumpentium cannot be shared.'

'I say no deals with Barker,' avers Cleo. "We'll save Sunsetwind in spite of him, and then remove him.'

'We should seek a less confrontational course of action. Is there a way to smuggle the medallion out of the country?' asks George. 'With Redman's device? It may be our only chance to stave off all out war through which we would all lose.'

'Cephren,' says Cleo, 'Let me take the Volcano; I'll go in from Anishnabe under Great Blue, come up at Mita's, take the medallion and device and leave the same way. It can be done.'

'Too risky,' conveys Cephren.

'I wouldn't be near Chicago.'

'No.'

'What then?'

Everyone looks at Cephren for some answer. He sighs and looks at the wall. The image of Flower Child appears in his mind. *Never make deals with*

Trashies, Cephren, she says. Then Jimmy Pidgeon appears plugging, *Go for it, man!* Then Redman pops into his mind: it is time to speak to Redman, in person. There is no other way.

'If you're asking me to make a decision,' he says, looking at George, 'Then I must go back to Sunsetwind myself.'

'What?' exclaim George and Anna together.

'Over my dead body!' snaps Cleo, her temper flaring.

'No one else can do what I must do,' insists Cephren. 'I can't elaborate just yet; it's just too risky.'

'Too risky! Of course it's too risky!' exhorts Cleo.

'It's too risky for anyone else, but me.'

'Why?' quizzes George.

'Jimmy's Chip,' he remarks. 'The X13. The Volcano.'

'All the more reason for someone else to go in.'

'Listen,' maintains Cephren, 'You just don't understand. I have this thing in my head, which makes me the only qualified person to do what has to be done. I can't say anymore. I can stop the war. Only I can make that sacrifice; besides, I must see Redman.'

'You said earlier trust must begin again,' recalls George. 'I have kept my side of the deal, but I don't understand why you're doing this.'

'Believe me, George, I know how it sounds, but this is exactly what I mean: trust me. Please.'

'And how do you propose to get into Sunsetwind?"' asks Cleo, peremptorily.

'As a candidate, of course.'

'But Barker won't permit it.'

'Oh yes he will.'

'Why?'

'He'll have no choice.'

'I don't understand.'

'Precisely what we've been discussing.'

'Cephren!'

Never in that contemporary world has there ever been such a show of force. A great proportion of the American Forces align along near the Chicago border south of Lake Ontario. Admiral Mckee, the American Supreme Commander, boldly makes the request to the Chicago forces whether they could escort Cephren Path into Sunsetwind. After a short wait, Trinny Burnamthorpe comes on the Admiral's monitor smiling ever so politely to say, 'He'll have to wait his turn, Admiral, after us.'

'All we want to do is get Cephren back in Sunsetwind, Ms. Burnamthorpe. He is still campaigning and reserves that right.'

'Really?' she trills cynically. 'Then he is a bigger fool than I could ever imagine. Don't you think I know why he wants to go there? Come on, Admiral, let's be pragmatic. No campaign ticket is going to buy his way back into the good graces of power. He is an uncommon dissembler who will stop at nothing to get his needs. What do I know? *Trust me*, I recall. *Trust me*, my ass! Sunsetwind is ours! So bug off!'

'The show is all yours, ma'm; permit us then to observe your fieldwork, so we may learn the art of stupidity. I do believe that is what will ultimately descend like a hawk on its helpless prey, you I should say. I beg you to reconsider and avoid the inevitable tragedy of war. Prompt release of Heyoka Yellow Tooth would suffice as an appropriate gesture of your good will.'

Ignoring his suggestion, Trinny disappears from his monitor. The Chicagos facing them are then supported by a flotilla almost equal to his own. Now they square off waiting for either side to move. Like a game of chess, all goes according to strategy.

Meanwhile, Cephren and Runaway in the Volcano have quietly slipped into the Atlantic as their escort goes west to parlay with the Chicagos. Emerging beyond sight of land they sped to Anishnabe and submerge again in Great Blue Lake to emerge on the Sunsetwind side. As soon as they are airborne, however, a flotilla of Barker's new Elite Corps emops surround him. Strangely, they all salute him by dipping their starboard side, then escort him south to the Pyramid. Upon final approach, hundreds more emops are airborne in a test pattern high above Clearview. They look like a huge flock of vultures waiting for a kill. Cephren barely notices: he is so emotionally caught up circling the Pyramid, though it isn't the homecoming he expected. He sees the familiar rolling hills and escarpment to the west, Great Blue to the north, the forests and vales of his life, and red-grey granite of his heritage in the Pyramid. Little does he know, he is in for the shock of his life. No sooner is he directed into the north entrance where dignitaries park their emops, and is led by a brace of smart guerillas in formal dress up the elevator to Survivor's Walk, he is greeted not by Del Barker, but a resplendent Chromolox, and beaming Board, who don't stand on ceremony and oblige his astonishment, but without a moment to spare conduct him in utter amazement front and center to an erected podium at the north end of the vast Survivor's Walk, to the sudden sonic roar of ten thousand gathered Sunsetwinders as far as he can see. The tears well uncontrollably and blur his eyes, tumbling freely down his cheeks. His emotion knows no restraint, and when he turns to them, the Board enjoins him to remain there and reap his just accolades. For extended minutes the reverberations of thankful Sunsetwinders do just that as his surprise and jubilation at this miracle of fortune knows no words. So choked is he, he feels utterly paralysed. And the continuous roar unabated thunders down the colossal thoroughfare, such that, at that moment in time no person present could ever forget the homecoming of Cephren Path.

There, on the brink of war and expecting the worst by taking a terrible risk, not only to himself, but concerning the future that lies ahead at a fork in the road – one way to hell, the other to enlightenment – Cephren finds himself redeemed to his world. This miracle has given him the chance to lead indisputably into the frontier of time. But true to his nature, modest and humble, all Cephren can finally say to Chromolox is: 'Where is Redman?' He catches Mita's eye standing to the side smiling. Vince is beside her cheering with the crowd, saying, 'It's all yours, Cephren!' And LeRoy, Olivia, and Gabriella waving her handkerchief with those wise, stubby fingers shine in the moment. And the Deerhills, even Strange is there, but no Treason. 'How on earth?' Cephren yells above the din. 'Am I dreaming, Chromolox?'

'No, Cephren, in good time, take it in, say something simple.' Chromolox then speaks into the microphone. 'Please welcome home, our beloved Chairman! Cephren Path!'

The crowd isn't about to decline its uproar, but slowly subsides when Cephren tries to speak.

'Sunsetwinders, Sunsetwinders! My, that has a beautiful ring to it!'

Another uproar.

'No amount of hardship can ever overcome our day of triumph.'

Uproar.

'We have overcome!'

Huge uproar.

'But we are not out of the woods yet! Are you prepared to defend us against our enemy?'

A resonating affirmative.

'I want to thank you all for your fortitude and perseverance, but especially those who at great risk to their own lives helped bring about the revolution. Please, a big hand to our President Chromolox and the Executive Board and the guerillas!'

Another huge uproar.

'Now, if you'll excuse me, we must get back to work; we are in the midst of a crisis, and an election!'

The crowd goes wild.

'Thank you! Thank you!' cries out Cephren, only to be drowned by the noise. He is then led out of Survivor's Walk back down the elevator to the bay and the Volcano, and whisked away with Runaway to the clearing near Redman's Bunker. There, his trusty Volcano is taken from him and replaced by another emop. He and Runaway are left standing in the vestiges of winter's snow in the quiet of the forest, stunned at what had just transpired as if it was a surreal fantasy. They look at each other smiling, still not sure whether to believe in it. What happened to Barker and the Free Radicals? How is it that no one from the outside had heard of the turn around? Only the old bent frame of Redman yelling at Cephren from his door fifty meters away brings him to his senses. He calls back, 'Redman! Redman! Is it true? We are free?'

Cephren cannot hear Redman's response, but sees his impulsive arm flailing in anger. He knows instinctively from Redman's reaction, that it is indeed true, and he'd better get over there quickly.

When he comes up to him, he wants to hug him; but the snide, old curmudgeon just turns his back saying, 'About time, son. We have business to attend to. Hello Runaway, help yourself to refreshment in the cooler. Follow me, Cephren!'

'Redman, for nature'sake tell me what happened!' beseeches Cephren, following him back to his study deep within the bunker.

Redman's only response is, 'Likewise!' under his breath and 'About time you came home!'

Once settled into his decrepit wood-lined study, Redman reclines in his old wood-swivel chair, his legs dangling. Cephren sits there across from him smiling in some confusion, stunned as to the fantastic reversal of fortune. Redman puts up his hand when Cephren is about to speak, as if their present solace is an exercise in restraint. After a moment, Redman gets down to business.

'Did you enjoy the reception, son?'

'You've got to be kidding!'

'No, I'm not the type; you should know that.'

'Redman, I came here ready to exercise my diplomatic immunity with the full backing of the American Armed Forces. I came here specifically, not to pontificate the abuses of power and Del Barker, though I probably wouldn't have been able to help myself, nor the wisdom of my being elected to the Earth Chair, but to see you! Redman, you have no idea how good it is to see you, and everybody, and that reception was out of this world; and I think I am qualified to say that, literally. Furthermore, I have something so unbelievably unique stored in this brain of mine aka Jimmy's Chip, there is an irony almost so outrageous, it makes me laugh. There is too much to say; where is the Board?'

'Why do you think we practice restraint, Chairman; slow down! Collect yourself! You sound like a damned fool blathering on like that! So, am I correct in assuming you cracked the X13?' he asks with a twinkle in his eye.

Cephren looks at him for a moment practicing restraint, then begins to nod slowly. Redman now loses his composure. He stands up with his gnarly fists clenched and jumps like a kangaroo. 'Yippee!' he squeals. 'Cephren, my boy, didn't I say you could do it? Didn't I?'

Cephren, never unimpressed by Redman's quirky side, shakes his head with a grand smiling buddha satisfaction.

'Well, now,' says Redman shifting back quickly to his usual persona, 'Let's get to the logistics. First of all, you are here with me, because it's safe, and there's an imminent invasion which will not succeed, thanks to all. I saw your speech on the monitor – touching, precise and eloquent . . . '

'Thank you, Redman; may I ask where is the Board; how did you overthrow the government, and where are Barker and the Free Radicals? Please.'

'I'm getting to it, Chairman; respect the temerity of your elders; hell, we must cherish moments like these.'

Cephren knows how sentimental Redman really is, but frustrating.

'Well, then, the Board: the Board remains at the Pyramid and is directing a counter-offensive, as you know from my recent discussion with Cleo on the shortwave when Barker was still in command, which was the case until just yesterday, mind you. At any rate, we are presently mounting the electromagnetic pulse device fuelled by a sliver of unumpentium – we have saved the mould by the way, as we most certainly must make a new one to give back to Heyoka and the Yellow Tooths. Where was I? Oh yes, then we will fly the device into Chicago under the pretence that you have decided to go to Windy City and campaign. There, high above we shall set the charge and render useless their entire electromagnetic network. We haven't told Cleo this. We want her to get someone else to invade the Bungalo to free Heyoka and Sam, if Sam wants to come. It is a dangerous mission: there will be casualties. Maybe they can capture Trinny too; wouldn't that be a coup?'

'But why haven't you announced the emancipation of Sunsetwind to the world? And where's Barker?'

'Why? What better smoke screen could we have created? If they knew Barker was deposed, they most certainly wouldn't hesitate to invade thinking the country was in chaos. The element of surprise, son, is one of the greatest proponents to a successful war. We must strike as soon as we are able. The Americans are lined up along their eastern border, just where we want them. We are going to send out a small decoy force to spread the remainder of the Chicagos' around to the north. The Anishnabes have agreed to the plan and they will take that responsibility. Then we will announce to the Americans that we are free and that you have decided to go to Chicago. Diplomatic immunity may at least allow you, the Volcano that is, as you are too valuable a person to send on such a dangerous mission, to get in long enough to set off the charge, at which time the Americans will attack; we will attack; everyone who wants to will attack.'

'Sounds awesome; they won't know what hit them. But how do you know this electromagnetic charge will be effective? We all have countermeasures for such a device. We have sensors. The Chicagos have systems that are the most advanced in the world.'

'We'll jam their sensors so they won't know they're down,' says Redman with fire lust in his hawkish eyes.

'With what?' queries Cephren. 'The electromagnetic device will have an amplitude that will fry their monitors like lightening!'

'What got us into this mess in the first place, Cephren, will get us out.'

Cephren looks at him quizzically.

'Scanners, man! A Resonant Scanner!'

'You mean you can jam electronic surveillance with them?'

'That's how we managed to destroy Barker! He had us all tagged. We would scan the tags with a device Vince and I rigged, that enabled us to remove them without their knowing. That's how we convened the underground Board! And we travelled at night! We jammed all their signals, only long enough to do what we had to. Our breakthrough came when Treason, bless her heart, brought Heyoka's medallion out of Chicago.'

'Where is she?' queries Cephren, worriedly.

'We don't know. We know she escaped. In fact, without Treason we never would have been able to pull off the coup so soon. She gave Del a severe blow to the genitals, then a concussion that also cracked a vertebrae in his neck. He is completely incapacitated. After his people exchanged the fake medallion with the Chicagos, we set off a small experimental charge on their return route from the Neutrals. The whole emop party crashed, though not severely. Our guerillas were ready and captured the Praetorian escort, then returned to the Pyramid in their place. There was no resistance, because Barker wasn't even there. He was at Mita's Clinic with his swollen balls on ice and in a neck cast; besides Mita put him out of his misery with some sedatives. When she told him the Free Radical party just lost the election, he was so drugged he hadn't any idea what she was talking about. He has since been moved to the Prison hospital in Penetang where he will remain until he is in better health, then there will be a hearing before Gabriella. He will be tried under Sunsetwind law, as will many others who participated in the usurpation of our province.'

'Are you sure Treason is all right?'

'She contacted her mother to get a scanner to remove her monitor tag and it was removed by some guerillas in the Neutrals. But she has since disappeared. Her mother claims she has gone to the wilderness with some of her Forager friends. She'll be safe there.'

'She deserves the highest honour. If and when this is all over I'll see to it,' avows Cephren.

He and Redman now speak in more sober tones. They caution against their earlier optimism. The war, as yet undeclared, presents little respite from the new freedom of Sunsetwind. Old Redman, looking more haggard and worn from the stresses of the past months, now resigns himself to a retirement of sorts. It is out of his hands. Chromolox and the Board are in full control under the smokescreen of Barker's tyranny. What a strange and deadly interlude. The Invasion, as it was called, caused lives to be turned upside down: a worse suffering among a growing number of poor people, terrible enmities and discord pitting Sunsetwinder against Sunsetwinder due to their allegiances. But the nightmare is not over yet.

Cephren now has to inform Redman about what he knows, an absurd notion in itself, when considering the enormity of information. And he knows there is no adequate way of downloading his peculiar little piece of software. Therefore, to justify his actions during those perilous months, he knows he must ultimately reveal the greatest gift to humanity ever known. In effect, it would be the endorsement of the universal spirit of humankind, pending the response. He isn't sure he knows where to begin. Redman observes him with his tired, red eyes. The anticipation is almost anticlimactic. Redman knows intuitively the import of Cephren's task, and quakes slightly at the notion. But Cephren's genius would flower in the advent of the spirit of the X13. But from a pragmatic point of view, Redman could never begin to empathise with the logistical rectitude of that meaning.

'Well, come on,' presses Redman, 'Let's hear it: in your own words. I'm no fool. They're about, aren't they? It has to do with them, doesn't it?'

'Yes and no, Redman; it has more to do with us.'

'With us?'

'All of us, us and them.'

'So what does Jimmy have to do with it?'

'I would say he was the greatest contributor, from our point of view.'

'For nature'sake, Cephren, what on earth do you mean?'

'This bunker had something to do with it,' says Cephren looking about.

'This bunker?'

'Yes, it was the Barnett's up to the Horror. Terrie Barnett and Old Scratch lived here afterwards.'

You mean Flower Child?'

'Yes, this was her family's bunker.'

'Fascinating, but what relevance . . . '

'We always knew her to be my ancestor, but so was Jimmy Pidgeon, and Perreault. Their daughter married a Barnett.'

'The chip revealed this to you?'

'Yes.'

'Why?'

'You know Jimmy's poem.'

'Of course.'

'There's a simple cipher and anagram encoded in it.'

'I half suspected. Something so simple, technology overlooked it.'

'The chip, I think, lives in a way and picks its host so-to-speak.'

'Go on.'

'Well, it picked me. What baffles me, is I wonder if it let me in because of me. Anyone else may have come up empty. I can't explain that; it's just a feeling.'

'How so?'

'I believe it communicates with me. There I was alone in the Volcano, having escaped from the Chicagos – it seems like a different lifetime long ago . . . the anagram is subsumed in Pidgeon's poem: *With an ocean blue sky I go* . . .

eleven The Emperor

Humming precisely
Like the wind in the trees

–Jimmy Pidgeon

Blind, white luminescence, the pure light of a proton mash pervades Jimmy's bedeviled mind, encapsulated by the sun, yet he stills feels nothing. Life in the universe emanates through its source. All formations, from pre-biotic life to the complexities of intelligence, pass within his sphere of consciousness. Then trillions of faces, lives and evolutions transcend where every single entity fits in a kind of perfection of dissonance – and life and death reciprocate in harmony. The proliferation of chaotic life is as elementary in essence as some battery powered train announcing: All aboard! Full speed ahead! Nothing stops creation, ever, forever, and Jimmy feels in that apogee of his experience, the very electro-chemical response his blindness endures: divinity.

The blindness, however, de-coalesces into a mottled kaleidoscope of luminosities. It thins remarkably before his emerging vision, where little breaks of darkness appear, and the light organises itself into a vast array of celestial bodies, each one placed according to its size and chemistry. Indeed, a galaxy of sprayed light spans his mind, in which the identity and quality of each proponent is evident. And the way across from each body consecutively or from one end to another, the navigational continuum through neutral gravitation channels, is quite spectacular – from the Orion cluster to Corona Australis, or Zeta Reticula to Itibi Ra, or the outer reaches of the Milky Way where life proliferates as abundantly as anywhere else. He finally sees himself sitting on a rock at the edge of the galaxy somewhere on a desert abyss gazing upon a brilliant blue pink nebular cloud in the darkest of nights. But as Jimmy begins to think about what he sees, a veil comes over his vision and shuts down the omniscience. It seems there is an aptitude or operation that he will have to master in order to access the knowledge. Whatever it is he has in his head is not a computer chip with command and retrieval accessibility; it is a living accessory that bonds with its host. In other words, he perceives that they would have to get to know each other before the "chip" would open up. Even still, he has no idea whether such a "partnership" is possible. He doesn't even know if he is awake or not. He can't feel his body, or see it. He thinks he must still be in some sort of paralytic state. All he can remember was lying face down on a warm, metal table while they put something in his brain. The gift. But what is it? A Trojan Horse to control his mind? He realises he must come to his senses! But how? There are so many questions to ask. He has to speak to the Reptoid. And Lilly. 'Help!' he utters. He feels a reassuring presence and opens his eyes.

He is lying on a bed. It is firm and warm. Turning to the presence, he sees in the dusky room sitting on a metal stool, Lilly. She is looking through him with those haunting orbs for eyes. In the weak light, she is dark and ghostly. Her long spindly arm is extended and gently settled on his stomach. He can feel the compassion through her touch. Without speaking she says, *You are in capable hands; try not to think or move your body; just lie still. Do not speak or the device might be rejected by your pineal gland.*

Jimmy does as she says and relaxes under her power. He believes in her goodness. She is part human and that alone atones for his insecurity. Yet there is a fatalistic pleasure in the scenario: he realises that if ever there would be a super-human scientific discovery, the pineal bonding with this device is the living embodiment of all those possibilities. Mercifully, he sleeps, with the notion that he might just have to stay there for some time while he healed. He smiles in a curious heaven.

He really slept. He could have died for all he knew. When he awakens, he is alone. His head pounds at the back with migraine-like symptoms. It is so painful, he has to get up and seek relief. He isn't sure what he can do. The thought of asking a freaky, grey alien for an aspirin or two doesn't seem plausible, yet they had to have something to help. Exiting the room, Jimmy finds himself in a long straight hall, so long in fact he can't see the end of it in either direction. His head begins to reel dizzily in pain as he stumbles along the wall to the next room and sees to his surprise a young human man dressed in a well-tailored suit, with a low cut collar and no tie. The man looks at him, smiles, and goes back to this small wireless computer device.

'Do you have any aspirin?' asks Jimmy, struggling to enunciate his speech and ignoring the oddity of his presence.

The young man looks up again, pressing some sequence with his device and says, 'Don't worry, man, I just sent for the Doc.'

'Who are you?' queries Jimmy.

'Darrell Lester; who are you?'

'Jimmy Pidgeon, MJ-12,' he says cautiously.

'Don't know that. You must be local.'

'That's interesting: local. Then what are you, a gringo?' winces Jimmy, ever ready to parry, even with his head in a vice.

'Very funny, Jimbo.' Darrel extends his hand. Jimmy takes it ever so slowly as he has trouble focusing. 'You really need an aspirin,' Darrell says. 'Soaked with codeine, or something heavy, man.'

'Are you from earth?' asks Jimmy, curious in spite of his headache.

'Genetically, yes, but born and raised right here in The Ranch.'

'The Ranch. But you now live on earth.'

'Correct,' jives Darrell, facetiously.

'How many others are there like you?' inquires Jimmy still reeling in his pain.

'Hundreds, all ages, it could thousands by now.'

'Thousands? What do they need you for?'

'Hey, we're a minority; we believe in Equal Opportunity, man.' Darrell laughs cynically. 'You know, affirmative action. We are the glue that keeps the world from falling apart; that's what I like to think; hell, I'm an earthy guy.'

'You must fit in admirably then.'

'Hey, I'm a class act.'

'Do the authorities know about you?' quizzes Jimmy.

'Which ones?'

'Any one.'

'Locals, no way, but the gringos, sí señor,' he intones.

'Locals, meaning earth authorities, and gringos meaning Greys and Reptoids,' assumes Jimmy.

'You said it, buddy, but don't say I said so; *I'm a spy in the house of love!*' he sings mimicking Jim Morrison of the Doors, the long defunct rock group who in turn had actually borrowed the phrase from Anaïs Nin, the writer of erotic literature.

Jimmy flashes on this fellow's uncanny human response. No one would ever suspect he is an alien; he is as human as the next person. He also reminds him of Danielle and her adolescent obsession with Jim Morrison. The thought strikes home: Danielle. The Gift as he then knew it would be the sort of thing she would die to get her hands on. Yet her practical strength is something he could really use right now.

'So what do you do on earth?' presses Jimmy.

'I'm in advertising.'

'Really,' says Jimmy, disbelieving.

'Yes, really, I specialise in technologies at Mayhew, Lester Advertising. If you have any money too, I could make you a millionaire. I have a knack of knowing what's hot and what's not.'

'I can't seem to think how that could be otherwise,' remarks Jimmy sitting on the bed and holding his head.

'Thank you, I take that as a compliment.'

'So why are you here?'

'Hey, give me a break, buddy; you can take the pressure for only so long. I mean, it's a rat race! And a helluva bore. Time out, man, just a little time out, back at the Ranch! We all do it – you know. Hey, what are you doing here?'

'This is all a little weird for me. They just put something into my head. I'm an ultra-classified government engineer orbiting Mars with a advertising exec. from . . . '

'New York, New York!' he sings imitating Sinatra.

'New York.'

'Hey, do yuh wanna know what's weird?' asks Darrell.

'I think this place is the Capitol of Weird,' replies Jimmy.

'Cocktail parties,' says Darrell, ignoring Jimmy.

'Cocktail parties,' sighs Jimmy. 'Okay.'

'Yeah, yuppie cocktail parties, where everybody's looking for something; know what I mean? After being here and getting what you want; it's not even what you want; it's just a kind of headspace where all desire is sublimated through each other immaculately. It is as if there is no morality because there is no evil, or cultural restraint, which on earth seems to always cause tension. Let's face it, down there as a race we seek to survive and build up vast networks both psychological and infrastructural that struggles to maintain civilisation. It's just plain silly sometimes: He wants Her, and She wants Egghead, and Egghead wants Mitsy, who wants the Dork, who wants the Bitch, who wants Slick, who wants the Prude, who wants the Prick, who wants the Tease, who wants . . . you know.'

'I get the picture, Darrell; but who do you want?'

'Nobody really!' he exclaims, then laughs. 'See what I mean? There's no truth. It's all pretense, superficiality, and hype. Nobody gets who or what he or she wants, and if one gets what they want, then they covet someone or something else. It makes for self-consummation en masse, although there are many exceptions. But generally people's energy is wasted in the Look. It's all in the Look. Evolution is perverted, man. It's takes a long time to sort it all out; that's why the Ranch is so great. We're all doomed, you know; there are too many bad apples. And do you know what they say to me?'

'No.'

'They say, "Fuck off, Darrell. Mind your own business." So I mind my own business and make people rich by promoting their thing and watch their eyes light up.'

'I think you are in the wrong line of work,' comments Jimmy.

'I'm no martyr, man.'

'What do *you* want?' asks Jimmy, squeezing his own neck in an attempt to relieve the pain in his head.

'I wish only that people could really understand the extent of intelligent life in the universe. It is fantastic, a real cocktail; but people don't really care; they're all too self-possessed; they're forced to be by the circumstances they create for themselves; or caught up in their narrow fundamentalism, thus limiting their views.'

'What choice do we have? Our history has been a battle for justice. We're still fighting the barbarians of our own nature.'

'You've got that right, Jimbo,' states Darrell.

'Perhaps, but I don't think you can fully appreciate the demands of freedom on earth in an institutional sense.'

'Hey, I know that. Listen, I'm a just a gringo. I tell the truth, and play by the rules or my business will crash. I never let anybody down, but when I tell them confidentially that I'm really not from here, they laugh at me.'

'So would I,' says Jimmy, 'But then I would ask you why you're here and as an advertiser of all things, rather than, say, a Peace Corp. worker.'

'Simple: the big picture. I represent the big picture.'

'Well, perhaps we don't want the big picture just yet.'

'Ha ha.' He feigns a laugh, 'But you got it. Think of it as big oil moving into town. Someone's gonna pump it, right? An' what are ya gonna do about it?'

The analogy startles Jimmy, but the sudden appearance of Lilly and Bart intervene. Bart looks with admonishment at Darrell who just says, 'Kiss my ass, Bart!' Then both Lilly and Bart help Jimmy up and out into the hall where they take him to another room down the other way. It is a more comfortable area with human sized chairs and a sofa. There is even a viewing window, though small. But before Jimmy can exercise his curiosity, they serve him a drink that is pearl-like in colour and tastes flat and repulsive. It seems to thicken in his stomach, but almost instantaneously begins to relieve the pressure in his head.

'Thank you, thank you,' he murmurs in bliss.

Bart shines a tiny light into Jimmy's eyes. Bart's own dark, full bug eyes like wrap-around shades are emotionless, almost primeval. The only quiver of communication comes when he stops and takes Jimmy's pulse like any doctor but with another instrument that shows some readings.

You are a good host, says Bart, planting the thought abruptly into Jimmy's head.

'And you're a good doctor,' says Jimmy, returning the flattery. 'But what exactly is this gift and what am I to do with it?'

We call it the Neteru. We desire that you know what they know so that you may better understand the cosmos.

'Where are the Neteru?' asks Jimmy.

You are the Neteru, he telepaths. *We know of no other.*

'You mean to say we are the last of the Neteru?' queries Jimmy, unsure of what he is hearing.

But Bart does not elucidate, and Jimmy looks to Lilly who doesn't seem ready to pick up the thread of Jimmy's inquiry. This makes him more confused than before. Who were the Neteru? Is humanity really the last vestige of an ancient race in the universe? muses Jimmy to himself. And why were they so damned important to the Greys? He decides to push harder.

'Let me speak to Big Cheese or that Reptoid,' he demands.

'Perhaps they will speak to you later,' says Lilly quickly, more assuredly.

'Lilly,' asserts Jimmy, 'This has gone far enough. I'm MJ-12 for God's Sake. You can't expect me to accept a gift as a hole in the head! Can you? Be reasonable. This Neteru and that Darrell leave me little choice but to blow the whistle on this cosmic Ranch when I get back, unless I get some satisfactory answers!'

Still, Bart ignores him and Lilly hasn't any compunction to transgress Bart's intransigence. They leave the room and lock the door. Jimmy goes to the viewing window and sees the massive reddish-grey hulk of Mars far beneath them turning, turning on its orbital path. This exotic trip makes him feel unusually claustrophobic.

A short while later Lilly comes back and unlocks the door. She sits down with a sigh putting one leg up on the heating element against the wall. Her spindly half-human leg still had a pleasant shape to it. Exposing it seems like a very human gesture to Jimmy. It occurs to him after speaking with Darrell that human traits are considered highly desirable; further-more, human character is given a wide berth and some deference in terms of their self-esteem. Is it possible that human passion for life is coveted by the Greys? Or Reptoids? Or is there some trait in human behaviour akin to the Neteru that they seek? The Neteru are indeed a mystery, and yet he has been told humans are the Neteru. But why would they implant the Neteru device in him?

'Lilly, thanks for coming; you seem like a really decent person. Two things,' he says showing two fingers.

'Yes,' she smiles, 'I'm here for you.'

'First, what is this thing in me?'

'The Neteru?'

Jimmy nods.

'It's a synaptic memory chip made from a rare, liquid mineral found only on planets in a red dwarf system.'

'This stuff is called Neteru then?'

'Yes.'

'Do you use it for other purposes?'

'No, it is so rare and its properties . . . are uncooperative, but we have found that through experimenting, it agrees with lesser synaptic frequencies. In other words, it does not benefit us.'

'Has it been tried before?'

'Yes, and we noted a pattern in its behaviour. It responds well in what we call aggressive types, not the ignorant kind, which can also be negatively aggressive. We deem aggressive to mean strong thinkers with superior resolutions, but intelligent and calm natures, like you with both your scientific and artistic skills.'

'How then do I make it work?'

'You just think. It really is a gift. We have little use for it. It will enable you to make great strides in the development of your technology and to travel in space.'

'But most alien species don't want us to travel in space.'

'You can't as a race, until you develop the technology which is a long time coming, but they welcome individuals like yourself. Believe me, they have tremendous respect for you. They would never harm you in any way. They see you as a progenitor and will watch out for your descendants.'

'What about this chip? Will they pass it on?'

'If they deem the subject worthy.'

'Well, in that case, I hope I live up to their expectations and the Neteru whatever it is or whoever they are.'

'Do you have other questions?' she asks.

'I'd like to know about Darrell. Is he for real?'

She laughs that high octave twitter like a chatty bird. 'Oh yes.'

'How many are there like Darrell?'

'You'll have to ask Johnny.'

'Who's Johnny?'

'That's what the Reptoid you met likes to be called by humans.'

'Why?'

'It's comfortable, familiar. I heard him once say children enjoyed very much the fable Johnny Appleseed.'

'I suppose then he identifies himself with the spreading of 'appleseed' metaphorically, unless he wears a tin pot hat.'

'No,' she laughs. 'I doubt it's as simple as that.'

'I doubt it too, but we're not talking apples.'

'You may make your own observations,' she says.

She removes her leg from the warm wall heater panel and beckons to Jimmy to follow her.

'Are you hungry?' she wonders aloud as they walked the hall side by side. He towers over her.

'Now that you mention it, I'm dying to see the menu.'

They walk the seemingly endless passageway – a tube like structure with doors at varying intervals. Lilly explains that the ship is about a kilometer long and a hundred meters wide – a tubular looking structure. Jimmy is beside himself with amazement. The sheer magnitude of that craft is a testament to the manifold versatility of anti-matter reactors. No longer is rocket-fueled thrust a calibrated requisite in ratio of economy to payload. Literally any size of craft could easily lift and propel itself on its own gravity wave.

A few Greys and a small number of humans are moving to and fro along the long deck. Jimmy and Lilly pass numerous facilities where human children at various stages of development are being taught and some are at play. There is apparently a tube shuttle beneath them, which is certainly more convenient; however, Lilly believed the walk appropriate to familiarize Jimmy with the ship. She explains that the chip in his head would be sufficiently fused already. The technique they use repairs the cells in his brain almost instantly, but about twenty-four hours of quiet is necessary to allow the brain, specifically the pineal gland, to accept it. The chip actually rejects certain people outright.

They arrive at a door, which opens to a lounge area furnished like a Howard Johnson with wooden tables, comfortable chairs and most everything supplied from earth. There is a buffet arrangement of food with many choices consisting of a predominance of exotic greens, some of which are alien vegetables grown on board, or local fare including bean dishes including: soy, black, white, red kidney, and garbanzo; also served are lentils, basmati and tur dal. Oddly, a soy roast beef and Yorkshire pudding are offered, together with pastas, Szechuan soy plum duck, garlic rosemary lemon lamb and poached sea foods including raw oysters; there are many dairy choices too. Hungrily, Jimmy tries a bit of almost everything. Lilly sips on some Miso broth and dips seaweed rice crisps into it.

'My compliments to the chef,' comments Jimmy. 'Quite a purveyor he must be to procure and prepare such a feast, especially while orbiting Mars. A regular soy Ponderosa.'

Lilly smiles and keeps her eyes fixed on Jimmy. He can feel her thoughts probing and teasing his voyeuristic side. Very definitely, he realises she is not adverse to further exploration of his propinquity. He quickly returns the vibes that he is not interested. Fidelity is the conscience of true love. Yet, to Lilly it does not matter. The concept of alien or even hybrid morals in sexuality are loose at best. Mating, though interesting, is an ephemeral thing to them. It is a stage in the evolutionary ladder that gives way to cerebral union far removed from possessive, primeval, territorial and conjugal mores. It goes both ways: male and female. Jealousy had died with the old races before clinical conception and their subsequent devolution.

Other ordinary looking humans, mostly young, come and go in the dining area. The extent of their usefulness to the aliens shocks Jimmy. He understands that well placed humans in various sectors of society are a perfect watch. What bothers him is the question as to what extent this was going on. And why would they let him in on it when as far as he is aware MJ-12 knew nothing about it? They didn't expect him to keep his mouth shut, did they?

'I've got to see this Johnny, Lilly,' he insists.

She averts her eyes that exude the look of a love-struck adolescent.

'Okay,' she says blithely, even coquettishly.

She gets up and he follows her to an entrance. They step into a tube similar to the one at X13. In seconds they stop at the other end of the ship and get out to take a lift. Getting out at the obvious "bridge" or command center, both Bart and Big Cheese greet them. They seem very congenial, and take him by the hand as if he is a child and lead him to what seems to be a smaller bridge with viewing screens and leave him alone. No sooner had the Greys left when Johnny Appleseed appears from an adjacent compartment. Jimmy is taken aback by his casual western apparel: dressed in faded jeans and a Greatful Dead T-shirt and bare feet.

'Hello Jimmy,' he says in perfect English, holding out his hand, adding, 'Don't be surprised.'

'Hello,' greets Jimmy, a little nervously. His hand has a cool, dry feel to it, like that of an old man. 'Do I look surprised? I suppose I should be with a hole in my head, but I assume you mean your earth hippy thing. How did you get out of that skin-tight suit?'

'Sit down, please,' Johnny says, indicating a built-in console chair that swivels.

Jimmy sits down.

'To answer your question,' replies Johnny, 'We dematerialise a seam. The suits are circuited to help aid telepathic control of the ship if need be.'

'Wonderful, then you must think our clothes truly simple, laid back even, though I can't say it puts me at ease to see you so relaxed,' remarks Jimmy. 'I think: *subterfuge*.'

Johnny laughs a very human laugh. 'In spite of how you feel; I'm not about to bite off your head like some of our primitive ancestors. We do condone the perks of your civilisation, you know, Mr. Pidgeon.'

'Well then, we shall soon put aside our differences and go our ways amicably,' purports Jimmy.

'I wish it could be so simple as that Mr. Pidgeon. But it is not a question of differences, rather common sense.'

'How so? You have hundreds of thousands of years on us,' states Jimmy.

'You need us to get over the impasse of technical emergence. The statistics of emerging civilisations are not in your favour. The majority self-destruct by ruining their environment, and killing each other off in wars of attrition to the point of regression into barbarity. There is a fine line of survival into the next phase of ecological harmony and technology. The have-nots will revert to primitive religious ways that will seek to destroy every vestige of advance. We are here to monitor and nurture that potential for advancement, yet I admit, it is tenuous at best. Earth has been for the most part a great disappointment with the exception of some wonderful distractions.'

'Do I detect an emerging vanity? Are we a novelty, a passing fad? Are we that irresistible?' asks Jimmy, a little put off when he was just beginning to appreciate him.

'Yes you are, but as I said, primarily for the wrong reasons. Of the half million or so star systems within our influence, yours is one of the least likely to succeed; that's why I'm here, as a trouble-shooter.'

Jimmy has to contemplate for a moment. It is his turn to laugh. 'Here I am speaking to a . . . human reptile, who speaks perfect English, orbiting Mars, wearing a Dead Head T-shirt! So you do enjoy our "perks" I gather.'

'I have learned to love you, and sympathise for your terrible problems. I have faith in your own particular ability to do much more for earth than we could ever do without revealing ourselves.'

'Well, I suppose thanks are in order for having some faith in me. This is an impressive 'ranch'. Very impressive.'

'Yes, you must find it impressive, but it is Reticulan. I am only a guest, or observer, if you will.'

'But in charge of Mission Earth: do you have an official position?'

'Some call me the 'Emperor', but that's just a euphemism for my authority.'

'But an Emperor nonetheless,' maintains Jimmy.

'Perhaps, but not one to impose authority: you do that all by yourselves.'

'You seem to be a very civil and almost human, dare I say it. But why am I really here? Why do you need me with this Neteru?' Jimmy points to his head.

Johnny looks at Jimmy, through him, with those yellow vertical-pupil eyes and with no eyebrows, hair, ears or pronounced nose. Jimmy returns the look. Johnny is obviously not human, and appears horrible as such in comparison; but in the eyes, despite their reptilian features, there is a deep understanding and yes, spirit, if wanting in warmth. He is about Jimmy's height but half as thick and probably ten times as strong. His hands are not clawed or webbed, but well-shaped and flexible, almost delicate, though with only three fingers and a thumb. His voice is soft, even gentle, but clear and syllables roll easily off his long, red tongue. His mouth, though small can be seen to stretch very large. He doesn't have teeth, but hard mandible-like gums. Despite Johnny's alien features, he can actually be described as good looking.

'We consider ourselves a civil race, Jimmy. Our own advancement has been long and arduous. We have come to see ourselves as caretakers of the universe, with the help of our friends, the Greys, as you say. The Greys are actually an older race than ours, but in decline and a minority. Our race, the Reptoids, as you say, have a modest portion of the galaxy within its indirect influence. There are many races out there, but ours tends to be dominant. And when I say dominant, or perhaps vigilant, for lack of a better word, I do not mean it so much in human terms, which may connote some empirical implication, but merely our technological leadership and ability to contain the divergent impulses of newer races. Reptiles, although given a bad name here on earth, are a very hardy and adaptable life form and usually defensive in nature. Mind, we certainly do not see ourselves as predators in any literal sense of the word, though will not hesitate to limit the progress of an emerging race if it brought its contagion with it out into space. We have to protect the environment by maintaining toxic-free and undisrupted gravitational harmonised systems; otherwise we will not interfere with its development. This is a natural and evident directive for most space-travelling species.'

'But you have interfered with ours when we've barely been out of orbit.'

'Marginally. As you know your containment is a high priority amongst us and other species. Everything we do is to that end. I should point out that we have consolidated your containment, rather than numerous races coming and going with no clear objective.'

'And the Neteru?'

'Is of no use to us; it is of an extinct race; but we always thought when someone of your calibre came along, we would give your Neteru as a token of our wish that you emerge from earth with some notion of the order of things out here, and possibly the sentiment or remembrance of that lost civilisation, which we see as an obligation.'

'Did you have anything to do with its demise, Johnny?' quizzes Jimmy, a little apprehensively.

'Yes,' he confesses without hesitation. 'Tens of thousands of years ago we were the antagonistic ones. It was a terrible time. The Neteru were enslaved against their will, but to our surprise and delight in fact, have emerged again in you and us to a lesser degree. I should point out that today as a race, we are much like you, thanks to the Neteru. Infusions of their DNA altered our race forever. We are truly grateful and not only wish to protect what you are, also in part to protect you from yourselves, as you are technologically adolescent, but from us, at least the fear of us. And believe me, fear is the last thing we would want for you, notwithstanding its importance as an impediment to your success. It takes a long time for undeveloped planets to shed their fears, their own homemade fear, prejudice, and ignorance. Certainly our presence could not allay that.'

'This is overwhelming,' states Jimmy, shaking his head. 'If the mainstream of our society was to know the scope and involvement of alien life here and in the universe, there would be tremendous pressure to build fortress earth. Fear is a built-in survival kit. We would immediately go on the defensive, not to mention the probable meltdown of our cultural institutions.'

Johnny ponders this for a moment looking at Jimmy and smiling with his eyes.

'You are fortress earth,' he finally says, 'Or Sol 3 as we refer to you; and you have been that way as long as we have known of your existence. No race that I know of would want to take your planet. Believe me, it's yours. Your cultural institutions, democracies, or religions that I think you infer, are the front lines of defence. All developing races are the same and very ardently scrutinized. Evolution is a curious thing. Many changes occur on many levels. Some species on earth are more evolved than others, not necessarily in intelligence but collectively. In nature, one life form doesn't preclude the value of another in terms of survival. In the final analysis there are no values. Your race defines intelligence as self-determination and your institutions seek to justify it in terms of values. In your religions for example, the embodiment of spirit is tied up in archaic tradition and ritual. Religions are in fact perversions that inhibit the freedom and essence of your particular kind of spirit, which ironically your religions sprung from. Rather than enhance your spirits, they victimize them. Do I need to cite examples? No. Your entire history is rife with them. Any attempt to suppress the spirit of creation is self-defeating and curtails your chances of collective survival as a race; in fact, it does the opposite by promoting conflict. I have seen it over and over . . . '

'Wait a minute,' interrupts Jimmy, 'I'm the last one to speak up for some of our cultural heritages; but even you must agree that our development has been contingent upon the virtues that religious fervor was built upon. Your very own ethical treatment of us, if I understand you correctly, is apparently virtuous, comprised of charity, compassion and mercy. So don't tell me we are too far off the mark to make good.'

'You are right, Jimmy; but you are one of a kind, peerless; and when I hear you speak, I only wish you could speak for all humanity. What I say about your race, however, is ineluctably true. There could be no reasonable meeting of minds. Your impediments are too vast. You are at a serious juncture in your evolution. You are pushing the limits of what your planet can do to sustain you. You must change or die. Your economies, politics, cultures and needs must change. Let me elaborate: in the universe, there are endless resources. There is no need to covet one thing or another, no need to trade, or sell, or fight, or anything; these are terrestrial things, petty, primitive processes. You cannot possibly expect a race still throwing itself before altars and superstitions to be met with open arms in the universe, even if you have the technology. It would be a disaster. Technology will eventually convert the way you behave, but over a very long time, maybe thousands of your years. But it is necessary to prod a little here and there, futile as it may seem in view of your burgeoning populations and ecological dilemmas. You will break with primitive nature one way or another, as you have begun to do to wrest control. You may interbreed with alien races to accommodate control. The sooner you realise as a race that God is Nature and vice-versa the more enlightened you will become. Your religions must bridge the two polemics of God and Nature as one. Inevitably, natural occurring phenomena will create great obstacles to your evolution – acts of God as you interpret them – perhaps for some divine purpose you believe. It's all meaningless, ultimately, as you will discover, not to say that our alien vigilance must not prevail. I know and generally those of my race know, as well as most cosmic civilisations, is that the universe is a chaotic promenade. It is an atomic struggle, blind in itself – a propagating organism living and dying all at once. There are elementary laws constantly redefining themselves at variance to our expectations. The universe is an ever-living wonder that we cannot take for granted, as you must now see happening on earth. Your uses are infinite, as are ours. So curbing your destructive tendencies is our obligation until your future is better guaranteed. It's as simple as that.'

'If so,' counters Jimmy, 'How is it that you have become such a dominant force? Did you not come up against other dominant forces?'

'Yes, but we recognised our similarities. We all use gravity waves; we all need sustenance and light; these are shared interests. Having attained these degrees of life, subjection is only a hindrance to passage. Freedom to move in space is impossible to police. Malevolence toward others is malevolence to one's self; this is a symptom, if you will, of self-destruction, therefore an anomaly to well-being.'

'But what of your purported desire to amalgamate our DNA with yours? This is offensive in the extreme to us.'

'That is only the natural evolution of your species. Eventually, if your race survives, there will be joining. Believe me, you will wish to. The desire to live is stronger than the desire to die. Your species, though gaining in longevity, would live ten times as long with infusions of extra-terrestrial DNA. We are all mixed. It's inevitable. We may become more like you.'

'That's very hard to accept. We romanticise our form. We idolise beauty in humanity. What of the other humans, the advanced human-like species, such as the Eridanis or the Itibians?'

Johnny laughs. 'We see your vanity as primitive. We are all beautiful. Beauty will become less subjective. These other races would concur with me; they are galactic members.'

'Should we not be seeking their friendship?' queries Jimmy.

'Usually a species such as yours finds containment easier with a different species. A similar species draws too many comparisons and can generate enmities.'

'Try telling that to humankind.'

'Precisely.'

'So,' says Jimmy, 'We shouldn't have much to fear from you.'

'On the contrary, you as a people have much to fear, and fear you will, until fear becomes nescient.'

'Are there evil Reptoids, Johnny?'

'There are those who are not so familiar with your species.'

'And?'

'They may anticipate greater understanding from you.'

'And when not complied with?'

'Casual death would be unlikely, but not impossible.'

'We have evidence of rapes committed against our women by Reptoids,' states Jimmy seriously.

'As I've said, there are those who deviate from our common goal – to protect your interests, as well as ours. We cannot let a few bad individuals dictate the fate of your world. I don't think my personal apology would suffice to allay victims of such behaviour. But to a Reptoid, such an act is intended to be complimentary; nevertheless "compliments" of such a nature are abhorrent. These perpetrators are a risk to both us and you. On the other hand, such risk is nature's wild card. As your society produces undesirables, so does ours, though perhaps we are not so intentionally deviant.'

'It is criminal. Please do your utmost to apprehend these deviants; and Johnny, one more thing before I go home,' utters Jimmy with conviction to indicate a sense of purpose, futile as it did seem. 'How do I use this Neteru?'

'Your synaptic link will interface with the Neteru and they will either reject you or receive you to do what your heart desires. As I've said, the Neteru were highly evolved and we all have some of them in us. The Greys tell of a split in their ways. Some chose to remain human in a sense, and others evolved, though we failed them in that regard. This was a long time ago. The human type have disappeared, as they were more like you of course.'

'Not a healthy prognosis for us then.'

'Yet humankind is an irrepressibly recurring species.'

'Yeah, like fodder for the gods.'

They both laugh – the Reptoid now making a clicking sound, but mirth in his eyes. Jimmy, sadly, can't help thinking of Johnny burning at the stake after having relayed to the earth authorities what he had just told Jimmy. For all his reasonableness, an intuitive alarm resounded through him. He isn't sure if it was the Neteru or himself. Maybe they had begun to interface with him already.

'You know your moon,' adds Johnny, 'Was not originally part of your solar system. The Neteru commandeered it hundreds of thousands of years ago from their own star system. They travelled through space in it before setting it up in earth's orbit. Today, as some of you know, it is a vast, derelict ruin. The hard titanium crust and hollowed core have served as a base of sorts for visitors for thousands of years.'

'Really! Incredible! I suppose that could be why the early moon missions were abandoned,' says Jimmy. He had read about the moon in the bible, but wasn't aware that it had been brought there by the Neteru. 'So, Johnny, then I assume you take great stock in the fact that the Neteru chose earth – such a beautiful little gem, and obviously much coveted. How long were they here before you found them?'

'Many thousands of years. But by then they had integrated and had been absorbed by the indigenous people, before the cataclysm destroyed their continent. Earth may be beautiful, but it can be unstable and dangerous. There are many rogue asteroids and crust anomalies.'

'Our best defence. Who else would want earth?'

'Indeed, then we do have an understanding. I want to extend to you, Jimmy, our sincerest regards to your advances. We have faith in you and wish you the most success.'

'But, Johnny, there is something I do not understand,' declares Jimmy.

Johnny looks at him impassively.

'Why,' Jimmy continues, 'do you need us – I'm referring to the humans – Darrell for example – to do the containing, if we do have an "understanding"? I feel you must have some ulterior motive, or you just don't trust us.'

'First of all, Jimmy, human is human, and as such can easily be misunderstood. We conduct our surveillance on the human condition, to understand better the human condition. It would be false to say we have nothing to gain by our eavesdropping; on the contrary, our understanding is very much behooved. You have toured the ranch; is it not a little less intimidating than say the cold sterility of a purely Reticulan vessel? We have been here for a long time and have learned to desire a greater understanding. Do not construe an ulterior motive by us. Our civilisation trembles at the notion.'

'You have no idea, Johnny, how the average person would do just that.'

'Or Hollywood.'

They both have a final laugh. Jimmy is momentarily allayed of any doubt regarding their intentions, but the old saying: know your enemy, couldn't help but present itself in his mind. There are too many unanswered questions. There are the nagging doubts that the Reptoids are more interested in humanity precisely because it is defenceless.

For three days after his experience on the ranch, Jimmy finds himself rather depressed. It should have been obvious why, but his heartfelt mood keeps evading his usual cerebral rationale. The experience has so shocked him, the reverberations of the encounter cloud the methodical aspect of his mind, disallowing any due process. Instead, he takes delight in the beauty of the desert at night in Dreamland. Even during the day, he would hike up a rocky outcrop where he could see down the valley for twenty miles. Although barren and devoid of much flora, the very faint pulse of nature there and old Indian spirits still signified awe and wonder at terrestrial existence. The comfort of earth should not to be overlooked. The specter of blueball earth looming invitingly as they had re-entered the atmosphere stuck in his mind. He realised that for whatever lay ahead, this bounteous planet would never be taken for granted as some cog of an alien agenda, no matter how many planets like earth there were in the universe.

Jimmy ruminated on his talk with the inordinate Darrell and the sagaciously reasonable Johnny. He doesn't care whether they are discriminating or not; humans too, are formidable and would stop at nothing to protect their own containment. That evening as he sits once again watching the blood red sky spill across the west, he understands what he must do, at least for himself, if not humanity. No alien program would stop him, and subsequently no local one either. How could they distinguish between a terrestrially raised human and an extraterrestrial one from the ranch? He knows why they had let him see the full picture. They wanted his compliance because the whole program is based on compliance, though mutually beneficial for the time being. The aliens know he wouldn't talk for fear of shaking the tree, and bring the locals down all over him. His people would exclaim in an apoplectic fit that an implant had taken over his mind! His credibility would surely be questioned.

The stakes are getting higher and higher. He must go it alone, play along as best he could and garner what he could from the chip which was purportedly of no use to the Reptoids. But he is of some use obviously; only now he sees how they could be of use to him.

That evening, he decides to push a few buttons. He and Colonel Good are seated in the lounge after their repast.

'Colonel,' says Jimmy, sipping his mint tea, 'I have a request.'

'Here to listen,' utters the Colonel with his coffee.

'I want to convene a meeting with MJ-12.'

'We're meeting next month, as usual.'

'We need to meet now.'

'Why?'

'A thought occurred to me: the Greys have been creating hybrids, such as Lilly for example.'

'Yes.'

'They have also been creating full-blood humans.'

'Not here they aren't.'

'I saw a great deal of human activity on the ship.'

The Colonel looks at him. Jimmy carefully gages his reaction.

'Humans,' says Colonel Good, 'You mean what looked like humans. We know that they use humans for various tasks. What they do with sperm and egg out there is not our concern down here.'

'But has the possibility of their using these humans here on earth ever been seriously scrutinized?'

'For what? Human then would be human. We shouldn't have a problem with that; they would be subjected to the same laws and restraints as any citizen. There are billions of us and few of them. It would take a great many imposters to control the vote, if that's what you're getting at.'

'Yes, but what if these quasi-humans get into positions of responsibility that could work to undermine our self-determination?'

'I see your point; we should know who they are and issue special visas that allow us to monitor their lives. However, we abide by democracy; people have rights. Do you think that these people would sue us? That'd blow their cover wide open, leaving them fair game,' the Colonel jokes, his tone a bit mocking, as if he really doesn't want to believe Jimmy. 'Besides, how in hell could we know the difference between us and them?'

'That goes without saying, but I'm not talking about legalities,' says Jimmy straight-faced.

'Then what?' sighs the Colonel, giving in a little.

'I'm quite concerned about our status, here.'

'Are you inferring MJ-12?' asks Colonel Good, doubtfully.

'Hear me out,' claims Jimmy intently.

'Believe me, I'm listening.'

'Could it be that our policy of containment has been unwittingly and dogmatically perpetuated to make us think we are controlling the situation, when in fact the aliens have inculcated our response in order to hasten their own agenda unhindered? The longer we hold out, the sooner they will have us. Just a theory, mind.'

'The absolute excoriation of the program, Jimmy, in the public eye, would ultimately bring us into conflict with the aliens, especially so if we learn to use their technology and start gallivanting through space. To them we're like the barbarians at the gate.'

'But remember the Alamo, Colonel: ultimately, the few sacrificed for the many. I don't think we have to guess the reaction of society once we throw in our hand, so-to-speak. I don't think nuclear war is any kind of resolution, mind you, but a helluva deterrent,' remarks Jimmy.

'True, but nuclear war is hardly worth winning; and how few is few?'

'No, it isn't, but they are smarter than us and know that. Therefore, we must be able to prove to them we have the resolve to destroy ourselves rather than to submit, if that is the only recourse we have.'

'But the aliens aren't threatening us in any way.'

Jimmy checks himself before answering. 'No, they play a perfect game: they play on our heightened sense of self-preservation and our being threatened by their technological superiority, our paranoia regarding our own security, and most of all our fear of integration. The sky is the limit to what the aliens could do surreptitiously if an understanding is established in which these fears have been assuaged.'

Colonel Good for all his loyalty and efficiency cannot make that supposition when there isn't any obvious threat. 'Don't fix it if it ain't broke,' he says.

'I just want to discuss this with the whole panel, Colonel. It warrants it.'

'But it's not an emergency, Jimmy.'

'I think infiltration of their humans among ours could be very serious. Our consolidation or position is eroding to theirs. Do you get my point?'

'I tell you what: let's think about it. We can write up a report and present it next meeting. Would that suffice?'

'I hope so. I just have a feeling the clock is ticking.'

'To what?'

'Domination.'

'Domination?'

'Yes.'

'All because of a few humans on the ship?'

'Not specifically.'

'What then?' asks the Colonel.

'The Neteru.'

'What do the Neteru have to do with this?'

'I think the Reptoids absorbed the Neteru.'

'Absorbed?'

'Dominated,' states Jimmy, getting up. 'I believe we are the surviving vestiges of the Neteru and they fear our re-emergence.'

'What exactly did they do to you up there, Jimmy?' wonders the Colonel a little too sceptically.

Jimmy laughs as he holds the back of his chair. 'They served me apple pie and ice cream. Did you know they, the quasi-humans, call the ship The Ranch?'

The Colonel smiles. 'No,' he says. 'What else did they do to you?'

'They served me a damned good dose of paranoia,' Jimmy adds, thinking perhaps he should say no more. Any mention of the implant or Johnny Appleseed could only impinge upon his standing with the Colonel.

'Well, we can rest assured that's precisely why we're here,' declares Colonel Good sincerely.

But that is exactly why Jimmy is worried. Who are we? Do we really know who is who?

Jimmy spends the subsequent days working vigorously on the Meteor, which he had begun to see not so much as an advance for humankind, because it would never be declassified, but as his personal safety valve if ever there comes a time he might have to bail out.

True to his word, Colonel Good prepares a report without using Jimmy's name that addressed some of the concerns he raised. Jimmy feels relieved that the Colonel still respected their quietude.

At the meeting held in an old farmhouse in Maryland near Washington, it is proposed that a think-tank should come up with a solution to deal more quickly with such a threat. They stipulate that a criteria of evidence be established to warrant any use of force. However, as a whole the committee is not prepared to back down on the containment policy. It is just too beneficial, mutual or not. It is a policy just too entrenched to safely find a way out; and with no visible or even credible threat, the present objectives are to be maintained. Ultimately, the only result of Jimmy's initiative is the creation of the code Blue Phoenix. This would be enacted under the most serious of circumstances dealing specifically with human aliens. There would have to be an obvious move by an alien or aliens to penetrate society and solicit some incumbent political power to open up for public viewing the reality of the situation, hence furthering the purported fear of transgression by aliens. By raising the stakes with Blue Phoenix, MJ-12 had effectively muzzled a window of opportunity to lift the secrecy and deal with the problem democratically. But now the free world was to be subjected to further punitive action. MJ-12 believes that by enlightening society, they would be playing neatly into the alien's hands. The aliens would be seen to be in control, and humanity in no way ready to deal with alien reality. MJ-12 just couldn't accept the consequences of that no matter how benign integration with aliens was proposed. The perceived chaos and instability to the status quo might well bring about mass hysteria if all the truth became known. Blue Phoenix was precisely the kind of response they thought appropriate to counter the gravity of the threat, the one problem being, they were not at all sure how they could differentiate between human and quasi-human, therefore making any implementation redundant. Jimmy is disappointed because Blue Phoenix cancels the true purpose of the threat that he had originally disclosed; the point was to enlighten humanity and bring the situation mainstream, not curtail it further. It appears to Jimmy that nobody in MJ-12 understands what he was really trying to say without revealing the Neteru. Needless to say, the gift had him muzzled if he was going to keep his position inside alien politics. He would have to bide his time until an opportunity arose.

While Jimmy is in Washington to attend a reception that evening, he hears over the news in his Willard Hotel room that Danielle was to address the General Assembly of the United Nations in New York the following day.

Using a pay phone, Jimmy calls Max Light's special line and leave a message that he would be in New York for the evening. He knows Max will book him a room near Danielle who always stayed at the Plaza off Central Park. They had had a few rendezvous' there before in years gone by.

The next day is a busy one for Jimmy. He books himself on a flight from Baltimore to New York for the early afternoon. Then he rents a car and drives to Sharpsburg, Maryland, early in the morning to get out of the capital before rush hour traffic. The season is fall and the leaves are beginning to change. The tranquil charm of the cultivated Maryland countryside relaxes him. His destination is a small farm adjacent to Antietam Creek slightly to the north of where the infamous Civil War battle of the same name had been fought almost one hundred and eighty years before. To the present day it remains as one of the bloodiest battles in American history, where over twenty thousand men, young and old were casualties on the field of battle. A haunting place for old Doc Williams – his predecessor in MJ-12 – to retire, muses Jimmy.

He pulls into the driveway that goes down an embankment and along the creek through a forest before emerging to a well-groomed lawn and new buff-brick dwelling. There is an older model pickup truck parked in the driveway and a woman on the walkway turns to see him park.

'Hello,' she says. 'Can I help you?'

She is in her thirties, buxom and blond.

'Hi,' says Jimmy, getting out of his car. 'Is this the Williams residence?'

'Yes.'

'I apologise for coming unannounced. I was a colleague of Dr. Williams, and I just happened to be in the neighbourhood. Well, I thought I should say hello. Jimmy Pidgeon's my name.'

The woman stands there and smiles, leaning on truck squinting in the sun. 'Sure,' she says. 'I'm his granddaughter, Sally. He's down in the garden. Just follow the path around front.'

Jimmy thanks her and follows her directions. The old man is on his knees in a modest garden clipping some herbs.

'Dr. Williams.'

The old man turns around, smiles and continues to work. 'If I don't get these out today, the leaves will lose their power,' he says curiously, almost lethargically, not seeming to recognise Jimmy.

'Take your time,' says Jimmy. 'Don't mind me. It's a lot of work, gardening.'

'There are only the rewards . . . pardon me,' says Dr. Williams, slowly standing and straightening. He turns and faces Jimmy. He is tanned and wrinkled with wispy white hair. Extending his hand, he adds, 'Actually, don't mind me. Have we met before?'

He doesn't recognise me, thinks Jimmy. This is strange.

Shaking his hand, Jimmy introduces himself in name only. 'Jimmy Pidgeon, sir, and the labours of the garden are in the bounty of it all. And yes, we have met on a number of occasions in Dreamland.'

The doctor does not seem to comprehend what was said.

'Call me Doc, Jimmy; yes, well, you know what they say around here: Civil War dead make great fertilizer.'

Jimmy doesn't know whether to laugh or commiserate.

'There was a field hospital here on this very site,' reveals the Doc. 'I found a grave of limb bones, boot soles and buttons. Gruesome, after all these years.'

'A bit of a shock, I'd say,' utters Jimmy, intrigued.

'So what can I do for you, Mr. Pidgeon?' asks Doc.

'I work in the Program, Doc. I need to speak to you about something confidentially.'

'And what program might that be, Jim?'

'The Program, you know MJ-12.'

'Never heard of it,' he says looking at Jimmy assuredly.

'I thought you worked there,' says Jimmy, confused. 'I know you worked there.'

'Worked in research all my life.'

'As a genetic engineer?'

'Yes, with the National Foundation of Science.'

'You were chairman of that and the Naval Research Committee and Institute of Defense Analysis.'

'Yes . . . '

'Lilly says hello, Doc.'

'Lilly who?'

'Lilly Grey,' answers Jimmy, losing his composure.

Dr. Williams seems genuinely unaware.

'Are you not familiar with X13?' asks Jimmy, really bewildered.

'Never heard of it. Who do you work for again?' he asks a little suspiciously.

'Ah, Leghorn Industries. I guess I was mistaken; well thank you for your time, Dr. Williams. I'd best be on my way.'

'Mistaken about what?' asks the Doc, now concerned.

'About your being able to help me.'

'You haven't asked for my help.'

Jimmy decides to go for broke.

'I need to know whether or not you were subjected to special treatment by the aliens.'

'Aliens? What aliens?'

'It doesn't matter; I'm sorry to have bothered you.'

Jimmy turns and walks back to his car. Doc Williams calls after him saying, 'Sorry, for the trouble, Jim.'

Sally is still on the drive watering the flowers.

'That was quick,' she says.

'Sally,' says Jimmy, 'How long has your grandfather been retired?'

'About ten years. But he still was being consulted up to a couple of years ago. Why?'

'I thought he'd been retired just last year.'

'He worked in research all his life.'

'With the National Foundation of Science.'

'Yes.'

'Do you recall any accident that may have happened to him?'

'Accident? No. Why?'

'Must be a different Williams. The one I'm looking for had some kind of accident.'

'What kind?' she queries.

'Something to do with his head; you'd know for sure, maybe a scar on the back of his head.'

'Granddad has a scar on the back of his head.'

'Yeah, from what?'

'I don't know; I've seen it when I cut his hair.'

'Is it right about here?' Jimmy points to the center at the back of his head.

'Yes, how did you know?'

'I was told.'

'Then you do have the right Doc Williams,' she says. 'Didn't you recognise him?'

'One of them.'

'Huh?'

'Sally, your grandfather worked on ultra classified matters of National Security. But he can never talk about it. Do you understand?'

'I never realised . . .'

'How could you? But everything is fine. I was just checking up on him. He's a great guy. And we never had this conversation, okay?'

'Okay,' she says nervously, as Jimmy gets into his car and speeds away. On his way to Baltimore, Jimmy knows there is only one explanation. If Doc Williams had retired ten years before, who was the Doc Williams who had retired just before his own promotion to MJ-12 this year? Could it be that the real Doc Williams was gone and the gardener was an imposter? Yet he had the scar. The scar could have been from something else or it was a scar from the removal of an implant. Perhaps the aliens retired the real Doc Williams ten years ago when he was rejected by the implant and was replaced by a clone. But how could the aliens replicate the same man and make him oblivious to the program? Supposing they could, they must then have had someone working on the inside to do what they did without MJ-12 being aware of the situation, someone who could cover for the cloning. Who could it be? Colonel Good? The Secretary of State? The Director of the National Security Agency? The Director of the CIA? Or even the President?

All the way to New York, Jimmy's mind keeps revolving in a frenzy of paranoia. He checks in at the Plaza. Max had reserved him a room. The first thing he does is look up Mayhew, Lester in the tele-directory on the room videophone. He finds it and calls to ask for Darrell.

'Mr. Lester is unavailable. Who, may I ask, is calling?' comes the reply. On the screen a lady in her fifties appears.

'Tell him MJ and to call me at this number at his earliest convenience.'

He gives her the number and waits, and waits. At seven p.m. after he'd given up, the phone beeps. Jimmy picks it up and Darrell appears on the screen.

'Hi Darrell, I'm glad you made it back in one piece. How was re-entry?' asks Jimmy smiling.

'Excuse me; do we know each other?'

Jimmy half expects the response after his meeting with Dr. Williams.

'We met on the ship, remember? The Ranch?'

'The ship? What ship?'

'The Zeta Reticulan around Mars. Come on, man!'

'Is that a club?'

'No, man, a space ship!'

'Listen buddy, I don't know what kind of fool joke this is. Are you some kind of game show promo for Tekwhiz?'

Jimmy sighs, but goes along with it.

'Yeah, yeah, that's what I am. Just checkin' up on ya, Darrell. Want to thank you for making me so much money.'

'What did you say your name was?'

'Piercemore, James Piercemore.'

'Are you one of those group investors?'

'Yeah, we like to remain anonymous, you know, reputations and the like.'

'I don't have a problem with that. So what about this ship thing. Sounds hilarious. Get me a few tickets, buddy?'

'Hell, ya don't need tickets; they'll just come and take you there for free.'

'Hey, I'm there. Could I bring my wife and kids?'

'Sure ya can . . . '

'How about this weekend?'

'Just answer this skill testing question.'

'All right.'

'Do ya love your mommy?'

Do I love my mommy?' he laughs. 'Why yes, sort of; she's my mother!'

'Sort of? What about your wife?'

'She's a peach.'

'I'm sorry Darrell, you lose.'

'What was I supposed to say, no?'

'No, I've got the wrong Darrell.'

'Give me a break, asshole.'

'Okay. The next time you make love with your wife, make a note of it and every time for a month and ask her to do the same. Then ask her how many times you did it that month. If it doesn't add up, don't blame it on her, blame it on the other Darrell . . . '

'Are you out of your fucking mind?'

'No, I'm doing you a favour. Aliens are abducting you and putting an imposter in your place . . . '

Click. You can't knock Jimmy for trying, although Darrell may have been better off not knowing. Maybe some good would come of it if Darrell suspected. Jimmy doesn't for a minute think imposter Darrell could have been that good an actor.

Ordering a meal in his room, Jimmy waits for some communication from Danielle. The call comes just past ten. She asks him to come up to her suite. Max knocks at Jimmy's door and escorts him personally past a number of security personnel into Danielle's rooms.

'Jimmy,' she says in her most cool voice, 'What a surprise!' She kisses him long and lovingly on the lips before letting him speak. 'You seem tense.' She adds, 'I'm the one who should be tense. Did you watch my speech today on CNN?'

'No, Danielle, I've been hard pressed lately.'

'You seem bedraggled. What's wrong?'

'Let's relax, okay.'

And relax they do. Both now in their early sixties, they have lost none of their youthful vigour when it comes to their hard-won loving. They conjoin in a passion, an envy of newlyweds.

Afterwards, blissful sleep closes their eyes before a word is spoken. Unfortunately for Jimmy, Danielle has be up at six and out to the airport on route to Europe. Groggily, Jimmy gets up too, and tries to explain what he knows.

'You mean to say aliens implanted some kind of device in your brain?' she asks aghast.

'It's okay; it doesn't hurt. Listen, we don't have much time. We'll have to talk about this when I come home at Christmas; just don't say anything to anybody, or I'm dead and perhaps you too for that matter.'

'Me?'

'Danielle, I've screwed up . . . '

'It's hardly your fault; they put a device in your . . . '

'Danielle, because of me there is a new emergency security code. I think I've inadvertently cornered us.'

'Jimmy, what on earth are you talking about?'

'The aliens know about us. They've known about us all along.'

'What makes you say that?' asks Danielle in an almost humourously matronizing way. She holds him close to her lily-white breasts.

'They must need us somehow. We fit into their big picture. They know how to manipulate our intelligence to make us work in their best interests.'

'How's your head, Jimmy?'

'You're not listening, Danielle! We must talk about this! Devise a plan of action!'

'All right, but first shouldn't you have your head looked at by a doctor? I know one who is very discreet . . .'

'Danielle, you're missing the point. This is only the tip of the iceberg. Everything I've told you about Dreamland is dwarfed by what I know now. We must talk. Our lives depend on it. But I need time to complete my project at S-4.'

'How much time?'

'Hard to say. Five years,' he says dejectedly.

'Five years! Jimmy, you're not making any sense. You talk as if the world's going to end tomorrow. Now you listen to me! In a nutshell, what on earth are you talking about?'

'They are a dispassionate race! I think they fear our emergence into space because we are the Neteru. We are innocent, basically; evolving naturally. They exchange technology for our compliance concerning their presence. Yet they slowly mobilise in various ways ultimately to absorb our DNA. We are a valuable resource to these people; otherwise they would leave us alone! We must speak out – eventually – and as a race resist them! It's up to you, Danielle; you have the power and the credibility to pull it off, but not before I say so or they will kill you and me. Then we're doomed.' He looks down at his older, naked legs on the edge of the bed. She lets him go and stands there naked holding her underpants, looking as if she is seeing a ghost.

'Jimmy, for God's sake, I think you need to come home for a while. You're ranting and raving about the most ridiculous things I've ever heard! What has gotten into you?'

Jimmy stands up and goes to her and observes closely her body. He fondles her breasts, sniffed behind her ears, feels her genitals.

'What are you doing?' she utters.

'I love you, Danielle and don't want anything bad to happen to us.'

'Jimmy, Jimmy, I love you too,' she says seductively. 'But I've never seen you like this.'

'I am in full capacity of my senses, Danielle. The aliens can replicate DNA and create identical people. I just want to be sure you are the real Danielle.'

'Well, am I?' she queries haughtily, though humoured by his seriousness.

'Yes.'

'How can you tell?' she says teasing.

'I'd know your scent anytime, anywhere. It can't be duplicated.'

'Oh, Jimmy, maybe we have time, just quickly,' she purrs mischievously.

He smiles and they both fall back on the bed, but are interrupted by Max knocking.

'Twenty minutes!' yells Danielle.

Later, on her way out, she looks at Jimmy sympathetically. 'Jimmy, you know the routine: wait here until I've gone down the elevator. Max will return and let you out. Now be vigilant and be cool. Love you!' And she is gone.

'That Christmas,' says Cephren to Redman, 'Jimmy told his daughter, Andie that she and her husband, Rob, must build an underground bunker system. He presented them with a set of drawings and showed them where he wanted it and how it was to be built down to every detail. They were shocked at the size of it with numerous passages and huge rooms. It was to have a secret entrance from a well that was to be dug in an addition to the house. There would be a trap in the forest and a door entrance also in the forest . . .'

'And my Bunker is the remains of his very plan?' asks Redman incredulously.

'Not just the remains, Redman; I believe the whole system is still intact.'

'You mean to say all these years, I've been living in the very same Bunker Jimmy Pidgeon designed and where Flower Child lived?'

'There's more: Jimmy . . .'

Redman's beeping monitor interrupts their talk. Chromolox appears on the screen as his link is open.

'Redman,' she says, 'Is Cephren there?'

'Right here, Chromolox,' speaks up Cephren, moving within the vision of the screen.

'There you are. We have Anna on our main line with an officer. We'll connect you. I should say, she is not aware of our liberation here. Due to the circumstances, do you think we should inform her?'

Cephren thinks about it. Redman shakes his head.

'Too risky,' Cephren finally says. 'What she doesn't know can't hurt her, Chromolox.'

'Good, how is it going down there?' asks Chromolox effervescently.

'Great, I'll fill you in later. Would you have someone clean up my Loft? And what time do you want to meet?'

'Your Loft is already done, scrubbed top and bottom. Be here at six. Our final preparations are in progress. All quiet on the western front. The Americans are giving the Chicagos something to think about. Others are moving in to beef up the resolve. We'll brief you later. I'll connect you. Good to have you back, Cephren, safe and sound.'

Likewise, Chromolox. Thanks. Put her on.'

Anna Gram appears on the screen.

'Cephren! You're all right. I've . . . we've been worried sick about you! Where are you now? Has Barker treated you well?'

'As well as can be expected, Anna. I'm incarcerated at present . . . in the Pyramid. Barker has relented and is going to let me speak . . . I don't know when, or to whom, but so he said, so as not to upset the Earth Federation, and as long as I stick to world issues and keep Sunsetwind out of my vocabulary. How are you?'

'Oh, Cephren, desperately in love of course,' she gushes. 'You should've let me go in. I'm worried they won't let you out. Should I go to Africa, or wait?'

'Anna, Anna, what would I have done without you? If you want to wait, that would be okay, I suppose. But I'm going next week, anyway. We're on the final stretch of the campaign and there are still some major contenders for the Chair. But do as you please.'

'Are you sure you are all right?' she reiterates, concerned.

'You have no idea how good it feels to be back home, in spite of the Free Radicals,' he adds, in case they're being eavesdropped upon. 'I can't wait to see you.'

'We're going to be the happiest people alive, honey. You have no idea what I'm going to do to you.'

'I'm there all the way, Anna.'

'Okay, I'll head off to Nairobi tonight with Captain Dave. George gives you his best. Cleo is chomping at the bit. Love you.' She puts her hand up to the screen. Cephren does the same.

'Take care, Anna. Love you too.'

Cephren turns back to Redman.

'So you were saying, Cephren,' says Redman. 'Better move along here: this Neteru chip is trustworthy, you think?' he adds suspiciously.

'As true as the air we breathe, Redman; now where was I?'

'Jimmy designed the underground complex here,' reminds Redman, 'Presumably to hide from the aliens if necessary, or the world.'

'Well, as it turned out, five to six arduous years did go by, before Jimmy could finish and test the Meteor...'

The Bungalo is buzzing. Not only are there ten battalions of emops (one hundred to a battalion which comprised a whole division of one thousand) in the air circling about Windy City, but a hundred more divisions spread out around the whole country from Minnesota to Upstate New York where they face off with the Americans. Trinny herself is having fits of rage periodically throughout the day. Ever since Treason had manipulated her way out of Chicago with Heyoka's medallion, the seriousness of this loss was compounded each day. After a horrendous world tour, where she had fumed more and more as it progressed, she came home to throw a final fit of uncontrollable acerbity condemning every living thing out to get her. 'They hate me!' she spat. 'They'll taste my venom!' After her foiled attempt to retrieve the medallion through Barker, she promptly withdrew from the campaign race.

Deep within the Bungalo at the communications nerve center, where her people survey and monitor the world, she nevertheless continues her plan to take over the reins of power in North America in the name of unification as she had been pontificating all along. But no more of that: politics are inefficient. Only action would suffice. She had planned phase one to reinvade Sunsetwind to annex and subjugate it this time and not hand over the country to another Barker. He had proved to be a bigger "ass" than she had anticipated and above all, she wanted to scourge the country for the unumpentium, which Treason had so cagily swapped with a fake. In fact, that was the stick that broke the donkey's back for Trinny. Before then she still resisted withdrawing from the campaign in the possibility that the medallion would be retrieved. Afterwards, she lost all sense of humanity. There would be no more façade of civility, no more political linkage, no more religious white washing. It was gauntlet time as was inevitable, it seemed, when desperation found an excuse for absolute despotism. Even the people of Chicago were appalled at her lack of consideration for their views and constitutional infrastructures. They were powerless, however, because the system was built on totalitarian principles, rather a benevolent feudalism gone awry. Unfortunately, the standards of living were so high that nobody had the courage, nor venue by which to oppose her hegemony. Any sniff of dissent was met with too steep a price. Besides, obedience had been bred into all the strata of society. But now it was show time.

There is one person, or perhaps two, who take great delight in the rapidly escalating predicament of Chicago. Uncle Sam, of course, is stuck in the middle of a very difficult situation like a hot kitchen and a grease fire and worried that he might not get out before everything blew up in his face. His mother doesn't seem to notice him at all these days, which doesn't bother him really, because he finds time to sneak out and visit Heyoka at her window, although it had been strictly forbidden. Someone is supposed to be with him at all times, but he is very good at getting about undetected, besides in the crisis nobody paid much attention. The security staff are frantic with their own problems. He doesn't have access to any open monitor, so there is little harm he can do but get in their way, which he is careful not to do.

He and Heyoka have become quite close. She, being thirty years of age, is just comfortable for him as a motherly figure. Yet, she is the type who can identify easily with his eleven years making their time together fun, notwithstanding the love she radiated.

The crisis that has being boiling now for the past twelve hours, has taken so much of Trinny's time that little Sam finds himself with more freedom than ever before. The first thing he does is to go to her window and lets himself in. Trinny never followed through by sealing her window that ironically was the link to all her present problems. Sam doesn't think a lot about the problems; all he wants is to go out on the campaign trail with his dad and Anna Gram. Anna Gram had become quite an obsession, at least from an eleven-year-old's perspective. In fact, his own mother unwittingly unleashed his youthful imagination, by forcing the Gospel Party, the municipal authority in Windy City, to allow the back-to-back showing of Anna Gram's early cinema classics. The Gospels, however, being a powerful lobby and ruling denomination within the power grid and a growing threat to Trinny's "democracy" (demockery as they term it), do as they are told and release the films through their licensing agency to the many outlets. It is perceived that if the world was to get an overdose of an x-rated Anna Gram in and out of the buff, the voting public would denounce her and Cephren outright. The human condition, of course being as it is, doesn't read it that way. Most of the world rights distributed through Chicago couldn't have done more to lavish attention onto her. Even the Gospels, who controlled the distribution, are impressed by the very redeeming qualities both Anna and Cephren express politically, albeit shocked by her early films. Meanwhile, Sam and Heyoka are treated to many an afternoon watching most of the delightful Piercemore masterpieces brought to the screen: the most notorious being Mount Serious, based on a novella by Piercemore, produced and directed by the revolutionary doyen of the cinema, Brázil Two Dogs. Two Dogs directed Anna during her first spectacular decade of superstardom, making them both immortal in that genre for their contributions.

While Heyoka would blush and put up her hands during the most sexual parts not before covering Sam with a blanket who nonetheless peeked to see for a moment the seduction by a hybrid female alien of a loyal and loving father and scientist. The terrible dilemma of the two central characters can't have been more poignantly expressed by their final impassioned plea to disembody each other from their separate realities. The final consummation seems to presage a sudden new paradigm shift in human evolution.

Heyoka then councils Sam about the movie in view of Cephren and Anna's relationship. She explains to Sam that although the movie was not appropriate for him and she had to cover him from time to time, it did nevertheless reveal to her through her own on-the-mark intuitions that both Anna and Cephren, although politically charismatic, are flawed as mates, so not to get his hopes up. This comes with no enmity or hidden motive; it is the sight of them together on the news, in the debates, and separately from various locations, where she observes them putting on an act. They are sincere in what they espouse, but are not natural politicians. Heyoka has a sudden flash that they have never slept together, though, at the same time something foreboding strikes her.

'Sam,' she says, while doing her pacing routine, 'Tell your mom she should visit me.'

'Why?' he replies.

'I fear she intends to kill Anna Gram.'

'No, she meant neutralise.'

'She's desperate. Your mom thinks the world will understand that she is most suitable to lead us into the 25th century.'

'By killing Anna Gram?' he asked incredulously.

'Yes, but she will destroy herself instead.'

'What should I do, Heyoka?'

'Tell your mom not to hurt herself. Tell her she must stop the hurting. Tell her Anna Gram is in danger. Tell her Heyoka said so, and that I called you outside the window.'

'She'll . . . she'll hurt you then, and maybe lock me in my room.'

Heyoka looks into his sad, frightened blue eyes with her strange, sunny brown-green eyes. 'We may never see each other again, Sam, but I doubt it; she's too busy to discipline you; besides you're already disciplined.' She kisses him on the cheek, gently.

Not an hour after Sam left with his message, Trinny shows up in Heyoka's room. She is actually calm, neither frothing at the mouth, nor cynical with invective. She is in fact almost morose, looking flat, even fatalistic. When she opens the door, she shuts it gently and leans back on it not saying a word. Heyoka can see that she is taking a time-out from her rage. Ever since the medallion incident, Trinny had disdainfully kept her distance from Heyoka, although she liked to stop by and get her little fix of Heyoka's peculiar spiritual medicine once in a while. Over time, the more hooked she became in these meetings, she reached the point that her time with Heyoka is the only respite she had.

'Is this the end, Heyoka?' asks Trinny finally.

'Yes,' says Heyoka quietly.

'The Yellow Tooths are out there too. The Texans. The Anishnabe. The Prairies. The Californias. O'Reilly and his Mujahedin. The English. The Americans, of course.'

'They wish to make peace,' says Heyoka.

'There can be no peace.'

'Why?'

'Because I . . . I cannot . . . abide by their terms,' she declares with growing venom, and then lashes out: 'I will fight to the death!'

Heyoka goes to her and comforts her.

'Why sympathise with your abductor?' Trinny weeps now, sickeningly schizophrenic.

'I sympathise with your pain,' says Heyoka.

'I am a murderer,' she cries.

'It is time to stop and face yourself. The enemy within.'

'It's too late. She's dead. The vain bitch is dead.'

'I am sorry.'

'Anna's dead.'

A shocking silence marks the tragedy.

'I am sorry,' manages Heyoka again feebly, beginning to cry too. They cry together. 'If vanity is life, Trinny, ineluctable life, given freely, why kill her? If need be, why not me?'

'I don't know,' she sniffs, 'I hated her . . . but I don't anymore . . . maybe I killed the hate . . . I could never kill you..I love you!' Trinny slides to the floor a sobbing, pathetic wretch. Heyoka puts her hand on her shoulder and kneels there beside her, head bowed.

Jimmy Pidgeon knows how to keep his mouth shut. He learns from working in the Program that obedience is a significant attribute. One could do as one wished within the parameters of one's field of work; but any deviance from policy directives is met with swift retribution. It isn't the people he works with who carry out this action; it is another authority completely, who hadn't any idea of what one did; as directed they just contain any potential security leak. They are a special group highly trained under the auspices of the National Security Agency (NSA). This team, newly code-named Blue Phoenix, is on the go anywhere and anytime. It would erase lives if the occasion warranted it just like the air-brushing of a person in a photo. Such a job would be made to look natural with a reasonable cover story that would suffice to cover their tracks.

So Jimmy understands the rules. He also understands the stakes, as well as the truth. But he cannot reveal the truth, because the truth is a lie as far as MJ-12 is concerned. Jimmy has tried to alert very carefully to his fellow MJs the duplicity of their so-called containment by the Greys and by extension the Reptoids. He knows of course that the MJ-12 policy is compliance. It is certainly easier to deal with the suppression of something people are hardly prepared to believe in any way, rather than open up the whole logistical nightmare MJ-12 envisioned if they knew the truth. In effect,this smokescreen is a policy of slowing down humanity's technical evolution as well as our biological, therefore to ease into the horrific future and buy time to catch up. But Jimmy knows that indeed this is not the case as reasonable as it sounds. Humankind is in fact setting itself up on a platter for the Reptoids, if not to be absorbed as Johnny intimated, but dominated. The Reptoid's amazing use of gene replication is a process of absorption, no one being the wiser. Eventually, humanity's will to self-determination would be bartered away by reasonable compromises. The only panacea to this, is of course, exposure – letting the chips fall where they may. Yet exposure can mean any number of scenarios including obliteration, which would not do. What is to be done?

For six years Jimmy fretted in the hope that just maybe with the completion of the Meteor he would have his safety valve. He envisions Danielle, being true to her word, making the exposition of the millennium, and then the subsequent denial by the general powers, and her repeated rebuffs, and his presentation of the living proof in the Meteor on the White House lawn and every capital in the Western hemisphere. It would be undeniable: no debunking, discrediting, or censorship could wipe the reality off a billion screens around the world.

The risk, of course, is Danielle's life. Her very expostulation hopefully would serve to protect her. To assassinate her would certainly point the finger at those most vehemently opposed to her allegations. And in the aftermath, they couldn't really explain away her credibility and write her off as a lunatic. Nevertheless, there is the possibility that her assertions would be downplayed and that any unified effort to eke out the truth would be stonewalled barring his showing off the Meteor, until the status quo grudgingly accepted the new reality. Jimmy knows alien exposure is a terrible risk and fully expressed his reservations to Danielle, who wouldn't hear of any backing down. For her, it is the *pièce de resistance* of her entire life. Remembering her roots, her adolescence out there on the perimeter with Jim Morrison and the big beat, (not to mention young Jimmy Pidgeon crafting into words and astro-physics his and Danielle's bizarre dynamics), then her political career and hard-won respect, she now has to do what she was chosen to do, what her whole life had set her up to do: defy the odds, ultimately, universally.

In hindsight, he sees his reluctance to go ahead with their plan as a last ditch effort to avert an unprecedented tragedy. Danielle, he fears more and more, would self-destruct. No matter how eminent her standing in the world, disbelief and shock would be the first manifestation of her revelations. Jimmy's Meteor would be passed off by the military as a skunk works invention gone awol. A classified project then would have been downgraded and after a few weeks all but old news.

For several years, Jimmy had been accessing the Neteru to the best of his ability. He had set up programs to make his interfacing easier to retrace and bring "on-line" things that by their elusive nature are lost in the vortex of its infinite variations or synaptic processes. He would ground himself to his old computer and plug in his own password code: The Midpoints. Only he knows whose midpoints they are on the solar zodiac as no one of any consequence knew about his relationship with Danielle, except his daughter and son-in-law who were out of the big picture and enjoyed their privacy. Then plugging in what he knew from the Program's "Bible" regarding the immediate space within fifty light years of earth and his knowledge from the Neteru, he had a holographic map of sorts. Stemming from Zeta 1 and Zeta 2 of the Reticulae star system, he traced the Grey's most frequently travelled routes. The sun is off their beaten track so-to-speak – a long thirty-seven light year span, but incidentally a stepping stone for interstellar travel from other precincts of the galaxy. What strikes him, are the series of local life-supporting star systems that begin from Epsilon Eridani, through Tau Ceti, 107 Piscium, 54 Piscium to Gliese 67. Then there is another route from Tau 1 Eridani to both Gliese 59 and 67. Alpha Centauri and Alpha Mensae are other systems but younger. He knows that Tau 1 Eridani had been adopted by humanoids though had succumbed to be completely dominated by the Greys and the Reptoids who came from afar, their nearest stars being Castor and Pollux more than 60 light years away. But on 82 Eridani, the so-called humans there, had held their own, though they had at one time been assisted by the Greys. In the Bible there was something termed the Eridani Frequency mentioned by 'abductees' or 'contactees' as some liked to be called. Jimmy often wonders how the Eridanis managed to avert the domination of the Reptoids, when they were helped by the Greys.

A few years back, after she had gotten back together with her husband, Billy the Navajo, Cora Little Feather once asked Jimmy if he would meet her best friend, a woman named Rhonda who had married into the reservation like herself. Rhonda was part Cherokee from Oklahoma, and had spoken to Cora about her experiences with aliens over the course of her life. Jimmy had agreed to the meeting, feigning ignorance, but was sympathetic to her consternations and listened to her story about the benevolent Greys, who were not like the 'others'. She claimed that Zeta 1 had resisted the Reptoids while Zeta 2 succumbed and that through the Eridani Frequency as she termed it, the Reptoids had decided to by-pass Eridani. Probed by Jimmy on what this frequency meant, though he had read about it himself, she replied that she didn't know, but that they were enlightened and technically advanced enough to deter somehow the Reptoids as long as the Eridanis left earth's solar system alone, which is why humankind had not been visited by them more often. Then there were the Itibians who originated near the center of the Milky Way and were well out of the Reptoids sphere of influence, but no one knew anything about them except their name.

Jimmy took the meeting in stride and basically said there was nothing to fear from the Sky People, and he couldn't imagine why they would want to harm humanity in any way. He thanked her for coming to him, but stated that there was little he could reveal to her other than what he had said.

Jimmy attempted to solicit Lilly on the issue of the Eridani Frequency, but she became uncharacteristically coy on the subject which naturally spurred him into thinking there was something to it. He concluded that Big Cheese, Bart and Lilly must be Reticulans from Zeta 2 and Rhonda's Greys from Zeta 1 of those star systems.

One time soon after Lilly's evasive response, she persuaded Jimmy to take a trip with her to the base in Antarctica. Under the ice shelf near the undersea entrance, she stopped the craft, a small Zeta 2 reconnaissance disc, and began to put on the airs of a naughty debutante. Jimmy, slightly humoured, began to worry when she semi-paralysed him with the stare. Immobilised, Jimmy was straddled by Lilly on his lap and she whispered into his sixty-seven year old ear, sweet nothings she had borrowed from every sexy Hollywood film she had ever seen.

'No, Lilly,' he struggles under her power, 'This is wrong.'

'No, it isn't,' she insists strangely.

'Why?' is all he can say.

'Because this is the only way we can conceive a child together,' she says.

'It is against my will; please Lilly, it offends me. Love must be mutual,' he pleads. But her mind control overwhelms him and she coerces a sexual response.

'No, no, no,' he says resisting hopelessly. His rejection is so powerful that she relents for a moment.

'I'm sorry,' she says, moving her little body off of him, but keeping him paralysed. 'I'll make you a proposition: in exchange for your love, albeit temporary, I will tell you about the Eridani Frequency.'

'And if I refuse?'

'I'll do it anyway.'

'But there are many men who would oblige you, Lilly; why must you force me?'

'I want to be human, but look at me!' she cries.

'But you are human, in many ways – these passions!'

'My mind is made up,' she pouts.

'I can't believe this is what you want,' murmurs Jimmy sadly.

'I promise you it is,' she squeaks. 'Wouldn't you rather have me than some complete stranger?'

'Is that the ultimatum?'

'I'm sorry Jimmy; we must not disappoint them. I promise you it won't happen again unless you wish it to.'

'Johnny has made you do it, hasn't he?'

'Yes,' she admits, 'But he believes our child will be of great importance and will be protected.'

'Protected from what?'

'Potential disaster on a colossal scale.'

'What kind of disaster?'

'An asteroid will be nudged by another to set it on a course for earth in 2126.'

'And how could he possibly know that seventy-nine years from now?'

'I don't know. That's what he said.'

And so Jimmy Pidgeon impregnated Lilly the Hybrid under the Antarctica ice shelf. What she told him afterwards, however, dwarfed that most personal violation of his self-respect.

'Forgive me, Danielle, forgive me,' he moans as they languish in the tepid after-shocks of their consummation.

'You love Danielle Perreault,' she says, still moving on him in agile little bursts, her thin, white alien legs entwined rigorously about him. 'But I know what you deem to call love is a deception, an illusion; but do not think on it now. I love you Jimmy, more than you'll ever know.'

Jimmy refrained from answering, so demoralised was he in his perceived weakness. She then trumpeted her conquest by ignoring his depression and soothingly spoke of what she knew.

'The Eridani Frequency is a highly calibrated artificially induced electromagnetic harmonic that is very unpopular with the Reptoids. It is harmless to us, but in their species, they have a built-in radar-like sense, which is seriously disrupted and causes vertigo to one exposed to it for any length of time. If humans learn how to use the spirit of the Frequency – that is to say, practice living life on as high a harmonic as possible – then at least the spirit of the frequency is achieved. Obviously, spirit is not a threat to the Reptoids, but highly evolved people will not be willingly absorbed by them and resist their hegemony. The replication of genes is easily transferred from enlightened people, or an evolved race, because they are more simplified to the point that the Reptoids fear their passivity; this is why they wish to keep you contained indefinitely.'

'But what of the technology?' asks Jimmy.

'Technology is the sugaring, Jimmy, since time immemorial. People are enticed, then subjected to technology. And power is in the hands of those who control it.'

'Tell me then how they replicate people like Darrell.'

'They simply neutralise his normal synaptic waves as we do with abductions, except this process is more complete. They rearrange his conscious memory . . .'

'But he was raised on the ranch.'

'Yes and no, his biological twin – and there may be numerous biological entities – are raised concurrently, one in Queens, say, and one on the ranch; but both are interchanged with identical memories, except that the ranch twin retains both worlds – when it is convenient – while the Queens original has only his terrestrial memories that are interfaced with his changeling during his own spate in that role. In other words, each one's experience is compounded as one in the other, with the one exception that neither is aware of the other and one of them has no memory of the ranch.'

'Yet, what of Doc Williams? He had a twin too?'

'Yes.'

'From that long ago? He's old.'

'He was a prototype.'

'Then why not me?'

'You were a discovery. There has been some discussion as to whether or not to use you for a new generation.'

'A discovery?'

'Once you entered the Program. Johnny really likes you.'

'What if he knew what I know now?'

'Believe me, no matter what you do he'll still like you. In spite of our agenda, there is deep compassion.'

'Does our . . . you know, being together, have anything to do with this?'

'I was to feel you out and . . . have you . . . reasonably, if possible.'

'So you really were put up to this?'

'I didn't want to; but I couldn't bear the thought of someone else doing it, so I volunteered and they accepted.'

'God, what will you do if you're pregnant? Give the baby to them?'

'Not if I can first give it away to a good home; but they will find out and deal with me. And I am pregnant or will be over the next few hours.'

'How do you know?' asks Jimmy.

'I just ovulated.'

'What will they do with you?'

'Send me to Zeta, probably.'

'So you're not against me, Lilly.'

'Against you? Never. Yet anyone of us would say the same. But I know what you mean. You wish to see the Eridanis, don't you?'

'I just want to rid earth of the containment,' says Jimmy, dejectedly.

'The Zeta 1s would contain you too.'

'But perhaps with a little more respect and consideration.'

'Their objectives are not so devastating, but similar.'

'You mean to say, the Eridanis are under the power of Zeta 1 too?'

'Zeta 1 beings are far more advanced, Jimmy, and enjoy their mutual benefit. There is certainly no racial discrimination.'

'And the Zeta 1s don't wish to dominate?'

'No,' she says, 'They are like our Neteru; some of us wish to be like them and remove the yoke of the Reptoids, but we haven't the resolve.'

The resolve. That was the question. How did one resolve the situation without bringing about chaos? For Jimmy, chaos was preferable to continued compliance. He felt that the great democratic institutions would very quickly get a grip on the situation. He didn't realise that a war, a world war would be the price to pay in just over thirty years into the future. The New Republicans or Radical Right, an emerging political force with teeth, would get a boost from Blue Phoenix and wage war on the United Front, showing the resolve necessary to destroy the vestiges of Reptoid containment which had been proven to have evil ulterior motives, as per humanity's self-determination. Blue Phoenix in this case was a horrible price, a Masadic response – to die rather than submit. Now that was resolve. And no one was the wiser, except the MJ-12. To the rest of the world, America had become a boiling cauldron waiting to spill over. A burgeoning and increasingly militant religious movement was to take a stand against the 'heathen establishment', which in many respects had come to control America through its impenetrable corporate hegemony over the average citizen and indeed the western world. The United Front was the 'establishment's' answer to the sectarian religious movement. It would be in 2072 that the New Republicans would finally win the Presidency, and the one after that. Their revolutionary policy-changes regarding everything from drastic socialisation of the corporate structure to mandatory ethical re-education, the complete shutdown of the bio-genetics industry and thousands of other initiatives would so polarise the country that the

United Front with the backing of the intelligence community would seek to do everything in its power to destroy the Radical Right. Catastrophe would strike when the President was assassinated June 5, 2077, along with about fifty men and women of his private guard, all microwaved by a flash bomb on a golf course. The panic that ripped through Washington and the Pentagon was both expected and dreaded. Within a year, the armed forces were divided, half backing the United Front out of Washington and the other half behind the Radical Right now based in Colorado with the headquarters under Cheyenne Mountain. It was thought for the first few months that reason would prevail, but war in Mexico, the Middle East, and South Asia precipitated a siege mentality. Terrorism reigned and the vicious circle of revenge perpetuated itself out of control. Then there was Colonel Jeremy Blaine, undercover in the Righteous, who under orders from his mentor General Good – both working outside the authority of MJ-12, which had been discovered to be controlled by the aliens – threatened a nuclear retaliation by citing New York, Washington, Atlanta and Mexico City as their targets. Most people had the chance to evacuate, but many refused to believe in the vituperative rhetoric and lost the gamble. Colonel Jeremy Blaine, of course, was the field commander of Blue Phoenix.

'I love you, Danielle; I love you,' says Jimmy, with a tinge of melancholy, 'More than you'll ever know.'

They are embracing on the simple wooden bed in a crude log cabin in the wilderness of northern Quebec. They had been camping there for a week at the end of August, just the two of them. Max had flown them in personally. The cabin had long been abandoned by the old Forest Fire Service, but had been discovered by Danielle and Jimmy on one of their many camping ventures. Camping, naturally, in the wilderness, is all the privacy they crave, except perhaps at the Park Plaza in Manhattan.

Their long enduring love for each other, over fifty years now, had been the very best and worst of times for each of them. Danielle's public life and intransigence regarding her past, and Jimmy's preoccupation with the Program had kept them agonisingly separated, but they learned to thrive in spite of it. Their needs both cerebral and physical, became so acute at times they literally burst into each other's arms when they got together. For days they would languish and saturate themselves in each other's love, to soon go their separate ways again.

This time is different. They had discussed it for years leading up to this moment. The Meteor is complete, and one of the great apogees of Jimmy's genius. All his life, he had been working for this day. The years of toil, trial and error, then breakthrough, could not have happened more perfectly. It seemed finally, the well-deserved light shone brilliantly down on the two of them now sunning on the rocks. It is the sun of the heavens bestowing the path of light to human salvation from its own turpitude and doom in the sights of the Reptoids.

The plan is simple enough, though Jimmy is still worried about Danielle. She is to address the European Parliament on the fifteenth of September. Jimmy will abscond with the Meteor and present it to the world, then as a precaution take Danielle into hiding once she returned to Ottawa if things became too difficult. Then she will address the entire world, and demand that people disassociate themselves with the Reptoids and seek some communication with the Eridanis, with whom they would accord their allegiance. Jimmy had made travel plans to escape with the help of Lilly. Once a formal agreement was in place for the world to accept, Danielle will retire from politics and marry Jimmy. They in turn would work together to facilitate this bold new venture for the human race. Humanity could then develop its own Eridani Frequency to protect people from any new threat from the Reptoids, if they were to persist.

Unfortunately, though, dreams have a way of running aground from a sea swell into the devastating shoals. Reality and dreams have their own tug of war. Often, the illusion of each gives false hope. What is left in pieces scattered along the wake, describes the calamity of best-laid plans. Usually, if there is a survivor, he or she will learn that only fate is the victor, and it will muster up a story all by itself to describe the events transpired with no beginning or end.

'Jimmy,' purrs Danielle with her legs wrapped tightly around him back on the cot, 'I love you too. And I want so much to marry you once I retire from politics.'

'As long as you don't see it as a new job,' he teases.

'Silly old man,' she contends.

The day is glorious and warm wafts of forest-scented air envelope them in an erotic embrace through the open window. They began to kiss. Before long they are once again enjoined in that indefatigable coupling that takes them soaring into their own Eridani Frequency. Releasing in a literal gush of emotional ecstasy, they eventually slumber magically for almost two hours. Rising naked, they take to the water and swim long and slowly across the pristine lake beneath the afternoon sun to bake on the rocks on the other side.

Later, around the evening fire, cooking beans and soup with baked bread, they talk a little shop.

'We have worked hard for this,' she says. 'People will listen. For almost a quarter century, I have devoted my life to the prosperity and well-being of Canadians and all citizens of the world. Through the proceeds of Hometech, we have done more for the third world, by far, than any organisation ever. There's one thing that I would still like to do – start up a Canadian Aerospace Institution. In fact when this is all over, maybe you and I can direct it. If the lid is blown off the containment, there will be some healthy competition around the globe for interstellar travel. We'll have a head start.'

Jimmy thinks about what she said. The firelight dances in their faces.

'If we're successful,' he says, 'A big if.'

'What could possibly go wrong? I've made a thousand speeches over the years. Most went over well, if not, at least noteworthy. This will be the speech of my life; hear me out: *Ladies, gentlemen, citizens of the world, I bid you to lend a keen ear to what I am about to say. I have come forward at this time not just to speak of our wonderful ally, the European Union, a shining example of economical thrift and civil harmony, but that your union both culturally and politically be seen as a standard to raise to the world, both developed and developing, so that we may push beyond the parameters of our beautiful terrestrial sphere into the new frontiers and wilderness of space. Now you may wonder indeed what I am driving at, but let me tell you this: it will not be easy for you all to accept or believe the revelations thrust into your lives today. But it must be done. And it has not come to me to callously or irresponsibly create fear and suspicion, no, not at all; in fact, it is this very notion that I decry most vehemently. We have nothing to fear, only our own base attitude if we decide to let loose the mongers of chaos. We must be calm, cool and collected. So, to the point: let it hereby be known: we are not alone in the universe! For many years now, certain authorities have been monitoring, communicating and trading, yes trading, with alien species. A predominant species known to us are the Reticulans or Greys, and there are others similar to us in appearance called the Eridanis; let me explain . . .* Well, what do you think so far?' she quips happily.

'It's a start,' he says smiling.

'A start, just a start?'

'I kind of thought you might warm up to it a little more. You know, not so know-it-all – a bit more humbly . . . '

'How do you mean?' she complains. 'Like, well I think we're being visited by Martians! I just want to tell you, but don't worry; it's all in our imaginations! Come on, Jimmy! I know how to do this: keep it plain. Tell it like it is.'

'We really are going awol, though; they're gonna come down on us big time with Blue Phoenix. And these people are my friends.'

'Hey, we're doing them a favour. Don't cold feet me now.'

'I'm not. It worries me, that's all.'

'And it will worry everybody soon. That's the point.'

'I know, I know, it must be. Let's just come through. Things will get out of control.'

'We have the Meteor, Jimmy.'

'Yes, I know, but I have to steal it first.'

❦

Redman's monitor beeps again and Chromolox appears.

'We'll be meeting in an hour, you two,' she announces. 'Just thought you'd like to know so you wouldn't be caught in the middle of something. More countries are lining up besides the Americans. Hooray! See you soon.' And she escapes.

'Well, I suppose we should head up pretty soon,' says Cephren, shifting his large frame in the old, wooden chair.

'Hell, with the emop we can be there in two minutes,' snaps Redman impatiently. 'You can't leave me dangling!'

'You know what happens. He and Lilly under the pretense of another test drive, take the Meteor into the upper atmosphere and wait for the speech. But no speech is forthcoming. All the signals suddenly jam, even the local ones, even the microphone on the podium, all blamed on an intense solar storm. No one hears a word she says. Frustrated as hell, she has to postpone the speech, but the ceremonies carry on and she loses her chance. She comes home an angry woman. Another opportunity would have to serve her purpose. But none came. Inside the week she is dead. But there isn't a single trace of any explosive material. It was as if the house had simply disintegrated including Danielle. Jimmy assumed it was Blue Phoenix, but realised that Danielle hadn't revealed a word before the communication links went down, which meant . . . '

'The Greys did it!' interjects Redman, his eyes fixed like a child on Cephren.

'Yes, but how did they know?' asks Cephren, rhetorically.

'Lilly?'

'No, Lilly remained loyal to Jimmy.'

'But who then?' asks Redman impetuously.

'This is what completely blew me away, Redman. You'd never guess.'

'Well, out with it, boy!' exhorts Redman, angrily.

Cephren pauses a moment to savour Redman's intensity. He really enjoyed Redman in such a frame of mind. He wants to preserve it: that face twisted in anticipation, veins working.

'The Neteru!' blurts Redman, pleased that he surely knew the answer.

'No.'

'No?' Redman appears destroyed.

'It was Danielle,' lets slip Cephren, looking at his feet.

'Danielle?'

'Yes, Danielle Perreault herself.'

'Why?'

'Jimmy didn't find out for a while. When their plan had been foiled, and he didn't return with the Meteor for fear that he would be caught, not knowing who was behind the trip-up, he and Lilly hovered around waiting to see Danielle, but she had returned home to a crisis in Quebec. For many years she had miraculously laid to rest Quebec's bitter struggle for separation with her anti-federalist ideology. Under her, Quebec achieved greater independence in all but a tenuous political link, which actually saved Quebec from a potential economic disaster. However, there continued to be extremists who hated her for taking all the wind out of the Quebecois nationalist's sails. Some extremists took the Federalist Mayor of Montreal and his staff hostage, and were going to kill them one by one unless she finished the job and severed Quebec. A special commando team raided the building, however, and saved the day. Finally, Danielle was able to get out to her Gatineau residence in the country where she would be free to meet with Jimmy. But she died before this could take place.'

'So what happened?' queries Redman. 'I still don't understand.'

'Later, up in orbit, completely despondent and disconsolate, a guilt-wracked Jimmy, thinking Blue Phoenix somehow got to him and Danielle, was surrounded by three Reticulan vessels which locked the Meteor in a gravity field and took them to the mothership. There on board, he and Lilly were taken to see Johnny, who to Jimmy's surprise was very happy to see him. Johnny and Big Cheese then took Jimmy on a personal tour of the ship, showing him the reconnaissance terminals and Replicant section where the groups of human school children were seen about. This tour was quite extensive, and Jimmy listlessly followed and listened. Towards the end, they came to some nice suites and beckoned him to enter one. Inside, he had the shock of his life, for sitting and staring out the window into deep space was none other than Danielle. Yes, Danielle. She was alive. She turned when they approached, and to Jimmy's double shock, didn't even recognise him. He stared at her stupefied. She basically ignored him, though greeted Johnny and Big Cheese coolly, shaking their hands. Jimmy, beside himself, blurted out, 'Danielle! You're alive!' She looked at him curiously, then back at the others. Johnny and Big Cheese smiled, at which time Big Cheese took out his neuron rod, or whatever it was, and directed its charge to her. In a split second, while she again looked at this strange man calling out to her and all but hugging her, she snaps back to the earth Danielle. With a heart-stopping cry she falls into his arms, crying 'Jimmy, Jimmy,' over and over. The others left before she saw them. They held each other for the longest time. Jimmy explained to her where they were and what had happened. The other Danielle, he had discovered was a clone and all her life Danielle had been interchanged with the double.'

'By gosh, that's unbelievable,' utters Redman.

'There's more, but let us head up to the Pyramid, Redman; you fly with Runaway; I want to walk. I want to see my homeland and feel the earth under my feet and breathe the air.'

'So they executed their own clone,' continues Redman, 'To foil his plan, but also to reveal to Jimmy their resolve. But what did they do to them?' he insists.

Cephren gets up and stretches. Redman follows.

'They let them go, including Lilly.'

'In return for what?'

'That they would never go back to earth.'

'So what did they do?'

'They went to Eridani.'

'And they never came back?'

'Right, at least Danielle, but it'll take too long to explain now.'

'Okay Chairman, lead the way, then.'

Cephren huffs and puffs over the rise out of the meadow into the maple wood and out into the field. He stops for a breather. There, in the distance is that vast edifice of reddish grey, that great sentinel to the wonder of humanity and endeavor, the Pyramid. It looms large in his vision, as it always had since he was a boy. The grey March day couldn't even suppress its magnificent luster and light. Large patterns of crusty snow and brown hayfields mark a surreal mosaic as he continues on his way. He thinks of Blondy Boy, hoping he was all right with the Honeys in the Kawarthas. Runaway swoops quietly nearby with Redman in the emop. They keep his walking pace.

twelve In the Universe

Waving invisible wings
Goodbye

                                                   –Jimmy Pidgeon

Cleo knows she will relish this attack: her very own Charge of the
Light Brigade, except without the infamous misreading of
orders. To her it is all honour and revenge, a fitting combination under the circumstances. The revenge is not part of the plan, but an
incidental plus. The important object of the mission is the absolute subjugation of the state of Chicago for obvious reasons, but also for reasons yet
to be disclosed by her brother. So with an elite clutch of American Special
Forces she makes her way to the border with Chicago.

There is something extraordinary going on, but she doesn't have the
complete knowing of what all that is. Her task at hand preoccupies her
utmost attention. Even news that O'Reilly al Khazzami and his Mujahedin are taking up positions on the western edge of Chicago barely
flicker in her mind. The pace of events that past day had been all too
engaging. The subsequent arrival of the Volcano without Cephren, but
fully loaded with an electromagnetic pulse charge and orders to proceed
to The Windy City to detonate it, just about makes her lose her famous
cool in anticipation. That cool, of course, is the most volatile cool known
among friends. She assumes that Cephren had gone underground or

made some temporary pact with Del Barker, as difficult as that appeared, but plausible in view of the circumstances. At any rate, her orders from Runaway Dumptruck himself, by extension of Chromolox and the Board, are to proceed to the Bungalo after the pulse should render Chicago's defences useless for a sufficient duration before the Chicago circuitry could be repaired. The one wild card is that Cleo doesn't know exactly how long it would take them to repair their downed systems and if there would be enough time to rescue both Heyoka and Sam. Exiting Chicago, she is to dive into Lake Michigan, head for Anishnabe and let the rest of the allied forces comprised of the many aforementioned powers contain the Chicago war machine.

In order to gain access to Chicago, Cephren was to be interfaced from his monitor at the Pyramid to the lead emop, the Volcano, piloted by Cleo. Using his diplomatic immunity and brazen naïvety as a cover, he will saunter into the jaws of the bear seemingly unaware of the Chicagos' intention to capture him or kill him. The mission is to appear as one with an olive branch. Only Cephren could be capable of doing such a foolish thing as to wave a peace flag to the Chicagos.

Naturally, Trinny Burnamthorpe believes that Cephren, being the fool that she deemed him to be, would at least make the perfect hostage to barter for the disbandment of the forces arrayed against her, little realising the Trojan Horse on her doorstep, or for that matter the dramatic turn-around in Sunsetwind. As it is, she has delayed her invasion because of the unexpected shift in the political climate. The news that George Washington had stepped down from the EF candidacy makes her all the more surprised and unsure of what to do. To make matters worse, the subsequent American threat along her border confounds her into a hyper-neurotic temper, which tips any vestige of sensibility into madness.

Madness can be a sort of understated euphemism for loss of control, or seeming desperation and last ditch effort to turn the tables using any means necessary, but in Burnamthorpe's case, she cracks. Afterwards it was said that she screamed in such a vitriolic manner that the veins in her head popped and lost their moorings. Her eyes were on fire, burning in their sockets surrounded by broken blood vessels bursting about her face. Her senior people abandon her, leaving only Babylon and the security staff. She raves that Cephren would die the second he lands. Babylon tries vainly to remind her that Cephren is their only hope, but she retorts that neither success nor failure, are options, only death. Babylon, to his credit, stays with her to thwart any undue harm she may cause either herself, or her child. Babylon is basically a good person in spite the loss of Treason; in fact, on account of her, he is a better man.

When Cephren's message beeps into Trinny's monitor professing the desire to make peace, she rather ignominiously shuts it off, but Babylon turns it back on, spurring yet another shocking tirade from his mistress. This time she doesn't shut it off, but takes her ancestor's semi-automatic handgun that she keeps in a cabinet in her office and aims it pointblank at Babylon's head. Babylon smiles in his realisation that he is definitely making the right decision and proceeds to send a message to all their Generals in charge of defences to return to their bases and await further orders. Before Trinny rebuffs that order, she pumps two rounds into Babylon's head. The Generals are thrown into such a state of confusion, they choose to hold their ground but step down from their high alert to one of caution. It is the voice of Cephren that ironically brings Trinny back to her frazzled senses. Oddly enough, with Cephren, she felt she had to keep up appearances so as not to admit her despicable actions.

'Well, now that you're here, dear, shall we endeavour to sit down and work out the fine print?' she asks leering into the monitor.

'I'm not quite there yet, Trinny; would it be all right to enter Chicago through Detroit?'

'Enter wherever you damn well please; do you really think I care?'

'I think you care about the welfare of all the Chicagos.'

'Oh, thank you, lame brain; as if this is about domestic issues, not that it is any of your business.'

'I thought I'd drop by to see Sam if it was all right.'

'Just walk in, numb nuts, and do whatever you please,' she spits, facetiously.

'Aren't you prepared to make concessions, Trinny? We want to prevent
a war.'

'Prevent one? With a hundred thousand emops stacked up on our borders? You bastard! It's all your fault! I dare you to land in my country!'

'I believe I can make a change, Trinny. Please don't do anything rash
until I get there.'

At that moment, Cleo crosses into Chicago ten kilometers above
Detroit. One hundred Chicago emops immediately surround her group
and escort them to The Windy City. She wants to tell them that their
gravity waves would be jammed shortly and that they would plummet to
earth. She just hopes their parachutes worked.

Travelling at over one thousand kilometres per hour, she will cover the
three hundred or so kilometres in about fifteen minutes. The weather is
clear over Windy City and she knows exactly where she wants to go.
There was a time when she visited the Bungalo under very different circumstances, as nauseating as it was then, too.

High over The Windy City, with the simple push of a button, Cleo
detonates the device Vince had made; Trinity Two he had named it. At
first, there is a stalling, then a skipping feeling as the Volcano's new
installed resistors kick in. Outside her windows, it looks as if it rains
sparks throughout the sky. The sight is extraordinary: everywhere sparks
generate an outward flow as far as the eye can see in every direction. Her
Chicago escort has just disappeared; they dropped like cannon balls, but
to her relief they released their safety parachutes. She then dives toward
the Bungalo.

Without an impediment to her offensive action, Cleo makes a close circling pattern around the Bungalo. Numerous security personnel are scrambling about in a disorganized fashion, astounded at the sudden collapse
of their "impervious" defences. Calling Admiral Mckee, she is told that
a squadron of Yellow Tooth Cherokees were on their way and that the

invasion has gone perfectly as planned so far. The Chicago forces not affected by the pulse are in disarray and for the most part offering little or no resistance.

Arriving at the head of the Yellow Tooth squadron with Sunning Snake their leader, is Runaway Dumptruck. Together, with Cleo's group, the squadron lands and begins to surround the Bungalo, appearing to be all but deserted. Cleo goes immediately to Sam's room to find it empty. Runaway joins her, and they go from room to room until they arrive at the basement area where Heyoka's room is situated. Sunning Snake appears on the scene and makes known that the compound had been secured. All the personnel had given up without a fight, having no weapons, their electronic circuits having been frazzled by the pulse.

Reaching the last room, Runaway smashes in the locked wooden door with palpable ease, to see Trinny, Sam and Heyoka sitting on the bed. Both Runaway and Cleo stand there gazing at the pitiful sight. Trinny holds her antique handgun to Heyoka's head.

'Hasn't there been enough violence, Trinny,' says Cleo, calmly.

'Hasn't there been enough violence?' mimicks Trinny.

'Are you all right?' queries Cleo to Sam and Heyoka.

'It's okay Cleo,' says Sam bravely. 'Mom is scared that's all; she won't kill us.'

'I gave her permission to shoot me,' says Heyoka with a smile, 'But I do not meet her requirements, it seems. Trinny, my sister, forgive yourself your anger, and there will be another day in the sun. You are a victim of your own fate . . .'

'Shut up!' Trinny screams.

'Do not speak so to our leader!' exclaims Sunning Snake angrily, positioning himself between Runaway and Cleo.

'Forgive her Sunning Snake; I am well. She is upset at the loss of her country, the great State of Chicago.'

Trinny stands up and turns the gun on Cleo. Cleo doesn't flinch.

'How does it feel staring down death, whore,' remarks Trinny with a smile. 'I'm just sorry Cephren wasn't man enough to face me himself.'

But no sooner has Trinny closed her mouth on that last snarly syllable, Cleo flings her cat-quick side kick directly into Trinny's gun hand with a thwack, sending the weapon flying to the wall; Runaway like an acrobatic bear leaps and takes it. Trinny, still smiling, reaches out with her other hand and sends it like a whip towards Cleo's face with her long reach. Cleo, however, has her arm up instinctively to block the hit. Sunning Snake and two of his men then move to Trinny, whereby she breaks into fitful sobs, her chest heaving wracks of anguish.

'Hand her over to the Americans, Sunning,' orders Cleo.

'Trinny,' says Heyoka going to her and putting her healing hands around her shoulders, 'I am sorry to see my warrior sister so distraught, but you must take my advice: open up your heart to goodness and heal yourself. The world will always go on without us. Let renewed love be your cure.'

But Trinny is broken in spirit and cannot respond. Her vision of life has manifested many a carcass on the road of humanity, wind-dried in the tepid sun.

The death and subsequent martyrdom of Anna Gram cannot have caused a greater shock in the Western world since the tragic death of Lady Diana, the Princess of Wales in the late twentieth century. The first report from Captain Dave himself, in tears, is met with disbelief. It was understood that she did in fact have an implant, a typical Chicago tri-c, a memory enhancer, and that she had been assassinated by yet again another transmitter whereby its proximity jammed her frequency and caused a massive embolism of the brain the same as Impala's. It was also revealed that the Chicagos had been eavesdropping on her brain by a micro bug in the implant. Every conversation she had had was monitored. To her credit, Cleo never for a moment actually believed that Anna was a witting spy for the Chicagos; thousands of people from all over the world went to Chicago for implants. Initially, the Chicagos thought that she might be useful, but her power and presence had outgunned any advantage her intelligence afforded them. The tragedy was all the more acute as it was on account of Trinny's perverse thinking that Anna's life had to be forfeited, because the longer Anna lived, the more insidious Trinny's own failure grew.

There is an unprecedented sorrow. Her body lies in state first in Paris, then Washington, then Sunsetwind, then finally at her home and ranch in the Texas panhandle where she was laid to rest. By the time she was interred on her ranch, Cephren had been elected Chairman of the Earth Federation winning more than 60% of the vote, Queen Jodie of Queensland and Wu Chen Ng of China coming second and third respectively.

Cephren suffers terribly on account of her death. Juxtaposed with the burgeoning weight of his new responsibility, he feels bound to a guilt he doesn't wholly understand. Suffused with this guilt his countenance is impervious to any notion of personal happiness to follow, because with Anna, there had always been the hope and stirrings of romantic involvement to which he put off. Through her love for him she had given him power and resolve when he had been at his most desperate. With the ideals of love, anything could be achieved. Now that he had achieved what he had set out to do, only the haunting beauty of Anna Gram remained as a visage to remind him of his debt to her. And he believes that her commitment was self-sacrificing, wholehearted and pure.

He had been sitting in his emop just after his conversation with Trinny during the invasion when Captain Dave interfaced with the tragic news. Anna had been preparing for a speech when a crowd of Kenyans, who had been cleared, were allowed to see her. Someone in that crowd who managed to get very close to her must have transmitted the deadly frequency. Captain Dave was powerless to help her, as she fell suddenly among the feet of the rabble.

The general elation and pandemonium that sweeps the world upon the demise of the Chicagos falls on Cephren's benumbed senses. It is as anticlimactic as the end of the world. All his hopes, dreams and desires fall flat. Even his soon-to-be presented knowledge of his Neteru experiences fall away from his providence as the inertia of a terminal illness. Only the sight of his son, Sam, and the ethereal Heyoka, make him smile, a dizzy smile as he goes through the motions but remains distant and cautious. The festivities that evening are as if in a dream in which he walks along the perimeter, senseless and melancholy. There too, is someone walking the perimeter who would not let him see her face, for the tears there too. He senses she understands. Thoughts are put into his mind mysteriously. He can see that it is Heyoka, almost desperate in sympathy, but standing aside respectfully. He sees her as teenage young, but knows her to be thirty. She tells him not to feel sorry for Anna's immortality, as her life was more precious than the legend. Cephren then sees her tears and some kind of love he knows is there but impossible to reach under the circumstances. Neither he nor she could allow it for the time being. That alone feeds his solitude. And solitude is the sacrifice he would live up to until Anna's ghost had been laid to rest.

The Neteru device is almost a cruel appendage, in a manner of speaking, by virtue of the fact that it keeps projecting Anna into the screen of his mind, especially when he slept. Sometimes in a dream, Cephren would even be able to see from her eyes, himself lustily sprawled and asleep. She would blithely entice his libido, fondle him and snuggle to look up into his eyes, open wide in anticipation. He would persuade her to stop, even under the circumstances, his restraint nearly breaking when she held him hard and ready, as he woke murmuring defiantly, 'No, no, no, we must not sully the honour of our pathos.' Then the soothing words of some interloper, none other than Heyoka, would put him back to sleep, letting him hold Anna and feeling the vibrancy of her peculiar love. Anna would fade then, unrequited as in life, yet willing to make that sacrifice over and over again.

From the moment Cephren heard the news of Anna's death, he engaged in himself a kind of autopilot in order to maintain his equilibrium. To sit in the Board room with the others was comforting on the one hand because he was among friends, but unbearable on the other because their province was in a state of emergency about to detonate a massive electromagnetic pulse over The Windy City that would hopefully render the Chicagos' electric circuitry useless. All he really wanted to do was to be alone and cry. Chromolox even suggested he might want to be alone, but he stoically declined the invitation. Mita even came over to him and crouched there with an arm around his shoulder and a hand on his forearm. She spoke to him in that soothing voice that he had once been so infatuated with. Now it repulsed him, though he tried his best to put up a show of strength. Redman had told him as they exited the bunker that she had had a torrid affair with Vince. Apparently, it had simmered, but was still agreeable. Vince and Mita were an unlikely match in that their differences were incompatible, yet once consummated a quirky symmetry emerged which seemed to benefit them both. For Cephren, his youthful dream was shattered. Mita's touch alone felt corrupted as he saw her and Vince together. He liked them both but not like this; his grief compounded all the more deeply. When Mita looked at him, he could see in her eyes the tactile gratification of her torrid affair, something she had probably long yearned for though never indicated as such to him before. Maybe it was Vince's vulgar openness that got to her, maybe the world turned upside down, perhaps the unique cocktail of chemistry or all of the above; it certainly had changed the Board's dynamics, mostly himself. At any rate, he could see Mita wanted to speak to him personally, but that would have to wait.

Chromolox then interrupts the searing silence waiting for news that the Bungalo had been secured. She receives confirmation and announces it is time to announce to the world the emancipation of Sunsetwind. So it is done and a cheer rings around the world with the subjugation of Chicago and Sunsetwind's hard won freedom. In the Boardroom there are congratulations and kisses and condolences. Redman and Gabriella even do a little folksy dance. He is so hilarious that everyone laughs, including

Cephren. Champagne is served and spontaneous toasts to all, every other toast to Cephren and a solemn one to Seymour and then Anna, whom no one there knew personally except Cephren.

When the celebrations settle down and Chromolox holds court, she asks Cephren to tell them in a nutshell what they are all dying to hear. What on earth did he find out about Jimmy's Chip? Cephren feels he must say something before he leaves for Paris where Captain Dave had taken Anna to have to lie in state there. Yet Cephren doesn't want to reveal the big surprise until after the EF election.

They all sit around the table, their eyes on Cephren and he looking back smiling in his happy-sad way. He wants to tell them that the chip is the memory of an entire civilisation long extinct and that its power in a sense brought them this victory, but that their supremacy is only a beginning, as there are forces so much bigger in the universe. Nevertheless, the question of supremacy is not what the chip is about; it's about us as people, learning to live in harmony with all life in the universe that is ever evolving, and that we must be up to the challenge of change in ways we cannot yet comprehend.

'Chromolox,' he begins, 'Should we not share our elation with the people? I think I would like to get into that at a more suitable time . . . '

Cephren is interrupted by a guerilla who monitors them to say that George Washington is on the line. Communications put Washington through to the large screen in the Boardroom. He too, is celebrating with his staff. There pass between them all a general toast as a couple more champagne bottles pop. General Dennis makes a short touching speech in tribute to Anna Gram. He apologises to Cephren for remarks "made in the heat of debate" and finally expresses his humility at "her greatness of heart and action" and praises her "beauty and grace". Cephren thanks the General and George adds that "If Anna complimented Cephren, it was also Cephren who complimented Anna, and your peculiar synchronicity had put us all to shame", furthermore, "Her stature shall grow when we are forgotten, such was her destiny".

'Here's to a rejuvenated United States of America!' he finally exclaims, 'And perhaps to the emergence again of the great Commonwealth of Canada!'

'Thank you, George, and I assume I'll be seeing you in Paris,' says Cephren, quietly.

'Of course, and I would like personally to bring the casket back to Washington, if Anna's family and the Texans would grant me that.'

'I will tend to the details myself, George, thank you.'

'Well, it looks like the gods have endorsed you, Cephren,' he remarks. 'I hope to hear from you in regard to some of your . . . election assurances. You know we have some interesting intelligence ourselves – fallout from the pre-asteroid years – I think, pending your success at the polls, which I believe imminent; we should compare notes. You obviously have what all of us wished to have had and that, perhaps, is what all of this fuss was about. Anyway, my most sincere blessings. See you all soon, and congratulations again Sunsetwinders; you have saved the world! Out for now.' And he is gone.

'Well, Cephren,' jokes Vince, 'We may depose you again, if ya don't come up with a damned good story!'

Everyone has a laugh.

'You're right, Vince,' says Cephren. 'You'd better reach down and hold onto your socks, because I remember your telling me once you thought aliens were invented in Hollywood.'

'Oh you know me, Cephren,' he retorts playfully, 'I'm not much of a bandwagon man one way or the other!'

'Rather he's the horse!' interjects Mita with surprising candor, beaming at Vince.

Everyone laughs again.

'Well, I'll say one thing, it's true,' confirms Cephren, 'They're here.'

'Who's here?' asks Chromolox.

'The Greys mostly, the Eridanis who are a lot like us, the Reptoids who are the most formidable, but there are hundreds, indeed thousands, of interstellar quasi-human species that they know of in the universe; on the whole most are decent and civilised, though some are intolerant of emerging species such as ours as they present a risk to "electromagnetic harmonics", which for example is like someone rudely interrupting a perfect perennial symphony. People like us have to learn to join in with our own distinctive sound to contribute to the whole concert. As I've been explaining to Redman, there is much to say. Once I gained access into Jimmy's Chip, I had to learn how to use it. Incredibly, Flower Child became my guide of sorts. She once carried this same implant. I 'remembered' what she remembered. Jimmy's Chip, or the X13, or the Neteru, (the name given it by the aliens), is indeed a synaptic memory chip holding the memory of not only Jimmy Pidgeon, an earlier carrier, but information regarding the navigation of the universe. The last of the Neteru adopted earth as a hideaway from the Reptoids who had all but exterminated them, and we on earth have in part genetically descended from the survivors. They had bequeathed to the inheritors of the chip super knowledge impossible to assimilate in a lifetime, or ten thousand for that matter. Yet, regardless of my own limitations, information is now more or less easily derived.'

'Have you established contact with these beings?' asks Chromolox.

'Yes, they in fact contacted me.'

'Who?' queries LeRoy.

'An Eridani, or Jah as they say, named Dewrzah, and some Greys accompanying him: the Greys, as some of you may be aware, are from either Zeta 1 or 2 Reticula, two solar systems almost forty light years from our sun.'

'No guff!' exclaims Vince, wide-eyed and turning to Mita who smiles back at her whiz kid. 'This is it, isn't it; this is really it!'

'Yep, in the real universe, Vince,' concurs Cephren. 'It makes Star Tripper look like Disneyworld reruns. The fact is that the truth is not so drastic as we have mythologised.'

'How long have they been here and what do they want?' asks Chromolox.

'Hundreds of thousands of years, even millions, for some of them like the Greys and the Neteru. The Greys have a great need for infusions of our DNA and have been harvesting it all this time. It was an arrangement we first became aware of back in the twenty-first century by the U.S. government – to trade technology for resources such as DNA – but it's far more complex than that. It was the Reptoids who took it upon themselves to police this sector of the universe, using the Greys to monitor our containment as a species for our own good apparently. We are considered to be a dangerous and unruly planet and a threat not only to our own survival but potentially to other species.'

'Incredible, but what on earth do they need our DNA for?' asks Bill Deerhill.

'The Greys have been around as a technologically advanced species for a very long time, millions of years in fact. They are one of the oldest known species who evolved originally eons ago not from primates but a form of cetacean or dolphin-like aquatic creature. They have told me the dolphin is the best analogy, but that they adapted eventually, like us, as a land-based mammal. Their skin is similar in colour and texture to dolphins, although more luminescent; and bone structure, the residuals of cetacean appendages, have evolved into a humanoid frame, but smaller. Their large, black almond or wrap-around eyes that encircle the anterior portion of the skull, have that protective shielding which many of our own aquatic mammals have developed, the difference being that their shielding is really a natural set of "shades" to protect them from the excessive sun in their twin though not binary solar system. But most striking is the Grey's ability to transfix or paralyse prey in a manner of speaking. Like the dolphin who uses a powerful ultrasonic emission from the anterior "melon" of their skull to stun prey like barracuda, the Greys can do the same to an "abductee". This is their most astounding feature. This "stare" can immobilise one and render them powerless. And naturally, being telepathic, they communicate in the same way, by putting thoughts directly into one's mind.

'Their problem is that they have evolved and cloned to the point where they can no longer reproduce sexually. Neither males nor females have functioning sex organs, although there are definitely feminine and masculine genders by virtue of their appearance and even behaviour. They must clone one another by genetic manipulation. But cloning generation after generation is like inbreeding and eventually the genes burn out, which makes it necessary to introduce new genes. This is where we come in. Our DNA chain is a fresh, unique genetic code and when it is modified to their own genetic material, hybrids are created which are rejuvenating their race. What's interesting is that the Reptoids, who in effect are masters over the Zeta 2 Greys, had them clone humans much as we have cloned animals and humans in isolated instances. They take a modified cell and fuse it with the egg to create an identical sibling. This was done with countless people before the Third World War; in fact, unbeknowst to historians that was a major reason why the war was fought. A certain individual, General Good, of the United Front directed his key subordinate and double agent, Colonel Jeremy Blaine, (military leader of the Radical Right), to fight against the United Front – though few knew it at the time – in the attempt to show the Reptoids that we were in charge of our own destiny and were prepared to actually annihilate ourselves to save ourselves from assimilation. There was a critical stand-off that resulted in the use of nuclear ordinance setting off exchanges in the middle east and South Asia. The United Front except a few in the know (thanks to Jimmy Pidgeon), had been not only dominated by these human clones but was behind the assassination of President Kimball the New Republican who supported the Radical Right; however the aliens had nothing to do with the actual assassination – yet in spite of the catastrophic results by unleashing World War 3, we most definitely would not have been the people we are today had not Colonel Blaine do what he did. The irony was deadly.

'Danielle Perreault was probably their most successful clone. She was assassinated of course, but the other clone survived and lived out her life on Jah! As you can see, there is much to tell; the real history is full of bizarre innuendos.'

The Board sits in stunned silence for a few moments while they seem to teeter in disbelief.

'As I said, it was Jimmy Pidgeon,' relates Cephren forging ahead, 'Who ultimately tipped off General Good regarding the purpose of the clones to expose the depth of our containment and control. World War 3 and the Big Asteroid, of course, changed all that; we were no longer such a viable resource – I suppose they had had enough of us; we were no longer worth the trouble. Perhaps they had attained what they needed; however, the Zeta 1 Greys and the Jahs such as Dewrzah were benevolent and continued to interact with humans on a limited basis. The Reptoids themselves I believe, were not inherently evil, but actually more like us than they were prepared to admit, and perhaps even a mite threatened by our moral purpose, and Neteru origins who long long ago were their superiors. They really wanted us to be more like them as there are several advantages, such as: five to ten times longer lives, greater intelligence, being more ecologically efficient, and able to exist peacefully; but who's going to take away our great passion for life, our inspiration, our beautiful planet, our self-determination? Are these antiquated skins to be shed? We are unique and resolved to do as we choose. And we survived against tremendous odds with no assistance from anybody. To our credit, we came to understand the criteria for universal survival and cleaned up our act on earth as best we could in view of the mounting crisis that faced us at the time. I don't think I need to extrapolate on that or the 21st century.'

'So where do we go from here?' queries Chromolox. She seems to be able to sustain a cool head, whereas the others appeared shell-shocked.

'I have to be ensured of a victory on April 2nd, Chromolox, before we can act. I will be making many speeches and directives if I win.'

'Who's this Dewrzah?' asks Yani Deerhill.

'Dewrzah is a Jah. They are humanoid, similar to us, only tens of thousands of years more evolved. Dewrzah is very old, almost four hundred of our years. What is fascinating is that he claims to have known Jimmy Pidgeon and Danielle Perreault, as well as Lilly the hybrid Grey, a friend of theirs, and hear this; Heyoka is the descendant of both Jimmy and Lilly's child who was raised by a Cherokee woman who married a Navajo. The grandchild of this child became the wife of Yellow Tooth himself. To top it off, both Cleo and I are direct descendants of Jimmy Pidgeon and Danielle Perreault, as many others surely are! Furthermore, Flower Child who was born as Terrie Barnett, is also their descendant. Isn't it incredible how things come full circle?'

'Almost as if it was planned,' observes Mita.

'Yes,' accedes Cephren, 'Thanks to Dewrzah and the Greys giving the Neteru back to us through of course Redman and his mother Bird-in-the-Sky both of whom were abductees.'

'So I would appreciate no more snickering behind my back!' demands Redman, with a mischievous smile.

'Just give us mere mortals a little time to catch up, Redman,' retorts Vince.

'Mita,' declares Redman, 'How do you weather such a scoundrel?'

Mita blushes with her hand to her forehead. 'He makes me laugh,' she says, embarrassed.

'So, if I may change the direction of this dialogue,' asserts Vince in deference to his woman and reputation, 'Our friend Jimmy Pidgeon, it seems, has been cheated of his place in history, due to his alter ego, James Piercemore.'

'Yes, Piercemore was of course Pidgeon,' agrees Cephren, unequivocally.

'What happened to him?' asks LeRoy.

'Do we really have the time to get into this?' speculates Cephren. He looks at Redman who winks. Cephren sighs and holds out his glass for some more champagne. Chromolox jumps to fill it. Everyone is all ears.

Dazed and confused, coming out from under the spell of that brain jammer, the magic wand, Jimmy discovers himself sitting face to face with Johnny Appleseed. His memory returns in jumps and starts; he remembers being corralled in the Meteor by the three Grey reconnaissance ships. He remembers Lilly twittering humourlessly, 'Time to give up the ghost, Jimmy!' Then once inside the ranch a touch of the magic wand by Bart puts him out of his misery by temporarily erasing his immediate memory. Johnny is there in a dull, silvery one-piece suit greeting him affably; Lilly is nowhere to be seen. Jimmy, having been suddenly relieved of some terrible weight in his mind by the subtle touch of the magic wand, looks around in wonder thinking he has lost his marbles. Johnny then leads him down the long corridor stopping here and there in various areas to view the quasi-human activity. They run into Darrell Lester, and Darrell politely nods, but can't resist saying, 'Jimmy, if you ever consider a change of occupation, give me a call.' Then he extends his hand as he departs, 'Here, take my card.' Jimmy takes it, and he and Johnny go on. Arriving at Johnny's quarters, Bart appears again but Johnny communicates with him telepathically and Bart goes away.

Now seated Jimmy looks at Johnny who returns the look almost sympathetically, but there is nothing there that reveals what he is thinking. Nor can Jimmy formulate thoughts in his own mind.

'You are an exceptional human being,' says Johnny breaking the silence. 'I want you to know that with respect to the fact that I must consider your uses better put elsewhere, I would also like to take this opportunity to thank you for your generous contribution to the program all these years. You have been our greatest asset, and this will not go unrewarded, unlike your compatriots on earth, who by your latest actions would probably have had you exterminated. I am also in your debt for your lifelong commitment to Danielle Perreault who deserved no less than your great love. I could never be your friend had it not been for your stewardship in that regard; and if I was a lesser person, I would envy yours, and Danielle's, superiority in ways of the flesh. Danielle chose you over me, you know!

And then there was your plan, which I am sorry to say had to be scuppered, though you must understand how I wish it could have been otherwise. You can't imagine how difficult it has been to watch the abject horror taking place in humanity, and my own collusion by proxy to yours and Danielle's demise. But I beg of you not to lose heart, for I have compromised on your behalf. I will set you free, though not to return to earth, but free to go anywhere you please in the universe. This will take on new meaning in a short while when I will reacquaint you with your true love, and I know that we have sedated you for the time being to relieve you of your pain. For your own well-being we will release you from this sedative just prior to this reacquaintance. Is there anything you would like to say, Jimmy?'

Jimmy is still too stunned to speak. Johnny's direct and eloquent speech has captivated him, but he is at a loss to know precisely what Johnny was talking about; yet, somehow it all made sense, if not for the reference to his "stewardship" and Danielle's choosing him. And where is Danielle? Something keeps gnawing in his mind that literally feels as if it is exploding.

'I . . . I suppose then thanks are in order, Johnny; you make it sound so easy. Ah, perhaps you could refresh my memory; in fact, what have I done, or rather, Danielle and I, to deserve this dénouement? And what is this stewardship you mention? And where is Danielle? How do you seem to know her so well?'

Johnny smiles, reflexing his handsome chops, and turns to his side to gaze out his window. Jimmy, looking as well, notices they are no longer in the orbit of Mars, but farther out. He thinks he recognises Neptune.

'In respect to your stewardship, this is your art, Jimmy,' declares Johnny bemusedly, still looking out the window, 'And your creative spirit. We are a stagnant species as compared to yours. To us, all the creating had been done long ago, and you as a species are just beginning. This entails your stewardship.' He turns back to Jimmy. 'Your stewardship unfortunately is too good and beyond what your species can assimilate for positive effect.

Look at the disparity of justice on your planet; it's perverted. Look at the religious wars, like acne spread over the surface of the globe. Power and possession are the compulsive drives for survival in a terrestrial sphere and will confirm my resolutions to contain you over and over. There are few antidotes to your problems, all drastic, given your proclivity to violence. Political solutions have little lasting effect. Natural disasters of great magnitude are usually the most humane solutions, rather than death by political attrition through starvation, war and disease. Asteroids are effective as well as ECDs.'

'You preclude then to assume our destruction?' queries Jimmy carefully.

'Personally, no. Naturally, yes. Nature has its own agenda, irrespective of ones feelings.'

'Are you hinting at some future cataclysm?'

'Perhaps,' replies Johnny cagily.

'Could you prevent it?' presses Jimmy.

'Perhaps.'

'But would you?'

'I doubt it.'

'But then you'd be out of a job,' expresses Jimmy managing to find his irrepressible sense of humour.

'Perhaps,' he says, standing, 'But come, Jimmy, let us not dwell on the future when the present has more than enough to keep us occupied. Let us proceed to your reacquaintance.'

Jimmy stands up and follows Johnny out. He is suddenly overwhelmed with curiosity.

'You never answered my question about our demise,' he states behind Johnny, who nimbly walks ahead.

'All your questions will be answered momentarily, but not before one request,' replies Johnny turning.

'What?' quips Jimmy.

'When you progress onward from here – I mean this milestone in life – please don't cease your great work. You will have much time on your side to extemporise both in science and literary art.' Johnny stops before a door and Bart appears again with the magic wand.

'Why would I do that?' asks Jimmy, not following what Johnny was saying. But Johnny passes his hand over the panel and the door dematerialised to reveal Danielle sitting in a room looking out the window. She turns immediately to see Johnny and Jimmy enter, with Bart hovering behind them.

'Danielle!' utters Jimmy stupefied, going to her having just recollected that she had been assassinated, because of the memory blanking. 'What on earth are you doing here?' But Danielle recoils in his embrace, actually pushing him away.

'For Heaven's Sake, Johnny,' she exclaims, looking alternately at both of them. 'Who is this guy?'

'Danielle, meet Jimmy Pidgeon,' he says.

She looks directly into Jimmy's eyes as if she thought him a ghost. Jimmy is too shocked to say anything and just stares back dumbfounded.

'I think you have mistaken me for someone else, Mr. Pidgeon,' she says politely.

Jimmy remains mute. All his insecurity regarding his experience with her roars to life.

'I have a distinct feeling I've met you before,' she comments, taking some interest.

'He's James Piercemore,' remarks Johnny, amused.

'James Piercemore? My God, why didn't you tell me? I know all your work Mr. Piercemore; may I call you James?'

Jimmy is still too numb to speak. He doesn't know what to think, his shock is so complete.

'He's shy, Johnny: why did you introduce him as . . . Pidgeon?'

'He has two names.'

'Oh, I see, something I should have done. So tell me James, have you ever been in a spaceship before?' she asks.

'Yes,' says Jimmy, 'But not with you.'

'There's something about you . . . something déjà vu.'

'We met once in a mall . . . '

'Where, when?'

'In Canada.'

She laughs. 'In Canada: can you be more specific?'

'Help me out here, Johnny?' insists Jimmy, with a sinking feeling. Jimmy is just too devastated to respond in any other way than to appeal to Johnny's compassion. He then realises all of a sudden what Johnny had intimated when they spoke for the first time years before. Danielle had had to have been Johnny's lover, his Empress to his Emperor.

Without a word Bart then steps forward and touches both of them with the magic wand engaging Jimmy and Danielle's lapsed synaptic frequencies. In that moment, sudden recognition and memory recall explode in a frenzy of emotional release. Johnny and Bart exit, sealing the door behind them.

'Jimmy, Jimmy..."

'Danielle! You're alive!'

Danielle and Jimmy cry, hug, kiss as Jimmy says over and over, 'Danielle, I thought you were dead! I thought you were dead!'

'I was,' she replies. 'Oh, Jimmy, Jimmy, you can't imagine what I've been through. Johnny told me everything! I know what happened! They killed me! I killed me!'

'What are you talking about? You're alive!'

'Jimmy, I'm a clone! We've been duped all my life! My twin is dead! All my life one twin played off the other like competing puppets to Johnny . . . '

'I told you about him before, Danielle! Don't you remember?'

'They've messed with my mind . . . ' She avoids his eyes.

'Danielle, were you his lover all your life?' he asks pointedly.

Danielle doesn't respond. She releases herself from Jimmy's arms and stares at the soft satin-like metallic floor.

'Jimmy, we are free now,' she announces. 'Please don't reject me for something I had no control of . . . ' She sits there despondently in her disheveled clothes, red cotton pants, white blouse and beige vest. She does up two buttons and straightens her long grey hair into its customary tied-back arrangement.

'Why didn't you tell me,' he asks stunned.

'Because I didn't know, Jimmy; you must believe me,' she says earnestly.

'I am trying to understand; I don't want to be angry,' he says slowly, partially to himself. 'I know we have both been subjected to forces way beyond our control; that's the only way I can rationalise it. I understand better, your life, now. Perhaps now we can put it behind us and carry on. I would like to try.'

'So would I,' she intones typically, a tinge insincere.

Space:

1:15 *If one deems that their religious belief to be God's truth, then it must follow that this faith rules their perception. If the parallel can apply to an infinite universe, one must then perceive the limitlessness of one's faith. Therefore, what could be more futile than to attempt to perceive the limitlessness of faith? It seems to me only an impossible truth, unless we know the limits within the universe. And if we know the limits in terms of energy, mass, and resonance, faith must be an illusion. Herein lie the limits: we sail rudderless in spaceship earth across the sea of the universe on a voyage ultimately doomed to founder in our present state on account of impending natural disaster or human error, like a colossal Titanic, and there are not enough lifeboats to save us all. This must surely be the reality quotient. And the revelation that we are one of a vast flotilla of spaceship earths – many of which are far more experienced or sea-worthy if you will – demonstrates we are in no position to exhibit our ego-centric superiority in faith. Preeminently, the desire to survive and make claim to our greatness, not only among ourselves but our sister ships, cannot be realised without further consideration to our own heedless passage, unfortu-*

nately purchased in blind faith. Any course of action like this kind of ineluctable foolishness will be met with self-destruction. This is the law of ultimate space...

Comedians:

23:756 I once knew someone who I envied tremendously. He was actually younger than I and had a young wife. They were a beautiful couple with beautiful children. They quit their jobs and moved to the country to practice their art. They had means to get by on and lived reasonably well. They didn't care whether or not they achieved any kind of material or popular success. They simply lived a pure and enlightening existence. I wanted so much to be like them, but my circumstances and drive would not and could not permit it. Years went by and nothing really changed in their lives. Their children grew up and moved away. They continued to live out their lives according to the design they had created for themselves. Then something changed. Everything they had practiced in their life ultimately came to a dilemma. They realised that what they had created for themselves was an illusion. Their happiness lay only in the idea of what it promised. In actuality they were not happy at all because their intelligence was far too acute to preside over the fantastic though limited produce of their art which turned out to be the rather mundane chronicle of their days, living organically and safely within the confines of their design. Their karma finally had come around to tell them they had led useless lives no different than perennial garden flowers. As a result they began to fight and challenge the terrible truth of their pitiful lives. They decided to free themselves of the bonds of their supposed prison. The man then wandered around the earth to assist others any way he could. The woman became a writer of social issues regarding love and relationships. Both became much admired for their charity. He was asked to lead delegations to the United Nations. She achieved an almost cult status as a wise woman who knew all about love and life. But as a couple they could never be together again. It was as if the more of each other they gave away, the more they grew to detest each other. Even the thought of being together and once again consummating as they had done so many thousands of times made them feel impure and depressed. It reminded them of their failure. The woman found out one day that her husband had died in some poor, faraway country. Sadly, she retrieved his body and had him cremated. She distributed the ashes across their old farm that she still possessed. In her final years, she ceased her publication and lived as she had with him before, yet in spirit. When she died of a sudden illness not long ago, I felt utterly devastated. Her tragic life, became my tragic life. To my way of thinking, nature had out-smarted our intelligence when we believed we were an exception. No one had deserved better, but we got what was coming to us. I realise now, the only one true happiness is in the laughter of the moment, the bliss of love whether between ourselves or for others. It seems happiness and sadness are equal partners in our present state. Both selfless and selfish love will become undone like power corrupted. All in all, I still see the man and woman standing there in their garden arm in arm on a pleasant evening looking to the sunset...

Space:

8:98 In the pitch black of deep space, light is the shade of darkness. Neutrino waves will ebb this way and that like foam on the sea. Our technological prowess is a lifeboat with a sail and oars making its way under our own volition. Our energy, our power, pulls us like strokes with the tide catching the wave and heaving us closer to our new world. Our sails billow in the electromagnetic winds, buffeted by our pulse, darkened by the unfathomable depths beneath, above and all around. It is a tight channel subjected to utter abandon, all hope invested in forged gravity. Woe is the ship marooned, far, far from light, enveloped in cold dark space. But we are encouraged by the streaking stars against the black of the abyss. We surpass them like one lighthouse to another . . .

Blessings:

4:441 The basic elements are the common denominators of intelligent life. As nature is undoubtedly a euphemism for God, or vice-versa – they should be as

one – all life therefore is given freely to proliferate everywhere in the universe
in an unimaginable magnitude, given the right climatic circumstances. This is
elementary. However the competing forces in life, no matter how diverse,
effect every life form to harmonise a symbiosis in which natural will is mani-
fested. This is survival. It is the collusion of instinct with rhythm in life and
death struggles that generates intelligence. Higher life forms in the mold of
humanity and far more advanced interstellar types are no different metaphor-
ically than adults and adolescents living under the same roof. The adult may
inform the adolescent but the adolescent will challenge the adult. Therefore the
symmetry is a mutual bonding of responsibility and refutation and respect.
We as a race are adolescent and must recognise the law of prerogatives . . .

Jimmy looks up again from his monitor and work-in-progress, which
he simply calls In the Universe. They are still a couple of days from Jah.
Danielle slumbers beside him on the foldout bed of the Meteor. Lilly, as
usual sits at the controls seeming to peruse endlessly the dark depths of
space. She is her usual spritely self though took what appeared to Jimmy, a
feminine caution to Danielle's presence. The situation isn't made easier as
Danielle treats her with little respect. Upon reflection it occurs to Jimmy
that all the ranch graduates – Danielle being one – hold their subjectors
with cautious esteem, therefore on the Meteor both Lilly and Danielle
carry on as if performing their routine tasks, each designed to keep them
occupied, Lilly at the console and Danielle resting in bed. Danielle is really
the odd one out. Having being thrust into this circumstance once removed
from her paralytic state at the beck and call of Johnny Appleseed and his
Zeta 2 Greys, she, even with her juvenile experience regarding mind distortion, is for a time concussed in a mode of shock. Jimmy, so delivered
from his own nightmare thinking she had died, is at best semi-solvent to
deal with their plight. Jimmy and Danielle's subsequent release, with
Johnny's bemused blessing, left them all dumfounded as to what to do.
Lilly, freed with Jimmy and Danielle, then set them on a course to Eridani,
at least to give them time to consider their options, of which only one

would suffice for Jimmy – to return from this exile as soon as possible. Being stranded away from earth is something he had definitely never entertained.

The ordeal has not been easy for Danielle either for numerous reasons. The most immediate is her lack of privacy. She cannot appreciate Lilly for who and what she is and deems her own relationship with Jimmy a private affair and so would not evolve beyond Lilly's supposed interloping for the time being. Subsequently, she shies from Jimmy, treating him not much better than Lilly. His futile attempts to arouse her sexual and emotional needs are flung back as improvident. And only after a couple of bizarre days in hyperspace does she begin to warm up to the idea again. However, this is not her main problem. After being exposed to Jimmy as a surviving twin clone, she has retreated into herself and would have bolted like an intemperate filly had she been given the chance. Danielle cannot bear to be discovered when all her life had been built as an impervious Keep, each stone meticulously placed. To have her darkest secret finally laid bare and to have no exit was a devastating blow from which she reels. She knows she has to confront herself with the truth about her sibling relationship, Johnny, Jimmy, and indeed her whole life, not to mention that of her mother and even father who had purportedly witnessed helplessly in a paralytic state her mother's original abduction by the Greys. The dawning reality is staggering in that her whole life has been a façade. She has tried in an ulterior sense to rectify her deception by conspiring with Jimmy, but realised the utter futility of their ultimate plan to emancipate the human race from the grip of the Reptoids. Not only is the human race immune to emancipation, but the aliens knew it better than she or Jimmy, and consequently were probably doing both of them a favour by releasing them from their struggle.

Danielle also feels extremely uncomfortable with a somewhat unfamiliar sensation: guilt. Before, her inner Keep insulated herself from guilt, and now she believes that her betrayal of the plan and infidelity to Jimmy hadn't been her fault, as her whole life had been beyond her control. Even her own conception keeps revolving through her mind. She finds contemplating her life from the very beginning to be therapeutic. She visualises Big Cheese and Bart taking from her newly conceived mother a cell from the tiny fetus and an unfertilized egg from the mother. They fused the cell with the egg and implanted it in a surrogate mother. The original fetus and the clone were then gestated separately, one naturally and one on the ranch, and born within two minutes of each other. Consequently, the two Danielles were routinely interchanged and interfaced with each other's lives. Exchanges occurred anywhere anytime mostly under cover of night. The Greys would transfix them both with the magic wand and using the gravity beam switch them in less than a minute. There were about eight exchanges per annum. The reconnaissance spacecraft would hover about ten to twenty meters above the house or apartment. Any people awake, either in cars, homes, or on the streets would be transfixed in a specific electromagnetic pulse that effectively shut down their sense of time and memory, known euphemistically as "missing time". Whole neighbourhoods were affected. The two Danielles knew of no other sibling self, except that one was made aware of her mentors, the aliens, and would do as they wished her to do, because she was powerless to resist. Danielle is now feeling a latent anger that her life had been played almost like a puppet. She wants to regain control of her destiny and feel that all of her achievements were her own. And now for the most powerful woman on the entire globe to have the rug pulled out beneath her, made dead to the world (at least her twin), and shunted off to a distant star system, annoyed her to the core of her being. But she is alive, though too numb to care anymore; it is the only escape she can use at present.

'What time is it, Jimmy?' she asks indolently, stretching from her bunk. Danielle likes to remain on Eastern Standard Time.

'Five a.m.,' he replies without looking up.

'Why don't you come to bed?' she suggests languidly, putting her rich grey hair behind her ear.

Jimmy, who is studying an extensive star map on the monitor, looks at her and smiles. Her appetites are coming back. 'Why not?' he says, quickly, leaving the monitor.

They cuddle in bed and manage to make love while Lilly stays purposefully at the main console minding her own business. Lilly had let it be known that hers and Danielle's awkward relations should not impede their hoped for friendship. Lilly had even admitted to Danielle that she had had Jimmy's baby but then given it away. The breeding was part of the program she had said, as Danielle knew it to be. She did not mention that she had taken the baby from the ranch where it was born and to be raised. Yet Danielle just tolerates Lilly because she and Jimmy need her. She knows they have to work together. Moreover, as it is, the turn of events are so strange for both Jimmy and Danielle, any ignominy either felt in respect to their infidelity is dwarfed by their banishment. Jimmy had lingering and suppressed anguish over both Danielle and his child with Lilly, and promised himself he would try to make amends.

'We will get back to the way we were,' mutters Jimmy defiantly, the love-making having not rendered him his usual comfortable repose.

'When?' whispers Danielle into the nape of his neck.

'After we arrive at Jah. By the time we get back to earth many years may have gone by. I think we could get away with it, as long as the Greys don't detect us. We could live in the bunker on Rob and Andie's farm.'

'Perhaps it's best we never go back,' she says wryly, 'Better than living in that giant catacomb you built. We'd turn into bats.'

'We have to go back, Danielle, to warn the government somehow what is happening.'

'There's no one to trust. I can't even trust myself!' she exclaims sadly. 'They've won, if you look at it that way. We must get on with our lives.'

'I made an oath, Danielle, to defend freedom. It's the least I can do.'

'God, Jimmy, you sound like a marine out of boot camp: *Roger Ramjet, he's our man, hero of our nation!*' she sings that old cartoon piece. 'Who cares anymore? The aliens will perhaps improve things at home.'

Jimmy doesn't answer. Her callous attitude makes him angry and now she seems unlike the terrestrial Danielle he knew. Since she had revealed to him Johnny had had regular sex with Danielle all her life, he is not completely the same forgiving man. But then he knew that it wasn't likely her fault; she did-n't even know, at least one Danielle wasn't made aware of the affair with Johnny, though Jimmy had a strong suspicion that this twin did know by her familiarity with Johnny. But how could the other not really know Johnny and the ranch? Could her memory have been that manipulated?

'I care,' he finally says, getting up and pacing.

'So do I,' squeaks Lilly, humourously.

'Shut up, Lilly!' demands Danielle.

'Danielle, cut out the hostility,' implores Jimmy.

'Well, if it wasn't for her, the little slut, we wouldn't be here right now!'

'Danielle! What the hell has gotten into you?'

'Jimmy, I've had enough of this charade. My life on earth is dead, dead! My life with Johnny is dead, dead! Good riddance . . . '

'You mean you're the Danielle who slept with him?' asked Jimmy, incredulously.

'No you fool, we both slept with him,' she lies, 'But I remember!'

'How can you be sure?'

'I don't know.'

'Danielle, I . . . I thought now we could at least be truly together . . . '

'Well, it seems to me we are, my dear,' she snaps facetiously.

Jimmy looks at her and she looks back haughtily and unladylike sitting there naked with her legs pulled up showing her grey mound, the sex that Johnny took all of Jimmy's life. It repulses him. He turns away. She con-tinues to eye him coolly.

'Jimmy, if it's any consolation,' she remarks softly, 'I much preferred you. I just wish you hadn't gotten so damned heroic. We used to rule the earth. Look at us now, and Johnny's still laughing. He thoroughly enjoys playing God.'

'You mean, you and Johnny ruled the earth,' corrects Jimmy, sardon-ically. 'He obviously enjoyed his greatest trophy, his Empress.'

'I'm sure he's found many an Empress to satisfy himself in,' she adds bitterly.

'Danielle, don't make it more difficult for yourself. Shortly, we will arrive at the Eridani star system; we must present ourselves to be worthy humans and gain their respect.'

'Poor Max,' she says.

'I know,' concurs Jimmy, commiserating. 'He was loyal to the death.'

Danielle closes her legs and refrains from responding. Her usual imperturbable expression shows a hint of remorse. Jimmy knows that she is suffering and gives her the benefit of the doubt in respect to her pulling herself together. Danielle has mental powers unparalleled with nerves of steel, yet she remains quintessentially – as she was known on earth – a woman of refinement and impeccable character.

They pull out of hyperspace just outside the Jah star system and begin their inward lap to the fourth planet from their star. They find it with little difficulty as all the frequencies led there. Soon they settle into orbit around the massive planet, at least twice the size of earth, but much warmer on the poles and hotter in the equatorial regions. The great globe is nonetheless beautiful and breathtaking in its unique differences. Their oceans are purplish-blue and massive and like earth cover most of the planet surface. Great swaths of green and brown and white towards the polar regions with dabs of rich burgundy made it look to Jimmy a little like a massive ball of spumoni ice cream with more blue. How similar, yet different it is from earth, but all the same forces of nature seemed to apply with vast high and low pressured weather systems. The Eridani weather, however, is as it turned out more stable than Earth's and indeed as it turned out artificially controlled. Within minutes of their arrival, an oblong ship comes along side the Meteor and secures them to it in a gravity field. A man with blondish hair, blue eyes, and lightly tanned skin comes onto their open channel.

'Hello Blue Planet people,' he says in perfect English, smiling, 'Welcome to Jah . . . or as you say – Eridani. My name is Dewrzah; we've been expecting you.'

'Greetings Dewrzah, and...Jah, or as we say Spumoni,' jokes Jimmy, smiling. 'I hope you take us in, 'cause we were kicked off ours through no fault of our own and have no place to go!'

'Spumoni?' says Dewrzah, a little quizzically. 'I am not familiar with the word.'

'Your planet looks to me a little like Spumoni ice cream,' quips Jimmy. 'I hope it tastes as good as it looks.'

Dewrzah laughs to their relief.

'You are welcome, friends,' he says, 'And I commiserate with your problems.'

'My name is Jimmy Pidgeon, this is Danielle Perreault, and Lilly Grey.'

'So it appears old Johnny ran you out of town,' says Dewrzah.

'How did you know?' asks Danielle, humoured by his familiarity with the North American idiom.

'We've been monitoring you. And I have spent some time there.'

'Really?' utter both Jimmy and Danielle together.

'Follow me,' says Dewrzah.

Dewrzah takes them down into the atmosphere that is almost identical to that of the earth. They fly over a vast ocean three times the size of the Pacific, huge snowy mountains, lush forests, deserts, large civilised areas, oddly antiseptic without any congestion or ugliness, then verdant rural areas and finally to a secluded lake where a few well kept homes are situated made from honed stone, beautifully crafted wood and unique satin-sheen metal alloys. Large windows adorn the designs of the homes and vary from round to rectangular, but are mostly round. There is a forest, fields of crops and meadows of wild flowers. A beach rings the lake of emerald green water. The scene and smells are all so similar yet different. The flora and fauna is unrecognisable. The flowers are brilliant but unnamable to them, including the birds and animals too. The scarcity of roads and commercial activity make it appear super-pastoral like some fantasy world in a fairy tale. There are no boats, nor cars or planes, just the occasional soft hum of oblong gravity machines. The purity of the environment seems almost sterile. Lawns and gardens are wild, yet unusually organised.

When they first stepped out of the Meteor onto terra firma, the gravity and air was obviously quite different. They veered clumsily, staggered and fell to the ground picking up the dirt and some flowers to smell.

'Amazing!' exclaims Jimmy, getting up and finding his balance. 'I feel lighter.'

'Wow!' peals Danielle in delight.

'We're on a new planet! With a sun! With water! Air! It's the most incredible thing! Dewrzah! Can you understand how we feel?'

'Dewzah and a woman who was also in his vehicle step out to them smiling warmly, witnessing their emotion. The woman introduces herself as Nutu, but otherwise remains silent and distant. She is darker than Dewrzah, tall, beautiful and young.

'Certainly,' he says, 'We cherish what you cherish. Now follow me to that house. You may live here. Your neighbours are also earth-human. Over there is Tommy Castello. He's second generation. Soon you may travel widely, but first we must settle you in. It will take your physiology a while to adapt to our gravity. You may experience discomfort for a month or longer. When you are ready we shall meet with the elders in the council to discuss your plans. I'm sure you will find it less chaotic here than on earth,' he adds.

But Jimmy and Danielle are too enthralled to care. Even the diminutive Lilly smiles in their unique happiness. She observes, however, that whereas Danielle is prepared to forget about earth, Jimmy is not at all inclined to do so. Their real differences were made painfully clear in that last segment of hyperspace. Lilly knows Jimmy could not love Danielle in the way it had been, though he goes through the motions in trying to appeal to his highest sense of compassion, but that's where it ends. Compassion is no competition for the passion that had once held them together. Danielle appears to be put off by Jimmy's adverse dealing with the slings and arrows of their fortune. 'Let's make the best of it, dear,' she had said.

'We are,' he replied. But the enchantment of Jah lets them suspend their problems temporarily. Indeed, their arrival is utterly the most incredible experience that they have ever encountered.

Over time they travel planet Jah, and visit its more densely populated areas, which seem scant as compared to Earth's; in fact, there are no cities per se, just widespread communities of the Jah who worked together, both individually and collectively on the multifarious tasks that occupy their society. Every major impasse either political or economic was put to a vote within the governing body, and sometimes directly to the people. Yet for the most part, each community is self-sufficient in every way. The communities grow their own food, generate their own power, educated their own children and govern their own constituencies. There are no political jurisdictions or borders, just geographic regions and bio-regions. The leaders are chosen by their communities for a specific duration in which a recycling of duty suffices to constitute change; there is no government per se that has executive power. Criteria for leadership with a candidate comprises usually a curious predilection for *carpe diem* – a rarefied sense of well-being and economy of time. Their race is so advanced emotionally, psychologically and socially that even the concept of power has no place in their vocabulary except as naturally energy. Every concept of life in our own human terms have little parallel there; even in race relations – and there are variations of race, although over the millenia they had more or less evolved into one – there is not a hint of discrimination. Their economy thrives on charity and a highly calibrated incumbency perpetrating itself in a kind of universal responsibility. From passion to philosophy, the Jah see all life as one well-tempered motivation. There is no competition in technology, commerce or art. All things are deemed to be of equal value. Jimmy likens them to supernatural beings living supernaturally, as compared to the many less desirable traits of an adolescent humanity.

After a time Danielle adapts surprisingly well on Jah, whereas Jimmy feels rather empty, though not wanting in scientific interest. One would think their reaction would be the other way around, but Jimmy yearns to get back into the fray of Earth's human affairs, and Danielle can't bring herself to care anymore, having spent her whole life in the thick of it. Jimmy can now understand implicitly why a species such the Jah do not want the Blue Planet People, as they call Earth's people, to travel in space and make contact. Humankind would see them as weak and for exploiting, if not at first, but surely in time. The Reptoids are not a threat because of the so-called Eridani Frequency and they had little to gain by harvesting the less complex Eridani DNA chain.

Danielle and Jimmy are soon at odds in most ways with their connubial arrangement. Jimmy has stated on numerous occasions his avowed intent to return home, though he procrastinates on an immediate depar·ture. He does, however, among his scientific and literary observations, have his preparations under way. Lilly has gone indefinitely to Zeta 1 having taken passage on a Jah ship. Danielle has told Jimmy she would stay and dared him to go home alone during their dissensions. This resolve became strangely desirable to both as if they knew it would be the end of their relationship, and they were testing the waters of such an about-face of their life. The old walls go up. At first there are no tears, just perhaps the consternation of unrealised dreams. But once actualised, the will now to proceed with their lives changes the chemistry of their affinity. The bond holding them together on earth had been a kind of competitive martyrdom like a charade of suffering and temptation, or a new challenge, or even a challenge in terms of discovery, whether it had to do with political power, scientific curiosity, or literary art. All of this came to a grinding halt on Jah. There is little more to achieve, only the quelling of a very human compulsion to do so. But a few weeks before parting tensions really come to a boil. They are doing their utmost to keep their emotions subdued in deference to their hosts, at least their neighbours who are far enough away but not quite beyond screaming distance.

'I am dead and gone to heaven,' proclaims Danielle one afternoon, as she and Jimmy are idling under a tree by the lake.

'I *will* miss you,' intones Jimmy, somewhat indolently.

'And I too shall miss you,' she says looking away, not wanting to face him as if going through the motions of duty.

'I have not out-lived my usefulness,' he claims, looking for her eyes.

She gives them to him.

'Nor have I,' she maintains.

'What shall I tell Andie?' he asks, after awhile.

'Tell her the truth that I have died and gone to heaven.'

'But that I didn't like it much,' remarks Jimmy, adding, 'But I will tell her...the truth.'

For some unknown reason when Jimmy says these words, Danielle bursts into tears. It is the first time in Jimmy's life he has ever witnessed her break down so completely. She shrieks aloud as she turns and twists in agony, with her chest heaving uncontrollably. It is a pitiful sight that catches Jimmy off guard. At first he can only look on in shock at this spectacle of emotion from a woman he had known almost his entire life, who usually smiled or gritted her way through any unpleasantness. Her usual strength now rebounds into a heart-wrenching show of guilt, remorse, desperation and everything perceived in extreme perturbation. Finally, Jimmy with his hand on her shoulder, speaks tender words into her ear and she soon lies there quietly inert in a seeming paralysis of fear. She then looks at him with swollen eyes and messy white hair.

'I've wanted to do that for a long time,' she murmurs haltingly between the involuntary sobs as her chest still heaves. 'For me,' she adds.

Jimmy patiently caresses her back and neck.

'I will survive,' she goes on bravely. 'On the up side, everything I've ever worked for in my entire life – to better the human condition – is realised here on Jah. What a fitting retirement project. I suppose I will simply become a foreign diplomat and help them better understand our earth. I think they probably understand it better than we do, though.

Perhaps, they could use some of my political skills, yet again they're likely to eschew them here. I will start again and work my way through their system and earn their respect, but I presume there's no need for respect because everyone here's so above it all; it's funny to think habits such as social graces are deemed to be affectations with little constructive value. I mean it's the norm, so they don't emphasise behaviour befitting certain situations as we do.'

She laughs at ease. 'My social skills on earth were forced at best. I think I'll fit in just fine here; I will feel comfortable in my solitude. There's no subterfuge, or 'look' to be made, just this naïve openness to our way of thinking. God, even their sexuality is shameless – I mean, I think it's okay – but public fornication seems a bit much; yet they do appear to make it discreet – I assume because no one bats an eye. It's as if emotions are conceptualised. Nothing sacred . . . '

'Danielle,' Jimmy interrupts, 'We don't belong here. Come home with me. Things will return to as before . . . '

'Living in your tomb of a bunker? Jimmy, Jimmy, love transcends. I like it here.' She holds him desperately.

'Jimmy, I have wronged you all my life . . . '

'No you haven't.'

'Jimmy, listen; I would wrong you again . . . '

'Danielle, you do not wrong me,' he states firmly.

'Here, I am actually whole, complete,' she asserts, not heeding him. 'I have earned this station. It is my idea of utopia; what more could I want? I am old, no? I feel older than you. You must go back. Take Lilly. It is my wish that you become whole too. God knows you deserve it. You belong to earth. I belong here.'

A silence befalls.

'I am whole,' says Jimmy, belatedly. Somehow the way he says it and the timing sends Danielle laughing.

'Look at us,' she says, with her eyes brimming tearfully. What are we doing here on a strange planet? How did we get here? What is this trip?

Do you remember the zoo?' Then in a sudden releasing, as if a mutual link flipped on cue, they both tumble into a fit of excessive laughter, and laugh, and laugh until it hurts. When it subsides they fall into each other's arms and make love passionately, almost ferociously under that tree like animals that is quite extraordinary for people their age. It is a desperate coupling as if they know they cannot stay together and is a last emotional hurrah to the senses. Afterwards, naked and subdued, they get up slowly and head into the warm emerald water for a swim.

'There's more,' she suddenly declares, as they walk back afterwards to their *palapa* as Danielle terms their funny round house.

'More of what?' asks Jimmy, calmly.

'I saw her,' she says.

'Saw who?' he wonders, turning to her while she continues walking, looking at the ground.

'Danielle . . . the other one.'

'You did?' utters Jimmy earnestly, which intimates his feeling that the other one was the one he might have really loved. But Danielle doesn't skip a beat.

'They put us together at our Gatineau residence before we . . . she died.'

'Really?' says Jimmy shocked, not knowing what to say.

'We never spoke. We didn't need to, or couldn't, somehow. We looked at each other through the French doors. This is it, the end, we said, putting our hands up to the glass; how cruel we must be to feel nothing! We knew then everything! Then they dematerialised her before my eyes, and finally the house.'

'But you must've communicated something more!' says Jimmy in exasperation, betraying his emotional fidelity in the hope that the other may have expressed some loving sentiment toward him.

Danielle is beyond reach.

'I couldn't believe how beautiful she was . . . we smiled and seemed to be thankful that we were special. She was smiling that kind of bodhisattva smile of understanding, as if to say, I can't say I don't know who you are and I don't really care; our lives must be one . . . when they . . . I, took her life, my life . . . she said one thing... "Jimmy" ...that's all I remember before being back on The Ranch.'

They stop in the doorway of the palapa and look deeply into each other's eyes. Danielle is tearful again. Jimmy holds her.

'Thank you,' he says. 'Thank you for loving me.'

'I killed her, Jimmy,' she cries. 'I killed my sister.'

'Then I killed her too; we had no choice; we only did what we thought best.'

'That's why I must stay, Jimmy,' she mutters despondently, 'To honour her memory, my memory; I would not know how to live on earth without her after that. They were cruel to use us like that . . . I am not like that . . . we . . . we were special.'

'Let us then pray for her, in you, in me, an offering of the greatest of all human essence, our meaning, our value, our love.'

'How?' she says, dejectedly.

'Our will to overcome the odds against us: we must survive to preserve who we were. People must know what happened.'

'Okay, Jimmy.' She keeps looking into his eyes, strangely submissive like a lamb.

'And a promise.'

'What's that?'

'That we keep in touch through the Jah.'

'Okay,' she agrees, hugging him and becoming tearful again. 'What on earth is wrong with me?' she asks into his shoulder. 'I can't stop crying.'

'You never cease to amaze me, Danielle,' he says.

'I will miss you, and Andie, more than you know,' she whimpers. 'I love you and I am dead.'

'Danielle?' asks Jimmy, as an afterthought.

'What?' she says looking into him now with eyes that burn.

'Which one of you gave birth to Andie?'

Danielle sighs before answering. 'I did,' she answers looking away.

'How do you know for sure?'

'Does it really matter?'

'I suppose not; I guess you both gave her away.'

'You have not forgiven me.'

'I have now.'

When Jimmy and Danielle finally separate, they simply smile and part, no hug or kiss or regret or recrimination or anything but a kind of existential happiness in their own happiness. Danielle seems to purge her demons and Jimmy still appears to be pursuing his. It has resolved as simply as that.

Jimmy exits the atmosphere with Lilly who had returned, and travels out beyond the solar pull before turning upside down. By pointing the Meteor's belly and source of the gravity wave, he could direct a more powerful charge to earth's sun, one in any myriad of stars. Then he engages the reactor confidently to its maximum and sends the charge like a lightning bolt deep into space propagating its gravity wave where the Meteor had no choice but to proceed with it far, far beyond any linear rate of speed, even the speed of light.

'What's interesting,' continues Cephren, 'is that Danielle became quite well respected in her new community and went on to become an elder. Dewrzah told me that she died in her sleep of old age. Her heart ran out. Some surmised she died of a broken heart, as she lived out her days increasingly and terribly remorseful of how she had betrayed Jimmy, although unwittingly. It wracked her with guilt and failure, although she never showed her feelings to the Jah, nor again to Jimmy in their infrequent correspondence.

'Jimmy lived out his life in and about the bunker, actually out-living his daughter and son-in-law, and died in his ninety-sixth year of a massive stroke. The year was 2077. He was cremated and his ashes were scattered on the farm by his grandchildren, the Barnetts. A sugar maple was planted in the place, as he requested, without any marker or headstone. Incidentally, there were some interesting stories about Jimmy's life in the bunker. He had been seen by other than family from time to time at his daughter's house and in the woods with his grandchildren. People inquired and were told he was a dear old friend of the family. Jimmy Pidgeon, officially of course, had apparently long since died of unknown causes in the southwest. When asked his name, the children just said Uncle Jimmy. But what really began the onset of the rumor mill, were the purported sightings, albeit rare, of the Meteor and the freakish, ethereal woman, Lilly, who obviously scared people half to death. Before Jimmy went back to earth, she had come back to Jah where Danielle, with her blessing, urged Lilly to join Jimmy and go to earth. Lilly did just that and remained his loyal companion for the latter part of his life. They both actually took a keen interest in their child, Rachel Little Feather, Heyoka's ancestor.'

'But what about Johnny and the aliens?' interrupts Chromolox.

'I'm sorry,' says Cephren, 'I didn't intend to sidetrack his, Jimmy's that is, dilemma. The world was just so frightening: the rampant terrorism with nuclear and biological weapons, mounting crisis after crisis, the disintegration of the great democracies, chaos and starvation, disease and epidemics, that I shield myself from his nightmare, all our nightmares.

'Johnny never found out that Jimmy had returned until years later. By that time Johnny had long since put Danielle behind him, and as she had not returned, considered Jimmy harmless. And harmless, he may have been; but he did manage to communicate with General Good. He actually abducted him in the Meteor when he was on leave at his cottage. It should be remembered that Jimmy lost some years, or gained some depending on how one looked at it, when he travelled to Jah and back. The time-space continuum was disrupted in hyperspace. By the time Jimmy returned back to earth it was 2050. At any rate, Jimmy related to General Good the whole story, from his early years with Danielle, to the present and explained why he had to take the Meteor. The General was actually overjoyed to see him and even told him to keep the spacecraft saying that they were making another one based on his data and customized engineering facility. Later, the second Meteor and all the recovered extraterrestrial ships were dematerialised at the outset of the war by General Good, for fear of them being utilised by the Righteous, who became aware of their existence when the New Republican party came to power. It should be noted, the General wished for the supremacy of the Righteous, yet only to defeat the United Front and the clones, but not with the use of the alien vehicles.

'The General revealed what Big Cheese had told him that Jimmy had been taken care of and was at least no longer a security risk, but would not elaborate. The General now understood how they had been manipulated, but he was stymied as to know who were the clones. How could Jimmy know that he, the General, wasn't a clone, or indeed himself for that matter? Jimmy explained by saying that he felt General Blaine was not a clone to the best of his knowledge, as Dr. Williams was the original prototype of that generation, and that consequently in the advent of Blaine's own death, Blaine had chosen General Good personally, with whom he felt obviously confident. But still they discussed ways to find out who the clones were. There was no way the General and Jimmy could download the alien's files, because they kept none. They couldn't possibly know if most of the MJ-12 were clones, if not all, including themselves! It seemed a hopeless situation.'

'So what did they do?' queries Chromolox.

'General Good asked Major Jeremy Blaine, General Blaine's grandson to tag everybody personally, I mean everybody including themselves, MJ, political people, thousands of people, with a microscopic implant. The Major used the magic wand – that alien neuron rod – which immobilised them and then he implanted the tiny device deep in their nasal cavity. Over a period of time, they came to know who the clones were from subsequent check-ups when many of them were found to be without the implant. So both the General and the Colonel (recently promoted), the only two apprised of the test study, had a pretty good idea who the clones were, although they could never be sure, whether the aliens could have been playing with them all along. The reason I say this is that it was possible that the aliens orchestrated the events as they unfolded, even World War 3, to bring about a house cleaning, as-it-were, because planet earth was self-destructing. War was an attempt by the Reptoids to do their dirty work and bring about some control necessary for their purposes and preserve the fertility of their earth-farm, as long as humanity did not nuke themselves into oblivion. This may well have demonstrated that Colonel Blaine, a man with an unblemished record prior to his siding with the Righteous and notorious nuking, was in fact undertaking to unhinge the alien stranglehold on earth.

'And to make a long story short, just prior to World War 3, it should be noted that Colonel Blaine was ordered by General Good to join the Righteous in the hope that he could persuade the aliens to let go of earth. When this proved to be impossible, Blue Phoenix was their only alternative. You would know of course from your history that General Good had been brought out of retirement by the United Front to lead their forces. By then, the United Front leadership was comprised of a majority of clones. Before Colonel Blaine nuked New York, or even considered it, General Good in his seventies had warned the Colonel that the new President Smythe (the United Front had usurped the mantle of government following the assassination of the New Republican President Kimball) was preparing to nuke Cheyenne Mountain that had been taken over by Blaine and the Righteous as their military headquarters. Blaine and Good were both in the predicament of both hating the Righteous and the United Front. Blaine dreaded what he believed he had to do. Today, it all seems so insane, but then it was deemed to be a war of survival. Blaine had to decide whether to stand down or use the opportunity to destroy the United Front, which meant destroying the government and everything with it. Old General Good did his best to monitor the crisis from the Pentagon and finally, uncovered by Johnny, revealed reluctantly to the President and Cabinet what was happening, despite the fact that most of them were clones. Then Colonel Blaine was killed by an infiltrator in the Righteous, but not before nuking first Mexico City, New York, Atlanta and almost Washington, in the vain hope the aliens would recognise their resolve and determination and leave them alone. General Good's dire strategy had failed of course, fatally misjudging the aliens' control; he was after all surrounded by enemies. The General was subsequently liquidated, but presented as the great war hero needed to help create the fighting spirit in order to defeat the Righteous, thus securing the illusion of victory for the people by the United Front. The aliens' vested interest in humanity was like a tenacious parasite. Johnny must have taken some kind of awesome pleasure in our squalor, although I believe he became consumed by his obsession with humanity, thanks possibly to Perreault, and really tried to effect change. He too failed ultimately. I suspect that that is why they have since never made any overt attempt to take over earth in an absolute sense, though remaining true to their concept of being our containers. Furthermore, when General Good had made it official about the clones, there was an internal housecleaning. It was precisely then that Johnny and the Greys realised they could integrate no more without overt action, and consequently within fifty years were gone.

'But the Third World war, of course, had changed irrevocably the geopolitical map. The ever-emergent Chinese saw the war as an opportunity to assert their control over Japan, Indochina, Thailand, Indonesia and East Russia, with little resistance. No one thought it possible since the Chinese from an historical perspective were not usually aggressors of that nature, with few exceptions such as Tibet and Korea. It is possible they too were acting at the alien's silent bequest. But the Chinese nevertheless smelled an easy victory; at the very least they couldn't help but increase their influence. Four long years lapsed before peace returned, at the cost of losing the Far East to Chinese interests and a couple hundred million dead worldwide. And although Johnny and his Greys remained for over forty more years until the Asteroid, General Good did succeed partially in extricating their hold on human affairs. The Reptoid's attempt to dominate us was then repaid in kind.'

'What do you mean, "repaid in kind", Cephren?' catechises Chromolox.

'In spite of their efforts to all but destroy us, we survived and within a few hundred years have far surpassed our previous expectations. An interesting anecdote is that as a last gesture of their "caring", the Reptoids deliberately altered the trajectories of the nuclear missiles fired at the Big Asteroid that were to pulverize it sending it to oblivion, which in effect meant that Johnny had hoped to scupper the earth. Knowing Johnny, I think, he felt he was doing us a favour, but by then their presence had diminished considerably. It would seem they considered it appropriate once again to send humanity back to the Stone Age as a form of suppression – hands-off control, if you will. Well, Chromolox, the point is: we have news for them. We are free.'

Some of the Board including Gabriella and Olivia can only shake their heads at the madness that had taken place before, down the labyrinth of their history.

'And Dewrzah?' asks Chromolox breaking the stupor.

'I met Dewrzah in Atlantis.'

'Atlantis? Are you serious?' she utters incredulously.

'The remains of Atlantis exist a couple of kilometers beneath the ice of Antarctica. Antarctica as a continent, shifted dramatically to the South Pole as a result of a major earth crust displacement over twelve thousand years ago. The ruins were discovered by the Americans with the help of the Greys in the 21st century. An undersea passage and tunnel lead to it. I went there when the Chicagos found me near Prince Edward Island in the Maritimes. Runaway and I travelled underwater there with them on our tail. We lost them under the ice and found the passage. It's the most fantastic thing, truly a wonder of the world; there are pyramids, statues, temples, all made from solid rock, crafted impeccably. It was the seat of an advanced civilisation that drew much of its inspiration from the Neteru.

'While there, I submersed myself back into Jimmy's Chip, which completed my indoctrination so-to-speak. On our return, we were shocked to see another craft entering the vast ice dome that surrounded Atlantis. The unique discoid craft hovered along side of us and then a man literally materialised inside the Volcano. Runaway stood between us and was immediately transfixed by the magic wand. The man then said not to fear him and introduced himself as Dewrzah from Jah. He was very similar in appearance to us, about the same height, but more delicately featured. He looked Nordic with short course blond hair; his skin colour was slightly paler and tougher looking as you could see the pores – a kind of ageless quality – but his eyes were a brilliant blue. He said later that he was almost four hundred years of age! And that his people had lived to five hundred of our years! He could speak English fluently, but also could use telepathy. It was from Dewrzah that I learned of Danielle's death in the Eridani system, also that it was Lilly who extracted the Neteru from Jimmy after he died, and in fact, finished the documentary in the X13 that we all know, which Jimmy had begun. Her people were also responsible for implanting it in Flower Child and then passing it on to Redman and Bird-in-the-Sky.

'Dewrzah told me that we would be welcome to join the Eridani Frequency, a galactic organisation solely construed to benefit all galactic species, to help those where possible and contain others that were dangerous to the natural harmony of the universe. He said the Reptoids had their own galactic commonwealth – his term – but were very particular about their own absolute hegemony. There was no longer a threat between them and the Frequency, as it had been worked out long ago, after our Third World War. In fact, the war spurred the two galactic organisations to work out their differences. The resulting accord had been a success, from what I understand; however, Dewrzah was quite firm in saying that there would be no welcoming delegation if our planet did not work out its tribal problems. He was trying to tell me that any power or force not compatible with the Frequency would be contained. He finished by intimating that if I were elected, and made good with our global "tribal" problems, preliminary overtures would be forthcoming. So, it's still up to me to win the Earth Chair, I think, for this to happen.'

The whole Board stands up and claps with a terrific accolade. More champagne is poured and Cephren toasted.

'Wait!' says Cephren, 'Let's not get too excited; besides, if we are to celebrate, I would like to wait until my son and sister arrive. I also want Heyoka and her warriors to be invited. Without her help, we would not be here today. And futhermore, please find Treason; she deserves the highest honour. Meanwhile, I must tend to arrangements regarding Anna Gram, so if you could forgive me and allow me to retire to the Loft; thank you everybody, bless you.'

Spring does not grace Sunsetwind until mid-May that year, a tardy month behind. But it comes with a munificence unparalleled: the ritual greening through forest and dale keeps one's faith in the infinite rejuvenation of life, and the swallows, robins, warblers, killdeers, bluebirds, blackbirds, orioles and many others sing their joy. The air smells of the fresh-tilled earth. Dandelions upon dandelions are spread as far as the eye can see across the expansive hay fields like galaxies of star-clusters. Nowhere is this more apparent that bright sunny day than surrounding the old Barnett ruins. A small group, the Board and friends, wait anxiously for the small earth-remover to uncover the old well from its centuries of detritus. Soon the wellhead is exposed and the cap removed. All the spectators crane their necks to get a peek down the black hole where water could still be seen. They set up a hoist with a platform that can be lowered. Cephren is the first to go down. He feels the chill of the cool, dank well as he comes to a stop beside the ancient door in the casing, which swings inward with a good push. Once inside the tunnel he reaches for the switch that he knows to be there, and beholds the wonder of lights turning on after centuries of disuse. Shortly, they are all in the tunnel with Cephren in the lead, and Sam at his heels.

'This is where it all happened,' says Cephren, still amazed. 'Flower Child created Sunsetwind from these subterranean spaces. This was her home, designed and originally inhabited by Jimmy Pidgeon himself!'

Cephren takes them down the long passage and retrieves the keys from their notch in the wall exactly as he knew them to be. They come to the first and subsequent doors and rooms to find them almost empty, but dry and cool. There are the remnants of supplies and equipment including dried foods and seed-grain. They all wondered if it was still possible to eat or plant both, if such an ordeal had to be done all over again. The uncanny catastrophe that had befallen those early Sunsetwinders dawns acutely on them. And here is the last resort, a haven and sanctuary hidden from the cruel world.

They continue their descent until they came to the fork in the tunnel. They take the passage to Jimmy's inner sanctum where he kept his computer and books and personal items. 'What a find!' they exclaim, gaping at the photographs, notes and troves of miscellaneous paraphernalia. There is talk of a museum.

The final passage down to the last door has them gripped in so much excitement that they are doing their best not to show impatience. Cephren had found the key to be among the assorted items in old Scratch's stash box that had been stuffed behind an original wood panel in Redman's lab. A ton of junk was piled about the wall, some of which had been there before Redman moved in. Again the stash box was found exactly as had been revealed in Jimmy's Chip. As phenomenal as all this appears to them, Cephren now inserts with some trepidation the key to unlock the last door into the room. No one else knows what to expect, as it is the final mystery. And the memory of it comes crashing down through Cephren's mind.

That day both Remy and Flower Child with their young son, a toddler of two, go for a drive in the Black Panther, the car that they had purloined from Darabak. They discover to their surprise that this sleek machine could also levitate, though clumsily, and even move through the air at reasonable speeds. For the past couple of years they had created a safe region within the boundaries of their immediate surroundings. Other outlying communities were soon persuaded to join them and they collectively administered the beginnings of a judicial sovereignty of which Flower Child as their leader ruled with a benevolent despotism of her own design. She was careful to pick able men and women who acted as her law enforcers as well as train a modest militia to counter any threat. They conscripted a motley assortment of vehicles, both land and air with personnel who were armed from the bunker cache, though only Remy and herself were privy to it.

Their reputation as a fair and just municipality radiated beyond the region, and over the decades their government grew into a large autonomous district. Although Flower Child created a justice system in which criminal behaviour was dealt with severely, and few dared enter her region with ill intent, there happened one day an incident that popular mythology recorded as the Rape of Flower Child. This incident had taken on these mythical proportions, because in fact Flower Child had never actually been physically raped, though the brutal episode had earned its ill estimation by its tragic consequences. That spring they began to construct a large field stone house on a high point of land where centuries later the present Pyramid would be erected. They were still living in the bunker.

A man has been watching from the woods. With him is Darabak's ex-mate, Dolly. They have evaded the security ring surrounding the hill that is patrolled around the clock every day. But the woman knows the shift and with the man easily dodges the security net. For a day the two of them watch from some dense bushes the front entrance to the bunker, which during construction is being used regularly instead of the camouflaged trap higher on the ridge. Remy has even cut a lane down through the forest to the entrance where they park the Black Panther. That night the man and woman avoid the patrol and stealthily sneak to the main door and go in unimpeded. No one is there. They look about and head to the rear where in the future Redman would make his lab and office. They notice that a wood panel in the wall is slightly ajar and peer behind. They see a passage that leads deep into the hillside. Following it they came to a door and hear voices. They burst into a huge chamber at least ten meters high and thirty by thirty wide. The toddler stands smiling in their way. The man smashes him over the head with his flash gun knocking him sense-less. Flower Child spins around in shock to see a face she thought had been erased from her memory. Standing there with a sick grin pointing his notorious gun is the malicious Gus with Darabak's ex-woman.

'David!' Flower Child screams, running to her son ignoring the gun. She kneels down and feels for a pulse. He is alive and breathing. 'Trashies!' she spits venomously, looking up at Gus and the woman.

But Gus says nothing. Still pointing the gun at her, he walks toward the fantastic object before them filling much of the room. It is Jimmy's Meteor. Gus gawks at it in his cynical wonder. His drawn, bearded face and rat-tail hair are a perfect compliment to his insipid eyes and sallow complexion. His ill-fitting clothes are smudged with dirt and grime, not an uncommon sight, but with Gus there is a putrid smell of fermented body odor in keeping with his squalid circumstances. Gus had led such a perverted life he could never be redeemed. It is known that even in his youth his rage and hatred were infamous and death seemed to co-opt his every intention.

'What in hell's name do you have here, Terrie?' he asks in his vulgar vernacular. 'A Flying Saucer?'

'You could have killed him!' she cries, thinking frantically what she could do.

'Where's that sap, Remy, Terrie?' he asked looking at her briefly while walking about the craft touching the cool, metallic grey hull.

'With the patrol, Gus,' she lies. 'You'd better put down your gun and get out while you can,' she adds coldly. She wonders where Remy is and assumes that he must have been in the bathroom, luckily for that matter.

'She's lying,' snaps Dolly. The woman stands there with a washed, glazed look in her eyes.

'What is this?' reiterates Gus motioning to the spacecraft.

'What do you think? A space vehicle,' she says facetiously.

'How did it get in here?' he demands.

'I don't know.'

'Do you know how it works?'

'No.'

'Then what are you doing with it?'

'Studying it. We don't understand . . .'

'Come here,' orders Gus.

'No,' she declares.

'I'll kill your son, if you don't.'

She moves to him haltingly. He grabs her and looks her up and down.

'Show me how to get in.'

'I don't know; there isn't a door.'

'Tell me what you do know!'

Gus points the gun at the boy lying inert on the cement floor.

'I don't know anything!' she insists.

'What are these lights?' he asks fingering a panel on a table.

'We think that it opens a door to the ship,' she says, defiantly.

'You know more than you're telling me.' He looks at the boy and appears about to harm him, but hesitates when he notices a large poster bed across the chamber. 'Go to the bed,' he demands, and beckons to Dolly to follow. 'Tie her up, face down,' he instructs.

'With what?' the woman says.

'Those coat hangers. Unravel them.'

Dolly unravels the coat hangers and twists them around Flower Child's wrists and the two posts so that her arms are extended.

'Now take off her pants,' he commands.

Soon Flower Child is naked from the waist down.

'Is this what he does to you for kicks?' Flower Child asks the woman. 'How can you stand this?'

'You murdered Julius,' she says morosely.

'Yes, because we didn't have any other way to deal with a criminal of his notoriety in this country. He murdered many innocent people, and you know it!'

'He saved us from starvation,' she declares, flatly.

'There can be no forgiveness for what he did!' says Flower Child.

'And I declare there is no excuse for what you did,' remarks Gus. 'We're all survivors; law is arbitrary, right Dolly?'

'Sure thing, Gus,' she says with little conviction.

'Now you listen to me, Terrie; you're gonna tell me what I wanna know or I'm gonna hurt you bad, understand?'

Flower Child does not dignify a response.

'Where's Remy?' he reiterates.

'On patrol, like I said.'

'What's the code to the Black Panther?'

'Jimmy Pidgeon.'

'Jimmy Pidgeon? Who's he?'

'He's my ancestor. He built the ship.'

'Liar. No one could build that. I've never seen anything like it. It's a UFO, right?'

'Maybe it is. Like I said, we can't make it work.'

Gus walks around to the end of the bed and leers at Flower Child. A bulge in his pants is noticed by Dolly, who turns away. He puts the weapon on the bed, and removes his pants to position himself behind her. Flower Child resists by attempting to kick him, making him laugh.

'Well, if ya can't talk, I'll just have to open her up a bit, eh Dolly?'

He is about to do his wicked deed when Remy fortuitously appears at the door of the chamber with a semi-automatic rifle aimed at Gus.

'Back off her, now!' screams Remy.

Gus coolly does as he is commanded. But Dolly, not as lost as she led on, quickly pulls a handgun from her belt, swings around and shoots Remy striking him in the shoulder and throwing him back into the passage, shooting wildly. Flower Child screams for him to get help. Gus grabs his gun, pulls up his pants and runs after him with Dolly close behind. Flower Child brings one free foot around and with her big toe managed to unwind the wire sufficiently to loosen it. Struggling desperately, she unties herself, puts on her pants, and checks quickly whether David is all right and runs back into the bunker. Remy had gone deeper into the passage up toward the generator and supply rooms, thinking that he could probably escape through the well and shoot them as they came out after him. But she doesn't know whether or not he could make it as there is a trail of blood.

She finds old Scratch's handgun that is handy, loads it, and races back up the passage. She can hear shots ahead up near the entrance. She passes the Meteor, reaches the generator, and then the supply rooms. A body is moving slowly on the floor of the munitions room. It is Dolly. There is blood everywhere. A bullet had struck her in the neck. She stops moving, her eyes staring vacuously. But Flower Child doesn't stop. She sees the passage ahead flash brightly at each explosion of the flashgun that sends its deadly voltage zapping everything in its path. She runs on fearlessly. They had exited the tunnel. She can hear a muffled cry outside above the well. The flashgun blazes away. She gropes for the ladder with the gun in one hand ready. Relieved, she hears return fire. But poking her head above the wellhead, she sees Gus standing over Remy lying sprawled across some rubble.

'Remy!' she screams.

Gus turns firing madly.

She empties her cartridge into his body as he falls shooting at the sky, cursing. In the dark distance, there are shouts. Flower Child goes to Remy and falls beside him crying his name; but he can hear no more. He is dead.

Cephren turns the key and opens the last door to enter that cavernous underground chamber. He feels for the light switch and flips it. There, sitting patiently in the hesitant flicker of its first light in centuries, is the magnificent Meteor. For several moments not a word is spoken as Chromolox, Redman, Sam, the Board and others assemble around it. Their awestruck amazement is shared in half syllables, uttering garbled expletives.

'Holy damnation!' exclaims Redman. 'How in hell am I going to get any peace and quiet anymore!' Yet he throws an admiring glance at Cephren, who smiling, ignores the old goat.

Cephren walks around Pidgeon's sleek craft by running his hand across its cool hull. At the touch he feels in it both the culmination of human achievement and the lynch-pin from which the wheel of pre-asteroid history ultimately revolved. Pidgeon in many ways was responsible for the eventual dissemination of the Reptoid hegemony over earth. It is an astounding revelation. Cephren observes in succession: the bed, a vault where over a ton of unumpentium had been stock-piled, the panel, and many other wonders of the redoubtable last bastion of Jimmy Pidgeon.

August 13. 2396

It is with some effort that I make this entry, dear reader, here in my cabin at Windy Island on Great Blue Lake. The hot, sultry air shifts outside my open window causing a slight trembling of the birch leaves. It signals the beginning of the end of the stifling heat wave in the full pulse of summer. For almost two weeks since the closing of the Summer Fête, which featured its largest extravaganza yet – a week long Fête of art, music, theater and song and dance – Heyoka, Sam and I have been languishing indolently on these rocks. It has been a euphoric occasion, in which ghosts have been purged and true love kindled like none other. Sam is the culprit. He has been insisting for three months that Heyoka come visit us. He compelled me to fly down to Cherokee – now a new state in the new union of the United States of America, which includes Chicago – and personally bring Heyoka back for the Fête and then stay with us on Windy Isle. She and I were both apprehensive at first, but soon became inseparable. I realised that Sam knew all along what would happen between us, and perhaps, probably, Heyoka too. Her strange, dignified manner, quiet speech, hauntingly angelic face, and nimble waif-like body, I have now fallen for, so desperately that she finally came to my rescue last night knowing I could never initiate the deeper connotation. One simply does not explore that possibility with such a person. Therefore, the absolute exaltation and surprise, for both of us, could not have consummated such utter bliss in the entire universe. The warm-scented zephyrs caressed our bodies through open windows like flowing silk. Entwined we slept, as if forever. And forever is upon us now. How transient the times have been. How melancholy the memories. How dangerous the resolve. And how divine the outcome.

We have no idea how we shall fare, whether here or there. Separation will not do us harm. We seem to read each other and know our deep fidelity to each other. She told me that she had seen me in a dream in her youth and had waited all this time. I replied I had no idea how our lives would turn out and that I seem incapable to reflect. Let time be our judge. She said she would live with me in Sunsetwind, if I would reciprocate in Cherokee. I agreed wholeheartedly.

That we consider ourselves a couple and will present ourselves as such enriches my post of the Earth Chair and our fledgling alliance with the Eridani Frequency. Initial meetings with Dewrzah, who came to the Fête by the way, unnoticed until I introduced him, have been very encouraging. He was most helpful in assisting us with the sub-space equipment and used his ship to illustrate how they could move through objects and render themselves invisible. He actually saved both Ten Mile and Penny Luck from their famous frozen mishap, due, we now know, to Redman's Resonant Scanner experiments the summer before that "opened the doors" Dewrzah said, with new electromagnetic frequencies. Ten and Penny are still very weak and recovering at Mita's clinic. It is hoped that they will be off mobile life-support before the end of the summer. Although severely shocked by their misadventure, they have recuperated enough to express embarrassment on the one count and unimaginable astonishment when informed that they had missed a rather auspicious year, though relieved no one had yet been commissioned to carve their marble coitus memorial.

There has been a tremendous surge of interest both at home and abroad in respect to the Jimmy Pidgeon-James Piercemore revelation and even Flower Child. Professors and students alike have been trying to gain access to Jimmy's personal belongings. But it will take some time before Yani Deerhill, who is in charge, can organise and catalogue everything for public use. At any rate, I have been too busy with my new responsibilities to help her, though I would like to very much. Eventually, I think I shall record for posterity my own experiences, and the Neteru, permitting. Vince has been very demanding concerning the Meteor; he wants to know how to get it out of the underground chamber and into the Pyramid to do some reverse-engineering. I told him that until everything in the tunnel, including Jimmy's personal things had been accounted for, I would not attempt to fly the machine. He is more than frustrated with me; but I promised I would take some time after this much needed vacation. I must admit to being a little hesitant to send a neutron wave onto the ceiling to make it permeable for the Meteor to be freed. The machine is old and if it broke as I was passing through the ten meters of ground and something went wrong . . . so much for that.

I feel a lazy afternoon siesta upon me. Cleo and O'Reilly will be arriving this evening for a few days. Chromolox said she'd come by for a night with Season Honey and her kids. At present I see Heyoka walking up the path having had a swim. Sam is at a friend's cottage. Heyoka quietly enters the cabin with her long wet hair smelling aromatically of Great Blue.

Before I shut my monitor down, dear reader, my final thoughts turn to Flower Child and yet another of her lost poems, all of which Mita has been compiling in a new volume. How does it go?

To euphoric death stands my beau

Leveling his big gun
At the behest of his fair love,
That must engender the fruit in the womb
Driving a dangerous dream to the tomb.
Oh, wonderfully sad this ecstasy,
The same all through the universe,
In essence a lethal temptation: life,
The epitome of the senses
To die for it –
I know I'll die for it
Woe is me happily –
My turn will come under the lilacs
And the spring rains will soak my remains,
Sweet-distilled back to earth,
To a starry vastness
Where I must pull my love to another . . .